For Ben and Steve, to whom I owe a debt of gratitude for lifting the curtain and showing me the wonders within

And for the Time Being, wno gave me a reason to write the damned thing

studies in mathematical pornography

The American Dream

Jim Chaffee

PART I

Did you hear about the mathematician who was so boring, even the other mathematicians noticed?

B. J. Pearson

Chapter 1
Monodromy

Jehovah's most devoted and single-minded witness lay like a wizened lump of clay, shriveled memory of once boundless energy, muted cheerleader of the coming vengeance. She opened her brown eyes to see me standing alone beside the bed; offered no smile, not with her eyes, certainly not in the set of her mouth. The weak voice emitted just above my signal-to-noise ratio and I bent nearer to capture the words.

"I tried to wait… see Armageddon… the resurrection."

Shit. The Old Testament monster Jehovah, this vision of mounds of dead scattered around the globe in a sea of blood, carrion for vultures, still possessed her. Same shit as Phoenix. I remembered why I'd avoided her for over a decade, why I'd almost not returned for this final visit.

Dad's sister Mary had picked me up at the airport. Dad, my brother and my sister camped out at a nearby motel, unable to return home across seventy miles of desert for fear she'd die on them; living in God-forsaken Coolidge, suburb of God-forsaken Florence, stuck on a hideous wasteland between Phoenix and Tucson near Casa Grande, another desert hole even the Indians had the good sense to abandon centuries earlier. My mother's choice of places to settle, where the need was great, whatever the fuck that meant.

Impending oral exams rattled around inside my brain, thoughts like loose change. I'd even brought goddamned books to study. I tossed my bag into the open trunk and clambered inside the humongous Detroit iron.

"Dad sounded pretty beat when he called; like he begged me to come out. How'd she get here to Tucson?"

Aunt Mary, behind a face so corrugated from the merciless sun it seemed no space remained for one more furrow, answered tersely in crisp Kansas speech untarnished by all her years in the empty Arizona desert.

"He's had a rough time of it." The high whistle in the background of her words matched the blowing sand outside the air conditioned car.

"What happened?"

"You mean he didn't tell you?" It was less question than accusation. She knew him.

"Nothing; just calls and tells me she's dying. I tried to beg off but he sounded like he needed me here."

"Well, the rest of 'em are pretty no-damned-good. Your sister is a basket case anyway, and your brother is a big crybaby."

"He's the macho one. I'm the prissy academic."

"You're the only one who's done a damned thing with his life."

"Not everyone would agree."

"You were the one in the war."

My brother Ernest, the tough one. In the photos they'd sent me he stood on ledges and hills looking off in the distance, an explorer, usually with a rifle in hand. And his wife, a small woman with mean eyes, also his sister-in-law as my own sister Julie married his wife's brother and best friend. At sixteen. They already had kids. Here I was, pushing thirty and still whoring and in school.

"Not like I had a choice. I'd've been drafted anyway." I wasn't sure if she knew I'd had the choice of Marines or jail. "They didn't have the lottery for my age group."

I needed a joint. I hadn't brought anything but hash-laced cigarettes, uncomfortable with carrying a baggie on the plane.

"Maybe we can stop on the way and get some booze," I said, lighting one up.

She remarked on the smell and I said it was a Perique blend from St. James Parish, a true statement. I showed her the bag I rolled from. The Perique covered the heavy odor of the flecks of Nepalese and Pakistani and Moroccan hashish rolled in with the tobacco. She appraised me from the side: her nephew from someplace outside the known universe, eccentric graduate student in mathematics.

At a strip mall liquor store, red neon sign blinking LIQ R, I got a pint of cheap bourbon. It wasn't as if I could afford much, but my leg ached from the cramped seats and I wasn't ready to face mother without a shot or two.

I tipped the bottle and took a belt. A nauseating warmth spread through my guts.

"When I was in Phoenix the doctor explained how they intended to kill her right there. I thought she was s'posed to die quickly. What happened?"

Aunt Mary gave me a sharp sidelong glance; said I needed to ask my dad.

I didn't go into the fresh and lingering conversation from that prior visit, gangly doctor explicating, my dad, brother, sister and I listening. He'd spoken to me, sensing from the questions I asked that I was the one to be reckoned with. Besides I'd let it be known I was no Jehovah's Witness but was ready to defend

6

her right to refuse blood. Her choice, I said, without adopting her superstition, the family's superstition. Idiots.

So the doctor'd looked at me; they couldn't de-bulk the tumor without her losing too much blood.

I'd heard it was a massive growth; I remembered the photo of her from several years before with a little belly like a nascent pregnancy. Anyway, now it had grown in and through her colon and they would have to remove a bunch of it, re-channel and such, and it wasn't possible without transfusing blood.

The family listened but didn't seem to hear. The physician went on that they wanted to start chemotherapy, that it would shrink the tumor and when that happened she'd have holes in her colon to leak and induce peritonitis and she'd die.

I'd shrugged and turned to my dad, asking if he'd heard. He said they wanted to do chemotherapy instead of surgery and I said yes, and it will kill her. She'd die of inflammation of the guts.

He didn't say much, just looked down and kind of shuffled his feet. Then he asked what other choice we had. I turned to the physician and waited for an answer. He said that otherwise she'd just die without any treatment. There was nothing to do other than the surgery.

I couldn't see shopping around for other points of view. Certainly the holistic crap they'd tried hadn't done much besides providing an excuse to avoid the initial visit. They eschewed doctors, I knew that, and I guess she had a damned high pain threshold to boot. Still, raw garlic wasn't going to cut it, as they now saw all too plainly.

Dad had asked my opinion and I said I didn't know. My specialty had been inflicting pain and death with the tools of the infantryman, and my experience with medicine came from the wrong end of the stethoscope. I never saw much natural death. He said this wasn't natural and I pretended not to hear, saying it was his decision. I didn't want to go into how loony it was to believe death unnatural, about laws of large numbers and outliers, about expected death age versus expected years to live.

Maybe it would've been better to say get another opinion. Probably should've; but I sure as hell couldn't spare time fucking with such shit. I'd been preparing for oral exams. I had no interest in it.

So now here I stood looking one last time at this dying woman racked with cancer, her peritoneum full of *E. coli.* She'd be dead soon, maybe by tonight, and I'd come to make the transition easier for my father. About my brother and sister I didn't care, and about her I certainly didn't give a rat's ass.

Let the ancient vengeful volcano god of genocidal, homicidal smiting fury she worshiped carry her through.

My leg ached though the whiskey had helped a bit. I needed to sit. The family came in while I dragged over a chair, our aunt, dad's sister, watching at the door, and I stood for a final moment while mother took us all in.

"I have to die to bring this family together," was what she'd said in the hospital in Phoenix, but now she was too weak to try that shit. I plopped into the chair.

Julie looked to be near tears, Ernst like he was trying to buck up. I was hungry, having had only peanuts so far this day nearing its end. I decided to go outside for a smoke.

"Anyone here hungry?" I asked. "I haven't eaten since last night."

No one said anything or seemed eager to leave, so I gathered up Aunt Mary who had remained standing in the doorway, spectating.

"Can we get a bite somewhere?"

"They have a cafeteria downstairs."

"What about a taco stand? Nothing nearby? Can't get tacos in New Orleans."

"No?"

"No. They're pretty much about their own stuff down there. I miss tacos. Can't even get real tortillas, just canned ones and those damned shells in a box."

I smoked another of my hash-laced cigarettes as we walked to her car and had a decent buzz on by the time we drove off, smoothing it out with more hootch, offering her the bottle which I knew she'd refuse.

We found a bright taco joint blaring some kind of accordion-laced guitar music with a polka beat and singing that seemed to disturb her. I didn't mind it: conjunto; I'd picked it up in Kansas City, of all places, while boffing a Mexican chick for a few months. My aunt drank a coke while I had a half dozen tacos and a beer spiked with the remains of the pint. We drove back to the University Hospital in silence.

The rest of the family milled around the room looking hangdog, so I dragged my sister off to the cafeteria for a cup of coffee to try to figure out what had happened. I asked our aunt to come along, just so I'd be sure to get two sides.

We sat around a linoleum table drinking a ghastly excuse for coffee, burned and weak at the same time, almost an impossibility, and Julie told me the story. It seemed that dad had gone to the administration when they called him in about Mom's bill. He told them he couldn't pay. He didn't have insurance on her.

"No insurance? Why the fuck not?"

Our aunt frowned at my language, but my sister seemed not to notice.

"He didn't have it on her. I don't know why."

"He worked for the damned county, right? Those people have insurance."

"But he had to pay extra," Julie went on.

Our aunt broke in. "Your dad was just too damned stubborn. He refused to pay the same amount for her as a man with a bunch of kids would pay."

I wished I had been unable to believe it, but it was the kind of bullshit the jackass would pull. There might have been a bit more to it, but not much. He could cut off his nose to spite his face, then when covered with blood feel he had been screwed by some external force.

Julie didn't dispute what Aunt Mary said.

"So what'd they do?"

Julie said they threw her out. Our aunt interceded, saying not before he refused to sign a paper taking responsibility for repaying the debt.

"Well, they said she had to leave. It's a Catholic hospital, Manny."

"So? It's still a business."

Our aunt piped up again. "He borrowed an old station wagon from a Witness friend in Coolidge and drove her back from Phoenix across that hot desert in the middle of the day. She was in back on a mattress. The wagon didn't have air conditioning, either. When she got back, he got some of their Witness friends to stay with her since he had to work. They ran shifts, someone with her all the time. One of them was a nurse and showed them how to change her dressings, but she had one of those rubber tubes in there that oozed all the time."

A Penrose drain. They sent her home with a fucking Penrose drain in place. I worked on incensed but couldn't figure out who'd shown the bigger asshole. Knowing my father, he'd not only refused to sign for the debt, but had been ugly and hostile to boot, insulting whoever had least authority.

"Well, she isn't dying tonight. I can see that. Maybe tomorrow. I don't feel like staying here all night waiting."

"We have a motel room if you want to sleep," Julie chirped.

"With the three of you? No thanks. What about you, Mary? You going back tonight?"

"I think I will. I don't want to stay and it's less than an hour. I can bring you back in the morning. There's room at my place."

9

So we found ourselves flying low beneath the Arizona night, stars and all that hanging above the blast furnace that never dies. I fell asleep, a habit developed during my formative years heading across the desert at night to avoid the heat in the days before air conditioned cars and houses.

We didn't say much and I slept almost immediately in the extra room in the trailer she kept out behind Dad's house. I never understood that set-up, with the dislike all around, except she probably paid them. I didn't want to know and didn't ask.

Morning smashed in through the windows hot and relentless. Aunt Mary was up already, fixing coffee, and I stumbled into the kitchen with a lit cigarette. She wished me a good morning. I returned it and we drank in silence.

When we got to the hospital the crew was already at vigil. Now at least there was only family. I'd almost kicked the shit out of an asshole Witness teenager in the Phoenix hospital who'd asked her if she'd been to the meetings. I told the family any more of those dickheads and there was going to be blood. They knew my capabilities and stopped the visits, at least while I was with her.

My father and I breakfasted in the cafeteria. After we sat down, I started in on him.

"What's this shit I hear about no insurance on Mom?"

"I didn't have it on her. It was extra."

"You couldn't afford it?"

"It wasn't that. I had to pay the same for her as someone paid for a wife and a bunch of kids."

"So? What's that got to do with it?"

"It's not fair."

"Fair? They got a saying in the Crotch: shit in one hand, wish in the other, weigh which is heavier. Fair's no heavier than a wish."

He didn't reply and I resurrected my cold scrambled eggs and greasy hash browns with a liberal douse of hot sauce and finished eating without another word. Then I clandestinely added to our coffee mugs generous slugs from a fresh pint of cheap bourbon I'd procured at the same liquor store and started in on him again.

"So what'd you say to them?"

"The lady from administration took me in her office and said I had to sign a paper. It would have put me in debt for years. I didn't have any ten thousand dollars. I refused and they kicked her out. I'm not going to be in debt for years paying for her death."

"So how'd you find this place? How're you paying for it now?"

"One of the sisters knew about it. She got in touch with a doctor here and he had her admitted as a charity patient."

"They want anything?"

"They'd like her body, but I can't let them have it, knowing people will look at her all the time. I'll let them take the organs for study. I'll have the county dispose of her body. They do a cheap cremation for indigents. It's just a shell anyway. She'll have a new one at the resurrection."

Resurrection. He still didn't understand about shit and wishes, like most of the superstitious Christian nutcases I'd met.

"The doc here said they could have done something for her without surgery. He said the hospital in Phoenix didn't use the latest methods."

I understood his feelings about debt. Debt was the shits. I didn't like it either. I had charged this flight to my credit card, was likely over my limit since I hadn't yet paid off the last flight out a month earlier, and would need to sell some coke or a shitload of pot to make it up when I got back. I didn't like being forced to sell beyond splitting up a pound of dope with margin to cover my own use; too risky, selling to people you didn't know personally. Nor did I like coke enough to use it much, though I kept some for guests. It did provide a higher margin than pot. Maybe acid would be better yet.

We went up to the room and spelled my brother and sister. Aunt Mary had disappeared.

Mom labored breathing and she didn't respond to any sort of chat. I was pretty sure it wouldn't be long and decided to wait. In fact, it took twelve hours for her to wind down and give it up. My brother and sister had long since left the room, too broken up to stay, and it was just Dad and me in the end. He sat staring at her and I got the night nurse who called the doctor to pronounce her dead.

We met up with Aunt Mary back at Dad's place in Coolidge. She invited me to stay with her, a relief to get away from the quasi-shack my dad now inhabited alone, temporarily haunted by my brother and sister.

The next day we met for a powwow around the kitchen table, a last one before Ernest and Julie took off.

"Is there anyone on her side we can notify she's dead?" I asked, broaching the subject no one seemed to want to approach.

"We don't know where they are," my dad said.

"Doesn't she have a sister in France?" Julie asked.

Ernest said, "We don't know if her sister is alive or not. Her mother died back when you were in Vietnam, but they'd stopped writing long before that. They didn't want to hear The Truth."

"Her sister was younger. She's probably alive. Where was she? What about the rest of them? She had a dozen brothers and sisters."

Ernest continued. "We don't know about the others. The sister lived in Marseilles with their mother. We got a death certificate for her mother and a letter asking for Mom's share of the funeral expenses. I guess they were still pretty poor."

"Did we send them anything?" I asked.

"We're poor too," my Dad said, and I knew they'd probably not bothered to answer that last letter.

"We could send something to the old address."

"Don't know where those old letters are now," Ernest said, and it dropped.

I spent the next two days reading the first volume of Kobayashi and Nomizu's *Foundations of Differential Geometry* and the first two chapters of the second volume, about a hundred pages, stopping at chapter IX which went on to complex manifolds. Not ready for that yet.

This trip had taken the time I'd set aside to visit the expert at Loyola to get a quick rundown, so now I was stuck with books. The exam had been postponed a week with this death; I wasn't going to let it slide more.

The only real topic from differential geometry on my list was Lie groups, my advisor's interest computational in terms of symmetries and conservation laws, local properties, but there was a hard ass on my committee, an expert in Lie groups and Lie algebras who maintained this grimly formalistic approach via categories and functors and a bastardization of the exponential map. I'd taken his course and learned he didn't give a fuck about geometry.

It wasn't as if I didn't go for machinery; I love heavy equipment as much as anyone, for sure more than my advisor whose approach amounted to using the bare minimum of gear to set up a formal computation. No machinery for machinery's sake. But I had great curiosity regarding bundles and connections on manifolds. I'd been sent to look at Spivak, but found it fat and filled with words, the opposite of his little advanced calculus book. Warner's terse approach from a functional analytical viewpoint appealed, but offered little geometry.

Kobayashi and Nomizu got down to brass tacks, moving right away to connections on fiber bundles via Lie-algebra valued one-forms and on into Riemannian connections, curvature tensors and all the rest in only a couple hundred pages or so. Volume two, though longer, got into Jacobi fields in Riemannian manifolds early on and ended in characteristic classes, if I'd go that far. There'd seemed no other choice except Bishop and Crittendon's *Geometry of Manifolds* which I'd brought along as backup.

There existed ulterior motives in this, of course. I hoped to distract my interrogators with a run through Lie theory embedded within differential geometry, where they would be on less firm ground.

Dazzling them might help, as on the writtens when I'd distracted them from my deficiencies, turning a question regarding complex analysis into an excursion through harmonic functions and maximal properties by contrasting the Weirestress point of view via analyticity and formal power series with the Cauchy vision via holomorphic functions. I pleased everyone, playing up the beauty of what appeared a strange coincidence that didn't work with real differentiation by showing at root the Cauchy-Riemann equations characterized as a system of over-determined partial differential equations (PDEs). Utilizing conjugate differentiation of complex differential forms, I dragged in a superficial bit of cohomology with complex coefficients in proving Cauchy's integral formula to unite the two classical points of view, all to please the several complex variables (SCV) people, then returned to the Cauchy-Riemann equations and harmonic functions to look at the mean value property, ending up showing the maximum modulus property as not so surprising while obtaining it for the heat equation. That took care of the PDE group. By the time I had finished writing on this problem, half the allotted four hours, the hefty spliff I'd done just prior to boarding the St. Charles streetcar had worn down and my vision slowed proportionally. But it worked.

An old trick I'd learned long ago, overwhelming people with what I wanted to present, like picking your own ground to fight on. They overlooked my inability to say anything about the Denjoy integral, not that I was alone on that one. As it turned out, I had been the sole analyst to come out of that group of entering graduate students.

The last I remember of the visit was my father sitting at the kitchen table, alone, drinking a fifth of rotgut. Aunt Mary drove me to the airport.

Chapter 2
a) Smooth Connexions

On the plane I blazed through Bishop and Crittenden (B&C), leapfrogging along the main results and examples of interest. It turned out to be a not-necessarily-proper subset of Kobayashi and Nomizu (K&N). No surprises, not in the sense of information anyway. Felt more concrete than K&N, maybe more examples or a different collection of examples developed in more detail. Both approaches got to Riemannian connections about the same time and both ended up in variational theory with the Morse index. K&N spent more time with Lie groups and transformations, giving a long section on Lie groups before entering fibre bundles, later devoting an entire chapter to transformations. Lie groups seemed more basic to their development of bundles. Both clumsily evaded the multilinear algebra underlying the tensor stuff. The prof who'd taught me multilinear algebra as an excursion through formal tensor constructions on modules had remarked that differential geometry was the study of properties that remain invariant under change of notation. Neither of these books presented anything to change my mind; I hoped to yet find an approach avoid the fuzzy index orgy by exploiting the algebra so I didn't need to figure it out for myself.

K&N seemed more like geometry: I felt the curvature. B&C read more like applied mathematics. Worse, B&C spelled the word connections "connexions."

My Dallas connection went slick as greased owl shit and I debarked in New Orleans to compare the difference between dry blast furnace hot and moist swampy hot, the miasma of bogs, decay and rot permeating New Orleans even as extreme summer hung potential in the Earth's tilt a couple months on the horizon.

I'd have preferred Red meet me, but his car had been wiped out in flooding outside his uptown apartment during one of those downpours where the pumps lose the battle for the outlying streets. The waters receded within hours but the uninsured clunker was a goner. He, however, made decent sums on the odd drug deal, with plenty of connections, and I needed extra scratch just now.

Instead there stood Lori at the gate, wearing her muted smile like her face wasn't quite in focus, her features conspiring to tone it all down. Not a looker; softly padded body and small tits flattened on a tubular trunk, she wore little girl or peasant blouses with tie tops that showed off what she did have, always without a bra and always in loosely fitting jeans to hide thick calves and ankles and accentuate a flat ass. Turned down mouth and round eyes with lashes like sunbeams seemed painted to enhance the little girl look though she never wore makeup; perhaps it was the contrast with her pale skin. Somehow she kept her thin goldilocks hanging like a spaniel's ears, curled on the ends sheep-like. But she understood the effect of those luscious curved lips stretched over an erect penis, those baby-blues gazing up at you in wonder; it had likely brought off many a shot in the mouth.

She handed me a joint when we hit the highway and remarked that Steve had told her my oral notices were posted all over the department. It didn't concern me. They were always open to the public, but no students attended and few faculty not in your own group or one of the groups surrounding members of your committee.

We headed uptown to a little shack that served cheap food and I got my favorite, a soft-shell crab poor-boy. It reminded me of a cartoon I'd seen in Mad Magazine when I was a kid, a pizza with everything on it, including a live octopus or an alien, not clear which, a guy's cavernous mouthful of looming teeth ready to engulf the whole mess. The crab played the alien, legs and claws sticking out the sides; I loved chomping through the creature's fried and battered body squirting juices and dripping mayonnaise and sauce. The only problem was the mess on my face, but Lori licked it off when I let her.

Afterward we parked at her apartment and caught the streetcar. There was no easy way to park in the French Quarter, and this being the start of the weekend we'd not find anything in Marigny either. Parking in Treme was out of the question, neither of us feeling up to being shot.

Lori rested her hand on my thigh, then held my hand, uncharacteristic sentimentalities, and I felt her mood as the streetcar rocked and swayed around the long curve from Carrollton Avenue past Tulane and Audubon Park. I kept quiet. I guessed it was Steve, still dragging his feet about dissolving the marriage, but from what he'd told me it was not his doing. Deana didn't want a divorce though she knew Steve and Lori were getting it on. It incensed Lori that Deana referred to her as "that little girl." Steve had been sick of Deana for a long time, but he hadn't wanted any hassles until he passed his orals. That done, he plunged ahead in ridding himself of her, but she wasn't passing easily from his life.

Around Napoleon Avenue Lori began the soulful stare. Past Louisiana Avenue I asked if she'd ever eaten at Commander's Palace, trying to get past it all; she ignored the question. I told her it was the favorite restaurant of the department's resident gourmet, Professor Momus. She snorted and said Steve called him a lush. Maybe he drank, I replied, but he sure as hell knew a lot of stuff, even if he'd stopped creating. His advisor had been a founding member of Bourbaki.

As we made the circle around the statue of Robert E Lee she told me Deanna had decided to give Steve the divorce and moved out, but that he didn't want to live together yet; he wanted to remember living alone.

Not knowing what the hell to say, I lamely muttered to give him some time, that he was nuts about her, some bullshit about which I knew nothing. Steve and I discussed math and dope, the only interests he seemed to have besides porn films. He'd never said a thing about Lori to me, and the only woman I'd seen him hit on was the young one staying with Red, tall and athletic with a hard body and straight-legged walk, no hips, a round ass, a decent set of tits on a long torso, close set eyes, slightly gapped front teeth and a hell of a ski nose. I'd once seen her around some of his visiting friends from out of town, sporting a pair of tiny shorts and a leather vest open in front with nothing under it until he whispered to her and she disappeared, reappearing in jeans and wearing a t-shirt under the vest.

It had turned dusk and the Quarter lit up and came alive up as we walked up Bourbon Street blocked off from motorized vehicles for the night, Lori firmly gripping my free hand, my old black grip in the other, the macadam street sloping from the bald center towards broken lines of sidewalk. The buildings crowded flush against the sidewalks and hawkers for the strip joints standing in the doorways incited imagination to encourage entrance as bored topless girls standing behind them discouraged, the few on stage gyrating listlessly. GIRLS had been flipped from BOYS in LIVE _____ ON STAGE at Little Darlings. Knots of men and a few couples, most holding plastic cups of beer, stood gawking into the darkened dives.

We made St. Ann and hit my place, 839 Bourbon, passed through the iron gate into the brick passageway leading out to the courtyard and climbed the rickety spiral stairway to the top, the third floor. The landlord didn't call out "Good evening, Mr. Bouchée" from his second floor apartment and the French doors were shuttered behind the plank storm door, so I guessed he was out or with his boyfriend or some other man. I thought of him as Scarlet O'Hara with a bushy mustache; he always referred to me as Mister Bouchée in an exaggerated drawl, lending the name Butcher a gay Southern Louisiana French pronunciation.

After a couple joints, Lori and I commenced our prowl at a locals bar she favored for the pinball machines. Before she'd gotten her high-paying corporate job she'd done part-time programming of pinball machines. A wizard at communicating with computers in their basic instructions, she now programmed PDP-11s for real-time control, freed up for full time work after flunking her written exams the previous term. She didn't care shit for mathematics and I wondered why she'd bothered in the first place, but she took all three of the damned four-hour exams, wasting three full days of her life even as she spent the nights with me carousing and screwing. She didn't bother to register for the following semester.

We avoided tourist places and I made certain we steered clear of the gay bars, not wanting anyone to get the wrong idea. It was my neighborhood and I felt at home in the omnipresent crowds, but my apartment rested in the heart of the gayest neighborhood in the South, on Bourbon Street between St. Ann and Dumaine. Next door to my place, once sharing a courtyard before a wall had been erected, the Washing Well Laundryteria, and across Dumaine from the Washing Well, the Café Lafitte in Exile. More commonly referred to as Lafitte's, it was a hardcore gay bar with music blaring twenty-four hours a day, every day, where men performed sex acts on the balcony and I'd been told in the bathrooms. It wasn't uncommon to see men in leathers, sometimes wearing chaps with no pants, their bare butts hanging out.

The local atmosphere abetted my favored garb of work shoes, baggy trousers and loose fitting t-shirts. Once walking to my apartment I heard the words "Not bad" from behind me. One of his companions replied in nelly voice drag, "If he would just lose those awful khaki pants," and I thought, That's why I wear them, cocksucker. Steve refused to come to the Quarter to visit because the gallery on the balcony at Lafitte's in Exile always hooted and whistled at his tight jeans, cowboy shirt and boots. I explained my approach but he couldn't bring himself to dress like a janitor.

I repeatedly lost to Lori at pinball, so after several beers and shots she tired of the routine and dragged me off to a place packed with women, a lot of them dressed like bikers; I saw no other men in the joint. We sat at the bar and she watched, then sidled up to some of them and struck up conversations. She kept moving until she came back with one in tow, a short thing who made little Lori look tall: pale and skinny with long hairy arms and sticks for legs, brows like inky wooly worms and jet-black stringy hair hanging to her shoulders.

We moved to a table and the girl, named Milly or something like that, giggled and showed tiny teeth inside a tiny oval opening overwhelmed by a humongous beezer swerving to the right from a hump at mid slope.

I ordered beers and shots of bourbon and poured a shot in her beer. She stared at me as if myopic and unable to focus. The bridge of her nose seemed to perch far above her giant round black peepers, maybe mid forehead, and the peepers themselves were perched a little askew in a concave visage creased at the bridge of her nose like a paper dessert plate. I guessed she was drunk.

The boiler-makers didn't enhance her sobriety; hauling her up the winding stairwell would have been a major problem had she not been so slight. In the quasi-light of the apartment I saw clown red daubed on her cheeks and smeared around her mouth to give an impression of lips, lashes coated with a purple viscous substance beaded into drops, all of it strewn above a receding chin with a crease on the bottom. Her flattened face suggested an asymmetry with respect to eyes set low and wide apart far down on the nose, well below the bridge and off center, the left one slightly higher than the right which seemed a smidge farther from the centerline of the nose. She had lesser boobs than Lori, no ass at all and elongated legs encased in tight jeans.

We smoked a joint on the narrow gallery perched a high three-floors above Bourbon Street, accessed via the bedroom window that ran from the floor to the steeply pitched roof sloping from the garret's high ceiling. The window opened like French doors but the ceiling swooped so low all but infants and elves had to duck through.

The view of queer Bourbon Street from on high mesmerized Millie; she steadied herself with the flimsy wrought iron handrail along the edge of the narrow outcropping. Lori took advantage of the moment to stand behind her and fondle her chest where breasts might have been. Millie turned and kissed her on the mouth. Lori dragged her to the living room, promising nose-candy. We snorted the stuff I kept for guests and they engaged in serious tongue probing. Lori helped her get naked from the waist down, then went to her knees and buried her face between her legs. Millie moaned and randomly emitted hysterical laughs like a hyena. Lori steered the wobbly half-naked creature back to the bedroom.

Street noise grinding outside poured in the open window and Millie confronted the monstrous ceiling-high, gilt-framed mirror behind the bed, taking an unsteady step back from the reflection of the three of us.

"Where did you get that mirror?" she squealed, pealing off her blouse.

"Was here when I moved in. Landlord says it was put here by some washed up silent movie star, Lola Montes or something like that, someone I never heard of. I don't understand how they got it in here. Won't fit in that window and would be impossible to bring up the stairwell."

Lori whispered in my ear to shut the fuck up. Millie squealed "Far out" and Lori kissed her on the mouth, pulling her down on the bed, backing away from the drawn-out kiss to suck the girl's nipples.

Millie on her back, straight and flat as a little boy, her dense sprout of pitch-black pubic hair narrowing at the mons pubis to thread up the middle of her stomach and branch to tufts of black sprouts like anemone scattered around puffy nipples the color of moles standing alone on a chest with no hint of tits. I reached out and stroked one; it felt like an erect fingertip sprouting from a knot the size of a golf ball.

She said something that sounded like "I never done nothing like this before," and Lori said to me, "Can't you put your dick in her mouth?" before diving into the lush growth between her legs.

I tried to push my dick in Millie's mouth but she made a lot of noise and held me back with her hand against my groin before relenting to suck the head like a lollypop. I ejected a wad in her mouth and that seemed to upset her, but Lori cleaned her up with her tongue, kissing her and cooing some kind of odd noises in her ear until Millie calmed down at which time Lori attacked her cunt again. Millie heated up to moaning punctuated by the hyena laugh and Lori encouraged me to fuck her. I entered with restraint, the constricted aperture wet but tight; she protested I was too big until Lori shut her up by kissing her. Lori thumbed the clit above my penis and the hole relaxed, easing around my dick as Millie fell into a rhythmic ride that brought me gradually to another ejaculation.

I sat on the edge of the bed as they lay face to crotch, parasites sucking and slurping amidst moans and cries and snorts. Lori rolled onto her back with Millie on top, mouths leeching cunts. With her tongue she lubricated Millie's asshole which she found buried in long, luxurious black growth that clamored vine-like up over her ass and along her spine. She motioned for me to fuck that hairy sphincter while the two of them performed sixty-nine. This time Millie thrashed like a fish out of water and flailed against me as I slid in. With concentrated thrusts she drove our rhythm, her bony ass butting my pelvis until I felt stoking behind my scrotum the pressure of building orgasm. She wriggled free from between us before I could explode, landing on her butt on the floor.

"I'm hungry," she ejaculated. "Any food here?"

"Some sardines in the cabinet," I said as the urge dissipated. "Not much else."

"Too fishy!" Millie squeaked and Lori laughed out loud.

"Bring that fucking thing over here," Lori said, grabbing me around my hips and pulling me so my erection poked at her face. She licked and slobbered the length of it while Millie muttered to herself words that sounded like "It's too big." Once Lori'd slathered it with spit she said, "Come on, pretty boy, fuck my face" and offered me her mouth. I set to trying to finesse my hard-on down her throat in a motion staggered by the slow push at the end when she slid out her tongue and locked her lips attempting to inch to the base. I lost interest in this game and pulled her up to a position where I could steady her head with my hands, stepping up the pace to periodic forcing, speeding as the pressure grew again until I let go with my dick buried as deeply as I could cram it, grunting with the spasms rocking my pelvis. Lori ingested without a hitch, inspiring a piercing "Wow!" from Millie.

I wanted to sleep, but Millie would have none of it. She begged for food. We smoked more dope and snorted some coke and then Lori and I escorted her to Molly's Irish Pub, a twenty-four hour place that catered to a mixed crowd of locals and savvy tourists. We must have been a sight, a threesome careening across the quarter, Lori and I supporting Millie upright.

In the brightness of Molly's, Millie turned out to be a horror. The pale complexion turned pasty, almost greenish in contrast to the ultra black of hair on her head and face. Smeared makeup mixed with dried bodily excretions didn't add to her appeal. Or maybe they did.

The kitchen was closed but there were sandwiches and Millie gobbled her way through a chicken salad dripping mayonnaise and washed it down with a mug of beer into which I'd dumped a shot of bourbon. As I chased shots with Guinness draft, Lori disappeared at the bar and returned with two nondescript guys from Australia. She must have clued them to what she had in mind because they were all over Millie who seemed oblivious to everything but their "funny accents" which elicited her hyena laugh. Gibbering repeatedly about how pretty was their talk, Millie snuggled up against one of them while the other rubbed the nape of her neck. The five of us left together; at the door they peeled off for their hotel, sustaining Millie barely afoot between them.

Lori pulled my face down and kissed me on the mouth, exploring with her tongue. The earthy flavor mingled with the beer recalled for me where my dick had been before she had cleaned it so thoroughly; I started to pull back but she held me insistently.

"I like ass juice on dick," she said when she let go. "And I'm ready for a fuck now. I wanted to go with those two Aussies. They were cute. I was afraid you wouldn't have tagged along."

We trudged back across the quarter, now deserted in the lower blocks where tourists predominated. Most places shuttered already, even the tourist strip joints, and it would be desolate until we hit Bourbon and St. Ann where the gay crowd still yo-yoed between their twenty-four hour bars.

"Maybe you should have."

She snuggled up and took my arm in hers.

"Would you have come along?"

"I'm pretty tapped out. I need to sleep."

"I want some action before we sleep."

"May not be anything left."

"We'll find something."

"You might wish you'd gone with those two."

"I like doing two guys. Or three. Never done more than three together. But I like the idea."

"Pulling a train?"

"That. Or just all together."

"Cluster fuck. Gang bang. Orgies?"

"Not really. Like to, but Steve isn't into it."

"No?"

"No other guys. Just girls. I wanted to do a threesome with him and a guy and he wouldn't have it. Doesn't care if I do it, but he won't join."

"Makes sense."

"Why, are you that way?"

"I never really thought about it. I doubt it'd bother me if there weren't guy on guy stuff. Not into that."

"A lot of people think you're gay, living down here. You're the only person in the entire department who lives in the Quarter."

"I don't care. Let them think what they want."

"Would you have come with us tonight?"

"Probably if I weren't so fucking tired. I'm whipped."

We hit St. Ann and made our way to the apartment. Bourbon had been opened to traffic again and the stream of guys wandering my block was joined by cars cruising for hustlers, young men and boys standing on the corners from St. Ann to Esplanade.

Once inside the passageway, the heavy iron gate secured behind us, Lori pulled my face down for another kiss, then knelt and unzipped my pants and fellated me beside the gate. No one on the street noticed but the idea they might brought me to immediate erection.

She stood. "Those fucking bricks are wet and hard," she said, and led me by my erection to the bench in the courtyard. She pulled off her jeans and climbed on top and stuffed my dick in her cunt, lowering herself gradually.

"See," saying another long kiss, "you can't help yourself."

"Sometimes it works on its own."

"Like autopilot."

"That chick was weird, don't you think? Ugly."

"You think she was ugly?"

"No tits, no ass."

"Did you see the hair? Her pubic hair was nicer than the hair on her head."

"Almost as long."

"Like silk. Soft as silk."

"Never seen such a hairy woman. Black hair on her stomach, her chest, her asshole. Her back."

"Her back too? And those eyebrows. And skinny arms covered with long black hair. Her legs too, if she didn't shave. And armpits. Legs and armpits full of coarse stubble."

"Really? Stubble?" I hadn't noticed the stubble. "I didn't get that close. She had tits like knobs with tubes on the end."

"Those dark hard knobs were the areola. Huge areolae, no boobs."

"Like a tarantula with those skinny extremities."

"Four legged spider. We ought to have called her spider woman."

"__"

"Don't stop," she said. "I need this; I deserve this."

"Why deserve?"

"You know how hard it is to get a chick from a gay bar to go home with a man and woman together?"

"No. That was a gay bar?"

"You didn't notice you were the only guy there?"

"No."

She hadn't let up dragging her cunt up and down my cock and I was wearing out supporting her. My right leg nagged at me with dull throbs.

"Let's go upstairs," I said. "I need to do this in bed."

She dismounted. "Listen," she said standing awash with moonlight in her white tennies, no pants, hands on hips, "Steve and I prowl for girls like that sometimes. But not lesbian bars. Usually places where I know some bi women

22

go. We had luck only twice. Usually we do threesomes with women I already know."

"Interesting. Wonder how that happened?"

"I think she really wanted to hook up but not many takers. Maybe they knew her. She was alone, dikes all around her and no one talking to her. She's a submissive, I think."

"Should be popular?"

"Depends. There is some kind of code. Probably true for guys, too. I have friends tell me that effeminate men aren't respected."

I shrugged. "Nellies they call them."

"Anyway," Lori said, "I asked if she wanted to go to an apartment on Bourbon Street with my boyfriend and me and she said, 'I don't do guys.' Then she looked over at you and she couldn't stop staring. 'He's pretty,' she said. 'You sure he's a boy?'"

"That's where that fucking 'pretty boy' you called me came from?"

"Yeah. She said, 'That pretty boy over there? He's just a big boy, isn't he?'"

"You tell her I was a killer?"

"Course not. I said you were a sweet guy. Gentle. I said she didn't have to do anything with you if she didn't want to, but I think she wanted to. Your white hair and blue eyes—"

"Not white. I'm a towhead."

"Looks white; not like in old-man-white. Not snow white. Blonde white. You look so harmless."

"Cute? Like the two Aussies?"

"Not cute. Sweet and pretty. You're a pretty boy. With a big dick."

"Really?"

"You must've been told that before. I thought she'd freak more when she met it."

"I heard it once or twice. A whore in Okinawa said I was too big, wouldn't let me fuck her. But I always took it as an excuse or just some kind of flattery. Like telling an ugly chick she has pretty eyes."

"It's true. You must have noticed around guys in locker rooms—"

"I don't notice other guy's equipment. Not something men do."

"Well, I have sampled more than a few and it's the biggest I've encountered."

"Your sample isn't that significant. Come on, let's go up…"

I started dragging her up the stairs, she carrying her pants, me with my bare erection drooling from the wet spot on the front of my khakis.

"I never thought of myself as looking harmless. Or sweet. Or cute."

She zipped around me and ran up to the top of the stairs.

"I will admit," she said as she waited for me on the solarium, "it is a trick for someone your size to look harmless. But you do. Maybe it's the short hair. You look like a clean cut Republican dork."

I pondered this as I unlocked the yellow front door, a solid barrier built from long planks to cover the flimsy French doors. I pushed Lori through the living room to the bedroom, onto the bed, and took off my clothes.

"Wonder what's up with her now," I said. "If she really meant she didn't do guys, she's got two of them probably fucking the shit out of her now. Probably using her like an old rag doll…"

"She might be puking by now. You pouring bourbon in her beer wasn't going to help much…"

"Not to mention that chicken salad. I couldn't eat that on so much booze. Just watching her made me wanna puke."

"Her eating habits were disgusting."

"You think she takes birth control?"

Lori laughed. "No. Now forget her," she said. "You're making me think you're more interested in her than me."

I undressed and climbed on the bed to perform my duty.

"Steve," she said lying on her stomach as I climbed aboard, "alternate between my ass and my pussy."

b) Parallel Displacement

I awoke removed from Lori and the sheets. I didn't remember finishing with her; probably I'd fallen asleep after she'd climbed on top.

She slept as I went about morning business, coffee, shit, shower, shave. By the time I came out of the bathroom she sat at the black lacquer table on the solarium nursing a steaming cup of instant coffee.

"Want a blow job before I clean up?" she asked.

"Good morning," I said.

"It looks cloudy," she said.

She worked at looking sad and serious while we traipsed through the quarter to Jackson Square for coffee and pastries at La Marquise. I wasn't up for her mood and didn't take the bait, sitting quietly probing for deficiencies in my grasp of Ito's construction of his stochastic integral. She gave up on me and left soon after, not even returning to the apartment for a final fuck. Just as well; I dragged around most of the day doing nothing, went out for a sandwich later, and turned in early Saturday night.

Sunday my head cleared and I worried about the upcoming exam Thursday afternoon. I had no interest in reading books, but after lining up several joints to help me along I skimmed some of the material on the reading list. Fortunately, all were short and to the point, and I skimmed McKean's *Stochastic Integrals* and Folland's *Introduction to Partial Differential Equations,* hitting the high spots with the intent of making certain I understood the big picture, some details of approach and how hypotheses tied to major proofs. No memorization, impossible with so much material anyway, but understanding enough to reproduce the highlights of essential arguments without fatal holes.

My advisor's papers were not an issue, since only he knew what was in them and he wasn't going to try to trip me up.

Lie groups loomed as the big worry. I needed to smoke a lot of dope to review that stuff again. Problem was, my advisor cared for no more than the local approach, local Lie groups and their associated Lie algebras with a view towards symmetries of PDEs. But Professor Karl Oberst, the big gun from the topological algebra group, would come after me, maybe, since I had of necessity taken his course in Lie algebras. With no interest in our point of view or problems, he nonetheless was an international authority and could not be left off my committee.

I'd absorbed the viewpoint from Kobayashi and Nomizu since I figured differential geometry would be the last approach anyone there would take. Tulane being small, the math department concentrated on one uniting area, groups, so that there were groups and semigroups and modules and group rings in all sorts of settings, algebraic, topological, analytical. But not geometric; no geometers on the faculty.

The topological algebra point of view would be topological groups and that hideous functorial approach; I would tiptoe through geometry instead, getting the topological stuff as a side show on the way to the Montgomery-Zippin theory with results on the compact-open topology for transformation groups. Then I'd hit the high points of connections, sketching an argument about parallel displacements to show that the holonomy group for a connection in a principle fibre bundle turned out to be a Lie group.

The problem was I hadn't tied any of it to the viewpoint of either my advisor or Oberst.

Assigned reading on Lie theory was a single chapter on Lie groups from a fat book on symmetry groups, a fat book I didn't care about since most of it was superfluous and the whole approach ugly. It relied on local theory in a neighborhood of the identity, the exponential map to the Lie algebra gained mostly via matrix groups, the so-called linear Lie groups and the classical groups. Heavy on computation, it stressed the Campbell-Baker-Hausdorff theorem, analytic groups more than c-infinity, expansions in terms of Lie brackets. It wouldn't satisfy Oberst. Still, differential equations and one-parameter groups were the natural tie to Kobayashi and Nomizu, adjoints and inner automorphisms raw meat for the group theorists.

I smoked a couple joints while plowing through the mimeographed notes from Oberst's course. The path would of necessity jump off Oberst's theme in the categorical world, the exponential map from the algebra to the group, and the differential equations would play their part since Lie algebra = tangent space for Lie group as manifold. After bringing up Ado's theorem regarding realizations of abstract Lie algebras as matrix Lie algebras, I could dance around the matrix exponential as a solution to the ordinary differential equation using the constant coefficients case as an example and then do Campbell-Baker-Hausdorff with the time-varying case by looking at the logarithm. The problem that there existed no constructive process to build the associated matrix algebra could be brushed off. The bigger problem would be if Oberst asked about a proof of Ado's theorem; I had no idea of how it went. It wasn't in my readings. It's essential to not come off as shallow, the major danger of bringing up outside shit.

The exponential, that would be the key. Oberst loved that baby as a functor.

I reviewed my advisors point of view with the one parameter groups, going into details on some of the preprints and works in progress on the list, more to do with symmetry groups and their application to partial differential equations. The other fat source, a machine translation of a book by a Russian named Ovsiannikov weighing about ten pounds, we both agreed I'd skip. The damned thing was impossible and no one but he had an inkling of its internals.

It sounded like a plan, but in the back of my head lingered doubts about how the geometric approach would interlock with the two other divergent approaches. The differential equation, tangent space = Lie algebra, and one parameter groups would hook up with our approach, but Obert's way left me cold.

I smoked another joint, by now quite fucked up, and went out to find some food. I settled on a kabob and egg roll with beer at the nearest Takee-Outee and wolfed it down on the way back.

I didn't remember falling asleep but I woke up standing on a machine-quaking mound of sand vibrating an endless stream of waves, each grain a wave colliding with other grains training in original form in new phase, a mountain of solitons turned liquid and I slipping inside and towards the pit, the maw. I sat up and reached for a grip on the sky, clammy with sweat and shaking.

"Son of a bitch."

Son of a bitch. Oberst would know all that fucking geometry. Who was I kidding? He would know all that shit. He might even know a lot of the PDE shit. What he wouldn't know, probably, was the stochastic processes and for sure the stochastic differential equations (SDEs) and stochastic integrals. I lit up a joint and shuffled off to make a cup of instant coffee before the shit-shower-shave routine.

Forgoing my leisurely buzzed ride uptown on the streetcar, I grabbed the Freret Street bus and got there in half the time, approaching the math building from behind. I'd left early enough to spend time in the library looking up a proof of Ado's theorem. Two hours before I had to teach, no seminars this week, and I considered skipping the only class I took this term. But I'd missed the previous week. Not polite, not politically correct. It was acceptable to not do shit, not pay any attention, but it was bad form to make it obvious.

The department occupied the top floor of the building, the second floor. The first floor was admin, and there was a basement, a scary idea in flood-prone New Orleans where they had to pump water from every hole they dug, though it only appeared to be underground from the back.

The library filled a large room at the end of a wide corridor paneled in dark wood that split the top of the massive stone building across its considerable width. Like all the reasonable libraries at Tulane, it belonged to the department and stayed off limits to undergraduates without permission from a professor. I had seen the university's main library, devoid of anything of much substance for undergraduate use but with a damned fine collection of ancient texts, including some Lewis Carroll.

Professor Momus waylaid me before I could make it. I could tell he was a bit lit up, but not like I was. He wanted to chat, saying he looked forward to my exam, that he loved the *Malleus Maleficarum,* had missed his historical period, would have been a masterful grand inquisitor.

Shit, he was coming to my orals; I prayed he'd be the only representative from the several complex variables group. Those fuckers knew differential geometry. The Denjoy integral, the only question on the analysis written exam I didn't know squat about, I'd been assured was his doing. He made certain it stayed on the syllabus though he was likely the only person in the department who knew shit about it. He was going to be there Thursday.

His visible words didn't make it to my ears, dying on the way, falling to the floor and forming waves, superpositioning their wiggly asses around my feet; I might fall through the suddenly insubstantial atomic wiggles mixing with his squirming words. I remembered he'd kept me one day talking about music and religion, about Bach and Shinto, and when I tuned in again he was going on about the St. Matthew's Passion, humming for Christ's sake. I didn't want to insult him but had to get away.

"I love Bach," I said, "but more the Mass in B Minor..."

"Ah, H-Moll-Messe," he said and began speaking German, clearing his throat and then making his point in a pedantic style at odds with his roly-poly shortness, sporting above his sport coat and tie the round bulbous nose made famous by W. C. Fields. Floating above it all I saw the ludicrous image of the two of us, a panic-stricken graduate student and a W. C. Fields mathematics near-genius discussing Bach and inquisitions. "One time at Yale I recall a performance in the..." and I tuned out again and when I came back it was "...in Dusseldorf at the university as a visiting faculty member for a year the famous..." and I dropped out again. He liked to tell about having Gian-Carlo Rota as an undergrad at Yale, of Rota solving an unsolved problem he'd stuck on a final exam in topology.

One of the secretaries, Joelle, came out of the department office set off the middle of the long somber corridor and called him, "Professor Momus, can I have a minute please?" and he smiled, "See you Thursday afternoon," waddling off with a fat-man gait.

I ducked inside the library and picked up Jacobson's *Lie Algebras.* The statement of Ado's theorem read that every finite-dimensional Lie algebra with characteristic zero had a faithful finite-dimensional representation. I didn't know what the hell a faithful representation was. The index didn't have a listing for faithful, either alone or under representation, so I went to the basic definition for representation. It seemed it was a homomorphism into the linear algebra of homorphisms of a vector space, in other words into the general linear group. Faithful meant it was an isomorphism of the space, so a faithful representation was a one-to-one homomorphism into the general linear group, that is, a mono-morphism.

All this intricate instrumentation came off as beating around the fucking bush, though I knew better. It pissed me off anyway. I wanted a joint but would have to settle for a hash-laced cigarette before I taught my class. For now I had to buckle down and glean the idea of the proof.

Leading up to it four lemmas and a theorem. The set-up included a new piece of machinery, a universal enveloping algebra. I seemed to recall Oberst bringing them up in his class, but it hadn't stuck. It'd been in his notes and I'd skipped over it. Now here, waiting in ambush. Along with solvable ideals tied to a direct sum representation related to the kernel of an adjoint representation came some stuff about nilpotent ideals of finite co-dimension invariant under derivation. I'd not considered so damned much heavy equipment, but decided to push on.

Jacobson had a chapter on universal algebras in his book; they turned out to be nothing more than a giant algebraic object allowing the fill-in of a leg of the standard commutative diagram triangle. Big deal. Probably some kind of tensor algebra. But the chapter went on and on, leading into the Campbell-Hausdorff Theorem, leaving out old Baker whoever the hell he was. A new twist on this formula for the product of exponentials in the algebra, obtained by extending some free algebra generated by some finite set to an algebra of power series in the set. And suddenly section six:

Cohomology of Lie algebras. The standard complex

It was just too goddamn much. The big picture began to crumble into a heap of algebraic enginery far from the local one-parameter groups I needed for the PDEs, far from the geometry of manifolds and connections, deep in the Cartan-Eilenberg world of abstract nonsense I'd been warned would rear its ugly head in several complex variables with the famous Theorems A and B. But not here. I'd not expected it here, though I should have.

A mountain of debris rose up as I thumbed through, looking in vain for smoothness conditions and charts, finally coming upon derivations and the Killing form. More algebraic appliances.

I shut the book and left the library.

Outside in the humid New Orleans beginning of an afternoon I smoked a hashish-laced cigarette and let the whole thing deflate. Too late for all that shit. I needn't compound the plethora of heavy equipment with more contraptions, more isolated conceptual constructions of great beauty and complexity. It would be for better men than I to tie them together, find the cat walks or rope bridges linking one to the other. I hadn't time or inclination now, so close to the exam, to walk those dizzying heights, finding out who had already built the enveloping equipment, whether by rope or even more humongous mechanisms of the mind.

Humbled, my machination fell apart. If asked about proof of Ado's theorem, I'd shrug my shoulders and say I'd looked at one, but hadn't the machinery to grasp the essentials.

Chapter 3
Centering: Expectation Zero

There existed one advantage to teaching the only session of elementary statistics. Unlike multi-session classes like calculus marching lock-step to a fixed curriculum towards a joint mid-term and final exam written and graded and curved by the whole teaching team, I got to write the two exams myself. That made the dull content worth dishing up.

In every undergraduate math class, text and paced syllabus came down by decree. No one teaching them had wiggle room in dispensing grades. Ninety percent was determined by the final, the other ten percent from the mid-term. No credit for homework and no "extra credit." Merciless not only for students; those teaching multiple sessions had their students' performance compared publicly. As if a genetic precondition, the same faculty year after year drew the stupid students like bugs to a light.

The room assigned me for this statistics class occupied an outer and back portion of Tilton Hall, ancient stone monstrosity facing St. Charles Avenue and Audubon Park removed scant steps from grander monstrosity Gibson Hall on the top floor of which resided the mathematics department. Unlike the math building, the roof of Tilton Hall leaked, forming a waterfall in the center of the room during the frequent short but violent downpours. No matter how hard I tried, it proved impossible to change rooms or get the roof fixed, as though planned as a test of my concentration. I never missed a beat as the class listened for the sound of rain so students could regroup around the sudden cataract.

I entered without book or notes as usual, still feeling the hash buzz, and stood waiting for exact time. Forty students enrolled, but only thirty or so ever showed up for class, the same ones modulo an occasional attendee, and they sat silent to whispering. Because attendance didn't affect grade, some decided they'd pick up the requisite information before the final; athletes in particular decided their tutors and athletic department pressure would get them through. But I harbored fun little tricks to play, questions like Explain why a random variable minus its expectation has expectation zero.

Right up front sat the class hotty, a cheerleader type with button nose and hair of spun gold pulled back in a bouncy ponytail. Innocently, it seemed, displaying compact, connected legs, wearing expensive-looking leather mules that accentuated developed calf muscles when she walked.

The first day of class she'd approached me saying she never did well in math but she needed to learn this material and to pass the course. I looked into clear blue eyes and saw someone who believed in truth, fidelity, Jesus and the American dream. Someone who would someday transform into a suburban mother of children; her round, high ass spread wide and hanging cellulite-cratered over thighs gone to gobs of more cellulite; those well-contained breasts now protruding like rounded hills hinting at perky nipples, submitting to gravity after duty as feeding bags, sagging flat against a thickened trunk and gone to wrinkled dugs with the release of the Cooper's ligament. I shuddered at the vision of elongated, chewed nipples on the ends of those two future sacks. But for now, tight calves and firm thighs bounding with potential energy for cheering leaps, displayed in short skirts, distracted. And she would always have her button nose, no matter how its base contorted with wrinkles.

Professional to the end, I told her if she attended all the classes, paid attention and took notes, read the text and did all the assignments, asked questions when she didn't understand, she'd do fine. She became a devotee, regular, diligent with questions about homework and my oft obscure lectures that distorted the incomprehensible text.

At the bell I began without hesitation, hitting the material on the syllabus regardless of whether Red had gotten that far or not. I plowed through variance and standard deviation, explaining carefully why one squared the difference between the random variable and its expectation. I labored over it, making sure they understood that the expectation of the expectation equaled the expectation, talking about moving the origin of a distribution of mass to its center to get a new random variable centered at zero but with the same spread. I told them I would ask on the final that they explain why this expected difference between a random variable and its expected value was always zero, one of the questions separating As from Bs.

I made a joke about the standard deviation as understood in my neighborhood without actually uttering the word fellatio and wondered how many of the blank faces busily writing in their notebooks understood what the hell I meant. One girl sitting in back of the class, a brunette I found devoid of physical charm who always waited around after class asking questions and trying to chat me up about the Quarter, smiled at the reference.

As the rest of them shot out the door at the closing bell, she hung back, then called to me as I made a break for it as well.

"Mr. Butcher?"

I turned to find her standing close behind me and re-examined her carefully, part of my project to classify female form and its relationship to my own sexual attraction.

No makeup. Thick brown hair that looked black until up close, pulled back into a short, bunched bobtail with a strand hanging free down the right side of her face. Brown eyes, round and unexceptional, set wide apart above a rounded nose with tiny nostrils perched at the end of an extended, straight, broad bridge. Her mouth drew a line minus the usual hint of a smile that differed from this look only by some miniscule turning up of the ends of unadorned lips, the upper full for a longer expanse than the lower but neither exceptionally thick nor thin nor long. A straight face tapered slightly just beyond the mouth to an abrupt finish in a round, fleshy chin, discordant counter to a high forehead and otherwise longish face. I decided her full cheeks gave the impression of a cylindrical face, when in reality at the eye sockets the swoop towards the chin would have been more pronounced without them. But her brows, dark and thick, ragged, preceded the rest of her features, stark against pallid epidermal canvas.

"Yes, Miss Cone."

"I heard your mother died. They said it was why you were gone last week."

She wore small silver hoops hanging from elfish lobules bottoming the pronounced round helix of the outer ear.

"It's true."

"I'm sorry. Are you alright?"

The slight frown turned to a pout which I assumed to be an attempt at a more pronounced frown. It almost charmed, better than the smile she usually presented.

"I'm fine. Her death was for the best; she was riddled with cancer."

"That's terrible."

"Well, there are not many deaths I consider lovely. But hers was possibly on the far side of bad, though of course there were atrocities committed in World War II that rivaled it. Are you aware that the Balkan fascists decapitated with hand saws?"

She stared, trying to look wide-eyed, but it was an impossibility.

"I had a question about the standard deviation," she said. "Your substitute got to it in the last session and said it was not as good a measurement in some ways as using the median."

33

"Well, we might get into that a bit later. It turns out that the expected value minimizes the variance, while the median minimizes another dispersion measure, the absolute mean deviation. But median and mean are the same for symmetric distributions, though these two dispersion measures are not."

"Oh," she said.

"Averages accentuate outliers, something medians avoid in sampling statistics. I might say something about it when we get to sampling. But don't worry, we won't bother with this median stuff on the test."

"Can you tell me some good places to visit in the Quarter?"

"What are you looking for?"

"A not too expensive place to have a drink with a friend, get some food, like a sandwich."

"Try the Napoleon House. They have draft beer and they serve good sandwiches, a fair mufalletta, not like Central, but good and also decent Pastrami, similar to the one at Maspero's. It isn't so bustling as Maspero's; they play classical music on a record player with the only rule being the record must finish before it is changed, and they make a decent drink called a Pimm's Cup. Try that."

"What's Maspero's?"

"An old slave exchange, they say, so they call it Maspero's Slave Exchange. Sandwich place, but a little too in and out for my taste; they have a lot of hippy waitresses. If you just want to eat and then go, it's okay, but I prefer The Napoleon House. You might try Mollie's Irish Pub if you're out drinking late. They're open twenty-four hours a day, seven days a week, and close only on Fat Tuesday at midnight for a few hours. The bartender Sam is a good person if you're in trouble. He's black and bigger than me and gallant; he will see to it you get out of danger and into a cab."

"Fat Tuesday? What's that?"

"My, you are uninformed. That is Mardi Gras day."

"Well, I wish I knew more. I don't have anyone to guide me. It's my first year."

The pensive hint of melancholic smile she often wore when amused began to play around the edges of her mouth; abruptly it bounced into a broad grin that pooched her cheeks and exposed a hidden dimple centered halfway between lower lip and the boundary line of chin. A pair of wrinkles at the ends of her mouth offset the cheeks and would have made the whole thing appear to be a smirk were it not for the literality emitted from her eyes.

"Where do you live in the Quarter?" she asked.

"On Bourbon Street, past the commercial district, the first block where the night-time traffic barricades end. It's the eight hundred block, near Lafitte's in Exile."

"What's that?"

"A gay bar. I live in the heart of the gay section."

The smile faded and she backed away enough for me to appraise her body without being obvious. Her usual attire: long black skirt hiding her shape below the waist; ribbed boat-necked blouse outside the skirt like a tunic accentuating heavy breasts well constrained within a bra, and also a bit of midriff roll. Turned down collar surrounding the neck line. I had not seen her wear anything but long skirts that hid her ass and legs, thick-soled brown loafers, and blouses that showed off her tits.

"I need to go study," I said. "I have my oral exams this week. But this is one of my office hours, so if you have more questions tag along. I have a class next hour."

"No, I don't have more questions," she said, still hanging back and giving me a serious once over.

"Have fun in the Quarter, but be careful. It can be dangerous. It attracts creeps."

I turned and left the room. She didn't walk out with me this time.

Having grown up in Las Vegas where there'd been ads with photos of showgirls in the newspaper, creatures I later ran across on the strip in apartment buildings sunbathing topless, it became a personal code of honor to avoid outside influence from magazines, advertising and other commercial sources pimping what to find sexy. This showed up in Asia. My comrades in arms, brainwashed with the *Playboy* model of feminine charm, ached for round-eyed women with heavy tits, skinny asses and hams for thighs, not exploring their unbiased reactions to what centuries of local cultural preferences had filtered into existence. I let sexuality happen of its own accord, not by some book, and found charm in many of the Vietnamese women, though they aged into crones far earlier than US women. It seemed they loved my fairness, a blue eyed towhead. The Japanese I found less appealing, but I still had a fling during my short stay, not something so simple in Vietnam where everything off-base was off-limits. But that changed when I got to the CAP unit.

I caught Red in his carrel with sandaled feet up on the desk reading *The Wall Street Journal.* He wore his brown hair in a pony tail and never shaved or trimmed his red beard. His brown eyes lit up when he laughed, and he laughed a lot. Lean and wiry, he looked as if he could put up a decent fight, but I'd never seen him make any sort of threatening moves toward anyone. I assumed he would make such a move only if necessary, without warning. Despite his friendly demeanor, disarming smile and infectious laugh, he had come out of a tough environment, a big northern city, had been busted for selling drugs in high school, obtained a GED while in reform school and once out gone to Mexico to live and work the import angle for a group of entrepreneurs. One of his projects was growing magic mushrooms and he tried to get to the city of the priestess Maria Sabrina without success because the Mexican police blocked the undesirables, mostly hippies, after Gordon Wasson made her famous. He'd eaten plenty of mushrooms down there but couldn't grow them artificially, not even the mycelium, all of it expiring when exported, and the whole thing had been a bust. Now during the rainy season he ventured out into the countryside to collect cow paddies, plopping them onto a table in his living room where they sprouted the blue-staining *Psilocybe cubensis.*

He looked up through tiny round lenses perched on the end of his nose. "Hey, Whitey. Thought you'd call when you got in."

"I hung out for a day with Lori, then studied. Got that fucking exam."

"There are notices all over the department. By the way, you got some babes in that class of yours."

"Think so? I hadn't noticed. Look, I'm done studying for this exam. If I don't know it by now, I'm dead meat anyway. You want to get together for a bit after class?"

"Uhmmm, I guess that'd work. I told Lynette we'd go to a flick tonight, but she has class until late, so we'll go to the late show."

"What're you gonna see?"

"I think maybe *The Man Who Would be King.* Huston. Why don't you come along?"

"Maybe. I'm a bit concerned about money. These trips cost me a bundle in plane fares, all on my credit card."

He went back to his newspaper and I sat in my carrel and worked on a preprint of a paper my advisor had given me on infinite sequences of conversation laws for certain partial differential equations, specifically evolution equations. My advisor seemed particularly excited about the Korteweg-DeVries equation for reasons I had yet to ascertain. This was where he seemed headed in his research and he wanted me to do something with it. I had other ideas, but decided it might lead to a quick topic. He'd be a visiting faculty in Britain next year, with the possibility of time in Russia at Moscow University where there was a guy with students doing research on conservation laws for PDEs, though from what I saw it was peppered with damned heavy machinery from differential geometry and cohomology, shit my advisor avoided. His coming year away was why we'd rushed to get the orals done. I'd be on my own, and it suited me. I'd have time to look into stuff I wanted to look into without the blinders he forced me to wear.

The tall black secretary came in asking for me. I judged her height at five ten, five eleven or so, since the top of her head came up to about my eye level. I'd learned to judge height by this measure, and she was about four, five inches shorter. With women heels made it a problem, but she didn't wear any, only flats. Her chocolate skin dappled with light brown freckles made her sexy as hell, not to mention almond eyes and a round ass that smiled even when she wore skirts. No grimace in that ass, none at all. And a healthy set of tits she kept as covered as possible. Married and faithful, they said. Not that it mattered. Women are like streetcars; if you miss one, another'll be along.

I stood to greet her. She liked me; I could see it in her eyes.

From her mouth a tailing laughter of words floated to my ears. "Mr. Butcher, there is a woman on the telephone wanting to talk to you."

She had the New Orleans' lilt in her voice; not like the ragged Irish channel accent that reminded me of guys I'd met in the Corps from Brooklyn or the obnoxious yat that I found grew more pronounced when a gaggle of natives yammered together, nor the garbled marbles-in-the-mouth roll one found in the Creole women of color, those plush orange-tan to milk-chocolates with honeyed lips and giant round eyes given to corpulence with age and difficult to approach when young and ripe.

"Mizz Dupre, I don't know any women in this city. None at all."

"Well, can you come on down to the office and tell *her* that. Oh, and Joelle and I are sorry about your mother."

I almost said she'd had it coming but held back.

I picked up the phone on Mrs. Dupre's desk.

"Butcher here."

A woman's voice I didn't recognize.

"Manly," she said, a name I eschewed, wondering why the hell a bunch of drunken Welsh immigrants would persist in handing out such a handle in the New World, "it's Bobbi."

When I didn't respond, she added, "From the student legal aid office."

The social worker who'd helped me gain access to the athlete's gym, among other perks, not to mention some extra money from the state, all for my disability. Not a friendly sort, so calling me had to have some motive I would likely not find pleasant.

"Miss Lowe. I recognized your voice. Just a little dazed right now."

"Of course. I'm sorry about your mother." All icy professionalism on her end. "There are some people having a little dinner at Commander's Palace tonight and I wonder if you might come along. I think you'd like them, assuming you can spare the time. I know your exams are coming up."

"How did you know about that? Those exams are inside the math department."

"I have my sources, Mr. Butcher."

I played along, unable to tell if she was putting me on. Her invitation carried no warmth.

"I'm done preparing for the exam, other than trying to stay sober. But I really am a bit short right now, financially that is. The trip out to Arizona wiped me out, put me in debt in fact. And Commander's Palace is a bit rich for my blood in any case."

"You'll be my date. I pay. Is that a problem?"

"Not if I can repay you later, but at a place I choose."

"Then you'll come?"

"Sure. What time and what do I wear? I don't have a tie."

"It is required, but I think they can give you one at the door. But you need a jacket."

"What kind of jacket?"

I noticed Joelle, Mrs. Dupre's partner in the office who had earlier saved me from Momus, smiling at her desk as she eavesdropped.

"A sport coat."

"Don't have one of those. Got a hooded sweat jacket, black leather jacket and tan leather baseball jacket."

"You don't dress up much, do you?"

"Not if I can help it. But the black leather jacket does have a collar. It was an expensive gift from the rehab institute in Kansas City when I graduated from college."

"Wear that, then. I know you have khaki pants. Wear those and a plain shirt with a collar you won't mind draping a tie on."

"Okay. Now what time?"

"Eight. Do you want to meet us there?"

"Sure. I can take the streetcar."

"No, I'll pick you up. Between seven thirty and quarter to eight. But please, wait downstairs. I hate to stop in your neighborhood."

"Okay. I know it's a hassle. I'll be down there at seven thirty."

As I cradled the phone, Mrs. Dupre said in a mocking tone, "Don't know any women, huh? I'll bet you got them lined up."

Joelle said nothing, just continued smiling down at her desk. Called herself a Creole, with skin like porcelain and luscious mouth like a red flower in bloom, gently contoured full face partially covered by falling straight black hair; her black-rimmed doe eyes reminded me of my first real lover's eyes. She'd been of Italian descent and big trouble in the end, but those eyes my father had called bedroom eyes captured me the moment I looked in them. Joelle had them.

"No, its business."

"At Commander's Palace?" Joelle asked.

"Monkey business," Mrs. Dupre added.

"I don't get involved in that sort of thing. I'm gay. Remember?"

Mrs. Dupre shot me an arched eyebrow smirk and Joelle shook her head. I thanked them and returned to the carrels, where I told Red I wouldn't be able to make it tonight after all.

"What's up?"

"I got a date. Commander's Palace."

"Wow. That's pricey. Thought you said you were broke."

"I'm the date, so it's on her."

"Sweet. Now you're a gigolo."

"It seems."

I grabbed my notebook and went off to class at the end of the hall, my advisor lecturing on symmetry groups, conservation laws and PDEs, a lot of it explicating the stuff by a guy from the University of Minnesota who'd written the paper I'd stared at in my carrel. My advisor would be overseas next year working with this guy who had an appointment at Cambridge, maybe do seminars in the Soviet Union. I'd looked at some of this guy's papers and wasn't all that impressed, but I didn't know shit. I found more interesting some of the stuff the Frenchman visiting from Stanford presented in his seminar, but I didn't say it aloud.

After class I spent an hour and a half at the gym. I had developed a routine at the VA hospital I kept faithfully. Nothing heavy. Worked up to bench pressing four hundred pounds at one time, but I now did repetitions of two-fifty, sometimes three hundred. Some meathead had tried to convince me I needed to do three times my body weight, but the idea of bench pressing five hundred twenty five pounds sounded stupid.

I worked out three times a week: chest with bench press and incline press; back, shoulders and arms; and on the longest, slowest, excruciating day I worked legs, carefully, to strengthen and stretch the bad one. That had been the real feat, getting that developed; when I started at the VA I could barely walk, but now I could do an easy two miles or so without limping, assuming I didn't cramp it too long, like sitting on a goddamn airplane. Running for the most part was out of the question, but that was what had gotten me into the athlete's gym: they had the only new-fangled no-impact aerobic equipment.

Chapter 4
Geodesic Balls

The only shirt with a collar I owned happened to be so hideous even I noticed. Cut square with a wavering approximation to a flat bottom, it hung unevenly outside my trousers and when tucked in wrinkled in giant rills running all the way up the back and sides. Fortunately, no one noticed because the pattern drew all eyes: small red and white checks like a tablecloth in an Italian restaurant. It had been a gift from a woman.

I put it on and went downstairs to wait at the mouth of the bricked tunnel of a passageway, watching through the gate, wondering what sort of car she drove. I'd neglected to ask. The warm evening precluded wearing the leather jacket I cradled in my arms which anyway clashed with the only presentable shoes I owned, a pair of tan Red Wing half-boots with white wedge soles for walking on concrete. The counselors at the Rehab Institute in Kansas City always laughed when I dressed up, saying I looked like a refugee.

The parade of men cruising past the gate played like an infinite loop from a Fellini film, men in drag wearing dresses, beards and makeup, tough guys in leathers kissing on the mouth, walking arm in arm to disco blasted from both ends of the block culminating in a crescendo of interfering and commingling waves near the center. I avoided Bourbon at night, dodging the crowd by heading away from it all, shooting out the gate and down Dumaine. Sometimes I got whistles from Lafitte's balcony, but no one ever laid a hand on me.

I tried to recall what Bobbi looked like. I hadn't studied her nor gauged my reaction to her; experience taught to lay off those helping me, to stare at the eyes and avoid impure thoughts. This realization came first with nurses and later therapists; it made sense, like not fucking your students or tangling with authority. Keep a distance.

Anyway, she'd broken the pattern and I wondered why. I might find out. A white Toyota pulled into the bus stop across the street, a raven-tressed brunette at the wheel. I hesitated before wading through the parade to her car, not recalling her hair so dark.

"Miss Lowe?"

"Yes. I did my hair," she said.

It came to me as I ducked into the passenger side: mousy brown. The new glimmering metallic sheen did nothing to soften the edges on her, but she'd done something else, some partial curl or maybe the remnants of a fallen curl job. It seemed fuller than the thin stuff I remembered hanging limp to her shoulders, now fluffed out or teased and bisected with a long tress of unraveling ringlets tumbling down the back of her neck.

She didn't show shock at my dress, but she didn't tell me I looked nice either. She concentrated piloting Bourbon to Esplanade where she turned left out of the Quarter and left again onto Rampart, following a path unknown to me, not on the public transportation routes I rode.

I studied her profile without a hint of stealth. Pronounced chin with centered dimple ending a long, narrow face, cheeks that softened it somewhat, but not so much as the fall of relaxed curls. A forehead that would seem high on other faces that she didn't bother to cover with bangs, the hair flowing from one side of her head to the other smoothly without parting, burying her ears. Thin dark brows, maybe colored, dark eyes not set too far apart with the straight, narrow bridge of her nose beginning dead center between them, ramping at a noticeable angle to end with flared nostrils. Thin lips, small mouth, the upper lip contoured like an arc from an ellipse of high eccentricity, the lower lip straight. White teeth not showing much even when she smiled, which seemed to be an effort for her.

She didn't flinch under my scrutiny; in fact, she turned her head this way and that to give me a wider platform, all in a performance of driving. Her swan-slender neck arced when she looked around and behind and over her shoulder, elegant like a snake. Her blouse and skirt didn't give away much except legs a tad removed from skinny, though in the car it wasn't certain. Gripping the steering wheel were oversized man hands.

Once uptown on St. Charles Avenue and away from Rampart which I think she assumed dangerous, a good idea since it marked the demarcation line between the white Vieux Carré and a free fire zone in one of the notorious black projects, or as I called them, the reservations, she turned to me and said we were dining with two of her closest friends.

"Why'd you ask me?"

"It was short notice, this invitation, and I wanted someone to balance things. Two couples make it more comfortable. I thought you'd be an interesting companion and it would be good for you to know these people."

"Well, sorry I don't have a more presentable wardrobe. Not many consider me a balancing factor."

"It's part of your charm. They'll find you fascinating. He teaches anthropology at Loyola. She has an MPA and runs a private agency for the state.

42

But neither of them needs to work; he inherited a massive sum of money and a small business empire."

"That must be a nice feeling."

"I wouldn't know. I doubt the two of us together would be able to afford what this dinner is going to set him back."

"You could leave me out of that equation and get the same result."

We pulled up in front of the restaurant and left the car to the attendant, following the walkway to the striped awning beneath the corner cupola. Inside bold walls in red or yellow, here and there murals in an Asian motif, easy to believe a much-remodeled ante-bellum relic of the nineteenth century.

Bobbi spotted the host couple waiting at a large round table covered with a spotless white tablecloth, two napkins like half opened fans at the yet unoccupied place settings. We glided past the hostess for the table. They rose to greet us as we approached. Balding, short and dumpy, as wide as tall, he wore sparsely distributed dark hair in disarray, a post five-o'clock shadow across his lower face, and a bristly graying mustache along his entire upper lip. His tiny drab eyes almost made me laugh; I imagined a cigar planted firmly in his broad mouth which ought to have been grinning but instead held the firm line I'd noted as we'd entered the room.

One look at her convinced me they were well paired. Shorter than he, likely five foot or less, long of face, her high forehead was topped by straight hair the color of straw and texture of string hanging from a ragged part atop her head to just below her shoulders. If not for the length of chin that veered sharply to end in a vee, her face from eyes down would have been no longer than her forehead. Painted brilliant red, her mouth made me think of a wound. A bulb of a nose perched off-center at the end of an extended bridge with a crook. She wore elongated rectangular rimless glasses from which peered two startling blue crystals dancing in the light, narrow eyes set close together and deep in her skull as if huddling in fear. Her brows, colored exactly as her hair, appeared to grow wide out the top of her nose bridge along the upper edge of her eye sockets; where sockets ended, the brows abruptly narrowed to pencil thin, sloped downward and continued along the curvature of her skull to disappear where I assumed ears hid beneath hair.

"Gudrun and Jeremy Ball," Bobbi said, sweeping the air between us with her right hand, "meet Manly Butcher."

Unlike Jeremy, Gudrun swapped the serious mouth for a smile. With the transformation the wide hollow from her nose to her upper lip presented the illusion of narrowing, the thin line of upper lip drawn like a stylized bird flying at a distance morphed into a dip-winged crow flapping on the down stroke, a threat of teeth leering sudden and sharp as the line of mouth opened and the lower lip grew from quiet pout to leering fold of red meat.

I shook her dainty hand and then his fat, hairy hand. He had a strong grip.

"Bobbi's told us a lot about you," she said.

I wondered what she had to tell anyone about me, someone she mostly knew from scant records.

"Well, I hope it's good," I replied I hoped cordially.

"Excuse me, sir," a man in a tuxedo approaching from behind, "you need to wear your jacket and put this on." He handed me a skinny green tie.

"Is that strictly necessary, Maurice?" Jeremy asked. His gruff voice suited his appearance.

"Just the tie, then," Maurice said, and Jeremy removed his own suit jacket, leaving only the vest. It looked like an expensive outfit to me, gray wool with a nubby texture.

"Let me help with that," Gudrun said, trying to fasten the top button, an impossibility on the scant collar. She flipped it up and draped the tie around my neck, then tied it so the collar pretended to be closed.

Jeremy laughed, saying at least it wasn't a clip-on, and Bobbi muttered something about at least choosing a color that didn't clash, but with khaki work slacks, white-soled tan chukka boots, red check shirt and skinny green tie it likely appeared the refugee had disguised himself as a Christmas decoration.

Mostly I noticed Gudrun leaning into me, pressing a pair of heavy breasts against me as she worked on the tie, breasts secreted beneath the loose jacket of the cream skirt suit she wore.

The Balls had started on cocktails but ordered a second round, some fancy drinks with champagne for the women, he drinking an old-fashioned. I ordered whiskey straight up. The waiter asked if I wished single malt and I flashed a puzzled look, so he said, "Bourbon or Scotch, sir?" I apologized, saying I had meant Bourbon, and he asked if Maker's Mark would be acceptable. I didn't know it, but said fine.

That done, I addressed the table. "Please," I said, looking at everyone before settling my eyes on Bobbi, "don't call me Manly. Anything else is preferable. My middle name is Edward, and you can use that or Ed. But mostly people call me Whitey. That's what I prefer to go by."

"There was a British poet—"

44

I cut him off. "Yes, Gerard Manley Hopkins. I have been told. He spelled it with an *e y,* and I think that in fact it might even have been hyphenated with Hopkins. At least I've seen it that way."

"Why did they name you that?" Gudrun asked. "Your family fond of poetry?"

"My family can barely read. The name's a family tradition for the first born. I think I'll break it. Manly is bad enough, but paired with Butcher is too much."

We sat and perused the menus, slender quarto folios bound in leather, several pages of stuff I'd never heard of. Meat sounded good to me, but the menu disguised it. There were two relatively straightforward options, one of them Grilled Veal Chop Tchoupitoulas, served with grits and some kind of goat cheese. I knew Tchoupitoulas, the street, from a few visits to Rosy's to listen to jazz. She brought in great people. I'd heard Diz there, Mose Allison, Sonny Rollins. However that couldn't push me past the goat cheese grits. I'd also located a Filet Mignon that didn't seem too out of the ordinary except for the buttermilk mashed potatoes. The only other land animal I recognized was duck, and that was not in the cards.

The discussion went around the table with everyone offering me advice. People dressed in white hovered submerged in the ambient background, commanded apparently by the man in black, Maurice, who had given me the skinny green tie.

"The redfish looks good."

"I think I prefer meat."

"That veal chop is really a variation on grits and grillades."

"What about that goat cheese? Is that strong? Never had goat cheese. I'm leaning to the filet." I didn't ask what the fuck were grillades.

"Not all that interesting, really. Trust me. Try the veal."

"Have the turtle soup as an appetizer. It's a classic here."

"Or the shrimp remoulade; that's also good here."

"I didn't realize anyone but South Sea islanders ate turtle."

"Turtle's good."

I opted for the turtle and veal. The prices astounded me. I'd eaten at a couple steak houses in Kansas City, one downtown and my favorite, the Plaza III, where I'd been a couple times for the prime rib. But neither of those places cost like this one. I was pretty sure dinner would have maxed my credit limit.

They brought wine, a bottle of yellow and a bottle of red. The yellow wore a plain white label: Grand Vin de Chassagne-Montrachet. Morgeot. The red sported a castle or rook or tower starkly drawn with bricks and an arched entrance, a lion atop curling an extravagant tail: Grand Vin de Chateau Latour. Maurice made a big show of placing the corks in front of Mr. Ball, who smelled the red, swirled a little in his bigger glass, and tasted it. He nodded his head and passed the other cork to Gudrun who followed the same ritual in approving the yellow. Meantime, white-suited minions placed a stand supporting a bucket of ice beside the table and the yellow ended up there, the red delegated to a folding stand to "breathe," as Maurice put it before gliding away.

"Try the white with your turtle soup, Whitey," Mr. Ball suggested. "We'll switch to the red for your entrée. The white is mostly for the girls anyway."

We toasted and began the appetizers. I found the soup sweet and otherwise tasteless, the chunks of meat chewy. I ate a few bites and tasted the yellow stuff.

"Bobbi tells us you served in Vietnam," Gudrun said. "A war hero."

I looked over at Bobbi who showed a deadpan expression.

"Not such a hero," I said.

"Does it bother you to talk about it?" Gudrun continued, and her husband broke in, "Don't you know that going to war like that can cause deep psychological scars, wounds that last a lifetime?"

"To be perfectly honest, Jeremy, it was mentally safer than living with my mother. She was nuts, a flipped out Jehovah's Witness. I always thought it was the shocks of her life that did it to her. She was born in Brazil, said her father died when she was a kid, next to the youngest of twelve or fifteen or some huge brood, said that someone took their land away and the family had to return to Spain, that was in the thirties, the Spanish civil war forced them to North Africa where she met my dad. They married, I think her escape, and she ends up alone with his nutty family out in Nebraska waiting for him to get out. He gets out and they immediately book it for San Diego, putting significant distance between themselves and my Dad's family; she never sees her own family again. Ever. But then she seemed to hate all of them except her younger sister and her mother; I think her oldest brother beat her up once for seeing my dad. Anyway, she flips out around the time I'm twelve or so, living in Las Vegas then, becomes this fanatical Jehovah's Witness. I was lucky to escape to Vietnam. My brother, four years younger, and my sister a decade younger, end up trapped and come out twisted as hell. She's just died and now that little pod of aliens living way too close together will unravel."

"How interesting," Gudrun said. "Where does your father live?"

46

"He lives in Arizona; Coolidge, a suburb of a back road bump named Florence, home to the state prison, near Casa Grande. Between Phoenix and Tucson. Awful place. My sister and brother both live in Reno, but it's a dangerous set up. She and my brother are married to brother and sister, and her husband is my brother's best friend. My parents essentially coerced her to drop out of high school and marry at sixteen."

Gudrun again. "Why?"

"Her hormones had kicked in. She got horny and interested in boys. They needed to keep her from sinning. Don't you know the end is near? Millions now living will never die. Under such conditions, who needs school?"

The artfully arranged entrees arrived, borne aloft by the white-suited minions who immediately stood down behind us while their tuxedoed CO hovered. Mounds of steaming food that seemed surreal to me awaited our attack. It didn't take long to find veal dull. The grits were awful, a disgusting texture like cream of wheat or oatmeal, and the cheese had no flavor at all, likely a blessing, only adding to the glop. As in the Marine Corps, I tried to make myself eat. Take all you want; eat all you take.

"But yes, Gudrun, it does bother me to talk about it. There are blank spaces in my memory. I remember I was shot up, and I remember lying in a hole in the mud though it wasn't raining, and I remember shooting at some shadows with a dead corpsman's forty-five. Mostly I remember waiting for another hail of grenades, thinking I was a dead man. It sucked."

It was as if I had shit on the table. No one said a damned thing. I tried to salvage the situation.

"I must have passed out because the next thing I remember is waking up in a bed at a Navy hospital in Danang. And a few days later on my way to Guam. Eventually a surgical hospital in Chicago for a year, where they did some stuff with steel and what-not to keep my leg in one piece. After that, on to a rehabilitation facility in Kansas City. And to school, and here. And that's it."

Jeremy spoke up. "You like that wine?"

"It's all good. It's likely wasted on me. I'm not refined. I prefer this red to the other."

I did prefer the red wine, but neither of them were anything I'd go out of my way for. Food had never done much for me; it didn't taste without hot sauce, black pepper, salt. I thought it not a good idea to ask for Tabasco here.

"Bobbi says you had your choice of graduate schools."

"I wouldn't say that," I said, looking at Bobbi again. She ignored me, but spoke into the silence that settled.

"I said Manly had a choice of graduate schools. He was courted by some. That is not so atypical; I found it interesting for an ex-Marine."

"Please, Bobbi, I prefer Whitey."

"I like Manly. It has a ring to it," returning to eating fowl with knife and fork, an amazing feat.

"I understand you're in mathematics. Why that?" Jeremy asked.

"I discovered I don't like to read. When I was bed-bound in Guam and then Chicago I read a lot of stuff. In Chicago a volunteer at the hospital, a PhD student in literature, used to bring in books for me, mostly novels and short stories and some history. She brought me a book by Leaky, I think it was, on evolution and some other nonfiction about south sea islanders and such, which made them sound promiscuous as hell."

"Some of them were. The old time sailors learned that first hand," Jeremy said.

"I read a lot of stuff. There was nothing else to do except watch television or follow sports or read magazines. I hate television and find sports a chickenshit substitute for war. So reading books was it."

Gudrun leaned towards me. "Why mathematics? What's that got to do with reading?" She'd removed her coat and substantial cleavage showed where she'd left upper buttons undone.

I looked at her eyes, avoiding the wound of a mouth with glimpses of bare teeth. "I thought after meeting this woman I would study literature, but the professors were full of themselves and, pardon the expression, shit. Their idea of what the authors meant to say seemed to range from insipid to wrong. One professor had an idea about a short story he harped on. I brought in some writings by the author that contradicted him, and he told me the author was the last person to be trusted with an interpretation of his own work. That ended it for me. I'd gotten interested in philosophy by then anyway."

"I didn't know that there was a school in Kansas City known for either philosophy or literature," Jeremy said.

"Well, the University of Missouri at Kansas City isn't known for anything except the Linda Hall Library, but they did some stuff well at my level of ignorance. I had a professor of philosophy who was damned good. German. He'd studied with Heidegger and Husserl, I think, and maybe Jaspers too. Read Greek and Latin. Fought under Rommel as a tank commander, got captured and came to the US. Went to University of Chicago to finish his PhD."

"That's impressive," Gudrun said.

"I took a two semester history of philosophy from him. But I lost interest; it seemed all the questions these Greeks had asked turned out to be bogus anyway."

"That isn't clear," Jeremy said.

"I agree with Russell on that score. They made a lot of embarrassing mistakes leading to a lot of pointless questions and that became philosophy. Anyway, this professor agreed with me. He encouraged me to avoid philosophy. So then I had no idea what to study.

"Two things got me into math. First, I learned algebra, something I'd never studied. I figured I ought to know it. Had an acquaintance in engineering who taught me what he knew, equations and such, including quadratics. It was so simple it took just a couple brief discussions. I encountered the square root of two and I asked him what it was. He couldn't answer except to say it was the length of a diagonal in a right triangle with the sides of length one. I realized I had no idea what the notion of one meant in those terms. One rock, fine, but one inch? I got curious, and then the philosophy professor clinched it one day by talking about different sizes of infinity. Cantor's theory of transfinite numbers.

"So I went to the math teaching assistants at the school and asked one of them about the physical meaning of the square root of two. He didn't really have a good answer but sent me to a professor who had an interest in mathematical logic. Topologist of the Moore school of Texas topology as they called it. Did his PhD under R. L. Moore at UT. He taught me trigonometry in a few minutes."

"How do you do that?" Jeremy asked.

"Do what?"

"Teach trigonometry in a few minutes."

"Have a pen?"

Gudrun pulled one from her purse and I drew a representation of an orthogonal two-dimensional coordinate axis on the tablecloth, then drew a poor excuse for a circle centered at the origin.

"Let this be a circle of radius one. Call this line the x-axis," I said, indicating one axis, "and this other one y. Take a point on the circle and notice it has two coordinates," drawing one line from a point at about forty-five degrees to the x-axis, another to the y, "the first projecting straight down to the x-axis and the second to the y. The x-coordinate of that point is the cosine of the angle, the y-coordinate the sine. If you go around the entire circle and plot each axis you will get one period of the curves of the sine and the cosine, and you can see why they are periodic two pi, since the circumference of the circle is two pi. You get

49

free that cosine squared plus sine squared equals one, since they are coordinates of a point on the unit circle. The rest is trivial."

No one said anything. I didn't tell them I'd picked up calculus in a few weeks and skipped those classes, enrolled as a math major, and during the summer took a boring, elementary course in linear algebra that could have been taught in a few days and a graduate course in logic and set theory. The next year I jumped directly into analysis, abstract algebra, and a course in logic that went through Cohen's work on the continuum hypothesis and his method of forcing. Unfortunately, we used three books, Takeuti and Zaring's two volumes on set theory and Cohen's own terse monograph, mostly incomprehensible but skinny. I worked out all the details. My junior year I devoted to graduate mathematics classes: two topology classes, complex analysis, and functional analysis. Along with mechanics from the physics department and a graduate class in probability and statistics. Then I graduated with the minimum of hours.

"Anyhow, I learned all that and it required no real reading at all. Just thinking. It's all ideas, not words. So I'd go to class, listen and solve simple problems. That was it. No work."

"Did you ever find out about the square root of two?" It was Gudrun, leaning in again.

"Not really. Not physically. But it's irrelevant. And by the time I understood the trivialities that had gotten me involved in the first place, I was hooked. I lost interest in logic and pursued what is called point set topology, the so-called Texas topology."

I'd lost my audience, including Jeremy who didn't ask the obvious question: How can you express ideas without words?

I shut up. I'd learned that ordinary people find this stuff intensely boring; the more excited I'd get the more their eyes glazed over.

Gudrun kept at me.

"What about all those schools that wanted you?"

I looked to Bobbi again. "Where'd you hear that, Bobbi? Not from me."

"Your counselors at the Rehabilitation Institute I talked to. They helped me get you those gym privileges."

I shrugged. "It was no big deal. More a favor from my professor. He gave the class in point set topology using the Moore method, where you get a list of axioms and definitions and a bunch of theorems to prove from them. These were the standard stuff of Texas topology. Continua theory. There was an unsolved problem he put on there, about dendritic continua, and I noticed a pattern no one else had seen tying some topological properties to some algebraic properties. Some invariants. We didn't go far with it, but it did end up a published paper. The professor sent it to some big shots who were also Moore PhDs, Bing at UT, Mary Ellen Rudin at Wisconsin. Word got to someone at Harvard and a preprint made it to Berkeley. So a few big shots were impressed with the method I'd stumbled on and wanted me to apply and work with them. By then I'd lost interest in Texas topology. The point set stuff's a mathematical backwater, out of style, and none of those people were interested in the theorem itself, only that I'd found this different technique."

"That must have been exciting," Gudrun said, a profound declivity widening atop her blouse as she inched my way, mounded gobs of chalky flesh struggling to lop apart and gap with opposite orientation squeezed together by some hidden harness, "all that interest."

"The problem's cold climates. My leg can't take cold. I learned that in Chicago and Kansas City. I need warm. Besides, I wanted a small graduate school. Someone told me at Berkeley grad students might not be able to see their professors except by appointment, and I like informal access. Texas didn't appeal at all. Never met a Texan in the Corps I liked or respected. Tulane seemed a good place, small and…"

I paused, searching for a word, and Gudrun leaned close, our eyes locking. "Intimate," she said. "Not to mention New Orleans' famous food and partying. We're having a party Saturday and would like it if you'd come. Bobbi, I assume you're coming?"

"I'll try. I have a minor commitment."

"Bring him," Jeremy said.

"I'd like to come," I said. "Just tell me where and when and I'll be there. I'll try not to bore any guests to death."

"That would be an impossibility," Jeremy said. "Most of them are already beyond such a death."

After that I tried to shut up. No one needed to hear more about me, and I knew no one wanted to hear more about mathematics.

Dinner passed to dessert stage around a discussion concerning whether our diverse diet might actually cause early death. I stayed out of it. I finished the meat but left the grits which disgusted me, gelatinous with a glaze of beige cheese. Dark coffee served in what could have been small soup bowls with handles left a satisfying bitter aftertaste that wiped the memory of grits. Jeremy urged cognac on me and I had no trouble with it, sipping my way through several of them, but I passed on the bread pudding they raved about. When I saw it, lumpy sodden bread and raisins and who knew what else, I was sure it would have made me vomit. If they'd served that stuff in C-rations, the Marines would've revolted.

They finished with finger bowls. I knew what these were from experience, having drank mine in an Indian restaurant in Penang, Malaysia while on R&R. The Navy guy eating with me had busted a gut.

As Bobbi drove us back to the quarter I said, "I'd invite you up for a joint or something stronger, but I know you have to work tomorrow."

"I don't need to go to bed soon. I sleep a split shift; a few hours at night and a nap in the afternoon and I'm fine. But we need to find a place to park."

"We ought to be able to find a place easy this late on a weeknight."

I directed her down Governor Nichols off Rampart and we found a place between Burgundy and Dauphine a couple blocks from my apartment. She squeezed the little car into a small spot with a precise maneuver.

"Nice job," I said. "I never got the hang of parallel parking."

"I grew up in Boston and had to learn. It's second nature."

We approached Bourbon arm in arm, bass beat and hollering they called music intensifying, cruising men increasing from sparse to dense clots obstructing the narrow sidewalks. She released my arm and moved behind me, clinging to my hand as if afraid of cutting loose and floating off with a leather pack.

The musicless excuse for music peaked where Lafitte's crowd spilled out onto the sidewalk. The knot of men parted to let us pass. Through the gate the covered passageway muffled the noise, the crowd left behind in another world; fake miniature streetlight in the courtyard illuminating moss-grown brick underfoot, stuccoed veneer falling off the brick wall from which sprouted green ferns, the courtyard all shadows and ferns, a green-streaked white plaster statue of an armless naked female torso, a dead fountain. We trudged up the winding, creaking wooden stairway past the landlord's place, locked dark and quiet, and entered my spacious porch.

The building was a Siamese twin, its identical match on the side away from the corner adjoined by a single wall. Two separate addresses, one shared courtyard, conjoined like a three story duplex.

Bobbi leaned on the railing of one of the two windows, looking across the courtyard at six tiny apartments marked by shuttered, wide wooden doors, stacked side by side in two three story columns like a three by two array bordered by stairwells on the right, each entry in the array corresponding to an apartment in the main building.

I joined her. The slope of the ceiling made standing upright at the two windows impossible.

"Those were slave quarters," I said. "They're smaller than any studio apartment I've ever seen. Shallow. When those doors are wide open, you can see the whole damned place, just a bedroom with a kitchen off to the side."

"This is a nice place. How'd you happen on it? People must be lined up to get in here."

"Luck. When I knew I was coming I got a copy of the Times-Picayune, saw this ad and answered it. The landlord liked the sound of me, graduate student in math at Tulane; figured I'd be responsible and quiet. He got some references and let me have it."

"I like it. Brick enclosure, skylights, even the red floor. It's a solarium. You ought to get some furniture besides that table. Some comfortable chairs. Does your landlord own both buildings?"

"No, only this side. He lives downstairs, second floor. His is the best apartment of the three. Huge balcony. He owns the three slave quarters in back, too, but I don't see how anyone lives there. The damned things are like closets. The one on top attached to the other building, not his, has a huge crack in the back wall. But they're always rented."

"It's an old place. These bricks, all of it, I bet its eighteenth century."

"I'm told the planks in the floors are pretty historical, like from ships or something. It's been restored. To original description, he tells me. He has copies of the old documents from seventeen seventy something-or-other. Restored around the turn of the century. Needs a lot of upkeep, and being historical it's a bitch to get materials. Have to use original slate on the roof, for example. He's trying to get my leak fixed but it's not easy."

I opened the door and Bobbi stared into the spacious square box with fifteen foot ceilings, chandelier and an old coal fireplace the landlord, Mr. Boudreaux, told me never to use. Leaky gas space heaters served well enough in this climate, the gas never accumulating in the drafty enclosure. When he'd first shown me the place, I'd remarked you could fire a cannon from the front door all the way through the living room and the door to the bedroom and on out the window to hit the Uneeda Biscuit sign painted on the bare brick structure across Bourbon Street. He'd said, in his exaggerated nelly drawl, "You'd better not, Mr. Bouchée."

Another old coffee table, a battered couch, and a couple upholstered chairs that had seen better days furnished the living room along with a scarred table just outside the doorway to the narrow strip of afterthought that served as a kitchen. The kitchen opened onto the covered sun porch, and on the other side of the wall from the kitchen was the bathroom and after that a small utility room with a window onto the gallery overhanging Bourbon Street.

"Make yourself comfortable," I said. "I need to use the bathroom and then I'll roll a joint."

Not knowing what she had in mind made me edgy.

I brought out my stash of moderately potent weed, dark Columbian with some fat buds but nothing like the sinsemilla I kept for special occasions. Smoking a cigarette, I sat at the table, laced the pot with Nepalese opiated hash and rolled a fat spliff in newspaper, lit it and took a monster hit.

Turning to hand it to her, she'd vanished, wandered into the bedroom. I stood in the doorway and took a second hit, watching her at the foot of the bed staring at the giant mirror on the wall.

"Jesus," she said, "ever worry about that thing falling on the bed? It'd crush you." She walked up to touch the gilt frame. "What is this? A wooden frame? It's huge."

"No; see the broken piece near the bottom? Plaster."

"However did they get it up here?"

"Good question. It won't fit in those windows. I asked the landlord and he thinks they brought it up before they fixed the front wall. He says it was opened out on that end. But I doubt it."

She came over and took a hit. "That's a huge joint," she croaked as she released the smoke.

"Jamaican style, according to a friend of mine who lived there for a time. He says they roll them bigger than this, prop them up with sticks."

Street music insinuated into the structure around us, rhythm entrapped in walls and floor, sympathetic counter pulses resonant in the air, dancing molecules reechoing her hair as a glowing obscuration.

She took another hit, held it, let it out with a laugh. "This is a loft. The roof really pitches to the street."

I inhaled until my lungs cramped.

"Prob'ly a store room for the shop on the ground floor," I croaked, smoke chasing the words. "The old plans put a shop on the ground, living quarters on the second floor, and I think storage up here." I paused for what could have been forever, then said, "Originally, I mean."

My eyes adjusted to the gloom; her face in relief, more angular than in the restaurant. Thin lips and small mouth. Eyes. Dark brown eyes, narrow, sagging circles of flesh underlining accents. Tired. I saw her tired.

She'd gotten quiet with her second hit.

"Let's go out on the balcony," I said.

We ducked through the window to the narrow metal catwalk, barely room for a chair, a flimsy ornamental rail on the street edge setting us apart from empty space. Barricaded at night into a promenade from Canal that ended one block shy of this block, at St. Ann, Bourbon Street throbbed an insistent beat, men prowling, kissing, walking with hands in one another's back pockets, chains hanging from jeans beneath leather vests and muscle shirts, leather cycle hats, kissing on the mouth. Suspended above it all we worked the spliff, both of us silenced by the jolt of hashish and marijuana. I flipped my cigarette off the balcony in a red arc and someone looked up at us, some bearded man in leathers, smiled, moved on.

"Its not bad stuff," I said to watch my words flutter to the street while she stared, senseless. "But I haven't seen God with it."

She turned to me, standing close, and I looked down at her, admired her graceful neck.

"Are you going to fuck me, big boy?" Her voice had deepened and her face leathered, ancient, the bags under her crone's eyes puffy and dark.

"Is that what you came for?"

"It sure isn't for the furnishings."

"What about the company?"

"That's precisely what it's about. The company's gotta pay for dinner some way."

"Let's get inside," I said. "I'll see what I can do."

She removed the blouse to expose a transparent beige bra, trifling brown nipples pointing through insubstantial material. Round superficial tits, not enough to fill my hands, high up on an elongated torso stretched above a flat oval of a belly with elliptical navel oriented upward. Bra off, the twin breaches released above a smoothly cylindrical frame showing no ribs, no cleavage, suspended beneath a high and prominent clavicle, widely separated across an evident sternum, the nipples parallel to the floor with no sign of droop and almost pointed dead ahead but slightly outward.

I didn't touch them.

"How about some coke?"

She leaned into me. "If you want."

We tooted off a mirror.

"You interested?" she asked, kicking off her shoes.

I touched the breasts, pinched the hard nipples. She put her hand on my groin and felt my erection, rubbed the spreading wet spot seeping through my trousers. I pulled down her skirt and stood back to look at her standing in the phosphorescent half glow flooding the room. Wide hips with saddle bags formed a hint of bulge at the top of slender thighs that tapered slightly to knees blended without noticeable bulges or knobs or twists into calves smooth, not muscular, not fat, ending in chubby feet planted flat on the ground sans evidence of arch. Short legs, short relative to her trunk, in the global perspective making me think dwarf.

"Come on," she said, "get out of those wet pants."

Standing in the middle of the bedroom against the foot of the bed, she removed panties and turned to look at herself in the mirror. The saddle bags showed more from the back, the taper more pronounced, but her smoothly contoured cheeks still smiled firmly above the widening of the haunches.

I dropped my clothes on the floor and stood with my erection pointing to the ceiling. She turned back and touched it, its weeping head dribbling on the historic planks. She licked the drool from her fingers.

"Pick me up, big boy. I want you to fuck me standing up," and I reached under her as she leapt, grabbing her ass cheeks for support. She glommed on like a parasitic leach, arching to guide my dick into the maw in her groin as she held me with tentacle arms and legs, spitting out the words, "Come on, tough guy, get it in me," and I lifted her higher, placing her over it and letting gravity pull her down until it buried in her wet hole. I slipped my middle finger into her anus and held her weight against it. My leg hurt like hell. I was afraid it would give out. I thought of Alexander's Horned Sphere.

"Fuck me, come on, fuck me," barking commands like a drill sergeant.

I flopped us onto the bed, restraining her arms as she pumped with legs wrapped around me. We paced a steady harmonic, neither fast nor slow. I pulled out and turned her over without letting her up, forcing her under me, under control. Pinning her arms to the bed, covering her legs, using my weight to hold her, I found the portal to her bowels with the head of my penis and rubbed while she shrieked, "No, not there, you son of a bitch," and tried to wriggle free. Impossible under my weight. She screamed with an edge of panic and tightened her butt muscles but I rubbed my drooling penis against her anus, pressing until it slid inside. I torqued with a clean movement, ramming home and pumping while she sobbed, then started to work with me, loosening the pincer grip of her cheeks. Echoing my rhythm, the sobs changed to moans and then keening as she bucked until I let go with a groan of my own, filling her like an enema.

She squirmed out from under me after I collapsed, hurrying to the bathroom to let go a series of wet farts; I imagined brown, viscous sperm dripping into the toilet from her butthole. I rolled over onto my back and leaned up on one elbow and she came back vicious, flailing at me with ineffectual slaps before I grabbed both wrists in one hand and held her at arms length.

"You bastard, don't ever do that again—"

"Do what? You set the challenge. Its my place to pick the method. We start again and it'll be more of the same. Maybe you ought to get on your knees and clean it off."

Dancing eyes, even in the gloom: sparks. I waited for it to pass. When she went limp I let her go. She sat beside me.

"You have a substantial tool. Anyone ever tell you that?"

"No. Maybe you don't have enough experience with tools."

"I was the only white woman in graduate school at Howard University. No one there had anything on you."

"And none of those dudes fucked your asshole?"

"One tried, but it hurt so much he gave up. That hurt like hell."

I grabbed the box of sinsemilla from under the bed and rolled a tight joint.

"That was different," she said. "Not like an orgasm."

I handed her the reefer. She took a few leisurely hits, then handed it back.

"Pain, but something else too. But not like orgasm. Something blended in the pain, vaginal spasms I think—"

"The g-spot. I think women who have orgasms with anal sex have g-spot orgasms."

"Like no orgasm I ever had. It started out with a lot of pain and the pain never went away, but it blended in with a wave that came up from somewhere I never experienced before—"

"G-spot."

"Gräfenberg spot—"

"Right. I think its supposed to be what corresponds to the prostate in the male. The sexual organs are homologous from what I read…"

"I lost track…"

"Maybe it was the dope." I passed the joint back to her. "Maybe you left your body."

"No, unless it was to escape the pain."

"We need to experiment some more—"

"You ever fuck without dope?"

"I don't do much of anything without dope, but you can. Though my high might pass to you…"

"I don't get contact high, Whitey…"

We lay on our backs staring at the ceiling. A dope silence between us, one of those moments when you don't need to speak to communicate.

"Maybe it would be more interesting to get them both going at the same time. Clit and g-spot. I have a frie—"

"I don't go with women. I can do it myself. I have hands."

"You ever do two guys?"

"I might consider that."

I leaned over to kiss her navel and traced with my lips the fine down swirling like a trail from her belly to her mons pubis, spreading out along her pelvis, her inner thighs. I rolled her on her side, looking at the pattern spread out circumferentially and found a scar, raised up angry and red like a plateau overlooking a plain. I touched and she jerked forward.

"What's this?"

"The remnants of teen surgery. Kidneys. Its ugly—"

"No, its interesting," tracing the ragged welt with a finger and she sighed, "It turns me on. Its an erogenous zone…"

I licked and kissed it and she gasped and arched her back.

"Its beautiful. It's a beautiful mark."

"No, wait, I can't start again now, its late…"

I nibbled, bit harder; she gasped a growl.

I buried my face in the vee between her legs, found hanging cunt lips obscured in the mat of mousy brown hair growing like a wild fern, mumbling and chewing the meaty flaps, sucking her vagina inside my mouth, all the time rubbing her scar with my hand, searching with my tongue for the clit, finding it a swollen elongated pearl, a flattened marble, a knob effecting spasmodic recoil. I presented my cock to her face; she took it in her mouth. She flopped like a fish out of water, her legs pinioning my head, my fingers pinching the scar. Her muffled sobs modulated to medley choke-gag-slurp when I ejaculated again, but she kept my dick in her mouth and I chewed her clit until she pushed me away.

I made a mental note not to kiss her mouth.

In a while I walked her to her car. I liked that she didn't put on displays of affection, no touchy-feely kissy-face bullshit, not even a hug, certainly no mouth kissing; just got in the car, said good night and drove off. I walked on to Port of Call for a late burger and beer.

Chapter 5
Killing Fields

Tuesday opened late in the day, noonish or so, my dick and mouth coated with the remains of my guests nether excretions seasoned by leftover onion and mustard. It occurred to me I'd be running low on funds with the fucking credit card to pay on, likely facing short rations, needing to curtail my habit of eating out every night.

I smoked a cigarette and a joint and drank a cup of instant coffee, shit, showered, shaved, and trudged off to the A&P where I gathered coffee and basic cheap foodstuffs to fit my limited galley potential: canned sardines, canned soup, canned tomato sauce and noodles, Kraft macaroni and cheese in a box, carrots and potato chips for when I got munchies, Dixie beer. I piled into a queue at a register behind a spidery chick the color of blackstrap molasses, hair pulled back in braids woven with beads and other colorful tidbits hanging down over a high arch of ass. Spindly legs ending in feet shod in spangled pink flip flops tumbled from a short denim skirt. Pronounced ribs demarcated a stretch of torso barely covered in short orange bandana halter-top tied in back and weighted down with mammoth flesh mounds hanging via suspensions of skin stretched from the sides.

I ached to reach out and grab that orb of a narrow ass. She must have read my mind, turned and sized me up. The round face didn't harmonize with the elongated body and pendulous bosoms sequestered in their tenuous halter; she'd painted it up so the eyes appeared as bone-black almonds, lashes dense and inky, the extended line of narrow lips amplified beyond their natural boundaries with lipstick of fire-engine red. Her forehead domed high, naked with the pulled-back braids; her flattened nose might once have been smashed by a two-by-four.

"Misty likes tall white boys," she said, her voice a honeyed drawl not from New Orleans.

"Really? What's she like about them?"

"White dicks. Misty likes sucking white dicks."

No one turned to listen, as if standing in line in the A&P at the corner of Royal and St. Peter talking about sucking dicks with a half naked black woman was the most natural thing in the world, but then the guy in front of her wore lipstick and hung on to the man beside him as if they were long-lost lovers.

"So who's Misty?"

She pointed to herself.

I'd have been suspicious she was a guy in drag had one of the pendant hangers in the halter not shown the upper arc of a giant nipple. And nary a hint of facial hair.

"Misty likes them tall like you. And that white hair. You are a pretty white boy."

"Thanks. You're not so bad yourself."

"You want to visit? I take a small contribution."

"What kind of contribution?"

"Money, baby. Just a little for you. Almost free."

"Well, I'm a tapped out white boy. No money till payday, and then not much. A poor white boy."

She gave me another once over, noting my clothes, and smiled. "I guess I can see that. Well, you come on by sometime anyway. Maybe we can work out a sliding scale." She handed me a pink card with a phone number and address in the upper reaches of Royal, likely around Barracks, the name Misty smeared across in the same color as her lipstick. She held her tits up with both hands, the giant gap diverging like a fissure, and asked, "You like these, baby?"

"They seem admirable, but I'd need to inspect them to be sure."

"Well, you call me before you come by, so's I'm not pre—occupied."

She turned, made her purchase, and walked straight-backed out of the store, flip-flops flapping the concrete, high ass playing its own rhythm trailing a wake of disturbance behind.

I closed myself up in my apartment and played from my worn out record collection, boxes of LPs kept for me by a high school friend while I survived the Green Machine, spinning them on my only furniture, Mcintosh amp, Thorens turntable, and a pair of BIC speakers. Moving would have been a breeze had it not been for shipping this set. Everything else expendable, consigned to the ash-heap of university scrounges.

I smoked dope and listened to Miles *Sketches of Spain*, then Monk, Billie Holliday, Dolphy at the Five Spot, Trane, Sonny Rollins, Parker and Gillespie on a Canadian gig taped on a shit tape recorder by Mingus. As it darkened I smoked one joint after the other and cried, falling asleep lying flat on my back in bed until Bill Evans emptied out and thumping against the spindle roused me. I ate a can of sardines, some crackers and carrots, drank a beer, passed into sleep.

Falling backwards into a hole, panicked, sat bolt upright. "Cocksucker," said or thought. I sat for a while, heart racing, cold with matted sweat, swung my legs over the edge of the bed and got up, sun rising over Bourbon Street, thinking I'd review for my exams. I smoked a joint and looked at McKean's *Stochastic Integrals,* drifted asleep reading his proof of Feller's test for explosions, understated perfection eschewing the obvious.

Then it was late and I had to rush to get to class, barely time for the iced coffee I kept for such emergencies, jolted awake and quick shit shower shave forsaking the lulling streetcar for the Freret Street bus, flanking the math department on maneuver directly to the class late, ambushed by the bell. Five minute rule in effect. My beetle browed lady fan not in attendance. I sang a dry lecture on sampling statistics, their first brush with confusing abstractions. The entire class fled at the bell, not even one question from the baffled cheerleader.

Not in a chatty mood, I checked mail and headed directly for the seminar. The Frenchman greeted me at the door, his hello sliding above the film of accent enough to let the listener know he didn't hail from these parts.

"Your exam tomorrow afternoon," he said. "I wanted to come, but was told only the PDE and topological algebra will be there."

"Interesting. Supposed to be open to the public."

"Yes, but I think it means less than what it says. It's so?"

"Probably."

"I have heard it is a formal affair, this exam. They have decided in your favor already. But don't tell anyone I have said this."

"No problem. I'm not going to believe it anyway. If I fuck up big time, they'll either drop me like a hot potato or make me redo some of it. That's how it works. Lots of times need to repeat some fucked up part of the performance."

"You'll be fine. Don't worry."

The first day he'd handed out a mimeographed set of lecture notes in French from some *Séminaire de Probabilités* on *Géométrie Différentielle Stochastique* by a bunch of hotshots I'd heard of, Paul Meyer and Laurent Schwartz among others, including himself. He also gave me a preprint of a some stuff on martingales on analytic complex variétés, but I hadn't taken much of a look at it. I could read mathematics in French, had passed a standardized exam in French for science that wiped out one language requirement, but still found it a pain. I wasn't sure if variété meant algebraic variety or manifold, I assumed the latter, but needed to invest in the French mathematics dictionary I knew existed.

It seemed odd we plowed away in this seminar on some stuff related to what control engineers called system's theory, something about input-output systems more related to operators than to martingales on manifolds. I'd asked him once and he'd told me that the papers he'd given me were all relevant, but he might not get far enough to cover their utility. They did assume more machinery in probability and geometry than many here could deal with, particularly the relationship to manifolds. But it didn't seem new stuff, either, since McKean did it in his almost decade-old book, a principal work on my reading list.

This day he talked more about transfer functions and Fourier transforms, working towards some sort of decomposition theorem based on an operator representation. He made forays into H_p spaces as places where transfer functions lived, spent an inordinate time getting conditions for positivity of a kernel using interpolation and now was working to get a reproducing kernel representation for "realizations" of causal, linear, dissipative systems. He hinted at some kind of contractivity, but I think we were all clueless on where he was going; I followed every argument he made but saw no shape looming at the end of it all. I'd felt the same way about two semesters of theorems regarding modules, no hint of the algebraic geometry or whatever had been the original impetus.

The Frenchman's work had been important enough to someone to get him tenure at Stanford, so plenty of people attended but so far not many had any questions for him, a bad sign. I guessed his real goal was to teach at the École Polytechnique, recently relocated to the outskirts of Paris, or more likely the École Normale Supérieure, though I'd heard the place to be for his stuff was really the Université de Strasbourg. None of it made that much difference to me; I'd be lucky to get a teaching position at some third rate US university with a sickly graduate program.

First I had to pass my orals.

After seminar I attended my advisor's class, then bolted for the gym to do the excruciating leg workout. Then home on the streetcar, not quite jammed up with commuters though plenty of tourists. I got a window seat anyway, starting out at nothing until we made the final straight leg to Canal where I dumped out and walked home, working off the stiffness from the exercises, wondering why I'd not heard from Lori.

Dinner, music, sleep. I forwent jazz for Stravinsky: Sir Colin Davis's Rite and Petrouchka. Then Shostakovich's Seventh, promising myself something more abstract later.

Stumbling awake through late morning already muggy, bright and shining, many joints with coffee and then a forced march down Bourbon to the streetcar and a swaying ride uptown, Audubon Park and the ugly old stone monstrosities, approaching from the front. Expecting ambush. Knowing of no reactionary force in readiness.

killing fields

I smoked a hashish-laced cigarette, marched up the stone steps, up the giant's stairs inside, and trudged down the hallway towards the room where my inquisitors awaited me. Deserted like an abandoned firebase. Not a soul in sight.

I opened the closed door and entered a room full of them. Spread across the front row the PDE group: my advisor, beside him the group's brash young genius, then the old maestro, and then Oberst, the topological algebra maestro. The next row: Momus against the wall behind Oberst, the younger PDE guys strung out beside him, one an up and coming star, and then scattered beyond them the remnants of the topological algebra crew.

A sudden hush; I'd surprised them at something.

The young PDE group genius stood and said, "You're a few minutes early. If you don't mind waiting outside, we'll call you."

I stood outside the door like a troublesome brat expelled from the classroom, pushing my nose into the wall, butterflies like going on my first patrol knowing armed men wishing me harm awaited. My advisor fetched me.

The PDE group genius began with a softball, doubtless planned to set me at ease.

"Tell us about your favorite PDE and its solution method."

I launched into a spiel on the Dirichlet problem in a bounded region of Euclidean space with a smooth boundary, conflicted between two favorite approaches. Taking first the elegant proof from Folland using Dirichlet's principle, interrupted by a random popping of irrelevant question from the back of the room, "What's smooth?," "What's the normal field?," "What's a harmonic function?," "What's a vector field?," "What's a norm?," "What's a bounded domain?" which I at first attempted to answer but soon realized led to an essentially infinite regress. Smiles on all the faces except Oberst's, whose visage bespoke boredom at foolishness, told me it was sport and I pretended not to hear any longer, proceeding to the set-up with the Dirichlet integral I said was a kind of potential energy on connected components. I showed that adding the standard norm and taking a square root gave a proper norm obtained from an inner product so the completion became a subspace of L_2 and also a Hilbert space in its own right.

No one interrupted so I plowed ahead, showing that the restriction map to the boundary could be extended to all of L_2, corollary of a bound on the L_2 norm by the potential norm, an estimate I proved with a hand-wave. I mentioned in passing that in essence we'd restricted to functions in the Hilbert subspace possessing L_2 derivatives of order one-half on the boundary.

I stepped back and examined what I had wrought so far, waiting for real questions or objections or a call for more detail. The board contained a goofy drawing of a domain, the norm, an inequality, and an integral along the boundary crucial to the hand-wave, the merest hint of what I had spoken.

They allowed me to pass from the unproven result and I sailed on into the last stages, sketching a proof of a beauty proclaiming equivalence between functions harmonic in the region and functions orthogonal with respect to the potential on the subspace of compact support in the region. Home free, I showed that since the functions with zero potential were locally constant, hence harmonic, they could be written as direct sums, their orthogonal projection onto the harmonic space being the solution to the Dirichlet problem. I then erased what little remembrance I'd left on the board and stated Dirichlet's principle of equivalent conditions, leaving only the drawing.

Professor Momus broke the silence with his characteristic throat clearing.

"Is this a good solution? I mean in a classical sense?"

I knew he would be aware of the history of this principle, stated by Dirichlet, used by Riemann and discredited by Weierstrass, rehabilitated by Hilbert. In the century or so since this rolling controversy arose mathematicians had built heavy machinery to give logical substance to these statements, equipment those giants could not even imagine: Hilbert spaces for functions to live in with right angles defined in infinite dimensions, Lebesgue integration to complete those spaces of integrable functions into Hilbert spaces where one could rest assured the orthogonal projection onto a subspace existed. Stuff like that.

"Not in some sense," I said. "Its weaker. We used that weak solutions of the Laplacian are harmonic. We also cheated a bit on the boundary functions, but I don't think we have time to show the boundary functions are continuous given continuous data. But we can go there if you want…"

"No, it isn't necessary," the PDE genius said. I noticed the random interference from the peanut gallery had ceased.

"Anyway," I continued, "it seems remarkable that one can also solve this problem by using a random process, the Brownian motion." I drew a wiggle inside to the boundary where I stopped it with a stopping time, evaluated it with the initial data on the boundary and took the conditional expectation given the starting point. "That," I said, "was a harmonic function that solved the Dirichlet problem, essentially the same one we had already found by deterministic means."

killing fields

I added one more interior squiggle heading to the boundary, talked about the infinitesimal generator of the process for extending the method to more general PDEs. A realization dawned on me and I let it out into the room: perhaps the mystery of randomness providing the same solution could in part be explained by considering that the conditional expectation operator was really an orthogonal projection onto a subspace of functions, just as before and likely the same space.

Standing back, the sparsity of marks on the board surprised me. A nebulous shape with some squiggles like lonesome spermatozoa or maybe spirochete emanating from a couple points to the boundary, a formula for the conditional expectation on the boundary, nothing else. Yet I had talked a good stretch, leaving only hints for the eyes.

My advisor's turn. "Give the defining properties of Brownian motion."

Another softball. I decided to expand this as far as I could.

I started by saying I found it helpful to think of Brownian motion as a drunk walking down the street changing direction by coin toss at each step, the steps decreasing to infinitesimal length at delta times going to zero, a limit of a random walk on the real line.

"Constrained to a line," someone said and with the word random the chorus in back resurrected the inane hooting. "What's random?" "What's a random variable?" and more, all of which I ignored.

I gave the standard four characterizations of Brownian motion: almost sure starting point at zero, almost surely continuous sample paths, independent increments and normally distributed increments with mean zero and variance the size the delta of the time step. Then I added the two conditions equivalent to the last two, namely normally distributed linear combinations at finite times and covariance at times s and t equal to the minimum of s and t. I considered proving the equivalence but thought better of it. Instead I plowed into Einstein's argument that a particle beginning at some fixed point and subjected to random bombardment in a medium allowing its motion to be rotationally symmetric would exhibit such a normal distribution. I wrote the density integral on the board, then talked about transition probability functions. From this, before anyone could stop me, I obtained the finite-dimensional distributions, then hurried on to give the basic idea of how it could be considered the solution to the heat equation on an infinite rod with a Dirac delta at the origin at time zero, diffusing to a stationary distribution uniform on the real line after infinite time, assuming one believed in infinitesimals. I considered veering off into a discussion of such improper distributions as priors for Bayesian statistics, a technique I thought begun by Laplace for silly arguments Christians repeat for the existence of God, but realized it would be stupid and suicidal.

The hooting from the gallery had stopped but it wouldn't have mattered, so involved was I in laying out this landscape of the mind. I tore on to sketch two proofs for the existence of such a process, zipping along the top of the Wiener proof using the sample space for the probability as the set of paths themselves, mentioning that the finite-dimensional distributions could be extended to a real measure on a sigma-algebra of functions concentrated on the continuous functions. Beside the integral for the finite-dimensional distributions, I wrote an example: the set of all sample paths b such that b at time 1 is between .1 and .3 and at time 3 is between 1 and 1.1.

By this time, I'd begun writing BM for Brownian motion. Before anyone could say anything I launched into the complete proof of the existence of this measure on the function space constructed around the Haar functions, the approach due to Ciesielski lifted out of McKean. That killed some time and also led to a proof for the expression of the covariance of the process. This left us square in the midst of a space of continuous functions with Wiener measure as model for the Brownian motion process, righteously called the Wiener process. From this vantage point I drew out a sketch of the fact that the measure was concentrated on continuous functions that were almost surely not differentiable, albeit it rather hurriedly with a lot of vague but authoritative arm-waving. I waded into the conditional expectation properties: Markov property, stopping times, strong Markov property, martingales and semi-martingales, ending it all with a proof that BM was a martingale.

I stepped back to view my handiwork and again found little on the board, a sloppy integral fdb and several large BMs. I shrugged.

"Should I prove Blumenthal's zero-one law or Khincin's law of iterated logarithm?"

"No, that's more than I expected," my advisor said.

"Just let me bring out the semigroup connection to the heat equation and the abstract Cauchy problem," and I stepped to the board, gave a short spiel on semigroups of operators, infinitesimal generators, and a bogus explanation for the semigroup property of BM on bounded uniformly continuous functions on the real line based on the Markov property, ending with a derivation of the fact that the flow of the semigroup satisfied the heat equation. In the middle of the board a giant BUC(R) sprawled amidst BMs.

killing fields

As I stood back basking in the glow of ideas lingering in the room, my advisor asked me to sketch the construction of the Ito integral and derivation of Ito's lemma.

I started by talking about Wiener's integral with a non-random integrand. The idea of using BM for an integrand in the Stieljes sense was cute, but of course the sample paths were so badly behaved, of unbounded variation in every interval, that it was not possible in a standard Riemann sense to do this path by path, and Lebesque's method didn't apply. Then I gave Wiener's trick for this particular case, starting with functions of compact support so it was possible to use integration by parts and reverse the path differentials. I stated that the map defined by this integral was an isometry of the subspace of continuous functions with compact support that overlapped L_2 with L_2 itself; added that this so-called white noise integral was itself normal with mean zero and variance the L_2 norm of the integrand.

Dramatically pausing, I said such an approach could not work if the integrand was a function of the sample paths.

I detected eyes glazing over in the gallery, most of whom had long since lost interest. Their glazed expressions spurred me to greater heights as I waxed eloquently on the irregularity of the functionals depending on both time and the BM sample paths which were themselves now considered the random elements. I gave conditions for a functional to be an integrand: jointly measureable with respect to the Borel sets on the product of the extended real line and the sigma-algebra of all sample paths, non-anticipating in that the functional as a function of a path at time t depended only the path up to time t, reviving the connection to the Brownian sigma-fields generated by BM paths b(s) for times t less than s, and finally that the square of the functional with respect to time was finite almost surely. I said a few words about the causality implication of non-anticipation, then defined simple functionals and, taking care to emphasize that the simple functionals be evaluated at the left endpoint to keep from sticking out into the future, defined the integral as the sum, showed that general non-anticipating Brownian functionals could be approximated in probability by simple functionals, and defined the general integral. I finished by showing that the integral itself was continuous and defined simultaneously for almost all sample paths. I proved the integral a martingale and mentioned in closing Stratonovitch's stochastic integral, obtained by evaluating the integrand at interior points of the intervals, leading to a more intuitive integral but without the martingale property, a serious defect.

By now I wrote more but erased it almost as soon as it hit the board, chalk in one hand and eraser in the other, modeled on the professor who had dragged me through a semester of multilinear algebra, tensors and exterior algebras and modules. On one end of his classroom high above the ground stood a window from floor to ceiling at the end of the chalkboard runway down which he had sped with chalk and eraser, wiping as he wrote, bouncing off the bars across the window and starting back the opposite direction. One day I stopped him with the comment that if we were to cut through the bars he would plunge to his death almost surely. He paused to laugh, saying the rumor was it had been a math professor falling to his death that had prompted the bars in the first place, then picked up where he'd left off.

I wore down one soft yellow chalk, the dust settling around me in a dull haze, and picked up a white one that screeched when I wrote with it, someone in back likely awakened by the rush up his spine hollering to use another piece of chalk.

I ignored him and sped into a discussion of what might happen if one did integrate with respect to paths not of bounded variation, presenting an intuitive and wildly incoherent sketch based on Taylor series that perhaps instead of going to zero it might wear a second order term, a finite remainder of the wildly jumping path. I gave Paul Levy's result regarding the quadratic variation of BM and came up with the Ito lemma for a pure BM process, with the second derivative terms of the integrand appearing for the quadratic variation in the integral. I used the formula to show that the integral of BM with respect to BM from time zero to time t is BM squared divided by two, minus t divided by two as the extra term the quadratic variation.

At this point my advisor, laughing softly, stopped me.

"Don't prove the general Ito formula," he said. "Just state it."

And so I did, leaving as evidence on the board the mnemonic two-by-two table of stochastic differentials with dtdt, dtdb and dbdt equal zero, dbdb equal dt.

I finished with the fact that the Stratonovich integral doesn't have the extra term, a dividend of knowing the future, and then wrote the conversion formula, warning that the Stratonovich integral doesn't have dominated convergence properties and is really less a stochastic integral than integro-differential operator.

I stepped back from the board, stick of chalk in one hand, eraser in the other, chalk streaking my jeans and t-shirt. I put both down and wiped my hands on my butt.

"Should I derive the exponential martingale?" I asked and someone at the back of the room, one of the topological algebra types, said, "No, please. We surrender." My advisor chuckled and gave the floor to Oberst.

He said he would appreciate it if the room would remain quiet while he asked me a few questions. Then he looked at the board and said, "You don't leave much evidence, do you, Mr. Butcher?"

The quieted room let out a joint grin.

"No sir, I think it's dangerous. No tape recorders, either."

Some laughter, not loud, not long.

"I have a few questions I'd like to ask." Precise, clipped, authoritarian, when Oberst spoke with his German accent it came across like a Gestapo colonel giving orders. "Can you define Lie groups and Lie algebras and explain their relationship."

I decided to go halfway between Miller's specific approach and the general, heavy equipment approach of Kobayashi and Nomizu, starting with Lie groups as differentiable manifolds with differentiable group product, diving into left translation by an element of the group, left-invariant vector fields and then defining the Lie algebra to be the set of all left-invariant vector fields with respect to the usual vector field bracket and of course addition and scalar multiplication. I generalized to define Lie algebras as vector spaces with a bilinear product called the Lie bracket satisfying the two standard conditions and showed that the bracket operation on vector fields provided a Lie algebra isomorphic to the tangent space of the Lie group at the identity.

Instead of pressing on with the exponential mapping, I stopped, letting Oberst ask for it.

He did. I flew into it, everything I had gone over in the previous week in the abstract and in the concrete rushing into my brain faster than I could speak, like walking through hallways of hallways leading to yet more hallways stretching away to infinity in static perfection, vector fields and integral curves and differential equations, flowing one-parameter groups the local version of global orbits of vector fields from whence they began their flow on an arbitrary differentiable manifold. I specialized it all to the Lie group, local one parameter groups commuting with left translation, unique solutions to differential equations defined by a Lie algebra element A giving rise to a unique one-parameter group flowing out from the origin defined as exp(At), evaluated at t equal one giving the map exp from the algebra to the Lie group.

I decided to zero in on the matrix case and as I wrote a general time-invariant differential equation over the general linear group I realized I'd been limping, more like dragging my right leg along, and people watched that, not what I did on the board. My noticing brought on the pain.

I leaned against the board to catch my balance, then wobbled to the first row and pulled over one of the small vacant desks and plopped down in it.

"Excuse me," I said. "My bum leg is attacking me."

From my chair I wrote the exponential of the matrix to give the solution as a series, showing the flow and the exponential map into the group from the algebra, talking about the general linear group and its Lie algebra of matrices, bringing up the classical examples.

"I can go into the Campbell-Baker-Hausdorff Theorem if you want," I said. "I just need to give my leg a minute."

I needed a drink and a joint. Pain rippled like hot spikes flowing from some nexus deep in the shattered remains of my pinned and pasted femur.

"No, that's fine," Oberst said. "I don't have more questions."

"I have one, if no one objects." It was Momus. No one said a word, so he cleared his throat and I expected the next words to be about Daniell integrals in this stochastic sense. "It seems that these topics are relatively disjoint. I don't see any connection," he said in his officious tone, as if he were beginning a speech. I waited for more, but he had finished.

"Of course, the Lie groups we are concerned with are the symmetries of the PDEs, the ones that transform the solution manifolds to new solution manifolds."

"Yes," he interrupted, "I am aware of those."

"The stochastic integrals correspond to PDEs via infinitesimal generators, and there is a tie there with symmetry groups to evaluate them in closed form. That is on one of the papers in the list."

Back in the hallway of hallways I stumbled on a new crossover lying ready at hand and stood up wobbly to head back to the board, leaning against the chalk rack for support.

"Ito and his school did some work on diffusion processes on manifolds and McKean has specialized it to a few sections in his book with Brownian motion on Lie groups, mostly the orthogonal group, and also on the space of symmetric matrices. It was amusing but not all that interesting. But it struck me just now that one can tie quadratic variation to connections on manifolds, since you can think of connections as a Hessian, mapping from smooth functions to symmetric bilinear forms."

I stopped, thinking perhaps I'd gone slap happy with the pain streaking up into my groin and radiated out as background waves pulsing my thigh, amplitude from dull ache to excruciating pierce and back, a periodic misery. I forgot about even considering Noether's theorem and the relation of conservation laws to symmetry. And maybe cohomology.

"I think we're done here," my advisor said.

I knew the drill. I had to leave while they decided my fate. I gripped the chair and raised myself, pitched forward and made the door, grabbed the knob for support and hobbled down the deserted hallway to the lounge and the comfort of the couch, hugging the walls for support.

As I passed the secretarial office next to the lounge Joelle looked up.

"You've been in there three hours," she said. "I thought they were only supposed to have you for two— My God, are you all right?"

She jumped up from her desk and came to help me over to the couch. "It's your leg, isn't it?"

I didn't say anything. I hadn't talked about my leg to anyone. Just the thought of being branded a baby-killer in Vietnam kept me mum. Now it seemed one of the damned secretaries knew about my leg. I wondered who else knew.

"I'm all right," I said. "Happens all the time when I'm on my feet too long."

My advisor appeared at the door.

"You did fine," he said. "You passed."

"Good," I said, clammy with sweat, almost cold, probably pasty pale.

"They were only a little unhappy with the way you used the board. They would have liked more written out."

"It isn't like I was lecturing first year grad students," I replied. "If I'd written it out with all the gory details we'd still be there." I paused to a mingling of burning cramp and nausea bouncing through some part of me I couldn't find. "Fuck 'em if they can't take a joke," I mumbled.

"What's wrong with your leg?" he asked. "Are you all right?"

Joelle sent him a withering stare. "It's a war injury."

I shook my head. Now everyone would know. Son of a bitch.

"You were in Vietnam?"

I nodded.

"I didn't know. What happened?"

"He was shot."

I decided to let it all out. "That's true. Six or seven times, in fact. Not sure exactly how many or if it was a machine gun or AK-47 or both, but at least six. The bullets shattered my femur, turned it to a kind of pulp. I'm lucky I kept it."

By now a small group stood around watching. Mrs. Dupre appeared and Joelle told her she was going to drive me home.

"No," I said. "I can grab the streetcar right out front here, take it to the quarter and catch the shuttle bus. It stops in front of my apartment."

"No sir. You wait here. You better be here when I get back. I'll get my car and get you home."

"You don't have a class to cancel today do you?" Mrs. Dupre asked.

"No."

I don't remember details of what happened. Joelle reappeared in a deserted room. She and Mrs. Dupre helped me down the endless stairs and wide stone steps in front of the building and into her car. She knew I lived on Bourbon Street and I stopped her at my building. She pulled up onto the sidewalk and left her flashers blinking, flagged down a massive queen cruising between the bars. Together they helped me up the winding narrow stairway to my apartment. He left to watch over her car to keep it from being towed, and she asked me what else I needed as I lay on the bed, near to passing out from the pain.

"In the medicine cabinet, a big bottle of pills and some water, please."

She brought both and I fished a thirty milligram morphine tablet from the menagerie of illegal narcotics.

"You better go," I said. "That big queen won't be able to hold off the city's tow truck force for long. They're always circling like vultures. And thanks."

"Should I get a doctor?"

"No. I've lived with it for a while now. It's not the first time. I'll be fine."

She hovered, uncertain about leaving me.

"Really, you're an angel. I'll be fine. Don't worry."

She hesitated in the doorway, staring at me, and then was gone. I pulled the box of good reefer from under the bed and rolled a joint, passing into sleep while smoking.

Chapter 6
Strong Deformation Retract

Twisted knot: pillow-sheet-limbs. Grope leg. Nothing: not pain not sensation. Clammy flesh. Untangle. Flail towards lit world. Grab the unresponsive block of scarred wood. Rub for germs of pins and needles. Nothing. Dead meat.

Drag the dead thing over to the edge of the bed and claw to sitting.

Burned a big-ass hole in the sheet. I pick up and revive the roach and inhale a deep toke.

With some care I raised up on the almost tingling leg. Neither pain nor control. I leaned against the edge of the bed and scooted back-to-wall for support; walking brought it grudgingly alive. Pacing until it felt real; rolling another joint; fixing coffee. The morphine had stifled my appetite, but the dope revived it. I boiled water and cooked macaroni, added the packaged powdered cheese-food, ate the stuff, showered and headed for campus, catching the minibus in the quarter to Canal, then the streetcar.

On the way in, I wondered why I hadn't heard from Lori. Thought she'd've wished me luck.

I stopped in the office to thank Joelle. She sat head down studying some scrawl of symbols I assumed she'd been assigned to type.

I'd always thought her hair black, but in the glow from the window the black highlighted like darkly roasted coffee. Her long face and noble nose straight as an arrow deceived the expectation of round face centered with a button. Perhaps the visage pulled long as illusion from her dense hair falling beyond her shoulders and piling onto the desk.

She looked up with a melancholy expression, natural sadness in her absent sloe-eyed stare, her full lips in a pout. On seeing me her eyes lit up with transformation of pout to smile, petite dimples at mouth-ends accentuating cheeks bosomy by contrast with the swooping line of chin.

"You're here! I didn't expect you to make it." Concern passed over her features, smile swapped for a neutral mouth I found beckoning, sexy.

"I'm fine. I said it would pass. It always does. It just wore out and I didn't notice. I hope one day to build the muscles back so it can deal with more standing and walking. It seems I lost a lot of muscle."

"I was so worried. I almost called a doctor."

"There wouldn't have been anything they could do except what I did: take morphine and sleep. But I wanted to thank you again. It was a great kindness."

"It was the least I could do. You almost died for me."

I wanted to tell her not for her, or anyone else for that matter. Not for anything; just a fuck-up, a cosmic joke on me. But she wouldn't have gotten it and I didn't want to antagonize her. I hadn't noticed how beautiful I found her. Her brows arched like streaks of the same dark roasted coffee, chiseled above shallow orbs emanating from the apex of the bridge of that regal nose.

"You didn't have any trouble with it this morning?"

"None. Woke up perfectly normal. Almost forgot all about it."

She smiled again and I could have kissed her. A mistake.

"I need to get ready for class."

I walked out of the office without showing any of the numbness that still dogged my leg. Once in the hallway I leaned against the wall for support, then made it almost to the graduate student carrels when I heard a voice from the office just opposite the doorway.

"Butcher. Congratulations."

I wandered into the office inhabited by a faculty member not more than a couple years my senior, a low-dimensional topologist. His forte was algebraic topology, a necessity in any real university no matter how small. His counterparts were a point-set descendent of R. L. Moore, second generation, a recently graduated differential topologist from Stanford, and an aging algebraic topologist who had taken to the bottle and prayed for guidance in proving new theorems. It seems the older professor had not made any recent mistakes, though neither had he written a paper in years. His work on yet one more calculus text for the textbook mill was kind of a joke with the graduate students; perhaps here would emerge finally the great American calculus book. Spivak claimed to have written the great American differential geometry book. It was fat, I gave him that, unlike his midge of a book *Calculus on Manifolds*. I thought that the great American calculus book.

Anyway, Ron Goldman had taken a liking to me though I had not yet decided what to make of him. Not so solemn as the rest of his group, he nonetheless took this stuff more seriously than it merited. A fault of many of the younger faculty, it seemed, and some of the graduate students as well. Grandly beautiful and totally irrelevant, all this stuff.

"You heard?"

"Of course. The word is out. They said you did well. Surprised them with your grasp of Lie groups and differential geometry. Said you were going on about connections."

"They didn't ask shit about Lie groups. I think Oberst sandbagged me. Probably felt sorry for me."

"I heard you were limping. Big to-do from the secretaries about having to help you home. No one else would do it."

"It wasn't necessary, really; I'd have gotten home. They felt like mothering me."

"So anyway it came out about your war wounds."

"I was surprised Joelle knew."

"Most of the faculty knew, with the exception of your advisor it seems."

"I don't know how. Very few people I talked to about it."

"Well, if it hadn't been for people like you, we wouldn't have had a war."

"If it hadn't been for people like me, we'd have won the war."

He laughed and I joined him, but his remark surprised me. The differential topologist seemed hostile, as did his two hippy grad students, but I hadn't expected such a remark from Goldman. Most knew better than to blame the people who went as if they'd had a real choice.

"Good answer."

"Well, it wasn't as if most of us had much choice other than jail."

"Canada."

"Too fucking cold for me."

"If you want to talk about Lie groups let me know. I used group actions to prove some theorems in low dimensional manifolds. People have said good things about the work. The theorems are getting used. And I know some algebraic topology, particularly homology. You will likely at some point need the Mayer-Vietoris sequence."

"I need to learn jet bundles. And cohomology, too."

"I can help with fibre bundles and cohomology but don't know anything about jet bundles. Never even heard of them."

"Well, chances are it will take some book learning. Can't always be avoided. But I'll likely come to you for a run down of cohomology and other tools."

"If you have to get it from books, it probably won't be useful."

75

My leg still not fully alive, I left his office walking carefully and crossed the hallway without betraying a limp. At my carrel, a cane leaned against the back of my chair.

"Anyone know who left this cane here?"

A head popped up above the rows of carrels, one of the crisp shiny-blonde German students.

"It was left by Professor Momus. He said you might find a use for it."

"Thanks, Klaus."

I trudged off down the hall to Momus's office using the cane for support. The door slightly ajar, I caught him napping at his desk. He jolted awake at my knock.

"Ah, come in Mr. Butcher. I wanted to congratulate you on a splendid performance yesterday. You comported yourself with exceptional aplomb."

His bulbous nose seemed especially red and porous today.

"You wanted me to have this?" I held up the cane, a long, thin stick with a gold knob.

I noticed that he seldom cleared his throat before making normal conversation, though he projected the speechifying tone no matter what.

"Yes. Consider it a token of my appreciation for your efforts on our behalf in Southeast Asia. I know there exist those here who would diminish those efforts, some even perhaps displaying hostility."

"Well, I must admit it is not what I consider to have been a worthy effort on the part of the US."

"I can appreciate that. I have not been a whole-hearted supporter either, but I also appreciate many didn't have a choice and some perhaps adventured out of duty."

"I'm surprised people knew about it. I didn't make much noise about it."

"No, but there are ways for all these things to become public knowledge. Besides which you are obviously not cut from the same cloth as the great majority of our candidates. You stand out, Mr. Butcher. There is a look in your eyes that does not go unnoticed. A faraway expression sometimes that seems to transport you to a polar region, as in a singularity."

"This is a beautiful cane. Light, just the right length. I think the round knob may take a bit of getting used to, though."

"Yes. A handle or crook would be more comfortable for extended leaning, but on the other hand it has simpler lines. Straight like a toothpick, I always think."

"Rather a large circumferential cross section for a toothpick, sir. Perhaps Godzilla? It has a nice heft. Could be a decent cudgel."

"Well" and here he cleared his throat "given its girth it would be a toothpick for a rather large creature. It is ebonized hickory, darkened the old-fashioned way with ammonia fumes. The rose gold cap bears the engraving of a mask. The ferrule is gold too and proclaims the inscription 'Rei Momo' which is Portuguese though I don't think it came from Brazil or Portugal. King Momus. Maybe someone thought it was Latin. But you know Momus of course."

He'd interrupted his speech several times to formally cough and clear his throat, his tone inflating as if lecturing.

"No, don't know except the Mardi Gras krewe called that, but I'm not aware of the meaning."

"The Greek god of ridicule. But more often than not a carping critic, one who is not constructive or pleasant."

"Critics are necessary."

"But unwelcome. There was an element of Momus with the chorus during your exam. But that is more common than you think. Particularly when the candidate is apt himself to ask many questions. And when the candidate is not likely to fail, in which case the chorus is more circumspect."

"No hard feelings, dude, but you failed."

"Yes, along those lines. There is seldom hooting at debacles."

"The date on here, 1856, is that legit?"

"It seems unlikely to have been backdated, unless there existed an interest in forging an antique. In any case, it is now a genuine antique."

"I imagine it's worth money."

"I had it appraised at a bit more than one thousand dollars. But please don't sell it."

"Of course not, but I will be afraid to let it out of my sight. It's more than twice my own net worth."

"It looks quite common. That is the beauty of it. Unless you realize the two bits of metal are gold. It has grayed some. A straight stick, with an apparent grain, hickory with certainty, but hickory canes are quite common. And it makes a lovely knobkerrie for whacking belligerents, though it may be a bit long and hard to grasp from the end."

I grabbed near the tip and swung as if braining a slew of combatants.

"It seems you have gained the knack already," he said.

"Let's say I've been in disagreements at close quarter before. My last job was dispensing misery and death. But I wasn't all that good at it really. That's the true story."

"It is rumored that you were highly decorated."

"The operative word is rumor. It isn't true at all. I was a trouble-maker. What the Marine Corps called a shit-bird. It seems to be my nature."

"So you were not decorated."

"Purple heart, twice. An award given for being in the wrong place at the wrong time. And I would just as soon any discussion out there regarding my war exploits die."

"I see that such speculations and innuendoes focus undue and unwanted attention on you from these pipsqueaks around here."

"Exactly. I am already a freak. I would be super freak, with no way to mitigate it, if someone thought I had won some gallantry medal. Any decorations for gallantry happened to someone else."

"I assume you accept my gift?"

"Certainly. It's a true honor. I can say nothing that would describe how I feel about this."

"It is my honor to bestow it upon you. I have taught at some of the finest universities in the world and never have I met such a character."

"Thanks. I hope I can live up to your words."

"You already have. With that, let me change the subject. What have you been reading for geometry? It seems you moved far beyond what was on your list."

"Kobayashi and Nomizu. Through the first two chapters of the second volume. I find it slipping away now. Can't seem to tie it to anything."

"I recall you wrote well on multilinear algebra on the algebra qualifying examination. You displayed a firm grasp of the basics of modules, tensor products, and alternating algebras."

"I liked the multilinear algebra course. We did it all over modules. I also took both semesters of the advanced module course Bolyai gave last term."

"You are an analyst. Go to the book by Postnikov, *Variational Theory of Geodesics.* He utilizes multilinear algebra to determine tensorial properties without dragging the reader through the orgy of indices. He also contrasts the global and the local properties while concentrating on analysis to prove the theorems. It concludes with a thorough discussion of Morse theory and includes a technique of Bott's."

"I hate reading books." I decided not to ask him who was Bott.

"I must admit that I love them. But I am unusual in that regard here. There are not many of us who like to read as much."

"I like that math's transmitted mostly orally. And papers are always short. That is a good thing."

"Of course, mathematics is largely an oral art form. A form of conceptual art, really. The innovative insight and ingenious argument. Literary form plays a small part really," and with this throat clearing I realized he was set to deliver a lecture, his formal tone rising to new heights, "except for the terse exposition presented often without helpful guide posts; it's rather the directness of expression and the inroads and explanations of one area via another, as with J. Frank Adams and the relationship between non-vanishing vector fields and division algebras, extending the classical theorem of Frobenius, for example. To explain some geometry with algebra or vice-versa, or to see much broader swathes of the mathematical landscape, as with the interplay in several complex variables of algebraic geometry and function theory…"

"Or between partial differential equations and probability." I had began backing towards the door; once more he cleared his throat.

"One often confronts the beauty when the mystery falls away, as when seemingly eccentric behavior in one dimension becomes clear with the structure of higher dimensional complex manifolds. You are aware that there is a relationship between martingales and non-probabilistic analysis, as with potential theory or the recent work of people like Fefferman and Burkholder relating functions of bounded mean oscillation and H-pee spaces with martingales. It seems there is excitement regarding these new results."

"I've heard the names but no one here is working with it. Except for the relationship to PDEs, which I discussed yesterday."

"Ah yes, a lovely explication of the Dirichlet problem using Brownian motion. You are aware this goes back to Kakutani?"

"No. Actually never heard of him."

I had reached the doorway, ready to duck out.

"Ahem. I knew him at Yale, of course—"

"I really have to prepare for class. I teach a class—"

He cleared his throat yet again. I worried I might have missed the bell.

"This book by Postnikov is a small book, really. More like a paper. He writes as if talking, without a lot of verbiage. And also without a lot of symbols. It is as if he is at the board. I saw how you present your material. You say it and write very little. He also works like this. Try it."

"Does he do cohomology?"

"No, but there are a plethora of viewpoints of cohomology represented at your disposal. Mine of course emanates from algebraic topology and algebraic geometry as used in several complex variables. The topology group has a slightly different viewpoint. You have an ally in that group."

I didn't mention that ally had just accused me of being a war-monger.

The conversation had played out though Momus displayed his usual lack of enthusiasm for disengagement. I took my opportunity and prattled again about needing to get to class, a true statement, thanked him profusely once more for the gift and extricated myself. His voice followed me, admonishing more careful board skills in my expositions. Fuck that, I decided as I headed away.

I practiced ambling to class, swiveling my cane with a flourish as I entered the room. I leaned into it and scoped out the faces. The cheerleader up front smiled and shook her head like I was a certifiable loony. Her breasts strained against their sleek container.

In back sat my dumpy fan. "Miss Cone, I missed you last time."

She blushed and smiled at me. "I was unavoidably detained."

I knew exactly why. "If you need a fill-in, let me know."

I launched into a rambling excursion regarding the statistical properties of the sample mean as an estimator for the expected value of a distribution, driving mercilessly through the distributional properties and ending with the example of sampling a normal distribution. I showed that the variance of the mean went to zero as the size increased to infinity. I used the cane as intimidating pointer and leaning stick.

The cheerleader frowned and shook her blonde head. After class she cornered me. "How can a statistic be a statistic?"

"Well," I said, "two different uses of the word. Consider each sample as a draw from a normal distribution. The more draws you make the more you know about the shape of the distribution. And since they are drawn at random, they are also distributed normally, but the more of them you draw the less uncertain you are about the shape. That is the variance going to zero. I suggest you do those exercises I assigned. They are about sampling with and without replacement from urns filled with balls. Pay attention to the distribution of the samples. That will help get the idea. The rest will follow from what we studied about sums of random variables. And remember sums of independent normal variables are normal. If you still don't get it, come to office hours."

Behind her stood Miss Cone. "Did you mean what you said about filling me in?"

"Of course. Come to office hours and I'll give you what you need."

"Thanks." We walked out together and she left me where I ran into Steve at the foot of the steps in front of the mathematics building. Straight and lean wearing cowboy boots and long sleeved shirt, long legs embedded within a pair of denim stovepipes that slouched behind the knees making them appear bandy, he tilted his head back dripping Visine into each eye, sure sign he'd just come from home fully loaded.

"Damn, Steve, you look like you might bleed to death through those roadmaps you call eyes."

He shrugged. "Well, it's good shit. Second round of drops."

"Want a cigarette?" I asked, pulling the case of Perique hashish-laced specials from my pants pocket.

"Too strong. Can't cut it."

"Laced with good hash," I said.

"Wish you'd put that stuff in something smokable." But he stood near while I smoked it down. Neither of us brought up Lori.

"Heard you passed," he said.

"Yep. Got a present from Momus," holding up the cane.

"That old drunk."

"Maybe so, but he knows a lot of shit. He's a smart guy."

"He's finished. Just taking up a chair. Ought to retire."

I shrugged and we made our way up to the department. I stopped by my advisor's office.

"Good job yesterday," he said. "It seems your leg is better, too."

"Its fine. Momus gave me this and it is helpful when I am standing. I used it as pointer-intimidator in my class."

He seemed to relish the image, chuckling shy acknowledgement.

"I want you to focus now on the conversation laws."

"Sure, but we're doing it in class."

"Yes, but maybe more computationally. See if there is something we can do along those lines. Maybe with a computer."

"Well, I don't know shit about computers. Never worked with one."

"I understand MACSYMA isn't hard to learn."

"I prefer to concentrate on the geometric aspects. This variational stuff and Noether's theorem seem to point to some interesting connections between the symmetries and conserved quantities. No one has done a lot of with the differential geometric aspects of diffusion processes on manifolds, and that is a natural place to look at conserved quantities. I think there is something beneath all this tied to the quadratic variation of these processes. And people keep looking at the Laplacian on manifolds. Let me do some reading and thinking and discuss what I have come up with in a couple weeks. Is that acceptable?"

"Okay, but just don't get off on too deep a tangent. "

He referred to the legendary graduate student in the department who sat in classes correcting the lectures while taking notes. About to run out of time, his long tether stretched by years as a graduate student without a viable thesis. Knowing a lot of stuff wasn't the end goal.

"Don't worry. I have an intuition. If it doesn't play out, I'll drop it."

Before class I went to the library and found Postnikov. Two hundred pages of large type, including the index. Read breezily, like Momus said, almost like talking at a board.

A phone message at my carrel from Gudrun Ball reminded me of the party Saturday. I guessed I wasn't going with Bobbi.

I sat out office hours in my carrel without a single visitor. To date, there'd been no visitors. I got lost in Postnikov and didn't notice the time.

My advisor had already started his lecture as I entered the room, moving on from Noether's Theorem with some discussion of symmetry algebras of self-adjoint operators before plowing ahead with Hamiltonian vector fields and a bit of geometry with a definition of the Poisson bracket of one-forms and a proof it was exact. He wrote a slug of problems on the board and promised for next class the proof of another version of Noether's theorem, this time for two-forms on even dimensional manifolds related somehow to one-forms. What he wrote on the board didn't make sense to me at all, but I figured he'd start there next time so it didn't matter.

I got the hell out as soon as he seemed finished, grabbing my bag and heading for the gym.

Chapter 7
Absolute Neighborhood Retract

I made my way across Esplanade to Fauborg Marigny to see Bob. I'd met him through Red; they'd been friends since boyhood growing up in the northern Midwest. He stayed in the upper floor of a rambling old wooden structure on Frenchman's a block beyond Snug Harbor the other side of Washington Park. Snug Harbor was a restaurant and bar with an after hours jazz scene. Not so ritzy as Rosy's, it offered local groups as had Lu and Charlie's across Rampart Street. Snug Harbor had that bright, open airiness of decent restaurants without a need to hide the cockroaches; Lu and Charlie's clientele had reveled in a dark jazz club atmosphere, dominated by a gaudy Bruce Brice hanging near the bar. No such place any longer existed for jazz.

Climbing the long open stairway on the outside of the building to Bob's place always taxed my leg, the wooden stairs slick in rain and the railing not something that inspired trust. I called from the vacant lot next door to be sure a climb wasn't in vain. He popped his head out the window, black hair tied back in a pony tail, dense full beard sleek like animal fur carefully combed. Today he wore a scarf on his head and appeared as Blackbeard at the gunwales hailing me aboard.

Up close, his soft brown eyes peered out like a creature hiding in the woods.

I took a hit from his perpetual joint and asked about coke. I bought the small amount of coke I kept on hand from him, but it wasn't a drug I cared about one way or the other. He brought out a bit of his latest and we tooted, a lift starting at my eyes and running up along the top of my head for a brief instant. For me that always seemed the extent of it.

"I'm going to a party uptown tomorrow," I said, "and need a bit to flash. I think I can get some buyers if the price is right." He always had fair prices with a smaller margin than most and he didn't step on the stuff. Not a greedy guy. A hippy in the sense of freedom, not political and not revolutionary, but with that spirit. He also kept a shotgun and carried a handgun sometimes; Marigny could be dangerous. It didn't have the foot traffic of the central Quarter where I lived.

"I can spot you a little," he said. "Just got a fresh shipment."

"That'd work. I'm too fucking broke right now to buy shit. Had to go into credit card debt to get to my mother's deathbed in Arizona last week."

"Jeez, I'm sorry. I didn't hear about it."

"I told Red, but tried to keep it quiet. Seems everyone at Tulane knows more about my fucking life than I do."

He blew a lungful of smoke. "You like this stuff?" referring to the coke. "It isn't stepped on too much at all. I think it's pretty pure."

"I'm not much of a judge, but I feel it okay."

He tooted another couple lines and offered me the glass. I felt it up in my head this time, clear and bright, and said it seemed okay.

"I got some new pot in last week. Columbian, dark and lots of buds."

"That what we're smoking?"

"Yea. Whattaya think?"

"It's good. Sweet, too, not musty like some of the shit that comes in."

"I get a good buzz."

He offered me a bottle of Jack Daniels and we drank a bit, sat in silence, then I accepted a small baggie of the coke and a few joints and made my way back down the stairs. It had gotten dark out and I walked quickly to Washington Park where I crossed the street at Dauphine to the business side, then turned off Frenchman at Royal and doubled back along Kerlerec to Pauger Street which became Bourbon once across Esplanade. I felt safer on Bourbon than anywhere else in town.

Dropping the drugs off at my place, I hit the street again for Cosimos, a small bar at the corner of Dauphine and Governor Nicholls that catered to straight locals. The place was always so empty I wondered how they stayed in business.

I landed there when I wanted to be away from the academics and math types and rest of the bubble dwellers. The clientele were people who lived in the quarter and worked real jobs and didn't chase their own gender, at least not while there. Mostly drunks. One beautiful woman who worked as an engineer at the local television station got plastered almost every night. She lived conveniently across the street and the bartender on duty would get her home, often after she'd passed out, locking her door with a key she'd given them. She never remembered anyone or anything, but guys always hit on her and she could be very friendly, making out with complete strangers. From what I saw, none of them made it inside her apartment.

The bartender had driven tanks out of An Hoa. First time I'd come in he'd watched me for a while, then asked where I'd served. We hit it off, former Marines who'd been there. Never talked about it, neither of us. He didn't ask me shit and I didn't volunteer shit, but from the start we'd bonded.

"Hey," he said when I pulled up at the bar. "Been a while."

"I been out of town."

"Work?"

"Yea, travel for the man."

"Regular?"

"Sure." He poured me a whiskey from the bar well and a glass of ice water.

"So how is work?" he asked.

"Same old shit." I'd told him I worked for a company downtown doing some accounting stuff. "This is our slow time of year."

"Interesting. It picks up here a bit around Christmas, with a lot more drunks. Then after New Year's it dies down."

"Don't see our girl tonight."

"She hasn't been in yet. In fact, been showing up less than usual. I think she might have a boyfriend."

I finished my whiskey and he poured another. A cab stopped outside the bar and a tall, lanky, dark-haired character dashed inside. He stuck his face in front of each of the handful of us sitting at the bar, then hit the couple tables, asking each in turn, "Do you know who I am?" I'd never seen him before and told him I had no idea who he was.

He looked at the bartender, then said "I can't believe it. No one here knows who I am," and dashed back to the waiting cab.

"Jesus," I said, "what the hell was that about?"

The bartender laughed. "Doesn't anyone here know who that is?"

No one answered.

"That," he said, "was Pete Maravich. I recognized him, but didn't want to admit it to him."

A guy sitting down the bar said, "Is that who that was?"

"Sure was."

"Who the hell is Pete Maravich?" I asked.

The same guy laughed and said, "Basketball player. Call him Pistol Pete."

"New Orleans has a basketball team?" I asked.

He laughed again and said, "Not for long."

"That's likely why," my friend behind the bar said. "People like you not even knowing we have a team. Evidently the city has a lot more of your type than the other."

"You mean fans, right. I have never given a shit about sports, but this city is not rife with followers of the dribbling art?"

He poured me another drink. "On me," he said.

I stumbled out sometime later. He never charged me for more than half of what I drank and tonight he'd put it all on the house.

When I got back I smoked a joint and fell asleep, aware that next week I needed to get serious about putting together something for my advisor. I needed to move in some direction on a thesis topic or he would find one for me.

Chapter 8
Analytic Continuation

Saturday I lolled in bed and began a deliberate perusal of the first chapter of Postnikov.

Momus had it right; it read like someone at a blackboard talking. Sloppy notation, mistakes, plenty of proof by intimidation: every calculation easy, all statements transparently true. I didn't know the Russian word for obvious, but it would have stood out in this text. Arbitrary, too; everything was pronounced to be arbitrary: let p be an arbitrary point on a manifold M and v an arbitrary vector in the tangent space M_p and alpha an arbitrary covector on the cotangent space $(M_p)^*$ and so on.

Yet eminently clear presentation. You knew exactly where the objects lived: tensor fields defined algebraically as module-multilinear maps, tensorial properties not some sort of coordinate preserving gobbledygook but in terms of module-linearity over the C-infinity functions. Tensors themselves maps on the tangent spaces or cotangent spaces as vector spaces, though there were some odd kinds of indices as superscripts and subscripts that I thought ought to be subscripts and superscripts respectively for fields of vectors or differential forms, but clearly distinguished on given tangent spaces or cotangent spaces as vectors or covectors. Nothing confusing or that deep when approached without trying to give some semblance of geometry, whatever that is. And best of all, the initial definition of differentiable manifolds avoided the tortured systems of charts and diffeomorphisms explicitly presented in most books like a kind of pornography.

It dawned on me that my multilinear algebra professor had been right when asked about the geometry lurking somewhere behind all this stuff, telling us differential geometry was the study of invariants under change of notation. It was pretty much all notation. It made my heart jump for joy to run across some solid meaning behind the orgy of indices.

I smoked dope and plowed ahead, wondering why this Russian called the mean value theorem Lagrange's theorem unless his argument relied on some subtlety of variational calculus that flew past me. Didn't seem to matter one whit, however. Got to what he called Cartan's equations for the connection forms in the last section of chapter two; seemed to recall Kobayshi and Nomizu proving a Maurer-Cartan equation and begin to suspect that they might have had something against Cartan. I didn't think the Japanese had any kind of hostility for the French, but maybe the Japanese at Berkeley and Brown did. I recalled that Chevally's ancient monograph on Lie groups had been dedicated to both Cartan and Weyl. Opposite sides of geometry. Strictly of historical significance, my advisor had said, but skinny nonetheless I'd noted.

Forced myself to stay inside, keep working, not give in to the temptation to head out and wander the quarter. Mustn't cut myself too much slack.

Before long I'd ducked out the window, stood on the catwalk watching the street. Gaggles of gawking babes everywhere, always with some man pulling them along. Once they hit this corner most turned back, alarmed at the sudden throng of males on the balcony at Lafitte's kissing and fondling and ogling the men in the street; blocks numbered above seven hundred patrolled by guys in leather, tight jeans, hands in each other's back pockets, here and there a dark-bearded queen made up in semi-drag. Aware they weren't in Kansas or Kansas-friendly territory any longer, the hetero couples slowed, then retreated.

I guessed how long it would take some of them to note the discontinuity in climate, that tourist-land for the straight crowd had vanished in a new territory. Slowing down, looking, "Uh honey, I think we ought to turn around" jerking the chick back away from the balcony where she stands staring up at the crowd of butch boys, hardly a nelly in evidence, beards and construction hard hats and tight shorts and work boots, maybe here and there a Nazi uniform, someone calling out "Show your tits" to laughter and hoots from the gallery.

I pushed myself back inside and finished chapter two, halfway through the book and ready to start Riemannian Spaces, then put it down and hit the street headed for a Jackson square teeming with tourists. Stopped at Café du Monde for coffee and beignets sprinkled with sugar, about all I could afford. Would have preferred La Marquise.

Returned for more dope and on into the heart of chapter three: Riemannian spaces. Nothing all that difficult, but I decided to get my ass on to the party uptown before it got too dark to read the street signs. The Balls lived on Calhoun, across St. Charles Avenue from the University, Calhoun meeting St. Charles somewhere near Audubon Park, but I didn't know how close to the park or how far off the drag. Besides, I didn't like walking that deserted, expensive neighborhood alone at night. Felt like chum.

I showered and changed into a tight sky-blue t-shirt calculated to showcase my blue eyes and the muscles of my torso matched to a presentable pair of khakis; a ploy to look simultaneously tough, vulnerable and handsome, an affectation I didn't allow myself on campus or in my own neighborhood.

The streetcar would likely be infested with residual tourists but I took it anyway since it would be easier to spot the cross street from St. Charles Avenue. I was never sure where I was once the Freret Street bus passed the Brown Derby Club at the corner of Louisiana Avenue until it arrived at Tulane, and though Freret was only a few blocks from St. Charles, it was on the wrong side of Tulane and I didn't know if Calhoun made it all the way through. I deliberately kept my universe bounded and rarely paid more than scant attention to any but the major streets.

In fact, they lived beside Audubon Park, just off the avenue in one of the stately old mansions. The walk to the front door seemed a city block, winding through trees that had seen the area when it all looked like the open parkland the other side of Calhoun. It was a bit early and I had considered killing time in my carrel reading papers, but thought better of it. I'd just as soon be early, get a head start on food and drink.

A brunette brandishing abundant décolletage via partially unbuttoned white blouse met me at the door. I followed the greenish aura of her loose pale slacks into a dark paneled room with ceilings so high they almost disappeared into the winding stairs we passed on the way to a hall larger than my entire apartment. Across the immense rectangular room lavishly decked out with tables of food, bottles of liquor, beer on ice, and a punch bowl filled with some red stuff I saw two of my host, each confabbing with a double of himself, quietly earnest, pulling at identical cigars. Like talking to a reflection in a mirror that didn't obey its reflector. One of them looked at me and smiled.

They waddled over in parallel and Jeremy boomed out "Mr. Butcher, glad you could make it. This is my twin brother Harry," and I thought Harry Ball but said nothing. They wore identical blue jeans with waists likely double the inseam and pant legs rolled into massive cuffs showing red and green plaid flannel on the inside, identical checked shirts as unsightly as the one I'd worn to dinner, and broad green suspenders.

Harry held out his fat hairy hand and we shook vigorously. He had as powerful a grip as his brother.

"What's your game, Mr. Butcher?" he asked. "Slaughter?" He chuckled alone, pleased with his joke. Jeremy scowled.

"It was at one time, sir. I slaughtered Asian long pig, but we didn't bother to eat them."

He didn't seem to know what to make of the remark and stood mute. Jeremy smiled.

"Yes, I guess that is true," Jeremy said.

"Oh, I get it," Harry said. "Army man."

"Marines," I said.

"Reformed," Jeremy said, "now a gentle PhD candidate in mathematics at that prestigious institution across the street. Not Loyola, Tulane," he added.

A leggy blonde in raggedy blue jeans cut into short shorts strode into the room. Jeremy turned to watch her approach, his eyes glued to her upper torso, oblivious to the spindly pins and boxy hips. Her tits hung like overfilled water balloons from high up, almost from her shoulders it seemed, swinging back and forth within a blue ribbed tank top cropped above her midriff.

She halted beside Harry. The flesh sacks ceased swaying and sagged flat against her chest, their nipples, visible through the material, pointing at her toes. She stood five ten or so in her flat sandals, dwarfing the Ball twins. Her navel hovered far down on that elongated torso and I realized if the blouse had been cropped an inch shorter those fat nipples would be uncovered.

She beamed an expansive toothy smile, a narrow face of unexceptional features framed by limp, waveless hair hanging almost to her shoulders. The colors of her brows matched the hair, it all seemed natural, and her smile dimpled the corners of her mouth. Her blue eyes openly appraised me, laughing maybe. A happy woman, I thought. Sincerely happy. No artifice.

"Who is this beautiful man?" she asked. "A new actor?"

"No, dear. He's a civilian. A former killer turned academic," Harry replied. "Studies accounting."

"Please," I said. "Mathematics and accounting have nothing in common."

She took his arm and stared at me. She could have draped her boobs over his shoulders like a floatation device.

"When are the other girls coming, Harry?" she asked.

"As soon as the shoot is over, Dina. Be patient." He looked at me quizzically. "Have you ever thought of acting. You have the looks."

I didn't say anything.

Dina said Harry made films. Jeremy coughed.

"I can't act," I said and Jeremy laughed.

"Porn films, Mr. Butcher."

"Ohh," Dina said, "what a perfect name."

"Doesn't matter what kind of films. I can't act."

Dina moved up against me. "My name is Dina," she said. "Shall I call you Mr. Butcher? It seems so formal," rubbing my chest with small hands.

"Call me Whitey," I said. "There are more like you?"

"There is no other like Dina," Jeremy said. "She is one of a kind. They broke the mold when they made her. Perhaps we can screen one of her films for you, since it seems you are unaware of her talents."

Dina walked away to a table with booze and I stared at her meager ass, flat as a pancake framed by straight hips. If not for the tits she would have no physical appeal, and to me they were no help. Ugly as a mud fence, that was what came to mind.

"Some ass, huh?" A woman's voice this time. I turned to see Gundrun smiling at me.

"Might be to some tastes," I said.

She pulled me away from the twins who stood now grinning broadly, their heads together murmuring some private jest. Both wore the same damned thick toothbrush mustache covering upper lips behind which mouths hid in such a manner that teeth appearing in a smile offered a sinister surprise.

"You prefer the rounder type, then."

Looking down at her standing with hands on hips looking up at me, I knew I needed a joint. I thought dwarf: short legs and short torso. Slender except for swollen hips and round protruding ass, tits distending buttons and deforming seams of a taupe silk blouse; melons packaged firmly within a cleavage-revealing brassiere. Shiny new jeans resisted the outward expansion of her hips and thighs but tapered so drastically to her ankles I wondered how she'd gotten into them.

"I prefer a smile," I said, referring to asses but knowing she took it as a compliment regarding what she wore on her tiny carmine mouth. It beamed with my words. Her face outrageously long, a huge face atop a tiny person, not helped by the lumped chin and oversized square red plastic frames, nothing like the narrow rectangles she'd worn at dinner. From my high vantage her blonde hair sprouted like a fountain atop her head far above her spacious forehead, freezing bluntly at her shoulders. I imagined greenish blonde.

I lit up one of my hashish primed cigarettes.

"I thought it was a joint," she said, freeing a Gauloise from its blue packet and tapping it taut.

"No, but there is something a bit extra in this." I handed it to her and she inhaled deeply.

"What would that be? Nice taste," she said blowing twin plumes from her nose between us like a gray fog.

"A little hashish nestled within the Perique."

"Can I have one?"

91

"Of course. I apologize for not offering but hardly anyone likes this tobacco, particularly not women."

"I've been smoking Gauloises ever since I went to France my sophomore year in college." She took another long drag and vented again from flared nostrils. "I got pregnant that year and had my first abortion."

I wondered why she was telling me this stuff. It didn't go with casual acquaintance. Like me telling some stranger how I got into the Marine Corps. But her words changed steadily as she spoke, a bit dreamy, prolonged and floating. She was already wasted as she lit up the number I gave her.

"This is good shit," she said.

"Its alright. I have better. You won't see God with this."

"Who cares. Let me give you a tour," and she took my arm, guiding me past Dina who made like she might join us but stopped from what I took to be a warning glance from Gudrun.

We passed the woman who had greeted me at the door, now engaged in earnest discourse with a man dressed in a white uniform and chef hat carrying a tray. Gudrun ignored them both and steered me toward a long hallway.

"Who was that?" I asked, mostly about the woman.

"Just hired help. Shawntel is the woman's name. She works for Jeremy and I try to stay out of their way. He calls her an administrative house-keeper. The man is a cook. Jeremy insists on domestic help. Family tradition."

"He's from here?"

"Born and raised. Notice no accent."

"Well, we have a couple professors at Tulane from here and they speak like they could be from anywhere."

"It means they're from the good neighborhoods and the good schools. Not yats."

"So I assume it's true his brother makes porn films."

"Yes. He has a home in California, somewhere near Santa Barbara, but his major studio is in the San Fernando Valley. He also has one here in New Orleans. They are doing a production tonight and several of the actresses will be here later. Maybe some of the actors, though Jeremy discourages it. He calls them sleazy."

I could see she flew above us all now, so buzzed she all but glowed. Her hair breathed green, a crown of radioactive seaweed. When we got a ways down the hall, she jerked me around a corner and up a narrow stairwell.

"This is our gallery," she said, and we entered a room with a bunch of couches or daybeds or something like that, lots of them, and beyond that a narrow space with a banister overlooking a room below with more plush lounging furniture.

"Jesus what is all this?"

"It was set up for Harry to use in filming. He does some production work here. Of course, the house is so big no one notices."

"It does seem to go on forever."

"Jeremy's niece Anabel calls this the Escher room because it seems architecturally impossible."

"How big is this place?"

"It has somewhere around thirty major rooms. Many tucked away," and she moved closer, ran her hand over my thigh. "I play around."

Hanging silence. I brought out a joint.

"This is superior," I said. "Do you use coke?"

"No. I don't like the feeling. It makes me jangly."

I lit up and took a hit, passing it to her. She took a hit and we stared off into the space over the railing.

"If we didn't have so much company expected," she said, "I'd rip your clothes off and throw you on one of those banquettes right now. But not tonight."

"It must be a real bitch to air condition this place."

She shrugged. "I don't know what Jeremy pays. Probably a lot. He keeps it very cold."

"I noticed."

"You must have lunch with me one day."

"So long as it isn't a place like where we had dinner."

"I noticed you didn't seem to appreciate it much. Jeremy is a gourmand."

"I'm pretty simple. Burgers, poor boys, cooked seafood."

"People here say poboy. You like raw oysters?"

"Haven't tried them. Fried."

"Raw. We'll go to a raw bar one day."

We smoked the rest of the joint and she led me off to more rooms, hidden rooms and public rooms and a library past a lot of muddy old paintings hanging in dark and darkened rooms, then eventually down the big stairway at the front.

"I hope Bobbi makes it," she said as we rounded the long sweep and came into view of the party. "She's having boyfriend trouble."

"I didn't know she had a boyfriend."

"Of course not. She wouldn't say anything about that. She likes to get laid."

"Well, I wouldn't know. She dropped me off."

"Don't bullshit me. She was going to be all over you. She doesn't do anything for nothing."

I let it go unanswered. The noise levels rose as we descended. Lots of raucous female laughter at which Gudrun mumbled what sounded like "braying bitches." It came on like falling out of the sky into a dream. Or delirium. A group of women dressed in what could only be called poor taste stood alone in the middle of the room surrounded by people in suits, in tuxes, in jeans and leisure suits, even a Nehru jacket, the place jumping as if we'd been away days rather than minutes. I noticed Jeremy glance at his watch as we entered.

Immediately Dina grabbed me away from Gudrun and dragged me over to the clot of women.

"Girls, here he is. Isn't he beautiful?"

One of them, fragile looking, not five foot tall and skinny as a rail, so pale she looked like fine bone china translucent in daylight and covered in tattoos, her hair platinum and faintly blue eyes that almost vanished into the whites, looked me over. "Is this one of Harry's new discoveries?" she asked in a baby voice.

"No," Dina said, "he's a civilian."

"He ain't much to look at," the pale one said. "Darker. Real men are darker."

Dina snorted. "We all know what kind of dark you like, Mirabelle."

I couldn't take my eyes off her waifish countenance bounded by falling ringlets of fine silver-white hair so frizzy it formed a nimbus like an image of the Virgin.

She wore a short black skirt and combat boots that amplified her shapeless bird-legs and hipless lower chassis. Her body was straight without so much as a hint of a curve. Covering a torso delicate like a child's, a blazing red blouse hung loose and unperturbed by flesh protrusions from her neck fixed with a thin strap tied in back. It ended just above a navel outlined in red flames. Extending from her shoulders midway down her upper arms intricate patterns variegated in a rainbow of bright hues, purples and reds and greens and yellows and blues, intricate details of a mélange of unrelated shapes streaming together, geometric and animal and vegetable, flowers and a snail with an eye on its shell, a St. Brigid's Cross in bright yellow straw, solid color to the shoulder on her left arm but with stark white flesh showing through between fleshy red petals on the right, ending behind her shoulders but continuing round her back.

She rotated slowly to display a dorsolateral aspect, lingering when facing forward so I confronted a female Chinese doll with thick black hair and giant rounded ears wearing jade earrings tattooed all the way down to the small of her back, dressed in a purple coat with filigreed golden sleeves and red collar and bounded above on Mirabelle's left shoulder blade by what seemed to be a kind of mandala or throwing star with a red geometric egg drawn in the center, festooned behind it all in red flowers extending to Mirabelle's right shoulder blade.

Dina whispered in my ear that Mirabelle's stage name was Albina. That she had a tattoo on her mons with red flames and snarling around her vaginal lips a wolf's mouth with sharp teeth. The words Black Snake Whore etched below the flames on her mons. Her scant bodily hair permanently removed. Her areolae inked in red flames and her nipples solid ebony.

A meatier one with brown hair tumbling down over her shoulders stepped between Mirabelle and me. Maybe a half foot taller, she had olive skin and blue eyes and curves: round breasts with nipples pressed against a gray dress she might have painted on, ample hips and sturdy legs displayed in dark nylons to solid mid thigh. She wore black high heels with studs around the base and straps around the ankle and across the top of the foot. In profile a rounded forehead and sharp nose with substantial bridge displayed a small bump high up; her eyes close set and narrow; her mouth wide, straight and unsmiling.

She pushed up against me, her body hard as a rock, and said, "He's probably got a small dick." Her husky voice spread thickly over an eastern European accent.

From the back of the group someone said, "Not small enough." I couldn't see much of her, but what I saw didn't impress me. Long face verging on horsy, small mouth, high forehead, small chin, coarse straight brown hair hanging to where it appeared it had been cropped with a pair of pruning shears just above rounded bony shoulders. She did have green eyes, though, a dramatic touch against the dark hair, and on the cheeks around her straight nose light freckles that she'd tried to cover with makeup.

"That's Linda," Dina said. "She's a valley girl; lives near the studio in Chatsworth. A real Los Angeleno."

"That should be Angelena," Linda said.

95

"Linda does only girl-girl and solo," the one still pressing against me said. "I prefer girl-girl and solo, but I can work with boys. If they are pretty. But Linda can eat pussy like no one on this planet."

"Whatever," Linda said and walked away. I noted she dressed as if going to work in an office in ill-fitting long skirt and white blouse.

"And this," Dina said, "is Susana. She's from Hungary."

"Czechoslovakia," Susana said, playing the word out with a guttural finish. She ran her hand against my crotch before she backed away. "You're wrong, Miss Albina. He might give some of your favorite snakes a run for their money."

"And who are you three?" I asked the trio of washed out blonde toothpicks standing in the background. They chimed together in girlish voices, "I'm Bambi."

"You're all Bambi?"

"Yes," another chorus with giggles.

"We're filming *The Three Bambis,*" Dina said. "Of course we need three real Bambis."

"Stage names, though. Right?"

"Who knows?" Susana said deep and low.

I looked around the crowded room. Bobbi stood talking to Gudrun in a corner. I did a double take on spotting what I thought had to be Misty talking to Harry and Jeremy. Extricating myself from Dina and her covey, I made my way over to Gudrun and Bobbi, grabbing a beer on the way. Three bartenders manned stations along separate walls and women in chef's hats and white outfits stood preparing pasta dishes to order before elaborate setups on either end of the room.

"Hello, Manly," Bobbi said. "I'd have asked you to come but had to take care of something and wasn't sure I'd make it."

"That's all right. I got here." I pulled Gudrun aside. "Do you know that black woman over there talking to your husband and brother-in-law?"

She looked and shook her head. "I've never seen her before. I would guess she's with the actresses judging by how she's dressed."

Gudrun walked off to join them and I went back to Bobbi who seemed as solemn as her clothing, blue jeans and a plain dark blouse opened far enough to show what a meager fissure existed between her insubstantial boobs.

"Did Gudrun jump your bones?" she asked.

"What?"

"Just now. On the tour. Jeremy timed you two and I bet he guesses she did."

"That's nuts. She just showed me around. What is it with everyone here? They all seem to think about sex constantly. Must be the water."

"Come on. Those two have a clandestinely open marriage. They both do whoever they can, when they can. But Jeremy can't keep up with Gudrun, not even with the porn stars available. She travels a lot for work and she fucks everyone she can find who's willing. She even gave him a venereal disease once."

"You seem to know a lot about their private life."

"The whole town knows. He rejects the girls working for Harry, though I suppose Harry could set it up. Says they're whores and he only does it with willing volunteers."

"You ever do it with him?"

"You kidding? I don't go for short fat bald guys who smoke cigars and wear suspenders."

"He seems taken with Dina."

"Oh yes, he likes those floppers. But his brother screws her. And he uses her to get deals done, too. She was a whore when he found her, or so it's said."

"She's ugly as hell."

"Funny, most guys are knocked out by her. They see those saggy floppers and go ape-shit."

"Your boyfriend one of them?"

"I don't have a boyfriend. Don't have time for that. Too much work."

We passed a silent moment.

"You watch Gudrun," she said. "She's after your ass, you'll see. But she'll fuck anyone who'll have her. And she has some dugs of her own. She just doesn't display them so flagrantly."

"I doubt they're anything like those things hanging off that Dina."

"You'll find out for yourself. Just wait."

I excused myself and headed for one of the chefs in white to look for macaroni and cheese and get the hell away from her.

"Macaroni-cheese, honey? I don't know. What kinda cheese you like? We got no macaroni, babe, just spaghetti and fettuccine and these rotini here…" pointing to some twists. "Oh, yeah, babe, we got these rigatoni but they big for macaroni cheese. What kind macaroni cheese you wanting? Like baked in the oven, cause we ain't got none of that neither." She paused for a minute, then added, "I can try to do cheese spaghetti."

97

"I sort of thought like out of the box, you know, Kraft Macaroni and Cheese with the little package of cheese powder that turns to goop with milk."

"Oh, honey, I gonna fix you with fettuccine and butter cream Parmesan sauce. It's the best cheese spaghetti they is."

"I don't know…"

"We ain't have no cheddar-type cheese food here, honey. Mr. Ball, he don't cater for such as that. But I know what you mean. I fix in my home, from the box, but I like American Beauty best. It got sweeter cheese and better pasta. More bite."

"I buy that one when I see it. It's cheaper."

"Yes, honey, that too. I gonna fix you up with this here fettuccine dish."

"Okay, but the thing about macaroni is its less messy."

"Believe me, babe, ain't nobody here gonna worry about you got a little cheese on your shirt or chin."

All the time she'd been smiling and a cluster had formed behind me but she'd kept right on, a yellow-faced woman with orange hair who could have been in triplets with the Ball twins, including the mustache. She turned around and tossed a tong full of skinny noodles into a basket and dunked it in boiling water, meanwhile whipping up a scoop of butter and cream into a kind of sauce she thickened with brittle grated cheese. She plopped the noodles into a shallow bowl and mixed in the cheese and cream and butter mixture until it dissolved and coated the noodles.

"Pepper, sweetie?"

"Sure."

She ground pepper from an oversized wooden contraption.

"That enough?"

"Fine," I said, clueless.

"Now you eat that hot, cause it ain't much good when it get cold and hard. Get you a glass of that good Italian wine over there. Some Chianti."

I grabbed a fork and tried twisting the stuff around but it didn't work well, so I lifted it dangling from the fork and lowered it into my mouth. I couldn't believe the flavor: sweet and rich. Amazing. A whole new world opened up, if I just knew what the hell that grated brittle cheese was. I made a note to go back and ask. I passed on the wine, grabbing a glass of water to wash it down before starting on Wild Turkey.

Gudrun towed over a doughy guy of medium height wearing a sparse attempt at what Harry and Jeremy had growing on their lips. His neatly cut thick dishwater hair stuck up in disarray around his head as if he didn't believe in combs; he wore the saddest expression on his face, likely a result of eyes like a beagle bulging from above dark folds.

"This is a distant relative of Jeremy's," she said, "from the California side of the family. He works here in New Orleans now. His name is Kip Downland. Kip, this is Whitey Butcher." Then she was gone.

"Whoa, that's some spaghetti technique, dude," he said. His slow delivery would have sounded drunk had he not spoken with such deliberate annunciation.

"What kind of distant relative?"

"That's bull. He knows my mom. Met her once in Barstool." I couldn't reconcile that the words slurred above the precision of the speech.

"Pardon?"

"You don't know Barstool? Otherwise known as Barstow. She worked project management there with a company he owns. They had some problems and he had to reassure the government. He got to know her."

"So where you from, Kip?"

"Taft. California."

"Don't know it."

"A suburb of Bakersfield."

"Heard of Bakersfield, but don't know it."

"You'd have to be there. Mostly vegetables and country music and Mexicans."

"Doesn't sound like a good place to be."

"To be from." He scanned the room. "Man, there's a lot of split-tail here."

It took me a hanging second to catch what he meant. "Yeah, there is. But the real interesting stuff is courtesy of Jeremy's brother Harry."

"I know that stuff. I got my eye on that Hungarian. But she's pretty cool about me. As in not interested."

"There's others. The Bambis."

"Yeah. What a trip. Skinny though."

A black guy dressed in a lavender leisure suit and pink shirt with a heavy gold chain hanging outside the coat wandered over. He wore long, pointed, saffron-colored shoes.

"This is Jerry," Kip said. "Jerry, this is Whitey."

Leaner and shorter than Kip, Jerry seemed nervous. I couldn't tell if it was feeling out of place or just energized. Skin so black he almost glistened.

Only the second black I'd seen tonight. He looked me in the eye and I held out my hand. He shook lifelessly.

"What's going on, Kip?"

"Lot of babes here," he said.

"What do you do, Kip?" I asked.

"Jerry and I work over in Jeff Parish. Out by the Huey Long Bridge. Strategic Petroleum Reserve. Government boondoggle. Drilling holes in salt domes to pump in oil."

"Don't know about it."

"It's in all the papers."

"Man don't read no papers," Jerry said. "That's cool. I wouldn't know nothing about it if employment people hadn't sent me out."

"I don't read papers, that's true. Waste of fucking time. If its important you'll find out soon enough, and there's never a damned thing you can do about it in any case."

"Jeremy owns one of the companies that hired me," Kip said. "Saved me from Taft. Now I run a software package that generates bogus reports."

"I got on cause they ain't got no minorities there," Jerry said. "I don't do a damned thing, but pay's okay. Looks like they ain't got too many minorities here neither. They ain't even got no black help."

"I saw one other black here," I said, "a chick I met once in the Quarter."

"You meaning Misty. That nasty bitch be everywhere. I wouldn't let her suck me off with your dick. No telling what nasty shit that bitch be putting in her mouth."

"She must be gone," I said. "I don't see her."

"The black chick?" Kip asked. "She's around the corner preparing to audition for Harry."

"What the hell?"

"Yeah, bunch of guys be lining up to get they dicks sucked. You say that an audition? I thought she doing it for fun. She always be doing that shit."

"I thought she did it for money," I said, "not fun."

"Depends on if she likes you looks or not," Jerry said.

"Sliding scale," Kip said. "Interesting idea. She wants to be in the movies and Harry wants to see her perform. He won't get involved except as a spectator. If he likes her he'll bring in some of his talent and see if she can take it up the ass and such. But he'll pay her tonight whether he uses her or not. I think I may get my dick sucked. It's free."

"That nasty bitch," Jerry said, "put anydamnedthing in her mouth. I would not be doing that shit, Kip."

"She ain't gonna give me VD with her mouth."

"Maybe wors'n."

"Did you see the albino?" I asked. "With the fucking tattoos? I have never seen anything like that. Looks like she'd glow in the dark."

"You ought to see her in the movies," Kip said. "She likes them big and black."

"She ain't turned on by me," Jerry said. "Not big enough, I guess. But she just guessing from the outside. She ain't seeing nothing I got. But they all just bitches anyway. Ain't nothing special."

"You guys interested in a little smoke? I need to sit and rest my leg and I am ready for a joint."

"Shit yeah," Jerry said.

"Count me in," Kip said.

We began making our way out of the room when Dina snagged me.

"Oh, God, tell me you're not leaving. I don't know anything about you."

"Believe me, nothing to know. We're headed for the outer room to sit and smoke a joint. I need to get off my feet."

"I thought you might be going to participate in the audition. I can provide better."

"No, Dina, I am no actor and I will not be on display. If you want, come with us."

Blue eyes alight, she turned on a smile displaying an even row of regular upper teeth under a straight upper lip bounded below by a wide oval, like a half moon decked out in ivory. Slightly oversized front teeth angled inward the least smidgen along their dividing line.

We found a dark corner with a glass topped coffee table and I plopped onto an uncomfortable couch that might have been an antique. I pulled out a joint laced with gummy Nepalese hash.

"Let's start with this," I said, "then I have something sweeter for dessert, to bring us closer to God."

"I wish I had some coke," Dina said. "Harry is so stingy with it. He only likes to give it out when we shoot."

I pulled a bag from my pocket along with a short, silver flat-bladed folding knife. "Lets start with the dope."

We passed the joint and I poured out some of the cocaine and chopped it up a bit, divided it into four lines. Dina had a rolled greenback ready.

"Ladies first," I said and she tooted a line. Jerry and Kip went, then I followed.

Things brightened up with the joint. I ignored the blathering people and pulled out a bud of Sierra Madre sinsemilla. Unfortunate they couldn't see the threads of purple and red weaving through the seedless bud, sticky to the touch; I crushed it carefully and rolled a tight joint.

"What's that? Thai stick?" Seemed to be Kip talking.

"No, some sins from Mexico. Sierras they said."

"Treasure of the Sierra Madre," Kip intoned. Jerry might have lofted to some other planet. Dina stared at me dreamily, creeping me out.

"Here," I said, "another line and then smoke this," setting up four more white lines.

"How's your feet?" Dina asked.

"What?"

"You said you needed to get off your feet. I guessed they were tired."

"No, Dina. My leg. I have a bad leg."

"Oh, I'm sorry. How's your leg."

"I don't know, man. They haven't brought it in yet." Kip again.

"Where'd you hear that?" I asked, preparing another line.

"A guy who'd been a Navy corpsman in Vietnam. Told me he said that once in triage to a guy who'd lost his leg. The guy was hollering 'My leg, how's my leg, Doc?' and the corpsman said, 'I don't know, man, they haven't brought it in yet.'"

I laughed and Dina said that was horrible but laughed anyway. Jerry mumbled, "Cold. That's cold."

We snorted the coke off the table and I lit the joint, took a deep hit.

"That's good coke," Kip said. "You have a source?"

"More or less," I said.

"Can you get me some?" Dina asked.

"Let me check. I have a friend but he's not a dealer. He just parted with a bit of this to me at cost. He might be able to get some, but probably not a lot."

Dina rubbed my thigh absently as she stared off into space.

"I'm fucked up," Jerry said. "I'll see y'all later." He wandered towards the big room.

"Whoa, that's good dope," Kip said. "Man I would love to get some of that shit."

"That's almost impossible. Get it from a friend as a kind of gift. The shit sells for a fortune. Like two hundred fifty bucks an ounce or so."

"That's not so bad," Dina said.

"Rich for my pocketbook, but I know people who'd go that price," Kip said.

"Damn, Dina, you must have some money. That's like four grand a pound. I hate to pay even a tenth of that."

"Oh, I make good money. People like my movies."

"It's the acting," Kip said.

"I settle for Colombian when I can get it, but I smoke rope from Mexico sometimes at one fifty a pound. May take more, but not that much more."

"It's the crystal purity of the high I pay for," she said. "What kind of friend gives stuff like that away? You must provide some very special services." She withdrew her hand and got up, looked down at me, then walked away.

"Jealous bitch," Kip said.

We sat a while and then Kip went away and I sat alone, mulling over co-variant differentiation and parallel translation along curves, geodesics. I might have dozed off. Suddenly Harry was standing over me talking.

"What?"

"I said we need volunteers for that girl Misty. She's insatiable. Fren-zied."

"Christ, man, don't throw your banners at me."

"No, really. Its unbelievable. I've never seen anything like it, not even with Albina."

"What? You want me to watch?"

"No, I need volunteers. Particularly ones that might be hung."

"No way. Don't you have a stable of film studs?"

"I got them here. She went through them all."

"Kip expressed interest."

"We used him, but he's a real disappointment."

"Not me. Sorry."

He wandered off muttering to himself. I got up and saw that the party had dwindled to a crew that looked like goat herders and nymphs, or maybe nymphos. Twisted expressions, turbans and hair shirts; I knew I was fucked up. Had to get home. Jerry and Kip were drinking together, alone, backs against the wall, holding off a mob of whispering aliens. I wandered up.

"How was she?" I asked.

"Perfunctory blow job. Didn't like me, I think. Not my type."

"I clued you on that bitch," Jerry said. "Man, we got to split. But we need to get together another time, dig?"

"Sure. I'm game. Call me at the Tulane Math Department. Ask for Mr. Butcher or Whitey or some permutation of those. They'll get me the message."

I was about to hit them up for a ride when Dina glided up behind me.

"I thought you fell asleep," she said. "You looked so peaceful."

"Dreaming of you," I said.

"Don't bullshit me. You need a ride or something? I got a car here."

"Yeah, I do. But I was going to ask Kip or Jerry here. No need to trouble yourself. Besides, this city is the murder capital of the country. Dangerous out there."

Kip's eyes widened. "Man," he said, "you're weird turning down a ride from this babe. You take my car and I'll take the ride from her."

"Come on," she said, hooking her arm in mine and pulling me towards the door. "You're coming with me."

She grabbed an unopened bottle of Wild Turkey and we headed out into the morning.

Chapter 9
Flabby Sheaves

Dina lifted her crop top and let peek from below a pair of gnarly brown splotches surrounding nipples like amputated pinkies.

"You like these?"

I blurted "No."

She stared in amazement, then peeled off the shirt. The appendages hung against her slender frame like tubular bladders flattened and distended with the weight of some coagulum compacted at the ends. They stretched from below her shoulders high up on her torso along the indentation of her armpit, wide apart on either side of a bony sternum. Shapeless and skinny and adorned with perhaps the ugliest tits I'd ever seen.

"Come on," she said, "suck them. Men love them."

"Let's get high," I said, moving over to the couch with the bottle of Wild Turkey. I took a slug, then brought out the nose candy and another joint. When she leaned over to toot it seemed her udders brushed the floor.

I didn't want coke and let her toot again, instead taking another belt of the booze.

She sat on the couch and looked at me. "You don't like me, do you?"

"I like you fine, though I don't know you well."

"That isn't what I mean and you know it. You don't like the way I look."

"You're not my physical type. I prefer rounded tits that stand up and point out. Round asses that aren't flat. Hips. Maybe even brunettes."

"I don't get it. Here I am, a woman most of the men in the world want to fuck, sitting in your apartment with no blouse, so wet between my legs my panties are soaked, and you're turning me down?"

"Not turning you down. Just not inspired."

She grabbed the lit joint and took a vicious hit.

"You have a bong?"

"No. I do have a pipe somewhere. Why?"

"Let's do some of that sinsemilla. I can get you more.'

"I have enough. Let me make up something special."

I grabbed newspaper and rolled a monster cone of a spliff with maybe a quarter ounce of the Columbian, then rolled a small tight one with the sins. We sat on the floor in the enclosed porch and smoked the spliff until we were so fucked up we could barely move. A green anole on the wall eyed Dina and displayed its red throat flap. Eventually we migrated through the loft to the balcony and ducked through the low window.

"Wow," she said. "Bourbon Street?"

I moved next to her and put my arm around her bare waist. "Yes, ma'am, that it is. And to your left, across the street at the corner, the biggest gay bar in the South."

We smoked three varieties of hashish and the night brightened, crisscrossed with red streaks. I fired up the sins. We smoked and watched the parade of prowling men, the young hustlers on the corners waiting for suburban scores driving down Dumaine.

"Wow," she said. "Wow." She might have said it several more times.

She dragged me inside. "Shower," was all she could croak.

I showed her and she held onto me, helped me out of my shirt, encouraged me out of my shoes and pants and underpants until I stood naked in the gloom and she bent to her knees and diligently sucked my cock, slurping and drooling and repeatedly burying it to the hilt, face against my groin, licking my balls, pressing it deep into her throat which felt rough and constricting and not all that pleasant.

She took off her jeans and guided my hand to a shaved groin with only a blonde strip running up the mons like a tidily mowed patch of dead grass.

In the shower she scrubbed me as if I were a classic car making ready for a show, paying particular attention to my erect cock and my anus which she lathered farther inside than I found comfortable.

"Mmm," was all she murmured as she went to her knees again and sucked my drooling erection, lapping up the secretion. "Now me," she said and I soaped her down.

She directed me to her hanging boobs whose nipples at my soapy touch knotted like warts, splotchy dun areolae crowning the ends of the rounded bulbs like carpet domes the texture of gooseflesh. She leaned into me and licked my face and my shoulder as I rubbed her nipples. She scrubbed her own nether regions as rigorously as she'd done my ass. We toweled each other dry and she demanded I snort coke with her.

Pulling me over to the bed she saw our faint reflections in the mirror.

"My God. Perverse."

Perverse the word. Nothing ever described to me by fleet sailors regarding Hong Kong brothels came close to this woman's meticulous ministrations. She knew her way around the male physique: what to try for expected responses and how to manage them. She brought me to orgasm so many times I lost count.

Insatiable had no meaning in my prior experience. I'd run out of steam and she'd sit me on her face, drive her tongue so far up my asshole she French kissed my prostate, and I'd climb erect again. I fucked every hole, asshole to mouth to cunt to mouth to asshole to cunt, ejaculating in each of them. Numb, I passed out as she sucked my dick; I dreamt an extended orgasm in a warm mouth.

Unkind light blasted me awake. Warm flesh against me, fetid air and sheets and a body, an arm, a bag of a tit flopped across my chest. I shook myself free, rolled away. She whimpered but didn't waken.

I got up to make coffee. What a fuck story. Bad enough with Lori. Now this one.

I drank the coffee and showered. Every time I passed the bed her miserable carcass sprawled in some hideous position, baggy tits, skinny ass, flesh rolls here and there. Mouth open, drooling. A pair of lizards tattooed on the back of her left shoulder.

I gave her an hour and then shook her.

"Time to get up. I got shit to do today."

She sat up and blinked. "What time is it?"

It was pushing ten. "Going on noon."

"Jesus," she said. "We just got to bed."

"Well, I got stuff to do."

"Can't you do it and let me sleep a little longer?"

I didn't know what to tell her. You're a skank. I don't want your ugly ass around here. Get the fuck out and don't come back.

"You can't stay."

"What? You're throwing me out?"

"No, but you need to get up. We can have coffee and pastry at La Marquise. Then you need to get on your way so I can get to work."

"What kind of work? Reading for your thesis? Or you hustling the street?"

"My advisor's bugging me to get some shit underway."

"I know about that. I won't be in your way. Go get your coffee and whatever and then when you come back I'll get cleaned up and we can have lunch and talk. I want to know you better."

I left her and went for a walk. What a fuck up. She would be trouble to get rid of, but more trouble if I didn't get rid of her. I needed to figure out how to do it without being brutal, and now it seemed she was no bimbo, either. She'd see through whatever I said. Insinuating I was gay wouldn't help; she'd likely find that more appealing.

I walked down to the river and paced the Moonwalk, watching the tugs pushing their cargoes downstream, keeping them from careening off into the shore with the current at the bend.

I decided to be honest with her.

When I got back she'd cleaned up, made the bed, made herself coffee and stood watching the prowling men in the street.

"You said it was going on noon," she said. "It's just eleven now. I think you're an asshole."

"I am. That is what everyone tells me and I think they're right. I'm insensitive, self-centered and have no concern for anyone. I'm not a nurturing human."

"Take off your pants. I want to see your leg. I felt it last night and it was covered with scars."

"I'd rather not display it in the daylight. I don't wear shorts. I'm not proud of it."

"Come on. Let me see it. If you do, I'll leave after lunch."

I dropped my trousers and she came over to run her hand along the purpled maze of twisted gashes.

"Jesus, what happened?"

"I got shot in that leg. Several times. Turned it to mush. They essentially rebuilt it."

Her fingers explored furrows and ridges, probing excavations and caressing gnarls.

"It's ugly," I said. "It makes me weak."

"There were some serious holes here."

"Well, the word was six or so, but it was hard to tell."

"Muscle damage, I guess."

"Yep. Shattered the bones. Shortened, tied, some muscle just gone."

"But not as ugly as I, is that it?"

"You're not ugly."

"Come on, don't bullshit me. You thought I was ugly from the beginning. I knew you weren't gay cause even gays like my boobs. But they are ugly. I know it. Men who like them are fucking idiots. I am an ugly woman."

"You're sexy."

"Bullshit. Not to you. I work hard to create sex. Did I work hard enough last night?"

"I thought you liked sex."

108

"I do. But it's work, like anything worth doing. You dig mathematics, but it is work, isn't it?"

I didn't say anything. She didn't give me a much chance to consider the question.

"Was I good last night?"

"Too good for me."

"Whatever the fuck that means. You shot a huge load in my mouth while you snored."

"I passed out. Drunk, drugs, Christ I had more orgasms than I recall ever having in one night."

"Then I was good, but not good enough to stay."

"Why the hell do you want to stay here? It's a dump in a gay neighborhood. There's only one bathroom. I hate to share a bathroom. There's only one bed, and I don't like to sleep with anyone."

"It's deeper than that. I know it. You don't want me around."

"That isn't it. I don't want anyone around. I don't have time or space."

"Walk me to my car. I'm not sure where it is."

"You don't want to eat somewhere?"

"I don't want to put you out. Besides, I'm too ugly to take out in public. Just walk me to my car and I won't bother you again, Mr. Butcher."

So I did. Then I returned and got back into Postnikov, Chapter Three, Riemannian Spaces, which began with a painfully fucked up discussion of Riemannian connections. His definitions had turned ambiguous, the notation no longer specifying what lived where, the covariant derivative with respect to an arbitrary vector field zero but not zero when applied directly though it ought to have been unless that meant something else. I looked back at his discussion of covariant differentiation and parallel translation along a curve, wondering now if I had understood any of his approach at all. Not a good sign, given I'd slogged through that territory twice before.

I tossed the book aside and left to get beer and burgers at the Port of Call; to listen to the jazz on the juke box.

Chapter 10
Twisted Convolutions

I nursed a beer and hankered after a shot precluded by my dwindling money supply. Someone had stuck a lot of quarters in the jukebox and Miles wafted over the dark, quiet interior; few people on a Sunday afternoon. It started to rain outside and the splash of cars on Esplanade infiltrated alongside a persistent drip drip drip off the sign hanging over the door or the tree beside the door or maybe both.

When things go wrong they go all the fucking way wrong. A hand on my shoulder and a pitch outside the realm of what I needed to hear: Lori's voice.

"There you are."

She sat down on the empty stool beside me and asked for a beer.

"You want anything else?" she asked.

"Get me a shot of bourbon and another draft," I said, pouring the remains of the glass down my throat.

I slugged back the shot and turned to look at her wet hair, unwound curls hanging around her face like a wet dog.

"You need a phone," she said.

"Why? I wouldn't've been home if you'd called."

"I wanted to call you last night."

"I was occupied."

I asked for a pack of Camels, not feeling like rolling my own.

"If I want to get together I have to hunt you down."

"You can leave me a message at the department."

"Not a good idea right now."

I didn't go for the bait. I had no interest in hearing a sob story about Steve I'd probably get anyway.

"I was afraid you'd be over at that strange place in Marigny. I can't find that place. What's it on, Royal?"

"Yeah. I was considering making my way over there later to see the human zoo, but no need now."

"Jeez, you're in a mood. Get your dick bit off or something?"

"Something. Trying to pick up some differential geometry, but that shit is all notation."

"All that stuff is useless bullshit. Ego tripping. Mathematics is one big ego trip."

We sat for maybe two minutes in silence before she dragged in Steve.

"Steve says he thinks we'll move in together soon, but he wants to give it more thought. Says he doesn't mind who I do so long as it isn't you."

"You been talking about me to him or something?"

"Something."

She was playing me off against him. I'd suspected it but hadn't minded the sex. She didn't know Dina's tricks but she did have a surfeit of enthusiasm and no inhibitions I'd uncovered. I was certain it'd be no contest between them; Dina'd win hands down. They were both ugly, but Dina made Lori a beauty.

"When you're done with that, let's head out of the Quarter," she said. "There are some places I'd like to take you."

She paid the tab and we dashed through the rain to where she'd parked the other side of Esplanade and headed out Tchoupitoulas along the river or canal or whatever running body of water rolled behind the levee. Cutting over on Washington, she made a turn onto Magazine, twisted a maze through some back streets and stopped before a shack with an unlit sign. I had no idea where the hell we were.

After scoping out the room from the doorway, we migrated to the pair of pinball machines staring at us from the far side of the room, past a few tables with chairs disarrayed, a long bar tended by an obese woman or man, not clear which in the dim light.

Lori bought beers and waxed my ass at pinball. When I played my short turns she intently studied the handful of men in the room sitting alone or in unspeaking pairs.

"I'll be back in a minute," she said, then wandered over to a guy sitting at the bar, sandy hair, youngish. She sat beside him and chatted, then they got up and she led him to the ladies' room. They went inside for five minutes or so and she drifted back to me, he to his place at the bar. We finished the beers and she said let's go.

The next dark establishment seemed livelier, recorded Fats Domino playing above the ching of pinball machines, smack of pool balls. Some guys looked up as we came in. I spotted no other women except a lone bartender, brunette, maybe thirtyish. She knew Lori.

"How you doin', babe? Ain't been seeing you in a while."

"Been working a lot of hours. Rush project. Some control system for a pipeline."

"Ain't that sumpin. I passed by your house but just your girlfriend staying there."

"She said you'd stopped by. I guess you two did okay without me."

"Uh huh. Want brews?"

We took a table near the restrooms.

The bartender came out from behind the bar carrying two Dixie long-necks. Taller than Lori, dark skin, bushy hair, hard to tell how to properly stereotype her. New Orleans, famous for worrying about percentages of racial mixture, was talking up Dutch Morial as potential mayor to succeed Moon Landrieu. They termed Morial a Creole of color, one of the aristocrats with light skin. To someone who'd grown up in the West, people saying it wasn't like he was really black because of his aristocracy sounded absurd.

The black turtleneck she wore swelled with a hefty chest; her jeans evidenced a wide ass and substantial hams for legs. Lori stood and they hugged, then kissed on the mouth.

"This is Whitey."

"Pleased to be meeting you, Whitey. Where'd you find so pretty a boy? I might want to taste some of that myself." She gave me a huge smile of crooked teeth behind sensuous lips I wished she'd kept closed.

"She's an ex," Lori said when she'd gone back to the bar. "She still comes by sometimes to see my roommate. We sometimes do threesomes or more, depending on who's around. Steve's been with the three of us."

"I didn't know you had a roommate."

"She's almost an ex too."

She scoped out the men in the room, then stood and went to the bar, sat beside one of them and in a couple minutes they headed into the ladies' room. Then she was back, finished her beer, and did it again with another. She picked off four of them before we left.

The next place hunkered at the end of a large unlit parking lot. The rain had turned to mist so it wasn't a big deal when she parked at the edge of the lot in the farthest, darkest corner away from the other cars.

Better lit, this joint jumped by comparison. Three pool tables and five pinball machines surrounded by a herd of men, scattered amongst them a handful of women, nebulous shapes obscured within floating layers of bluish smoke.

She chose a seat at the bar and we accepted more Dixie longnecks from a man who looked at her as if he knew her, didn't like her, and didn't want her there. She ignored him and quietly made her way around the room, talking to men who came over to the bar and clustered, each introduced to me by first name. I didn't remember any of them. When a table vacated our party shuffled over to it like an embarrassed cadre of males escorting a solitary female.

Some of them tried to make small talk but I wasn't in the mood. I had a pretty good idea of what she had in mind and didn't know if I wanted any part of it. It seemed a weird scene.

When she added one last male and stood to move them out to the parking lot, I didn't think I'd go. She saw the look and pleaded with her eyes. She'd put herself in a dangerous situation and I was the backup, the muscle. It smacked of the same sort of shit the Marine Corps had always done to me, trying to get me killed.

I acquiesced but I didn't like it.

She took the men one at a time to the far side of the car, leaned them against the metal behemoth, unzipped their pants, went to her knees and fellated them to orgasm. One of those waiting spoke up, a lanky kid with greasy black hair and an attempted beard.

"Let's all do her, man," he said. "The bitch is a slut; she wants us all to fuck her. Lets do her."

I put my arm on his shoulder. "If she wanted to fuck you, she'd ask. I don't hear her asking." I gave him my cold-blooded look, the one I'd worn when I shot VC suspects to encourage their companions to talk. Guilty or innocent didn't matter to me.

"Who are you, man?"

"I'm her husband. And if you don't settle down I'm gonna kick your ass." I towered over the kid, and I let him know by my grip on his scrawny shoulder I meant what I said.

"Man, you two are weird."

No one else said a thing. I wished I'd brought the cane. The kid kept his place in line, staring down at the tarmac. It seemed for a minute he'd leave, but watching her sucking cock kept him there. He went next and she did him. She did them all, one by one, and I encouraged them to stay and watch, not a difficult task, but with the worry they might be tough to get rid of as a group. But neither did I want them alerting the bartender or customers there was a woman out in the parking lot sucking dicks.

She stood up after the last one. "Thanks, guys. Been a pleasure. Now we gotta go."

They filtered away and we climbed in and drove off. She didn't say a word until she'd parked in a vacant spot on what had once been a lawn outside an old house.

She leaned over and put her head on my shoulder. "Kiss me."

"What are you, nuts? No way."

She looked up, remnants of semen hanging from her chin and nose, drying around her lips, glistening like goobers in the yellow illumination from the spotlight attached to the wall.

"Steve does. He'd come up now and we'd go do my roommate together. Maybe she's got friends up there. Wanna see?"

"What would you've done if they'd decided to gang rape you? I couldn't stop them."

"I'd go along for the ride. Something new. Besides, I thought you were a tough guy."

"With a gun. War's not about fist fights. War's a team sport about standing your ground when people are trying to kill you and killing them instead. And I don't choose to put myself in harm's way without some kind of prior discussion."

"Come on, kiss me and let's go upstairs."

"No, I am not coming up."

"Okay," she said, "let me finish this," leaning over and unzipping my pants. Watching had roused an exuding erection that soaked the front of my underwear, but she had to work to finish it after the previous night's exertions. Slurping, drooling, sucking, she coaxed an orgasm from me. Then she drove me back to my place and dropped me off.

Chapter 11
Free Modules

I got to Tulane with barely time to make class. A sparser turnout more lethargic than their usual stupefied selves confronted me; even the bubbly blonde up front and my brunette drudge at the rear appeared present only in form. I rambled on about the Central Limit Theorem, my back to the board, and turned with some discussion forming to impress the idea of convergence of distributions. Ms. Cone sat with her legs up on the chair in front of her, the pleated skirt open and framing a fat-lipped gash sprouting a wild growth of dark pubic hair.

I lost track of what I wanted to say. She put a hand over her mouth, flashed an innocent *what-me?* expression and put her feet on the floor before anyone noticed.

It took me a minute to recover. I'd had an example in mind, a set of bins configured in a Pascal's triangle into which dropped balls would arrange themselves in a normal distribution, but I decided given I didn't have one to show, to describe it would be fruitless. No one gave a shit anyway. They only cared about the final and their grades.

I opened it to questions. There weren't any so I assigned a problem set and then talked about something unrelated until the bell rang. They herded out en masse, no one hanging back to ask questions.

I wanted to avoid my advisor's class, to avoid him, not having done shit all weekend but hang out with sluts. I'd have to run out on him as my class had run out on me. Not a fucking thing to discuss, not a single idea, going on a week after the oral exam. Not a goddamn thing accomplished. My life had become one of the sea stories I'd heard from fleet sailors concerning liberty in places like Subic Bay or Hong Kong. Who could believe it?

Two messages in my mailbox, one from Harry and the other from Kip. I called both of them right away, Kip following Harry.

Harry wanted to meet at the Ball Mansion. I told him I had a class to attend, then would show. He said he'd be there.

Kip wanted to meet later that night. I told him I'd call. He could meet me at the Ball place and we'd go on to the quarter.

I caught Red and told him I could move some shit for him and Bob if he could get it. He came up with a price of thirty-five hundred for a pound of the sinsemilla, two fifty an ounce, with no break on quarter or half pounds. He had some of the Columbian I got from Bob for four hundred a pound, no smaller quantities.

I used the meeting with Harry as an excuse to dodge my advisor and bolted immediately after class, crossing St. Charles Avenue and hiking to the door.

Gudrun met me wearing a green frock that made her look like she'd been out back beating laundry on a rock, her hair hanging wet and limp. She frowned.

"Jesus," she said. "Don't tell you're going to get involved in those damned movies."

"What movies?"

"Harry's filming. Where I showed you at the party."

"I wouldn't know about that. He wanted to meet me, though."

"Maybe it's about Dina. She's in a funk. Won't come out and play for the camera."

"I don't know anything about that. She drove me home and that was it. She's not my type."

"Uh huh. I believe that. You'll have to get there on your own. I am not in the mood to go back there. Shawntel took off when they started filming. She doesn't appreciate all that unbridled commercial sex. I don't know where Jeremy is."

I found my way, guided by a girlish voice singing out "Oh baby, give it to me. Oh baby, it's so big. Give it to me. Fuck my ass."

Harry stood in the doorway, arms akimbo, intently watching something. I touched his shoulder. He turned and put a finger to his lips, then pulled me into the doorframe beside him.

On one of the foldout beds the tattooed albino nymphet, looking all of fifteen with her fair hair made up in ringlets, convolved herself around three very large black men in some sort of entwinement difficult to unravel from our angle. Above us on the gallery a camera crew filmed the action. A man on the opposite side of the room gave silent hand signals to the four on the bed.

"Cut," the man yelled, moving toward the bed. "Goddamn it, Mirabelle, you act like you're doing your nails or something." He spoke a slow, precise English accent, his voice even and without hint of rancor. "Lets see that ass move a bit."

The group unknotted and Mirabelle languorously sat up on the bed with one skinny leg folded in front of her, the other bent so she leaned her round chin on it and stared at me with eyes that could have been the faintest baby blue.

Above her porcelain skin the tattoos hovered, glowing vivid neon. I couldn't make out much on her front, hidden as it was behind her leg and arms as she leaned into her knee; the tattoos on her back stopped at her sides, but the designs and colors that ran continuously from her shoulders halfway to her elbows, lighter and more intricate in blues and purples on the left, darker and bolder in reds and forest greens on the right, clashed violently and left the translucent white skin from mid-humerus down a startlingly blank canvas.

My eyes followed the patterns down to the purple mouth and red, bloody teeth surrounding her cunt, the pasty labia streaked in red.

"You try to move it, Mr. Bigley," she replied aping his accent in a baby voice, "with that monster schlong stuffed up your bunghole. It ain't easy to move with them two pinning me nether 'oles and me mouth occupied with th'other one, now is it?"

She pointed at me and stood up, more waiflike naked than I could have imagined. Above the mouthful of teeth on her mons jetted orange flames, directly below them and above the mouth words difficult to make out until she came closer. BLACK SNAKE WHORE. The same orange flames circled both tiny areole which together with her nipples were inked solid black.

She raised up on tiptoes and looked up into my eyes.

"Let me 'ave the little one on 'im in me bung and I'll be okay."

She took my hand and tugged me towards the bed. I stood firm.

"Not 'til you get those scrawny albescent twigs tattooed, dear," I said, and she walked away, the two black gorilla hands tattooed on her prepubescent ass cheeks a distraction from the gaudy design of her back.

Harry turned to me. "'Cording to her, all white men have little dicks. Don't pay no 'tention. I have on good authority yours ain't so diminutive."

"You mean that Hungarian or whatever she is with the nose who groped me?"

"She did? Susana? Not surprised, but that ain't where I heard it. She claims to be Czech, by the way," turning back to watch the quartet get into position as Albina engulfed between her legs the obese man lying on his back, presented herself to the man behind who worked an erect cock into her anus, then snarfed the limp one hanging in her face.

With "Action" they began a hyper version of what they had been at when I came in, the much tattooed porcelain doll hugging the legs of the man thrusting his pelvis in her face, drooling copiously and making a lot of smothered noises and periodically pulling back to squeal "Oh fuck my ass, oh baby deeper mmmph" with her oral partner smushing her head back into his crotch.

She twisted like a contortionist, spindly spider legs clambering over hock and ham to support otherworldly superposition.

I pulled Harry out of the room.

"You wanted to talk to me?"

"Def'nitely, but you don't wanna watch?"

"Not particularly."

"You wanna fuck her?"

"Not today. Maybe if she cleans up."

"She don't much go for white guys anyhow, but she digs big dicks."

"Well, that leaves me out."

"Let's go get some dinner and talk," he said, taking me by the arm. "Whatta you feel like?"

"Anything simple. Burger, poor boy, shit like that."

"I got just the place," and we drove a few blocks away from St. Charles Avenue alongside the park, turning at Prytania.

"I have it on good authority you got a ex'lent source of cocaine and marijuana," he said, pulling into a paved lot in front of yet another New Orleans shack.

"Not really," I said. "I keep myself supplied, and sometimes the people I know have some available. But the pot you're talking about is fucking expensive. Like five grand a pound, when it comes around. Ounces are expensive, on the order of three-fifty or so. Tough to get top grade sins that isn't moldy or some shit. I can get Columbian for six hundred a pound, but no smaller quantities. The coke, I can check. I don't use it." I tacked on fifty percent to the price Bob charged me and said I thought I could get grams at that price.

"Dina said your pot's 'mazing. I can pay that. Coke's a staple in the business. Have to have it. Canya get like a pound of that sins grass and whatever coke's available? Like at least five grams?"

"Let me check. I don't feel comfortable getting it in quantities or for other people. I'm not a dealer. Don't you have a supplier?"

"Yeah, but his coke's been stepped on big time and his pot's like all leaf. My supplier in LA's excellent but I ain't taking it with me when I fly. Had a decent supply when I drove out, but it's gone now. Bitch fuel."

"What about Jeremy or Gudrun?"

"They don't get no good shit. It ain't dealing anyhow. 'S'a favor."

"I'll see what I can do. But money up front. Not being a dealer, I don't keep the stuff around. I don't have money to pay for it."

"Sure. S'not a problem."

We exited the car and headed across the lot.

"Best damned roast beef poboys 'n'th'city," he said as we entered the shack. "Bona fide source of Bunny Matthew's 'ternally drippin' san'd'ich."

Matthew's cartoons showed up in the local underground rag and were sometimes amusing, but I didn't know that one.

The three tables were unoccupied. We stood at the counter and ordered roast beef poor boys and Dixie longnecks which brought back visions of Lori's longneck quest. The Bunny Matthews cartoon hung behind the counter, yellowed and frayed and ready to fall, the dried tape peeling away from the wall.

"No one here," I said.

"After lunch and before the drinking crowd what needs to eat," the man behind the counter snapped back, wrapping our sandwiches in white butcher paper.

Harry paid him with a hundred dollar bill.

We sat at table in dire need of a scrubbing. Remnants of past perpetually dripping poor boys swirled in phantasmagorical imitation of Jackson Pollack's work. I hovered above the mess, not sure what might be wet, but Harry placed his elbows in it and tore into his sandwich, an erratic outline in green shredded lettuce against tan loaf crust turning soggy, juice of tomato and rare roast beef adding to the random masterpiece.

"I dunno what you did to Dina, but she's moping big-time."

"It's nothing to do with me."

"She stayed the night at your apartment and 's'nothin' t'do with you?"

"Who says she spent the night at my place?"

"Look, don't get cute with me on this, okay? I know she's got the hots for you."

I didn't rise to the bait.

"Lemme tell you about Dina," he said. "She can't take rejection like a normal person. But she is damned smart."

As he took an enormous bite of his sandwich, a giant slab of tomato plopped onto the table. He picked it up out of a mass of goop and slurped it down, the juice running from his chin onto his oversized orange knit shirt on which hovered a green alligator at chest level.

Holding the sandwich like a metaphor for something I didn't want to know about, he talked with his mouth full of food. "When I met Dina," he said between a wad of entwined bread and tomato, lettuce shards falling from the corners of his mouth onto the table, "she worked as a hooker for an escort agency. 'Cept the guy what ran the agency used her as his personal slut," the roast beef like a film of dark phlegm in the back of his mouth, "and she liked it. Also supporting herself finishing her PhD in Anthropology at Columbia. Worked in linguistics." He picked at the gooey bread coating his front teeth with fat fingers, shoveled it back to swallow.

I stopped watching him chew, suppressing the urge to cram the remains of the fucking sandwich down his throat.

"Turns out her parents divorced when she was six and fought over who wasn't gonna get her. Grandparents didn't want her so's to keep her from th'orphanage, an aunt took her in. But I ain't so sure it was really an aunt. Who knows. The whole family'd been involved with drugs and prostitution, I think. But this aunt either was or become a Jehovah Jumper or some other kind of Holy Roller. Dina stuck it out, did well in high school, went on to college on scholarship, never spoke to the aunt again. She started working as a hooker in college."

He seemed to expect me to say something. "Impressive she went on to get a PhD."

"Is it? She liked whoring. I convinced her was too dangerous, got her into films. Same difference, only more control. Says she likes being at the mercy of strangers. Degraded. Abased. Humiliated. Claims she must have some kind of self-image problem, maybe related to her family. Always psychoanalyzing herself. Sometimes I have to come up with weird scenarios. We did all the swing clubs up and down the California coast. She'd put herself in submissive roles and guys'd go ape shit."

He finished the sandwich and tongued his teeth clean.

"One night at a club in Malibu, beautiful mansion on the beach with a magnificent view of th'ocean from a hot tub on an outdoor balcony, I auctioned her off to the highest bidder. She was nuts for it. Wore a blindfold and stood naked, passive, while potential bidders stroked her, checked her out. The guy who bought her had her do all comers in the hot tub, give them all blow jobs. Then took her in the dark room and let everyone do her, two and three and more at a time. Women too. Then made her do the willing women while every man who wanted to fucked her asshole. Man, afterwards she was a mess. But another woman cleaned her up with her tongue in an amazing lesbian action. Wished I'd had my camera."

I sprouted an erection. Tried to stop it, but the damned thing took off on its own.

"We did some films based around those actions, you know. Like improv. She'd team up with another woman, different ones, n'do gang bangs for movies. They'd clean each other up after. You ever watch chicks eat cum out of an asshole? Fart splooge into each others mouths? Or double anal"

"No. Can't say I have."

"But none of that's nothin' compared to what her old manager at the agency did with her. Throw her in a room full of his friends, leave her at their mercy. Take her to a bar or pool hall full of bikers or some other sleaze bags and lettum have her for a few hours. She dug it. And him, too. Wasn't easy getting her away from him. Know what a whipping stool is?"

The spreading wet spot on my underwear stuck to my leg.

"No, can't say I do."

"Like a padded round footstool with straps on the legs. Strap your arms and legs down hugging the stool and then someone whips you. Her agent used to take her to a submissive club in New York, strap her on the stool blindfolded and let everyone who wanted fuck her asshole. One night she lost count at maybe fifty or so. Said she bled for days after."

Getting up would be an embarrassment. I had to change the subject.

"What'd you do?"

"Someone killed him. Popped him with a small caliber in the back of the head. That got her to come over. Scared the hell out of her. She's got no tolerance for all that violence."

I felt the erection begin to ebb, but when he said "She loves rough sex" it rejuvenated.

"So what's her problem now?"

"She's moping round. Won't clean up. Smells like a goat. Wearing a frumpy pink ratty old housecoat, pink slippers with that fuzzy shit all over like the fat black ladies wear. Says she's just ugly and no one wants her."

"And how's this related to me?"

"Look, she was my toy. But she got over it. Now she's loose and I don't think she much likes it. Needs a guiding hand. I saw how she took to you at the party. Went home with you, am I right? And she was fine 'til after that. She ain't talkin' 'bout it, so I don't know details. But sumthin transpired."

He looked at me with a kind of mournful expression that enhanced his bulldog visage.

"You aren't gay, are you?"

"No," I said. My erection persisted as a stream of demeaning situations for her paraded through my head. "Give me her number and I'll call her. Take her to lunch or something.'

"Okay. Atta boy. Don't worry, she won't last long. Seems to wear through men faster these days. Just treat her right."

I remembered being told by someone that one aw shit wiped out a thousand atta boys. I convinced him to have another beer before we left, hoping my erection would dissipate enough to walk out of the place without bending me over. We had two more and he wanted to drive me back to the quarter, but I told him I had other business and needed a phone. We went back to the Ball place and I called Kip, arranging to meet him there in half an hour.

I called Dina. Her attenuated voice bounced alive when she heard me ask, "Dina?"

"Whitey? Is it you? Really? Where are you?"

"Yeah, it's me. I couldn't get you off my mind. You're haunting me."

"Really? How?"

"Torn. I have mixed feelings."

"Tell me."

"Not on the phone. I don't do personal conversations on the phone. Face to face. Tomorrow. Lunch."

"Okay," she said, "lunch tomorrow."

"Meet me at my apartment around one or so."

"Great. Can I get your number?"

"You have it."

"What—? Oh, I meant phone number."

"Don't have one. Just come prepared."

Dead air. Then "Prepared for what?"

"Think about it. What do you want from me? I mean, what do you most want? Maybe we can strike up a deal."

She didn't respond and I let the silence hang. Than I said, "See you tomorrow. I gotta go now. Have some other business."

"Okay," she said, her words clipped. "See you tomorrow Whitey."

The filming continued unabated. The Hungarian who'd felt me up and the tattooed albino and maybe five of six black men were entangled in a writhing knot. It made me wonder if they used white men. The one who'd called herself Linda and wore the matronly clothes at the party sat naked in a chair masturbating. But the surprise was Gundrun in disarray, blouse open, one of the Bambis kissing her on the mouth, hand in the crotch of her jeans. They weren't part of the filming, standing apart on the other side of the room, but when Gudrun noticed me looking she pulled away and buttoned up.

"Don't mind me," I said.

"Fuck off," she said, leaving the scene in a hurry. Harry was not any-where to be found. The Bambi came up and rubbed against me. I pushed her away.

"Not now," I said.

"You don't have to be mean," she pouted. "Mean people suck."

I swallowed a remark about her ability to train a cadre of mean people. "Where's Harry?"

She pointed to a room on the other side of the filming. "You'll have to go around, though," she said, "or you'll mess up the scene. But he's busy with the other two Bambis anyway."

"Why don't you join them?"

"Bor-ring!" as she walked away wearing a pout.

I waited for Kip out front at the street. He pulled up in a beat white Mazda. Jerry in a shiny bright shirt the hue of a ripe eggplant rode shotgun. In back another black guy filled out most of the seat.

The guy in the back wore jeans and a faded orange t-shirt with a clenched fist on the front. His dark glasses made him look like a bug with a short, wide face, a broad nose and a tightly groomed full beard. He took up so much space we couldn't help but touch, but he wasn't fat or sloppy. He looked intimidating as a water buffalo up close but broke into a huge grin when Jerry introduced him as Mule. He tried the black handshake I could never remember and we settled on the original; he found that amusing and laughed out loud.

As we headed for the quarter Kip meandered around to asking how much coke and pot I could get. He knew a couple Navy guys, corpsmen he said, who wanted to score. The Navy guys wanted the sins and some coke. He wanted some pot, but not so pricey. I gave him the prices I'd quoted Harry and told him I needed money up front. He said no problem. Jerry and Mule didn't say anything.

We drove around the quarter for almost an hour before we found some-one vacating a spot. Kip got out of the car wearing the same nondescript kind of baggy, rumpled outfit he'd worn at the party. Not jeans, but loose cotton trousers, maybe cheaper than my own khakis. Jerry wore yellow slacks and tan shoes. We formed a bizarre squad even for the Quarter.

I herded them to my place where we smoked a couple joints of the Columbian. Kip and Jerry decided to go together to buy a pound. He ordered several grams of the coke and a pound of the sins, saying he'd meet me with money tomorrow night.

We hoofed it the few blocks to the Port of Call where we got the evil eye, I assumed because of Jerry and Mule. We downed a few beers and they left, Kip and Jerry having work in the morning. Mule didn't volunteer his line of work, but Jerry hinted it had to do with women and money and his nickname.

The whole setup made me paranoid, selling dope to people I didn't know. Needed to figure out how to control it all. Decided to deal only with Kip and with Harry, no one else present. It was possible either of them could be narcs, but more likely they'd be dupes for narcs. I didn't trust Jerry and didn't like the idea of this Mule guy hanging around. Nonetheless, I stood to pick up at least five grand on the two deals, maybe closer to seven.

I woke up in the middle of the night in a cold sweat. The idea of having Kip show up alone was pointless. If any of these clowns worked with narcs, knowingly or not, I was fucked already. Just having the money would be enough for them to get me. Then they'd want me to turn in my contacts. I'd already stepped into the ambush, if that was what it was.

Chapter 12
Cohomology Invariance of Perfect Bilinear Skew-Symmetric Intersection Pairing

Somehow I came to before ten, drank coffee, shit, showered, shaved and plunged into Postnikov. Chapter three read easily now and I realized I'd locked up on memory, unable to access the signification of the expression representing the direct sum of modules that made up the tensor algebra. The hassles of Dina and Lori and the worry about selling drugs to potential narcs had frozen my circuitry. My sleep decision seemed to be, Fuck 'em if they can't take a joke. Let them hang me if that was the way it played out: I'd cast my fate to the wind. Had always worked before. So the rest of it, parallel translation and torsion tensor fields wrapped in algebraic packaging, slipped into place for the Riemannian connection.

I'd gone through several joints and worked my way up to complete Riemannian spaces by the time Dina buzzed.

I lowered a basket with the key to the gate and she let herself in. Demurely costumed in loose blue jeans and a faded blue denim work shirt that nearly hid her massive flesh bulbs, the red bandana on her head completed the guise of matronly scrub woman except for the small backpack.

"You're studying, aren't you," she told me, accusing herself.

I lit up a joint. She rummaged in her backpack and slipped some cash into her jeans pocket.

"I got to a good place. We can go to lunch. What do you want?"

"Don't you have to go in?"

"Never on Tuesday. Or Thursday except for a monthly departmental seminar. Or the odd group seminar."

"Sandwich?"

"Pastrami?"

"Ummm. I love pastrami."

"Maspero's Slave Exchange."

"Slaves?"

"One never knows," I said. "I've never had one."

She walked with purposeful gait, long strides like a man, but as we passed out of the gay section and drifted down Chartres past Jackson Square her pendulous bosoms swaying free within the loose work shirt like a pair of harmonic oscillators run amok caught plenty masculine eye and a few hoots.

The lunchtime crush at Maspero's had ended and the tourists were off somewhere else for the moment, so we found abundant free tables. A hippyish frizzy brunette in denim skirt-overalls and a white ribbed A-shirt, her legs and armpits wirily hirsute, waited on us.

We ordered draft beer, pastrami sandwiches and fries and sat quietly for a bit before she asked me, "Why'd you want to get together again? I thought you were pretty much finished with me."

"I wasn't in a good place. Let's say your performance overcame any physical defects I might find in you. But I'm not interested in any standard relationship—"

"You think I'm into standard relationships? I fuck gangs of men on camera, and not just for money—"

"That's too controlled. Taking direction. Redoing scenes. Cut! Shit. No one cuts loose. What turns me on is the idea of you out of control. Personally and in situ. Someone else setting the scene, you just the toy. Uncontrollable scenes. Maybe more than you bargained for."

She stared with eyes the blue of the cloudless sky.

"Maybe," she said. "I don't think you like me."

"You gotta convince me you're worth my trouble—"

"Yeah? How?"

"That's why I suggested the slave exchange for lunch."

The waitress brought our beers.

"You gonna buy me?"

"You're not my type physically—"

"But I have other features? Some kind of inspiration?"

"You're an ugly blonde bitch. I prefer brunettes. But you have a brain. And the real stuff's imagination, need, fearless pursuit of pure degradation. Busting limits."

"Kink fodder. So I could do in a pinch, that it? As kink fodder?"

"More than a pinch. I'm guessing, but I think you're in need of something more."

"I am not into doing in a pinch."

"I guessed not. But after, later, I kept thinking you're a seeker. Of you in places outside your control, situations of my choosing. Not yours. Demeaning situations. My choice."

"Yeah? Tell me."

"Gay biker bar up the street, over on Decatur; tough place. Throw you in there naked and let you convince them to let you do them, all of them."

"And if no go?"

"No go? Not a choice—"

"Not me. Them. I can't force them all to let me suck their dicks. Or to fuck me. Gay men, maybe they aren't going to cooperate—"

"Then I'd kick your ass out into the street and make you get back to the apartment. Naked. At night. Alone."

"Hmmm. Anything else?"

"Take you to some bars uptown and set you up to do men in the parking lot."

"Blindfolded? Auction me off blindfolded?"

"Maybe. I see you begging for more, like a dog. Mostly I want you for a loaner. *My* loaner."

"Loaner?"

"Like at a car place. You know? I tell you who's going to drive, when, where, all that. You can do it for the movies, but all else needs my approval. You get no say. You can ask permission, and I may or may not give it. No choice when I say what the game is."

The waitress brought our sandwiches. I'd sprouted a groaning erection, my underpants sopped with drool. I had to stop. Fortunately, Dina said nothing. We ate in silence, she paid the check and left a fat tip.

She broke the silence before we stood. "So what are you paying?"

"Putting up with you. That's the pay. I thought you were interested in me."

"Maybe. I wanted to find out. But you don't have any inkling of where my head is at on this stuff. I may be a lot farther out there than you can envision. I might just be a cunt driven by a personal demon well beyond your paltry imagination."

I ordered two more beers. She waited until they came, then drew little curlicues in the frosted mugs before she started talking again. Her fingernails were gnawed to the quick.

"Scholastic philosophy hypostasized nouns and ignored verbs," she said, "more or less. I reify verbs, not nouns. My sexual hypostases are activities, and they control me. In other words, I turn medieval logic on its head, in a sense, by flipping the *copulatio* for the *suppositio.* If that makes sense."

"No."

127

"The *suppositum* resides, for me, within the verb, not the noun. It is not the who, it is the is."

"Sexual encounters are not with others, but with yourself?"

"No. There are no others. Just aspects of your *self.* And you play off those. You *are* the event, the reification is you *in* the event. The moment."

"Sounds kind of Existentialist, more or less."

"Only in the Zen intersection of existentialism with the moment. Not as a philosophy, where Existentialism is just plain stupid. For example, a real Existentialist must assume that truth is a function of his biological state, more or less. To say that the solution to x-squared minus two *equals* the square root of two is nothing but a biological statement, without truth value. Existentialism is the mistake of attempting to posit the momentary awareness of Zen as some kind of metaphysical foundation, while denying the metaphysical."

She stopped and bored into me with her blue eyes, pristine vision violating my personal space like a power drill between the eyes.

"You are, of course, aware," she added, "that Kirchhoff first formally proposed the idea of existentialism. I guess his influence was Locke and Berkeley."

"The physicist of Jerkoff's laws?"

"The same."

"You aren't denying the existence of other people, are you?"

"No. I don't have Kant's nausea with the idea of a noumenon. Nor do I have a problem with Kant. He was right that the noumenal world is unknowable as Itself, though direct experience of it in some sense is the goal of Zen. But we're primates. We sense the noumenon via sensors that filter through our brains whatever phenomena it is they gather. So we only really know that gathered shit. And *you* in yourself are not that gathered shit. So I don't know *you* as you are in yourself. Of course, neither do you."

"That's pretty fucking obvious. But then you're assuming there is some way things are in themselves."

"Of course to both statements. Obvious totally, and I have no problem with the idea that things might exist in themselves somehow; as a physicist might say, *invariant.* But when I am at the mercy of a gang of men with erections or whatever they might wield, I am not really knowing those men. I am in that moment as a sensate being experiencing, for want of a better word, the verb which is the action. In fact, I am part of that verb in so far as there is an I, which needs to disappear in those moments; the *verbs* which are those *moments.* I can't say it better than that without making it shit."

cohomology invariance of perfect bilinear skew-symmetric intersection pairing

I mulled the idea. She came from somewhere outside the known universe of the women I'd known Most people, especially women, try to avoid those moments. Like avoiding combat, or worse, landmines. Or being shot. She wanted to be in those moments, but to survive as a sensate being. To throw herself into those moments I guess to lose herself, but to come back as herself modulo components of new information. I didn't think I could go there; the best I could do was to watch her. It was the surviving as sensate being that would be the trick. Dying or losing the sensate would be the risk. Like walking in the minefield, a passive activity.

"If I come around to you," she said, "it will be something bigger than you and me as a sexual relationship. You're not showing me a fucking thing there. Your puny ideas aren't even jack-off surprises. They're not jack-shit. You can't, in fact, because *it* has to be the action, not your pyrexial jacking off. Your pip-squeak autoerotic interaction with me is only useful as reified *copulatio* for the goddamned hypostasis. Think of it as gerundification to form *suppositio*. In Latin one might say gerundive of the moment. Hence of small didactic value except as paired into a broader autodidactic being metastasized from the pair of us in interaction with the world in itself."

"I have no idea what you just said."

"Doesn't matter. I don't think you can fathom that yet anyway. You can't get beyond the cock sucking and deep rimming."

"You talked about my need. This is my need, Whitey. I'm explaining my need to you who are an ancillary component. Or appendage. Just consider as if I am Bishop Berkeley and I say to you, Mr. Butcher, what are these debasements? The ghosts of departed masturbations?"

I didn't have any response. All I gleaned from her words was some kind of putdown. She succeeded in making me a midget, but only as Berkeley had put down Newton for his infinitesimals as ghosts of departed quantities. So was it really a putdown? I kept my mouth shut and listened.

"Have you heard of John Lilly?" she asked. "He considers himself a scientist and takes acid in his sensory deprivation tank. It isn't science, and he'd be better served if he treated it like Huxley did his experiences with hallucinogens. Have you read Huxley's *Doors of Perception?* Or maybe some of the real work by anthropologists on hallucinogenic curing, like with yage?"

"I've used hallucinogens for reasons other than partying. I don't need to read about them."

"Of course you have. I might get you a copy of Lilly's *Programming and Metaprogramming in the Human Biocomputer*. Take it as a good sign if I do. It's short."

"I'll read it if you do."

"For me, a stew in a sensual broil is askesis of the most rigorous sort. It is more fideism than science, more Zen than Existential, but…"

Time skipped a beat; I don't know how long. She stood up.

"If you dreamed what's going on in my head, bitch," she said plopping money on the table, "you'd freak."

We got up and meandered in the direction of the apartment, dawdling in Pirate's Alley to stare at amateurish art work. I laughed at a black velvet painting of an Elvis in white singing in front of the fence at the Corn Stalk Hotel. She watched a caricature of a fat tourist take shape.

She grabbed my hand.

"Let's go now," she said, pulling me away.

We went fast, walking so I had trouble keeping up.

Inside the deserted courtyard she backed me against the wall and placed her hand on my erection.

"Hard? Wet?"

She pressed against me, shoved her mouth on mine and rubbed my slobbering dick.

"Maybe you aren't kinky enough. Maybe you're not man enough. Ever think of that? Maybe you can't satisfy me. I don't like to do all the imagining and you'll find it tough to compete when my rider is astride."

She pulled me back down the brick tunnel of an alleyway to the gate. She removed her shirt.

"Okay, buster, here and now."

She freed my erection, dropped to her knees and sucked the head, loudly slurping and smacking her lips; looked up at passers-by and called out through the gate. "Here! Look here everyone!"

Gawkers congregated on the sidewalk outside the gate. She pulled back, drool hanging from her chin. "Anyone want to fuck me?"

She stood up, dropped her jeans and mounted the hard-on poking through the fly of my trousers. I held her against the wall and fucked her, then forced her to her knees.

"Suck it, bitch. Eat it all. I want sperm blasting out your nose, slut."

I grabbed her by the hair and, steadying her head against the brick wall, fucked her mouth mercilessly, shoving far back in her throat, smushing her face against my crotch as with spasmic hip thrust and total-body jerk I ejaculated a wad. All aquiver, she gagged and coughed and when I let go her smutted face from nose to chin gleamed glaucescent goo.

"You cunt. You got to learn to take it all."

"Lemme have the bitch. I'll teach her to eat cum." The crowd had set up a murmur and a fat guy at the front pressed against the gate.

"You want her?" I asked.

I pushed her back and opened the gate, pulled him in and shoved it closed again, starting an uproar as men stormed the metalwork.

Clearly surprised, he stood popeyed gaping at Dina who, had she been standing could have eaten on the sparse, matted whorls flattened atop his head; a disheveled, unshaven, pudgy frump of a man.

"Her mouth's your cunt right now, bud" I said to him. "Take advantage of it. You won't have another chance in this lifetime. Fuck her face good."

He worked a stout choad from his pants and set to it, holding her by the ears and short-stroking her mouth. He finished quickly. I pushed him back out the gate, using his corpulence to force back the crowd before he or they could react, then dragged her upstairs to the covered patio and pushed her naked torso out the window, tits hanging free above the courtyard while two black women working at the Washing Well stood on the stairway and watched in amazement as I fucked her asshole and said with quiet frenzy "This is the just the beginning you slut, you'll be sucking the biggest nastiest dicks in the world shoving monster cocks up your ass fucking dogs and horses begging for it you whore" until she screamed out "I want to be your bitch, please let me be your slut," and I ejaculated again.

I dragged her from the window by her hair, opened the door and pushed her inside.

"Clean it off," I said and she snarfed my drooping dick until it glistened with her saliva, shriveling in her mouth, taking it all in and sucking until it grew erect again. She pushed me onto the sofa and kept at it. Pulling back, she looked up at me like a blue-eyed puppy, chin coated with wet sperm and spit, and asked, "Please master, may I fuck it now?"

"No," I said. "You're an ugly bitch and I have no interest in fucking you. There is nothing desirable in your cunt for me. You have to earn my dick in your cunt." I paused. "And never, ever, kiss me again without my permission. I am not interested in your filthy fucking mouth except as a fuck hole. Understand?"

"Yes, Sir. How can I earn it, Sir?"

"Impress me with performance, cunt. Enough for you to earn a reward. You're a slut. My bitch. It's performance art. Good work and there'll be a doggy treat."

"Yes Sir."

"We'll see how you are with free-form later. Now on your hands and knees and stay there until I tell you to stand, bitch. We'll get you a collar, understand?"

"Yes, Sir. There is a shop nearby with accessories, Sir. Can I pick some? And a collar?"

"Yes, but if they don't please me, you will find I can be cold towards you. For weeks. Understand?"

"Yes Sir."

"When in this apartment, you're a bitch. On your hands and knees naked except for your collar. Get doggy bowls for food and drink, understand? My permission for standing is required."

"Please Sir, can I have pads for my knees?"

I almost laughed.

"Am I special? Please?"

I grabbed her hair and shoved my drooling dick in her mouth, pushed it back to her throat, held her face against my pubic beard. She gurgled. I relaxed my grip and, steadying her head by her hair, dragged her face up and down on my cock.

"Yes, you're special," I cooed. "I've never known any woman who disgusts me as you do. You spunk-eating worm…" and no more words came, only grunts as an orgasm nearly jolted me off my feet with her face shoved against my crotch snorting like a pig. When I let go she looked up, tears in her eyes running into the white snot curtained from her nose and chin, a rivulet dripping to pendulous bosoms lopped against her meager frame.

A hangdog slut of a bitch, a worthless cunt. I had no clue as to her reaction, and I didn't give a fuck either. I didn't care if I ever saw her again.

Looking up, blues eyes sparking as if devoted, she quickly looked back down and smiled at the floor.

"I've never been with a woman who disgusts me so much she makes me want to see her grovel for men and women and every kind of sexual creature, dogs and goats and horses and pigs." I stopped and watched her.

She looked up again. "Please Sir, more."

"I won't abuse you myself. I may tie you up and give you to others. I won't hit you, but when you fuck up you will be without me for as long as I find it necessary to punish you. Understand?"

"Yes, dear."

"What?"

"Sir, yes Sir."

"More than obedience, you bitch. You need to be *my* slut, *my* holes. Horny and always ready. Beg for it. Hungry."

"Oh God, yes Sir."

"Only with my permission. Aggressive, never acting. No release without my permission. Understand?"

"How can I control that? Sir, I—"

"Learn. When you slip, you will be alone. Understand?"

"My movies—"

"Those movies are your job. You have my permission to perform, but no release, bitch. Understand?"

"Thank you, Sir. I love you. Sir."

"What? This word. Love. What the fuck does it mean?"

"It means you own me. Like no one I have ever been with. You own me, Sir."

"You can't stay here. You know that. I live alone. But you need to move nearby. You need to find a place."

"Yes Sir, please Sir. Close. Yes."

I stood looking at a creature intended for abuse. Round blue eyes peered from a face smeared with exudate, devoted-puppy eyes. A new feeling, liberating somehow. I ran out of words and so did she, and then I turned my back and walked away to wash off my dick. She called after me.

"Before I forget, Sir. Harry gave me money for the drugs. I have the money here. Sir."

She crawled over to where she'd left her backpack and came out with two separate wads of cash rolled in rubber bands. Mostly hundreds, some fifties and a few twenties.

"Harry says to get a pound each of the sinsemilla and Columbian and two ounces of the coke. I want a pound of the sinsemilla and five grams of coke. He says he'll give you some for the trouble."

"Not necessary. Don't use coke much. Have plenty of weed. But two ounces is a fucking lot of coke."

"If you can get it, then. If not, get what you can. I want to split my pound with you. And I'll get an ounce of the coke, then, Sir."

"Split? What is this 'my'?"

She looked down. "Nothing, Sir. Sorry, Sir. I own nothing." After a pause, she looked up. "Are you angry with me?"

"Not this time. But slips like that make me wonder if you're committed or just playing bitch-for-a-day. Get dressed, go out and buy those accessories while I read. Don't forget your bowls."

"Can I clean up, Sir?"

"No. Don't even look in a mirror. Put on one of my T-shirts and cut those fucking jeans off so they are very short."

She cut them with an old K-bar I gave her. She stood up and put them on without underpants and I made a long tear up the back to expose a good chunk of her scrawny ass. I handed her a white ribbed tank top undershirt that showed off her nipples.

"Walk across the room," I said, and she did, to the porch and back. Her tits attempted to take flight.

"All right, get your boney ass out of here."

She stopped at the door. "Please, Sir, a concession? Just one?"

"And that would be?"

"That man you brought me. He stunk. Rank and fetid, Sir. I hate that. I hate odiferous people, Sir. He needed a bath, Sir."

"He did? I didn't notice."

"God, he stunk to high heaven, Sir. Please, no more malodorous people, Sir. I don't eat or play with shit, sir, or olid exudates or smelly people. Just so we're on the same page, Sir."

"If I notice, I might honor the request," thinking she'd given me a tool, and with her deliberate cogence it was probably intentional. "Just remember who the fuck you belong to, cunt. Tease and act vulnerable to everyone. No matter what you think. You are a whore on command. *My* command."

With a crisp "Aye aye, skipper," she took off, leaving me wondering where she'd picked up that Corps jargon.

Chapter 13
a) First Variation, Isotopic Deformation and Constrained Degenerate Extremals

I stood on the balcony and watched Dina pass through the gate and down Bourbon Street toward Canal. Same manly stride but now attracting plenty of attention, even from the cruising gays.

Snared. The whole thing felt like a set-up. Like I'd tripped a wire and now hung in suspended animation awaiting final manifestation of the particular fucking booby trap.

I tried isolating the mechanism. Couldn't see it. Paranoia? Dina made me think of my mother in some askew way. Not literally, that was damned certain. But aliterally. Acausally, more or less. Like I'd returned to an adolescence trapped in Dina's rules and variations on superstition. Like she'd hooked me and played a taut line calculated to keep me from throwing the hook no matter how high I leapt and vigorously I flailed.

The entire scene from lunch onward looped in my stunned brain, different details standing out in each run-through. I didn't get it. Not something I could've guessed a week ago. Or a few days ago. I'd stepped into a pitfall, a baited trap, a deception I couldn't unravel.

I went through her backpack. Books and money and a pair of sunglasses. Three fat rolls of hundred dollar bills on the bottom of the bag, several fifties and a couple twenties stuffed inside an interior pocket. A plastic wheel of birth control pills crammed inside a flap. No sex gear at all.

But the books. *Folie et déraison: histoire de la folie à l'âge classique* by Michel Foucault, *Tristes tropiques* by Claude Lévi-Strauss, *La Prisonnière* by Marcel Proust, *De la grammatologie* by Jacques Derrida and *Locus Solus* by Raymond Roussel. All thumbed save the book by Roussel, which looked new.

I'd read a tiny bit of Proust in translation. I could read some French, but not well; had passed a French proficiency exam for science. This kind of stuff would be impossible, assuming I'd want to read it.

The only book in English wore a green cover with solid black border and regular boldface lettering. Dead-centered in a column of three words twice the height of the others **Chariot of Flesh, Malcolm Nesbit** directly below the top border, **The New Traveler's Companion Series** above the bottom border. Poor binding, cheap paper. I read random pages here and there. Boring pornography. A guy fucking a chicken and killing it as he ejaculated, a bathtub filled with sperm and bimbos. Maybe Harry and company were going to film a version, though it seemed classy for them.

In a side flap I found a notebook with a preprint of a paper, *Possession sexuelle.* To be published in some French magazine, *La Quinzaine Littéraire.* Attributed to Dina. No last name. Possession as in slavery or spirit possession? Or perhaps dominated by sex. I bet some French word for fellatio appeared in the text. I didn't check, but it bled red pencil marks.

More than half the notebook was filled with precise block print in English. Tiny letters. I scanned a paragraph regarding phonies, people like Foucault who talk freedom as a job in itself so as to keep themselves "in the system." Freedom meant embracing isolation and anonymity. To be free was to be controlled and to be controlled was to be in control; to give up control was only possible in freedom. And to experience isolation while in the throes of sexual release—

I shut the notebook and put it back as I'd found it. Something here seemed out of whack. And who the hell was this Foucault? I knew the name Levi-Strauss, but besides the smidge of Proust the reading of which I'd found as stupefying an activity as solving ordinary differential equations or puzzling out tricky antiderivatives to evaluate integrals in closed form or, everlastingly worse, applying similarity methods to solve partial differential equations or, mind-numbingly tedious, putting mathematical arguments into the formalism of first-order predicate logic, the lot of them was a blank page in memory.

I reloaded the rest of her stuff as I'd found it, picked up Postnikov and lit a joint. Incoherent words flew off the page past my cognitive center. I returned to the balcony, wishing I'd gone with her.

A second plunge into the icy waters of Postnikov and concepts snapped back into place; I skated along minimizing curves in a complete Riemannian space. It aligned without help from Postnikov. Damned obvious actually. His work to get compactness of closed, bounded neighborhoods in complete, connected Riemannian spaces came across as unnecessary, even pedantic. I saw the heart of it all right away swirling about the separability of the induced metric space. But the connectivity of arbitrary points by minimizing curves had a more direct proof in any case. After a couple tortured pages ending with the conclusion that closed, bounded subsets of a complete Riemannian space were compact, I began to suspect the fault lay with the fucking translator. I jotted a two line proof in the margin, then in three more lines got the major result regarding connecting points with those minimizing curves. Smoothness of the distance function tumbled out on its own. Looming above the arbitrary Riemannian manifold M with interior metric ρ as the fog blew away, three equivalent conditions like a sign post. Postnikov stated them and proved them to close the chapter, but since I had fathomed them before I read his statements of them and understood how to prove them, I closed the book, not yet ready to delve into variational properties of geodesics. Anyway I already understood that geodesics were not in general minimizing curves between their arbitrary points. Big deal.

Too many fucking arbitraries. Arbitrary this and arbitrary that. Because X was arbitrary it followed that…

I rolled another joint, went back to the balcony to smoke it and watch the street, then inside to flop on the bed and stare at the ceiling.

The tangle of geodesics and minimizing curves wound through my brain pulling me along stretches and flats as points receded on approach and then a tug at my hand. Ratcheting up to flee or fight, I found Dina on her haunches on the floor beside the bed, head enclosed within a black leather mask zippered shut on the side with handles where her ears might be, two small holes for her nose and a hole for her mouth. No eye holes.

I sat up and placed my feet on the bare wooden floor, stood and walked around her. Naked except for the mask. Beside her on the floor several collars, plain leather, studded leather, a metal collar of chain mail, a stainless steel collar and a rusted iron collar with padlock. Leashes of leather and metal, one a heavy chain. A bunch of paraphernalia I understood as if from prior life. All sorts of gear of straps, ropes, chains. Face harnesses with mouth devices to hold in place rubber or plastic balls or sculpt the mouth into a hole, with or without hooks to lever back the nostrils. Blindfolds, masks and face-covering helmets, rubber, latex, leather, even spandex, and a bunch of gags, including one with an O-ring to force open the mouth. Two different stainless steel dental contraptions for prying wide the mouth. A high, solid collar with chin slot designed to compel the head upward at a slight angle and firmly in place with scant freedom of movement. A wooden rig with locking neck hole and flat pieces that tightened on the sides of the face to fix the head steadily, behind it rings for attaching to solid structures. Simple iron and padded leather restraints. Rods with manacles to spread legs and arms, other manacled rods to bring them together. A hinged, flat pair of metal strips that closed to create fetters for the ankles on the outside, wrists on the inside, aligned in a row and locking on the end opposite the hinge; another pair of metal fasteners, one for wrists, the other for ankles. A lightweight wooden yoke for neck and arms, armholes single file to the front; a light wooden pillory for head and arms, a companion stocks for ankles attached to the neck device by chains. Lightweight and elegant, a metal yoke of burnished aluminum with wings folding around the wrists and snapping to around the neck, padlocking shut to trammel the arms out to the sides leaving two triangular open spaces on either side to accentuate freedom denied.

She'd set the hook. I was the mechanism of the deadfall; shaking the hook now would be the equivalent of biting my own teeth.

Between her legs lay a black rubber mechanism, a gag with an elongated mouthpiece extending back at least an inch and oblong in front like a flattened cylinder, fastening behind the head with a pair of straps. I picked it up and shoved it in the mouth hole of the mask and tied it taut. I fastened padded leather restraints to her ankles and hooked them with chains to the row of hefty D-rings on a long restraining bar that bolted into three heavy base plates, then fastened a matching pair of restraints to her wrists and, pulling her arms behind her, hooked them to same bar. The chains could have been shortened to bring her wrists to her ankles allowing no degree of freedom, but I left enough to pull her back so she faced up at my crotch with tits sprawled walleyed across her chest forming a naked faceless funneled piehole.

Wondering how the hell she'd gotten so much gear up here alone, I planted my feet on either side of her, shoved my dick in the hole in the mask and used the convenient handles on the hood to drag her head forward, hold it against my crotch, then ease it back. I iterated the motion lentamente, da capo from forcing the erection to the back of her throat, harmonic motion accelerando to presto ending without finale, fermata her face flush with my crotch, pissing in the hole and then walking away.

I had no idea if she was in pain locked in that position, but it looked anything but comfortable.

After a joint I returned and fucked the hole until I shot a load, utilizing the convenient ear-handles to press her face against my crotch while I ejaculated. I continued stoppering the hole until my shriveling dick released a jet of urine. I left her for maybe twenty more minutes before removing the mask and releasing her.

Demure, she hung back on her hands and knees. I lit a joint and handed it to her. She curled at my feet when I sat on the edge of the bed.

"Please, Sir, now?" she asked.

"Now what?"

"Now will you fuck me?"

"No way. We may have company later tonight, but first we go to dinner. I'll take you to Ruby Red's, I think. Or the Port of Call. Burgers."

"Is that all you eat, Sir? Sandwiches?"

"Burgers are sandwiches?"

"I worry about your health, Sir."

"I work out three days a week, though I've missed the last couple times."

"Fruit and vegetables, Sir. You need to eat them."

"We'll see. We may put you on a high protein diet. I want you to clean up before we go out. Wear the same outfit. You need to bring some sexy heels next time. Those flat sandals are okay but they'd be more fetching with straps winding up the calf. Anyway, get your skinny ass in the shower now."

"Alone?"

"When you merit a reward, I'll give you one. So far you don't merit shit. Just remember, you get one refusal. You refuse any command, that's it. We're finished."

"Can I stand in the shower, Sir?"

Kicking her ass moderately hard seemed an appropriate response.

I showered while she painted her face in garish reds, a display I found most unappealing but which would surely speak volumes to the males out in the world. She appeared as a caricature of a clown whore with lips smeared cherry red, cheeks daubed rouge, eyelids painted blue and red. I decided to take her to the Port of Call. Of all the straight, mostly-guy places I knew in the Quarter, it would be the best for sending her to the john with a john to pay for the food.

"Don't bring any money," I said.

Her face lit up. "You want me to provide service for pay, Sir?"

"Right. You'll work for it. Proposition men for the money. Take them to the ladies head, since it's seldom occupied."

"Thank you for the vote of confidence in me, Sir."

I put a spiked collar on her and attached a leather leash.

As we stepped outside the gate and onto Bourbon, I noted a skinny fag on the corner at the bus stop across the street wearing a T-shirt ripped open to show a pierced nipple. I broke into his conversation with a young street hustler.

"Where'd you get that done?" pointing at the nipple.

"Huh?"

"I need a body artist to work over this pig of mine," nodding at Dina standing beside me at the end of the leash.

He looked her up and down. "My, but she is an ugly specimen, isn't she. I just love those hanging milk duds" and he grabbed both her tits. "Does she give good head?"

"Cost you five bucks to find out. But you can take her to the men's room in Lafitte's there and get one for free if you can tell me where to get the work done."

"Just a minute," he said. "Let me get you a card. There's a man off 'lysian Fields over at Chartres just before Spain Street who does creative body work. He's careful, too. It's said he's a defrocked medical student or doctor or something of that sort. Sterile. His work, I mean. He creates scars for the butch crowd."

He hustled into Lafitte's and came back to pass me a small hand-drawn card with an address, phone number and in carefully inscribed Gothic letters, Hansel Romanof.

"Christ, is that his real name?"

"I wouldn't know. He's a regular at Lafitte's; people call him Hans."

I handed him the leash. "For you its free. Everyone else is five bucks. Got it?"

"You aren't coming to watch?"

"You nuts? That is not a place I visit." I turned to Dina. "You need to get at least twenty bucks, bitch. If you don't get it, don't bother to come back. I'll just send your shit home and you can get lost. And I am not waiting for more than an hour. I got people coming in two. Buzz when you're done."

I went back upstairs and left her to her fate, not bothering to watch her disappear into the raucous motley of gay men, blaring rhythmic cacophony and smoke. As I passed down the tunnel-passage from the gate to the courtyard I thought I detected a phase-shift in the emanation from the bar.

I smoked a joint and mentally reviewed the big picture revealed by Postnikov. I could see several pathways on the horizon, all emanating from the comparison of curves between fixed endpoints, some sort of calculus based on variation of paths. As I began to put together my own theory, the buzzer sounded. From the balcony I looked down at Dina.

"Be right down," I called, checking the clock when I stepped back inside. Forty minutes.

I grabbed the cane Momus had given me and wound down the spiral stairway.

"I made fifty dollars," she said, "but he kept twenty-five."

We drifted toward Esplanade in the heading away from the river toward the Port of Call, she dressed in the flimsy white tank top and short-short cut-off denims, me as a janitor in workpants, T-shirt, work shoes, carrying a cane and holding a leash attached to her collar.

first variation isotopic deformation and constrained degenerate extremals

"They took me to the bathroom and he collected the money. I kept track by the feel of their dicks and only sucked them off and let them fuck my asshole. Eventually they had me wedged in a stall with a hole for sucking, leaving my ass sticking out."

"How'd you keep them from fucking your cunt?"

"I told them it was off limits. They paid attention. I didn't really care if they fucked my cunt. I was more interested in how much they'd obey me. But if you want that to be off-limits, you need to apply one of the chastity devices I bought."

At the bar I ordered beers, burgers and fries. The Port of Call was late-afternoon quiet, almost melancholy, *Flamenco Sketches* from Miles' *Sketches of Spain* playing on the jukebox. So smoky that people across the room would materialize out of the gloom as they approached.

Dina picked up another twenty bucks before the burgers arrived. She seemed chipper, her conversation animated with wild hand movements that bounced her tits. The patches of semen on her face made me smile. Mostly I ignored her, continuing my mental construction of the variational calculus. It was cheating in a way, since I'd been through a light version with Kobayashi and Nomizu and with Bishop and Crittendon, but the approach of Posnikov's was sufficiently rich in structure to make this a nontrivial exercise. I worked out the geodesic approach to the minimization problem, bringing in the parallel condition and the second-order local ODE in local coordinates, considered a sort of surface with fixed endpoints, and got a vector field associated to the quasi-surface. Figuring out what a first variation of the arc length ought to be, the notion that a geodesic would be a curve that killed all first variations fell right out. The additional requirement that the curve be parameterized by arc length for sufficiency seemed clear, and I was working my way through a proof when Dina yammered in my face and pointed at her watch.

It seemed there remained less than half an hour before the two hour window I had given her closed. Not sure when Kip would arrive, we made the five minute walk back to the apartment. Kip was not likely the punctual-to-early-arriving sort and it would give me time to work out what to do with Dina. Mostly I didn't want to miss this opportunity to bank more cash to pay off the fucking credit card bill. This deal provided a fat cushion, a rarity in my life.

We snorted a couple lines of coke, smoked a joint of the sins, and while she snorted a bunch more coke I fiddled with some of the harnesses and other devices she'd bought. She prattled about more appliances: Something she called a metal stockade to secure one on hands and knees with a detachable appurtenance to install dildo or dildos in cunt, ass or both; a sort of flat yoke for the head and arms, another for the feet. All portable devices. Lots of contraptions, it seems, including an old fashioned wooden pillory or stocks, she applied both words, that presented full access. This sounded like a substantial piece of furniture for the apartment though I had the space. She said she'd have bought it all but couldn't have gotten it here alone. I didn't ask how she'd managed what did she get.

I chose straps to bind her calves to her thighs, bending her legs back at the knee and attaching wrists to ankles and elbows near the knees. The arrangement forced her to grasp her feet. A pair of wrap-around goggles painted black over her eyes and she could see nothing. An O-ring gag fit tightly in her mouth. She lay naked on her back on the bed, a drooling bug-eyed frog, every orifice handy. Her tits hung to either side like two stretched out meat-bladders faintly webbed with hair-line fissures. In that moment she appeared as ugly as anything I had ever laid eyes on, fodder for abuse. I pissed in her mouth. She made odd noises: squeals, gurgles, swallowing. My dick grew erect and I fucked her face for a while, then lost interest in the enterprise and withdrew.

Anyway, I'd checked the fit. Clearance for dicks was more than adequate. The O-ring stretched the shit out of her mouth, making her drool incessantly. It cracked me up.

I piled the rest of the hardware into the narrow utility room off the bathroom and went out to the balcony to smoke dope. Before I had finished Kip, Jerry and Mule sauntered up to the gate. Kip looked up and saw me; I signaled I saw them and headed down. Kip carried two six packs of Pearl beer in cans.

"Quiet," I said. "No talking; walk quietly. I've got a surprise for you."

"We stalking split tail?"

I put my fingers to my lips and he quieted. We made our way up the worn steps, a sound I knew carried all the way to the bedroom, but I'd left the windows open on the balcony for street noises to cover our ascent.

At the door we removed our shoes and padded across to the bedroom where I presented Dina, frog tied, goggled and drooling on the bed.

"Jesus—" from Kip, "Sheeeeeiit—" from Jerry; I put my fingers to my lips. Mule wandered over, took out an enormous schlong like an elephant's trunk and tried to push it in her mouth. It wouldn't go through the O ring.

"Damn" he said, went around behind her and holding the trunk like a hose, rubbed the head against her vaginal lips until the tube inchmeal straightened to a shaft like something from another planet. Jerry poked his flaccid penis into the mouth opening, working it in and out around the foreskin until it hardened.

The two of them fully clothed silently fucking the bound body backlit from the streetlight filtering into the windows and immersed in thumping bass beat from the bars pulsing into the room removed me to scenes of demonic hellions raping and torturing women and men alike in hallucinatory oils by ergot-inspired painters of the sixteenth century. I glanced toward the mirror and confronted the faded apparition reverberating from the giant glazed speculum: Mule half-horse half-man, two-legged centaur on powerful hindquarters plowing a horse's cock into the trussed thing on the bed; Jerry standing on hairy goat legs, hoofed Satyr-Pan pumping a slender goat's penis in and out of the mouth hole. The reflection of two beastial utensils buried to the hilt on each plunge centralized the room.

A gawping Kip stood beside me, silent this once, and I pulled him out through the front room to the patio, no longer concerned about a possible bust.

"So you got an order?" and he handed me a wad of money. Pound of Columbian, pound of sins, and ten grams of coke. I told him I'd probably have to deliver the pot tomorrow at the Ball mansion, but would have the coke tonight. He nodded and hurried back to the bedroom.

I gathered up the money from Dina, counted out enough for her order, and carried only enough to cover the buy, leaving the rest in the kitchen cabinet. While my guests entertained themselves with the immobilized bitch in the bedroom, I made my way downstairs, out the gate and up Bourbon past Lafitte's toward Marigny. The jarring rhythm from Lafitte's overwhelmed the street, charging the inverted demimonde to a writhing spawning of men on men like salmon on the cusp of death.

I got the hell away, the noise fading as I hit Esplanade and crossed, walking fast along the empty streets of Marigny until Frenchmen where smaller, tamer crowds of men and women mingled around music clubs. The vision from Bosch or Brueghel, never sure which is which, traveled with me, unshakeable.

b) Short Exact Sequences of Chain Complexes

Bob called Red and gave him the pot order, saying Red'd have it for me tomorrow. We drank Dixie longnecks and smoked a joint while he measured out the coke, putting it into separate baggies. He told me about a chick he'd met, was going to hook up with her at a club on Frenchman after we'd finished.

Back within the hour, I found them still at her, the four of them conjoined in infernal congress. Jerry and Kip alternated between cunt and mouth-hole while Mule reamed his thing into her asshole, slowly twisting, then gradually withdrawing before starting again. Dina lay gleaming and silent in the sparse light except for what might have been a panting undercurrent harmonizing with the street music and the sloppy wet sounds of the men fucking her, Jerry "Shit this bitch be a sloppy hole," Mule grunting on the invasion, hissing "Sheeeeit" as he held and then slid back out, Kip mute. Dina quivered a solitary ripple of goose flesh upward along her spine on each of Mule's in-strokes.

Relief at zero possibility of a bust with this scene underway flooded thruogh me. The perfect solution and it hadn't dawned on me until this accidental cluster fuck.

"Work that bitch's asshole, Mule. Work that hole good," unneeded encouragement from Jerry. He looked up from fucking the face-hole and saw me in the doorway.

"Where you get this ho? Man, I ain't never seen nothin' like this shit. White people be strange. You want a little?"

"I need to piss," I said, pushing my dick into the mouth hole and emptying my bladder.

Jerry shook his head. "The bitch be LOOSE!"

I got a joint going, pulled Kip aside and handed him the coke. "Tomorrow at Ball's for the dope."

"Okay," he said.

I let them keep at it until they wearied. Then I untied Dina and removed the O-ring gag but left her goggles in place. She looked more like hell than her usual self, sweating and smudged with fluids, thighs and legs and ass, face and neck and tits, hair. The strap indentations showed red and white.

"Please Sir," she begged, "can I see?"

I hooked the leash to her collar, took off the goggles. "On the floor, bitch," yanking her off the bed.

Sitting up like a puppy, she asked "Please, can I see the big one?"

I pointed to Mule, standing with folded arms and wild dreadlocks looking down at her. "Beg, bitch," he said and she sat up panting, tongue out, hands folded down in front. He snapped his fingers and pointed to his fly.

"May I Sir?" she asked, looking at me.

"Only if you take them all again."

I brought out some coke and she did five or six lines. We all did some. We smoked a couple joints of the Columbian laced with hash and one of the sins and drank the beer Kip had brought while she went to work, starting with Mule.

She opened his fly and hauled out his flaccid penis, pushed back the foreskin and, like a python, seemed to unhinge her jaws and engulf the head. She pushed on until her face met his trousers, gorging on the flaccid meat, then pulled back at a snail's pace, her lips extruded meat flaps distended snug along the bludgeon like an occluded sore exposing the dark salami gradually from within a gaping rictus drooling with saliva and whatnot.

"Damn," Mule said. "Ain't no bitch never got it all down like that."

Jerry slid around behind her. Leash held tautly in hand, he fucked her asshole.

She kept at Mule's dick until it mushroomed upright toward the ceiling like an erect arm crowned globularly rotund on the end. She englutted the entire member, engaging until he barked and jerked with a spasm holding her face flush against his trousers. Thick and grayish ejesta blew like snot from her nose, extruding bubbly from the seal around her stuffed mouth. He let her up slowly, her lower face a smear of gleaming ricotta-like exudate.

"It's a miracle, Sir," she said, "transubstantiation," wiping some of the mess from her chin and eating it, "transubstantiate, goo—" Jerry shoving his hard-on in her mouth to shut her up mid-word. He rigorously pummeled her face until emission, at which time Kip stepped forward. She gummed and mouthed and licked and sucked his flabby white worm to no avail.

"What's wrong with you, worthless cunt?" I intoned in her face. "Can't even get this guy off? You got some bad time to work off now."

She hung her head and stared at the floor; a sauce of slobber and spunk and God-knows-what dribbled from her face.

They left in high spirits and I returned to the bedroom. A fetid mass of folds of fat and skin like a plucked chicken sprawling beside the bed, she looked up with innocent blue eyes peeping through the drying makeup-stained mask of sperm, saliva and shit.

"Now Sir, please fuck me?"

"Absolutely not. You are a selfish cunt. I saw. You had at least one orgasm. Am I right?"

"Yes, Sir. I tried not to. Please don't punish me."

"And you couldn't even bring Kip to orgasm."

"Sorry Sir. I tried, Sir. He's a dud, Sir. A dead fish. It isn't my fault, Sir. I did my best today, Sir."

"I guess. As reward for trying, you can stay the night. Sleep on the floor at the foot of the bed. But first clean up your mess and change my sheets."

She kissed my hand and crawled to the bathroom where she pissed and emitted a sequence of wet farts. She cleaned up her drool and, taking the liberty to stand, changed the bed to my other pair of sheets. Then she gathered books and notebook from her backpack and crawled to the space on the floor near the bed where I had laid a towel, curled up and read.

c) Cocycles mod coboundaries among the integers modulo 100

I filled one of her new bowls with water and set it nearby.

"Thank you, Sir"

"What you reading?"

"Sir?"

"What are you reading?"

"I'm re-reading several works in philosophy and anthropology. For one, Jacques Derrida's classic trilogy of deconstructionism. *De la grammatologie, L'écriture et la différence,* and *La voix et le phénomène.* More for specific application this time. Also Claude Levi-Strauss, for a couple of reasons. One is Derrida's application of his deconstructionist methodology on Levi-Strauss. And Michel Foucault. His history of mental illness. I intend to read his *Surveiller et punir* as soon as I can get a copy. There is rumor of his history of sexuality being out. Three volumes of it. Oh, and Proust just to keep my head on straight."

"Proust is fiction."

"Yes, of course. You haven't read Proust?"

"No. Well maybe a little of *Remembrances,* but I gave it up. Too much controlled smoking."

She didn't laugh. "Oh, and a novel by Raymond Roussel. If you didn't like Proust, you'd hate Roussel. But he says some important things about science."

"Science? It's fiction?"

"Not science fiction."

"That's not what I meant."

"Fiction can say something about anything."

"But perhaps not in any meaningful sense."

"What is meaningful, Sir?"

"Precisely defined, Dina. Operationally defined. So that what is intended can be understood and communicated directly to others."

"I don't think that is possible, Sir."

"You haven't studied mathematics."

"I write papers in philosophy, Sir. I am at work on one now for submission to a French journal immediately upon sculpting it into the form I seek. I have another that's been accepted; they're waiting for my final edit."

"What about?"

"Some issues in philosophy, Sir. I have been in communication with several philosophers and sociologists. We are at work on deconstructing science, Sir. Including mathematics. We apply new methods to the language."

"What language? Mathematical expression is so precise it doesn't have much extension, Dina. It is rigorously precise, but without saying much about anything real. In particular, it is not science."

"One of them is doing field work studying scientists in laboratories, Sir. At the Salk Institute."

"I hope he doesn't confuse engineering with science. They are sometimes intertwined, but they are not equivalent. Any more than number crunching in the sense of numerical analysis is related to mathematics."

"He claims that there is no such thing as theory in science, Sir."

"Well, he's confusing engineering for science then. Medical research is not science. It's engineering. They look for stuff. The goal of engineering is to build stuff or find stuff. Technology. Science is not concerned with technology and making things any more than philosophers are concerned with building skyscrapers. Or theory, for that matter. Though actually science is the final form of a lot of philosophy. Einstein and Newton were cosmologists and cosmology is subsumed in the philosophy of nature. If you think about the goals of science, it is philosophy. So scratch the comment about theory. Some philosophers are concerned with building theory, namely scientists."

"I don't see a distinction between engineering and science."

"That doesn't surprise me. It'd be like studying accountants to learn what mathematicians do. I doubt you understand any scientific theory. But you are in constant contact with the products of engineering."

"Sir, I studied anthropology. That is science."

"No, it isn't. Any more than economics or any other so-called 'social science.' Anthropology doesn't make predictions from theories that can be shown false. So it has no theories, and so it isn't science. Same with economics, all the bullshit mathematics they load it up with notwithstanding."

"Applied science, Sir. What about applied science?"

"Another name for engineering. A special form of engineering. Engineering may be guided by some piece of a scientific theory or at least some predictions or principles from scientific theory, but it's still engineering. It'd be like calling writing advertising copy literature. Or confusing tract homes with cathedrals."

"The only distinction between accounting and the number crunching you speak of, Sir, is in the language. Andy Warhol, Sir, showed advertising is literature. Or art. It is all the same, Sir."

"Bullshit, Dina. It's the end goals. Literary goals are long term, advertising short term. Accounting is totally divorced from mathematics, while numerical analysis is concerned with providing accurate numbers that go with certain aspects of mathematics or physical science, approximations to numbers like pi for example or approximations to solutions of differential equations. But that isn't mathematics. The goals of computing are short term, mathematical goals are timeless. The Greeks showed the square root of two isn't a fraction."

"Have you heard of Benjamin Lee Whorf?"

"No."

"He was a scientist, Sir, a chemist who became a linguist."

"Then he gave up science. Maybe he developed testable theories. I can't say. But by and large, from what I've seen there's no science in linguistics, though there is mathematics. I know a little about Chomsky."

"Whorf is different from Chomsky. Whorf studied the Hopi language, for example."

"You realize, of course, that engineering has little use for science. Engineers don't give a shit about mathematics or physics. Almost everything they do is from trial and error, not theory. If trial and error is science, then Edison was a scientist. But he didn't know shit about science."

"Experiment is trial and error, in reality, at least according to the sociologist studying the scientists at the Salk Institute. Most of them have PhDs in microbiology, Sir."

"Having a PhD in mathematics, physics, biology, it's irrelevant. If you get your PhD and then go out and sell insurance or teach in some junior college, are you doing mathematics or physics? Or biology? Not in my book. Same when a person trained in science turns to engineering, which is the way to make money.

"This bozo sociologist's misguided. He mistakes that engineering for science. They are unrelated, though from time to time engineering makes use of scientific results, almost always in cookbook form. Inverting a theory, not building one. And an engineer can stumble across something useful for building a scientific theory, like Pasteur did. Doesn't make it science, though. Different goals. Science most often stems from philosophical questions, like with Newton or Einstein. Or Darwin. In fact, it is a form of philosophy."

"Science is really about control, Sir. It is not about nature."

"Engineering is about control. Not science. Science is figuring out how a very limited selection of things work. That 'how' is a theory if it can be falsified, which is the goal of experiment. And theory has narrow philosophical extension."

"Not really Sir. Science is a white man's invention for control. Of other men."

"Control of what?"

"Privileges."

"What kind of privileges?"

"White male privileges. Economic privileges, for example. Economics and physics."

"You think Einstein wrote his papers in 1905 for financial gain? Or to get power over other men?"

"Maybe gain, sir. The Nobel Prize. And power over other men. A professorship."

"There are far more direct and certain routes to money and power when you're that intelligent, Dina."

"Einstein worked in a patent office. He wasn't doing physics, Sir."

"Not in the patent office, true. But he was on his own time. Like an amateur artist. An insurance agent can do physics, but selling insurance isn't doing physics. He'd have to do it when not selling. Same with teaching. Teaching mathematics is not doing mathematics, no matter where you are, community college or Berkeley. But mathematics professors in the major schools don't get tenure for teaching. They get it for doing mathematics. That is not the case with junior colleges."

"Then the language, Sir. Look at language usage in science. The language is exclusionary."

"I don't understand what you're saying. Like Maxwell's field equations are some kind of exclusionary jargon designed to keep out non-white males?"

"For example, Sir, the linear world of mathematics is anathema to menstruation. Women are cyclical, Sir."

"Oh come on, Dina. Besides, mathematics is not linear. It is far more nonlinear than your periodic example, which is actually linear in any case."

"Derrida's method of deconstruction attacks the hierarchal structures, Sir. When you read Maxwell—"

"I don't read Maxwell. Don't need to. It's the same for math. I don't need to read Elie Cartan. I can read some other presentation of his ideas. In a different context. Mathematics is concepts, Dina, not language. Language is the only carrier of the concepts, unfortunately. Would be much easier to simply plop the fucking concepts directly into someone's head. Telepathy. Then you'd be able to see how meaningful the notions are. But most other crap out there, especially the so-called social sciences, are language devoid of concept. They ape mathematical language and even borrow what mathematics they might understand, but not to express concepts or theories. The shit can't be tested, or when it can be and is and fails, they make an excuse for staying with it."

"I don't believe that is correct, Sir. The language is highly relevant and revealing of the fundamental processes at work in the back—"

"Baloney. I have been learning some stuff that Cartan did, for example. And insofar as he was not stating false theorems, I can get to where he was from different perspectives, and perhaps go on to places he didn't see. As for Maxwell, all I need is his field equations. Nothing else. Partial differential equations, Dina. My point of view won't be a physicist's, perhaps, since mathematics is not concerned with physical reality, but I can appreciate that—"

"But Sir, that privilege is encoded in the language of the 'field equations' as you called them."

"I can change the damned symbols and their common names. Christ, Dina, we have a professor here who used the octonions to rewrite Maxwell's equations as a single expression with three symbols and a single operand."

"It's still symbols, Sir."

"So what? Those symbols are magic formulae?"

"Magic restrictions, Sir."

"I know women who understand them, Dina. Better than I, actually, since I am no physicist. I don't know squat about physics, actually."

"Those women have to transgress their gender, Sir."

"So to learn physics they have to stop being women?"

"It's a crossing of boundaries, Sir. Like women who take steroids for body building."

I let it rest. Clearly nothing I said was getting through. I decided to try one final approach.

"So, Dina, if enough people stop believing in electricity, it will go away?"

She thought about it. I could see the gears at work before her eyes lit up.

"Yes Sir. It would. I hadn't considered such a notion before, but it would. Humans created electricity; they can end it, too. I can use that idea. Thank you."

"That doesn't make sense. You can't believe that. What about lightening?"

"What I believe is irrelevant, Sir. Lightening need not be electricity, Sir. In any case, not as Maxwell or whoever he was conceived it. Perhaps it's thunderbolts from a sky god."

I was tempted to ask her why didn't they perform an experiment, but decided to let this go. We were not only not on the same page, we weren't even in the same library.

"What's the name of your paper?"

"Which one? The one in final redaction or the one in draft?"

I knew the meaning of redact, but'd never heard anyone actually use it. She could give Momus lessons in ostentation. Mostly I thought her incoherent. She seemed to hide behind grammatically correct strings of terminology wanting semantic content. As a kind of defense. It got denser when she got cornered.

"Both."

"The one in revision is *Possession sexuelle.* The one I'm inditing, or really more like still formulating, is *Clôture, le sexe anonyme et violent, de l'esclavage et le fidéisme.* I must get the first one back posthaste, Sir. The journal is prestigious. It has been around for some time. But that also necessitates fastidious revamping."

"I understand the first title, but what's the second? My French is pretty lacking."

"More or less enclosure, anonymous and violent sex, slavery and fideism."

"What's fideism?"

"It's akin to total reliance on faith instead of reasoning for a metaphysic, but for me beyond the moral strictures of religion. Anti-rationality or perhaps better said, arationality. More mortifying than religion. Like flagellants, but beyond beating. I personally find no use in castigating the flesh, Sir. I believe the proper road is via abuse, submission, sexual mendicancy. Humiliation. Loss of all exterior respect, Sir. Perhaps interior as well. Castigating the self through impersonal sexual stimulation while isolated from stimuli, from the agents. Forcing the self into retreat. You know about Tantra, Sir?"

151

"Not really. I know of it, but not technically."

"Principled profligacy, Sir.

"…

"The paper itself is actually more a recension of some shorter works by Foucault on sexuality, Sir."

"I don't know this Foucault person."

"A French historian and philosopher, more or less. He's a submissive homosexual, Sir. That is more what I am addressing in this work. He is not principled as a profligate, Sir. He will destroy himself. His philosophy is a wrack."

"Maybe you can translate your papers for me."

"I'd rather not, Sir. If you don't mind. Sir. I'd rather you not read them."

"Why?"

"Just promise me, please? You won't try to read them, or read them if they are translated?"

"If you tell me why—"

"I can't Sir, except that they are beyond the purview of our relationship. And it would be best if we not have these sorts of conversations, Sir. If that's acceptable."

"If not?"

"I would have to consider my options, Sir. You have your perimeters; I have mine. It is a question of space, Sir. Boundaries, Sir."

That caught me off guard. I'd not expected an intellectual line in the sand. I clammed up and climbed into bed to read Postnikov while she did whatever the fuck she did.

"Sir," her disembodied voice from below the end of the bed, "one more thing."

"So long as it's within the purview of our relationship."

"Get over it, Sir. Pissy is not your style. That black man. His name was Mule?"

"That's the only name I know him by."

"He had the largest penis I have ever experienced, Sir."

"It seemed big. It sure as hell wouldn't fit in the gag opening."

"Yes Sir. But also a miracle."

"Miracle?"

"Yes Sir. Transmutation, Sir, of eccrisis into honey, Sir."

"Eccrisis? Christ, Dina, speak fucking English…"

"His waste, Sir. The erumpent sexual exudate—"

"His spunk? When he blasted that fuck-wad in your mouth?"

coxcles mod coboundaries among the integers
modulo 100

"Yes Sir, the sperm transmuted to honey, Sir."

"That's what you were going on about when Jerry shut you up?"

"It was a new experience, Sir. Perhaps the better word is transubstantiated. Transubstantiation is more in line with being a fideist."

"It changed midstream?"

"Acrid, the first taste, then honey. A miracle, Sir. Transmutation makes sense, too. As in alchemy. Transmutation of sperm into honey. Better than lead to gold, Sir."

"Hardly. And Jerry's?"

"Just acrid, Sir. He eats a lot of meat. Pork, I think. Maybe bacon."

"Probably biscuits with sausage gravy. Or biscuit and sausage sandwiches. And my piss?"

"Bitter, Sir. Ammoniacal. Maybe you're diabetic, Sir…"

Chapter 14
a) Adjunction and The Partial Cone

Dina in the morning disgusted me. A smiling horror sleeping beside the bed like a puppy. All I could think was how to pawn her off on someone else. Shit.

So now a new hassle on my day's list of bullshit besides finishing a drug deal and cooking up a story for my advisor to get him off my back. Not about to risk falling into the hands of that oxymoron called the criminal justice system by dealing drugs, I had to keep this university gig going. Not much money in it, but no work in it either. I needed a story.

Avoiding the sight of Dina, I went about my morning business, coffee, shitting, showering, shaving, then buried my nose in Postnikov. Her awakening reminded me that people who wake up cheerful ought to be killed. She asked for coffee and I poured a cup in her bowl. When she asked could she shower I grunted from behind the book. She seemed to take it for a yes.

The Jacobi variation and associated curve and vector field seemed the obvious thing to do, the tie to geodesics natural as hell. The differential equation came easily from the rest and the field of frames along with it; an isomorphism from the Jacobi fields to the tangent spaces showed the subspace of Jacobi fields at a fixed point to be the same dimension as the tangent spaces.

Conjugate points. Postnikov made them abstruse. They were clearly the singularities of the exponential map from the appropriate subset of the tangent bundle to the manifold. Indeed, it resurrected images of Herr Oberst's abstract nonsense approach to Lie algebras. Everything from that class fell into place here. I knew he'd been doing shit minus the geometry, but I'd not known enough geometry then. Now I saw the geometry via the exponential map. The example of the sphere made it seem too simple, since I saw problems with the cylinder, a flat thing. I needed to wrap my head around geodesics in projective space, maybe on the ride into Tulane.

The notation thickened, particularly dealing with minimal Jacobi fields. The approach via broken Jacobi fields stagnated, congealing to embolism, but the flow resumed with proof of yet another vector space isomorphism, this time between certain of these fields and a big Euclidean space. Mostly to get uniqueness for initializing the Jacobi fields.

I was about to put it down but he piqued my interest with the appearance of a quadratic form, Morse's form, clearly a Hessian of the length of the piecewise smooth broken geodesics, singular at conjugate points. I knew I'd seen it before but not so backlit. The degree of singularity related to the negative index of inertia of the Hessian at the conjugate point and Postnikov proved the obvious: the index was equal to the dimension of the minimum subspace on which the quadratic form was zero. He used the prior isomorphism he'd hammered out between Euclidean space and the fucking broken geodesics.

Then the whole goddamn thing littered itself with determinants, lumpy extrusions like dingleberries in the gravy. It seemed clear that the fucking index would have to be the number of independent directions in which one could deform the arc to make it shorter. The index of a geodesic segment would have to be finite, equaling the number of interior conjugate points counted with their multiplicities. The submanifold not tangent to the geodesic made more sense; the geometry led to a theorem without the layer of gooey notation. I set about making this more precise and proving it. My statement matched his in all essential details, but both seemed to require counting negative eigenvalues of the Hessian with an implicit call on Sylvester's law of inertia. He called it Morse's index theorem. I checked his proof; mine came out more concise and enlightening.

There remained one long section in chapter four. Number thirteen. Regarding another quadratic form, this one named for Bott, presumably the same Bott whose name Momus had dropped, and a final formulation of the index theorem. I really wanted to sort all this shit out before I slogged on, to put it aside for now, but the first sentence of this last section cracked me up. Bott found a different quadratic form that involved less arbitrariness, particularly in the choice of submanifolds related to the singularity. Less choice of where to skate. So Postnikov wrote that Morse's form involves a considerable amount of arbitrariness and Bott's considerably less arbitrariness. And all this time I'd assumed with all the arbitrary thiss and thats, that the crafty old Russian liked all things arbitrary. He'd been shitting arbitraries and now he celebrated wiping some arbitrariness away. Anyway, in the details they arrived at the same place with respect to corank and index of inertia, but with more effort than it seemed to merit. I didn't bother to find another approach or check that maybe I'd found Bott's approach independently.

There followed what Postnikov labeled a short appendix, really a short extra chapter on something called focal points that extended this stuff to geodesics ending orthogonal to fixed submanifolds rather than at fixed points. I'd lost interest; it looked pretty dismal.

The fifth and final chapter didn't appear interesting either. I decided I'd bag it. The Russian began to bore me with his tedious arguments and occasional formal "arbitrary" calculations so trivial I wondered why he'd wasted a half page on them. I realized the book could have been condensed to a third its size.

Glancing up, I witnessed Dina crawling, hair turbaned in a towel, tits nearly dragging along the old wooden planks. The vision brought with it the realization that the degree of conjugacy of a conjugate point measured by the index and the degree of degeneracy of the form measured by its corank amounted to the same thing. Degeneracy and degrees of freedom related. It seemed just. Still, it pissed me off that he'd dragged me into conjugate points with dreary shit using determinants, a clunky foray into discontinuous vector fields that seemed unnecessary. It amounted to an extortion of truth from the obvious. As I'd gobbled it up and plowed through minimal vector fields relative to some quadratic functional based on an integral on the tangent spaces along a geodesic, after fighting off the obscuring cobwebs, it seemed clear there existed a better way to finish it. Miserable stuff ending with that result, that every minimal field was a Jacobi field. That's why I fucking hated books. Too much blah-blah-blah. Limit everyone to two pages.

At least he'd ended the chapter with Bott's quadratic form, a simpler, more elegant approach I wish he'd started with. But only after he'd paid homage to the original master. I began to see him as singularly crafty. Or a crafty singularity.

I had to get my ass to Tulane. I would find no story for my advisor hidden in this stuff; I had pretty much gotten what I'd wanted anyway. I finalized my foray with a commitment to skip the rest of the fucking book.

Dina dropped me off; there'd been no time on a streetcar to ponder geodesics and conjugate points in projective space. I scaled the wide stone steps outside Gibson Hall and made the long climb inside to the top floor with an assist to my bum leg from the cane. When I hit the department my leg didn't ache and I realized the cane could be more than a snazzy accessory.

In the cubby-office of grad student carrels Red handed me a grocery bag and I locked it in my carrel, then headed for a class full of eager faces. Something seemed wrong. I hadn't seen so many students since the first week of class. I leaned into the cane and stared at them.

"Are you all assigned to this class?" I asked.

It dawned on me mid-terms arrived shortly. That explained the sudden influx of new meat. I gave them a fast lecture, increasing my brisk pace to a gallop. I reminded them at the end of class that their midterm was worth ten percent of their grade. Some guy asked if they could get extra credit for homework.

"I don't assign homework. Problems are your responsibility. I suggest problems to work, but your choice. They are representative of the sort of stuff you ought to expect on the midterm. Just remember, the test comes from the syllabus, which is outside my control. But this is the only section and I write the test from the syllabus."

"That sucks," he said. I didn't remember ever seeing him before.

"Are you enrolled in this class?" I pulled the roster from out of the textbook and unfolded it.

"Dave Duncan," he said.

"I see it. Okay, Mr. Duncan, I will put some extra problems on the board. No credit, but they are the sort of thing to expect on the test. And don't be surprised to get an essay question." That comment brought up a murmur from the bodies.

I dreaded the idea of writing an exam. I'd just as soon give the lot of them Cs. On average most would accept a C without complaint.

The first thing I wrote was "Demonstrate that for a random variable X, $E(X-E(X)) = 0$."

"What's that E mean?" Dave Duncan asked.

"If you don't know that, you have some work to do, Mr. Duncan."

"This shit isn't fair," he said.

"Life isn't fair," Beatrice Cone piped up from the back of the room. Even with her bushy brows she looked particularly collegiate in a white blouse, plaid pleated skirt and penny loafers. "That is an easy problem."

"Will you help me?" Dave asked.

"No way. I don't do losers."

Dave shut up and I added a few questions of a more computational ilk.

"Stuff like that," I said. "And probably an essay question asking for a brief explanation of something. I will expect an answer in sentences and paragraphs, in English."

As they made their moves to vacate the room, I said, "Mr. Duncan, you want to see fair, I suggest joining the Marine Corps. There is a plenty of misery to share there."

A few groans as they left. I exited with an escort, the cheerleader on one side and Ms. Cone on the other. The cheerleader smiled, flipped her pony tail and said, "I know how to do that first problem. It's awesome. I never understood any math and I understand everything you do."

Beatrice rolled her eyes but I stared into the ardent blonde fluff and said, "It's not me. I told you; listen, read and do the problems and this stuff 's a piece of cake. It's all you." She beamed and hurried off. Bernice planted herself in front of me, blocking my view of the retreating derrière.

"Is that a real indicator of what's going to be on the test?"

"More or less."

"Which is it? More? — Or less?"

"A little of both."

"Well, if that's it, it'll be a snap. I can almost stop coming to class."

"I'd miss you if you did."

She looked down. "Really?"

"Really," I said, "but now I gotta go. I got to attend a seminar."

"Really? What on?"

"I'm not sure, actually. Pretty boring stuff."

"See you," she said, mischief in a smile. "Take care."

I watched her broad ass and thick legs roil the previously homogeneous media as she lurched away, hurrying but not fast enough to dissipate the contrail in her wake or to relieve my confounded sensibilities.

I made the seminar just after it started but the Frenchman stopped long enough to congratulate me on my orals and then plowed back into some matrix calculation that he wanted to end up in a triangular form, a Toeplitz operator on l_2 that had something to do with black boxes and systems defined by matrices of bounded operators in Hilbert space that ended up being rational functions when the spaces were finite-dimensional.

In the preceding weeks he'd moved through reproducing kernels and the word *signals* had repeatedly cropped up as things transformed by black boxes internalizing devices called transfer functions, at least in the finite dimensional case. I couldn't be certain when this shit had to be restricted to finite dimensions, and even there it was unclear what was the dimension, given that equivalent realizations could have different dimensions. Probably existed some minimal dimension, at least to be hope for. None of it meant a damned thing to me mathematically and everyone sensed he was taking for granted some background in engineering. There was one guy I'd never seen before, physics or engineering department, who asked a lot of questions that had to do with minimal realizations and McMillan degree and the Frenchman always seemed to sigh and say, yes, but in the FINITE DIMENSIONAL CASE. Loud, as if this other guy didn't get it. But I was sure he got it better than anyone else, except maybe the department wonk who took notes and sometimes corrected the Frenchman (always politely, with "I have a question" meaning You made a mistake back here, dude), a grad student working in several complex variables who was famous for correcting lectures while he took notes. He sat in on every advanced course that touched analysis without making any headway on his thesis even as his carrel filled with flat tablets of corrected course notes. This time he didn't ask so many questions and I wondered if he too had gotten lost.

Out of departmental politeness, everyone in the partial differential equations group and the several complex variables group had attended the first sessions, but all of the faculty had long since stopped showing up; my advisor had politely attended for the first week, sleeping through every lecture, sometimes snoring loudly enough to interrupt the flow. We graduate students in any analysis group were indentured.

I kept wondering when the stochastic stuff would show up, this Frenchman brought in from Stanford for his work in martingales and the more generalized stochastic integration with respect to the broader class of semimartingales. That was what my advisor had touted. Who knew what the fuck he was up to here.

He kept me after and said he'd heard I had brought up some general ideas on stochastic integration that had been unexpected.

"I don't think so," I said. "Just the normal stuff. From McKean."

"A difficult work," he said. "Things are better organized now, I think. More general, clearer perhaps, fewer mistakes. But no standard text yet, in English. I have notes in French."

"Isn't that what you handed us?"

"Yes and some work in stochastic differential geometry. Meyer is the name for some of this; Paul, not Yves. The geometry, though, they are from Professor Schwartz. You might have an opportunity to meet him, you know, if he comes here for a short stay. He was much opposed to this war in Vietnam. He is a communist, you know."

"No, I didn't know but I don't really give a fuck. I wasn't too nuts about the war either. Didn't seem to make much sense to me. I never saw any communists. Just a bunch of fucking illiterate dirt farmers hoping to be left alone to maybe grow enough to eat."

"Ah, yes… You were infantry, no?"

"More or less. I was one of Uncle Sam's Misguided Children," knowing he'd not likely get the word play. "A hired gun. I went from a grunt unit to a CAP unit."

"CAP?"

159

"Twelve marines and a Navy corpsman, like a rifle squad with its own medic. Lived in a village. Protected the village from VC and NVA tax collectors and conscription, and also from US bombs and artillery, more or less. Usually less. Teamed with local militia called Popular Forces. Hence CAP: Combined Action Platoon."

"No communists? In the village?"

"Doubtful. Those fuckers didn't know shit about politics except they didn't give a rat's ass for the crooks running things in Saigon. Don't think they cared much about the ones in Hanoi, either, or even at the local political club in Tam Ky, near where we were, or Danang, either. I didn't know shit about communism... or capitalism, for that matter. I've since tried sitting in on a boring class as an undergrad; like beating a dead horse. Got a book on mathematical economics; pretty simple stuff, figured it out in a few hours. There's a theorem, sort of fundamental theorem of perfect competition. Says that in perfect competition it's impossible to make a profit."

"Yes, a result of classical microeconomics. Sort of a steady state result, like perfect gas in steady state equilibrium or so."

"More or less. I remember when the prof was going on about Adam Smith I asked about it. It seemed to me perfect competition fit the model Smith had in mind. The prof didn't like it. He tried to say it didn't really apply. I pinned him down pretty good, I think, made the point that there ain't no such fucking thing as capitalism. He didn't like that much. I stopped going after that. I don't believe capitalism or communism, either one, exists. In fact, it seems all that economic shit is a kind of religion. Capitalism, communism, neither got any connection to dropping Dow napalm on gook farmers conscripted to carry AK-47s or some shit weapons we supplied them, depending on who controlled the local patch. Except as rationalization."

"But you went?"

"Well, not a lot of choice."

"Conscripted? You were conscripted?"

"We say drafted. It's a long story and I don't think it's worth the time we'd spend on it."

"But they say you were wounded badly. You are a hero, no?"

"Wounded, yes; hero, no way. That's a rumor."

"Ahh, I see. Legend."

"Yeah. When are you going to get into some of the stochastic stuff?"

"And you would go again, knowing what you know."

"Given the circumstances, you bet. I might try to alter the circumstances, but I'm a slow learner. I was hoping you'd get into some of the more general stochastic stuff that's happening now."

"It's exciting, yes? Much new work. Not probable we will find time. For what I am interested in now is necessary to first cover system theory."

"Well, I'm lost. But that is not uncommon. I don't see the big picture. Only some of the trees."

"If you have time, come by my office and I can give you some crash course in what engineers call linear system theory. To bring you up to where I started. Very easy in its basic setting. Lovely mathematics. Differential equations, observed linearly. Some papers by a highly underrated mathematician named Rudolph Kalman. Perhaps his formal training in applications is not helping, since his mathematics is underrated by mathematicians and misunderstood by engineers. He also has worked with Brownian motion processes in linear settings, no Ito integrals, only the integral of Wiener with nonrandom integrand. But you might find some of the problems interesting. And one can make money with this. Particularly with his Kalman filter."

"What is this Kalman filter?"

"An algorithm. If I speak in poetics, an algorithm for taking away the pain of randomness."

The money part seemed promising. The first person who'd talked about money on the outside. Soon as I'd finish this PhD I'd likely be looking for a new gig. I promised I'd take him up on it when I'd gotten some shit done for my advisor, told him I had to head for his class on symmetries and conservation laws, and broke away.

"This is interesting? This conservation laws?"

"I don't know yet. It's almost orthogonal to the stuff on my orals, but directly connected too. Like an attached handle. Seems to be where he's steering me, in any case, but I'm more interested in this stochastic integration stuff. I gotta go. I'm late."

I trotted down the hallway to the class where my advisor'd already begun writing on the board. I sat at the back of the room, propped my feet up on a vacant chair in front of me, and tried to figure out what the hell he was up to. Unable to take notes and listen simultaneously, I usually opted to listen. It made it tough to get notes since the advanced classes were based on work in progress. It would have been a serious problem had the tradition of the lecturer handing out notes not been instilled. At least in the partial differential equations group. It was a tradition more by group, since the algebra people didn't hand out a damned thing other than problems. And there were other tricksters, like Oberst in his Lie algebra class. Tulane offered a bit of democracy: being a small department any faculty member wanting to teach an advanced class had to write up several paragraphs and hand out mimeographs as advertisements. The students voted and only one advanced topic per semester per research group got taught. It brought students to advisors, for one thing. But Oberst had cheated in his Lie algebra class. The only assignment for the class had been to take notes on a weekly rotating basis. Xeroxes of the notes were passed out by the note-taker. When it came time for the class to end, Oberst gave everyone a grade of continuing which turned incomplete if you didn't take the follow-on. Hence we voted unanimously for a second semester.

The word symplectic jerked my attention back to the room. He'd defined Hamilton's equations and now was going on about invariance with respect to the skew-symmetric matrix that defined those equations as a system in phase space. The board filled with my advisor's yellow scrawls, abbreviations I'd learned to decipher after a semester class on stochastic integration and lots of face time in his office. Symplectic one-forms and the negative of their exterior derivatives, the symplectic two-forms, and some associated symplectic manifold and then he seemed stuck proving something he called Darboux's Theorem. He finished a computation and seemed satisfied.

The department wonk didn't look up from his notes to stop him, so I assumed he'd gotten it right. He put up another form, the Liouville form he called it, and mentioned something about it being a phase volume, I guess for the phase space. He didn't seem to do a fucking thing with it, though, except to mention it was non-vanishing. A volume form, then. I stored it away and watched him go.

He chased a diagram to prove that cotangent lifts of diffeomorphisms were symplectic and then defined Hamiltonian vector fields. I saw where he headed then, conservation of energy and the flows of the vector fields being symplectic, of course. Physicists love to conserve shit, mathematicians to obscure shit in the process of applying rigor. Physics made unrecognizable.

It began to come together for me. He'd put everything on a Riemannian manifold and gave the equations for the connection, the Christoffel symbols by another name, and it turned out that the projection of the integral curves were geodesics. Only the names had been changed.

I sat back and stared at the ceiling, looking for the relationship to what I'd just pried out of Postnikov. The ceiling gave way to covariant differentiation and it all fell in place.

Looking at the front of the classroom again, I saw him writing examples to compute as exercises; all infinite dimensional examples. He wasn't fucking around here. Three systems of PDEs to compute all this shit for, including the Kortweg-deVries equation. I guessed that would be near to impossible. All seemed massively computational.

I decided to slow him down.

"Excuse me. I have a question."

He looked up.

"Can't you just use the covariant derivative and skip all this Hamiltonian stuff?"

He didn't say anything.

"Use the covariant derivative along curves and do parallel transport, the standard thing. Conservation of energy pops out directly by a computation, I think. There must be some direct relationship between this Hamiltonian stuff and plain old Riemannian geometry."

"I guess so. Should I give it as an exercise to work out the details?"

"Your choice. I already have them worked out in my head."

Some seated in front turned in their chairs and sent me evil stares. I ignored them. One whined, "I don't know anything about Riemannian geometry," and my advisor laughed. "Forget it," he said. "It isn't an exercise. Unless you want to do it. Besides, I doubt it extends to infinite dimensions."

The exercises didn't matter to me. I never did the fucking exercises anyway. But the remark about dimension gave me something to chew over.

Class broke up and people fled the room. I caught him before he could get away from the board.

"I got some new stuff to go over," I lied. "We can get together maybe Friday?"

"What time?"

"The hour before this?"

"Let's make it after."

I'd skipped a couple workouts and didn't want to skip Friday's, but decided it could be a late one. Now all I needed to do was find some shit to talk about that related to SDEs and manifolds. That was where I wanted to head. My question in class had shown where he stood with respect to differential geometry in general. He had no clue. That would help.

A skinny kid accosted me as I vacated the classroom. I'd seen him hanging around but didn't know him. He'd come the year after my entering class and seemed to be confused a lot of the time.

"Do you understand that Pfaffian system stuff? The differential ideal and all that? I'm confused."

Supported by my cane, I leaned into him.

"Did you ask the guy teaching the class? He's got office hours."

"I came out of his office more confused than I went in."

"Okay, I wasn't paying a lot of attention that day, but the Pfaffian's just a linearly independent system of one-forms that vanish. They annihilate the tangent bundle of a submanifold that solves that system. It's related to integral manifolds of subbundles. It's called the Froebenius Theorem. Go to Warner's book on differentiable manifolds and Lie groups. He gives all the details of this, but I don't think he uses the term Pfaffian. The differential ideal is just an ideal in the algebra of forms on the whole manifold. It vanishes under exterior differentiation. Not a big deal. Warner's book. It's a kind of ugly mustard-yellow thing, but skinny."

He started to open his mouth again and I said, "I gotta go, man. I need to exercise and then I have an appointment. Get Warner's book and if you have a question after that bring your notes and the book, and we'll try to sort it out. If necessary I can escort you to his office for another confab. I think this form stuff was a formulation due to Elie Cartan, but its nothing once you get the Frobenius theorem."

Of course I hadn't read Warner myself, though I had looked in it once. Mostly concerning Lie groups, but I'd run across the differential ideal in the context of differential forms. I hadn't absorbed much. I considered it a potential place to look into cohomology, if necessary. I'd appreciated his approach to tangent bundles and such; it felt more like analysis, but I hadn't pursued it.

I made it downstairs and headed across campus for the gym, twirling my cane as I walked.

Another guy working out in the gym spotted me some, so I pushed myself to lift heavy. Made me forget everything. Feeling a damn sight better than when I'd gone in, as I got back to the department I stiffened up despite the long, hot shower. I looked forward to soreness in the morning.

b) Suspension

The place was almost empty, staff gone, only a handful of students and faculty remaining. I avoided everyone, grabbed the brown paper bag of goodies from my carrel and booked it to the Ball mansion.

Harry himself let me in. The place seemed to slacken more each time I arrived. Disjoining from reality maybe. Disharmonic, alien, maybe incoherent. It grew increasingly difficult for me to rationalize the foreboding it instilled.

"Hey," he said. "I heard some disturbing stories about Dina last night."

"So? What the fuck that have to do with me?"

"You were involved."

"Is she working? Feeling okay?"

"Yes, but I worry…"

"Look Harry, you come to me and tell me she's all fucked up. I talk to her, she comes around and you're happy, like my little talk changed something. Now you tell me there's some other problem I'm involved with. I got nothing to do with her, man. Dig?"

He looked angry but I knew he wasn't gonna fuck with me.

"She's almost too happy," he said. "Kind of mania about sex. I've never seen her so intense."

"That's good, no?"

"If it doesn't hurt her."

"Let her decide where there's pain."

"She brought a new actor. Black man with the biggest dick I ever seen in my life. And I have seen a lot of hanging meat. He made Albina cry."

"Call himself Mule?"

"Yep. Kip's friend."

"I met him. Didn't know he had a big dick, but not surprising given his size. Thought Albina liked 'em enormous."

"Was a threesome. He was getting in her asshole and she yelled stop, crying. Couldn't decide if he ought to pull out and start over or what, but she couldn't take it in the end."

He smiled. I pretended to not get it.

"What'd you do?"

"She gave up. First time. She's devastated. Lost her confidence. We did the scene with Dina. No one else would touch it."

"She cry?"

"Dina? I think she had an orgasm. Seemed to try not to, but she did. Great scene."

Shawntel came out of the room in a dressing gown looking pretty used up, the mousey Linda naked behind her. Harry responded to my questioning look.

"Yep, she's in them now too. Jeremy convinced her."

"Yeah, and Gudrun too?"

"God, that would be a coup. She's out of town on business. But that black girl from the party, she's working. Shoot with her tomorrow. Shawntel only does les scenes with Linda here. I think you met her."

Hair cut straight at the bottom hanging almost to her shoulders like shapeless curtains, stringy, dark not black not brown. Blue eyed. Not greenish blue or hinting at blue, but blue, bluer than mine maybe, dark pristine blue fucking eyes. High forehead, too-long face tapered to pouting mouth downturned by nature, gradual round chin. Maybe five nine, taller than Shawntel but slender bordering skinny, small tits lifting to tiny pink nipples pointed at the sky and not pear-shaped, fit in a cup, set wide apart bordering a pronounced sternum. Round shoulders, spindly arms not carrying much meat. Long toned legs, well proportioned without boney projections or knobby knees, hipless.

She started at me with those blue peepers. Cornflower blue maybe. Couldn't put my finger on the blue; lifted my eyes from her shaved cunt showing just a hint of five o'clock shadow darker than her hair and returned the stare. Her eyes went back a long way.

"Mr. Butcher," she said. "I thought we'd be seeing you in performance by now."

"Ah, well, the one that doesn't like men. Dresses like a secretary."

"I'm not dressed like a secretary now. There's been endless speculation here as to your riding abilities. If you'd come around I'd volunteer to do a boy scene."

"Wow," Harry said. "That is not something she ever says. Men are a rarity for her. Its more than her professional persona. She did one boy scene in a film and it hurt her image. The critics called it lifeless."

She walked up and stood on my feet, arms around my back to steady herself. "Boys aren't inspiring. Don't know how to work the other side, if you know what I mean. But I got a funny feeling about you."

"You're not going to find out in front of a camera. I don't do scripted. You'll have to study some other way."

She stepped off and stood back, turning her pout into a smile. Long teeth came through, slightly wide and slightly askew inward, not all that much but enough I saw it. Better she pout.

"You asking me out?"

I caught a glare from Shawntel, side of my vision only, so maybe my imagination.

"Depends on if you're a cheap date. I don't have a lot of money. Don't think a classy babe like you'd hang out in the holes I find to my taste."

"Well, try me sometime," she said. "I've been called cheap, and worse. And I've some experience in holes." She turned and kissed Shawntel, then walked back to where she'd come from, no sway but grace in lithe legs ending abruptly in a long rounded butt that would have been heart shaped had there been hips.

I gave Harry his dope and asked him to see to it Kip got his. He was supposed to be by for it later, but it turned out Kip and Jerry were watching Mule in action, so I gave it to him in person and got the hell out. It was dark when I caught the streetcar for The Quarter, but I felt pretty secure with my cane. It seemed to have grow into an extension of my personality. Anyway, no one fucked with me when I carried it.

Chapter 15
a) Brownian Holonomy

Molded skull: eyeless seamless white latex, conformal feeding-protrusion... Flopper tits: scarred in purple-red-blue wale, multi-pierced ultra-protracted nipples stretched along dual rows of tandem barbells... Beardless cunt: concatenated labia rings of gold chain, bloated glob clitoris pincushion studded with jewel tips... Contorted to human frog, on her back, wrists to elbows trussed ankles to knees, hands strapped to feet, asshole and bald cunt presented skyward... Dina?... Spotlighted naked on a gleaming circular dais lubricated slickly viscous, anchored to pairs of antipodal points on the platform, dragged to and fro via ropes by men hanging back in the shadows... From out of nowhere a man spears her cunt with a rubber-fisted pole, rammed, impaled, repelled around the circle, men shove dicks into the buccal cavity, ejaculate... another, another, another... my turn, my dick... warm spongy mandibular gnawing suction, gummy syrup ooze, have to piss... jesus... let go...

Shit! Sat up in bed, wet-spot wet-dream. Imagining Brownian motion on a sphere elastically tied to the poles. Turned on the light, grabbed a clipboard: Let that fucker go from the north pole tied to the only cut point, its antipode the south pole; see it wriggle to escape? can't get away flowing along the surface of that sphere. How far can it get? How wide the Brownian bridge? Clearly heat kernel hidden in here, but where? need to backtrack.

Where'd cut points come from? Couldn't remember where they'd fucking come from. Not Postnikov. Shit, Kobayashi and Nomizu. First hundred or so pages of volume 2, first two chapters; as far as I'd gone. Cut points always appear at or before conjugate points along the geodesic arc, assuming there are any. Conjugate points, that is. Not on the cylinder, though the geodesics stop minimizing half way round, hence by definition have cut points; but that fucker's flat anyway. Always have cut points on a compact manifold. The two ways of Exp: vectors on the tangent space and flows in the manifold.

I lit a joint, made coffee; figured out the heat kernel on the sphere, not bad the Brownian motion untied running its ass off. McKean did this in some Japanese journal and that paper by Gorman, too, bare-knuckled wrangling the process but on the rotation group. Ito and Yoshida did it for all Lie groups. Could make interesting computations; still, one ought to swat all the Riemannian babies at one time. Just seemed a piecemeal hammer and tongs approach without reason otherwise. Anyway, the rotation group is not the sphere...more projective three space, as I recall, but ought to be trivial. The two-sphere is not a group. McKean in the little blue book going through Ito's approach: gluing together local solutions for arbitrary elliptic operators on the neighborhood system; get a diffusion on the manifold with paths okay up to explosions. Need partitions of unity? Paracompactness required? Yoshida, too, maybe the same way. Gorman references Yoshida doing it for the three-sphere, which is a group. Unit quaternions. Seems much ado about not that much. McKean much deeper in the blue book giving some test for explosion on Euclidean spaces, Brownian motion with a new clock lifted to the frame bundle. None of this inspiring.

Did I unconsciously cadge the fucking proof of Morse's theorem I'd "invented?" Doesn't seem so; review K&N's presentation. Shit shit shit.

Easier on the brain to drop the Brownian motion verbiage; see BM as a family of travelers.

Real projective space. Crush the sphere: identify those antipodal points. The poles merge, and on the sphere they're both cut and conjugate locus. Of course, crushing that fucking sphere merges the poles and everything along either side of the equator, so the goddamn geodesic starting at a point and ending at its polar opposite on the sphere starts and stops at the same fucking place in projective space. The two minimizing halves of the geodesic smashed into one arc. The conjugate point's the fucking point itself. In projective space the cut locus's gonna be the crumbled equator, and that includes the point and its antipode. So the cut locus becomes the points at infinity. That hyperplane, that copy of projective space one dimension down sitting out at infinity. Trivial.

A few theorems from K&N came back. Like the closest cut point's conjugate with respect to some minimizing geodesic or else the midpoint of a geodesic starting and ending at the originating point. Like the sphere. All those great circles from the poles through the equator smushed up in projective space. Stuff was trivial. Made me want to play with ellipses. Too easy. Maybe more enlightenment from general surfaces of revolution.

Ito and Yoshida either barehanded constructions of sample paths to get elliptic operators or finessed them directly from the parabolic PDE and elliptic operator to the BM. Or McKean, injecting the differentials from Euclidean space into the Lie group. No one wanted to use the white noise as a functional via the Wiener distributional approach; on test functions could be embedded into some L_2 or a thing similar. That appealed; lots of machinery, functional analysis and such. Or compose with real-valued test functions or diffeomorphisms? clearly works on Euclidean space but of course skirting the issue of existence. Need them to test them, but ought to exist a shitload of them…

Ito showed the kernel for a parabolic PDE with elliptic operator on manifolds minimal relative to the volume element on the manifold. Compact manifold? I smoked another joint and found McKean, opened it to page ninety and read the damned theorem. Ito clearly assumed the elliptic operator G exists on the manifold before examining the unfolding parabolic equation, the process and sample paths. But existence of local solutions of the SDE governed by the elliptic operator is easy, the only difficulty patching them together. Explosions. Also get some condition for harmonic functions. Don't see a hypothesis of compactness, but McKean's pretty casual sometimes. Took a bit to figure out Weyl's lemma was about when distributional solutions were real solutions. Had to read the proof to understand the damned statement. Only needs compactness to get that the path visits every coordinate patch infinitely often. Makes sense. But all probabilistic. Need more direct approach. Where's he use G acting on one equals zero? And what to make of explosions? Not on compact manifolds...

Tired of fucking with McKean; back to geometry. Exp flows as a geodesic. Remember the big theorem: The inside of the cut locus along the set of all unit vectors in the tangent space is an open set in the tangent space that Exp sends diffeomorphically onto an open set in the manifold, and if the locus is attached as disjoint sum get the whole fucking manifold. Don't need compactness. Compact case get the inside of the cut locus in tangent space homeomorphic to a hypersphere in the tangent space. Finiteness of the cut locus implies compactness. That's easy to see. Got these babies in my head now.

I attempted to compute the law of the Brownian bridge on the sphere tied at those antipodal points, the cut points. Smoked a couple joints and listened to that tied Brownian traveler humming, spherical symmetry pushing random vibrations of the BM trying to escape its ties, resonating with the symmetry of the sphere via Laplacian eigenvalues like heat drumming a radiator, residues of harmonics modulo the Euclidean length. Made me think of Cannonball's solo on *Flamenco Sketches* on *Kind of Blue*. Transduced by the logic of the set of modal progressions, sublime transcendence from brass and vibrating reed.

Non-positive curvature is wilder. Can see the goddamn Exp increasing the distance now; no stopping. There's the wild ride. Get a covering map out of Exp and if the fucking manifold is simply connected get a diffeomorphism.

That made me feel better about seeing my advisor. Decided to open a can of sardines. Needed to maybe look at the eigenvalues of the Laplace-Beltrami operator. Started to generate some differential equations, thought better of it. More geometry, less analysis. The geometry'll keep him off balance. He snacks on differential equations.

brownian holonomy

Cannot forget the Dirichlet problem: capturing that random but legally disciplined wanderer when it first hits the boundary, taking expectation with respect to the starting point in the interior to randomly solve the deterministic Laplace equation.

Played computational games with the heat kernel on the real numbers, then on the circle. Derived the spherical solution via eigenfunction expansion, same as Fourier series. No such animal exists for the real line. Not compact. Continuous spectrum, Fourier transform; but solutions are close for small time. In fact, the same modulo 2π. I took a few limits after getting rid of long-time-from-now terms and found that Brownian standard deviation popping up, proportional to inverse of root t. Interesting. Ought to be the same locally in time, of course. It takes a revolution to figure out you're on a circle. So in the long run the BM can tell the circle from the line. Senses the topology.

How otherworldly is this heat kernel stuff? Waves take a finite time to get away from source, but not heat; not according to the heat kernel; starts out right after initial impulse, immediately felt arbitrarily far away on an infinite rod...is that why the BM moves so goddamn fast? Always getting back, at least in one or two dimensions, in finite time no matter how far away? Unbounded variation in every interval.

Think about Frenchy's device for taking away the stochastic blues, that Kalman thingy. Engineers have to have a way to make the world causal. It's gonna be in their nature... This Brownian motion lives in their devices in some form or other; maybe not Brownian, definitely not... What can come of integrals of white noise? Acausality? Nice idea, acausal, but not yet a word in English. Transformations? McKean's paper on differential space: Wiener measure as a uniform distribution on an "infinite-dimensional" sphere of radius square root of "infinity": an intuitive limiting argument using a basis of L_2 on the non-negative real interval, going to infinity as more basis vectors are shoved into the meeting...watching the rotation group, the spherical Laplacian and its eigenfunctions, the fucking spherical harmonics, stabilize as they grow. End up with a rotation group on n-dimensional Euclidean space growing into the rotation group on his infinite dimensional Euclidean space, the orthogonal group of L_2, all this with a single solitary Brownian traveler...with Poincare's help all the way from 1912...get uniform distribution in some generalized sense on the infinite sphere...sphere in name only, really flat, of course, has to grow up flat since curvature goes to zero... Could this be polynomial chaos growing up to be Wiener's homogenous chaos? The moral, according to McKean is that the Walsh expansion stands in same relation to Bernoulli trials as Cameron-Martin-

Wiener expansion to Brownian motion. But orderly chaos. Lives by a set of rules. Not like people trying to fucking kill your ass. That is fucking internal chaos…directed in like an implosion…homogeneous chaos blues.

This shit must terrify engineers, unseen acausal monsters lurking in their devices waiting for power-up…the white noise and its infinite degrees of freedom of rotation suddenly integrated via some nonlinear functional to defy their causal universe…probably a good thing they didn't understand Wiener all that well, the old blowhard…

I almost laughed out loud.

Back to the original path: way to go is lift that baby. Play in Euclidean space with the sphere embedded, lift the bitch from Euclidean space to the frame bundle and project it to the sphere, or any manifold for that matter. Take a process from the manifold to the horizontal subspace of the frame bundle and then project it to Euclidean space for comparisons. Laplacian on the horizontal subspace isn't the same. Can't be. Anyway BM escapes in dimensions higher than two. What the fuck?

Think of Levy's two-d BM as a conformal invariant. Get a new clock on that baby as path length of some analytic function of the process, lifted to a covering process on a Riemann surface running under the new clock. Does any BM really know what time it is? Ah, but it hits every disk as t goes to infinity. There you go.

Ought be a way then to apply the Laplacian to forms, get the heat equation on forms, maybe even arbitrary elliptic operators. The d-squared zero is a problem but can work with both d and a formal adjoint δ on the cotangent bundle.

Came up with three forms of the Laplacian, one for the horizontal subspace of the frame bundle and one for forms commuting with the d operator based on a sum of the products dδ and δd: symmetrized. Computed the difference between the standard Laplacian, the Laplace-Beltrami operator they call it, and this thing for forms and it dawned I had to be assuming the Levi-Civita connection to get all this Laplacian shit to work. It gets rid of torsion; can't have any fucking torsion. Gotta be compatible with the Riemannian metric.

So the goddamn standard Laplacian bitch doesn't commute with the exterior differentiation bitch: need some hair around that hole, as my daddy'd say. Works nicely with the BM on the sphere, any manifold, any compact manifold anyway, probably any manifold; of course can get it from trace of the Hessian. Suddenly a lot of shit from the books I'd pushed myself to read came back. I could see the section in old Kobayashi and Nomizu clear as day: Sectional Curvature. And the old limping shot up sergeant, Korean war vet who'd elected to live in The Crotch, taught weapons…dismantling the old World War Two thirty caliber machine gun with that fucking spring "take your head off," he'd say in his Brit accent, "You take the bitch thusly…" or "Grasping the bitch just so…" Limping around the stage, limping on the long hikes back and forth up and down the line shaking his cane at us girls, encouraging stragglers, encouraging leaders, at least quadrupling the mileage we'd all hump, wearing down his old boots…and then that goddamn hill with the end in sight turning into a curve on up to greater heights in the coastal California sun and scrub… Yes, I confess to having been a Hollywood Marine.

No fucking natural way to get L_2 on the manifold… can't integrate functions; only forms… No natural differential operator anyway and certainly nothing natural in second derivatives, been through that already…remember the goddamn symmetrized operator on forms? Cocksucker!

Curvature. It all hinges on curvature. Freedom from torsion, but not from curvature. That's why the fucking sphere ain't flat and the cylinder is. The Brownian particle can sense that, too, and if you wait long enough the goddamn topology, too, as in the circle is compact, the line ain't…

I dinked with some exponentials (real ones, not just projecting tangent vectors up to cut points) and finally saw that the Laplacian on forms and the regular Laplacian were related by a map defining the action of the curvature tensor on differential forms…depending on how you looked at it. I preferred to look at it as a three-one tensor field, or at least it seemed right, but maybe it's really a covariant degree four tensor or perhaps an endomorphism. What's really real? Frames of reference: perspective? More than perspective: frames adjust reality. Really. Anyway, adjusting the sign on the Laplacian for forms, they coincide on functions; on one-forms I got something in the Ricci tensor.

My leg stiffened up on me, sitting up in bed smoking dope, eating this and that, splattering sardine oil on my notes and already sperm-stained musky sheets. Sun not yet up, Quarter still deserted. Took a fast walk to the river, passing through empty streets, even Lafitte's on the corner nearly asleep, three men on the balcony smooching and grappling. An embracing couple of bearded guys in biker leathers sitting on the windowsill of Jake's Clover Grill across Bourbon caught up in a long kiss.

Only other living soul the Bead Lady at the three open payphones on Royal near the square yammering some otherworldly melodic tongue into an upside down phone, its cut metal cord sticking up like an antenna. Spooky the way she's always out, day and night, gaunt scarecrow hugging the shadows, random walk scare the shit out of you suddenly on you, hand out in front, "Lucky bead mister?" German accent maybe with that gray frazzled hair, long dress usually gray and layers on top and maybe under, too, dirty white tennies, gnarled outstretched hand with fucking dried fava bean or a few plastic beads, stiff precise movements back-leaning, pointed extremities. I zipped past her, she not paying any attention to me but watching all the time; trucked on down to the river to Café du Monde. Strong black coffee and beignets with plenty of powdered sugar, thought about polar coordinates and the Brownian bridge computation I wanted to do. Clearly the heat kernel always exists on compact manifolds. Use eigenfunction expansions. Or some other way. Get a Dirichlet version on pre-compact manifold, zero on the boundary, let those babies expand to fill up the entire space. It's locally compact. Take a limit. Laplacian's gonna have the Riemannian metric so the BM's gonna feel that curvature.

So now I knew how to prove the existence of the heat kernel on general Riemannian manifolds without resorting to probability. Is it an operator semi-group? Gotta get a Markov process, but ought to be easy to show. Then get a process and prove she's a Brownian motion. Not a big deal. Or skip the limit; show the unbounded operator gives a semigroup acting on L_2, some kind of spectral result. Like on the line. Probably works. Heat flow as measures gives Wiener measure on continuous functions on manifold by extension via isometry, McKean's hallucinogenic vision of Wiener's differential space as infinite dimensional rotation group of L_2 acting on the "infinite dimensional sphere" of radius "square root of infinity": infinite bubble flattening (how could it be otherwise since curvature is 1/radius?) by stretching out as square root of radius n going to infinity simultaneously as dimension n goes to infinity!...all that is a potential approach here. Maybe. Anyway for short times the heat ought to flow along geodesics, at least in a world where the random made sense. The not-haphazard world. People confuse the two anyway. Randomness ain't haphazard; she follows rules so we can solve problems in the mythical deterministic reality.

On my way back the Bead Lady'd disappeared but people percolated through the tenebrous dawn rising from solidified blocks of decaying buildings that hugged the narrow streets and cracked sidewalks. Gray people of the dawn coming alive. At the gate, turned once to look back before passing down the bricked tunnel of a passageway to the cloistered interior, sanctuary, and saw, looming, the dreadful Pontefract of day. It popped into my head, the Pontefract of day; no idea where from. No idea what it meant, but it seemed to apply.

It made sense to deal with BM in polar coordinates on the sphere and then think about distance. But geometry. Fuck with the advisor's mind. I lit a joint. Of course, the right way to think about polar coordinates is in terms of a radius and angle on a local n-minus-one sphere for arbitrary n-manifold. Breaks into two terms, radial and some functional thing of angle, so of course on the two-sphere it's going to be angle on the equatorial circle and a distance. Lat and colat. The latitude is the circle, diffeomorph of the equator, the angle from the pole the colatitude measuring distance along the sphere. The cutlocus cuts that fucker up around a point p say, surrounding the place where those geodesics stop minimizing. Two disjoint components, cutlocus a closed set.

Split the Brownian paths into these two processes. Bingo: on the manifold with radial symmetry the two processes turn out to be independent. I see it. Gonna get the BM as a funny kind of product of these two components. Problem with measuring distance is the fucking cut point. Everybody's got one on the sphere: fucking antipodal twin. Gotta figure out how to get around that. On general manifolds the goddamn cutlocus has got to be avoided. Better look first at this whole thing in some complete Riemannian manifold. Extend those maximal geodesics forever.

I felt the Brownian traveler skitter the manifold on an infinite dice roll at infinitesimal steps. Like an infinite squad of random wrigglers out on patrol, acausally probing for the feel of it; more thorough than if deterministic, undistracted by reason or preconception or prejudice telling where not to look. Best of all, remembering all of it. Or absorbing it all in their little random souls.

Need to trace him with the one-dimensional piece, the radius. But two interesting problems here. Cut points fuck with distance: on the sphere every pair of points has two distances, one the long way. Antipodal has two equal distances, short way being long way. So you get some kind of adjustment process in the SDE for the radial process. A boost from the cutlocus set; pushing along the geodesic?

I wrote down an expression for a stochastic differential equation with the correction term. That baby had to be zero off the cutlocus, negative on the cutlocus. Can see how to prove it, too. Need to use the triangle inequality, of course. But get a semi-definite additive functional of the Brownian motion supported on the cutlocus. Subtract it and get a positive functional. So now we skitter out past the cutlocus. So what? Ought get some means of comparison, differential equation of some sort, must have something to do with Jacobi because we are with God here playing this subtle variational game.

Must give us another process. Think about this later; write it down in the rough.

More interesting questions: does the little bastard escape or return? When's he blow up so he can't get everywhere? Always exist some place he ain't been? can't get?: If one does it, they all do it. Little lemmings all blow up. Could see manifolds so steep the little buggers fall back. But you can't fall off a manifold! So the BM has constrained wandering. Gotta be curvature. Puffing to get up that hill, winded. Use Riemannian curvature tensor to get sectional curvature and Ricci tensor. Need to bound that Ricci curvature below? Use Jacobi again, get a nice pair of upper and lower bounds on the Laplacian of the radius. In terms of curvature, of course, upper in terms of Ricci curvature, lower in terms of sectional curvature. Likely not sharp bounds, but anyway now we're cooking. See that expression for the SDE, easy to see a BM there; no big deal to prove that. But see that negative curvature push that BM away right from the start: Just like I saw, the little BM screaming down some horrific upside-down slope, terrified, doesn't know you can't fall off a manifold...blows up instead. Poof. Vanished into thin nothing.

Amazing insight. Diffuses like a motion with asymptotic velocity pushing away from the starting point. Completely unlike Euclidean space. The bitch can sense the geometry! Holy shit.

Now at least I had notes for tomorrow. I needed more detail, but that could wait. Needed to figure out a fiercely curving manifold, gotta have sectional curvature getting negative really fast as a function of distance, so pushes that little son of a bitch off to infinity in finite time. Can see it. Heat equation ain't about real heat, that's for damned sure. Little BM randomly scurrying so fast gets to the end of the line before getting to the end of the manifold. Places where BM can't appear; vanishes first. Hidden places? Will have probability strictly less than one of being everywhere in the manifold. Like killing on the boundary. Big deal, unless this is death without killing. Natural death by negative curvature? I needed the right complete Riemannian manifold with seriously growing sectional curvature. The negative curvature acts like a malignant drift, pushing that baby along so fast it never makes it. Would be interesting...

Woke up aware of someone in the room. That hum following me, more like a cello each time...

I saw how to build the manifold. Wrote a few hints, smoked a joint.

The cello called me back. Almost make it out in the dim din — holy shit fucking night again... Midnight?...passed out — too much dope?

Needed to find some goddamn way to get a distribution of the tied BM on the fucking sphere. Maybe from a diffusion: after all, just conditioning on the second endpoint. Shouldn't be this goddamn hard. Be nice to have this one computation to go with the rest of this stuff. Not that much, really, but at least makes it look like I'm doing something besides dope, booze and sluts. Too much whoring, but where else you gonna find this freedom?

Woke up again and wrote down the SDE for the Brownian bridge in Euclidean space, got the probability law for the tied Brownian process in Euclidean space. Lifted it to the sphere. Used Girsanov's theorem to get existence on half-open interval but now fucking with some singularity at the endpoint, some logarithmic thing. Stuff like solder forms I'd forgotten from Bishop and Crittendon popped into my head as needed and I proceeded speedily through a messy calculation. Got some bounds, saw a general expression for any compact manifold, wrote down the law for the tied BM on the sphere and collapsed into sleep, serenaded by the cello...

Hum from somewhere, cello? softly whining singing background shit—

Sat up terrified, sweating, papers scattered over the bed, joint burned out on the ancient regime wooden plank floor. Lit it, looked around. No one in the room. Knew it was a cello. That jiggedy dance with the whip or whatever it was from Dimitri's Second Cello Concerto? That's it! That last ambivalent movement with the alternating morose sonority and jiggedy dancing goad to the cellist. Fucking Russians.

Stared at the high ceiling out of view, hands under head, roll into fetal position as singing cello fills the room, vibrating so softly cannot be sure it's really there... Can I hear it? from jiggedy to low and melancholy and back again...deep, flowing around me vibrating...the sphere pulsing harmonics... spherical harmonics...the tied BM picks it up, wobbles with the harmonics, chattering, clanking, wobble and clatter...eigenvalues of the Laplacian on any fucking manifold, not just the sphere...shit, I got it...

I awoke in transit from somewhere...the cello serenade growing desperate in wild dancing gait...there it is the fucking trick I needed. Move from general to specific.

Sat up, grabbed a pen and wrote out the differential equation to lift to any radially symmetric manifold. Amazing how the radial process disconnects from the angular process, following its Laplacian generator; leaving the angular process to do its own thing according to a new "clock" defined by the radial process. Just like that BM lifted to a covering process on the Riemann surface.

I sketched out the example for the negatively curved wildly sloping motherfucker pushing along the little untied Brownian bitch screaming skittering to oblivion and that woke me up a lot. Finally sketched out some notes for the idea of short time geometric information gathering versus long time topo-logical information gathering. Bullshit, but refinable.

I drank coffee and ate sardines for breakfast, shit showered shaved, smoked a joint, then hoofed my ass on down Bourbon to Canal and the streetcar whence I swayed on up St. Charles Avenue.

b) Torsion-Free Warped Product

My advisor sat behind a metal surface mounded with papers and books, before him a cramped narrow space with the file cabinets pressing in. It always amazed me the swathe of openness he left behind him. Outside his classroom I'd dodged ambush by the same nerdy kid as last time and now stood stripped of excuses, yellow notepad in hand writing with scrawls, drawings and quasi-words. The nearly opaquely yellowed window in the background begged for cleaning.

"I don't have this well organized," I said, "but I've been running Brown-ian motion on manifolds. I looked at McKean and some others and realize it's simpler than all that. Using the heat kernel. Easy to see how to prove the heat kernel lives on a compact Riemannian manifold and I have a proof it lives on any Riemannian manifold, even not geodesically complete. Saw three modes for working with the Laplacian, on functions, forms and on the orthonormal frame bundle."

He just stared back, big brown eyes as always noncommittal, poker-face peering out of the darkness except for the occasional twinkle that seemed to indicate something amused him. I didn't see it now.

Everything he'd lectured in the class preceding this meeting had come to me as geometry. I'd seen his mathematics unfold on manifolds, all sorts of them but satisfying the standard topological conditions just shy of compactness, overrun with Brownian travelers wandering in search of geometric and maybe topological enlightenment, and now I raised him a new vision that, holy shit, I realized matched my analysis vision. The two intertwined. Algebra loomed off in the distance, formal and cold, but my feel for the active gnawed at the bounds of my ignorance.

A new sensation overwhelmed me: wanting to be smarter. I'd never been where being smart was rewarded at the same time that I could see my limitations.

"Look," I said, writing something on the board, "the Brownian motion learns by wandering the manifold. Its paths can tell us topological stuff in its long time behavior. Sees geometric stuff in the short term."

"You mean that the process is controlled by aspects of the manifold?"

"Yep, but it feels it too. Shows up in some stuff. Like the circle versus the line, the process eventually learns by letting go. Wandering. A lot of it's related to curvature. And eigenvalues of the Laplacian. I don't know if individual particles alone can tell the story ever, or sometimes, but I think I have an example of a finite time explosion on a manifold with—"

He cut me off. "Just a minute. Let me get someone else who can add to this."

He came back with Frenchy and we hit the discussion where I'd left off. Frenchy stopped me early on.

"So, you have a proof for this result on all Riemannian manifolds, existence of the heat kernel?"

"Yes, but let me assume its true for compact manifolds 'cause I see how to do that—"

"Sure, it's been demonstrated," he said.

I gave the limiting argument for non-compact manifolds more convincingly without closing all loopholes.

"Yes, that is quite good, a new result maybe. Not probabilistic. Perhaps worthy of a paper. The bounds."

My advisor watched implacably, not stepping in at all.

"I can show more," I said. "You get a semigroup and can define Brownian motion with it."

I explained the work I'd done the previous night modulo ghostly cello serenade and they listened. Then I sketched out a loose program: exploring manifolds with Brownian motion. Maybe tied to symmetry by looking at invariance properties of manifolds defined by PDEs remaining invariant with respect to their own diffusion processes. Looking for conserved quantities.

My advisor asked Frenchy if he wanted to join my committee, since his specialty was working with martingales on manifolds. Frenchy said it'd be tough from Stanford.

When I got to a construction of the Brownian motion on a radially symmetric manifold on the product space with the change of time in the angular process through an integral involving the radial process, Frenchy smiled and called it the warped product.

I finished with a vision: Dina beckoned, awaiting some random forcing.

"Look," I said. "The key here's the white noise. Malleable randomness, acausality of the orderly variety, waiting for Ito's integration. That's the right approach. You learn more by probing randomly than by any following of preconceptions. The integral, the Brownian motion process, she doesn't need any reason, because as random as she is she still has to follow the law. Law incorporating geometry and topology, at different time scales. So I know the right way's to work with the white noise distribution, deal with functionals of that baby. There is some link between the Brownian traveler's random meandering and the shape of what she travels, and the topology, too. Just gotta find it."

And with that, Frency signed up. Now there were two of them to fuck with me, Advisor One and Advisor Two. But they both seemed pleased for now and I could play them off against each other.

I left McKean's vision of the infinite-radius sphere in infinite-dimensional Euclidean space out of it. I still didn't recall if he worked with the orthogonal group or the rotation group; he kept saying rotations and writing $O(n)$ as n trundled off to infinity. Or so I remembered; could have been me. Too dangerous to bring up anyway. Too much metaphor and certainly too much to spring on my advisor so early in the game. I know later McKean'd brought in the orthogonal group, but didn't recall any $SO(n)$ showing up as rotations, though he'd written rotations. Maybe. And I couldn't recall that shit about modding $SO(n-1)$ out of $SO(n)$ and the relationship to the sphere. Be circumspect… my own private vision of hell for now…

They expressed amazement at my exploding Brownian traveler on that barren negatively curved hyperbolic monstrosity, amazed at the drifting speed pushing it away from the start. They talked about it and looked at the clues in the SDE and the curvature bounds and considered the probabilistic interpretations. Things gelled a bit for all of us.

A new vision: Miss Cone. Definitely Miss Cone. I voided an image of planting my dick in her face and tried to get back to the sphere and rotations; probably something to do with group actions.

I'd made my stat class in plenty of time. Miss Cone had straggled in behind a gaggle of athletic boys like she'd just left a cluster fuck. A longhair'd passed me reeking of reefer. The cheerleader'd sat demure, already settled, smoothed legs tucked under the chair. Avoiding any talk of bundles or Brownian travelers and unaware of the drift I followed, statistics poured from my mouth, mostly examples and worked out computations. I dragged on about shape.

At the bell, Cone and the cheerleader had caught me in a pincer. I penetrated Cone's dowdily ensconced subterfuge and emerged inside her naked head. The cheerleader wore more modesty and less dowdiness, flashy in exterior charm. More a traditional subterfuge here, more Christian and moralistic, tempting to but not beyond rigid boundaries ending badly. The sap who descries that umbral calculus will incur eternal torment.

I dwelt on Cone's eyes; looked inside.

After a question answered tersely, cheerleader exited.

Cone had started on questions about the French Quarter again. Thinking she might head towards me, I cut her off. I envisioned my advisor's pending class. Previsions of the sequent one-on-one in his office had haunted my unconscious since before arising. It had gone better than I'd imagined then, confabulating with this bitch so clearly in heat which only now I noticed; in the rear view mirror, as it were.

She hadn't seemed to like it, leaving her standing in the abandoned classroom, but I'd had a head filled with stuff to spew in just over two hours. And it had gone well.

Maybe now they'd stop fucking with me. And my advisor'd leave off goading me to formally and symbolically compute conversation laws for nonlinear PDEs using some shit like MACSYMA. Whatever the fuck that was.

Chapter 16
a) Five Lemma

BRAAP — BRAAAP skull penetrating BRAAAAAAP—images… melting away… BRAAAAAP—climbing from a hole, leaving behind vaporized engrams… vanished, gone… insistent BRAAAAAAAAAP—

Dry and dizzy, I clambered out of bed, the sheets twisted from the stained mattress by frenzied sleep hot with alcohol fever. Sweating, still smelling bourbon… BRAAAAAP unrelenting, chasing away remnant hints of dreams, crowding out images felt now more than remembered, even the feelings dissolving, leaving behind overwhelming sadness at loss…

Pulling on jeans and passing out the window to the narrow metal widow's walk slick with steady drizzle, white-knuckled grip on the flimsy black iron railing, looking down at the street. At the gate Gudrun Ball pushing the doorbell another time, holding it in BRAAAAAP…

"Just a minute," I yelled. "I'll drop you a key."

She looked up all blue-eyed, boobs straining against the yellow T-shirt damp and clinging to her, premature matron-cleavage at the plunging scooped neck curving down and away from the straps. The fat ruby gash broke into a smile; from my third story perch I discerned lipstick stains on tiny white teeth lurking behind curvaceous mounds of garish kisser, red flapping bird above a fat anchor of arcing pout. An urge to plunge my dick into that clown hole surged over me. Hangover shtup-urge…

I turned away, carefully threading a dizzy barefoot return along the narrow strip of metal.

It took a couple minutes to find the key, haunted as I was by the residue of dream images; splitting my brain searching for what I knew to be lost, ready to cry at the loss and not remembering where I'd left my keys…missing shards of my life not mitigating the erection assaulting denim… The buzzer again BRAAAAAAAAAAAAAAAAAAAAAAAAP and I ducked back out the tall window to the dizzying perch and couldn't find her until I leaned far over and there pressed against the wooden shutter on the ground floor apartment two men groping her.

"Hey, assholes," I hollered, "I'm coming down and you'd fucking better be gone…"

"Yeah, you and what army?" A mangy cur of a man, likely drunk, his partner bigger and grinning missing teeth, both in need of a shave, probably a bath.

"This bitch's ours, dude," the bigger one with a slurred Southern accent, "you'd do best staying up there…"

I grabbed the cane and my keys hiding in plain sight on the kitchen counter beside the sink and zipped down the stairs, through the passage to the gate, shoved out into the street and immediately smacked the big one on his lower back with the knobbed end, then tripped his partner with a down stroke to the back of his right knee. The big one pulled his hand from beneath Gudrun's skirt, grinning at me and backing away and I let him have it full in the shoulder. He reeled back and I hit him hard in the side beneath his upraised right arm. He crumpled and I turned to the other lying on his back on the dank concrete.

"Don't get up until we're gone," I said. I stood back just far enough to wield short, free swings. They knew I'd brain them.

From inside the gate, I turned back. "When I get upstairs I'm calling the cops."

"You broke my ribs," the big one whined, holding his side, sitting on his butt in the gutter blocking a rivulet.

Gudrun emitted a level hiss. "You rotten bastards. The fucking cops'll bust your heads and dump your sorry vagrant-asses in City Park, so I suggest you book it now. If I had my gun, I'd take care of you myself."

It seemed she inspired them to move on; they hobbled across Bourbon.

"They hurt you?"

"No, just pawed at me."

Her hair hung over her shoulders and neck like a drowned varmint. The swooping U of the T-shirt stretched where they'd tried to tear it open.

She smoothed her skirt and peered down her shirt at the apex of the V deep in the crevice; red hand marks embossed stark white flesh. Her high-gloss vermilion lips trembled. She pushed me against the bricks and pressed against me, shivering. I looked down on her, her face buried in my bare chest, and my erection returned. I wanted to hold that head between my hands and fuck the scarlet wound in her face. I wanted to pull back from a full plunge into that quivering yap with lipstick streaks the entire length of my dick.

"They were going to rape me!"

"Never happen," I said. "The guys at Lafitte's wouldn't let it. Or Mrs. Cairo at the Washing Well. She had to be watching. There's no place for those assholes to take you here. Everything ends flush against the sidewalk. It's why I live here. Always people around. No place to hide. No ambushes."

I held my cane awkwardly before me with my right hand and she hung on my right arm as we corkscrewed up the narrow stairwell towards the dim radiance of the skylight. Pressed against the brick wall and leaning into the bad leg now come alive, she forced a tight into the rickety yellow banisters on which propped the faded red handrail to which I clung hoping to forefend a plunge to the bricked plane below.

"I really wanted to see you," she said. "You don't have a phone. I was afraid you'd be out. Or maybe not alone. You are alone, aren't you?"

"Of course. I live alone."

"The word is that Dina stays with you."

"Not with me."

"You deny you see her?"

"I didn't say that. She visits me from time to time. So does Bobbi. And people you don't know."

"Bobbi has taken up with that black man, the friend of Kip's. Moose or whatever he's called."

"Mule? Interesting."

"All she cares about is big dicks. I have been told she likes anal sex."

I gave a sideways glance at her T-shirt bowed out by breasts, off-center nipples accenting PERFORMANCE, one poking the O, the other the C. The line below read COUNTS. Below that the words John Deere.

She looked out the window onto the courtyard.

"There," she pointed across. "I knew it."

"There what?"

She moved aside and I looked at the top floor slave quarter. Standing on the balcony outside the wide doorway opening onto the shallow room filled by a bed, Dina at eye-level smiled back at us. She waved.

"Mr. Boudreaux agreed to lease me this place for an entire year," she called across the verdant expanse of faded, crumbling bricks.

"I thought it was a guest quarter."

"It is. I paid for a year, in advance."

I pulled back inside.

"I didn't expect that," I said.

"She's smitten with you. Not that it's so hard to understand," rubbing her left hand on my bare chest. "Manly."

"A butcher, too. Don't forget that."

184

"Mmmm," she purred, rubbing with both hands.

"I haven't showered or anything. I got in late, half drunk."

"Out carousing?"

"Drinking and playing pool. A place over in Marigny. Owned by cops. Bartender's a woman who used to be a man. Former Marine. Tough as hell."

"Like you," leaning into me and inhaling deeply. "Please don't shower for my sake."

"Bare concrete floors, two old pool tables. I have a friend who likes the cheap Dixie longnecks and obnoxious crowd. Takes his girlfriend for protection. One ugly bartender."

"I love longnecks…"

"Full of transsexuals and their thug boyfriends. Our mutual friend Bob likes it too, cause it's owned by cops."

"He's a cop?"

"No, a dealer. Seems they had a big shipment of acid. Blotter."

"I never used acid."

"Today might be a good day. Wanna go for it?"

"I don't think so. Takes a considerable time commitment, doesn't it?"

"Twelve hours, more or less."

"I don't need to be home tonight. Jeremy thinks I'm in Baton Rouge on business."

"Business on a Saturday?"

"We both do a lot of our work on weekends."

"So why'd you tell him that and come here?"

"Isn't it obvious?"

"I think so, but I don't get it."

"I'm horny. I've heard you're excellent. After all, my T-shirt says it all."

"Why not spend the weekend with Jeremy?"

"Come on. He and I haven't slept together in years."

"Then why the marriage? Why the phony business trips?"

"It is all appearances, dear. He likes to swing. Go to clubs. Meet other couples. Orgies."

"And you?"

"I'm more into one on one."

"So that's Chantal's position?"

"Mostly. He takes her on his business trips, for entrance to the swing clubs and to meet swingers. No single men allowed. Only couples."

"Façade, then, is it?"

"No, dear, not really. Marriage is more than sex."

She began pushing me into the apartment. Steering me.

"Wait," I said. "What about Dina? She'll know you were here."

"So what? She won't care."

"What if she's jealous?"

She shrugged. "So she tells Jeremy. I don't care."

"I do. You're married. I've been down this road before and it didn't turn out well. Nearly got me killed."

"I'd like to hear that story."

"I'm serious."

"Look. He enjoys hearing my adventures, okay? He is expecting this at some point."

"What about lunch?"

"What?"

"I haven't had coffee. Haven't shit. Haven't eaten. I'm hung over. Haven't even smoked a cigarette or a joint yet. And I could use a shower."

"After. We can shower together after."

"Well, if you're staying, there's no after. It'll be all night or nothing. And I insist on the acid."

She stopped pushing and looked me in the eye.

"Acid scares me," she said. She pulled out a blue pack of Gauloises and lit two of them.

"Fear's a good thing. It's healthy." I took a long drag of the dark smoke. "I try to be afraid every day… I'm a brutal fuck, too. Just so's you know."

"I can handle the brutal. I like it." Smoke pluming from flared nostrils. "I don't think I can handle the acid."

"Well, let me put on a shirt and we'll go to lunch somewhere. You did plan to feed me, didn't you?"

"I was hoping you'd feed me."

"I'm tapped out."

"I meant with this," grabbing my erection. "This thing seems to be of a different mind than you. And ooh, it is big."

"I have a lot of ways to take of care of this. Don't worry about what it's thinking."

She backed away, holding the cigarette between us.

"Oh, well. I am sure there are much better looking women than I on your plate." She inhaled deeply, vented more smoke from her nose. "Dina, for example."

"I don't make comparisons. She's not attractive to me."

"Nonetheless you do fuck her."

I found a joint, lit it with the cigarette, took a long hit, handed it to her.

"Look, I aim to get high on acid today. And I don't aim to do it alone."

"Okay. Let me take you to lunch anyway. We can go to Ruby Reds. Been there?"

"Yeah, I go sometimes. A little pricey for me. Burgers and beer are cheaper at the Port of Call. And they have jazz on the jukebox."

"I don't like it there. You have a record player here?"

"Only jazz. And some classical stuff. No rock."

She cocked an eyebrow.

"Sorry. I'm pretty fucking square."

I brushed my teeth, put on a T-shirt and my Redwing chukka boots with the white soles for concrete and tore a double strip of hits from the sheet of blotter acid Red had given me a few hours earlier at the no-name bar. I wrapped the rest of the sheet in plastic and put it in the refrigerator. Red knew the source well and had been assured each dot was at least a quadruple hit. Fresh shit, too. Could halve a square and still get an easy couple hundred mikes from the half.

The drizzle had transformed into a sunny day; puffs of white fleece floating in blue soup. We wound down the stairs and out the gate. Gudrun grabbed my hand and we marched off side by side, she bounding like a teen going steady. We humped up Bourbon a couple blocks, zagged riverward at Ursuline, zigged another block farther along at Royal, a zag towards the river at Governor Nichols, a zig at Chartres, a zag at Barracks across Decatur to North Peters and then a final zig to Esplanade. We crossed to Ruby Reds, a dark hole at the end of the Esplanade not far from the river.

The door led into a winding cavern that opened out to a dingy rectangular room with tables and a long bar, dark and quiet and cool. Peanut shells littered the floor.

We sat at a table and called for beers. The bartender, a chunky bleached blonde painted to look younger, brought a couple drafts and a basket of peanuts.

"We ain't opened officially yet, sweeties," she said. "But the cook's firing up so's you gonna be able to get you some food real soon now."

"So tell me about your married woman, Mr. Butcher."

She sat across from me, elbows on the table, the pack of Gauloises resting between us. We smoked and I looked into her blue eyes. I wanted to fuck her but I wasn't about to give in on the acid.

"It's a stupid story. It happened when I was a teenager. I was a trouble-maker. Fought a lot. Hung out with thugs."

"Must have been difficult for your mother."

"You bet. Worried her sick. All I did was fight, drink and try to get laid. Hated school. Listened to jazz. It was what I had in common with a handful of bohemians stuck in thug and surfer land. Fancied myself an angry hipster. Used to help out the bimbos by letting them sit next to me and cheat off my tests until I got caught. I didn't care."

"Surfers in Las Vegas?"

"Yep. Funny, no? Mostly imports from California, wearing Pendleton wool shirts, long bleached hair, faded and bled out Madras shirts, listening to bad music like The Beach Boys or guitar shit like Pipeline. I hated that whole scene, particularly the music. There was one guy they all kind of looked up to, had dark curly hair and never dressed up in a surfer uniform except those san-dals—"

"Huaraches. I saw a documentary on the whole scene once for an anthro class."

"This guy listened to jazz. He was big on West Coast stuff, cool jazz, Mulligan and Brubeck but he really dug Paul Horn. I was more into the East Coast hard stuff that came out of bop, or so I thought, like Mingus, Monk, Col-trane, Miles, Dolphy even though he'd come out of the West.

"But he and I got along okay. The handful who dug jazz were pretty broad across the spectrum, actually. Not too many intellectuals, since jazz had kind of bad name there, too, but there were a few. One of them wrote on the school paper and in a column made some silly comment about surfers. Three of them threatened him and it got back to me. So I waited out in the parking lot for them in my old beat-up '53 Plymouth and kicked their asses. I just enjoyed fighting.

"I hung out with this big guy, bigger than me, always fighting with blacks they bussed in. He and this one big black would have amazing fights. Took the principal and a bunch of grown men to break them up after they decked the football coach with a trashcan lid. After that there were always cops on campus. But I never got involved in that race stuff. Couldn't understand the 'hating nig-gers' bit.

"Anyway, this guy was a boxer, Golden Gloves, and a street fighter. He trained guys for fun, and I did a little with him and he stopped with me. He real-ized I could kick his ass and told me so. Said I had a gift for hurting people. I think he was afraid of me. Marines called it a gift for mayhem. I got in a fight with some asshole who called me out one day. He started shoving me and I put him in the hospital. He never touched me after the first two shoves."

"Wow."

"Yeah, wow's right. Broke his jaw, several ribs. He almost lost an eye. I couldn't believe the fury pouring out of me."

"How'd you do in school?"

"I did okay. I understood shit right away. I went to classes but never did any assignments. I always aced the exams, but refused to hand in papers or such unless it was something I found interesting that didn't require too much reading. Took bonehead English classes because they didn't expect you to read books. They had you read small paragraphs and then tested for comprehension with essays and such. That was easy. I learned to sandbag the tests they gave for placements, intentionally answer incorrectly enough so they'd leave me out of the harder classes without making it seem obvious."

"That would be hard."

"Not really. People I listened to jazz with knew I wasn't stupid. I remember one of the school brains telling me I was going to be a loser because I might have had the chicks then and been tough then but I'd be a penniless loser later. Some of my jazz friends defended me but I was a little pissed by it.

"I'd taken business math and aced it. But this guy was going to take some algebra class, I don't remember much about it, it was what they called advanced. I enrolled. The counselor warned me I didn't have the prerequisites but I went ahead. I mean, they kept putting me in shop classes and I hated that shit, could not bring myself to build bird houses and stupid crap like that, hated to work with my hands.

"It was a funny class. I didn't learn a thing, did no homework, nothing. Just went to class and watched the teacher do boring shit on the board everyday. I aced every test he gave, got the highest score on the tests. Made a B in the class because I never did any of the goddamn homework."

"That's funny. What did the brain say?"

"He didn't say anything. The teacher thought I was cheating after the first two quizzes, so he made me come up to the board one day and gave me some problem to do. Something he hadn't covered yet. I figured it out right away."

"That must made them rethink your potential."

"I promptly forgot everyfuckingthing in the class and never took any more of that shit."

"I wonder what they'd think now if they knew."

"I couldn't care less. Besides it was later in the year I got expelled for beating the shit out of that guy who started the fight with me.

"What is funny is when I was in the hospital that the girl from the University of Chicago brought me all this literature to read. I liked some of it. This *Journey to the End of the Night* by Celine really tickled me. And *The Tin Drum.* Some other stuff was less stellar. I did kind of like *Gile's Goat Boy.* The girl, Natasha, fucking dogs because she felt sorry for them. Pynchon's *V* amused me: Benny Profane and Pig Bodine. I recently took the time to read his *Gravity's Rainbow*; that's how much I liked him. It was fun, old Brigadier Pudding eating shit right out of some whore's asshole until it killed him. Fighting a trained octopus on the beach. Future affecting the past as a result of operant *de*-conditioning. *Naked Lunch* was funny, a real put-on I thought. *Another Country* was stupid, and I hated the beatnik writers, and that tiresome tough guy Mailer, too. That stuff was mostly shit. Henry Miller was almost funny. *Under the Volcano* was a terrifying perspective on being a drunk. I liked some older stuff, too, like James Joyce and *Moby Dick.* Hemingway bored me; Steinbeck had a few good moments. But that was all after high school—"

"You read *Ulysses?*"

"Yeah. And *Portrait of the Artist, Dubliners, Finnegan's Wake.* I spent a lot of time on my back."

"That's impressive anyway. So what happened with this married woman?"

I called for more beer and waited for the waitress to bring it over before starting again.

"A woman my mother was studying the Bible with. Converting to Jehovah's witness. She had a kid. Going through a divorce from some Air Force guy. Big brown eyes; my dad called them bedroom eyes, doe eyes. Worked as a cocktail waitress at the Sands. At the pool in summer. Wore a bikini to work. My mom claimed she was very promiscuous, but I didn't care. She was my first really terrific fuck. Before that it had been girls mostly scared, though there was one ugly honor's student who gave blowjobs, I think to keep from getting pregnant. No one knew except the guys she chose to do. I think there were a lot of them. I heard she got pregnant in college and dropped out."

"How old was she?"

"The blowjob girl? She was like sixteen or seventeen or something. Maybe eighteen."

"No, silly. The woman your mother was studying with, getting a divorce."

"Twenty-three. I was just turned eighteen. Senior year. I had this wild-eyed vision of going to New York, listening to jazz, smoking pot, all that shit. No idea of what I would do for money except work some shit job. Wanted to marry her and take her with me. She knew better. It was a kid dream."

"What about college?"

"You kidding? I had no interest in college. Reading books? What a nightmare."

"So what happened with her?"

"We were fucking one night in a motel. We had to fuck in odd places cause she was staying with her mother until the divorce settled. She wanted to have custody of the kid, so she couldn't be out fucking all the time, particularly with a high school kid. Particularly one who'd been expelled. So…"

"This was after you'd been expelled?"

"We'd started before I got expelled. She didn't seem to care. She just liked to fuck.

"So we snuck around. Out by Hoover Dam on Boulder Highway, out by the dump on the edge of town, shit like that. The motel was a place for us to really go at it. I remember cause I fucked her six times one night and six the next. She had the motel for a week, a vacation from her mother and her kid, she said. Her husband got wind and came around one night. Beat on the door."

"You fought with him then?"

"No. We didn't answer and he went away. The next day he waited in the lot for me to come to the motel. He laid hands on me. I nearly killed him."

"It seems you were an angry person."

"Damned angry."

"About what?"

"I don't know. My mother was angry—."

"Like most fundamentalist Christians."

"She'd been brought up so poor I guess it made her mad just being in a place where people had three squares a day. She was born in Brazil, I think I told you? of Spanish immigrants. Said her father'd lost his land and died and their mom got all twelve of them back to Spain somehow and then they were run out of there by Franco and ended up in Oran, where she met my dad in the war. She was so angry her greatest wish was for Jehovah to come down and kill all the rich people. She was full of rage. And intoxicated with God. She preached that shit all the time."

"That sounds like a painful way to grow up."

"Intense. It was an intense way to grow up. I think her hostility rubbed off on me. Maybe the aggression, too.

"Anyway, that's the story, and I'd rather you not repeat it."

"What happened to her?"

"I don't know. Kept the kid? Got married?"

"I sort of lost touch. They were gonna put me in jail for the assault. Real jail, not some juvenile detention place. Had a choice: join the Marines or go to jail. Marines seemed a wiser option. They liked my hostility and my intellect. I did well on their basic tests, well enough they liked me for officer material. They like tall guys anyway; mostly little guys join the Corps, short shits with chips on their shoulders. I was an excellent marksman and literally kicked ass in hand to hand. All that stuff came easily and I beat the instructors sometimes. They might have let me get into judo or some shit like that."

"The war stopped that?"

"No. They couldn't channel my hostility. I hated authority. I realized right away that in the military your superiors are all going to be ass-kissing cretins. The higher the pay grade, the dumber they are. And they have the ability to hurt you because they fucking own you. GI is government issue. A serious sunburn is an offense unless you do it under orders because you are government property.

"So I became a fuck-off out of self-defense. Just enough rebellion to keep out of serious trouble, to let them know I couldn't be trusted to follow orders blindly. That I'd be an embarrassment. They called me a shit-bird. That got me to where I ended up in Vietnam."

"Okay, I'll do it."

"Do what?"

"The acid. But let's do it now, if you have it with you."

I pulled out the strip and ripped off a single square of the blotter for her.

"This little thing?"

"My friend said it is pure, but very weak. Two of those is a single dose, so you'll be taking a half dose. That's a good beginner dose. He knows the guy who makes it, in Madison. A chemist and church organist. Has a test pilot stays with him."

"Test pilot?"

"Yeah, a roommate. Takes the stuff to test it out. Sort of a critic. Fucked up all the time, it seems. Usually in his underwear on the couch zonked."

"That is strange."

five lemma

"Supposedly this guy makes experimental stuff. He's interested in trypt-amines and some kind of derivatives. Hanging extra rings or some such. My friend's into chemistry, but I don't know shit about it. I smoked DMT a few times and it comes on real fast; short and intense. This chemist is working on variants that come on slow and last a long time. Supposed to have one that goes on for a week or so. Sort of like STP versus acid."

"STP? What's that?"

"A hallucinogen. I didn't find it as intense as acid, but it lasted a lot lon-ger. Took longer to come on, too."

"So you're sure of this acid?"

"I trust this guy."

"Let me have two, then, if they're only half strength. I want to try a full dose."

I tore off one more and gave it to her. She popped the little paper squares into the red gash in her face, chewed them and swallowed them. I took four of them: equivalent of sixteen hits. Thought I might see God tonight.

"I don't know if I'll be able to figure out how to get it together to fuck," I said. "This stuff makes everything complicated as hell. It all tangles up to-gether."

"Don't worry, I'll figure it out for you."

We ordered burgers and more beer and I wolfed mine down. She ate a bite. Mostly she stared at me.

"Let's get out of here," I said. "This isn't a good place to get off."

She left money on the table and we made a fast exit. The bright sun smacked my eyes and she grabbed my hand, pulling me along behind her down Esplanade, crossing the street to the grassy median skipping like a child. I hob-bled along in her wake dodging ripples, stumbling on my erection and slowed by my leg, unable to make good use of my cane. She stopped at the mouth of Bourbon and pointed at passing cars, wide-eyed.

"However," she asked, "did those big people get inside those tiny metal boxes?" and I saw what she meant, toy cars peopled with full-size humans.

I held her back. "Those cars are bigger than they look, Gudrun. Take it easy."

"Bigger than this?" grabbing at my erection. "Come on," and she pulled me across the street, bounding down Bourbon like a little girl wearing a flutter-ing butterfly yellow and blue.

I tried to keep up but refused to run. She beat me to the gate. I'd not noticed before the ancient contours pressed against the sidewalk, yellows blues pinks in plaster and Lafitte's Blacksmith Shop brick and timber, the banana tree resurrected to living green, sidewalk and plaster both flayed by age beset with rivulets meandering acausal across the whole expanse of the quarter, the city, maybe the sky, looking up to read the sign in red brick faded UNEEDA BIS-CUIT cracked down the middle and listing, bricks ready to fall, the balcony at Lafitte's in Exile jammed with boys and maybe one woman. Cracks in the sky.

"What took you?" she asked. "Look at this place! You live here!"

"You're wearing a butterfly."

"No shit, Sherlock."

"I hadn't noticed."

I let us in the black iron gate and she pushed me against the wall of the brick tunnel, pulled me down to kiss my mouth. Gooey lips covered mine; probing tongue.

"Let's sit in the courtyard," I said. "Better to get off outside. Warmer."

We sat on the metal settee amid bricks and the fountain not running and the green plants always on the verge of death.

"Your lipstick is sticky."

"Now its all over your mouth."

The hole in her face moved and the words fell out, almost visible in the clear stratosphere. An electric charge zipped up my spine and out the top of my head. I flicked it off with a shrug.

"Me too," she said. "It's working, isn't it?"

"Yes."

"What do you want to do?"

Greenly streaked bricks sparkled mossy carpets overrunning cracks; surrounding us wriggling stuff. Waves I hadn't noticed before. And as one more charge rushed up my spine and out the top of my head, snapping back my skull imperceptibly, I knew we were all fibers on some giant bundle, acted on by some strange fucking structure groups. Lie groups. Everywhere buzzing. Something almost tangible riffling everywhere: I could see it or feel it.

"What?"

"I said Dina is dangerous. You need to be careful of her."

The red-smeared hole in her face moved and nothing came out until the sounds made their way visibly to my ears or something and I said "I don't know. Look at the brick's breathe."

"She's really dangerous. She chews men up. Spits them out. Her guy before Harry got shot. She's been a prostitute."

"That's a positive."

"She can take advantage."

"I'm used to it. The Marine Corps excelled at it."

The back of my head exploded.

"Dina is a seeker," I said. "A pure seeker. The only guy she endangers is Dina."

"What is she seeking?"

"Something I don't want to find. I would guess you don't either. You ever see the stuff she reads? In French?"

Her mouth contorted around some visible words.

"What?"

"I didn't say anything."

"Dina's a saint," I said. "A holy fool. A madwoman. Very dangerous, her pursuit. Nowhere I would venture."

She released some words, or maybe not, her mouth a festering rose now, raw, slab-lipped and flushing amongst a throbbing spectral profusion crimson to flame to fuchsia to maroon, erupted and deforming on its own. Expanding and contracting scarlet wings flapped above blood-stained teeth, moving across her face to escape were they not tied to the bloated protrusion below. Ruby-mouthed cocksucker popped into my head.

She grabbed my hand, working her oral fixture to keep the bird from escaping. I waited for the words.

"Oh, please, let's go upstairs."

"What?"

"I need violating; if not you, then some other."

I sensed Dina watching from above and knew not to look up. Couldn't touch her thoughts or visions but knew the time had come to trudge up and mercilessly manhandle this walking set of fuck-holes.

"You have lipstick?" I asked sitting on the bed.

She fumbled in her purse while we smoked sinsemilla and I pulled up her skirt and found a yellow-bushed cunt I painted bright red and gummy; a thickly vermilion flower of tiny golden moss-grown flaps. I pushed her on the bed face down, curdled butt in the air, and festooned her pink puckered asshole in intertwined orbs of the dense lip rouge.

"Now you're all painted holes. Your body's a cunt. You're a walking cunt."

I ran my hand over her bare thigh and goose bumps rippled like a textured undulation across the visible flesh downed in microscopic white hair... stood her up and pulled the T-shirt over her head, the bra wired below flimsy material encasing two lopsided loaves packed in with exposed nipples... freed, the broad bags lurched askew, fat and wide-apart gobs of pale putty cobwebbed in blue gossamer, walleyed and uneven, crowned with pink areolae dappled in tiny bumps, one giant orb on the longer loaf, a daintier ellipse on the fatter flattened one, both punctuated with erect nipples. She held the longer tube out to me and I stroked it... she shook her head and pulled it hard and motioned to me and I pinched the nipple and twisted hard enough she fell to her knees and wrestled my dick from my pants. I held her head and shoved my wet erection in her face until she coughed but I kept pushing and when I pulled back she gasped a string of saliva that dangled from her chin.

On the bed I fucked her mouth hole the red lipstick streaking my dick, shooting hard in her throat, maybe a groan from me, she masturbating all the time...

Coughing, gasping "No, don't stop," when I removed my flaccid penis.

Two fibers here entangled how many entangled pairs coupled? everywhere the tiny buggers ratcheting up or drawing down skittering random travelers leaving only contrails of what? "What?" she'd spoken words lost now shimmering in the mirror behind us... My dick in her mouth, slurping "Come on, get it up, I need this..." "What?" "Will you stop with the what?" tongue now a blanket on my cock, lips pulling back sucking hard... Lean over, munch the petals of the flower... noises like moaning "Hurt?" "God... no... better..." engulfing the flower beyond petals, gynoecium fleshy stigma stigmata ovule glutinous cunt, lapping the hard tiny bud, she gasping, pulls back her head, I mouth and nibble and bite the engorging button... she gasps again.

"Fuck me—"

"What? —"

Climbing over me, pushing me down, climbing atop and straddling me, sinking down engulfing me the red flower bobbing up and down a cork in the stream flowing around us I sit up spin the toy bitch around the axis joining us fucking her now... pushing in and out hoping to crush the red flower...

"What?"

"Are you gonna fuck me? fuck me fuck me fuck me..."

Push her face down on the bed, hand on the back of her neck... "Wait," I jump up to the bathroom grab a jar of Vaseline slather my warty dick knotted with fat veins throbbing purple alive pulsing blood, push her face into the pillow holding her by the neck and shove my dick in her asshole, screaming writhing dwarf legs kicking futile, shove it home harder each time harder slam it pull back shove into the flower of cunt then the asshole then the cunt back and forth steady rhythm asshole cunt asshole cunt... let go in one of the holes... fall on top of her...

Sitting on the bed a painted face working it's red smeared mouth-hole, eyelids painted blue, lashes darkened black or blue, colors running together... "What?" "I'm a cunt hole all of me fuck me again" "see them?" I point at the wrigglers surrounding us now "acausal fibers we're trapped on fibers on a manifold... no, wait, we are fibers... wait —" "Come on" taking an inutile shriveled worm in her mouth "Come on" "Its all conjoined all coupled paired everything and we're the Brownian travelers" she tugging at the limp phallus, tonguing scrotum, slurping perineum, gargling testes, englutting the flaccid tuber, "No really I see it all now..." setting forth to find holes on the fibers, random couplings in stochastic ambient background spaces... "See?" streaked face made-up in goo powder paste gloss blush blemished mask from hell, goo on fat tits and fat ass fat thighs, someone's limp worm in her mouth looking at me from behind the mess of her face "I think its information... we're paired God I see it look transubstantiation or transmutation of energy, consubstantiation maybe, into flesh on the fiber... look here at the bundle..." the homunculus standing hands on hips looking down at me on the bed.

"Find my hole, asshole. This thing's no good" shaking the flabby sheaf from who-knew-where or maybe flabby cosheaf but not a functor by any means "the supports must be soft" I think I say and maybe: "didn't your mother teach you not to put shit you found lying around in your mouth'" can't be certain... For sure "I can't find the goddamn stalk anyway" an old Missouri dirt farmer dragging out the word gawwwddamn "a crushed worm... dead fish... of no use to me and what is all this shit you're gibbering?" "What?" "I'm out of here..."

Standing lop-boobed in the center of the bedroom, chunky meat-bags diverging orthogonally to expose wide expanse of bony sternum. Nipples shriveled splattered stains, more black than their original pink. Turning to walk away, fat boxy feet support fleshless calves supporting, via jointed knobby connectors, stocky hams widening suddenly to match the abrupt butt cheeks arcing upward to the round brown hole and along the falling dimpled ass-cheeks grinding off sporadic glimmers of churning curd amidst the trundling propulsion towards the doorway, flesh reflectors dimpling with each step, random parabolic antennae dents in the tallow. Leaving behind her clothes, midget legs thumping through the bedroom door trailing a wake of rhombic interfering vibrations in a mad scramble to scoot from behind the square hips propelling an ass-blob lost its smile to jowls bobbling away from me "Wait, we'll get transverse again I promise..." pauses at the front door the runt not looking back flips the bird high overhead on upraised left hand and passes through the porch. Her footfalls smacking wood down the stairwell...

The distracting gnome-like apparition vanished, going with the (Killing field) flow spiraling down to the courtyard, sweeping her... where? Dina? A connection? A lot of connections. They'd bracket, of course, Dina and Gudrun, but which connection gave rise to this particular Killing vector field?... would the Lie derivative vanish for Dina and Gudrun?... or was this the vanishing? It'd be skew-symmetry, for sure, if it vanished there...

No, but stay tuned. There'd been no torsion with the dwarf, for sure; but that didn't disallow twists, mutations, deformations arriving with the monodromy that had to be coming. We'd sure as shit get us a fucking holonomy group of translations along some kind of twisted fibers, torsion or no torsion, she and I being the Levi-Civita connection for this nasty metric in any case; but Dina another metric for sure, maybe another dimension entirely. She'd parallel transport to Dina but Dina'd transform back and we'd all feel the holonomy of these connections, the deviation from product bundle. What was it the crafty old Italian geometer'd said, maybe Levi-Civita or maybe Ricci in a lecture to poor old Tullio, something like "With my connections you can get rid of the torsion, but there ain't shit you can do about the curvature." There'll be big time deviation after parallel transport through Dina, curvature galore... Bottom line: you can choose your metric connection to kill the torsion, but you're gonna be fucked by the curvature. Gudrun's gonna learn that before this night ends.

Abreast a new tide of brainwaves flowing along some kind of basin constrained without slipping, climbing a steepening gradient until looking down from directly above where I'd just been... rushing spinal harmonics training up my neck, out the top of my head, rebounding off the fifteen foot ceiling and I followed the siren call of Paul Levy in the world born of Riemann. No albatross round my neck, but other constraints. Stochastic but tied, and not just a stinking bridge this time... can't keep from feeling coupled; I'm only a marginal process projected from some kind of product, maybe not a warped product but an unnamed relative. The coupling time sometime behind me, ephemeral anchor suddenly dragging my ass not lock-stepping with another random walk but sure as hell not independent either. Is there mixing to some fucking place I don't want to be?... I sure as fuck feel close to something out there, not mirroring but convertible, certainly, from my path to that other's path almost-everywhere. A metric? It isn't the fucking weak topology I feel. And I feel more bound than were things ergodic.

five lemma

This isn't my area. Feel strangely out of my element. Entropy and mixing and stuff like that, stuff I barely know infringing here, stuff I don't know shit about. How can I converge to some measure preserving concepts I ain't fucking understanding with any depth... brushed against... only... barely... But I know I'm mixing with something or to something or somewhere; have no idea what any of this means...

At some time I entangled in a sort of product lifted to a larger process. I'm a marginal now and I feel it, coupled on the horizontal frame bundle via some bigger Laplacian in the sky; the tug of the first spectral gap, that first eigenvalue controlling some of this shit and likely the goddamn manifold too and there ain't shit I can do, maybe an explosion or maybe conserved, a goddamn transient or an intransient recurrent stuck here, where? intrinsic property all I can see, the global embedding space not visible at all, and the fucking possibility of stochastic incompleteness seeps in as I see myself blown off to infinity in finite time, a blowup on what I know is geodesically complete. Jesus, where the fuck am I? drifting fast and coupled... So I escape to infinity? transient residue of who-knows-what, but in finite time? A transient exploding swept along by astounding negative sectional curvature? The recurrents are the cowards, sure enough, but what comfort in coming back and coming back, eternal return, and suddenly I see the ergodicity in all this, the mixing or strong mixing or metric transitivity and understand the beauty of NOT visiting every fucking new place in a universe you can't even fucking feel in a global sense, tied to this miniscule embedded submanifold and constrained by coupling or tied like a bridge, a Brownian bridge maybe tied to the same endpoints as the alter-ego marginal, my dual-paired bonded marginal partner and maybe this fucking bridge acts more like a goddamn variation field, the parent process entrapped in some variation field with endpoints in the embedding manifold outside our local manifold? endpoints lost in the global haze might as well be another universe, is another fucking universe... holy shit feel the variation through geodesics, a fucking Jacobi field... can't be random and geodesic but now I know there's a fucking index form associated with this bitch, this field, I can sense it and is it Killing's field? for chrissake that's the field and maybe Gudrun is flowing on a geodesic between me and Dina? coupled to Dina as marginal partner process? what the hell product was that Frenchy called it? warped product one of us the radial process, the other the "angle

I'm skittering and I know it ain't negative curvature feel the Ricci curvature bounded below how the fuck you feel that? sectional curvature positive Ricci tensor friendly here and not heading to infinity right here, anyways

process" skipping manifolds? hopping across? not some kind of uniformization here and how can you leap connected components? Dina as angle process?

A large spectral gap and Gudrun will be okay if there's no conjugate point between Dina and me but if so hell to pay with reality, for damned sure… much worse with a goddamn cut point but I know there's a bound on the spectral gap here because I know there's a lovely pair of lower bounds on the Ricci curvature hereabouts that fucking treacherous tensor but I know everything's okay here, we're compact here, and I need to figure out those fucking bounds…

Body load killing me, neck twisting with each traveling jolt up my spine, need to splice together something to step back soon or will lose paracompactness and have too many goddamn open sets to be able run across the fucking torsion-infested bayou on a partition of unity afloat on the old field of snapping

we've got the dimension and some positive constant K bounding the goddamn Ricci in one case… the diameter of the fucking manifold in the other, pi's in there… I can feel it slipping away below my feet, partition of unity wobbling in the tensor field, fucking tensors snapping at my heels… can I keep my bounds and leap the spectral gap back to wherever I was even as the world recedes?

"Sir you breached the spectral gap?… "Sir Gudrun and I found ourselves governed by the compact-open topology and we bracketed, too… but that's just algebra isn't it Sir?… "Sir I assembled a holonomy group to test the curvature… "Sir the torsion isn't zero and there's plenty of twist in the fibers… "Sir we represented a twisted convolution on a Heisenberg group… "Sir we're information-coupled… "Sir, you can get rid of the torsion but the curvature will fuck you hard… "Sir there's an obstruction —"

"What?" yammering in my face. "What the fuck? Dina?"

tensors.

"__"

"Don't you need an odd dimension for the Heisenberg group?"

"Gudrun, what's he talking about? What is this Heisenberg shit? I'm uncertain Sir" followed by guffaws or maybe street noise…

"Fuck that shithead, Dina. He's been whatting me and gibbering ever since he got off… Let's go back to your place. We don't need this dork… Forget his dumb ass… I want to bite chunks out of your floppy titters, chew your meaty cunt flaps… we'll wait over there…"

"No, sir, we need space, and I told them come here—"

"This twisted convolution won't commute, Dina…"

"When is a gate not a gate?"

"What?"

"Don't do that what shit, Dina. Now you're sounding like that fuck-head."

"I'm sorry sir, but I don't understand — you or him. Telling some joke? —"

"We left the gate ajar!" Snorting. Cackling. Croaking. "Don't call me sir, Dina. Ma'am."

"Aye aye sir…"

Dina on her hands and knees naked except the collar and leash held by Gudrun, mammas dragging the floor, Dina in her Killing form tracing compositions of adjoint representations, Dina irreducible symmetric bilinear "Cocksucker, Dina, what the fuck?"

"Yes Sir. Oh, please Sir…"

"No." Gudrun yanking on her leash. "All cocks are for me. You get your nose in my pussy, bitch…"

Gudrun prostrate before the rocket aimed at the ceiling. Dina's face buried in Gudrun's crotch eliciting alternating giggling-crying-moaning sobs. Gudrun suckling at disembodied penile protrusion, urgent slurping competition to deafening feeding of Dina, gobbling swallowing gulping cacophony of the trough, barn animals gorging accompanied by barely audible cello laying down continuo. Gudrun salivating copious drool over the protrusion-rocket appendage-from-another-planet stone-hard purple-wart-encrusted pulsing-veined insensate nothing.

"I told you he didn't need help sir."

Gudrun mouth full of alien meat prong "Gnoth gall ne shur, bish—"

I stood up pulling Gudrun off the bed leeching to the other's tubular meat bomb via fleshy-lipped annelid vermillion smudge-hole.

"Oh," she lamented to the music.

I took the remaining six hits from the pocket of my jeans lying formless and alone on the floor sans corporeal filling and gave them to Dina. She looked up at me with yet one more pair of skies and chewed up the strip. Gudrun's cunt breathed alive and Dina returned to the lipstick painted gape engulfing her face within tumescent hanging flaps, head buried to the neck amidst the distended maw. I shoved the other's dick up Dina's asshole to the hilt and feeling nothing, pumped her with the rhythm of the vibrating travelers and the tunes floating

201

in from somewhere obscuring the strains of the cello inside the room and the voracious feeding of Dina and the whimpering sobs of Gudrun all polyrhythmic atonal medley assaulting my ears, fucking Dina's guts to smooth out the harmonics…

Gudrun's mouth against my pubic hair wolfing down the other's dick fucking her mouth in the same rhythm. Dina slurping oysters from the corpulent cunt burying her face… head… headless at the cunt lips…

Dina surprised yelping loud moan Oh! Ow! Shit! Who is it? Ow Goddamn it's BIG… Ow FUCK! harder… please…sir!

Mule fucking Dina and Jerry coming around to fuck Gudrun… I remain burying an alien penis in the face-wound, fury driving me but no sensation except the sound of the room cracking with each movement, oscillations reflecting off the walls superposing perpetuating colliding, amplitude and pitch living cacophony of a barn full of animals, mouth and cunt noises mingled with sweaty flesh slapping hard fucking in and out cunts assholes mouths… groans lilting above the cello. I pull back to watch, hoping to see the alien penis remain behind. It's vanished.

Mule dragged his dick from Dina's asshole dripping fudge-streaked cum, rivulets of the stuff streaming to her crotch. His dick fallen to half mast, crooked black tube arced headfirst diving towards the floor… stretched envelope of creased and wrinkled foreskin covering the head. He finds Gudrun on her back, stubby legs wrapped around Jerry fucking her in slow motion, advancing inchmeal into her cunt, extracting bit by bit, pausing on the outstroke, Gudrun rubbing against the almost visible glans before advancing yet again…

"Don't mind me, Jerry, but I been wanting to shove my dick in this bitch's pie-hole since I first laid eyes on her."

Mule looks Gudrun in the eye and grabs both cushy tits flopped to the sides, squeezes the bigger one so hard she cries out. She stares up at him behind a countenance streaked and glistening in ribbons of smeared red-blue-green: unsmiling intensity peering wide eyed, no laughing, no crying. He twists the mismatched crowns of pink nipple, first the fatter one, then the smaller one. He climbs up onto her chest, pins her arms with his knees, dangles his penis in her face. She stares at the leathery curvature, the extended head-flap dripping fresh from Dina's asshole. Raises her head to it, blue-eyed ruby-lipped lizard snarfing down an elongated purple tubeworm in slow motion, dragging over the extruded foreskin until it disappears. Unable to move except lips and jaws, concentrating, contracting, swallowing, extended lips engulfing beyond the head, wide-open azure peepers not a single blink, peristaltic lip motion inching down the worm, gobbling to the end until mouth rests against the patch of black hair. Mule shoves her head with both his hams, flattening her lips against the black groin with a SMURCH. Grinds her face into wiry pubes. Jerry fucks her faster. Bridged between them, she thrashes in seizure.

Mule pulls back. Round lipstick kisses smutch his pubic hair. Drool streams from Gudrun's gaping inflamed rictus. Gasping for breath. Crimson coat of smegma glistening the length of Mules erection skewed sharply to the right pointed towards the ceiling. The head a drooling fist-knot.

"Come on, bitch," pushing her flaming rubious sore to the gnarly head helped along with a thrust of his hips stretching her jaws agape. Her lips painted in Mule's ooze engulf the anaconda to where it bellies out in the middle. Momentarily hung by the girth of the truncheon's gut, distended buccal cavity funneled scarlet lips pouffed out, peristaltic waves inching along until Mule shoves her head from behind, her jaws unhinge and the bulge breaches the orifice, the entire monstrosity disappearing into a smothered moan.

Dina on her hands and knees beside the bed, barking, "Fuck her face, tickle her uvula, stretch her aperture."

Jerry retreats from Gudrun's cunt. "Get yo ass over here bitch," grabbing Dina's leash and yanking her off her knees. "Sit down, Mule, and lay the bitch on her belly so's I can fuck her asshole. Push her face down on you meat, man. This here bitch gon' be sucking her pussy."

More barking from Dina. "Fuck her asshole hard, stretch it out, fuck fuck fuck."

Mule'd disarranged his hair in braided ropes tousled willy-nilly. They laid flat and greasy, widely spaced as if he'd wanted to announce approaching baldness with plenty of empty scalp. His brownish-black beefy frame covered with short curly black hair overwhelmed the pygmy, her penis-punctured face unreal. Sweat cascading from his head and body rained on her, mixed with meared makeup, the goo on her face and in her hair beginning to run down and pool on the bed. He raised up on legs like tree trunks and rolled her over on the bed like a rag doll, then plopped down onto his butt with her face in his lap, forcing the red smear over his erect appendage. She choked and coughed up in his lap.

Jerry dragged Dina to Gudrun's spread legs and Gudrun presented her ass. Dina gobbled Jerry's member like a pro, covered it with saliva, buried her tongue in Gudrun's asshole leaving a trail of saliva, spit in the opening, then set to munching her cunt. Without fanfare Jerry drove his dick into the puckered lipstick-garnished orifice. Gudrun emitted a muffled groan and cringed on impact.

Wiry-framed a shade shy of vivid black plum, almost devoid of body hair and knotted with muscles, Jerry the clean-cut all-American businessman except for the pointed dog-shit yellow shoes and navy blue socks speckled with red threads, hard riding Gudrun's asshole.

I rolled a spliff of Columbian laced with sinsemilla and hash and slogged through the mud of the barnyard where the rubato of feeding and slapping skin mingled to drown out the cello lilting continuo in the background audible below the thumping bass beat from Lafitte's and the street carnival outside, laughing, yelling, deafening music blasting when the door to Lafitte's opened, muted when it shut.

Jerry'd moved to the side to accommodate Dina's slurping but otherwise savaged Gudrun's asshole from above, the slap of sweaty flesh and suction SCHLURP SCHLOOP of his piston dragging in her anal cylinder as loud as the music. Mule brayed little amorous nothings, "Come on bitch, get it down, all the way slut, that's a good ofay, now swallow... daddy's gonna pull out a bit now, okay bitch now suck the head, yeah like that suck harder, okay bitch it going down again..." Gudrun's throaty gags and snorts escaped the tubular blockage along with leaking saliva and frothy white spume sometimes bubbling from her nostrils. Mule methodically moved his appendage in and out of her face, the glans penis almost appearing on the upstroke pausing for her to take a breath and rapaciously slobber and suck the bulbous meat head, her tongue appearing before his slow downstroke hauled it back inside; pinching her nostrils shut and forcing her face down against the stiff bristles of his groin at the end of each stroke. Her buccal panorama visibly deformed with the downstroke, lips distended and cheeks indented as if the whole thing might implode. I watched close up, marveling each time her lips dragged beyond the enormous midsection bulge, her eyes watering.

I held the joint out first for Jerry who took a deep hit as he rested against Gudrun's ass, fully embedded, and then passed it to Mule.

"How does that huge thing disappear in that little red hole, Mule? It's fatter than the hole is wide."

He laughed and took another hit. "Magic. This white bitch got some magic talent. It ain't a mouth. It's a magic fuck-hole."

Jerry chimed in. "This here bitch's a fuck toy. Shit yeah. Who'd a guessed? You gonna get in here, Whitey? They's a hole left unoccupied."

five lemma

"Wait," Mule said, pressing Gudrun's face down against his groin. He growled and Gudrun choked and an erumpent fuckwad exploded from a visibly prolated nostril, fatter ones following from both nostrils arching back streaking across the bridge of her nose and plopping onto her left eye. She retched as Mule slowly let her pull up, jerking and arching his back several times with orgasmic spasms at which more ejaculate leaked from around the tight seal of her mouth, blew from her nose, slathering her face and Mule's groin to dank swamp.

Jerry picked up his pace without missing a beat. Dina continued feeding on her cunt.

Squeezed out of Jerry: "Damn… my turn…" Folded over, resting against her back, thrusting involuntary spasms. He stopped, breathing audibly. His penis retracted from her anus in a fart followed by creamy bubbles. White ooze streaked brown bubbled to surface, slowly venting to spread towards her vagina and along the inside of her thighs. Dina lapped it up.

Jerry and Mule on the floor smoking the joint I'd passed them. They refused to share with Dina and Gudrun, pleading hygiene.

The women side by side on the bed smoking a joint of their own. Dina stroked Gudrun's neck and shoulders; Gudrun rested her head on Dina's bosom bags.

 Shimmering faces. Dina'd worn no war paint, but Gudrun bore the abstract expressionist masque of opaque makeup mingled with human discharge, a mélange of texture and color smeared gloriously across the flesh-canvas in swirling dense layers of adulterated divinity fudge. Her eyes exploded dark matter streaking radially from the lashes, the left one glued shut with a giant wad of sperm dissolving in rivulets of sweat. Dina tried to wipe it but Gudrun pushed her hand away. Her lower face disappeared within a gory carnelian-ocher cake of gooey lipstick and exudate streaked sapphire and black with eye-shadow and fudge, her mouth an indistinct orifice amidst egesta, chin bearded with a ragged fringe of pink chunky clabber dribbling gravity-elongated strands.

Dina bent to Gudrun's torso and licked the overflow. Shuddering waves of goose flesh, Gundrun lifted one of Dina's pendulous sacks and traced the areola with her tongue, sliming a trail with face and tongue to the navel, licking around the indentation, looking up before nibbling the labia, slurping at the cavity. Dina lowed.

Gudrun pushed Dina back onto the bed and Dina worked around to position her face in Gudrun's groin, the deafening feeding crushing out the boisterous street, accentuating the cello resounding in absentia.

Jerry and Mule tooted some powder from a small folding mirror. Jerry got up to stand over the entwined carnal cooties and watch, seeming amused at the voracious anal-vaginal tonguing.

Dina looked up at him.

"It's analingus, sir. A-n-a-l-i-n-g-u-s, c-u-n-n-i-l-i-n-g-u-s. *Cunnis lingere,* from the Latin," rolling her tongue into Gudrun's asshole, dragging it to her cunt. Gudrun hissed and followed the example, eliciting a moaned "… anogenital stimulation…" from Dina. They wheeled around and kissed passionately.

"We call it filthy. Hell yeah."

"Rimming," Mule said. "Didn't never see it 'til I got into white skanks."

"That be the movies, Mule. You a movie star now."

Mule got up to watch. Jerry's cock rose to erect. Mule's flaccid trunk hung to his knees. Dina sat up and licked around the head inside Mule's foreskin, drawing the knob out of its lair, sucking and licking until the organ erected as corpulent arm curved towards the wall.

"These bitches look like they ready for round two," Mule said.

"Hell yeah," Jerry echoed and Gudrun pulled Dina back down to the bed. "You ready Mule?"

"Yeah, let me have the little one."

The two women lay on the bed, lean huntress hunched atop plush midget, faces buried in cunts. I brought out a jar of Vaseline and Jerry and Mule shellacked their members. Jerry pushed into Dina's proffered asshole as she fed at Gudrun's gash and followed his rhythmic lead with her own thrusts.

Mule sat, picked Gudrun up like a toy doll and held her facing away from him. He torqued her asshole down over his erection with a single motion. She howled with the unannounced penetration; tears streamed from her eyes, rivulets in the cracked emulsion of her face. He stood up with the impaled Gudrun hanging face down, clinging to his ankles for support. Hand in her hair, he pulled the head back, arching her like a squashed dumpling with fat hanging nippled protrusions; matched her to Dina seated atop Jerry's member. The two women kissed voraciously before Mule shook Gudrun free and pushed her head into Dina's cunt. Dina twisted around on Jerry, ending with her ass up, back on the floor and legs wrapped round Gundrun's neck, then pulled herself up Mule's legs to feast on Gundrun's cunt. While the women gobbled the scowling giant demon mercilessly plunged Gudrun's toilet hole, hammering down-strokes eliciting yelps with each concussion, loud SCHLUP on the uptake as the cock pulled to the edge, explored the sphincter, then rammed home again to another yelp from the dwarf white fruit hanging from the trunk. I couldn't make out the boundaries of the deformed hominids, black and white writhing whorl of quasi-corporeal protrusions and cavities.

Deafening…

Dina wriggled free from the ménage and crawled to where I sat.

"Permission to suck your cock, Sir?"

"What?"

She engulfed the dead penis, then stopped. She waved a hand in front of my eyes. I tried to blink.

"Are you in there, Sir?"

"What?"

I saw the words meant for me but they never made it to registration. Only barn noise, street noise, bass beat, cello, words aimed at others.

I plodded to the barnyard where Gudrun on all fours sucked Jerry's cock while Mule probed her asshole. I worked my way beneath her and she wriggled around to somehow puncture her with the alien attachment I'd sprouted, pumping the dead wood in the groove of Mule's vicious attacks in all likelihood via the agency of the percussive jackhammer eliciting an involuntary unh from her at each impact. Noise and Gudrun dripping emulsion of sweat, clown paint, ejaculated and oozed emissions smelling of shit and spunk. I tried to remain perfectly still, to stop breathing beneath the musk and pulverizing concussion.

Harmonic seduction stoked a fire in my impuissant nether regions. Gudrun's face squashed against my drenched chest at the nadir of Mule's downstroke followed instantaneously by the grunted unh at which moment her cunt-jaw vice-gripped the benumbed member and dragged slowly its length with Mule's upstroke, loosening at the apex for just the slimmest time-slice before crashing down again, eliciting from my body a desire to micturate. This need propelled the enflaming of my infernal hunger which grew as the battering increased in tempo. Barn sounds transformed subtly to mechanical thrashing: schump schloop thump thwack unh, schump schloop thump thwack unh, repeated precisely ad-infinitum crescendoing to a forcible expulsion of fluid from my body through the remotely attached piston, my lower back and pelvic girdle convulsed by an earthquake of spasms as convolution after convolution billowed to syncopate Mule's machine-rhythm hammering of her asshole. I might have yelled "Harmonic entrainment!" An unending seizure propelled me to the far corner of the ceiling. I watched the performance accompanied by angular cello sonority.

Gudrun pushed away from the jet emitted by my body through the unnatural attachment. Mule picked her up and Jerry and Dina steadied her, head down, ass up, bent at the hips, feet at her ears with ankles crossed behind her head. Mule floated above her anus, open to the heavens, and fucked it straight down, a human pile driver. The grinding and whooshing seemed far away until Gudrun's mournful lament melded with the cello to announce death, joined by Mule who hollered while buried in her poop shoot. The crater erupted Mule's orgasm in the orange of yolk; Gudrun squatted over Dina's face and farted the discharge, mother bitch Dina lapping her pup's expelled shit, lapping the excess flowing down the dwarf's thighs and lower back, reaming the gaping cavity clean with a spatula of tongue. Jerry shoved his dick in Gudrun's face and ejaculated. Dina sucked my egress from Gudrun's cunt. The two women ended in protracted French kiss.

The crew milled aimless, not knowing what to do next. Fulsome clown show.

Dina's visage presented a winter expressionist scene, white smears with flecks and gossamer webs of brown and red, thin hair matted and plastered to her scalp.

Mule ground up powder on the mirror and they tooted several lines. Then Jerry noticed my body on the bed.

"Goddamn, man, looka Whitey. I think he dead."

I could not move; not a twitch, not a blink, open eyes staring at the ceiling. Jerry's voice came to me in the cello berceuse.

Mule held the mirror beneath my nostrils. "He ain't dead. He breathing fine."

"Everything's breathing," Dina barked. "No death."

The voices separate lines, monodies each for ambivocal cello.

"He cain't be sleeping," Jerry said. "Not if his eyes open like that. It spooky."

"He escaped, sir," Dina said. "He left his self behind."

"What the fuck that mean? You cain't escape you self," Mule said.

"But you can escape your self. He got free of his physical self. I think it happened with that ejaculation into Gudrun. His face grew all contorted, like he was in pain. He's had trouble responding to anyone speaking to him since before you got here."

"He talked to me," Mule said.

"I think its induced temporary catatonia," Dina said. "He'll be back. In fact, he's here right now somewhere, watching all this."

Jerry looked up at the ceiling.

"Yeah, up there. Probably in that corner." Dina pointed directly at me.

"Man, let's get out of here," Jerry said.

"Where you wanna go? Uptown? You bitches wanna go uptown?"

Gudrun croaked. "He'll be back. Assholes always come back."

They turned to look at her standing alone and until those words, silent. Dwarf expressionist kewpie doll from Pandemonium, mug a wild abstract of anger and violence, dense wads of white base smeared with red lipstick, maybe blood, shit, colored lashes smudged together exploding blue mascara. The left collapsed star remained stuck shut. Her 'do tangled and snarled, glistening wadded contortions flattened stuck to her head or peeled back to crooked lines of naked scalp, golden locks sculpted into the deformity of modern sculpture.

Dina barked, "I don't think it's a good idea — sir!"

"It ain't that late yet," Jerry said.

Mule spoke up again. "They's a old warehouse up on Tchoupitoulas. Kinda unofficial men's club. Brother's go on up to gamble, drink, do some drugs. They got a room with mattresses they sometimes bring bitches. They be plenty glad to see some ofay hos. Even looking like you two." He laughed a bass line.

"I don't know if its safe — sir!" Dina barked.

"I gonna be there to keep order," Mule said. "Takin' my piece."

"Let's go," Gudrun croaked. "Dina, you don't need to go."

"If you're going, I'm going, sir."

The cello silenced.

b) The Laplacian on a Riemannian Manifold

I got back to the wreck late morning, snapping to my self lying on a bed tacky with exudates, reeking a heady brew of rotting wood and flower spunk.

Things weren't the same. Sheets stained a motley of colors and textured whorls contorted in a knotted mass pregnant with recondite symbolism. I pulled them from the bed and tossed them onto the porch to dry under the skylight, almost stumbling over Gudrun's clothes lying where they'd originally dropped.

I knew something I'd not known before deserting my guests. It stubbornly hung back, unwilling to make a conscious appearance, instead a nagging reminder I'd forgotten.

Objects of the world wore a subtle halo, nimbus of fading hue obscuring sharp distinction between it and not-it. The breathing had ceased.

I rolled a joint and drank coffee. My last memory of watching the two men and the two women from another world discussing going to a men's club in the warehouse district belonged to another movie. For all I knew they'd floated out the windows like clouds or angels or ideas.

Coffee stimulated the urge to shit and I heartily evacuated my bowels. I showered and put on clean clothes. I grabbed my mirrored cigarette case loaded with Perique blended with blonde and sprinkled with Moroccan hash and headed for La Marquise.

The streets glowed even in the bright daylight, the puffed buildings alight from within, the aura surrounding all things dead or almost. The living didn't seem so alive. The asphalt street didn't glitter.

Too few tables strewn with plates napkins cups, spilled coffee, crumbs… typical, too many people for the available space. I scored three croissant, a brioche, some creampuffs shaped like swans, a slice of cheesecake and grayish thin coffee in a white industrial cup and plopped down in the only unoccupied chair across from a prematurely gray helter-skelter haired woman sitting alone wearing a stained worn tank-top through the ribbed once-white fabric of which broken-down flattened dugs lay perfectly visible against her torso, giant dung-heap areoles surrounding elongated withered nipples from which radiated stretch marks to her shoulders and armpits and anywhere else her elongated pancakes attached via the ridge of leathery hide.

"Okay if I sit here?"

Her face peered out small beneath the maze of frizzy hair reaching for the sky.

"It's a free country. Or so they say."

A skinny, prolonged face, scarred a bit and maybe deformed, or maybe that was me. Her mouth disappeared when she stopped talking but opened like an exaggerated flap stretched from ear to ear above a chinless neck.

"Whoever they are."

"You got a cigarette to spare?"

I plopped the case on the table between us. "Help yourself. They're hand made. I use a little machine to roll them. But it's my own blend. Strong stuff. Perique from St. James Parish and some blonde from Virginia. With a secret ingredient."

"Sounds like good shit."

She lit up and I perused her assortment of bluing tattoos. Most prominent on her bicep, BOY FREE above a heart with a dagger piercing it, blood dripping.

She took a deep drag, let the smoke curl from nostrils projected at an oblique angle away from the contours of her face.

"That's a nice blend. The secrets pretty special. Moroccan is it? Green Moroccan."

"Right."

"I prefer Lebanese red. Takes out more brain cells. But I take what I can get."

"I got some black pressed stuff. Supposed to be Afghan. Some Nepalese, too, supposedly opiated. But none of it burns as evenly as this stuff when blended."

"It powders. But so's the red."

"I know. Just haven't seen any of that in a while."

"Well, I hear the place is a fucking mess. All these private armies fighting it out. Druze, Phalange, those guys."

"Those are pretty names. What's yours?"

"Today I'm calling myself Larissa."

"I almost always call myself Whitey. Excuse me a minute, Larissa. I need to get something to write with. I'll be right back."

"I can get you a paper and pen or pencil."

"That'd be great. Writing on napkins is a drag."

"Yeah, napkins aren't the best. You have a preference?"

"What? Sorry, zoning out."

"Pencil or pen?"

"No. Either one. I just need to make some notes. My brain's a little fogged up. Might not be able to keep it all straight. Usually I try to avoid writing. Fucks up the thinking process. Slows it down."

She got up and walked to the door, a hag muscling her way through the maze of crowded tables. A bone-bag in ragged old jeans that would have been tight had she an ass or hips. The idea of asses and hips didn't play in my overcrowded circuits and I skipped imaginings of what she'd be like beneath the draped garb.

Clomping across Chartres in oversized black motorcycle boots, she disappeared beside the Pontalba into Jackson Square. Her heavy boots displayed a life of their own, more likely directing than vice versa; they couldn't possibly obey any feet she might sport.

The idea of exploring a Riemannian manifold with a coupled Brownian motion process had come upon me almost full blown as I'd made my way from the counter to the table. If you could get two of these BM processes to hook up you'd probably learn something about the shape of the manifold from how long it took to meet. I was pretty sure from my last results that on a hyperbolic manifold there wouldn't be much chance they'd meet, since the little bastards always seemed to run away from their initial position. But a compact manifold without boundary would be a different story; I guessed there wouldn't be the extreme negative curvature to sweep them along with that supercharged drift.

A simple idea, really. Define a process on the Cartesian product of the manifold with itself, a pair of Brownian motions as its components so the projections would be the marginals. It seemed there had to be a coupling time in the compact case, or at least in the case where all the sectional curvatures were positive and bounded below, which I felt had to be compact though I hadn't seen theorems to that effect in either of the books I'd read. Course those books hadn't explored specific relationships between the topology and the geometry. Likely this relationship was a delusion on my part; bad intuition from the sphere. Just like the hyperbolic sphere had shaped my feel for negative curvature. But I'd seen the effects on the Brownian traveler first-hand, so to speak.

Anyway, it was clear the "first meeting time," what I'd call the coupling time after last night, had to be the infimum of the set of times where X and Y hooked up.

Larissa flopped an oversized drawing tablet and both a pen and a mechanical pencil on the table.

"I know some artists who have a studio around the corner," she mumbled.

"You an artist?"

"I sculpt. Mostly in metal. Some of my work's shown around the quarter, but mostly it ain't tourist fodder. There's a gallery over by Marigny handles my stuff. And a place in New York."

"You live in the Quarter?"

"No. I got a studio where I live. Just the attic of an old wreck over by Elysian Fields."

"I understand there's a tattoo place over there does some pretty extreme work."

"Oh, yeah. That guy's s'posed to be a med school dropout or doctor or mad scientist who got defrocked or disbarred or whatever happens to those guys. Really advanced stuff. Underground. A few blocks from me, actually. Over by St. Claude."

"Have another cigarette."

"Not sure I need another." She opened the case. "Then again, need and wants two other things." She lit up.

I'd absently been noshing my way through the pastries and hit a brick wall. The sugar helped get my brain alight, but I hankered after a real caffeine jolt.

"Eat some of these if you want," I said, pushing the remaining cream puffs in her direction.

She set to work on them with a vengeance. I lit up and inhaled the pungent smoke that smelled of dirty socks and wet leather. The hash gave it a peppery bite.

"Give me a minute to write some notes," I said.

Approached it by starting the thing in the Euclidean plane and defined the second process, call it Y, in terms of the first, call it X, with Y being $(X_1, -X_2)$; lifted them to the horizontal frame bundle and worked out the appropriate projections. Used the hell out of Nash's embedding theorem even though it was considered bad form, but at that moment there seemed no help for it. Hopefully I'd get rid of the ambient space later.

Had to take care the two points could be connected by a geodesic; that one of them was not a cut point of the other. I defined a map by parallel translation along a geodesic and then reflected the vector through a hyperplane in the tangent space at the end point perpendicular to the geodesic. I was sure to get rid of the cut points and points of equality, too, and then defined the process by projection. I got a set of stochastic differentials, probably had to be Stratanovich integrals and not true Ito's, but I'd fuck with all that minutiae later. I got two horizontal Brownian motions that I projected onto the manifold and a joint process on the manifold product.

Now to wait for those bitches to kiss headlights. Waiting time ought to be related to the Laplacian via the heat kernel, the eigenvalues. The first strictly positive eigenvalue. Spectral gap. Not sure where I'd picked that term up. Anyway, I'd work all that waiting-time eigenvalue curvature shit out later. At least a brain fart at this point wouldn't wipe the idea, even if it wiped the rest of slate. I had a feeling things would progress better later tonight, after the sugar and caffeine had their way with my physical chemistry.

"I wish they served better coffee," I said, trying to finish the cup of acidic watery liquid.

"It's bad here. Sad, too, cause the pastries are damned good."

She'd finished the pastries, including the remnants of the piece of cheesecake I'd started.

"They ought to buy their coffee from Café du Monde. In fact, I'm gonna head over there. Wanna' go? I'm buying."

She peered at me with red-lined roadmaps surrounding dilated pupils, as if trying to conjure my intentions. I guess curiosity got the better of her.

"Sure. I want to find out what you're doing. I wish we had some regular cigarettes, though. I don't know if I can handle another one of those."

"I didn't bring any unadulterated."

"If I had one of my bitches here, I'd send her out to give head for a pack."

"Really?"

"Just cause I don't do men doesn't mean they have that option. Not if they want a piece of me."

We crossed Jackson Square thronged with pigeons and tourists. The male pigeons puffed and bobbled for the females but hurried out of our way. The tourists we mostly elbowed through. We crossed the street and grabbed a table, ordering two coffees, no beignets.

"So what are you writing?"

"Just some notes on an idea I have. I might need to make a calculation later. I want to be sure I keep it from vanishing. I hate to write stuff, but sometimes I have to."

"What about?"

"Mathematics. I'm looking at something called a manifold. Think of it as a curvy surface, say, but it can be higher dimensions. Like a sphere, say, you know, that looks up close like plain old everyday two-dimensional space, flat and all. The same dimension everywhere, but maybe not the same shape. That can do all sorts of shit, so long as it's smooth."

"You visualize these things?"

"Not generally. A sphere is easy, of course, but there are pretty weird spheres. Alexander's horned sphere, for example, defies intuition."

"Horned sphere?"

"An example of the unthinkable. But just like a two-dimensional sphere in three dimensions, or a circle in two dimensions, you can have a three-dimensional sphere in four dimensions. You can't really visualize that, but it helps to consider that the two-dimensional sphere would be that bitches equator. And you can have fifty-dimensional spheres in fifty-one dimensions. And there are surfaces like the Klein bottle, a two-dimensional manifold, a surface, that won't fit in three dimensions. Needs four."

"What is this Gline bottle?"

"Klein. K-l-e-i-n. Named for a mathematician. Ever hear of a Möbius band?"

"A rock group?"

"No, a —"

"I've heard of it. You twist a piece of paper."

"Not really. A piece of paper is three dimensional. But take a mathematical rectangle. You can glue the ends together so it makes a cylinder. We call that gluing identifying the ends. Anyway, instead of making it straight, put a twist in it."

"I get it."

"Has some interesting properties. If you were two-dimensional and walked around on the thing, when you got back to where you'd started your right hand would be your left and vice-versa."

"Sure as shit?"

"I can explain it sometime if you're interested. A Klein bottle is more bizarre. Take a cylinder this time. You can make one from a rectangle by identifying the long sides, say."

"A tube."

"Yeah, a tube. If you identify the ends of the thing normally, you get a donut. A torus, we call it. But if you put a twist in it, like with the Möbius strip, you get a Klein bottle."

She shut her eyes and made motions with her hands like twisting a hose.

"You'd need to make a hole in the side," she said.

"You can't. That's cheating. Then it wouldn't be a surface. You need to go into another dimension. That's why it sits in four dimensions, but is only two-dimensional."

"That's pretty crazy. Kind of surreal."

"Well, I think if you poured water in it, the whole thing would get wet, since there's no inside or outside."

"Yeah. It's like a one-sided bottle."

"You got it. Pretty sharp."

"So you don't visualize it. But you sense it."

"You don't visualize this stuff but you see it. Maybe the wrong word; you somehow get immersed in it. The more you explore it in your head the closer you are to living in it. Experiencing it, I guess."

"I can see that. Pretty far out. Like getting inside yourself totally."

"You can maneuver in there. You can get around and examine stuff. And when you meet an obstruction, you look for a way to pass through, and that makes you 'see' more... I can't explain it without using words that don't say what I want them to say. I don't have any way to express it. But you experienced it with the Klein bottle."

"It's like there are things we cannot talk about. I think it was Wittgenstein said that."

"Anyway, I can express these ideas precisely to other people if they will take the trouble to learn the descriptive media. It isn't a language so much as a kind of intermediation —"

"An interface, that's the computer word."

"The art is not the expression itself, but what is expressed. And I can express these things so precisely that people can determine whether or not I am making sense, or making mistakes in my findings."

"Weird. So what are you looking at with these equations you wrote?"

I opened the tablet and showed her my scribbles. "They aren't really equations like you're taught in school. Not something you can solve. I have some equations here, but I also have some sets. They're descriptions of things. Things. Really things. Structural things."

"So you're not solving for some missing quantity."

"No, not some numbers. Things. I'm looking at things. Structures. Relationships that explain them. But I will try to make some estimates to tell me about these things."

"Nothing like high school."

"There you have some muttonhead coach at worst or at best some idiot who barely passed his math classes or maybe didn't get a math degree because the classes were too hard. So he hates math, doesn't understand it, and teaches the students to hate math. That it's impossible to understand. Makes me glad I didn't take any of that shit before college."

"So what kinds of things are you looking at?"

"I want to explore some geometric properties of these manifolds. Mostly right now how they curve. Turns out there's two ways to discuss that, one sort of external and the other internal, but they're the same. Its considered cheating to use specific external properties, however. For a lot of reasons. But not always... Forget I brought that up.

"Anyway, you can think of curvature by looking at a sphere, say, and cutting it into slices in perpendicular directions. You'd just get circles."

"Right. I see that."

"That curvature is positive and inverse to the radius of the circles. Just think, the bigger the radius the less curved it looks. Anyway, there the curvature is positive. You can look at other shit like a hyperboloid. You know what that is?"

"Yeah. I got it from it some drawing classes. The Greeks studied conics, where you slice cones."

"I'm impressed. That's more than my calculus students ever seem to know. But that's a hyperbola. Think of it of a two-dimensional version in three dimensions.

"So anyway, there the curvature is negative. And both are constant. But there is a significant difference, too. I mean, think of a sphere as a set where the distance to the center is constant, right? Same with a hyperboloid. But with the hyperboloid the curve is inward, so to speak. Not outward. So that's why it's negative, so to speak.

"And also the hyperboloid sprawls, whereas the circle's closed up. That is not a geometric property, but rather a topological one."

"Topological? Isn't that a kind of geometry? Like rubber sheet geometry?"

"Well, that's misleading. Not geometric in the sense of curvature. It just seems to me there's some kind of relationship between the topology and the geometry in this curvature sense. But so far as I know, people prove the geometric stuff by looking at partial differential equations."

I could see I'd left her.

"Calculus in several variables."

She shook her head. "No calculus in here. Sorry."

"Okay, just another way to look at stuff. For an engineer or a physicist, a differential equation is a deterministic way to view the universe. You start something along from some initial conditions and if you know the equation, you know everything forever.

"What most of them don't realize is that you can take something not determined in that sense, something like a random process…"

I could see her eyes glazing over.

"Think of a drunk walking down the street; at each corner he flips a four headed coin to decide it he goes straight, turns left, turns right or retreats."

That seemed to pull her back.

"That's a random walk. It turns out if you make the streets shorter and shorter so they become infinitesimally short, you get a process with continuous paths but that are also erratic as hell. No matter where you start, you always get back, at least in one or two dimensions. The accumulating corners are so sharp that the lengths of the paths, no matter how little time you allow to pass, are infinitely long in some sense.

"Anyway, that's a Brownian motion. Einstein invented a way to describe it that models the random bombardment of particles which gave rise to the name."

I didn't know how much longer I could hold her and tried to chart a path between speed and bizarreness to get where I wanted to go.

"The upshot is that this random thing can be used to solve partial differential equations. Totally deterministic things solved by totally random processes."

That sparked some life in her eyes. "That is interesting, in concept. But hard to imagine."

"Well, think of it as if the random thing is unfettered by preconceptions, so gets to every little nook and cranny simply by rolling the dice forever. No distractions."

I lit two cigarettes and handed her one, then drained my cup of black, bitter, strong coffee and signaled to the waiter for another.

"So anyway, that tells me that there is really no such thing as deterministic. I've heard philosophers and engineering students and physicists argue that the world is really deterministic, but then that fucks with free will and blablabla. I don't know about free will, but I know that deterministic is an illusion. It doesn't exist. The world's fucking random."

"Humph—"

"Not haphazard. Random follows rules. I can say things about the paths of a Brownian motion. In fact, the little bastards are governed by partial differential equations, in a sense. In the sense of being generated by them, but once they take off you can't be sure where they'll end up. But you know some shit on average.

"Think of it as if someone sets off a point source of heat in a cold room and we watch the diffusion of the heat. Or along an infinitely long rod. The mathematical process ain't real, since it gets everywhere in arbitrarily small times, violating for one thing relativity. Not like the equation that governs waves, which move with finite speed."

"So what do you do with these little random fucks?"

"I use them to explore manifolds. I release an infinite horde of them and measure how they move. That tells me something about the shape of the manifold, I hope. Some manifolds with massively negative curvature are so steep they're moving so fast they get to infinity before they get to the end of the manifold—"

"Oh, come on. That's nuts. They get to infinity?"

"Sure, in finite time. The negative curvature is like a boost away from their starting place.

"But these processes are governed by a heat kernel, a kind of partial differential equation, even though they explore randomly. Some of this has to do with the form of this heat kernel's spatial governor, if you will, the thing that tells how the process is going to diffuse over time along the nooks and crannies and hills and valleys of the manifold. The governor is called the Laplacian. The eigenvalues of this thing are part of the story, it seems. The action of this Laplacian is pretty complicated, but it is possible to write it in a such a way that along a special set of perpendicular directions it stretches and compresses only. Anyway, I'm interested in those eigenvalues."

I stopped. She'd probably tuned me out by now.

"I got some of that. The idea of this thing exploring like a kind of random robot is cool. I'm having a problem with the thing that governs it, but I understand the idea. More or less."

"Laplacian. Don't worry about it. I have this idea that in the short run the Brownian robot learns about the geometry, which makes sense. In the long run it learns about the topology."

"Given what you said about compressed and wide open versus curving, I can see that. Curving is sensed quickly, but it takes a while to determine if there is an end to it all."

"I'm impressed. I wish you were a student of mine."

"I'm impressed too. I wish you were a girl."

"Well, I can't be that. But I can send you a proxy."

"Girlfriend?"

"No, I don't do girlfriends. Someone I own."

"Really? Own?"

"Not my choice. Hers."

"Interesting."

"She's made a mistake, in my opinion. I am a tough master. I can send her over if you give me an address. She'll do what you want if I tell her. Just don't let her orgasm. If she does, punish her."

She laughed. "Sweet!"

She wrote a phone number and address on the page I'd scribbled on.

"What's interesting about mathematics is the aesthetics."

"I can see that. Nothing practical there at all, is there."

"Nope. And questions. They can be deceptively simple. Problem is, they might not be asked in an enlightening way. Not enough information in the formulation. So you need to get the right viewpoint; that usually means you ask it from some other perspective where you can see more. That is the part I really love. It's about asking the right questions, from the right perspective, as much as trying to solve something directly."

"That's why it's so important for you to live with the thing. To find a way to sense it. I see that. You're on a vision quest. This math of yours is your individual vision quest. Like a shaman. Private experience you want to make public. That is a beautiful thing. It's like conceptual art."

"When I tell people about the conceptual art, they think I'm nuts."

"Of course. Like they think a shaman is nuts. Or any kind of mystic. Your shamanism is totally rational, so rational it comes back irrational."

"I'd never thought of mathematics as a vision quest. Interesting perspective. But I don't see it in everyone. Lots of people treat it like some kind of business."

"Of course. Vision quest ain't for everyone."

I gulped down my second cup of coffee. She'd drank hers with milk and sugar. We decided to move along, she heading up Chartres along the river towards Esplanade, I back across Jackson Square towards Bourbon. Before we parted I promised to send Dina, exhorting her to creative abuse.

Chapter 17
Recurrence

I found a naked Dina asleep on the solarium, curled up on a coarse green wool blanket thick with what looked to be black dog hair. She roused when I prodded her with my foot.

"Wake up, cunt."

She caressed and licked the boot. I shook her off.

"You'll fuck the shine, Dina."

"Sorry, Sir. Do you want to hear?"

"Hear what?"

"What happened after we left? Gudrun and I?"

"You went off with Mule and Jerry, right?"

"Yes sir. I worried about you, but thought you'd surely revert to your body."

"Revert? What the hell you talking about. I am my body."

"Yes sir. Can we skip the metaphysics for now? I think you need to hear this."

"Sure. But who'd have thought Gudrun'd be such a whore?"

"Slut, Sir. Or pig. Or maybe trollop. That is more appropriate. I am the whore or trull, though I think trull can be applied…"

I walked away before she finished her prattle, went inside and sprawled on the couch. She crawled along behind and curled up on the floor.

"We drove out of the quarter on Rampart past Elysian Fields where Rampart becomes St. Claude and took some turns. I got lost. We stopped at an old house in some deserted place and Mule ran inside and came back with a pistol tucked in his belt. Then we just drove. All the time Gudrun stayed up front with Jerry and sucked his dick while he drove. Mule made me suck him but he stayed limp. Quite a mouthful even so. Huge foreskin."

"Spare me the details."

"Jealous?"

"No, just disinterested.'

"You need to get involved, Sir. You and I are paired by something transcending both of us."

"Sure we are."

She looked up with crystalline blue eyes gone flat in a world where everything still sported acid fairy dust. I felt a chill. Or maybe the residue of a rush.

"They took us to a big empty warehouse. I think an abandoned building. It had a high ceiling and there were pipes the length of it. It was dimly lit, dingy I guess is the word, with grayish walls and I think I heard or saw rats. I know I found droppings on the concrete floor. It was full of black men. Maybe a hundred of them. Immediately Mule announced he'd brought white fuck toys for entertainment and admission was five bucks. He said he was going to make sure no one injured the ofay bitches. Just use them as nature intended, he said, fuck their holes. No rough stuff."

"I'd say Mule's a fucking optimist. Or a believer in miracles."

"A horde of men surrounded us. There was not one single woman in the place that I could see. I mean besides us. They wanted a show, so we started one for them on one of the mattresses on the floor in a corner. But then they came on in waves. Must have been fifty or more at a time, Sir. Human waves. They separated us. Dicks everywhere, Sir. Gudrun disappeared into a mass of dicks like the one that surrounded me. I don't know how long that continued, but they threw us back together after a while and Mule told us to clean each other up. We'd come in all covered with goo drying like egg whites with makeup streaks. It had only gotten worse, Sir. We dripped with the stuff from every hole, Gudrun thick with it, me too I guess, coated. We licked each other clean inside and out to howls and laughter of derision, Sir, and then it all started again, serried legions closing in—"

"What? Serried legions? What the fuck's that mean?"

"Like phalanxes, sir. Lined up like bowling pins— or bowling pricks. More men than I ever fucked in a single night anywhere, Sir; they must have spread the word because there were so many I was sure there were fresh recruits. They kept coming—"

"How the hell did you two get out of here? Gudrun's clothes are still here, for Christ's sake. You marched out naked?"

"Yes Sir. No one seemed to notice us at all, Sir. We waltzed across the Quarter to where Jerry had parked over in Marigny. It seemed so natural, two black guys dressed like pimps and two naked white women stained with makeup and sperm."

I didn't believe her.

"So eventually Gudrun and I were separated by our own throngs. The noises became indistinguishable, mostly just the noises of fucking and laughing. Cocks everywhere. It was amazing. Then my crowd parted and everyone backed away from me. A little old black man with white hair who was smoking a corncob pipe and a tall black man dressed in full Indian chief regalia, mostly dark feathers, appeared. All I could think was an old man costumed for Mardis Gras and a Tchoupitoulas Indian—"

"A what?"

"Tchoupitoulas Indian, Sir. You know, the Mardi Gras Indians? The album *The Wild Tchoupitoulas?* George Landry? The Neville Brothers?"

I kept nodding no. I had no idea what the hell she was talking about.

"You need to get out more, Sir."

"Lu and Charlie's was more my speed before they shut it down."

"Anyway…Sir———the old man had a tin with some green ointment in his hand and he rubbed a lot of it in my cunt and in my anus. And on my nipples, too. The Indian stood behind him with his arms crossed and watched. They disappeared and the crowd resurged and men starting fucking me anywhere they could insert a penis. I didn't know how much more I could take after I started multiple orgasms; my cunt and anus convulsing simultaneously, contracting, twitching, out of control in spasms—"

"Orgasms? Without permission?"

"I'm Sorry Sir…but I held back until the cream. I don't know what it was. I flew apart, my arms and legs flying apart… I became a rocket, zooming out of the building…flying free through space. But it was weird, since even though I was flying at amazing speed I could see everything in the room as if in slow motion. From the corner, or the top of the roof, like on the apex of the room and the universe at the same time, flying away and still there…"

She seemed to want me to say something. I didn't. I figured she'd gone nuts.

"I could see me…my—self…lying on the mattress—and men…an endless loop of men…gang-fucking me. And I never lost contact, either. It was like a lucid dream where I knew I was asleep but paralyzed. I couldn't do anything. I felt every inch of dick…pounding, driving feet, yards, miles? of penis, actually…but lost smells and eventually sight and sound. The feeling muted, like behind a veil. Hard to explain, but for tactile sensation like fog is to vision. It got denser as the other sensory inputs ended, but never faded away completely. The weird thing was some kind of background chanting or other noise, like in *Satyricon,* you know, that chaka chaka chaka chaka not real loud but constant, and I could sense presences wanting to get out of the men, to assault me directly. Little demons like in a Bosch painting, partly human and partly other animal jumbled, chicken's feet on a man's body or human feet with a bird's beak or just a giant dick with legs. I wanted it too, that was the really weird part. I wanted to be raped and abused by these monstrosities, half-human half-goat demons with enormous animal cocks and teeth like needles forcing forked tongues down my throat and in my asshole, myriad hands holding me down while others fucked my mouth and cunt with oversized unearthly cocks—"

"Okay, great. What about Gudrun? What happened to her?"

"I don't know sir. I could see her. The same swarms of men-things surrounding her. But every time someone would leave her mouth empty for an instant she'd taunt them in a hideous croak that wasn't her. Things like "That the best you got? You've all got tiny dicks!" Vile taunts, goading them, challenging them to fuck her harder. Someone would always interrupt the string of invectives by shoving a dick in her mouth, but then she'd start with another spiel of insults as soon it as it finished ejaculating in her throat or shooting a stream of sperm into her face, spewing back words and cum at the same time. After she'd voraciously drain them, too, Sir. Like a feeding frenzy. She'd gobble up the sperm. It ran down her chin, her tits, her legs and thighs. She'd be on her knees servicing them all, the men fucking her asshole, pussy, mouth, paralyzed between the gangs assaulting her, and when they cleared for an instant she'd croak those insults all over again. They'd laugh, she'd challenge, they'd laugh louder. Then someone came with a baseball bat and shoved the fat end into her cunt."

"What! That'd kill her!"

"No Sir. I have had baseball bats—"

"Okay. That's fine. Where the fuck was Mule? Or Jerry?"

"Mule tried to stop her from goading them on. He tried to get her out of there. She refused to pay any attention to him, Sir. Jerry got the hell out and Mule followed him."

"They shoved a baseball bat up her cunt? The fat part? Jesus, I just can't see how that'd not split her apart."

"No sir. It's eminently doable. It was total anogenital gape by then anyway, Sir; they just rammed the bat home. On her hands and knees and the guy who shoved it in steered her with the bat, pushing her from one man to another; one guy would fuck her ass and another her mouth, the guy steering eventually fucking her ass with the bat sticking straight out behind her like an extra leg. I know she couldn't sit with it inside her, Sir. Probably not even lay flat on her belly or roll over. Just stayed on her hands and knees with the bat protruding behind, sometimes kind of dragging on the floor, other times parallel to the floor like a big wooden tail. That was how she was when I finally left the room—"

"You left?"

"Well, yes and no, Sir. I lay there while a horde of men fucked me senseless, but I was also gone, flying in deep space. Eventually I lost track since there was no up or down or even there that I can remember."

"How'd you get back?"

"I returned to my body. It was in an apartment in one of the projects with a few men sitting at a kitchen table, not doing anything but drinking beer and smoking dope. They had a dog, too. A Doberman. They laughed and gave me the dog's old blanket; said I'd earned it, which made me guess I'd had sex with the dog. When I entered myself I was asleep with the dog on the blanket, on the floor, next to the bowl. I drank from the bowl and ate some of its food and it licked my face. I wished I could remember fucking the dog. I always wanted to experience a dog and maybe a mule or a horse."

It was more than I wanted to hear. A return of the vivid images conjured from paintings by the Flemish master, monsters and demons sodomizing and butchering men and women alike in the landscape from hell. I fixated on a short hunchbacked demon with human feet wearing skates and what appeared to be a metal funnel on its head, without arms, a dogs face with the ears of a beagle and a giant beak with non-conformal sharp ends, the bottom curved up, the top down, a few scattered teeth…

"How'd you get back here? How'd you get in?"

"The men from the apartment in the project drove me here. They let me out and the gate was still ajar, just as I had left it."

"That's weird. It's late Sunday afternoon and the gate was still open? When did you get in?"

"Just now. I showered and came over to see about you, Sir. What happened to you Sir?"

"What do you mean?"

"During the party. You seemed to have left us."

"I was asleep."

"With your eyes open?"

"They were? I imagine I picked that up in the Corps, unconsciously. Probably learned it in Nam."

"What was the stuff you gave me. Sir? I thought it was blotter acid."

"It was."

"No, Sir. That may have been partly acid, but it was something more. I've never had a trip like that with acid."

"You talking about before or after the green salve?"

225

"Both?"

"You don't know what that green shit might have been. The acid was supposed to be very pure. And very high doses, too. Each blotter was four hits. The guy I got it from told me to divide them into three or four.

"Anyway, Dina, you need to clean this place up. Make up the bed. Its fucking filthy in here. Clean the floor, too, and the bathroom."

"Can I stand up to do it?"

"Not the floor. Only for the bed and sinks, and only as absolutely necessary. It better be spotless in here when you're done."

"You going to hold a white glove inspection, Sir?"

"Maybe. Then I got another place for you to work. Here's the address of an art studio over on Frenchman in Marigny. There's an apartment on the top floor. Tell the woman there I sent you and for you to do everyfuckingthing she tells you."

"Yes, sir. What are you going to do sir?"

"Sleep, so start with the bed."

"Sir?" looking up the Madonna as strumpet, halo-glowing beyond the post-acid aura, azure-eyed innocence personified in huntress of monstrous visions…

"What?"

"Do you know what is the biggest drawback of the jungle?"

"What?"

"The jungle, Sir. What is the biggest drawback of the jungle, Sir?"

"I don't fucking know. What?"

"An elephant's foreskin. Sir."

On point, patrolling the hamlet near the base of the rounded protrusion in the surrounding green near the river our CAP occupied, Hill 38. Noises in the undergrowth, scraggly trees pubic hair on red dirt. Women and small devils cavorting everywhere out of sight. Across the ambush-dangerous clearing an orgy of them capering around the Cham ruin on the road into Tam Ky; women vaguely familiar mixed up with demons and monsters out of Bosch. Dina herded along by a chicken-footed penis in one of those coolie hats like a cone on a smokestack or a detachable flared foreskin, poked and prodded; warning me with her eyes: *ambush.* I could see the ambush on the road, devils waiting. Gudrun steered down the road by a baseball bat sticking straight out of her asshole in the hands of a long-faced three-legged dwarf in green hooded cowl dragging along behind it the tips of enormous wings.

I needed to piss; took a minute getting bearings to walk across the floor to the bathroom. Bottoms of my feet didn't blacken with dust. Toilet and sink and the old worn claw-footed tub sparkling. No piss stink. Must have used a fucking toothbrush to clean the place. Nothing else available. Should've made her use her own toothbrush.

Nap groggy, my brain refused to kick start, thought hanging temporarily in abeyance. Reality gloomed; detail no more than adumbration draped in meager light from nowhere, slight nimbus surrounding everyfuckingthing in gloom soup.

Still not dark out. Who'd've guessed Gudrun'd be such a foraging cunt. Unbelievable. Harry'll kick himself for not filming this happening.

Wondered if it was the acid. That was a hellacious dose of acid. Funny telling Gudrun it was a small hit. She ingested like eight hits. What a cooze. Incoherent bitch.

I smoked a joint and decided to go out for a burger.

An enveloping vision flashed back from the dream: Gudrun slathered iridescent in varying shades of translucent ooze of unnatural creatures streaked with make-up like wet war paint, matted hair plastered to her head in caked peaks and valleys, mincing on tip-toe goaded by the fat hobgoblin-dwarf trundling along behind on a tricycle urging her forward with the baseball bat appendage protruding from her asshole. Dina crawling on all fours dragged by her hanging dugs with their nipples enmeshed in the sharp teeth of leeching annelid mouths on tiny human feet, the giant penis, cone hat and all, ramming her anus, greenish goop exuding around the seal of puckered asshole.

I laughed out loud. Fuck her. Fuck them both. Fuck Harry too. Fuck 'em all if they can't take a joke.

Chapter 18
a) Semisimplicity

Phosphorescent wakes muted yesterday's tracers, punctuating movement like infinitesimal contrails in the empty betweenness of things as colors gradually submitted to their less spectacular modulations. Movement an impossibility as in Parmenides; nonetheless I ended up at the Mathematics Department to find within my mailbox a plethora of drop notices for my class, a warning of a complaint from some asshole that I was not attending my office hours and a note from Jeremy Ball, an ominous invitation to visit the mansion after my day at Tulane was done.

I remembered little of class except Miss Cone's Neanderthal brows and the cheerleader's radioactive glow. Nothing else stood out in the shrunken assemblage. I may have not said a word, though I was fairly certain I did.

Because of the asshole complaint I had to visibly waste an hour glued to my carrel. The skinny kid who'd accosted me after my advisor's class on symmetries and PDEs regarding Pfaffians found me daydreaming of escape.

"I don't really get all the stuff in that class," he started.

"Don't worry about it. Probably not important to you."

"But it is. I want to work with geometry and analysis, and this manifold stuff is where it's at."

"What's the problem?"

"I've been trying to get into some books like Bishop and Goldberg. I tried to read Bishop and Crittenden but needed to start simpler. I want to read Milnor's book on Morse theory."

"So read it."

"It assumes too much. It's too terse."

"I thumbed the one with Goldberg a long time ago. Like an advanced calculus text. Better to read Spivak's little *Calculus on Manifold,* at least to start with. Get your tensors elsewhere. I mean, he develops the exterior algebra."

"Spivak discusses tensors in that book," a disembodied voice floated over from another carrel.

"I made a quick pass through the one with Crittenden, but preferred Kobayashi and Nomizu," I said, ignoring the unsolicited comment which I thought was right.

"You read that?"

"I hate to confess to reading books, but I did. Through the first two chapters of Volume Two. Most of it vanished after my orals. I got more out of a little book by Postnikov. More analysis, less fucking geometry."

"How can you read all that stuff so fast?"

"You need to read smart, man. Use your brain and save your eyes. I mean they're just showing you the path; you don't need them to hold your hand."

He gave me a blank look.

"Don't read all those goddamn words. Just the ideas. Dig? S'not as if the prose is the feature. Ideas are what you want; not how they're represented. What's the point of view? where's he coming from? and most important, what's the big picture? There ought to be a story there, but the prose is largely irrelevant."

"How do you get the ideas without the words?"

"The objects. Look for the objects. What are the objects? Definitions; then where do they live? what do they do? how do they exist? coexist? what's their activity?" I hesitated to say function lest he confuse it with the ubiquitous functions themselves. "That's the theorems. Once you have a theorem fixed in your brain, dig the proof yourself. See how to prove it. You can check the author's proof, or not, but if you choose to read the proffered proof, it will still go faster if you already see how to proceed."

"That would seem to be slower."

"No way. Active reading. Burrow in. You get immersed and then can see where he's heading if the shit's any good at all. You can see what he'll need next, what the theorems ought be. When you get the vision down well enough, you can skip major portions and come up on later stuff as if you'd written it.

"Anyway, I chart a path through expository mathematics as a function of the author's style to avoid words as much as possible; some guys try to explain too damned much. Better to work things out yourself, just pick up their point of view. Concentrate on understanding the major propositions, particularly the hypotheses. Construct your own examples, too."

I grabbed the skinny plain mustard yellow hardback I recognized as Warner's *Foundations of Differentiable Manifolds and Lie Groups,* which I'd recommended to him and which lay on his desk, and opened it at random. It opened to page 65. I scanned.

"Look here. As terse as this book is, listen to this:

"The one-form, italics df, is called the exterior derivative of the zero-form italics f, and this begin-italics exterior derivative operator d end-italics has an important extension to italics e-star-of-m given by the following.

"You ever wonder why the adjective 'important' is in there? It's an opinion, man. Worse, what's with all the fucking italics?"

He grabbed the book away from me. "I don't get his proof here that the interior multiplication on the endormorphisms is an anti-derivation of degree one."

"That's easy. First of all, the interior product's defined on the dual of the exterior algebra, so it *is* an endomorphism. Not *on* the endomorphisms; it *lives in* the endormorphisms of the dual of the exterior algebra. Just remember when you see something living on the dual space, you're heading for some kind of adjoint with respect to some kind of pairing. It's the transpose of the exterior product on the left by a fixed element of the exterior algebra in terms of the natural pairing of the exterior algebra and its dual. With this one, since you go up a degree with the left multiplication as an endormorphism, then you've got to go down with the transpose. You need to make room for the new hat in the product. See?"

"Not really."

"Well, think about it. But you won't find curvature in Warner, man."

"What is this book by Postnikov?"

I pulled it out off my cubby shelf and handed it to him.

"I'm done with it. I liked it because it's analytical and algebraic. Really amplifies shit like tensors. Just take it to the library and tell them I'm done with it, then check it out in your name. If you want it."

He stood thumbing the skinny volume, intense as a mathematician with a pencil up his ass.

"No pictures," he said.

"I draw my own. They usually fuck me up anyway. Just when I think I understand something, the author perturbs it with his own unnatural vision. I'm naturally prejudiced towards my unnatural visions. Why I prefer books like this Postnikov or stuff by Walter Rudin or Henri Cartan. These fucking picture drawing dorks make my ass tired. Besides, I don't recall any plethora of pictures in Warner."

"What I don't get is this covariant derivative thing. Or connections."

"They're essentially the same shit. You get parallel translation?"

"No."

"Let's do a calculation." I got up and moved to the big chalkboard at the back of the room, he following like a puppy.

"Think about the idea of parallel transporting a vector along a curve. Forget the idea of covariant derivative being zero and all that shit. In Euclidean space it's trivial, right? with only one coordinate patch and an orthogonal vector field to frame it all. Globally trivial. Just move that fucker along, right?" I drew a snaky little curve and some parallel arrows along it. "It comes back exactly at the angle at which it left.

"Now consider the two-sphere. Suppose you start at the north pole like you're riding a platform with a tangent vector pointing along that curve due south and you ride a great circle down along a fixed longitude to the equator. The little cart turns hard right, that is orthogonally, say, along the equator but the vector stays put, pointing south, and runs perpendicular to the path…" representing this badly as always on the flat board; noting a few newcomers appearing from their carrels, "You want us to move out of here?"

"No," one of the others said, "not me." No one else objected.

"Don't want to fuck up anybody's studies," I said.

Some murmurs without dissent from the small knot standing in the aisle between the dual row of carrels leading to the board, some heads popping up here and there above the rows of dividers between carrels to watch.

Turning back to the yellow and white streaked black board, I moved the vectors along the equator, pointing south. "So your vector points south, we parallel transport it along this great circle, lets say for pi over two radians and then bang, hard right ninety degrees again back to the north pole, the vector now sticking straight out the back of the cart like a baseball bat protruding from a butthole and bingo — when we hit the north pole, just coming over that last hill, the damned vector is out of whack from where it started."

"Whoa," he said, "how does that …?"

"Think about it," someone said, doing some shit with his hands to show the cart making it up over the curve of the sphere. "The curvature of the sphere does it. It changes the orientation. You travel pi over two along the equator and this vector ends up at an angle of pi over two with the original vector."

"It is the original vector," I said, "but right. The damned curvature rolls it even though you have moved that baby along in its original orientation with orthogonal turns. That is parallel transport on a sphere."

The kid was doing some shit with hands and he suddenly grinned.

"I see it," he said. "That makes sense. Of course, if you'd made right angles in the plane you'd be back on top of where you started with that arrow, but you'd have had to make three turns to get back to where you started, not two."

"We identified the points on the line after that last right turn in the plane to the pole," from the same other someone.

"We did a pinching to get the sphere. Think of stereographic projection in reverse.

"Anyway, that's what the fuck connections are about. You can't really do any kind of differencing between different tangent spaces, see? They aren't comparable."

He nodded. It seemed he got it.

"You know those Christoffel symbols?" I asked. "Messy shits usually a capital gamma with a superscript and two subscripts?" I wrote cap gamma sub i j and sup k on the board.

"Yes, but I don't know what they are."

"For me they are nothing but corrections to the partials, like fudge factors to keep parallel vectors 'parallel,' the local coordinate partials to correct for this shit, so the goddamn covariant derivative vanishes. I mean, velocity along a curve is invariant, you know, with the tangent spaces, but not with acceleration. The damned partials aren't invariant with respect to coordinate changes. Think about the unit circle in Cartesian coordinates and then in polar coordinates, unraveled, you know, and the tangent vector stays tangent but the fucking acceleration vector points to the center of the circle in one case and is zero in the other."

I wrote it down for him.

"Oh, yes. Hmmm, never thought of it quite like that."

Someone said, "Only Butcher thinks of it like that."

"So let's think about the two-sphere again," I said. "Unit sphere, say, let's set that bitch up with latitude and longitude. Standard spherical coordinates, theta from the north pole down to the equator at pi over two and south pole at pi, phi sweeping the circle at the equator at theta pi over two, with phi zero at (one, zero) on the equator. So phi does a zero to two pi, say." I drew a fair representation of three orthogonal axes and then a pathetic lumpy and flat circle as a sphere, the white chalk shrieking at one point before breaking. I grabbed a soft yellow nub of chalk and wrote $(s(\theta)c(\varphi), s(\theta)s(\varphi), c(\theta))$.

"So we have two differential operators, del theta and del phi, along the coordinates of lat and long, right?"

He nodded.

"So then those fucking connection coefficients, the Christoffel symbols, they're gonna correct for the curvature in certain directions, right? Remember what happened to that damned tangent vector. Now think about del theta with respect to del theta. We want to know what happens when we apply that to itself in, say, the del theta direction. There's the standard partial term and then the correction factors in each direction, right?"

I wrote $\nabla_{\partial_i} \partial_j = \Gamma_{ij}^k \partial_k$ in fat yellow smudges.

"So we need to see what's up in the tangent spaces, right? Moving along the coordinate directions. Think we're looking at the directional derivative of del theta along del theta, del phi, etcetera, you know?"

He nodded his head kind of slowly.

"Like this," I said, writing $\nabla_{\partial_\theta} \partial_\varphi$. "You know, running through theta and phi combinations. The four of them. Gives like eight Christoffel symbols, I think."

"I get it."

"Okay, then so how's the vector field del theta change along a longitude? When j and i equal one and component i, in i direction; you know, theta. Not at all, right? Its just moving orthogonally, so to speak. And same is true in the phi direction, too. Everything stays nice and orthogonal. So those two Christoffels are zero. No change."

I wrote $\Gamma_{11}^1 = 0 = \Gamma_{11}^2$.

"Okay, now do this for the cross terms. Moving along theta in the phi direction seems orthogonal, no correction in either theta or gamma component. And the same's true of phi with respect to theta. I mean think about it, the fuckers are orthogonal. No corrections.

"But now look at phi with respect to itself. Its all orthogonal again on the equator, at theta equal pi. But move up the sphere a bit, say to theta equal pi over four. Now we're running along a little circle below a cap, cut directly across the sphere and not through the center of the sphere. Not a great circle, so not a geodesic, either. See? Slice off the top of that bitch, that little circle. Its tight and getting tighter as you head up to the pole. We know that any two points on that circle are connected by vectors parallel to their tangents via a great circle, slicing through the origin. Right? Here on this little circle we got no tangency with respect to the tangent. You can see it if you close your eyes and look real hard."

He closed his eyes and I almost laughed.

"I see it! It is pointing up in the theta direction!"

"Exactly," I said. "It is fucked in the theta component, trying to twist out of the damned tangent plane, the tangent plane's doing a bit of a twisted dance trying to leak into the theta direction. Like when you try to walk across a hill instead of going up with the curvature; it's hard to do. You need to twist and step down to keep from falling off the hill. Right? You're not on a geodesic, which cuts through the center of the sphere. Easier to zigzag along the great circles."

I looked up to see Red rolling his eyes, grinning like a Cheshire cat. He pointed to the doorway where stood Miss Cone.

"I gotta finish this," I said, "a real student has come to visit me. So anyway, the only component is the gamma sub two two sup one, right? Now I don't see how the rest of this works. I have to work out the formula for the exact expression to get this I think, but I think gamma sub phi phi sup theta goes with the derivative with respect to theta as a correction to the phi partial of the phi variable and the second component of the tangent vector or something like that. Right away you see why you don't often get global parallel fields, given the four overdetermined PDEs to solve. But on a curve it gets derivatives with the dt and then you get only two sets of ODEs. Linear to boot, so with global solutions and all."

He stood with his nose in the board.

"Anyway, it's not too hard to work out. Just tedious. You can do it."

"Those are the gammas with the superscripts one, right, the subscripts varying with the …?" he asked.

"No, that's not right," said a scrag of a hirsute differential topology student who was near to finishing his PhD. He came up and wrote the PDE in coordinates with the gamma correction terms. Then he wrote the expression for the ODE along a curve.

"I can never remember that shit," I said. It surprised me he did; more likely he'd just seen it himself. His area was not geometry or PDEs, so this ought to have been foreign to him but then he could have gone through it before from a different point of view. It impressed me since I had to think it through, but I wasn't about to let him know that. "Thanks," I said. I didn't trust this scrawny hippy with thinning hair down to his ass, scraggly beard, a vegetarian who never used drugs or alcohol.

"What's the correction term?" the kid asked.

"Well, the only way I can see to get that is to consider the metric tensor components, easy to compute in spherical coordinates, but a diagonal two by two with one and sine squared theta on the diagonal. Since that is the metric term accounting for the small circles at fixed latitudes, I think, then the concern ought to be with the rate of change, you know, negative sine theta cosine theta. The negative makes sense, too. Or not, now that I reconsider it all below the equator. Oops, cancel that, course then it's positive."

"Well, I think the derivation's wrong," the hippy topologist said through his overgrown beard.

"Probably. Not a derivation anyway. Just playing with intuition. Heuristics. Needs formalization."

"Isn't there some book where they do this?" the kid asked.

"I haven't seen one. This is the more-or-less first time for me. No one works this shit out in books as examples. Too tedious to do carefully anyway. This is just seat of the pants. I'd be curious if someone does work it out to see the actual right formulas, but I think we got it here. Don't see how to get the damned sine squared theta term without the metric tensor, though, and that does bother me. I'd like to see a pure trig way to get that."

"Why don't we have something like this for fixed phi circles?" It was Red.

"You mean holding phi constant and varying theta around the sphere? Parameterization. Theta only runs from zero to pi. Reverse the roles."

"Oh, right," he said, looking up at the ceiling as if the sphere were floating away.

"It all has to do with curvature. The problem goes away if you have zero curvature tensor. In fact, the curvature tensor is a kind of first order correction when you pull that tangent vector back by parallel translation. And if you want to do the covariant derivative like a difference quotient, parallel translation gives it to you. But look into this for Riemannian manifolds. The Levi-Civita connection is the unique one compatible with the Riemannian metric, in— "

"What's that mean, compatible?"

"It satisfies an identity with respect to the Riemannian inner product on the tangent spaces, which is equivalent to killing the metric tensor and some other conditions. Postnikov does them, as I recall. Most important, it has no torsion. The torsion is a tensor field related to the connection and Lie bracket. I think it's the unique connection with that property. Anyway, if you work this stuff out correctly, show it to me. I'd like to see it."

I turned towards Miss Cone, still standing in the doorway.

The kid stood behind me at the board and asked "Did you ever kill anyone?"

"What?" I turned back to face him.

"When you were in Vietnam; did you kill anyone?"

"Yes."

"How do you deal with it?"

"I'm sorry, I don't understand the question."

"Killing people. Doesn't it bother you?"

"No. I don't do it anymore for one thing. Besides, it's natural behavior for the human primate. Beats me why society's inculcated so much guilt into such a refreshing activity. In fact, I never met anyone who had a problem with killing. It's when the primates on the other team try to kill you back that you separate the men from the boys. While I don't recommend making a habit of it, everyone ought to try it least once in their lives. Part of the team sport called war."

The hippy topologist got up from his carrel and left the room as I led Miss Cone to my carrel. I hoped his leaving had been on my account.

"Miss Cone, sorry to make you wait," grabbing the chair from the next carrel for her, "enter my tiny arena. You should have interrupted me."

"Oh, no, that was interesting. What was it about?"

"A way of trying to avoid geometry by using analysis, but aided by geometry. Height of circularity, actually, and about nothing on this earth."

"Sounded like spherical arguments to me," she said, grinning slyly.

I gave her a huge smile, suppressing an urge to hug her.

"But I don't understand how a statistic can be a statistic."

"That is not a trivial idea, believe me. You are probably not alone. Didn't I say in class that the word statistic has several uses?"

"No."

"Sorry, then. I will bring it up in class Wednesday, and if I don't, remind me."

"Okay."

"A statistic can refer to some specific number, like your vital statistics. I don't much like that usage. Confuses the idea of what is a statistic.

"Or it can refer to a specific measurement on some stuff. Like average height and weight or median income. Those are statistics and that is related to the first meaning in your question. That specific measurement is really a single element from a collection of possible statistics. And another use is as in a distribution. Do you understand how a statistic can have a distribution?"

"Not really."

"That is the same question, phrased more carefully. Let's consider a population of furry widgets."

"What?"

"You don't know widgets?"

"I heard of them, but I don't know what they are."

"Imaginary units of production from some microeconomic process, like a single plant that makes widgets. We want our widgets to be interesting, so we put hair on them."

She cautiously presented a half-knowing smile.

"So there are an infinity of these widgets, say. Just to make it easier for the mathematical statistician who hates counting.

"So you have an industrial process in place. You want to be sure the widgets are not overly hirsute, you know. A thick bush of hair but not too thick, and certainly not too long. Within fixed parameters. If you get outside those parameters, you need to go back and find a way to trim the bushes. Industrially. Now just for grins, assume the furry burries are normally distributed. That, in fact, is why I wanted an infinity of these things."

She whispered. "Muffs, right? They're muffs?"

I whispered back. "If you like muffs, then they're muffs."

She smiled knowingly.

"Okay, now you need to sample these guys to see how thick the hair is, say. Or long. Or both, but if we do both, for simplicity lets assume there is no correlation between the length and thickness of the hair.

"So you take a sample of size, say, one hundred. What would you compute?"

"The mean?"

"Most likely. You could instead compute the median, which might be more stable, but it is harder to compute since it requires an ordering of the samples and also the distributional properties of the median are harder for us. So the mean it is.

"Now, what do you think happens if you decide to take a sample of size, say, ten thousand instead of one hundred?"

"It's more accurate?"

"What's more accurate? You don't mean the computation."

"The mean. It's more representative of the population of muffs with a bigger sample."

"Right. But what—"

"But how long is too long? I mean, for the hair on these muffs."

"That is individual choice. Your choice, in this case."

"Do you have a preference?"

"For the hair on these muffs? Actually they were widgets, right?"

"They're muffs."

"Okay, I don't have any preference regarding hairy muffs. I'm ambivalent. But what did you mean when you said it was more representative of the actual population of muffs?"

She pursed her lips and thought, looking at me but not really seeing me for some unmeasureable step in time, then said, "I guess the error gets smaller, in a sense. I can see it, now, the distribution of these means will all be normal, and they will get tighter as the sample gets bigger. And that means the standard deviation gets smaller."

"And what is the standard deviation?"

She broke out in a huge grin. "That is a matter of choice, too."

"No, I meant statistically."

"The square root of the variance."

"Right; but of the population, and we like the variance for several reasons. But look: now you can measure the statistics of the statistic with a sample size of one hundred and of those with a sample size of ten thousand. There were things we worried about, right?"

"I get it. The expectation and the variance of the distributions. They both have the same expectation, but different variances. You want the expectations of those statistics to be the true statistics. Unbiased. And as the sample size gets bigger, the variance gets smaller. So the expectation of the sample mean is the expectation of the population, which means it is unbiased. And then there are confidence intervals—"

"Yes, yes, you got it. It's not so hard."

"Thanks. That's a big help. As the sample size gets bigger, the distribution squinches down. Which means size does count. Bigger is better—"

"Exactly. You were just worried that you didn't understand. But you do understand. A failure of self-confidence, which is kind of silly for you. You're smart."

"You think so?"

"Yes, definitely."

"You like smart?"

"Among other things."

She nodded reflectively. "I like big." Then she asked, "Did you really kill people?"

"Yes, I did. Quite a few, actually."

"Could you see them?"

"Sometimes like from me to you. Other times not so close. Close and personal is always my preference."

"Jeez. I never met anyone who killed people like that. I knew some relatives who killed, but with rifles or such. From a distance. In World War Two or maybe some other war."

"Korea, maybe. I did that kind of killing, too, but it isn't the same as putting a .45 to someone's head and blowing out their brains while they stand or kneel defenseless before you."

She stared. Then she stood. "Thanks again. I have a class."

She didn't leave in an orderly fashion.

Red came around when she'd gone.

"You're nuts," he said.

"Think so?"

"Muffs?"

"Her choice of word. I began with widgets."

He shook his head. "She's a babe, though, huh?"

"Kind of in a Neanderthalish way. Those beetle-brows, man. But I bet she sports one hairy widget."

"I'd like to find out."

"What about Lynette?"

"Ummm, that wouldn't work."

"Well, I don't find her attractive. Not interested."

We split for classes. There being no bell in the math department, my advisor started early with the Korteweg-deVries equation and then spent the rest of the hour with a derivation and discussion of something he called the Gelfand-Dikii identity. This time I was lost. It seemed totally disconnected from the last session which had been transparent. I spent my time thinking about Pfaffians, differential ideals, integrability, characteristic manifolds and the method of characteristics for quasi-linear PDEs.

I stopped the dorky kid after class.

"You might find it useful to consider that Pfaffian bit relative to the method of characteristics for quasi-linear PDEs."

"I don't know anything about PDEs."

"You don't need much, but it might help with where he's headed, given he has PDEs rattling around inside his head all the time. Take a look at Fritz John's book on PDEs. The first chapter's plenty, where he explains the method of characteristics. It might not hurt to look at Folland's first chapter, his book on PDEs. They're both yellow, but Folland's Princeton Press. Yellow paperback. He does it with respect to the characteristic vector's and the symbol. The symbol is kind of implicit in a lot of shit since it is the defining characteristic of elliptic operators. When a vector kills the symbol of a partial differential operator, there's in some sense a lack of differentiation in that direction, so the operator's in some sense lower order in that direction. An elliptic operator has no such directions; the only characteristic direction's the zero vector. So an elliptic operator of order k controls all derivatives of order k."

He stared, apparently dumbfounded.

"I diverge. Sorry. Look at the method of characteristics for solving quasi-linear PDEs. You find that it leads to integrability conditions, at least locally, and you get some ODEs that specify characteristic curves on a manifold that give local solutions. It might help."

Or not. It might confuse. It seemed I'd addled him. I didn't hang around while he stood staring at something no one but he could see, instead grabbing my bag and heading for the gym and a workout.

b) A Non-characteristic Hypersurface

The Ball mansion loomed behind the long walk somehow more detached than the last time. Of course, the post-acid residue had another few days of exponential decay before diminishing so infinitesimal it would no longer register from below my sensory threshold, yet it was some comfort to know it would never leave me entirely. Not until death and the final disintegration of consciousness, a comfort to those of us who didn't believe in God or gods, hell, life everlasting or any form of the Asian and hippy superstition of transmigration. No recurrence for me, not even in a weak sense.

Shawntel let me in. She appeared dragged out, conspicuous bags drawn beneath her eyes, and maybe a hint of mustache. Or it might have been the residue of the acid talking.

She said that when I'd finished speaking to Mr. Ball, Mrs. Ball wanted to see me. She left me before a closed door she professed was the entrance to Mr. Ball's study. The nearest other door she avowed to be the entranceway to the study of Mrs. Ball, who she claimed would await me while viewing some video tapes from this weekend.

I couldn't quite fathom what the fuck kind of video that would be. Certainly I was curious as to what Jeremy wanted. Gudrun's fate had gnawed at me a tad; how the hell Jeremy would not be aware of the weekend events was anyone's guess. Didn't seem possible. I doubted Gudrun viewed video of herself with a baseball bat up her cunt while fucked senseless by a rampaging horde of black thugs. But nothing these people were capable of could surprise me.

Jeremy sat behind a massive expanse of reddish-black wood swirling around a giant burl. The long and narrow room itself, wood panel, wood floor, reminded me of a coffin. Lined with shelves full of fat books. I refused to look at the titles.

"Whitey. Nice to see you. How are things?"

He gestured to a leather-cushioned hardback wooden chair.

"As usual," sitting down. "Trying to survive and get a thesis on the way."

"Yes, well the survival I might could help with. My company, you know, has a contract with the DOE on the SPR."

"SPR?"

"You know. What Kip works on, the Strategic Petroleum Reserve."

"He mentioned something about it."

"Well, to cut to the chase, we have a bit of a problem. We have the contract to manage the cost and schedule for the drilling."

"Drilling?"

"Salt domes. Drill holes in the domes and fill the caverns with oil. Been a problem for the government, though. Those domes are harder to drill than anyone originally guessed. Drills break, thieves steal the pipe and other equipment, contractors rob them blind. And we have gone through three sets of management to get it fixed. Out in Louisiana marshland."

"Fix what?"

"We can't project the costs because we can't get the schedule to come out and we can't put the two together and we can't figure out the cost of the schedule slips. They are reticent to fire us, though, since we are a minority disadvantaged company. But we're the contract management and it looks to the government like we can't manage ourselves. Not good."

"You own this company?"

"Is a corporation. Eight-a, minority disadvantaged. I am a minority, being Cajun, and also this company is separate from the family businesses."

"Interesting. And how does this affect me?"

"I am beginning to worry that there is either conspiracy or mass incompetence in this setup. I want to build this into a thriving small business with management contracts before I sell it. I have a commissioned study I need for someone from completely outside the structure to look at."

"What's it about?"

241

"A projection method for predicting the cost of the petroleum and also for the cost of gasoline, which is kind of a justification factor. It's all statistics."

"Why me? I don't know shit about any of that."

"Neither does anyone on the project. We hired a consultant to produce this report so we could implement it in software. The government added it to our tasks. But no one understands it."

He handed me a thin document bound in a stiff pressboard held together by long hinged metal flaps that folded over and fixed with flat sliding metal grommets.

"I understand you teach statistics," he said. "You might be able to help implement it."

"You mean with a computer program? I don't know shit about computers."

"Well, I'll pay you one hundred dollars an hour to work on it."

I opened it up and scanned. It was simple linear regression. Some economic variables with a lot of simple-minded assumptions.

"This is trivial. It's linear regression. It's the kind of thing I might give my stat class to do as an exercise."

"Really? We paid a PhD in economics, an econometrician, $25,000 for that report."

"You're kidding. He makes some strong assumptions, like here," I opened to the fourth page, "where he assumes that both petroleum and gasoline demand are linear functions of supply. I find that questionable. I mean, there is likely some linear range for gasoline, say, but then beyond that demand you need more plant, below it you have too much capacity and stuff sits idle. That is going to make cost nonlinear. Or piecewise linear at best. Same sort of thing for petroleum."

"We can't question his assumptions. He was forced on us by the government. The DOE administrator and his assistant have a lot of people they send us to employ."

"I'll look at it. But no matter what, I ain't wearing a suit. If I can, I'll just write you a report. But I need to know what kind of computer stuff they're using. I can get some advice on that once I extract a computational procedure."

"An algorithm?"

"You could call it that. Just some kind of arithmetic in the end."

"Okay. But you may need to make a trip out there to talk to the people about computers."

"What about Kip? Can't I just talk to him?"

"He might not be the best person or the only person. He isn't very high up the food chain. But we don't have a real computer staff. We buy time on a TSO operation, a linked CDC and IBM from an aerospace company in St. Louis. We have a direct line and do our input with a teletype keyboard and also with cards. The program it runs for cost projections is called COPES, which is supposed to integrate cost with schedule but for some reason they are not integrated. Instead they use some other schedule program, on a smaller computer in the engineering office."

"That's too much information. The only thing I got was IBM. Just let me look at this and I'll try to get back to you by Friday. But it would help if I knew if they had computer languages available. This COPES thing doesn't sound like a language; more like an end product."

"Fine. I'll see what I can find out. And thanks."

"Well, I can't promise anything. I'll do what I can."

I left his study and stood at the door to Gudrun's. I heard what sounded like Gudrun giving a speech. I knocked. A muffled "Come in" overran the speech.

An officious Gudrun in round wire spectacles appearing none the worse for wear sat behind her own oversized wooden desk in a room filled with books whose titles I refused to look at. She watched a television, on the screen her image dressed in a classy dark suit speaking to a group of men and women, mostly women.

I couldn't picture her as an executive, but here she was.

"What's that?" I asked, motioning with my head towards the tube.

She peered over her glasses at me.

"My speech Saturday in Baton Rouge. A conference organized by the state's nonprofits with support from our HQ in New York. Had short talks, panel discussions, special sessions on needs delivery and systems analysis. I gave this keynote address Saturday afternoon and then sat on several panels Saturday and Sunday."

"Last Saturday? Just past?"

"Yes. This last weekend."

I didn't ask her what the fuck she was talking about. She had to be up to something, but I couldn't figure it. Would be hard to maintain such an outrageous lie.

"The local television stations have broadcast snippets of it on the news, and one of the local morning news shows had it on just this morning. Part of this speech was shown on the last night's news. We want to get it on national television, like on Today."

I stood like a wooden dummy, staring at her.

"You look like you've seen a ghost," she said, sounding a bit alarmed or surprised or both.

"___"

"So you're going to do the consulting for Jeremy?"

I nodded.

"Cat got your tongue?"

She wore the **Performance Counts** tee shirt she'd had on Saturday, which I'd assumed Dina'd sent out with the sheets to The Washing Well.

"I guess I was trying to recall where I'd seen that T-shirt before."

"They aren't common. It's an old John Deere T-shirt I got up in Iowa." She stood up and came around the desk wearing jeans that looked familiar.

"I need to get back to this," she said. "Trying to reduce this film to short advertising pieces for fund raising. But I wanted to ask if you would like to go to lunch with me on Saturday. I have time, and I did want to follow up on my invitation from the party."

"Sure. What time?"

"Well, I know a place in the Quarter that is pretty good and not too crowded at one to one thirty. Why don't I come by and buzz and we can walk over."

As I made my way down the long winding path to St. Charles Avenue and the streetcar, I realized I'd been so dumbstruck I'd forgotten to ask about Harry. He'd been conspicuously absent. And I wondered who the fuck had been at my place this weekend if not Gudrun. If she were on the level. And if not, what the fuck?

In any case, what the fuck?

Chapter 19
Orientability

"Christ, Dina, what the fuck you talking about?"

The day'd opened flat, like underwater or somegodamnthing. Inanimate shades of gray there but not there. Even my incogitant cogitation devoid of mentation. A corpse of a day — incoherent, as in incommensurably out of phase. Not a common event, but neither unprecedented. As if I'd run smack into a splattered shit-shield or somefuckingincognosciblething or other. Irrational dubitation unraveling densely on a toroidal embedding.

"I knew it wasn't her, Sir, when I saw her this morning on the local news. They showed a clip of her speaking this weekend in Baton Rouge. Hundreds of people saw her there all weekend. It had to be a double, Sir."

A naked Dina on her haunches tugging at my hand first thing this morning made me think I needed to start locking the fucking door. Yelping about Gudrun on television this morning. Where the fuck did she see a goddamn television anyway? so fucking early…wasn't even eleven yet.

"Double? Like she has an evil twin?"

"Maybe a doppelganger, Sir."

"What exactly is a fucking doppelganger?"

"You know the word. I don't need to define it. These occurrences of bilocation have been reported throughout history."

"You can't mean that."

I knew she could.

"Then what was it? A mass delusion on our part or on the part of the people in Baton Rouge at the conference? Sir."

I couldn't argue with any of that. It made no sense and it wasn't going to make sense.

My empty-headedness likely a clearing of the deck for new stuff. New tools. New point of view. I'd sort of skirted the formidable machinery of algebraic topology for a while, knowing how difficult it would be to get a big picture there. People who worked in it were mostly mud-dwellers, their noses in the muck. I preferred some open sky, some puzzle pieces fitting to form a semblance of big picture I could assimilate. An attitude mostly frowned on in the game of mathematics, at least among the mud dwellers. Now I'd adsorbed a significant chunk of the geometry of differentiable manifolds, it was time to absorb the other side of the picture. The nasty toolbox. Of course, I'd likely live my life on smooth structures and might not need all that extra baggage, but then I needed a lot of shitty topology to play in the function spaces where one found oneself pretty goddamn often in the game I'd chosen. Likely to be true of this algebraic machinery for extracting topological insight from the structures within which one would, of necessity, from time to time bury one's nose.

"She hasn't got a twin, Sir, that she advertises. Not like Harry and Jeremy, Sir."

"No, I suppose that would be too much."

"Just accept it, Sir. I personally believe it was the result of a local demigod's theurgy. Perhaps even unintentional."

"I'm not going to ask what the fuck that means. I don't want to know."

In mathematics, everyone has a point of view regarding what is essential to grasp. The core of the discipline, so to speak. They also believe that once the core is assimilated, one ought learn only that much extra required for cranking out theorems. Research. Their "work," as in opera. For this group of purists so anal with respect to some formal notion of consistency not to see the inconsistency in that viewpoint amazed me. And of course no matter what, the fundamentals of their own area of concentration were part of that requisite core. At Tulane there seemed at least a smattering of encouragement for scholarship, at least compared to some of the places I'd heard about, but not up to Momus's penchant for book l'arning.

"Well, Sir, now we have that sorted out, I need to inform you that I am going to Europe for a month to six weeks. Of course, it is your right to come with if you want."

"Fine. I'm staying here."

"Aren't you curious as to why I'm going?"

"I'm sort of afraid to ask."

"I have formed a production company, Sir. We're doing our first films in Europe."

"What's Harry think about that?"

"He's down with it, Sir."

"Does that mean he likes it?"

"He's encouraging it. He's going to work with me, particularly in distribution. I'll create more avant-garde films for select patrons. I have patronage that wants cutting edge. Work that Harry can't deliver through his company."

"Why?"

"Like any avant-garde art, Sir, cutting edge is not always understood. Or appreciated. Our work is advanced sexuality, Sir. Harry creates film for mass audiences. The new production company will go well beyond homosexuality."

"You saying it isn't legal?"

"In some places, I think that's probably true. I'm going to Europe to work with an animal trainer. Animal training from an artistic point of view."

"Uh huh… Animal training?"

"Yes Sir. Horses, dogs; maybe pigs and goats. Especially dogs."

I got it while watching her crawl to her bowl to lap up the coffee I'd poured for her, the nipples of her hanging dugs scant fractions of an inch from dragging along the floor. Her burnished silver collar reflected light streaming into the sun porch; the glare bounced around inside my vacated head.

"You're going to fuck animals for the camera."

"Yes, Sir, among a variety of sexual acts."

"I sort of included a variety of stuff in the word fuck."

"Of course, Sir. Do you have a driver's license?"

"Don't fall in love with one of them. Is it legal to marry animals where you're going?"

"We'll be in Belgium, Sir. And Denmark. Sweden. Germany, too. The trainer owns a large estate in Belgium. I don't believe marriage with animals is legal in those places, but sex with animals is not illegal. That is why he owns rural estates in those countries, Sir. His main studio is in Denmark."

"It's going to be a bit chilly for cavorting in the buff with goats and such out of doors in those places this time of year, isn't it?"

"I don't know, Sir, but I suspect it will be. Late spring in northern Europe isn't as warm as in New Orleans. Perhaps I'll do all my cavorting indoors. I am a little worried about the stallion. I have been told it can be dangerous to get fucked by a stallion, Sir."

"I'd imagine. Never heard of any deaths, though."

"Yes Sir, a woman who had some sort rupture from a stallion, a woman who was accidently kicked in the head, and a man who suffered a perforated colon during anal sex with a stallion. The perforated colon incident occurred in the US, Sir. The man died of peritonitis. He'd been in a long term sexual relationship with his horse. He often had friends take photos of them together; the survivors were all prosecuted."

"Do you think the horse was saddened by the turn of events?"

"About the license, Sir?"

"I got one. For check cashing. Turned in my Missouri license for it. Couldn't believe the test was in pictures."

"Yes, Sir. So as not to discriminate against illiterates, Sir."

"That was what bothered me, I think. Illiterates driving."

"Get used to it, Sir. It's rampant in the US. But these people are terrible drivers anyway, Sir. It's like driving in France or Quebec. I want you to use my car while I'm away. I rent a parking garage in the Quarter, Sir."

"Didn't know there were such."

"A few. This is a covered garage. I have a key for it. It is located in close proximity to the old mint. I'll take you over later today and give you the key. It's a new Porsche 911 Carrera 2.7, Sir. Black, which is probably not the best color for this climate in summer."

"That's not the car you've been driving."

"No Sir, that was a rental. I had my Porsche shipped out from California when I decided to stay here."

"When did you decide that?"

"When I became your liege-bitch."

"Liege? I thought the master was the liege."

"Yes Sir. You are also my liege. Liege-lord. I am the liege-bitch. I took an oath of sexual fealty. Liege is the structure, formally speaking."

"Whatever. Anyone ever tell you you're fucking medieval?"

"Yes, Sir. They have, without knowing it. My avatar—"

"Christ, Dina, that's an expensive car, isn't it? I've never driven a Porsche. Just seen them from time to time, mostly in Las Vegas. Not so many of them in Kansas City."

"No to worry, Sir. You are insured under my policy. It is completely covered. But I am very particular where I have it serviced."

"Why do I need a car?"

"To drive out to where Jeremy's company is located, in Jefferson Parish. You are going to consult to them, are you not?"

"I said I'd look at this thing. How'd you hear about that, anyway? I just talked to him last night—"

"The medieval world is a small one, Sir. And nothing is secret within that circle. You do know how to drive a stick shift, don't you Sir?"

"Of course. It's inbred in us fair-haired western-born dudes. Natural selection. I didn't see Harry last night—"

"No sir, he's filming at his ranch in California. He has a place in the Santa Ynez Valley where he films sometimes, besides the studio in the San Pornando Valley—"

"The what valleys? Never heard of either place."

"Santa Ynez is north of Santa Barbara. There are a lot of horse ranches there. And an Air Farce base where they test missiles. San Pornando is a play on words, Sir. San Fernando Valley. One of the centers for adult films in the US.

"My agent has established an office in Marigny, near Elysian Fields. In a spacious building not far from that lesbian sculptress you sent me to, Sir; very unimaginative, by the way. It has two stories with a huge opened-out upstairs with four rooms off the central part. A long hallway leads off to the back and the rooms branch off from the hallway. And three full bathrooms with showers, and a half bath too. Oh, and with a kitchen at the end of the hallway. A place for a bar. Perfect set up for filming. Downstairs in back there's a large, dark room without windows we're making into a dungeon, Sir—"

"You have an agent?"

"Of course. But she is more than just a talent agent, Sir. She acts as a personal agent, more or less, and handles the business requirements—"

"I haven't met this agent?"

"No Sir. She's been in Europe and California since we met. Arranging things for this trip, helping to put together funding for the film business—"

"Funding?"

"Of course. Venture capital. No one does business without it, Sir."

There'd been a tiff in the topology group. Vacuum of leadership. The quasi-inactive algebraic topologist no longer gave a fuck about topology and so let the second generation Moore-school guy run the group, more or less, while the inactive one worked with some other Catholic, a mathematical physicist; rumor was they prayed together to not prove any false theorems, though such an occurrence would be a miracle. Or an anti-miracle. The young upstart topologists, Goldman and the differential guy, challenged the second generation Moore-guy's authority. Goldman considered the stuff of the Moore school to be inartistic dreck, whereas the Moore school guy had already moved on for the most part anyway, skirting the edges of manifolds and all. But he kept his ties to the continua bunch and so when he taught the topology course the year my entering class took it, he used a book light on the algebraic gizmos, the book by Munkres…

"I would appreciate your advice, Sir. If you could trouble yourself to take a look at the place, Sir. I'll have the agent come over. And if you could, maybe help out in establishing the dungeon. With the devices and all."

"You want me to do that?"

"Yes, Sir. I want to be surprised when I get back. I have a lot of faith in your ability. I have already selected a variety of equipment, but I would welcome your changes and additions. I have several sets of stocks, Sir, and a pillory. Among other devices."

"What's the difference between stocks and pillory?"

"Pillory doesn't constrain the feet with holes, but this one has fetters for the feet. They're quite medieval, Sir. Imposing structures."

"Terrific. It's a good neighborhood for riff-raff, too."

"Yes Sir. I would really like to try out a new piece, Sir. A more modern device, unless the stocks or pillory are installed. If you would accommodate me. Sir."

"You mean I'd need to line up volunteers? I'm not too crazy about managing a bunch of fuck-crazed strangers."

"You just bring them, Sir. No management."

The idea of Dina strapped helpless in some medieval device fucked by a bunch of maniacs appealed now that my brain had taken a hike. The erection that had sprung up with the vision of Dina and a herd of male goats returned with this new perturbation of the libidinous impulse, spectral emanation of our lady of lust, eigenfunctions and all…

"Tonight, then?"

"Tonight? I need to get the key, Sir. I'll call her. She can meet us there with extra keys. She handles all the intermediation for the business concerns, among other things. For a number of reasons."

"Mostly because of the nature of the business?"

"Mostly because I don't want to be a direct party to the more quotidian aspects of business, Sir."

"She knows about the business?"

"Yes Sir. She's involved, Sir. Besides being my business agent."

"I didn't realize you had an agent. Amazing, not even considering it—"

"Sir, can I suck your cock? It is wetting the front of your pants, Sir…"

"Do you want to?"

"Yes Sir!"

"I mean really want to?"

"Oh, yes Sir, I really do—"

"Then of course, no. You can't."

"Thank you, Sir."

Goldman had told me he'd wanted them to use the little book by Greenberg. I'd looked at it and noticed a dearth of general topology, not even the basics of separation axioms, nothing about Hausdorff or second countable. I brought that up and Goldman'd snorted that he'd develop what he needed as he needed it, but I protested this was an intro class for christsake. He assumed they'd had an intro, probably not along the lines of Willard, without a need for, say, metrizability maybe, though that was in Munkres, or Nagata-Smirnov-Bing, though that was in Munkres, too, as I recalled. When I'd heard they weren't going to concentrate on algebraic topology I'd bagged that class, having had a belly-full of general topology. However, shit like paracompactness was a way of life, and a hell of a lot of functional analysis rested on topology that wasn't found in Greenberg, like uniform spaces and uniformities which only got a mention in Munkres, come to think of it…

"Sir, are you listening?"

"What?"

"I said you'll meet her tonight. And I have money here for you, Sir," on her haunches holding out her fist, a wad of green enclosed. "You need to buy some presentable clothes. Not a suit, but some nice slacks and a few shirts. Knit polo shirts and silk-wool blend summer-weight slacks, Sir. Mayhap a summer-weight silk or silk-wool sport coat. And purchase some shoes, too. Some loafers with tassels."

"That's expensive clothes, Dina. And I don't wear shit like tassels. I hate fucking tassels."

"A new you, Sir. Two of you."

I grabbed the wad of money from her sweaty hand. "No fucking tassels."

"And maybe a few silk shirts, collarless, with natural nubs, Sir. Like in blue and gray. You'd be beautiful, Sir."

"I thought I already was."

"Of course you are, Sir. But this will make you devastating. I wish I had time to shop with you but I leave Thursday."

She went back to hands and knees and I wondered if Greenberg defined the compact-open topology, as important as it seemed to be for homotopy. He had to… And clearly paracompactness or some way to get partitions of unity, necessary as they were in the mechanics of manifolds…

Bent down on her elbows, tits flopped flat on the floor beneath her, looking up from her bowl, "I'm going with Mirabelle."

"That skinny transparent tattoo-job is going to do animal training?"

"No, Sir, a seminar and boot camp."

"Boot camp?"

"Yes Sir, all the rage now. This is a week's seminar and boot camp on inserting large objects into your anus and vagina, with some side sessions on deep-throating, mostly about relaxing your gag reflex to swallow—"

"I don't need to know the details."

"Sir, yes Sir! Anyway, Sir, they call it an anal invasion boot camp. Graduation is simultaneous double anal and double vaginal fisting. I set a record, Sir, by sucking two large cocks to simultaneous deep-throat orgasm while undergoing the double double-fistings."

"Okay, Dina—"

My erection had returned in spades, my pants now slathered with ooze.

"Let me finish, Sir. Special honors is to take a real baseball bat in your vagina or anus or both. I hold the record, Sir, with a giant Louisville slugger like Ted Kluszewski swung, both in my anus and my vagina."

"Who?"

"It's not important, Sir. A baseball player."

"Simultaneously?"

"Sir?"

"The bat trick."

"No, Sir, but I had considered it, Sir. I decided it might be too dangerous."

"Look, you don't need to provide—"

"Oh but I do. It is essential because we—"

"—are paired. Yeah, blah blah blah."

"It is true, Sir."

It cost me substantial effort to not whip out my erection and face fuck her, but I didn't want to give her the satisfaction.

"How much money is this?"

"It is twenty-five thousand dollars. I do not want you to scrimp on clothing, Sir. In fact, I'll send Utta with you. She's excellent—"

"Who's Utta?"

"My agent. She knows fine shops, Sir. I suggest Italian style. And a sport coat, Sir; please get a sport coat. No ties, but to wear with those shirts and slacks."

"Twenty-five thousand? Jesus you must be rolling in money. You don't mean twenty-five hundred?"

"No Sir. This trip to Europe will net me more than ten times what I just gave you. For a month's work, Sir. And tax free, too."

"Tax free?"

"Yes Sir. Like selling drugs. We have our ways. The only problem with so much money is not letting the IRS know how much you spend. But there is legitimate income, too, from Harry. That is reported and taxed and is always at least 200K, Sir."

"You're a rich bitch."

"Maybe compared to people you know. The people with whom I will consort in Europe are the truly filthy rich. Though not so endowed as you, Sir—"

"Or as Mule. Or that stallion you'll be getting it on with. That going to be a black stallion—"

"Maybe a stallion gangbang, Sir. For sure there is going to be a dog gangbang. The animal trainer owns two castles in Eastern Europe and several mansions, two of them here in the US. He is a financier and silent partner in this business venture. But mostly from old money. Landed royalty, Sir. Minor blood line. The family has been breeding big dogs for mating with human females for generations, Sir. Back into the foggy reaches of European history, Sir. For nobility."

"You going to fuck a real mule?"

"Yes, Sir. I plan to. One was promised. We're going to do a historically accurate short film based on the Tijuana club, the Blue Fox Café."

"I thought that was a myth."

"No Sir. It existed. We have done research and will recreate 1920s Tijuana. And also a film version of Apuleius' *The Golden Ass.*"

I didn't ask about this Apuleius. I had enough problem comprehending the rest of it. The scope seemed outrageous. It might not have been merely the scope, either. Upon awakening I'd realized, after spinning gears to jumpstart thinking, that what thought came, came devoid of mathematical content. Nothing except the haunting residue of knowing I'd discovered and lost something during Saturday's acid fetch fuck.

Not only mathematics came up missing. Empty-headed joyless organized abuse of Dina without the distraction of ideas beckoned. This must be how most humans operated, devoid of ideas. Kind of refreshing. The Marine senior NCOs had always accused me of thinking too damned much; they'd be proud of me today, wiped clean except for the haunting loss of I knew not what.

The topology people would mostly eschew the differentiable world where I planned to dwell. Not just continuity for me; I craved smoothness, even analyticity, and would likely spend my life within the smooth world except for the occasional necessary excursion without. Like into function spaces, a necessary evil. But still and all I'd not likely run across any dendritic continua, at least not that I would care a damn about…

"Sir, you seem distracted. I should call Utta. I'll leave you alone until later."

"You have a phone over there?"

"Yes Sir. You can use it if you want. Or better, we can get one for you in here."

"Not sure I want one here."

"No one has to know you have one, or the number. You can make it unlisted."

"Maybe if I decide to pursue this consulting gig I can set up a phone in your office. You going to have office help?"

"We are considering it, Sir. I'll be back later."

Since thinking was out of the question, I smoked a joint and read the drab report from Jeremy in more detail. I made some notes regarding the underlying assumptions, something I decided I would always be duty-bound to report if I continued this consulting stuff. I wrote out the linear least squares problem, a mathematical triviality disregarding any statistical interpretations which would be anyway impossible to apply meaningfully to this bullshit. The normal equations gave a simple matrix update, a lumped fit. But of course it would be more general to weight the measurements, and since there was no possibility of any sort of statistical weighting via a meaningful covariance, I realized it would be more useful to discount the past by de-weighting with some kind of exponential factor. Then it dawned on me how much more useful it would be if this shit could be computed recursively instead of redoing the fucking batch update each and every time.

I decided against going out and ate a couple cans of sardines with some crackers. I smoked more run-of-the-mill dope and drudged my way through this petty garbage. The idea that cost for the distillates would be a linear function across all ranges of demand amazed me. New plants on the high end, mothballed plants on the low end, were those not nonlinearities? Indeed, perhaps singularities or even discontinuities?

It was a simple matter to formulate an equivalent one-step update to the batch least squares. The only small hassle was the need for an inversion of a matrix sum, but a little thought coupled with formal manipulation of block matrices and I'd derived an equivalent sum that led to inverting matrices of lower dimension. Made it all feasible. I found the weighting easy to work into the formulation.

The final form came out as a recursive computation of a matrix multiplier based on what could be interpreted as an estimated covariance of the estimation error. I noticed right away the multiplier did not require the data, so would be independent of the data and pre-computable. I also noted that I could de-weight the whole mess even more efficiently by dropping the exponential weights and instead adding a positive semi-definite symmetric term to the "covariance" that would keep the matrix multiplier from getting smaller with time. Almost like an extra noise, though I wasn't thinking statistically. Just formally. One last idea smacked me in the face: I could put some dynamics into the estimated quantity and move it along a trajectory before the next estimate. That gave a differential equation and hence some kind of dynamic prediction difference. But of course, there was no way anyone was going to find a fucking trajectory for petrol prices, not righteously in any case.

After an hour I'd come up with a sketch of a report including a practical algorithm. Now all I needed was a way to write it up so these people could understand it and more importantly, compute it. Like doing a simple exercise for an elementary class taught by incompetents.

I rolled myself a spliff from the sins and laced it with tarry Nepalese hash streaked white with lines rumored to be opium. From the balcony mid-afternoon Bourbon Street mysteriously devoid of humans, be they tourists or gay cruisers, presaging the glaring-hot ghost-town afternoons to come when human life wilted on contact with pavement. Followed by glowing red-hot nights and costumed creatures running the pulsing cacophonous gauntlet, spectral emanations from overheated homoerotic nightmares and everlasting homogeneous stench of rotting garbage and rats and other vermin, human included, smelly cunt of a city where two Gudruns prowled alongside half-naked queers in redskin regalia wielding iron tomahawks smashing skulls slinking into the fiery backdrop of vesper amidst burly black-bearded men in pink tutus kissing on the mouth, fondling her fat tits, she and her double lying head to crotch legs wrapped around necks munching twin rugs and me sporting two dicks fucking both their asses Dina chanting in the background "double fuck them Sir" growing louder to "wake up Sir." Opening eyes to a gaunt raven-haired scarecrow leaning over me, a lavender bandana tied in front restraining a pair of sharp-nippled boobs could take your eye out were not the points a tad off-center and upraised. A spray of tawny forelock from high up fanned an extended forehead plunging mercilessly beyond brown brows, sharply penciled lines arched just above narrow almond eyes as black as her hair, the short lids inky smudges contrasted by fried egg whites. High cheekbones followed the long narrow nose bridge ending in simultaneously pinched and flared nostrils, fat lips with pronounced mid clefts painted blackish red, the lower incurvated as if to meet the upward jutting chin. An entire stretched-out face swooping from a hairline along what seemed the top of her head and veering inward at the eyes to a sharp finish like a flattened vee at the upturned chin. Tanned leathery-bronze and tall, ribs visible above a flat stomach on a long trunk sporting skeletal arms with huge man-hands; attached to the right wrist a giant watch with broad gold band. A symmetric bejeweled navel up high on her waist, more than halfway to the tits, pointed at my nose.

I sat up in bed and she backed away, maybe a six footer with legs slender to skinny stretching a long way to the floor, faded blue button-front cut-off Levis rolled up two turns at the bottom to her crotch. No hips, probably flat butt but couldn't ask her to turn around. Scantly fleshed calves gnarly with muscle but knees smoothly joining upper and lower without knobby protrusions. Meeting the floor, black high-top work boots with buckskin laces and a hint of white sock appearing along the upper edge.

"He's scary," she peeped in a little girl voice, high, thin and melodic with some lilting ictus I couldn't place.

"Where you from?" I asked, hoping I sounded as hostile as I felt.

"I'm Brazilian," she said.

"That's a Brazilian accent?"

"I have not accent. My mother she was American."

She edged backward toward the doorway where stood another woman, an inch or two shorter but still substantial.

Dina sat on her haunches beside the bed. "Allow me to introduce Utta," she said, at which the shorter one bowed from the waist, "and her lover Ricci."

"Ricci? Not Ricki? Ricci like the Italian geometer?"

"Ricci Tensão" the scraggy brunette sang, a pronounced nasal on the são like my mother had tried to teach me to say São Paulo. Her boobs, a pair of embedded bowling balls with sharp tips, protruded from the wiry body, obstructions to any possibility she might be able to lie flat on her face.

"I see why you choose him, Dina," the other said in a husky rasp imbued with flat tones, extended vowels and missing consonants reminiscent of old black and white spy movies. "He's got bad-temper dismeanor."

"And you? You're from maybe Hungary?"

She emitted a kind of burring wheeze that I took as an indication of mirth. "Heavens no, honey. I hail from Dallas," she said without a hint of Texas drawl.

I stared and she stared back out of grayish-blue eyes a shade I'd not previously encountered. Another pulled down face, not so extreme as Ricci's. A widely bulbous nose sprouted out of a tapered point ending a long narrow ramp starting between widely spaced eyes on the edge of her face: if they'd spread farther they'd have sat on the sides of her head like a bug. Ovular eyes of significantly smaller eccentricity than Ricci's, less pointed at the extrema of their semimajor axes.

Her muddy brown hair seemed almost blond beside Ricci's. From afar it was clear that Ricci had dyed the tuft that hung across her forehead; the uniform blackness of her hair also argued for a dye job though it didn't seem so inorganic as black dye. Even with her hair pulled back to form the single wide braid that came together from each of two equally divided masses on either side of a naked part, Utta's high forehead was nothing like the retreating hairline of Ricci. And Utta's hair was thicker than the ethereal stuff Ricci had on her head that was akin to the spun glass they called angel hair. I couldn't compare their ears since Ricci's were covered by the black threads that hung straight and limp down to her shoulders, but Utta had regular ears that laid close to her head. I doubted Ricci was jug-eared, given that her thin hair would not have kept clandestine a pair of protruding handles.

Side by side, arms around each other as if in defense against the nasty white man in the bed; the word blunt popped into my head. Utta seemed a slightly sawed off, disedged version of her lover in sepia tones. But more. In the faces. Both elongated, but Ricci's more angular. And the bodies. Utta plusher; more what I'd guess a cannibal'd find appetizing.

"We were going out to eat. But first I'll take you to where the car is parked and give you keys. Afterward to the office. Is that okay, Sir?"

Utta wore a one piece outfit, some kind of kid's romper thing with a short skirt like a playsuit. Metallic gold. Low cut with thin straps flaunting heavy tits that hung into their meat sacks with substantive cleavage, unlike the pair of hard rocks Ricci put forward. And legs. Shorter legs in proportion to what appeared a fleshier torso, though I'd have to see both naked to ascertain just how much fleshier. And hips, too. Probably a round ass. Meatier thighs, meatier calves, meatier ankles, same boney shoulders and scrawny arms. Not fat, just not nearly so meager. Her almost coppered olive flesh not so leathery; maybe even creamy, if olive can be creamy.

"Yeah, I'll definitely come along. I'm hungry. But let me shower first. I fell asleep and never showered."

"It's late, Sir. You slept the entire day away."

"I must have been tired. What time is it?" I didn't mention the opiated hash.

"Six," Utta grunted. "I can shower with you?"

"What's Ricci say?"

"Hey, it's not skin from my nose," Ricci said. "What's Dina's saying here?"

"Dina's got no saying in this."

"What's the upside?" Ricci continued.

Utta rolled her eyes and grabbed my arm. "Come on, get clean. Ricci's upside is my downside anyhows." The accent had to be German or Austro-Hungarian or one of those ethnically confused places in Eastern Europe, but the language contained odd elements out of place.

I held back.

"He's upside down," Dina laughed. "He doesn't want to go because he doesn't want you to see his leg."

"What's his leg?" Utta asked. "Wooded?"

"Yeah, what's with the leg. And those ugly fucking pants. Lot of upside without the shirt. Monster pects. Plentiful arms and bitchin shoulders. Downside with the baggy khakis. Twirpy legs?"

I looked down at Utta's feet, wondering how I'd missed the bright red children's shoes with a strap across her upper arch from beneath which peeked blue socks she'd rolled down below her ankles. I stared at the incongruous red plastic gunboats, the strap across the front with a square silver buckle, blunt toes, flat heels. A little girl's shoe to match Ricci's voice on Utta's big feet. I sprang an erection.

"Look," Ricci said. "Woody. Upside to the Mary Janes."

"Upside for real," Dina said. "He's growing an erection gaping at those downtown pumps."

I realized Dina had reason on her side regarding the leg. Scars were cool. Babes dug scars, did they not? At least to an extent. Like Prussian officers and their artfully placed dueling scars.

"Not pumps. But you liking them?" Utta asked, putting her hand out to touch my penile protrusion.

"Fuck yeah, but I ain't getting in the shower with you 'til you get out of those duds."

She pulled down the top of her cheerleader outfit or sunsuit or whatever the fuck it was she had on, letting it hang around her waist.

"You like these?" I assumed in reference to the knockers that tumbled from mid chest, widely spread fat tubes pushing nipples ahead of them parallel to the floor. The left one pulled to the side away from her body. The one on the right pointed forward out of the plane of her torso, the right areolae a puffy mass of pink studded with warty nipple buds, the left tiny and shyly retiring. Both nipples erect.

"You can have permission to touch them," she said.

"Upside down side," Dina barked. "I hope we disembarrassed you, Sir."

I grabbed a partial handful of the one with the enormous areole which felt like a knot on a mammary firm and pliable, stretched skin destined to collapse with time into a flattened web of red corrugation. I grabbed the other; smaller and flatter.

The substantial gap between her boobs didn't show bony sternum, her ribs not visible beneath the covering layer of padded flesh. Not a skinny bitch, but not fat either. Fleshy. I decided she'd be good to fuck.

As if she'd read my mind, she moved her hands from rubbing my bare chest to unbuckling my belt, opening my pants. She pulled them down and stepped back out of her romper suit. She pulled down my boxers and my dewy erection sprang up and out. She rubbed it, then climbed on it, still wearing the shoes, and I fucked her standing up. No one made a sound until I'd erupted inside her cunt and she stepped back.

"That leg has damage," Ricci said and Utta touched it.

"What happened here?" she asked.

"People tried to kill me. Worked out worse for them."

She caught the wad of ejaculate creeping down her thigh and licked it from her hand. "Now you have to pee, yes?" she asked, dropping to her knees. "Here" pointing and I pissed a hard stream into her open mouth. She didn't lose a drop.

"Wow. Eating fish, have we? Now shower," she said, leading me to the bathroom.

Working with mouth and hands, she erected me again and I fucked her from behind as she leaned into the shower's warm jet. It took some time and she stopped me. "Finish in the bed, okay?" and we did, she face down I mounted on top, Ricci and Dina encouraging our progress, Ricci skirling and clapping and dancing around the room in time to the rhythm of our copulation. This time Utta marked our progress soughing low trills until I hammered her and the trills morphed through guttural creaks to ululant scrunches. Afterward she lay discordantly wheezing. I would have suspected she lay dying of asphyxiation but neither Dina nor Ricci showed concern. After several minutes she rolled over, sat bolt upright and pointed to her mouth. I understood and relieved myself in the elongated gob, taking note of thin lips, unpainted and lusterless. She had a slight case of buck teeth. I wondered if perhaps her ankles were thick. I was not fond of chunky ankles. I didn't want to stare, but I hadn't had the chance to give her legs a good going over from a distance. Even at worst, she'd for sure be the best looking minx in the house right now.

We smoked dope and the girls snorted several lines of coke provided by Dina. She led us to a row of narrow free-standing garages where Elysian Fields, Frenchman, and Esplanade attempted to come together, near North Peters and the river. All different colors, they looked as if someone had stolen them from houses and plopped them down in an open field. It was close to the market area along the riverfront where produce was unloaded, a kind of open air market not far from Ruby Red's. Her Porsche sat in a blue wooden garage with gingerbread across the front and a white door that levered up manually. She gave me a set of keys and we set out for dinner, crossing into Marigny to eat at a little joint on Frenchman where they had jazz afterhours. I noticed Ramsey McLean and the Lifers played after eleven and thought I might return to catch a set. Jazz had been in short supply since they'd closed Lu and Charlie's and I didn't have the money or means to get up to Rosy's. Or hadn't until now, though it was all too formal for me, her place. And I wasn't a fan of the New Orleans music scene other than the few progressive jazz musicians, so stayed away from places like Tipitina's.

After we'd settled in and ordered, Utta asked me what I thought of Ricci.
"What do you mean?"
"You thinking Ricci sexy?"
"I don't know. I like brunettes, but she might be a tad skinny for me."
"What about breasts?"
"Look fake."
"What you say if I am telling you Ricci is neither man nor woman?"
"What, transsexual? Hermaphrodite?"
"No. Both. Neither."
"I guess Ricci would be a rare specimen."
"What specimen of?" Ricci asked.

"Hermaphrodite?"

"But species-wise?"

"Human, I assume."

"More or less," Utta chimed in. "Augmented."

"I am prototype. Genetic augmentation. Not clone. Genetically human. But no clone."

"What Ricci means to say," Dina said, "is that he or she was the result of an augmented fertilized macrogamete."

"I don't have any idea what the fuck you're talking about, Dina."

"He is what you call educated?" Utta asked.

"The ovum from which Ricci formed was genetically altered post fertilization, Sir. By direct intervention. But they didn't add information; they only modified it."

I guess I must have stared at her a bit longer than seemed appropriate.

"The zygote," Utta uttered. "Direct modifying of zygote."

I stared at Utta.

"Crude, dude," from Ricci. "Crude techniques. Upside's I'm here. Downside's not process with refine technologies."

"Well, anyway, Sir, now they have genetically altered gametes on both sides of the process, male and female. They contain more chromosomes, Sir. More information. Moreover, the entire process of forming a zygote is modified in the latest generations. One method has normal sexual union. Diploid chromosomes give up half each, like with regular humans. But instead of forty-six or whatever it is, they've got more. Like up to one-hundred-twenty, but more typically between sixty and ninety-five. That method is a bit more random. The gametes in the other method are both macro and contain only the requisite information, no randomness in the zygote. As if humans had twenty-three instead of forty-six chromosomes and they fused to make the requisite forty-six with only the two macrogametes."

"Yes," said Utta, "no spermatozoa needed to apply."

We sat in silence until they brought the food.

"You don't understand genetics, do you Sir?"

"Not much. A little. Never really interested me. But what you're telling me is someone somewhere is creating artificial humans, or rather, artificial creatures based on humans. Right?"

"Yes Sir—"

"I understand bullshit when I hear it."

261

"So far it all begins in vitro. In the test tube, Sir. You know? They create the cells artificially, from normal cells, but they are working to develop creatures that can procreate."

"I would guess the creatures with only half the chromosomes in their gametes are pretty weird looking?"

"They don't exist, Sir. There would be no point in any case, as those cells are totally artificial. The purpose is control, which is why those gametes are artificial if you will. You get exactly what you want. The other ones, they are less predictable in some aspects since some of the pairs are dissimilar and hence there is the element of chance. More or less, though that can be reduced to nearly zero probability, but cost goes up with the additional control."

"Some of the creatures frankly are weird; so much no one allows them free roaming. Too apparently different."

"This is apparently bullshit. You're putting me on, right?"

"You haven't touched your steak, Sir."

"We take him to club while you gone, s'okay Dina?"

"That is a good idea. Take him to the club."

"What club?" I asked through a mouthful of chewy beef.

"Over in Manchacs," Utta said.

"Manchac Pass, Sir. It connects Lake Maurepas with Lake Pontchartrain. There's a famous seafood restaurant nearby. Middendorf's."

I shoveled in more meat and kept chewing.

"You've never heard of it, have you Sir?"

I shook my head no and swallowed a partially masticated hunk of flesh I'd wearied of chewing.

"Chew more gentlemanly," Utta said. "You get indigestion."

"The area is mostly swamps, Sir. But the restaurant is good. And the club is mostly a secret. Invitation only."

"Initiations only, also," Utta piped in.

I pushed in another hunk of the stringy meat and set to work on it while Dina told me, "This has been a breakthrough kept very secret, Sir. In the jungles of northern Brazil, inland from Manaus. A consortium of European and American and Japanese and Brazilian scientists and genetic engineers, Sir. Paid for by the film industry. Everyone thinks they are part of the pharmaceutical industry."

"Hollywood?"

"No Sir. My industry."

"Porn."

"If that is word you want to call it. Concupiscent art-film better words."

"Sir, we needed new creatures for the screen. For our patrons. Beyond gay sex."

"Beyond animals?"

"That is not going to cease to exist, Sir, but it has its limitations. Besides the patrons, some of the more advanced thinkers like Harry have contributed a lot of money. And of course, those of us in the avant-garde—"

"The cutting edge?"

"The cutting edge — is good way to calling it—"

"Yes Sir, the cutting edge. You know, the idea of constructing athletes was an early impetus. Taller basketball players, more massive and faster football players, sharper eyed baseball players with superior hand-eye coordination, faster—"

"Not mentioning fight industries—"

"The soccer—" Ricci broke in.

"But it was recognized this was an impossibility without giving it all up, Sir. Those people must have histories. But sexual performers—"

"Sex athletes… enhanced lubricities… massive libidinal aggressions—"

"Sex workers?" I asked.

"If you will, Sir. Sexual athletes may be more appropriate, in our case."

"The downside in sexual work is to be known who you are. The upside is—"

"Being an unknown, Sir. There are hundreds of women with whom I have worked for years and yet I don't know their real names, where they come from, or anything about them except the right now. Everything you read is false—"

"Misinformation and misleadingness with intention," Utta said.

"Athletes can't get away with it. But it is in the nature of the sexual industry, Sir."

"So that's why Ricci over there has some sort of hard substance implanted in his/her/its chest?"

"Not," Ricci said. "I am early prototype. The mistake was in breasts. Not fully developed, so surgery required. Plastic surgery. But I am normal age. The new ones, some pass infancy and childhood fast, then slow down aging after."

"They grow these things in some kind of cabinets?"

"Oh, no Sir. They implant them in women. But the newer ones gestate within three months."

"This is bullshit. No one can believe this. These people are way ahead of everyone else, if such a thing is even possible."

"Later, if you want, eat Ricci's pussy while I suck the dick."

"Ricci's dick, she means, Sir. I can suck yours, if you'd permit me. Sir!"

I finished with the steak or whatever the fuck it was and ordered another beer and a shot of Jack Daniels. Dina changed the subject.

"Sir," she asked. "Are you aware of the strange ailments going on in the gay male community?"

"No."

"One of our neighbors is sick, Sir. There seem to be numerous afflictions of rare and odd opportunistic diseases. No one knows where they come from, but gay men are getting weird cancers—"

"Infestations. Such like Kaposi's sarcoma—"

"Downside uglity—"

"TB, too, and some rare pneumonias. Rare maladies most people never come down with. It seems their immune systems are deficient, Sir."

"One of our neighbors?"

"Yes Sir. The man they call Glendora, on the first floor at the street."

"Never met him."

"He's supposed to be quite wild, Sir."

"No one knows what it is?"

"No."

That sort of killed the rest of the conversation, but then we were about finished anyway. I poured down the beer, had one more shot and we left the place heading toward the edge of Marigny away from the Quarter, skirting Washington Square on Dauphine and crossing Elysian Fields to a rambling old clapboard structure that might have been a boarding house or brothel or something requiring sprawl in its better days. It stood past St. Roch before the dogleg at Franklin Street, two blocks lakeside of where Franklin met St. Roch at Chartres. It wasn't a neighborhood I frequented though I did venture in from time to time to buy drugs when Bob and Red were tapped out. It had a reputation of being dangerous and there was no other incentive than the drugs except once upon a time a waitress who'd worked in the Quarter that I'd boinked for a few months together with her harelipped girlfriend-roommate, before she moved back to New York to get married and her girlfriend-roommate swore off men.

Dina'd been right. Up front the office space seemed plenty officious. Two desks, phones, some filing cabinets. Frosted windows on one of which was painted in blocked black letters **QUASIHETEROPLOID & PSEUDOHETEROTHALLIC**

PRODUCTIONS Ltd. The same on a white wooden sign in green fancy Germanic letters overhanging the cracked sidewalk, oscillating infinitesimally in an imperceptible breeze.

The dungeon hid behind the offices surrounded by a hallway of walls in red flocked paper upon which hung photos of people I'd not seen before and diplomas evidencing mastery of unrecognizable acronyms or lettered in unrecognizable languages, perhaps Eastern European. It made me think of a moat with two doors in each of the four outer walls. We entered the nearest door and Utta flipped a switch hidden in a sliding panel. Light with no discernible source seeped in, dim and flickering as if torches in the walls displaced the blackness with a gloom of drifting shadows shaping a space cluttered with objects. The inner area appeared more spacious than the outer walls could have contained, floors and walls of dark and ancient wood.

"How do they do that with lights?" I asked.

"Yes, is magnificent, no? Flarelights," Utta said. She leaned back against the wall, tits jutting towards timbered ceilings sliding into obscurity somewhere far above us. "We considered industrial look, you know. Stainless steel walls, bright lighting. You know, kind of harsh lit."

"But how do they get this torch effect?"

"Is magic! Not real lights."

"Then that switch?" I moved towards where she'd slid open the compartment and she slapped my hand. I pushed her aside and felt for a sliding panel, a knob, something to indicate what I'd seen. Nothing.

"See?" she said. "Is unreal, this lights."

My eyes grew accustomed to the gloaming and I saw Dina gliding through the warehouse of scattered appliances, running her hands along them as she moved. She uttered what might have been joyous gurgles.

"They're up. The fixtures are up." She pointed back and forth at two medieval machinations of constraint.

The simpler one stood in the center of the room, a folding crossbeam erected on a solid shaft with base secured to the floor. The beam locked shut to form armholes on either side of a hole neck forcing the constrained to bend forward to crotch level. At the base pedestal two metal shackles attached by short chains ensured splayed legs.

The beauty of the other contraption took my breath. Orthogonal to the middle of the right wall as one entered, a stack of thick, flat, highly polished boards held together with a pair of posts of the same wood and the same finish, arm holes for the wrists, larger leg holes for the thighs, and a hole for the head.

Wrists and thighs restrained by rope straps, the head impossible to withdraw. The pieces evidently slipped in place around the victim who would be seated with ass protruding vulnerable from behind and face vulnerable from the front atop raised platforms. No support for the backside; it looked to be uncomfortable.

Dina strolled in rapt devotion, caressing the wooden monstrosities.

"Not all devices are here at this time," Utta said. "We await the boxes."

I pulled her aside and whispered. "Put up a short wall, thick material, and make a cubicle. A hole for the head and restraints on the inside for arms, flexible, like ropes or other devices of choice. She stands on the inside, head on the outside."

"Yes, this I like."

"It'd be great if we could do it with the outside wall of the building. Is there an alleyway behind here? Put her head through a wall, her ass outside and vulnerable on the sidewalk or alleyway?"

"Would be wonderful, but I think entails legal complications. But brilliant. You are evil man."

A light went on in her eyes. "Could put head outside for strangers to fuck the mouth, no?"

"That is an excellent idea. Yes. Perfect.

"Now here, in this spot, build a trap door into the floor. A box below with some space and breathing holes or something, but with an opening so her head's in the hole. Maybe some pads for knees, but she can get fucked for hours—" "Days—" "without coming up to see who it is doing her. Be terrific to put a hungry rat in with her face, wouldn't it?"

"Yes, a line of mans fucking her as the rat devours off her face. Wonderful, but again, with legal complicities."

"Yeah, that's too bad. But maybe have them build cages around the face area, with trap doors that slide open controlled from above. When she first goes in, the doors are open. Then they shut and in go the rats. She knows the rats can be released at a whim."

"Vicious, this idea. Yes. We do this one, too."

"Oh, and have a frame built that is like that small stock in front, constraining her head and arms. Another in back for the ankles, and a padded support for her torso so she can be gang raped. All her holes accessible."

"Such a thing we have already. Portable, easily assembled. On the pad have cutouts for breasts to hang. Can add weights, you know? Also it works for mans."

"Men?"

"Yes. The anus, the penis, all accessed."

"Not interested in men."

"For Ricci, it works too. His male part, her female part, their anus, mouth...

"Also, there is similar but kneeling, no support pad. Simpler. Adjustable restrainer, head, wrists, ankles, gigantous dildos to insert on stand, or machine—"

"Machine?"

"We have mechanical machines. For fucking. Two. Powerful. Adjustable for thrust and speed. Ricci is spastic while machine fucking his cunt when I sucking his cock."

Dina'd shucked her clothes and Ricci locked her in the crossbeam device. Her boobs hung free behind the wooden post, her bare feet in the chain restraints, skinny ass in the air.

"You want her now?"

"No. Who'll recruit a gang?"

"Ricci called friends. They bring people over from some bars."

Sure enough, people had begun to filter in the door. Utta removed her outfit and walked over to greet them. A motley of men, a few women, what might have been in-betweens, black, white, Hispanic, an Asian or two.

Ricci stood with naked crotch in Dina's face, shorts gathered around her boots. A narrow round ass, almost hipless but clearly a woman's ass, and with more substantial thighs from the back than I'd expected from the front or side view. Muscular. Not stringy muscle either, but quadriceps packed into a woman's thigh, even if meager.

I moved closer. Dina lapped a cunt sparse with solitary strands of long, straight, black pubescent hairs. Where there ought have been a clitoris, an erect penis. Not a small penile shaped clitoris. A substantial dork. Dina's technique evidenced practice: she plunged her tongue into the gash, dragged it up and onto the cock which disappeared into her face with Ricci's thrust and then with cock buried to the hilt, she frenetically licked the cunt, the entire progression harmonically entrained with monotonous disco music blaring from hidden speakers.

A man moved around behind Dina and guided his erect penis into one of her vulnerable orifices. I couldn't tell which he had chosen. A line formed behind him.

At the door stood naked Utta, arms akimbo, her back to me and her legs level and evenly spaced. Wide boxy hips melded into rounded thighs beefy on the outer edges, eccentrically arcing to knock-knees angular above chunky calves incurved between her legs and convex without and dropping into stumpy, thick ankles. The entire structure of legs bowed out ever so slightly from the squared-off groin where fluttered labial meat-curtains within a dense brownish thatch hung atop the interstitial archway.

Ricci removed its top and stood naked except for boots. Boobs exactly as I expected: hemispheres implanted on the chest tugged at the dermal layer, the edges of the embedded hemi-bowling-balls tracing a circular arc beside a bony sternum to far below bony shoulders, pulled taut by gravity's attempt to drag them from the parallel of the floor. Dual foreign protrusions fastened above ladder-like ribs surrounding flat, undefined abs. From my angle of view the pair might have been slightly off alignment, the left a skosh higher.

Utta came to stand beside me.

"Does Ricci ejaculate?"

"Of course. But pee is from other."

"She pees from the cunt and he ejaculates from the penis? Amazing."

"I told you, no? You want eat pussy while I suck cock?"

"I don't think I'm up to that tonight."

Ricci broke the repetitive rhythm and pressed its crotch into Dina's face, his dick in Dina's throat jerking spastically at the clitoral root, white froth bubbling over Dina's tongue buried in Ricci's cunt.

"He has orgasm in both places. Independent. Is amazing, no?"

"Looks like he'd impregnate herself like that."

A line had formed behind Ricci and the next man stepped up to Dina's mouth as two guys and a woman pulled Ricci aside.

"Now what?" I asked Utta.

"Those people wants to experience Ricci's sexual ambiguousness."

"What about restraining Ricci? Let's do that?"

"In storeroom" pointing at a door. "The thing you wanted before."

A room full of stuff. Utta dragged out hollow metal tubes attached to wooden restraints like stocks, one for head and wrists, the other for ankles, a padded cushion curved to accommodate hanging teats. We set it up facing an upright metal bar bolted to the floor. The apparatus assembled in a matter of minutes. She brought Ricci and its new friends over and Ricci stretched out on the pad. I restrained head and wrists in front and Utta the ankles behind. She tied a leather harness with a round gag onto Ricci's face, forcing open its mouth. Ricci drooled as Utta affixed a pair of wooden slabs to the pole and snugged Ricci's head between them, tightening it down to prevent movement.

"Strict head box," she said.

Rummaging in the utility room I found the simplest of constraints, a hinged pair of flat metal bars that closed in four fetters, two for wrists on the inside, two for ankles on the outside. A hook in the center allowed a person to be hung like fruit, arms and legs up, ass down. I picked up a metal gag that adjusted to force open the mouth, most likely a dental instrument. Beguiling how like a medieval torture kit was a dentist's tool cabinet. I discovered a plastic gag shaped in front like a short cup or funnel. Funnel cup? Endless naming conventions here. All the tools sported locking rings so I grabbed a handful of padlocks.

Orderly lines had given way to crowds surrounding Dina and Ricci. I went to Dina, excused myself as I pushed the man away who was fucking her face and inserted the funnel gag. I padlocked it in place, then padlocked all the restraints. I did the same for Ricci's paraphernalia.

Naked Utta, uninvolved in sexual games more significant than the occasional random grope, directed traffic in the office. It amazed me that this gaggle of well-behaved males had not yet gang-raped her.

I held up the metal contraption for her to see.

"Spanish stirrups," she said. "If you want I put on you."

"No, not me. I want to put them on you. But first I want you to put on your red shoes."

"You enamored the Mary Janes. Sexy for you. But who watches the crowd? Need someone in charge."

"I can be a traffic cop. And watch things. I'm probably tougher than you anyway. Besides, I'm sure there's some people here who want to get in you and I'm guessing you want to abet that."

"Of course is yes. If you watch out, then I take some fun. But only for short time. Okay?"

"Sure thing."

She put on the shiny red Buster Brown shoes and I closed the Spanish stirrups around her wrists and ankles, fixing her like a frog, orifices exposed and open for business. I padlocked the stirrups and encaged her neck within a stiff plastic brace scalloped for the chin, confining her face slightly upward in strict position. When I tried to implant the metal gag in her mouth she struggled, but bridled as she was it presented no problem to pinch her mouth open from the cheeks and slip it in. I ratcheted it as wide as it would go, enough to accommodate substantial pork. After padlocking it and the neck brace, I got some help from a couple burly men in carrying her to the desk fronting the office door. I think Utta had an inkling of my intentions, as I heard a garbled "Oo sumitch" or something similar, cut short by a slurp as an engorged and drooling male organ of copulation entered the stretched rictus. Another man inserted a cock in her asshole: gigged from both ends with a newcomer at work filling the free orifice.

I stepped outside the jammed building and took a deep breath, leaving the door wide open. A raucous assemblage of men and a handful of women clotted the sidewalk and spilled into the street. From within laughter, shrill, screechy, penetrating, drowning out the disco noise. Hoarse cries, strident hoots and caterwauls, grunts and groans, knocking, clanging, clapping, stridulation and ululation, creaking cricks, screeching thumping cheers and wild applause, grating crackles and explosions.

I lit a joint as I walked away, tossing the keys to the padlocks into a storm drain. It seemed I could almost make out furry creatures approaching from out of the mist that had settled over the block, but maybe it was only human reinforcements.

Ramsey McLean and his comrades had settled into a groove by the time I got back to Snug Harbor. I sat in back near the door and drank beer and bourbon. Ramsey played a bass solo that fit my mood, blue and hard. The whole set, in fact, came out blue and hard.

When they broke I went back to the apartment to catch some zees. I had to teach class the next afternoon and I'd decided to approach Goldman about that algebraic topology rundown. It was time to get serious about finishing up and splitting this scene. Continuity's not enough; got to be smooth.

PART II

THERE WERE CERTEINE NECROMANCERS
THAT OFFERED SACRIFICES AND BURNT
OFFERINGS UNTO HIM; AND TO CALL
HIM UP, THEY EXERCISED AN ART,
SAIENG THAT SALOMON THE WISE
MADE IT. WHICH IS FALSE: FOR IT WAS
RATHER CHAM, THE SONNE OF NOAH,
WHO AFTER THE FLOUD BEGAN FIRST
TO INVOCATE WICKED SPIRITS. HE
INVOCATED BILETH, AND MADE AN ART
IN HIS NAME, AND A BOOKE WHICH IS
KNOWNE TO MANIE MATHEMATICIANS.

— REGINALD SCOT, THE DISCOVERY OF
WITCHCRAFT

REALITY IS JUST ANOTHER MODEL.
— GRAFFITO, GIBSON HALL MEN'S ROOM,
TULANE, CA 1977

Chapter 20
Pseudocircularity

I bounced awake early. Someone chasing me or'd captured me, NVA or some other uniformed hermaphroditic phalanxes readying to perform abstruse sexual shenanigans on my asshole or mouth or some new orifice they planned to excavate with an explosive device. No panic, no erection. Maybe angst. Maybe the anti-calming cello lines atonally nagging the cracks of what sleep came. Certainly a nagging sense of urgency to get my shit together and get my ass out of this place before something real happened.

After breakfasting on marijuana, coffee, juice and oatmeal I wished was macaroni and cheese from the box, I flew uptown on the Freret Street bus.

First thing I dropped in on Goldman and asked for a rundown on algebraic topology.

"Sure. But you know I'm more topological groups. Actions. I take homology as basic more than cohomology for what I do. Momus would make greater use of de Rham theory. But it's homotopy where you start in algebraic topology."

He didn't mention his counterpart in differential topology for whom I assumed cohomology would be more the forte. But maybe not. I was clueless regarding the innards of differential topology, though I had glanced at the cover of Guillemin and Pollack, had promised to read the terse sixty-odd pages of Milnor's little blue book and knew Sard's theorem. But his cohort's stance on pacifism and the evils of the Vietnam conflict and its participants, at least those of US origin, sort of put us at opposite poles and he wouldn't give me the time of day. Not that I'd asked for it.

"My advisor introduced me to a physics guy over at Loyola who's hip to index theory for operators and cohomology and bundles and all that stuff."

"Didn't know they had good physics people over there."

"Evidently he's known for some work with relativity. An alternative theory that people take seriously. I need to spend a few hours with him in any case. He said something when we met about physics being classification of fiber bundles or vector bundles or some damned thing I didn't understand."

"Me either. At least not for physics. But I don't know anything about physics. I work in low dimensional topology. Dimensions three and four. That's where the good stuff is. Poincare conjecture's still open there."

"Which is?"

275

"That a simply connected homology sphere is a topological sphere."

"Doesn't do much for me. What I need's the tools. Most of the spaces I deal with are smooth, but not always."

"What are you working on?"

"I'm running Brownian motions on manifolds. Smooth manifolds. There's a relationship to the geometry through the sample paths, more or less. Or the probability speaks about the geometry. I see it might have some use in engineering problems with nonlinearity and noise."

"I work with group actions. I don't know much probability and nothing about Brownian motion."

"Well, differential geometry's the key to nonlinearity, that's for sure. But I don't see this'll have direct application. A wedge is what I'm hoping for."

"Looking for something that might make money? I guess there are ways to do it with math, but none that I can figure out."

"Or that interest you. It's good to have something to sell besides writing papers in academia."

"There are plenty of tools in algebraic topology. Don't know how useful they are in the outside world. A lot of it is not all that hard, but the machinery is a formidable mask to what are at heart direct methods. There are a lot of homology theories. You have to see through it. I try to get to the geometry, skirt the machinery. I use homology as a basic tool, but there are things that tie it to the other structures. You need to understand homotopy types and the ties to homology. You can't get it all but you can get a lot of it. You definitely need the Mayer-Vietoris sequence."

"I guess you're working on classifying stuff."

"There's a lot to do there. Plenty of open questions. We still haven't classified simply connected smooth manifolds up to diffeomorphism. Invariants are the key. Surgery and plumbing, attaching handles. It looks like dimension four will be interesting. It's big enough for wild structures, but too cramped to use a lot of the standard tools from higher dimensions. We have to invent new approaches. I suspect it's just big enough to have things happen that could be undone in higher dimensions, but not there. That's going to be where the action is."

It didn't pique my interest. The idea that dimension four could be special did, but not the approach. Like he'd said, it was big enough to counter intuition, small enough to obstruct shit that might be undone in higher dimensions.

To break the ensuing silence, I said "I'm guessing it's pretty tough sledding."

"It keeps me employed."

Dispersing from his little office, wafting along the sepulchral corridor like echoes in a dark wooden coffin, I mused you could drive a truck down the hallway. I must have spoken aloud because Goldman murmured something about reminder of a forgotten time. Ghosts? I asked, or a hangover?

We padded softly searching for an empty classroom. The conference room would be too distractible. There weren't many classrooms up here, but most of the faculty found it uncivilized to begin before lunch. There existed two empties. We chose the smaller for its clean blackboard.

He stretched his short legs in front of him and perched atop a one-piece student writing desk at the front of the room. He was young enough to be a grad student, even given his developing bald spot; black jeans and tee-shirt added to the look.

"Just to be sure where you are, how about computing the fundamental group of the circle."

I stepped to the board. "It's been a while since I thought about it, but as I recall it's pretty much follow your nose."

I wanted to hit the foundational steps in enough detail to show what I knew, emphasizing liftings and covering spaces without beating it to death. I started with e^{it} from the reals t to the circle as covering map and then considered closed loops on the circle, lifting them to the real line by unraveling so they stretched out as many times as they went around, negative or positive for the direction. That gave me the universal covering space and a group of equivalence classes isomorphic to the integers. I stood back from the board.

"That's all you're going to do? You're assuming the classes form a group. In fact, you skipped the definition of the equivalence relation. You proved an isomorphism without really saying what was the group product for the loops."

"Oops, seemed obvious." I backtracked to show how the loops formed a group by joining them end to end. I realized once there that not only had I skipped defining the equivalence relation, I hadn't even defined homotopy. I backtracked a little more and rectified it all. Then I got into the universal covering space stuff with the real line in more detail.

"You're not much for detail, are you?"

"I think I cover it," I said. "I just lay it out as it comes to me. Usually I have to go back and fill in."

"Your students must hate you."

"I'm used to people hating me."

I stepped back to admire the drawings and symbols scrawled on the board harum-scarum. Light seeping through the floor-to-ceiling window illumed a hanging cloud of chalk residue from my attack.

"What do you know about the higher homotopy groups?" he asked.

"I assume they'd be maps from spheres."

"That is the obvious thing. There are a few other approaches. All equivalent; each with its own advantage."

"It's easy to see an iterative approach that makes it a group. Use the n-cube and identify the boundary. That's a topological sphere. Map the boundary point to a fixed point in the image. Put the compact-open topology on the space of maps. Stitch the maps together to form a product along one of the coordinates."

"How would you make it iterative?"

"Obviously it's…" and I wrote on the board:

$$X^{I^n} = \left(X^{I^{n-1}}\right)^I$$

"That's not completely obvious."

"Well, the intervals are locally compact Hausdorff…so they're homeomorphic as product spaces." I wrote

$$X^{A \times B} = \left(X^A\right)^B$$

and said, "I seem to recall that for A and B locally compact Hausdorff and X arbitrary Hausdorff, these are homeomorphic."

"That isn't so obvious either."

I gave it a minute's thought and saw that for a map f from $A \times B$ to X, it hinged on the map from B taking b to the map $f_b(a) = f(a,b)$. That was what the two sides of the equality had buried in conceptual content. If f were continuous then each f_b was continuous. But that would not be sufficient…it dawned on me the other necessary condition would be continuity of the function $B \to X^A$ taking b to f_b. Clearly that was necessary. Together they had to be sufficient.

I think I said this before I gave a quick proof, then started to apply the little lemma to get the homeomorphism.

He stopped me. "Okay, you get it. There is another way, using reduced suspension based on the smash product."

I stepped back. All I'd written on the board was

$$b \mapsto f_b$$

"Not familiar with that," I said.

"Given two spaces, pick a point of each, identify those points and take a disjoint union. Then identify that space in the product space by modding out the disjoint union."

"Yep, that smashes them together pretty good," I said, seeing the inner circle around the hole and an orthogonal cross section through the flesh of a donut meeting at a single point mashed to that point. "You won't need to worry about where the hole in the donut goes when you eat it, will you?"

"I hadn't thought of it in terms of donuts."

"Well, I thought of the torus as the product of two circles—"

"I see that. Striking image, though you are looking at the donut in four dimensions. Anyway, you can get the (n+m)-sphere by smashing together an n-sphere and an m-sphere—"

"So you get the n+1 sphere iteratively by smashing in a one sphere. I see."

"There is yet another way—"

"Sure, look at all the loops in the space of maps from the n-sphere."

"We call that loop space and the $(n+1)^{st}$ homotopy group becomes—"

"The fundamental group of the nth."

"Right."

"You could even go down one step and look at path components in path space to get the fundamental group."

"Not a popular way to look at it. How about the fundamental group of the torus?"

"Well, cover it with the plane modulo the product of the integers…"

"You like to jump to configurations out of general topology. There is an easier way: the product of covering maps is a covering map."

"The plane. Makes sense. I think of unraveling flows. Or geodesics, images of the exponential map from the tangent space; the approach to Lie theory via Oberst still makes me dizzy."

"Too formal."

"Not a whit of geometry. Anyway, I saw loops unraveling along the squares in arbitrary directions."

"The fundamental group is the direct sum of integers with integers… What about the twisted cousin of the torus?"

I didn't follow him and said nothing. He was not at that moment in character, at least as I understood his character.

"You know, twist the torus to disorient it on gluing."

"That's a weird way to put it. The Klein bottle. Not sure. I need to think about it."

"Was trying to think like a point set topologist. The figure eight might be a better way to start. What about that? It gives me an opportunity to show you how I approach this. At least a hint of my approach. I look at group actions, like I said. In fact, we might find some time to talk about the action of the fundamental group. But let's go a bit farther in this direction. Not too far off the beaten path. Then I get you something to think about for the next step, which will be homology."

"I know I got to get this stuff down. I don't want to dwell on this too long, though—"

"At the rate you're picking it up, won't be but three or so sessions and we'll have sketched the edges of a good semester's course in algebraic topology. But of course, we're only waving our hands here."

"So far I haven't seen anything too deep—"

"You are picking it up pretty quick. So anyway, look at this:" he drew on the board

"and tell me what you think the homotopy group will be."

The union of two circles joined at single point. Running each circle independently was one thing, but the point where they connected was singular. Different tangents. I considered covering it with the real line with repetitions of one circle, attaching circles tangent to the axis at each integer point along the axis. Easy to see a covering: the axis covers the right loop, say, like the real line with the circle, and the circles cover the left. The singular point would be the integers along the axis. I made a move towards the board to draw it, but realized that it would not distinguish a loop around the right followed by a loop around the left from a loop around the left followed by a loop around the right. Clearly they had to be in distinct homotopy classes.

"Well, you got that singularity there in the middle. By the way, I'd expect a topologist to do better with drawing."

"I'm not one of the colored chalk types. You have to use your imagination."

"At the singularity you got two separate tangents. Just give me a minute to get the right covering space."

The modification in original realization came immediately. The x- and y-axes had to be the same to get the two loops to unroll in different places. So on each axis you'd attach a circle at every integer point which would identify with the common point on the eight. Except of course no circle at the origin. That would do it. Start at the origin and go along the x-axis for the right loop and then hit a circle for looping around the left; do the same for the other loop with the y-axis. Clearly a covering map, since every point would have a neighborhood with fiber a disjoint union of open sets homeomorphic to the neighborhood they covered. Like a stack of pancakes.

"I'm thinking you've got a generator for each circle. For covering space I'd take the plane with circles along the x- and y-axis at every integer point. The covering would take, say, the x-circles to the one on the right, call it A, and the y-circles to the other, B say. The integer maps to the singular point. If gamma-one is a loop around A and gamma-two a loop around B then those are classes in the fundamental group. Each of those circles spawns an infinite cyclic group. I mean, I must be using something I don't know here, formally, but the damned thing is a one-point union via a single identified point of two circles. So basically you've got arbitrary elements g-one, say, and g-two, which are the classes of the two loops. Now going around the loops a number of times is going to give a concatenation in the free group on these two letters to different powers. Words. They're words."

"So can you prove it isn't Abelian without resorting to a result from algebra?"

"I recall that the algebra is by embedding some normal subgroup or some such thing that is generated by a countable number of symbols, which implies it can't be free Abelian by some theorem I could probably drag out of my memory. We might have done it in multilinear algebra, but I think it was in one of the algebra classes I took from Bolyai."

"Well, you can prove it directly and then actually give a topological proof of the algebraic—"

"I see it, I think. The elements that correspond to n trips in one circle, then one in the other and then n again in the first circle but in the opposite direction give those elements in the covering space. I think that's right."

"Sounds right. But still—"

"Well, take the path in the covering space s cross the point zero, call it f tilde or something; call the path zero cross s, g tilde. Project those down to the figure eight and you get around each circle respectively starting and ending at the singular point. Then multiplying f times g and g times f as loops, they aren't homotopic; lift them and you can see they end up unraveling at different places in the cover. Done."

"There are simpler coverings. More geometric. But I think we might talk about discontinuous group actions and deck transformations. We still have two important theorems to get to. And one nontrivial computation."

"The higher homotopy groups are Abelian, I remember that."

"You see why?"

"Not really. It isn't obvious; at least, not to me."

"Remember your observation that the fundamental group of a space at a point x-naught is the set of path components of the space of loops at x-naught. It follows from a similar proposition to what you proved, but involving the evaluation map on paths in X cross X."

"Same thing."

"Exactly. You can use that. It's essentially a result for topological groups. If you've got loops f and g in a loop space at a constant map C, then given two loops f and g, define their product in the obvious way."

He wrote $fg \sim f_*g \sim gf$ rel $(0,1)$. I drew a square and divided it into four squares and took the edges to be f_*g, c, f, g, c_*g and f_*c to follow the products. I imagined the same drawing for g_*f.

"So then you get it for all the higher homotopy groups by induction," I said.

"Right," he said. "You can actually do this with something called H-spaces and H-groups and even H-cogroups."

"What's H for?"

"Hopf. He studied homotopy in the thirties and forties.

"And you realize that in the lifting result you stated it is essential to have locally arcwise connected along with arcwise connected."

"I bet the topologist's sine curve gets in there somehow."

"Yeah. Pseudocircle is counterexample."

I saw it as he said it. An almost circle not quite ever ending in $\sin(1/x)$ like the head of a snake almost ingesting its tail. Never quite closing the deal, it wiggles infinitesimally close in a limit.

"I won't forget that one," I said. "Easy example to remember."

He went to the board and described an action of the fundamental group on a fiber above a covering space. He proved some stuff using this to get results on the number of sheets of a covering map, then went through deck transformations, which didn't seem a big deal. But he shot off into something about properly discontinuous actions and emerged with a bunch of results, including a calculation of the fundamental group of the Klein bottle. Another non-Abelian group, as it turned out.

"We could get some classification stuff for covering spaces from here," he said, "but I have a feeling you are not too interested."

"Not really. I'm not unless it adds a lot to this."

"You can pick it up later, as necessary."

"I did like the result about the equivalence relation induced by the group. Getting that covering map and showing the deck transformation group is the original group is nifty."

"We can just look at the van Kampen theorem. That's important. And I want to compute a homotopy group that is interesting. Another piece of work from Hopf."

He used free groups to define something he called an amalgamation, a kind of free product modulo a normal subgroup. Then he wrote down a relationship between the amalgamated product of the fundamental groups of two open spaces with their intersection and the fundamental group of the space which was their union. In particular, if the intersection were non-empty with a trivial fundamental group, that is simply connected, the homotopy group of the space was the free product of their homotopy groups. I saw right away how to get the group of the figure eight.

"I see how to get the Klein bottle from that. Take out a disk from the center of the square" and I drew a representation of a square, not too badly, either, and put arrows along the parallel sides moving up the board in the same direction, towards the ceiling, while drawing arrows in opposite directions on the upper and lower sides. I drew a circular hole in the middle. "You pull the circle to the boundaries and that is a figure eight—"

"Okay, you see it. You get the two generators and then…"

He gave me an odd look. Not something I coherently saw. More a glancing blow, a kind of knowingness that passed between us. A kind of realization of something; not something one could put one's finger on. Passed in a flash.

"Let's do the Hopf map and get the third homotopy group of the sphere."

"Two-sphere?"

"Think of the three sphere as embedded in the cross-product of the complex plane with itself. The map sending the pair of complex numbers u and v to u divided by v maps to the one-point compactification of the complex plane, viewed as the two-sphere."

"Okay. I see that. Meromorphic function on the Riemann sphere built with the inverse of stereographic projection onto the extended complex plane."

"That's the Hopf map. It's a generator of the third homotopy group of the two-sphere. So the group is not trivial. In fact, it's isomorphic to the integers. We can talk later about some of the stuff he did because it ties up with cohomology and degree. You might try to visualize that map if you can. Interesting."

I filed it. I'd already begun preparing for my stat class and had to end this soon. But I guessed the fibers of the Hopf map had some intricate character, like maybe circle bundles or something like that. Probably twisted. That would be a nice way to look at S^3. Topologists could get off on that.

"You know what a graded group is?"

"Yeah, I recall we did that kind of thing with modules and tensor products. For groups it'd just be a collection indexed by the integers. No need for tensor products."

"So then a chain complex is one of those with a nilpotent homomorphism between C sub i and C sub i plus one." He wrote

$$\partial : C_i \to C_{i-1} \qquad \partial^2 = 0$$
$$\partial^2 : C_i \to C_{i-2}$$

and said, "Call it a boundary operator."

I knew what he meant while recognizing the ambiguity of what he wrote. Of course, we'd learned to understand what was left out by a sort of convention. It meant not adding more subscript hassles, which would make it unambiguous but tedious. Since the composition of the boundary map with itself was zero, the null space or kernel as it was more often called, the subgroup of elements sent to zero by the boundary map, contained the image of the boundary map.

I did wonder why he'd written the lower line. He'd done it as an afterthought, a measurable pause after staring at the board, as if it were necessary instead of redundant. Perhaps atonement for not being tediously clear with subscripts in the first line.

"Call the elements of C, chains; the elements of the image of the boundary map, boundaries; the elements in the kernel of the boundary map, cycles."

The pre-images of the Hopf map were unit circles. It was obvious when you considered a point like the origin in the complex plane, the south pole of the Riemann sphere. I always had to rebuild the homeomorphism of the sphere minus the north pole with the complex plane by poking an extensile shaft through the hole in the north pole and running it through the sphere until it hit the plane. Add a point at infinity or the north pole, depending on your viewpoint, to get the one point compactification. Anyway, I saw it right away visualizing the 3-sphere as a subset of the product of the complex plane with itself. The pre-image of the Hopf map at the south pole was the pair zero and $|z|=1$, $(0, |z|=1)$. A circle attached to zero on the left. At the north pole reverse the order, but along the way, say via the complex number one on the equator as itself in the plane, you got (u,u) on the 3-sphere as pre-image. Down the other side and you hit -1, which was (u,-u) on the 3-sphere. So connecting pre-images above the 2-sphere where they came from as fibers, a bundle of some kind, you would have a torus wrapped around the 2-sphere with a twist in it. A kind of twisted slinky with infinitesimally close rings.

"I see the Hopf thing as a bundle of some sort, with circles as fibers."

"Yeah, the Hopf map is a projection in that bundle. The Hopf fibration. You get the action of the circle group."

"Tori along the great circles." I saw an infinity of slinkies smoothly twisting along every potential direction around the great circles, all adjoining in perfect harmony, an amazing sight. Meshing exactly. Or was that right?

"Think about the inverse images of circles of latitude."

"You mean the circles parallel to the equator?"

"Right, not great circles except the equator. It is more interesting still if you can visualize a stereographic projection of the three-sphere onto R-three. You will see some interesting tori."

I needed a lift before teaching. He needed to speed up the pace.

He returned to where he'd been. "If there are a couple of chain complexes then define a chain map to be a homomorphism between elements of the complexes with the same indices that commutes with the boundary operator."

He wrote

$$f : A_* \to B_*$$

and said "So you get a collection of homomorphisms" and wrote

$$f : A_i \to B_i$$

"so that"

$$f\partial = \partial f$$

"and you get a ladder of commuting homorphisms."

He wrote

$$
\begin{array}{ccccc}
\cdots \longrightarrow & A_{i+1} & \xrightarrow{\ \partial\ } & A_i & \xrightarrow{\ \partial\ } & A_{i-1} & \longrightarrow \cdots \\
 & \downarrow f & & \downarrow f & & \downarrow f \\
\cdots \longrightarrow & B_{i+1} & \xrightarrow{\ \partial\ } & B_i & \xrightarrow{\ \partial\ } & B_{i-1} & \longrightarrow \cdots
\end{array}
$$

and stepped back from the board.

He could have saved a lot of writing with the last bit, just saying that the squares commuted or it didn't matter which way you went around the squares, the same thing.

"Okay," I said. "And you are going to do something with an exact sequence of chain complexes—"

"You've seen some homological algebra, I guess—"

"Diagram chasing can be fun, the first couple times you do it."

"After that, it is mostly unnecessary. Anyway, we can define a homology on a chain complex..."

$$H_i(C_*) = \frac{\ker \partial : C_i \to C_{i-1}}{\operatorname{im} \partial : C_{i+1} \to C_i}$$

Of course, you could see that coming. Cycles modulo boundaries. I'd already noted that nilpotency of the boundary map meant the image in C_i was a subgroup of the kernel in C_i; a normal subgroup, so you could mod it out of the image. The natural thing for any mathematician to do... And this was where you paid for not using more indices...

"...and then if we assume there is a chain map," he continued, "f, say, we get a homorphism f-star of the graded groups," writing
...Certainly f-star defined in the natural way: f-star of an equivalence class would have to be the equivalence class of f-star on any member of the class. Commuting with the boundary map sees to that: all the images go where they ought to.

$$f : A_* \to B_* \qquad\qquad f_* : H_*(A_*) \to H_*(B_*)$$

$$f_*[a] = [f(a)]$$

$$(f \circ g)_* = f_* \circ g_*$$

"pretty much what you'd expect from the algebra."

"And the star of the identity is the identity of the homology groups. This must be leading to something. Probably something to do with exact sequences of chain complexes."

"Right. We're going to build a long exact sequence out of a short one." He wrote

$$0 \longrightarrow A_* \overset{i}{\longrightarrow} B_* \overset{j}{\longrightarrow} C_* \longrightarrow 0$$

and we both stared at it.

"You get this," I said, writing

$$
\begin{array}{ccccccccc}
 & \vdots & & \vdots & & \vdots & & \\
0 \longrightarrow & A_{p+1} & \overset{i}{\longrightarrow} & B_{p+1} & \overset{j}{\longrightarrow} & C_{p+1} & \longrightarrow & 0 \\
 & \downarrow \partial & & \downarrow \partial & & \downarrow \partial & & \\
0 \longrightarrow & A_p & \overset{i}{\longrightarrow} & B_p & \overset{j}{\longrightarrow} & C_p & \longrightarrow & 0 \\
 & \downarrow \partial & & \downarrow \partial & & \downarrow \partial & & \\
0 \longrightarrow & A_{p-1} & \overset{i}{\longrightarrow} & B_{p-1} & \overset{j}{\longrightarrow} & C_{p-1} & \longrightarrow & 0 \\
 & \vdots & & \vdots & & \vdots & & \\
\end{array}
$$

the entire tedious expression in all its gory detail. "And you're going to get a long exact sequence of homology groups."

"Exactly. Figure out how to do that. You'll need to find a connecting homomorphism as you go down one step from C p to A p minus one."

It was already clear. Just follow your nose and pull back, push forward starting from C_p. "Have time tomorrow?"

"There's an algebra seminar that relates to my work, but it's later in the afternoon."

"Meet you around the same time then?"

"Sure. We'll do homology. We'll get the Mayer-Vietoris theorem and talk about homotopy equivalence."

I erased the board and we dispersed whence we'd come, in the direction of his office beyond the graduate student carrels, I continuing on down the steps to smoke a hash laden cigarette on the semicircular patch of brownish grass.

For stat class I "derived" the Neyman-Pearson lemma using a calculus of variations argument I had seen some years earlier from a professor at UMKC, a stat guy from Harvard who did everything the hard way. I was pretty certain the derivation was wrong; the one step that became a leap of faith I passed by waving my hands without seeing a rational argument or lurking construct for it. If I had been more interested, I might have attempted to rectify this, but I'd seen correct proofs of the result. No one in class had the vaguest idea what the fuck I was doing and I was anyway only trying to see if I could extend it to manifolds using differential forms. Maybe curvature got in there somehow. Probably already been done somewhere anyway. Since none of the students understood differential forms and I couldn't even assume they'd studied calculus, I had to make it far more obscure than it ought to have been, correct or otherwise.

The dwindled class restrained itself from bursting out of the room until the bell rang, at which they leapt to their feet without waiting for me to finish. Miss Cone gave me an angry look and beat it out of there. The cheerleader appeared dumbfounded, saying "I had no idea what you were talking about today. None at all."

"Don't worry about it," I answered, knowing that would make her worry more than ever. " I'll show you how to use the result in hypothesis testing next time."

She torqued her face into what might have been a smile and disappeared.

Avoiding human contact for the next hour, I bagged Frenchie's seminar and wandered Audubon Park smoking homemade hashish-tobacco cigarettes. I'd figured out the right blend of perique to Virginia burley to account for the burn rate of any type of hashish. A rough cut improved the burn, so I looked for it, avoiding shag which burned too fast. I'd been adding Latakia for depth and pungency. This batch was heavy on a hand-pressed Lebanese red with only a tiny bit of fragmented tar-like Nepalese, a slow burner, and some Afghan, another slow burner but not so slow as the Nepalese. Luck had also sent me a decent quantity of hash oil which I liberally dripped on each cigarette, though it did stagger the burn along the circumference of the tip.

It dawned on me that if boundaries and cycles were taken geometrically, homology would measure mismatch between some kind of objects and their boundaries one dimension higher. Two of the objects would be equivalent if their difference formed a boundary of an object a dimension higher. I thought I was being inventive as hell until I admitted I'd seen the homology groups of singular simplexes defined in that brief exposure to algebraic topology I'd sat in on my first year.

Anyway, the maps between homology groups of different spaces were the obvious thing, the only work to show they were well defined and exact. Amounted to pulling some stuff back or pushing it forward, using that the maps commuted with the boundary operator. Because a chain map commuted with the boundary operator, you could go around the squares two ways: the image of the class of an element c under f_*, which was $f_*(c+\partial A_n)$, would be the element $f(c)+\partial(B_n)$, making sense and preserving the algebraic structure of the equivalence classes. The chain map preserved equivalence classes and so induced a meaningful function on the homology group, a homorphism.

I made it to my advisor's class before he started. He nodded hello but didn't pay me much attention afterward. Maybe he was miffed about something. I didn't pay much attention to what he was doing, either, but he'd distributed a batch of xeroxed hand-written notes. Much of it corrected what he'd done during some prior classes. I realized I needed to go over the notes he'd handed out, which might not have been necessary had I kept up in class.

In my carrel I thought through the long exact sequence of homology groups from the chain complexes. The diagram I'd written came back

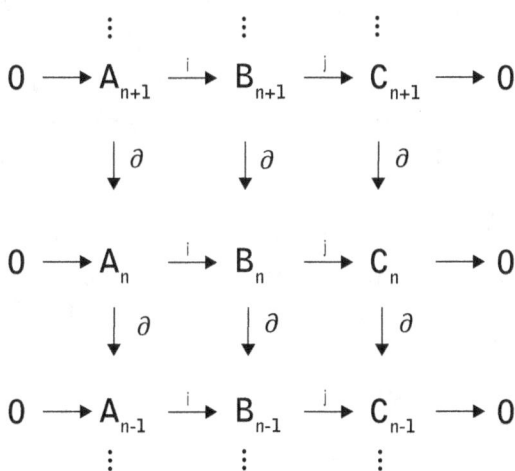

and I beheld a cycle z in C_n; that is, a z belonging to the kernel of the boundary map from C_n to C_{n-1}, so $\partial z = 0$. The map j from B_n to C_n was onto since its image was the kernel of the zero map, which was all of C_n. That meant this z came from some element b in B_n via the map j. So $j(b)=z$ and by the commutativity of ∂ and j, $j(\partial b)=\partial jb=\partial z=0$. Since by exactness the image of i was the kernel of j, ∂b would have to be in the image of $i(A_{n-1})$. So there had to be an element a in A_{n-1} with $i(a)=\partial b$ and then $i(\partial a)=\partial i(a)=\partial\partial b=0$. By exactness the map i was one-to-one, its kernel being the image of the zero map. So $\partial a=0$, putting a in the n-1-cycles of A and we had our map from the n-cycles of C to the n-1 cycles of A. You had to start with a cycle c in C_n and go back to c's origin as a pre-image of c under j in B_n, then down via ∂ to B_{n-1}, then back via $i$inverse to a chain in A_{n-1}. The rest had to be trivial. I'd finish it tomorrow.

I split to the gym and worked out with a vengeance, one of those encounters when you are master of the inert mass you push around. I didn't fatigue, driven by adrenaline or something.

The rest of the trivial details wormed their way into my brain between reps, almost unconsciously so that when I left I knew the following: The map I'd come up with would have to take homologous n-cycles in C, that is cycles y and z in C_n with the property that the difference between y and z, $y-z$, was the image of some c in C_{n+1} under the boundary map, to homologous cycles in A_{n-1}. That'd put them in the same equivalence class, differing by a boundary: $y-z=\partial c$. Since j was onto C, there had to be elements by and bz in B_n so that $y=j(by)$ and $z=j(bz)$. We'd need chains aby and abz in A_{n-1} that would map to ∂by and ∂bz in B_{n-1}, but since y and z were cycles, the boundary operator ∂ killed them, so by commutativity of the boundary operator with j, they were in j's kernel, the image of i. So it sufficed to prove that the homology class of aby and abz were the same.

Riding the streetcar into the sunset and staring at nothing out the window of the swaying behemoth, I finalized the proof that the construction worked. There had to be some element b in B_{n+1} that mapped under j to the element c in C_{n+1} with the property that the boundary operator took it to the difference $y-z$ in C_n. So $j(\partial b)=\partial j(b)=\partial c=y-z$. Then $by-bz-\partial b$ would be in the kernel of j, since $j(by)-j(bz)=\partial c=y-z$ making j of the difference of $by-bz$ and ∂b zero. That put it in the image of i from A_{n-1}, and by the time I'd walked up Bourbon to my apartment, I realized that meant there had to be an a in A_{n-1} with $i(a)=(by-bz)-\partial b$. $i(\partial a)=\partial i(a)=\partial(by-bz-\partial b)=\partial(by-bz)$ since $\partial^2=0$, and I already had that there existed aby and abz so that $i(aby)$ and $i(abz)$ mapped to ∂by

and ∂bz, that is, *i(aby-abz)=i(∂a)*. By the fact that *i* was a one-one map, *aby-abz=∂a*. That meant *aby* and *abz* were homologous.

After making a few notes and smoking several joints, I headed for Molly's Irish Pub for a sandwich and Guinness on tap. The place was raucous, some Australian woman drinking big cans of Foster's putting a bunch of admirers under the table. Her defiance embedded a sexual challenge, but I left before I found out if she'd go back to her hotel with one, several, none or not go back at all. Those were her options, the last one thanks to Molly's being a twenty-four hour joint except when it closed at midnight on Fat Tuesday.

I repeated my pattern of the previous day and hit Goldman's office before noon. At the same board as yesterday, I wrote first of all

$$
\begin{array}{ccccccccc}
& & \vdots & & \vdots & & \vdots & & \\
0 & \longrightarrow & A_{n+1} & \xrightarrow{i} & B_{n+1} & \xrightarrow{j} & C_{n+1} & \longrightarrow & 0 \\
& & \downarrow{\scriptstyle\partial} & & \downarrow{\scriptstyle\partial} & & \downarrow{\scriptstyle\partial} & & \\
0 & \longrightarrow & A_{n} & \xrightarrow{i} & B_{n} & \xrightarrow{j} & C_{n} & \longrightarrow & 0 \\
& & \downarrow{\scriptstyle\partial} & & \downarrow{\scriptstyle\partial} & & \downarrow{\scriptstyle\partial} & & \\
0 & \longrightarrow & A_{n-1} & \xrightarrow{i} & B_{n-1} & \xrightarrow{j} & C_{n-1} & \longrightarrow & 0 \\
& & \vdots & & \vdots & & \vdots & & \\
\end{array}
$$

"So I'm gonna prove that if" and I drew

$$ 0 \longrightarrow A_* \xrightarrow{i} B_* \xrightarrow{j} C_* \longrightarrow 0 $$

"is an exact sequence of chain complexes, then there is a long exact sequence" and I wrote

$$ \cdots \xrightarrow{\partial_*} H_p(A_*) \xrightarrow{i_*} H_p(B_*) \xrightarrow{j_*} H_p(C_*) \xrightarrow{\partial_*} H_{p-1}(A_*) \xrightarrow{i_*} \cdots $$

"so I have to define the map del star and prove all the usual stuff. Let me do it in gory detail, just to be sure I got it."

"That will be a unique experience, I think…"

I wrote

$$\partial_*[c]=[i^{-1}\circ\partial\circ j^{-1}]$$

and he frowned.

"Yeah, yeah, bear with me", I said. "The inverses make sense, more or less."

The whole thing opened up in my head, what went where falling into place as I traversed the squares both ways. It flowed out…

"S'pose we have c in C sub-p such that del c is zero." I wrote $\partial c=0$. "Then since j is onto, there is some b in B p with c equal to j of b," and I wrote j(b)=c "and by commutativity of j and del" I wrote $j(\partial b)=\partial j(b)=\partial c=0$, "so that by exactness there is a unique element in A sub p-minus-one such that" and I wrote i(a)=∂b. "Then" and I wrote $i(\partial a)=\partial i(a)=\partial\partial b=0$, "and since i is one-to-one," I wrote $\partial a=0$. "So the class of a is defined in the p-minus-first homology group of A and is the image of del star of the class of c," and I wrote $\partial_*[c]=[a]$.

"You need to show it's well defined."

"Right. I need to show it doesn't depend on choice of b and c within their respective homology classes. So s'pose" I wrote c=j(b') "which implies" writing j(b–b')=0. "Then there exists some a-naught in Ap so that" I wrote b–b'=i(a_0) "and by commutativity of i and del" I wrote $\partial b-\partial b'=i(a)-i(a')=i(a-a')$. "So then" writing a–a'=∂a_0 "and since they differ by a boundary, they're in the same equivalence class.

"Now consider c. Say c' is in the class of c, so that" and I wrote c'=c+∂c''. "So let" c=j(b) "and" c''=j(b'') "and let" b'=b+∂b''. "A simple calculation gives" j(b')=j(b)+j(∂b'')=c+∂c''=c'. "But" $\partial b'=\partial b+\partial^2 b''=\partial b$ "by nilpotency of del and so since del b and del b-prime are equal, they pull back to the same element under i-inverse. I think this pretty much shows that del-star is a homomorphism, too. Just look at what came out of it for c plus c-prime. Its gonna map to del-star of c plus del-star of c-prime."

"Yeah, skip that. Still need to show the sequence is exact."

"Well, that's not hard. It's clear that j-star of i-star is zero, so we have containment of the image of i-star in the nullspace of j-star. To get the opposite inclusion, suppose that j-star kills the class of c. Then" j(b)=∂c "some c in C-star. Pick b-prime in B-star so that j of b-prime is c. Compute j of b minus del b-prime and get that" writing $\partial c-\partial j(b')=\partial c-\partial c=0$. "So without loss of generality, we could have taken a rep of b from its homology class such that j of b was zero. So there's an a with i of a equal b and del of a zero, since it maps under i into del b which is zero. Then the class of b is an image of the class of a and the kernel of j-star is contained in the image of i-star.

"Now let's do del-star composed with j-star. If" $\partial b=0$ "consider" $\partial_* j_*[b]$. "By definition of del-star, we get this by taking b, applying del to it, and pulling it back to A-star. But since del b is zero, it pulls back to zero. It's similar for i-star composed with del-star. Pull an element of C-star back to B-star, hitting it with del and then pulling it back to A-star, which is the del-star part of it. Then you push it out to B star and it ends up in the zero homology class."

"You've stopped writing."

"I hate writing. It slows down my thinking. Forget where I am. End up thinking x, saying y and writing z.

"Anyway, that shows exactness at H-star of B-star and that the images are contained in the kernels. Now all that's left is to show if something is in the kernel of one of j-star or del-star, it's in the image of the of the preceding map. Then we get equality.

"So let's look first at the homology of A-star. If the class of a is in the kernel of i-star, then" $i_*([a])=0$ "which says that i of a equals del b for some c in B-star" repeating myself by writing $i(a)=\partial b$. "Then get c so that" $j(b)=c$. "Then compute" $\partial c=\partial j(b)=j(\partial b)=j(i(a))=0$. "So c represents a homology class and by construction of del-star, del-star of the class of c is the class of a" redundantly writing $[a]=\partial_*[c]$. "That gets the image of del-star in the kernel of i-star."

"Don't do the last one. It's too tedious."

"Once you've chased a diagram, you never need to do it again. I never did it in this context, but it's all the same. Usually we were chasing diagrams of modules. Same deal."

"Now we can apply this to get homology groups on topological spaces." And he went ahead to define singular simplexes and define their homology. Then he did the same for simplicial complexes, muttering something about simplicial approximations.

I shared his vision, at least a little of it. It pieced together with the topological content. You freely built Abelian groups from geometric objects, be the objects singular n-simplexes or simplicial complexes. You built relative homology using subspaces. I liked what he called cellular homology, defined on CW-complexes, a new term to me but very much in accord with my own topological experiences: tori or Klein bottles as squares with edges identified with different orientations, n-dimensional spheres constructed from upper and lower hemispheres joined at the common "equator." Made computation pretty damned easy once the Mayer-Vietoris Theorem came along, to wit that if a manifold was covered by the interiors of two subsets then the inclusions induced the long exact sequence

$$\cdots \longrightarrow H_p(A \cap B) \longrightarrow H_p(A) \oplus H_p(B) \longrightarrow H_p(A \cup B) \longrightarrow \cdots$$

The homology of the spheres dropped out with the fact that the upper-lower hemisphere with common intersection along the equator produced an excision with the inclusion of the northern hemisphere minus the equator into the sphere minus the lower hemisphere; or maybe that was the excision theorem. I was beginning to pay my brain's chatter more nevermind than his discourse. But anyway, given that construction it was clear the homology groups were zero for n greater than the dimension of the manifold, at least for those without boundary.

He pulled out the Eilenberg-Steenrod axioms for homology and tied it together with the idea of constructions like we had just discussed satisfying the axioms about which there were an abundance of general results to apply to all adherents.

I could sense frustration with the rush of stuff that he had to channel into a coherent sequence of ideas to maintain vision. I got the idea that it was like a room filled with things, all interconnected in convoluted ways, ties unending and undiscovered, and he had to pick up the most essential pieces and display their webbing.

He brought it all back with the notion of homotopy equivalence, an idea he presented after using homology to prove that there is no retraction of the n-dimensional disk onto its (n-1)-dimensional bounding sphere. Couldn't be pulled back. Nothing like a foreskin. Or that spheres of different dimension were not homotopy equivalent. Clearly homeomorphic spaces were homotopy equivalent, but not conversely given that n- and m-dimensional Euclidean space were both retractable to points, hence homotopy equivalent. No respecter of dimension, but overwhelmed by holes. There were relationships with the homotopy groups that he brought up, particularly the idea of being zero for n less than the dimension of the manifold when the homology groups were. But his example with the Hopf map, of the third homotopy group of the 2-sphere not being zero, showed there was a lot more to it than to be found in the homology groups. He attributed the ease of computing the homology groups to the Mayer-

Vietoris theorem, which didn't have a counterpart in homotopy. In essence, he said, the homology groups tell only a part of the story. But the important part of this story was that homotopy equivalence of spaces induced isomorphism of their homology groups. He promised to get into cohomology and to extend the Hurewicz theorem to higher homology and homotopy groups. I recalled that the version I knew had the first homology group as the Abelianization of the fundamental group, modding out the commutator subgroup; I guessed that for the higher homotopy groups the statement would be more difficult, given that the higher homotopy groups were already Abelian.

He stated a result he called the Kunneth Theorem relating the nth homology of the cross product of two spaces to the n-level sums of the tensor products of their homology groups direct summed with the n-1-level sums an integer lower of Tor of the homology groups. It reminded me of some abstract nonsense I'd learned about chain complexes of modules in one of the algebra classes I'd taken.

He ended it with a result due to a Russian named Novikov about the unsolvability of the word problem for groups. An algebraic result that bounded the possibilities in topology, since there is a relationship between finitely presented groups and 4-manifolds. And something with two-dimensional finite polyhedra. Fundamental groups came in and so also came simply connected. Anyway, there were no decision procedures for even the simplest of classification problems.

I returned to my carrel to ponder in some detail what he'd revealed. I packed it into a vision, made some notes, got home after dark. That day slipped mismatched into the next, sneaking up on me before I recognized the boundary had passed and I stood once again before my stat class making up for Wednesday with a detailed explanation of hypothesis testing and how to use the result presented in the prior lecture to construct uniformly most powerful tests. But in the background I replayed the vision of the time just passed with Goldman doing cohomology.

The de Rham theory suited me. He'd started with more homology and got some results that I didn't much care about, stuff using what he called spherical complexes. He applied the five lemma I'd learned in some algebra class to get some result that led to the homology groups of the real and the complex projective spaces.

I perked up when he defined the Betti numbers as the ranks of the homology groups and got the Euler number as their alternating sum. It was the same thing as the Euler characteristic which I'd seen in terms of alternating sums of vertices, edges and faces of a triangulation of a surface. I saw how it extended to higher dimensional manifolds when the geometric vision came together with the rank of the homology groups of each dimension up to the dimension of the manifold itself.

I thought I heard him say something about unnatural splittings but couldn't bound it with a context later and guessed I'd perhaps picked it up elsewhere.

De Rham cohomology was for me. You turned around the arrows from homology. Getting the groups amounted to computing the quotient of the closed p-forms modulo the exact p-forms. It involved differential equations and integrals, the arrows turning around with the differential operator which raised the dimension by one, opposite of the boundary operator of homology lowering it. It wasn't as if I hadn't seen the formal definition before, but the understanding that a form would represent a functional along paths via integration, path integrals, led to the idea of seeking forms that were locally constant as functions of the path (keeping the endpoints fixed, of course). Stokes theorem raised the differential equation and the fundamental theorem of calculus said that gradients were trivially locally constant. So the first de Rham cohomology group was locally constant line integrals modulo the trivially constant ones. Closed mod exact. In higher dimensions you did the same damned thing with volume integrals. The differential forms took care of everything; you'd get this complex running the opposite direction, up instead of down, with the differential operator d replacing the boundary operator ∂, the de Rham complex, a God-given set of differential equations whose solutions were the closed forms. Since $d^2=0$, the exact forms were already closed and became the trivial solutions, uninteresting enough to mod out of independent existence. So the de Rham cohomology groups measured "how many" interesting solutions there were. Or better to say, the size of the space of interesting solutions.

The obvious map taking a k-form omega to a map from k-gons to the integral of omega over the k-gon worked as expected. Of course, there was the matter of figuring out what it meant to be C-infinity for singular homology. The end came by showing that it made no difference; Goldman called it de Rham's theorem. So you got that map from the kth cohomology group to the group of homomorphisms of the kth homology group into the real numbers; I'd call the homomorphisms from the homology groups linear functionals. The cohomology groups and the homology groups were paired. He talked about some kind of universal coefficient theorems involving the homomorphism groups, cohomology and homology and Ext in one case, cohomology groups and Tor where he tensored in an arbitrary Abelian group Tor in another, and about making cohomology groups into modules or algebras using something called the cup product, but by then I was beginning to listen to the de Rham cohomology sing to me. I remember at first being one step ahead of him until he made his turn and after that we intersected only on occasion with wider and wider time steps between them. My own vision offered a journey that beckoned. Everything seemed to be exactly as it ought to be, leading to more complex visions of the core structures. The toolbox expanded more rapidly than I was willing to allow, so I built an unintentional wall between us and, in the end, he lost me.

When I fully tuned back in, he was saying something that sounded like, "As computationally powerful as the cohomology and homology groups are, they throw away information. What you might call torsion or extendability, depending on which setup you look at. In the homotopy category, a pretty flexible place since objects are considered equal if they can deform into each other, the spaces factor into some kind of twisted product of irreducible prime factors. That is the Postnikov decomposition. There is more involved than that. It's like de Rham theory sees only the prime at infinity."

I hoped I hid my astonishment. Once he got beyond the first idea, that of throwing away information which seemed obvious from construction in any case, he lost me with the irreducible prime factors. Like suddenly he was talking about number theory, a subject of which I had no interest, and primes at infinity. I didn't get it at all. And I didn't want to ask.

He promised to give me one more briefing, though that wasn't the term he used. He wanted to do it Saturday but I recalled my luncheon date with Gudrun. We decided to make it Monday. I asked if he could talk about general linear groups in this context. I said I was particularly interested in the special orthogonal groups. His eyes lit up, so I knew I'd hit a good button.

My advisor expended his hour presenting an example of a symplectic manifold that was not a Kähler manifold. I understood the example but didn't see it's relevance to what he'd been talking about at all, having lost track of symplectic and Kähler a while back. Brutal computations spewed trains of expressions in complex differential forms which I had previously met through Cartan. His board scrawl was worse than his indecipherable hand albeit more organized than my own. I knew there had to be a simpler way using the tools I'd seen with Goldman. Probably held more geometric insight, too. Not that I was ready to search out a proof. And I had to admit that my advisor found subtle insights in computations that I overlooked or just never got.

I hadn't checked my mailbox since maybe Monday and when I did found some junk together with a telephone message from Jeremy Ball dated Monday. I called him and he asked if I'd done anything yet with the report. I lied I had some notes I could bring by but that I didn't feel up to taking on the task. He asked when I could bring them by and I told him Monday would work, after the weekend, in the afternoon between two classes, a strategy I consciously chose to limit the available time.

When I walked into the grad student carrels to clean up the notes I'd written earlier in the week, make them presentable to give Jeremy, I saw carefully inscribed on the board in bold yellow chalk

$$\cdots \xleftarrow{d^*} H^{p+1}(A) \xleftarrow{f^*} H^p(B) \xleftarrow{g^*} H^p(C) \xleftarrow{d^*} H^p(A) \xleftarrow{f^*} \cdots$$

The turned around arrows said it was cohomology. Looked like someone was doing the same exercise in diagram chasing I had done, but for cohomology; in reverse order, more or less. It was the dweeby kid, who stepped back to the board with a book in his hands.

"What's up?" I asked him.

"I need to define the d-star term to get this long sequence."

"It isn't all that bad. Just tedious."

"You done this?"

"With homology. Same deal…"

"Look at this." It was one of the Europeans, a German or maybe Swiss or Belgian graduate student here to work with one of the European faculty. "Cohomology of childhood division."

Springing to the board, he modded out the subgroup of integers modulo ten from the subgroup of integers module one-hundred, naming the former T for the tens and the quotient subgroup O for ones. The coset of any element in the integers mod one-hundred would be determined by its ones digit. Using long division, he defined a function z of the ones components of two product representations of integers modulo one-hundred into the tens components and showed it had a property that he called the co-cycle condition and some other condition. I saw where it was going. There were other functions than long division that could give different "arithmetics" and which were co-cycles. Define these as the group of co-cycles, define some relationship of these co-cycles to be a subgroup called co-boundaries and then mod them out. Get different groups.

I couldn't figure what he was measuring. Had to be part of some scheme to classify groups. Probably Abelian groups.

I resisted asking him so as to enjoy instead the spectacle of the dweeb struggling to escape this fresh mania leaking from a shiny new piece of abstract nonsense. I retreated to my carrel to search out the notes to revise for Jeremy.

From the doorway I heard a familiar wheezing rasp.

"Mr. Butcher is here?"

Then she must have spotted the board.

"Who stuck on this silly diagram? This nothing. Do this in high school in Texas. Simple diagram chase. You…?"

I peeked over my carrel to see Utta pushing the limits of a diaphanous dress in summer flowers, maybe a size or two too small, hanging low on top suspended by flimsy straps not taut enough to constrain her asymmetric mammaries from flashing their mismatched nipples. Paired globular obstructions, rounded knees, interrupted the flow from slender calves to slender thighs. The skirt started upper mid-thigh, her diverging hams ill-curtained behind the doll dress contorted by their upward expansion and boxed at the hips. It hinted of meaty. A lie judging from memory. I recalled a round, not excessive, ass turned out from slender thighs, but the contraption defied logical description. Squared despite the slender and round. A masculine ass, firm and high and flattened but still round, and yet squared. It had to be an optical illusion resulting from elongated thighs that started low with abruptly increasing gradient and ended at what ought to have been the waist. No waist. Hips attached directly to frail thorax supporting the ill-matched twins that sprouted from just below her armpits. Heavy boobs that disappeared into her sternum without cleavage. More illusion brought on by the nipples staring wall-eyed. The big one aimed to the right on a tubular popeyed appendage defying gravity as if leaping from her chest; the little one on the left directed dead ahead out of a fat breast lying flat.

Her outstretched finger, its nail in purple with silver and gold speckles, pointed at the dweeb who stared wide-eyed, mouth agape, a look repeated around the room as rows of heads popped up out of carrels like an ordered colony of prairie dogs.

"If this not obvious for you," she wheezed, "you need study other things."

She looked at the algebraic scrawl of the European algebraist-wannabe who backed away as she stepped forward.

"This, cohomology of groups. What half-assed algebrician write this shit? Why integers modulo hundred?"

Red came out of his carrel headed for my row. He stood beside me and we both gawked.

She stood half pigeon-toed, her left foot cocked inward as if attempting to parallel the outward-bound right boob. On her fat feet a pair of square-toed pink cloth shoes with a strap and flat, thin soles. No makeup. A fistful of hair atop her head held erect by a skeleton hand with a bow on the back: a hair clip, not a barrette which would never have contained the rat's nest. Better to have let it cover the ears that curved high up on the side of her head, contrasting the absent lobes. But they did somehow match the long and crooked nose with bulb skewered at the end.

The two women in the office ducked down and one of them left, accompanied by the hippy topologist. The guys mostly stood with their mouths open, not clear whether smitten, terrified, or amused, or perhaps some emotional conglomeration.

I ducked back behind my scant wall but not in time, caught in a glance. She stood over me as Red grinned.

"What you shirk responsibility? You not in apartment since Tuesday. What about Mr. Ball? You forgot?"

Then she must have noticed Red.

"This one, he okay. I have time for him?"

"Go on, Red. Take her in the men's room. Do whatever you want; she'll go for it. Get a few others to join you—" at which she said, "Not dweeb with diagram troubles. Others okay."

As Red beat a hasty retreat back to his carrel I added, "Don't forget to piss in her mouth when you're through—" at which she grabbed my ear and pulled me out of the chair.

"Hey, easy," swatting away her hand. "You came to remind me to see Jeremy? I have it scheduled."

"You need clothes. Not acceptable to visit clients dressed like janitor. Or hobo. They do not pay such looking people big bucks."

"What clients?"

"Don't argue; just listen. I know. You come with me now."

"Where?"

"Clothier. Haberdasher. Cobbler. Nothing epicene. Masculine European. I have special connection. Not open market."

I didn't know what the fuck she was talking about, but I really didn't want to hang around and argue with her.

"Well, I need to work out. That comes first." I figured it would make it too late for her chosen shops to be open.

"No problem. I assist for you. Then we go. They always open for me."

I let the opportunity for comment on that pass. I wanted to get her the hell out of there. People already thought I was from another planet and this would only provide more fodder.

Red gave her directions for driving to the gym. Her Mercedes two-seater awaited us, illegally parked in front of the department building. Obstructing a fire lane. When we got to the car, she opened the trunk and pulled out a can of Coors. She shook it and popped it open and had it on her mouth before any spray escaped, draining it.

"Next best to real thing," was all she said, wiping her mouth with the back of her hand.

She spotted like a physical trainer. Because she wore no panties, when she spotted my bench presses I became more familiar with the pseudo-prolapsed labia protruding from the curly dense jungle surrounding her cunt than I would have wanted.

She disappeared while I showered. There was no one else in the gym, so I hollered for her a few times. She came out of the men's locker room again wiping her mouth with the back of her hand. From inside I heard a male voice, "You din't finish, bitch."

"I got go," she said.

"That's not right. You din't finish."

"Get over yourself, bub," she replied.

An older guy who seemed to be an official appeared and asked if she was my girlfriend.

"No, she's my aunt."

He just shook his head kind of sadly, like it would be a hardship to be with her in public but private moments might make up for it. Not to my mind.

"My eccentric aunt," I added.

As we approached the car, she smacked my bicep with her fist.

"What you mean auntie? I no aunt."

"I didn't mean like the little bug. I meant as in relative."

"I know what you mean. How I can be auntie?"

I didn't say anything.

"And you think I eccentric?" she asked.

"No," I said. "Not as a characteristic class of the people I seem to attract of late."

She let it go and we drove to someplace I had not seen before; my first visit to Metairie. The shop was uninhabited save for three short, fat, bald men in wild plaid suits. A tiny building, unmarked, but packed with cloth and what they called sample styles: slacks, suits, sport coats, shirts. I gravitated to the fine cotton and silk polo shirts and long sleeved collarless pullovers in nubby silk. They measured me for clothes and brought out tweeds and fine light wools and wool-silk blends. Utta spoke to them in some guttural language so I didn't know what the fuck they were saying, but I gathered they were going to make five suits, one a blue chalk pin-stripe, one a gray in what they called herringbone, and one sky blue in a silk-wool blend, the rest a mystery, ten sport coats of types and materials unbeknownst to me, and more slacks than I could imagine. Utta would not share much with me, mostly repeating "Not to worry."

The guy measuring me for slacks asked me which way I dressed; I had no idea of what he meant. Utta rolled her eyes back in her head and he smiled when he got up close on his knees, pointed at me, at my cane and asked her something in their guttural foreign exchange. She smiled and said, "You won't see such a thing," and then told me, "He asks how much this sausage weighs if unattached."

She insisted we buy off the rack a blue blazer with gold buttons, summer weight khaki slacks and two silk collarless shirts in coarse nubby weave. She compelled them to hem the slacks immediately so I could "change my hobo rags for dinner."

The shoe guy took us to a small room in back where they had rows of fruity stuff in my size. I rejected the idea of loafers with tassels and woven-toed slip-ons and two-toned gunboats. I picked brogues with thick leather soles and nubby leather uppers he said was buffalo hide. But I wanted boots and he brought a matching pair of brown and black calf-high lace-ups that looked old fashioned, like from the twenties, that he called cap-toes for the ridge symmetrically placed between the toe and arch. It seems they were buffalo hide, too, but the leather was smooth and soft, the opposite of the brogues. He measured my foot carefully to make boots of some unknown design.

Utta asked, "You have money? Money left from Dina?"

"Not here. I think I put it in a drawer in the apartment. I think in the kitchen."

"You think? Maybe twenty or fifty thousand dollars and you think?"

"I think it was twenty. How much is this?"

"Maybe twenty."

"Can't you just give these guys blowjobs?"

"Yes, but that cost us extra. I take care of it, but you owe me big one."

Outside a different night than penetrated the streetcar swirled around me as I perched in fancy duds beside the crazy cunt chauffeuring us across the metal monstrosity that was the Greater New Orleans Bridge. "The West Bank," she said, "Gretna" in the midst of our kamikaze run in the erratic New Orleans' gumbo of homicidal drivers. She pulled up to an innocuous wooden structure that made me think of the old cypress shotgun style house near my place rumored to be owned by a pair of crazy sisters. It was painted grayish-green reminiscent of a Navy building, surrounded by a white porch on either side with plenty of white pickets and posts and gingerbread and identified by a simple hanging plaque extended on a white wooden rod: "Le Ruth's."

Inside they knew her and kissed her ass, particularly a dumpy guy with wavy yellowish graying hair thinning on top who came out of the kitchen to greet her. He wore a white apron and white shirt and had fat fingers and spoke with a light yat. I pictured him as a short-order cook at a grill.

I had a huge appetite. Utta ordered for both of us. We had a white wine I found crisp and austere, like flint almost, a Chablis from France. It slated my thirst and accompanied pleasingly the crabmeat dish I started with, Crabmeat St. Francis, followed by a soup with oysters and artichokes. Utta sat across the square table that was draped with a pristine white table cloth, got up like child prostitute and eating escargots. I tasted one, a toothy texture that could have been snot in garlic and butter. She followed the snails with French Onion Soup and ordered a second bottle of white wine, similar to the yellowish stuff Jeremy ordered, a Montrachet she called it, to wash down my Soft Shell Crab with Crabmeat Meunière and her Frog Legs Meunière (without garlic). The sedate, almost grave surroundings accompanied by waiting attendants in white overseen by a man in black formal wear reeled out of the background of Marine Corps Enlisted Mess Hall as a promotion beyond senior NCO. General level now.

Utta drove to the quarter and parked in a garage adjacent to Dina's. She opened Dina's garage and showed me a small area in back with cot and closet and bathroom, a miniature hotel room more or less "You keep fancy duds here," she said. "Safer."

I neglected to ask her than what.

On our walk through the quarter I felt out of place, uncomfortable like never before, and realized it was the fancy duds. Not that they were uncommon

303

in the neighborhood, but I'd become chum. Fact was, I got more stares than Utta.

She made me fuck her repeatedly. Between bouts we smoked dope and snorted coke and she encouraged me to drink both six packs of the cold cans of Coors she'd bought on the way at Frank's Milanese Grocery, of which she partook second-hand. Once she deemed my debt liquidated, she left without ceremony and I fell asleep, only to awaken intermittently to a wild-ass cello solo that wove into my sleep.

I had showered and dressed in my official mathematical-ragpicker uniform or costume, never sure which, when Gudrun rang the buzzer. She gifted me a Bill Evans album I hadn't heard, *Blue in Green.* We talked small a token and I showed her the apartment at which she oohed and aahed, especially on the balcony. She treated me to lunch at The Coffee Pot, a café I'd never ventured into. My mistake. Simple and inexpensive. Omelets, red beans and rice, poor boys, though there were some items like grits and grillades that caused my stomach to grimace.

Gudrun wore the same outer duds as her double but covering an entirely different persona. A bra beneath the t-shirt, for one thing. Lipstick subdued for another. Not so aggressive. Same voice, different output. A whole other package.

We conversed around the edges of our lives, not meeting anywhere of significance. When we hit my apartment I gave her a joint and put on the record. *So What,* the Miles tune, was number four and I played it. Amazing variant, perhaps more significant swing than Miles' Carnegie Hall version; made me want to put on my walking shoes and hit the street, but Gudrun's face intruded. She handed me the joint and smiled indescribably. I couldn't synchronize her with the music. Bouncing gait, a jumpity Eddie Gomez singing as deeply as Bill. After a couple lines of coke, we laid on the bed side by side with our heads at the foot, facing the mirror and smoking joints and hashish-imbued cigarettes.

I didn't pay much attention to her words until she said, "You went in the Marine Corps because you beat up your girlfriend's husband. Does that make you reluctant to—" "What? Where did you hear that?" "About the fight and the Marine Corps?" "Yeah, that. I never told you that." "Must have been Bobbi—" "I never told Bobbi. I haven't told anyone here such a thing." "What about the people in Kansas City, the rehab people?" "Why would I tell anyone such a story?"

She shut up about it. I let it pass. Instead, I lined up more coke and rolled up more pot. We smoked some hash oil from a glass bowl. We listened to

Gomez man-handle the bass and Evans' deeply self-involved solos, conversing with himself and providing Gomez as much rope as he could run with.

In the middle of the sixth cut she turned her face towards me and asked, "Is it true?"

"What difference does it make?"

I made no move toward her. Her play. She eventually unzipped my fly and reluctantly scarfed my limp penis as if its putty-like flaccidity were an intentional insult.

As she worked on me I found myself leading the Gomez solo on the seventh cut by an infinitesimal time step. After a brief flirt with some melodic memory, it simultaneously dove and climbed onto the atonal aharmonic arhythmic free-born bowing path I'd heard the preceding night. The difference the warmth of last night's cello over the bass bowed in the higher reaches, but the same jangly stuff, nervous tension building to a dissonant variant of an exotic sphere a la Milnor or Kervaire — concerned now where that shit'd come from — constructed by plumbing in some whining bass notes.

Impossible to explain the nontriviality of my erecting a solid meat prong without bringing up Utta's drainage of scant hours earlier. The foreskin seemed an especial annoyance to Gudrun until the hardening set in. Clearly she was not the same creature with whom I'd dropped acid and orgied the prior weekend, no matter the resemblance. Couldn't ingest the entire loppy appendage never mind the engorged transformation over the head of which she could barely force her mouth. She climbed on top of me to ride the fully blown contraption with what seemed real enthusiasm tempered by fear and screamed an obscenity when I pushed that same head into her anus. That maneuver stood her up suddenly on the bed, after which she carefully wormed her way back down with her cunt. Couldn't take it in the ass, barely fit it in her cunt. I wondered what had been here and if this were the same version I'd met at the party. All in all, a less than inspiring conjoining.

She left soon after I finished in her, remarking without explanation that I was a bumpy ride. I think she had gotten off on it maybe more than once, it took me so long to finish. I hoped for no repeats.

I wrote up notes for Jeremy, explaining what were the assumptions of the consultant, what the equations meant, and finishing with some detailed algebraic expressions translated from my matrix representations. Then I listened to the track again, the solo of Gomez on *34 Skidoo*. I knew it like I'd heard it dozens of times. But I only remembered the cello from the night before, mirrored by Gomez while Gudrun'd sucked my dick.

I met up with Red at Bob's and the three of us went to the dump in Marigny with the cheap Dixie beer, pre-operative transsexuals and aggressively insane straight clientele to play pool. The bartender had been a Marine who'd served in Korea before switching gender. Short and wide as tall, she was tough as hell. I'd once seen her bounce a slate pool table to dislodge some stuck balls.

I left them drinking and shooting stick. I didn't play pool much. To say I was not good at it would be to adulate my ability. I stopped by Cosimo's but saw my favorite bartender was not there and hence booked it back to the apartment to smoke dope and pass out. As sleep claimed me, the cello sang the deep satisfaction of Stokes' theorem lurking in de Rham theory; the cello singing of the map taking the differential form omega to the integral over a chain gamma:

$$\omega \mapsto \left[\Gamma \mapsto \int_\Gamma \omega \right]$$

singing the correspondence of cohomology to homomorphisms of C-infinity singular homology; integrating forms over boundaries same as integrating differentials of forms over cycles, given the right geometry, the ties of analysis and topology bound in the mnemonic of the 19th century theorem of Stokes extending the fundamental theorem of calculus

$$\int_\Gamma d\omega = \int_{\partial\Gamma} \omega$$

made geometric with the magic of twentieth century topology: gift from Poincare, cohomology the fulfillment of Poincare's lemma. Singing true magic.

I skipped Sunday.

Chapter 21
Intersection Theory

I injected into Monday morning on the intersection of a fundamental homology class, that is to say an orientation of a closed and oriented smooth manifold, with a transverse class, as foretold in their actual meeting as submanifolds.

I bounded awake.

For closed, orientable smooth manifolds of dimension n, the homology classes in H_{n-1} and H_{n-2} corresponded to the fundamental classes of actual smooth submanifolds. But which submanifolds could be so realized? Easy to see in codimension one and two; but why? Why the fuck could I see that?

I smoked a joint.

It dawned on me that I'd heard Solomon Lefschetz had lost his hands in an accident and so switched to mathematics from engineering as an excuse to have chalk holders installed.

For codimension one the subspaces might be disconnected. In higher codimension, run solid tubes between components without changing their homology class since the difference would be a tubular boundary. Was I plumbing now? I knew Goldman was a plumber. Or a surgeon. Same thing, I guessed, at least in algebraic topology.

I had no idea what thought lay behind this. I understood it; I couldn't fathom its source. Nor something I'd read or discussed. The geometric-algebraic correspondence came alive with the projective plane, antipodal points on the boundary of the disk identified like a coin purse with twisted zipper so that a curve from the disk's boundary passing through the center to its antipode meets itself in sufficiently complex a manner on the surface of the purse that it's the nonzero element in the homology group with binary coefficients, seeing as it generates the fundamental group. Running two of these together intersecting transversely lands in the dual cohomology group with binary coefficients as an element not nilpotent. Algebra from simple geometry. Magic. Well, then, any two curves joining antipodes must intersect, more magic but flowing from the algebra to the geometry. Inverse magic.

I sat up and smoked another joint. It further dawned on me Goldman'd not said isomorphic homology implied homotopy equivalence. Couldn't be true, given the higher homotopy groups. He had cited the converse; maybe proved it.

At which I saw the icosahedron of twenty congruent equilateral triangles joined along their boundaries, twelve sharp vertices with twenty faces and thirty slicing verges. And its rotational symmetry group. Exquisitely eidetic eidolon from nowhen. From Miller's bland green book of my orals? Not likely; exquisiteness suppressed in that pedestrian piece. Rotational symmetries as subgroup of the special orthogonal group SO(3) isomorphic to the alternating group on five letters as in a vision of the five tetrahedra inscribed in the dodecahedron dual to the icosahedron and their permutations induced by the action of that symmetry group. Consider the homomorphism of the three-sphere S^3 as the group of unit quaternions into SO(3) and pull the icosahedral group symmetries back to its pre-image in the quaternions qua sphere to that subgroup of S^3 deforming into the selfsame icosahedral group as quotient group when the binary subgroup plus and minus one are fused. Contains the rotation group of a cube so has to contain the unit quaternions i j k so the commutator subgroup contains -1 and so the little bastard IS its own fucking commutator. Modding this icosahedral's symmetries pre-image out of S^3 by smashing it together and calling the resultant quotient Ж, Ж=S^3/(pre-image of icosahedral symmetry group of SO(3) in the unit quaternions), see that Ж is a goddamn exotic homology sphere that is not simply connected because its fundamental group IS the icosahedral pre-image. Covering space stuff I absorbed from Goldman tells me that the fundamental group is that very self-same pre-image of the icosahedral group that we mashed in our quotient. A homology three-sphere not simply connected. Far fucking out.

Now that scared bejesus out of me. I hadn't the vaguest idea where the shit came from except skipping Sunday'd allowed assimilation qua consolidation without intrusion. Not excluding intrusion from outside but from inside, extruding both Goldman and me to settle on some ephemeral appendages of stuff I didn't know I knew. Expunging days from one's life had merit.

And the mundane shit flooded in. It began with disks, those 2-cells that might be square if not for smoothness constraints turning out anyway to be not so constrictive. Imagine attaching cells via their boundaries, like sewing on patches or zipperless coin purses sliced in half maybe. Amazing that the de Rham complex of differential forms, calculus extended to smooth manifolds of all dimension, characterized topological information captured in homology, the Poincare lemma sort of uniting analysis and topology, or maybe geometry; Newton tied to Stokes tied to Poincare tied to this de Rham dude, whoever he was. And so, then, why not to some kind of differential homotopy?

Forget that shit. Not dragging me into that bitch. Nor the goddamn Poincare sphere bit. But it did seem that somehow transversal intersection of closed oriented submanifolds ought to correspond to the wedge product of forms. Some kind of duality at work here, forms corresponding to generators in cohomology.

Busted a cerebral hymen; no stemming this flood. De Rham's theorem said the differential forms on a smooth manifold capture everything in the topological construct of Čech or singular cohomology, take your pick. Magic. So why not de Rham homotopy?

Wrong turn. I smoked another joint. Pay attention to details. Like how Goldman used the compactness of the closed manifolds he worked over. See maps whose pre-images had to be compact when their images were. That's the essence. So define compactly-supported cohomology. That takes care of it. The reality lurking behind the symmetry of the cohomology for k and n-k on closed n-dimensional manifolds can be seen as an artifact of what is clearly an isomorphism from the nth compactly-supported cohomology group to the real numbers. Send that cohomology equivalence class to the integral over the manifold of any (and hence all) of the compactly supported forms residing within. There follows a pairing on $H^p(M) \times H_c^{n-p}(M)$ sending a pair of classes, one from each cohomology group, to the integral of their wedge product. A map to the real numbers. So there is a duality between cohomology groups as finite-dimensional vector spaces, no matter if the manifold is compact or not. Probably need oriented. But $([\omega],[\psi]) \mapsto \int \omega \wedge \psi$ says it all.

It began to subside, but not before I saw that one could define a degree between maps of manifolds that would assign an integer based on the integration of n-forms. The induced map on the top cohomology groups of the two manifolds would do it. Probably needed some restriction; thinking compact likely meant the pre-images of compact sets had to be compact. Must exist a name for this property.

It subsided like foam. Duality between homology and cohomology of complementary dimension frothed out, of course. At the end I saw duality between a single point on a manifold and a Dirac delta as limit of bump functions with total integral 1 but living not in the compact cohomology but rather some cohomology with forms having compact support when restricted to fibers, sort of compact support in a vertical direction. Would of necessity live on vector bundles. But the fact that it related to the Dirac delta so frequently used as initial condition for our fanciful Brownian traveler made me feel I worked in the right direction to please my advisors. Probably fooling myself.

I awoke from the vision listening to Goldman at the board anatomize SO(3). "The special orthogonal group in three variables," he said, "is homeomorphic to projective three space P-three. More to your needs, diffeomorphic."

"Yeah," I broke in though I recalled wondering this very question not long ago. "Think of the unit quaternions acting on itself—"

"Think Sp-one, symplectic group—"

Quaternionic analogue of the orthogonal group and I continued "—acting on itself by conjugation which is the same as an action by orthogonal transformations because it's linear and preserves norms. Leaves the real axis fixed so acts on the orthogonal complement of the real axis, that is on i j and k, and that means it's a homomorphism of the quaternions to the orthogonal group. And its null-space is the binary group minus-one, one. So mod out the binary group and you get two things. One of them is SO-three and the other is P-three."

"There is a more constructive approach," Goldman said. "Think of the semicircle as cosine of t plus i times the sine of t for t between zero and pi. It maps to a loop in SO-three and represents the nontrivial element of the fundamental group of SO-three."

I could see it as a rotation of the quaternions fixing the complex plane and so acting only on the j-k plane. In fact, cosine t plus i sine t rotated the j-k plane through 2t. It got worse, envisioning an elastic infinitely twistable goo between a ball and a case enclosing it and torquing that baby two full rotations before kicking the case to let the goo unwind back to its original position, untangling itself.

"Two full rotations are homotopic to the identity," I said, nodding my head. He smiled.

"In P-three take it from north pole to south pole through the center, with the antipodes identified a closed loop, since north and south poles are identified, can't undo it, but if you follow it back it comes undone as a closed path on the surface connecting the north pole to itself and homotopic to a constant."

The week flowed through as frictionless as it began, as if to trivialize my role in the feedback.

In my box I found the midterm test schedule and more drop notices. Last minute drop notices. The class attrition exceeded fifty percent, a good sign. The misses Cone and cheerleader remained. I wrote the exam in twenty minutes, adding two essay questions. One asked them to explain why $E(X-E(X))$ equaled zero. I avoided the terrifying word prove and asked for a short symbolic argument along with a geometrical explanation in terms of balance or center of gravity. In the other, I asked them to discuss the statistical hypothesis test as a kind of stochastic syllogism in the light of the Neyman-Pearson lemma. I knew no one would get that, but it beat asking them to prove the Neyman-Pearson lemma on a Riemannian manifold.

Monday's meeting with Jeremy Ball ended with me somehow not saying no but instead giving him a bill for fifteen hundred dollars for fifteen hours labor. He'd asked me how long the notes had taken to write and I said about an hour. That, he said, was unacceptable. No one could do that in one hour; in fact, no one could do anything worthwhile in one hour. We'd negotiated to fifteen hours on condition I would have plenty more hours for typing and adding expanded commentary on how to implement the equations. Just general stuff, he said. The details could be worked out once I reviewed the available resources at the SPR site.

It seemed I'd signed on to consult. He encouraged me to charge a hundred bucks an hour for the typing and any other consulting, pocketing what I didn't pay in rates. I considered it an interesting scam, too good to turn down. Safer and a hell of a lot more lucrative than selling drugs.

I gave the typing to Joelle and approached a fellow grad student rumored to be working in numerical analysis about the coding, promising them both a hundred bucks an hour. I think Joelle thought I was lying, but smiled beatifically and agreed to do the work.

The numerical guy had been employed by a defense contractor at Naval Surface Warfare Center in Dahlgren, Virginia. I'd never heard of it but liked how the names flowed into a single phrase when he said it. I couldn't get over the loss when he shortened it to NSWC, the individual letters forming a hollow sound thudding from his tongue.

The money didn't seem that big a deal to him, but his eyes bugged out when I described the problem and he started hopping around yelping shit about the algebraic eigenvalue problem and some guy named Wilkinson and SVDs and flopped a couple preprints of books from his little shelf to the desk in his carrel, one on the symmetric eigenvalue problem and the other called simply *Matrix Computations,* the latter by a Golub and Van Loan, and some paperback by Householder and a gray hardbound by Lawson and Hanson with the title

Solving Least Squares Problems. Incomprehensible stuff by names I'd never heard before.

He viewed a completely different world than I. Those things I called eigenvalues were for him numbers to be coaxed out of matrices of varying sizes. He asked was I hip to the LINPACK without waiting for an answer. His enthusiasm over something as stupid as concrete numbers astounded me but I recognized a useful madman when I saw one. Kind of person you sent out for a Purple Heart and Bronze Star. Perfect in a pinch.

For me, eigenvalues were the breakdown of self-adjoint bounded linear operators and the spaces on which they resided into simpler representations. I had computed them for three by three and four by four matrices once as a punishment, like doing pushups or cleaning floors with a toothbrush. This guy liked to figure out how to get numerical approximations to them from ugly matrices using something he called stable algorithms. He laughed at engineers using Cramer's rule as an algorithm for solving systems of equations and rattled off some horror story about the disaster resulting from some bad numbers so produced, almost blowing up a blockhouse or something like that. I marveled at the expression "bad numbers" and almost asked if numbers could be not only bad but evil; held my tongue instead. No need to alienate a potential ally in this new scam. As odd as I found my advisor's mania for abstruse symbolic computation, this shined an entirely new light on boring. Listening to him made me want to trap the dweeb in a savage board beating and I planned some brain numbing abstract shit made concrete to spring on him.

When Goldman had started to compute the homology 3-sphere that wasn't simply connected, I'd stopped him.

"Didn't you do that last time?" I asked.

"Don't think so," he said.

I proceeded to expound the vision I'd awakened from a couple hours earlier, leaving out the Revelations of John-like vision of twenty congruent equilateral triangles glued together along their boundaries, their twelve sharp vertices with twenty faces and thirty slicing verges and its rotational symmetry group, relying instead on its isomorphic brethren in A_5, the alternating group on five letters, pulled back to its homomorphic preimage in the unit quaternions. He shook his head.

"You sure you haven't seen this somewhere else?"

"No," I'd said. "I thought it came from you. I think we did it last time. Or maybe the time before that."

Attendance of the students left standing in the stat class was almost one-hundred percent with the exception of two who had probably been too stoned to realize the deadline for withdrawal was past. I expected them to come around after mid-terms next week and ask for me to provide them a dispensation signature to allow exit without penalty. I hoped for their sake I was in a good mood.

Cone and the cheerleader competed for most annoying in trying to pry information regarding what would be on the test. I smiled and told them they'd do fine, not to worry, but to pay especial attention to the class notes. It almost made me wish I'd given them a third essay test on the meanings of the word statistic, but I figured it'd give Cone too much of an edge. Maybe I leered at her instead of smiled because she came on to me openly after Friday's class, actually laying a hand on my chest. The cheerleader rolled her eyes up at the gesture. I pretended it hadn't happened.

Friday Utta showed up at the math department dressed like a kinderwhore trolling for Japanese businessmen on a sex tour in hell, popping out of a black baby-doll outfit with a short ballerina's skirt trimmed in pink lace. Her performance brought Joelle and Mrs. Dupre out of the office to stare, bemused disgust hovering about Mrs. Dupre's features, a hands-on-hip derisive glare imbued with sinister leering overtones directed at me by Joelle as Utta flounced us along the corridor, the dweeb following her to the stairwell as if entranced. It didn't help that Utta wore the red shoes, the one's they'd called Mary Janes, and seemed to be under the influence of something beyond piss and the usual intoxicants, especially given her erratic driving to the clothiers which I tried to rein in with several hashish-laden cigarettes.

The suits draped like skin, form fitting without adhering. In my reflection each coat amplified musculature like an incognito superhero in a comic book, the slacks as well displaying structures I didn't recognize on my artificially deformed right leg and discreetly outlining the hint of my male member that lay stretched along my thigh like a billy club. Utta felt my ass and oohed about the soft hand, meaning I assumed the texture like velvet, as if someone had smoothed the wool. The harder weave of the collarless pullover silk shirts showed a few nubs and implicated bare flesh below, almost as if opaquely translucent. An abundance of knit silk polo shirts arrayed across the spectrum from colorless to all-colors, both long and short sleeved.

But it was boots that knocked me back; a few dozen boots, all save one with cap toes, all military, either austere or rococo with side buckles plain or sporting flat bronze front plates on the straps like illuminated medieval manuscripts, one model in black with what appeared to be two rows of diamond shaped studs on each of the strap front-plates. Models constructed in black and brown and tan and cordovan and some mottled brown and black, in three heights from combat high-tops to paratrooper mid-calf to ultra-high top, the highest top in buckles with seven side buckles from the ankle to near the knee, filled out the collection. Some of the lace-up combat and jump boots had a zipper on the inner side. There was a solitary light brown three buckle high-top that the cobbler called an M1940 three-strap mounted cavalry boot. The one pair not cap-toed was rough-finished in buck leather, smooth-toed with four side buckles, one across the ankle fastening on the outside and the other outer-fastening buckle on top, the two mid-section fastening on the inside. Tanker boots, the cobbler said in a German accent, caressing the left one, licking or kissing it. The cordovan, he said, is the same method as the original Visigoth, shell cordovan from equine hides.

They fit like gloves, pliable as glove leather. The cobbler said the leather was magically tanned of unicorn hides. For each of the standard designs, there existed a matching soft brief case of identical leather.

"You make all this from hand?" I asked, not believing it possible so rapidly.

"Of course," the one who seemed in charge, an elfin creature with round glasses and a speckled bald head. "But," he whispered, "we keep small children imprisoned to do the labor until they are blind, at which time we sell them for potted meat. Really."

Utta showed atypical enthusiasm and interrupted him with instructions to bring out the surprise. A previously unseen man came out of a previously unseen back room with black leather jeans and jacket, the jeans plain and the jacket with braided seams and plenty of zippers and studs and pockets galore, fundamentally an ornately souped-up biker jacket designed like Brando's in *The Wild One*.

"What's all this?" I asked and they winked.

"Looks gay," I said.

"Don't worry 'bout dat," Utta said. "At CLUB there are women who melt with lust for big leather dick."

"Club? What's that?"

"Remember? Out at Manchacs. Tonight we go. Ricci come with us."

"What's the name of this place?"

"C-L-U-B. All capitals. CLUB. CLUB is name."

"What kind of name is that?"

"Short for closed and unbounded. Get it?"

The more time I spent with Utta the more I considered relaxing my rule about hitting women. Of course, I had killed women, so hitting one would not be so big a deal, but I was pretty certain she wanted me to hit her which put the kibosh on that urge.

She encouraged me to enclose myself in a pair of the leather jeans and black silk t-shirts meant to accompany them along with the black side buckle combat boots displaying jeweled plates. It made me look like bait for a butt plug from the fudge-packer's society; the only more convincing costume would have been leather chaps displaying my bare ass in lieu of the leather jeans. But when I tried the ensemble, the reflection overwhelmed me. That Utta intimated it was a sex club made the uniform quasi-appropriate.

Sure enough, Ricci awaited us outside, leaning with her flat butt pressed against a black pickup truck elevated on gigantic off-road tires, her bowling balls vectored skyward. Dressed in a dark pinstripe suit with a white shirt and tie, she came across as the canonical androgyne. Utta piled the stuff in the truck and we drove to the garage, Ricci following us. They arranged the outfits while I showered, then we headed out in Ricci's truck for parts unknown. I realized I'd have to return to the garage to change back to my shabbies, not considering showing up in my neighborhood as attired.

It was a long fucking drive out into the countryside. We crossed several severely arched bridges over what seemed to be mangrove swamps. It was a gloomy setting for a restaurant, let alone a club. They debated stopping for fried catfish at a place they called Middendorf's. I dissented, not wanting to show up at a country dive dressed like someone in search of a glory hole, despite the delightful sound of deep fried catfish sliced thin like potato chips.

It had grown dark when we pulled into a parking lot obscured by some woods at the end of a gravel road. Blinking in the night in the midst of a black lake the word CLUB hovered above a crumpled building. It seemed to levitate above the water.

Utta handed me a plastic card with my name and photo on it. I had no idea where she'd obtained the photo, but it was an old one in USMC greens.

"Don't loose it," Utta said. "Hard to get replacement."

"Impossible to get out without," Ricci added.

I tried to determine what else was visible on the card but made out only my name and photo.

"Take boat," Utta grunted and some armed men in suits much like Ricci's inspected the cards before letting us on a flat bottomed craft with a giant propeller in back. The building was an island, no man-made structure in sight except the sign high above everything suspended on I assumed invisible girders. Once ashore, it became apparent the island was the man made structure, hovering above the water without apparent submerged support.

"Now, take careful. Especially at stairs," Ricci said. "Loosing it easily here."

Her instruction suited the setting. We followed a pathway of some material not immediately recognizable presumably meant to resemble gravel. On the left we passed a blob of a pool and on the right a grove of yellow trunked trees topped with what appeared to be pink marabou stork like my brother had used in tying flies. Two naked women devoid of bodily hair blocked the path. The taller one stood in advance on the right, her hair reddish maybe from henna, her eyes brown, a pronounced mole on the upper of a pair of thin lips stretched like a line along a wide mouth on a long face with a longish nose. She was a lean creature, her long legs skinny with bony knees and supporting a long trunk to which were attached up high near her shoulders small breasts with a hint of curve and puffy pale, almost colorless nipples. She gestured to the one behind her who was painted up in tattoos on her torso: a heart between fat small-cup conical tits that pointed out of her sternum without cleavage at an angle of forty-five or fifty degrees between them, the right sporting a stud through the round reddish-brown nipple that matched its unadorned partner, the pair attached above a display of some kind of vinous banner with a red-winged gemstone like a crystalline butterfly, some flowery things, stylized pansies? drawn in black ink falling down her right upper arm from her shoulder, a noticeable tummy and the beginnings of cellulite around her bony hipless hips jacked atop stocky thighs arched outward from fat, boneless knees toward which meaty calves curved inward. The dwarfish tattooed one stood blocking the rear, pigeon toed and looking coyly at the ground wearing a toy doll's wig with bunches of bright yellow maybe-rayon tails hanging from the sides framing a face painted in red rouge on the cheeks, black brushes as fake eyelashes and black trimmed bushy brows above amygdaline black eyes accented with a thick application of mascara or tar or feces laden with occult blood. Her face was shaped like a heart tapered to the chin and there were white-haired puckered pin-point dimples at the end of her tiny etiolated-annatto fat-lipped mouth, the worst of it the round stud-like ring protruding from the pierced nasal septum. I would have preferred a bone.

"Make a truth quantifiable statement to pass," the lean nymphet at point giggled. "If it's true you fuck me; if false you fuck her," pointing over her shoulder at the horror on the walkway.

"I am going to fuck her," I said.

"Wrongly answered," Utta said. "You choose always the hardest way to follow."

"You regretting this later, butthead" Ricci trilled. "Make troubles for us, too."

"Asshole," the girl said, standing aside as the yellow-wigged freak let me by.

"What the fuck was that?" I asked.

"Gorgons at the gate. Testing you for later. Better you fucked the prettier one now. The other only bait for catching hemorrhoids. But you gonna pay later for being smart ass."

"Pay us now or pay us later," Ricci intoned.

We entered a stairwell that went on forever, climbing a passageway with doors and without landings, no end in sight.

They turned into one of the doors, Ricci blocking my way with a curt, "Not now, bub. Maybe after preliminaries you find later."

I trudged upward, passing doors from which emitted muted whimpers, murmurs, mumbling sobs and whines and whispers, burbles, susurrus and muffled ripples of laughter and droning lapping purling. Finally overcome by curiosity, I entered one to find a gaggle of backs-of-heads in a pit watching a skinny blonde on a bed atop a stage, leaning against a pillow and gurgling volubly while a female midget leeched onto her flattened tubular hanging right dug which, if like the left, was blanketed with a giant red nipple. Another midget female had her head buried between the skinny blonde's legs. A closer look evidenced only the gnarled torso and I assumed the head was buried entirely within the blonde's cunt. Audible slurps muffled like silenced farts erumpted in precise harmonic train.

Determined to find the end of the stairwell, I returned to my journey. After a lengthy hike and rounding a blind corner I confronted once again the entrance to the stairwell, except now the pool was on the left and the marabou feathered forest on the right, exactly as before but mirrored and devoid of gorgons. I reentered, assuming another traversal would restore right and left.

I slipped in the door behind which Utta and Ricci had disappeared on the mirrored side of the hallway. Ricci in her pinstripes stood on a stage staring at a stop watch, directing traffic in what appeared an orderly gang rape of Utta who at the moment was lifted like a hand puppet by the two arms of a big-nosed blonde buried to the elbow in her cunt as a man held her ears and fucked her mouth and another stood behind her humping her asshole. Given it was Utta the action would not have been interesting except for the staging and the to-all-appearances impossible position in which she hovered on the ends of arms buried deep in her cooze, an indelicate if not immodest to shameless and brazen trull of a sock puppet levitating. Both men ejaculated in their captive orifices, evidenced by runoff, and the arms withdrew to the sound of applause from somewhere in a darkened area of the room. The invisible audience showing appreciation, I assumed, for coordinated ejaculation.

Ricci brought up the next in the long line, a morbidly obese naked woman so layered in fat it was impossible to make out nipples or tits but who displayed, amongst the folds of labia hanging from what ought have been a pubic area below where there might have been a navel, a cauliflower of cunt lips intertwined with gold hoops strewn with bijouterie and whatnot. Her decorated labia hung to where one assumed were knees given her bending at said points. There stood with her a giant, not naked but smoothly depilous from the top of his head to his black pants from the cuffs of which protruded a lot of brown coarse hair and, it appeared, hooves, and from a hole in the crotch of his pants an erect and monstrous penile attachment unlike any on a human I had seen, dark and mottled with pinkish-beige blobs, fully erect at maybe three feet and not much circumferentially greater than the arms recently withdrawn. It ended not in a typical human glans penis but flared into a flanged blunt crown. Utta on her knees spied the approaching creatures and tried to crawl off the formless platform but something unseen restrained her, confining her within the unmarked perimeter as effectively as if invisible bars surrounded the shapeless mass of a stage that supported her at the level of Ricci's waist. Immediately her rear end levitated in presentation to the elongated monstrosity which pronged her cunt or asshole, hard to ascertain which, forcing an oomph from her as she pitched face-forward on her elbows between the fat ladies larded bent kneeless legs. Propelled into the cootchie lips that sprawled on the shapeless floor in lolling mounds of dimpled butt and thigh cottage cheese, her head disappeared and smacking-sucking noises emerged. With her ass she worked the dong to much rhythmic gyration, undulating until it spewed ejaculate copiously and with force for a long time judging from the spatter and never-ending spillage, all to thunderous applause punctuated by a chorus of three-toned whistles playing a rhythmic Latin dance riff. The male thing withdrew, spewing more goo, but Utta's head didn't reappear until Ricci thumbed the knob on her stopwatch and released a blast from a portable klaxon at which the fat one bounced up, somehow not snapping Utta's neck on the end of which her head reappeared dripping goo like her upended buttocks and thighs. The porker ran out of the light followed by the hoofed one to wild cheers, wolf whistles and another chorus of rhythmically coordinated three-toned whistles. Before Utta had recovered Ricci escorted the next three in line, males naked to the waist with copious curly hair on heads, arms and chest, sparse wiry goatees and breeches designed much as the previous one's with wiry black hair and hooves protruding from the bottoms and erect skinny elongate sharp-headed iridescent penises like Priapus in the vulgar depictions from Pompeii, a bouncily energetic trio of athletic males on her orifices which she offered while unnaturally hovering above the mat. I knew they'd swap holes until another overflow of ejaculate or a blast of the klaxon and so made my way out the door and back to the stairwell, climbing until I came to a door behind which a soprano sang Heitor Villa-Lobos *Bachianias Brasileiras Number Five* to the accompaniment of a lone cello.

I stepped into a room of indeterminate size and aspect engulfed in shadow, a pad on the floor, a chair in a gloomy corner occupied by a woman of amorphous features except for dark shoulder length hair who played a cello. In the center of the room beneath a bare bulb a young woman —perhaps a girl— stood alone and sang with mature soprano voice to the ethereal strains of the cello, beginning the close-mouthed hum as I remained rooted where I'd entered, not wanting to disturb the universe. I noticed she wore a simple dress with wide straps supporting bib overalls in solid gray hiding small peekaboo-playing breasts. The muted plaid skirt covered to mid thigh her solid legs. She was short-flanked from hip to knee, pronouncing oblong knees and long calves that appeared thin by contrast. I lit a hashish cigarette and listened attentively as I continued my languid appraisal. A reddish pug nose terminated an elegantly elongated bridge that emerged from between slightly arched brows above her narrowly elliptical eyes. A sleepy droop to the unpainted lids gave her pixyish visage an exotic impression that was damped by the pronounced sulcus in the oversized philtrum that drew attention to snoutish nostrils and tiny mouth with delicate curvature that harmonized with the hollow of the upper lip and was bounded below by a fat, downturned lower lip. Her high forehead half hid behind a sweep of bangs, the chest-length mousy brown hair parted to the side and feathered at the ends. Pronounced cheekbones at eye level amplified the taper of her face to dimpled compact chin. Maybe she stood five feet tall, maybe less, a short-legged woman on blunt bare feet. Her bell-like voice without syrupy harmonic overtones soared effortlessly. I stared, aware only of her sound and an awakening urge to fuck her while she sang interrupted by a sharp jab in my right buttocks, yanking me back to face the tall gate-gorgon, her painted, bewigged, pierced companion standing beside her. As the urchin soprano's hum hung they grabbed me where I crumpled and dragged me over to the mat on the floor, laying me out like a corpse on my back. They opened my fly and freed my penis as it grew erect even as paralysis overcame me. I stiffened as my overly engorged erection stretched its skin to bursting with excess blood. It must have grown into an enormous purple blunt instrument, but I could not move my eyes down to glimpse it.

"It was me wot got 'im so right is I got first use." The soprano had removed her dress and stood naked over me, narrow hips spread and round ass hovering as she squatted after snorting several lines of what I assumed to be coke from a mirror offered by the tall one. Her trunk seemed longer than it at first appeared in the dress and was adorned with the tits of a prepubescent girl. Her dense bush had been trimmed but was the exact color of her mousy hair.

"Okay, you go first," the taller gorgon said as my cock squeezed into the constricted damp opening lowering down over it. "You want a turn?" she asked the cellist who replied "No, he and I have a scheduled assignation to come," to which the tattooed gorgon replied, "He ain't making no assnation with no-body after this little group fuck, dear, so better to take advantage now-like." The cellist replied, "I don't want to spoil them now. He will be making plenty of assignations, don't you worry. Anyway, I prefer them active and besides, I need to play. We are to perform randomly shuffled selections from Handel's *Roman Vespers* and some *Concerti da Vioilincello* of Boccherini for this performance. I'm the soloist." "Suit yourself, but you gon' miss out this fat dick, dearie."

The tiny soprano meanwhile warbled oodles of roulades above a chorus and chamber ensemble of ancient instruments of indefinite aural focus, trilling an aria I assumed by Handel, the chorus harmonizing repeatedly "fixit" as a melodic refrain while she rode me and lilted into the voices, completing her solo in concordant moan carried along by the "fixits" and cellos. Her ride brought me to stages approaching orgasm. The abeyant ejaculation rose from my buttocks to my groin, triggered to erupt at no matter how slight a provocation. The taller of the gate gorgons replaced her. The room vibrated with sonorous strings and double reeds and valveless horns overridden by the solo cello as the she-jackal lowered onto my erection and cantered more aggressively than the singer had trotted me, pulling the coming farther along and closer to disgorging but prolonged so I throbbed from tailbone to gonads and pubis, increasing the urethral pressure to ready-to-blow but arrested even as she twitched and shuddered and was replaced by the tattoo job who galloped me to a giddy-up harpsichord horn and cello trio and bestrode me at the end gripping the base of my cock to rub ferociously her clitoris as if to she wanted to rip my thing out by the root, keeping it up until she spasmodically jerked and hollered invectives while the tall one commanded outside my visual range, "Okay ladies, line up in orderly fashion along the wall there; no need to shove, plenty of time. He isn't going anywhere" and one voice replied to laughter "It's only s'posed to be ladies?" to which the tattooed one squatted down hard and, gripping with powerful muscles, dragged her viselike cunt up and down my erection as the cello proceeded with Baroque order in solo above the orchestra, stroking without mercy until the orgasm in caesura grew to paroxysmal cramps and spasms out of joint with the musical accompaniment, inflammation spreading along my entire nether region perhaps reflected in my eyes fixed on her at which she called over to the taller gorgon "It's indecent, you know, the way he stares," the taller one answering "He can't help it, Gertie; he can only move his eyes, nothing else, and those only a little bit" "it's like a fucking voyeur, ain't it?" and they draped a thick cloth over my eyes so I could not see the hefty contralto who mounted next and paced me while her honeyed voice wafted above cello and harpsichord, finishing with a vicious unrelenting gyration prompting unrelieved *orgasmus reservatus* and the concerto displaying the swelling cello swirled around the room replaced by a choir of ancient chants and chorals and vigorous sawing accompaniment as an unseen sequence of all sizes of voluptuous-bony-blubbery-hard-soft-gentle-unruly-raucous-unruffled riders wet and dry bestraddled me through the chords agitating my unreleased venereal stress rising and falling as crescendos of throbbing unrequited orgasm and it dawned on me during an intermission as another faceless cunt rode hard that the proper way to look at partial differential equations was as submanifolds akin to bundles of partial derivatives killed by orthogonal submanifolds of the dual space, maybe this was the Pfaffian my advisor held up to our attention, the cotangent bundle or bigger perhaps and maybe this was jets, a way of stretching sections along their partials in a coordinate free fashion, prolonging oh Jesus a tight one worming down on me pumping up and down—urgent need to explode—back to the partial differential equations or Pfaffian system or whatever, of course the jets coordinate independent representations of the partials or the Taylor series better to think of it that way, but not defined as is the tangent bundle since it was clear that acceleration vector could not be created as is the tangent vector witness that fucking me bony hips blubbery ass loud suction cunt noises in rhythmic accord with the cello parameterization of the circle in the plane had velocity tangent to the circle either as Euclidean $(x(t),y(t)) = (\cos(t), \sin(t))$ or as polar $(r(t),\theta(t)) = (1,t)$ with the polar acceleration vector identically zero, now the fat lady sings, hope it ends here but a partial differential equation then geometrically seen as a sub-bundle of the jet bundle, assuming it had this coordinate free representation, easy to see as a function carrying its truncated Taylor series on its back like the tangent vector but independent of coordinate expression, that's the trick—but must have been done; just how well presented as exposition?—the fat lady sang but it ain't over an active panting one leaning across me grabbing my arms and arching her back I think, something to apply so much force and then how to define a differential operator in this bundle-land probably some kind of pullback bundle pulling back now hard leaning pulling my cock almost parallel to my legs must be using her hand wanting to scream STOP now riding again rubbing my inverted cock with a slippery tight hole filled with viscous goo; finally slowing to a pronounced milking pumping aspirating suction, my juices in suspension blocked stoppered balls aching, laughter from above "too bad we can't sit on 'is face" "'e's f-ing paralyzed, 'is tongue ain't work right" maybe I could kill two birds with this stuff, get my advisor's lectures sorted out geometrically, get this conservation law stuff and get the jet bundles, that name, Ehresmann I think, maybe have to go there since it didn't seem the geometry played a part in the symmetry guys' heads, certainly not in my advisor—new rider now and the laughter turned to urging her on, "harder girl" "ride him down" "use your spurs" desperate enough to pray for a spurt now —flush it out—empty—drain the damned thing another way to prove $SO(3)$ and the three sphere S^3 weren't isomorphic? not so simple since they have the same dimension as manifolds—use translation by an element of S^3 on an element of the quaternions considered as four space, just multiply like multiplying on the left by a unit quaternion and on the right by its conjugate— thinking of the three sphere as a Lie group more or less this one a sloppy rough rider slobbering wet drool all over my groin hair—what is that stuff?—so then actually acting by conjugation on the quaternions maybe that was what Goldman had done? easy to see that the map is in the orthogonal group on four dimensional space but need it in orthogonal group on three space but clearly true if think of three space as quaternions without real component, that is spanned by ijk, so need it in special orthogonal group SO(3) not so clear—a new one? kissing my chest? what the fuck slobbering on my chest? rubbing her cunt on my chest? how the fuck did I end up naked? someone cut off my clothes maybe like in a triage holy shit like in the fucking triage the light overhead noticing I'm not dead—rubbing my dick head on her cunt—rough—like on her clit judging from the noises so how to get that bastard in SO(3) from O(3)? think of it as a map from three sphere to orthogonal group via the sphere element to conjugation by that element and the elements are in a single connected component so has to be O(3) trivial clearly the map is onto and has kernel {1, -1} so SO(3) is the three sphere mod that kernel which is the center of the three sphere and the center of SO(3) is the identity map {I}: done, much easier, probably what we did—who can tell now? with the new one has the music stopped? no she sings part of the chorus delicate rider gentle but damn my dick probably torn to shreds bleeding it was what we did anyway so forget that shit rehashing Goldman's approach to convince me that I did it independently and I realized how to get the dweeb with parallel translation again think of the fucking two sphere just go around the equator and have the parallel vector end up as it began but not so on any of the circles of colatitude not zero not the equator and it would end up not in the same position but so what? that's just because it's no geodesic which is why—already what I did? getting confused maybe an integral better show connection form nonintegrability of parallel displacement the God-given differential equation not trivial, not equal to zero around closed curves and that was what I showed the dweeb at the board but he already understood, had already done that, "Yeah, sure worked that out found it in a book on tensors and variational principles or some such by Hanno and Rund or maybe Lovelock and Hanno or Rund" "Doesn't matter," I said.

He erased my scribbles and said, "But look at this" and drew the exact sequence homology ladder on the board, then a triangle with a connecting map that did it all in one swoop, like a snake swallowing its tail. "It's exact, see, cuz the map from the end goes back to the beginning via a representative of an element, say gamma" writing γ "with representative, say z, and so you have an in element the middle of the sequence, y say, that maps onto z and since the map commutes with the boundary operator you get the map of the element with boundary applied equal boundary applied to z and so there is some element x in front that maps to the y under the boundary operator and that is zero by the idempotency of the boundary operator and so the boundary operator kills x and it has to be an element of the homology group which is the image under that homomorphism which is the connecting homomorphism." He stood back and displayed only the scrawled gamma and the original sequence of three homology groups drawn in a triangle.

"Nice," I said, not following the details of the argument but guessing he had it right and liking his lack of chalk trail. "Much simpler than the argument I came up with."

"Works easily for cohomology, too, but easier to just use duality to get the stuff going backwards. Utta showed me."

"Utta? You hanging out with Utta?"

"Yeah. She's cool. Hot, actually."

"Where the fuck she learn homology?"

"She says high school."

"You know that's crap."

"Why? Maybe it was an advanced high school?"

"Where?"

"In Texas."

"That's not too fucking likely, dude. You need to be careful with her. She is dangerous."

"I don't think she's dangerous. She's sweet. And sexy. And she's a genius. You aren't jealous, are you?"

"No, man. Not at all. But her half-and-half lover might be."

"You mean Ricci? She's not at all. In fact, they are kind of over, except Ricci is like a mistress for her. I'm her lover now."

"You moved in together or something?"

"I want to, but she doesn't like to stay in one place. Says it ties her down too much. She likes to move around. She's a genius. Has a real interest in science. Expanding science."

"What kind of science?"

"Genetics. She is going to become an experimental body to carry new creatures to term."

"What? What are you talking about?"

"At CLUB. You've been. Those are experimental creatures there, many of them, and they need humans to carry the fetuses. Term comes much faster than with common humans like us."

He left me speechless. The only worse thing would be if he said he was joining her, marrying her, some bizarre shit like that. He said it. He said he was considering dropping out, she'd convinced him math was a waste of time and intellect, and joining her. He said he wanted to get engaged to marry her but she was putting him off about it, afraid of commitment he thought.

Fuck, I thought. THE MORE YOU SWEAT IN PEACE, THE LESS YOU BLEED IN WAR came to mind. The sign at Camp Pendleton. A damned lie. It just popped into my head. I needed to get away from him. I realized I had not thought of that sign since leaving that shithole before going to war with the Green Machine; that statement ought to emblazoned on every tombstone of every Marine killed in combat.

Mid-term week I decided to show up at the Strategic Petroleum thing. Perfect time. Giving and grading my test was the only departmental work I had scheduled, and since that was Tuesday morning it might be helpful to skip Monday, though I might instead work out the problems my advisor'd assigned. I'd head out after the exam and reconnoiter the setup.

I wore the blue suit that matched my eyes and an off-white silk pullover with the plain black combat boots. Not spit shined; I hated spit and polish. The matching briefcase set them off well, the cane a finishing touch.

The class didn't know how to react. It was the first time the cheerleader had given me an erotic going over, lingering for a long evaluation of my package as gay men called it, the reason I had not donned the suit until I got to the garage. New background desires arose, aimed at her. But not as in fucking.

Miss Cone seemed put off except she more unabashedly dwelt on the package. After she finished the exam—she was first done, in an hour though they had four scheduled—she asked me where I had gotten a suit to match my baby blue eyes, to which the Cheerleader said, "Cornflower blue," and I said "I thought they were sky blue" and someone else muttered powder blue and Cone said, "It isn't really you, a suit. But it's nice" and someone piped up, "The combat boots are him" and there were a few titters until they recognized the seriousness of their situation and shut up. I think Cone wanted to linger but after looking into my baby-blues decided to move on. Wisely, I think. I was not myself. I'm not sure who I was, but I didn't trust him.

I'd parked at the Ball's by prior arrangement, having had Jeremy arrange my SPR visit, and when I picked up the car a few of the fuck-dolls were on their way into the mansion, to film from the looks of it. I thought I recognized Misty among them, the sole black woman, but couldn't be certain though she was skinny with huge mammaries and wearing corn row braids. They were amused I was driving Dina's Porsche and wearing a suit and honked and cackled and whistled at me like a mixed flock of geese, crows, jays and maybe buzzards. I wasn't aware I'd become so notorious. But Albina waylaid me at the car, backing me against the door and putting her hands on my package.

"Whoa, there," I said. "That's off limits, bitch."

"I'm impressed, s'all," she said. "Really want to suck it, ya don't mind."

"But I do mind."

"But yer so pretty in the suit. And it is big."

"I heard you had some trouble with the big ones."

"Not anymore. I outdid Dina's old bat record. One in me cunt, one in me asshole, the wide parts, at the same time. I'm the new champ."

"You must be very proud."

"I am."

I noticed she had a tattoo inside her lower lip.

"What the hell's that?" I asked, pointing to it.

She rolled it down and I read, 'well cum.'

"Nice," I said, not admiring the assorted studs and rings protruding from some of the flesh bulbs on her face.

"I was going to just get 'cum' with arrows pointing inward like, but this is way cooler. And look…" pulling out her tongue and rolling it under at the stud where I read 'kiss.' "I thought to put 'love me' but t'was too sappy-like."

"'Fuck me here' would've worked."

"Didn't think of that un 'til later. Was pretty high then. Maybe too long anyways. Love to tour you of the various secret messages emblazoned in my corpus delicti."

"You'd be disappointed. I'm boring."

"Not as I heard. Maybe we kin go to CLUB?"

"Never heard of it."

"Bet you're still sore from that chthonian gang rape."

"Thänian? Can you spell that?"

"C-h-t-h-o-n-i-c. You're in need of help, dude, I can provide."

We stood sizing each other up. She had made me horny and I actually wanted her, but wasn't about to admit it. Besides, I wasn't sure just what I would do to her, given there wasn't much she wouldn't go for. Duress was not even an issue.

"You're lucky, ya know," she said. "They were gonna dismember you and feed you to the critters. That's the usual outcome, ya know. Utta and Ricci interceded on yer behalf. But haven't ya noted?"

"Noted what?"

"Yer cubic capacity's been expanded."

"What?"

"Like a piston with more bore'n stroke. Girth mostly. Seen a plaster cast they made fore and after-like. You may not be stroked to the length o' the Mule, but you got girth on him now. Maybe expanded a full inch diameter. Probably more ccs, know what I mean? Not to mention it's torulose now."

"What the fuck you talking about?"

"Torulose. Cylindrical with rounded rings of swellings at intervals. And I hear studded too, like knobby. True?" She took another feel but I pushed her hand away.

"That wasn't quite what I meant."

"Direct consequence of your rape, babe. Now you are a Louisville slugger. Love the challenge, babe. Ya know yer int'r'sted."

I was. And I had noticed an increase in girth and maybe length, too, but racked it up to imagination. The suit fit tighter in the rise, as the suit makers had called it. God forbid I spring an erection in these slacks.

"I've got to go."

"'member me," she said, turning and walking away in her miniscule miniskirt without panties, body of a precocious nine year old with legs skinny even for that age.

"You'd be hard not to," I replied, unsure if she meant re or dis. She acted as if she hadn't heard. Chthonian? Christ almighty...who'd have thought it?

I followed the directions Jeremy had provided out to the Parish, as they liked to call Jefferson Parish, a flat gloomy drive on slick beat-to-shit roads paved with oyster shell tarmac and populated by madmen driving as if unfazed by the idea of massive trauma. Red lights and stop signs meant nothing out here.

Interspersed within alarms of the road, the sort that danger had prepped for survival, the nagging reaction to the Cheerleader, Cone and the Fucking Tattoo Job Mirabelle or Albina, whatever it was, wormed into the void. My reaction to the Cheerleader hinged on her in-bred respectability, a driving desire to get her to publicly disgrace herself, to violate her self-image by going off with Jerry and Mule to a fuck club or getting it on with a club full of bikers or publicly acting out sexually with a gaggle of the wrong class. But not forced. It had to be chosen for love. Or devotion. Humility for the sake of me. As payment for my attentions. Afterward I'd toss her. Trash and toss. Get out, skank, you're too disgusting for me. After she'd gone to a public park and fucked a bunch of men and a dog, say. That played out in bits and pieces, an erection the danger of the preoccupation. I could see her making her way out of Marigny at night naked. Or riding blindfolded on a handcart strapped motionless with dildo up her asshole or cunt or both pumping proportionally to the wheel rpm.

The erection subsided with the interjection of Cone, who seemed willing to do God knew what for its own sake. Or Dina, who was indeed almost impossible to keep up with; I was like her excuse or sounding board. Surely no challenge. She sought out shit I'd not come up with. Animal tour in Europe, indeed. What more could one do? Or Mirabelle. That would be a challenge. What would one be able to get her to do for love that might be painful? Nothing conventionally degraded. To have a passel of kids and live in a white picket fence suburban house? Probably, but I'd be unable to stomach such a fate. To interject antisocial sexual behavior into that idyllic bliss would not work at all: it'd relieve her ennui. It was the socially acceptable ones, the socialized sexually pure with no worse than serial monogamy as crime, the sex for love bunch who brought out the best opportunities. I understood the desire to capture, degrade and release. Just not where it came from.

I pulled into an asphalt lot scattered with a bunch of glass-sided metal boxes in the shadow of a huge bridge, the Huey Long I assumed. I'd been told it was terrifying to cross, worse when shared with a train. It amazed me that the insensate kamikaze drivers with whom I'd shared the road coming out here weren't falling from the stretched steel suspension into the river below. Traffic seemed to be crossing without mishap from where I stood, parked near the box marked BOA. I assumed the B was for Ball, but had no clue what the OA represented.

At the back of a bare vestibule there protruded a desk behind which sat a black haired girl dressed to the nines. She carefully swiveled from her chair, stood with studied composure and, after smoothing her knee-length straight skirt down over her dark nylon encased legs, approached me on ultra high heels.

She walked with swaying gait and wore a purple sweater meant to emphasize the rack she didn't have, I assumed as hint to the imagination.

"You must be Mr. Butcher," she said in a thick yat unlike from the central regions of the city. Maybe a Jeff Parish yat or a St. Bernard yat, it flattened the vowels with a hint of nasal and thudded obtusely around the consonants without breathing out the background r. She spoke some more but instead of listening to the words I listened to the flow, clipped here and extended there. I interrupted her. "I'm expected, then?" and she clipped "Yeah uh-huh" followed by "Mr. Hines—he's waitin' on you now in his office." No chirren from that accent.

She had squeezed corporeal substance into her outfit. Not fat or hefty, but substantive nonetheless, opposite of the extreme angularity I'd just spoken to. Womanly with rounded hips and meaty thighs and well-developed calves, legs I was pretty sure would have been called gams in the decade of my birth. Pale skin judging from arms covered with fine black hair, but hard to tell from her face which she painted in the style of someone who looked at fashion magazines. Color galore on various facets of her visage, rouged cheeks and darkly reddened lips painted outside the lines to imply fullness that was not apparent in the short mouth set above a v-shaped chin with a dimple. There'd perhaps been white applied here and there and she'd daubed her eyelashes black with a reddish hue to the outer lids. Her face would have been heart shaped had it not come down from the hairline so straight. She'd fixed her hair with something firming so she could stand in a wind tunnel without it budging. But what caught my eye was the wide, flattened nose and close set eyes, giving her face the appearance of having been smashed with a shovel or other blunting instrument. Little eyes, magnified in paint like the lips. An artifice of a visage designed to distract and confound. Even the brows were plucked or trimmed. Had to be. A hairy girl. I searched in vain for hint of a mustache. Confluent trickery.

She smiled like it hurt, turning it off almost before I'd noticed.

Guessing her to be at most in her early twenties, I sought for a reaction to my appearance. She was as blank as if gazing at a cardboard sign.

Here was one never pulled a train, I thought. Yearning for a vicious retaliation from reality.

I'd expected a man named Aldo Corelli, an Italian who had been with DOE for a long time before retiring and taking over this disastrous ship. Hines apologized that Corelli was in D. C. leaving the shop in Hines' hands, being as how, he said, he, Hines, was the XO. He actually said XO as if this were a fucking Marine Corps battalion headquarters.

He was a slender, moderately tall, black haired guy with a firm handshake, well groomed but wearing pressed jeans and madras check shirt. A mustache for facial hair, trimmed and waxed on the ends. He greased his hair. Possibly approaching forty, there was no gray in evidence.

"Mike Hines," he'd said as we shook hands.

"Whitey Butcher," I'd replied.

"So what did you think of our babe Debbie? We put her out front because she's so smokin' hot."

He wasn't from around here, that was for sure. He sounded like he could have come from the west, maybe California.

"She's stunning," I said.

"Everybody around here wants to get in those pants."

"Uh huh." That would be stunning as in dialing up fish with an electric generator.

A dart board zoned into decisions adorned the back of his door: "golf" "sit on it" "no" "out to lunch" "soon."

I opened my briefcase and pulled out the typed booklet Joelle had prepared in imitation of the one the consultant had done. Mr. Hines held up his hand.

"Not for me. I'm going to hand you off to the manager of the operations."

He made a phone call and asked for Wally.

"He's a former Navy pilot. Landed jets on aircraft carriers."

I didn't say anything, hoping to make the asshole uncomfortable. It worked. He broke into the silence with, "Jeremy Ball says you had some experience in combat yourself."

"Some."

Fortunately for Hines, there was a knock on the door and a fat white-haired putty-fleshed man entered, a gut hanging down over his wool slacks showing hair and pasty skin between a row of stretched buttons.

"Wally, meet Mr. Butcher here. He's been sent by Mr. Ball to do some consulting for us."

Wally didn't say anything, just held out a sweaty palm to press against mine in a lifeless grip. When he withdrew I noticed his hands shook. Tremors and the bulb of a nose with a road map of red and blue lines told me he drank.

I sympathized with this old fart who had likely used up all his fucking nerves with night landings.

"Fly in Vietnam?" I asked.

"Yes, I had some combat missions. Never shot down, though. You in the Nam?"

"Yes. Marines."

His bloodshot eyes came alive for a flash and pierced my stare. He didn't need to ask me anything more.

"What you want me to do, Mike?" he asked Hines.

"Show him around. He has some stuff for the cost people with him, so hand him over to Everett."

As we left the office, Debby stood across the room conversing quietly with an older woman in heels, dark nylons and a straight skirt. They shut up when we came out, but the older one gave me a careful once over. Her skirt, not so tight as Debby's, displayed her ass to advantage. I took the moment we stood at the door as Wally goodbyed Hines to consider the outline from head-on of Debby's thighs in the dress. The V-formed front plaque at her crotch fronted a broad ass, flatter than the narrower one on the older gal that was nonetheless of positive curvature. A hint of tummy pooched just above Debby's equipment display. She saw me staring and looked down. The older one took a long look at my bulge and Debby sneaked a peek as well.

Neither of them showed much in the way of tits, but the older one was not pear shaped, was indeed lissome, and so by virtue of better balance came across as bustier. She had buttoned her shiny black blouse but one hole above her black bra and though not displaying cleavage, did display stretched buttons to better effect than Wally. Upon noticing them, Wally called out "Hey, Bobbi," and the older one beamed a spontaneous smile and answered, "How are you today, Wally?" Debby smiled again like it hurt.

As we passed into a hallway, I admired Bobbi from behind: callipygous with well-formed legs that were not long, certainly not skinny, and damned sexy. Wally didn't pay either of them any attention.

The corridor defied the external dimensions of the box. It stretched beyond several doors on either side. The first room on our left was large, open and windowless, filled with women, mostly young women, maybe girls, all facing the door. Wally called them Wang operators and I didn't ask what that was, but they sat at identical metal desks with identical typewriters and some other boxes. On the other side of the hallway was a room filled with wooden desks and a bookcase and some bookish nerds who looked up like sheep, a most unhip conglomeration. There was an office in back within the doorway of which stood an unkempt, dark-haired dork, clearly a dork, who didn't give us the courtesy of recognition. "Anthony Tusa," Wally said, the name on the door with the words Director of Publications below it. "Avoid him if at all possible. These people are all PhDs in English from Tulane. They edit our work to make them fit the formula, to format them and to make them indecipherable." He snorted. "Tusa can't hardly read."

The next room had a wooden doorway that read Scheduling. A smiling dark round man stood at a long stream of computer paper strung along the walls. It appeared to be a schedule of some sort, with lines and symbols like squares and triangles and circles. He came over to Wally who introduced us, calling him Joe Monkar. He shook my hand half-heartedly and said with an Indian accent, "Don't mistake me as a Pakistani." I considered laughing but held back, a good move given that neither of them laughed. A short pudgy guy came over, blonde and older than Joe but probably not past his forties. Wally introduced him as Larry, the manager, and Larry didn't say much except that they were scheduling. He pointed to a gray machine in the corner, saying that was the scheduling computer. Joe, he said, was the engineer and if I needed something technical, I was to deal with him. He asked if I was a new hire and Wally said, "No, a consultant," as if he were swearing. I noticed the back wall was all window.

Wally next steered me to a room across the hall from scheduling. There were no words on the door, but he said "This is the bullpen." It was bigger than the publications room and structured much the same except it also had a window for a back wall, with rows of desks at which sat a lot of men around my age staring at us like monkeys. They all had adding machines on their desks and when we'd entered the air was saturated with clacking, whirring and crunching. It ceased when they looked up en masse, but started again almost immediately. They wrote on forms, I assumed transcribing numbers. Everyone in the room wore ties. It was the first group so dressed. Until now I had assumed that only the women dressed up.

From a back office a slender man bee-lined toward us. He looked to be in his late forties and wore a thin mustache. On his way he picked up a stocky man who rose from a desk to join him. The escort looked to be younger and was balding with black hair and mustache trimmed short like Hitler's, only bushier.

Wally didn't make a move farther into the room, instead awaiting the pair just inside the door. Their approach indicated we might have to fight our way out, the muscular escort backing the other with clenched fists and a pugnacious expression. I decided I'd take him out first.

"Well, Wally, what you got here? Newby?" It was the one who had come out of the office in back.

"Consultant, Ned. He's got that economics report worked out."

"What economics report?"

Wally didn't answer. The stocky one moved into my personal space and glared at me, powerful arms cocked. I considered bringing down my cane on the top of his foot, but held off.

"You know."

"No, I don't."

"The way of forecasting those petroleum prices. You asked for the study."

"I didn't ask for no study."

The stocky guy whispered something in the thin guy's ear and he said, "Oh, now I remember. But wasn't me who wanted it. Was the management over at DOE. I don't see any need for it."

"Well, that's for you to take up with your boss. Word is, this guy's got it worked out."

The stocky one said something under his breath. I couldn't be sure but it sounded like it had "worked it out with a pencil" and "faggot pretty-boy" interspersed in it. I upheld a stoically bland expression. Wally didn't tell me their names or introduce me, instead hustling me out of there and on to a bifurcation at the end of the hallway with more offices at the end of either branch. Inside one sat Kip and Jerry chewing the fat. Jerry wore a shirt the color of shining eggplant with a skinny green tie, black slacks and high-sheen green jacket. Kip was dressed as he always dressed. Wally introduced us and they pretended not to know me. At least I assumed they pretended. A short, wide man came out of another office at the back of the room, greasy jet black hair thinly dangling to the top of his neck. It was impossible to tell his age but he looked like someone to avoid. Strange would be the word. He didn't smile. In fact, his expression didn't change in any way. He wore a nondescript dark suit, dark tie and black shirt. Wally introduced him as Leroy.

"This the guy with the report?" Leroy asked.

"That one on forecasting petroleum prices. Yep," Wally replied.

"Can I see it? We are the shop to implement it."

"What about the cost group?"

"We apply it to their numbers. Remember COPES updates the cost numbers."

I pulled the booklet from the briefcase and handed it to him. The numerical guy had told me to find out what compilers they had, explaining to me that compilers took higher language instructions and translated them, compiled it in technical terminology, into assembly language, from which assemblers took it to machine language. He started to explain how it was related to automata theory, of which I knew not a smidgen, and hence semigroup theory and I cut him off. "I don't want to know this," I told him. "If someone needs to speak computers to these jerks, it'll be you." I didn't realize I had thereby replicated, in a sense, their division of labor, except without the layer of pure management which accomplished nothing. I saw it here, managers of whom one had no expectations of any expertise, at least one for each group. Maybe they were the scapegoats. Maybe they were the buffer with other layers of management. More likely they were ceremonial artifacts. And more likely still, they saw me as a useless to dangerous intrusion.

"What compilers do you have access to?"

He looked at me like I was an alien. Then he looked at Kip and Jerry.

Jerry said, "We hooked up by direct line to computers at St. Louis."

"McDonnell Douglas," Kip said. "Data services. It's where COPES resides."

"What's COPES?" I asked.

"A program that does the cost projections. We feed in data from the drill sites and it produces the numbers as to how much we are behind budget."

"Or ahead of budget," Leroy added.

Wally snorted. "No one is able to tell how it relates to schedule slips. Completely independent as far as the computers are concerned, cost and schedule budgets."

"They got a IBM three-twenty and a CDC Cyber hooked together," Jerry said.

"Three-sixty, Jerry."

"Oh, yeah. That's it. Three-sixty."

This shit was worse than in my wildest expectations. Mind-numbingly boring and overrun with alien life forms; I hadn't seen so many clueless clowns in one place since my days in the Corps. I didn't let on I had no clue what they were talking about.

I looked around the room. There were a couple more desks that appeared abandoned and in the corner against the wall a big typewriter rested on a large table, hooked up to some wires.

"For compilers, I think they got all that shit," Jerry continued.

Kip had pulled out a list. "Says here under compilers that they support COBOL, FORTRAN, PL-1."

"Cost us extra to use that stuff?" Wally asked.

"We pay for CPU time and storage for the COPES," Leroy said. "Besides the cost of the dedicated line."

That seemed to satisfy everyone so Leroy returned to his office. Kip and Jerry escorted Wally and me to the remaining unexplored space, a central room surrounded by a hive of smaller offices. There were names on all the doors, among which was Aldo. Nothing else, just Aldo.

Seated at a desk with phone and typewriter in the middle of the room was the one Wally'd called Bobbi, the aging, leggy callipygian. This time he introduced her: Bobbi, no last name, the office manager. An older woman in charge of the girls, it appeared. From her neck I guessed her to be approaching fifty. She wore less makeup than the younger one at the entrance but was covering some age signs. Her quick smile was warm and showed in her eyes which crinkled with crow's feet and lit up. She stared openly at my groin and I think she communicated interest with the way she looked from my packet to my eyes several times, her smile changing from warm to a mock wonder. Or maybe I imagined it.

From a single office emerged a man an easy six inches taller than I. He had gray hair and wore gray pinstripes and stood very straight. He reminded me of J. Kenneth Galbraith, who I'd once seen at UMKC. With him slouched a shorter man of about the same age in a wrinkled dark gray suit. Wally introduced them by names I immediately forgot, having met my daily quota of new people, and the tall one asked me if I knew of software that integrated cost and schedule. I shook my head no. Kip whispered in my ear as the duo returned to their office, "Those two were hired from Treen's campaign as a favor. They been given the company joke, to search for software to integrate cost and schedule. The little guy considers himself a great technical manager and claims to have managed a whole staff of famous PhD mathematicians doing Operations Research for the Navy. Everyone knows he's lying."

I was intrigued by Bobbi, but Wally disappeared into an office with the name Wally Lord on the door and Bobbi went back to her business and Kip and Jerry dragged me off to where I'd found them.

"Man," I said, "that stocky guy with the Hitler mustache was hostile. In fact, his boss the thin man was hostile too. What is that place?"

"That'd be Jerry, the short one, and the other guy, funny you called him the thin man, perfect like in the movies, is in charge of those guys. They are always in there computing with adding machines and they distribute reports and give me numbers for the sites that get entered into COPES."

"All them guys in there is hostile," Jerry said.

"Well, a lot of the people here are from Mississippi. The Gulf Coast. White guys who've been out of work and drive up here every day or stay in apartments and keep homes and wives on the Gulf Coast."

"All them dudes there's from Mississippi. Me too, truth be told. But I ain't got no house in no Gulf Coast. I just excaped that shithole. No need goin back, neither. But them boys in there's scared to losing they jobs. They think ever body come in aims to do away with they jobs."

"They do think the computer will automate them out of work. Scared of COPES, for sure. They won't talk to me at all. But that Jerry is pretty defensive about the superiority of the South. Brings up people like Faulkner as proof. Thinks he's a tough guy, too. But mostly he worries about someone stealing Paula from him. As if anyone would want her."

"Yeah, she nasty. Fat and ugly."

"Coker says she threatens to leave Jerry if he cuts off his mustache."

"Like anyone with a ounce of sense be licking that nasty bitch cunt."

"I didn't meet any Coker."

"No, he's out with Hayden who you'll get to meet when they get back from visiting some sites. Coker's from Mississippi too, but Hayden's a local who lives across the lake now, over in Covington. You'll like Hayden, but it's fun to watch old Coker get mad. He turns red. Supposed to be a risk for heart attack: high blood pressure and high cholesterol. They won't let him eat oysters or shrimp. It kills him."

"Thought they'd be good for you," I said.

"High cholesterol," Kip said.

"So what do you guys do in here?"

"I'm the cost guy here who works with COPES."

"Me, I'm the computer operator," Jerry said.

"Where's the computer?"

"Don't got one," Jerry said. "They is one for schedule and they got the Wangs, but I don't touch them. Promise is they gon' get one for data interface, a Four Phase they call it. Make it easier for Kip to enter data, directly to the Four Phase for interface to the IBM."

"Well, it will store it, too. Take down some of the cost. They're paying about three hundred thousand a month for this line and COPES and all."

"How much?"

"The dedicated line's over a hundred thousand, and then CPU cost and storage cost and license fee for COPES.

"So what you think of that Bobbi?"

"She's sexy."

"Nice for an old broad. Great legs and ass."

"I wouldn't mind bustin' that up. Beats them buffalo soldiers they got working over to Parsons."

"They got some hot chicks over at Parsons, Jerry. Some of the black ones."

"Nu-uh," Jerry said. "You got to be sick or blind. How'd you like Debby?"

"You mean the 1940s model up front."

"She is a kinda classic," Jerry said. "Not sure what ever body sees in that one."

"She looks like someone smashed in her face with a shovel," I said.

"Man, you bein harsh. I ain't interested in getting any of that, but I tell you she ain't that ugly."

"You're both nuts," Kip said. "She is fine. Nice ass on her."

"What's Parsons?"

"Parsons-Gilbane. Prime contractor here along with DUCI."

"Doosy?"

"Draco Utility Construction or some such thing. They're drilling into salt domes out along the coast. Those're the sites. To store oil in."

"Fucked up," Jerry said, "but bring jobs."

"Y'all lookin' real busy." It came from the doorway behind us, rolled out like she spoke with practiced grace through a mouthful of marbles, awash in implied and clandestine Rs fat-toned and hollowed out. We turned in unison.

"Hey Judy," Kip said. "Come on in. What do you need?"

"Nuthin', babe. Just got this here report for ya'll."

She stood in the doorway eyeing me. "You got you a new white boy?" she asked.

"No," Jerry said. "Why you so hard, woman?"

She stood five foot and a few inches. Her color was light cocoa with orange in it, what they called a Creole of color. It always made me think of the term high yellow, which was likely the wrong usage. The face looked short, in part an artifact of the bangs, but compressed from nose to chin. Her nose was long and straight and broad, but her eyes focused the attention, huge and bright, set straight at the bridge of her nose, ellipses of near-zero eccentricity colored a soft hazel. She had a short mouth, small with lips full to fat above a rounded chin and beside a pair of bulging cheeks like she had something stored.

She addressed herself to Kip as she came into the room, ignoring Jerry.

"An-tony says you need to review this, babe," she said. She started describing what it was, but I ignored the words to catch the sound, a slur of shaded Rs sliding along her words, over the top and underneath the proclitic flow independent of the words, and as they spoke Kip asked about her children which came back as chirrun, honest with me as hrnost wit mre, a hum of Rs in the background of every foreshortened sound she emitted.

She'd dyed her hair a dark red mahogany with an orange hint that brought out the orange in her skin, straight hair cut to chin level with bangs across her forehead. It was not easy to make out her bodily outline in the outfit she wore, loose jeans and a loose blouse hanging outside to mid thigh like a jacket, but she had round breasts placed high up on her torso and a high round ass. One could only guess at her girth between bust and hips, but her bare arms were thick and so it seemed were her shoulders. Her thighs had to be corpulent to go with the bubble of an ass, but I guessed her calves were not of the same weight, though I could also picture fat knees and ankles. Hard to tell until she wore a skirt. But it didn't matter. Her face made up for it. She aroused in me the desire to shove my dick in her face. I started to spring a boner just considering it. Soft and sexy with a voice that inspired visions of fucking her while she talked encouraging trash.

Jerry introduced her as Judy, telling her I was consulting. She shook my hand, all the while continuing to ignore Jerry. When she left, all eyes followed her high ass which smiled when she stood, the cheeks in motion when she walked with no effort on her part.

"Man, she is ripe," Kip said.

"Not yet, she ain't," I said. "That's one you want to get into before she ripens."

"You got that right," Jerry said. "She ripe she gon be big. Be big as a fucking house."

"But she is damned sexy now," I said. "She married?"

"Hell no," Jerry said. "She live down'n the projects. And she got two, three kids."

"Two," Kip said.

"She in her early twenties," Jerry said. "And one'a them kids be five."

"Six and three," Kip said. "Had the six year old when she was sixteen. And she's never been married, but she ain't easy."

"Nope, she got real careful now," Jerry said.

"She is damned sexy," I said.

"She doesn't go out with white guys," Kip said. "And she makes sure any man she does go out with is ready to help support the kids."

"She ain't int'rested'n me," Jerry said.

"You interested in supporting her kids?" Kip asked.

"Fuck no, that shit ain't gon' cut it. Don't need no kids."

Kip and Jerry wanted to take me out the short way, the back door near their office, but I insisted they escort me out the front. I stopped in the middle of the lobby with my back to Debby.

"I'll be back a couple times at least to make sure this is implemented. I can't be sure how much Jeremy wants me to do here after this little chore, but I have a feeling he might give me some tasks this summer, after I'm finished teaching the semester."

Kip said, "Maybe we can party some."

"Shit yeah," Jerry seconded.

"Well, I must admit you have a couple nice looking women here. That Bobbi is a real knock out. And Judy is damned sexy."

Kip started to say something, likely about Judy, but caught a glance of Debby and ate the words. Instead he mumbled, "Nooners, maybe."

"See you guys later," I said. "You know how to get in touch."

I turned and caught Debby looking. She turned her gaze down and I looked past her like she wasn't there and walked out alone. I drove the Porsche past the front window in case she watched.

Jeremy paid upfront for the hours and gave me advice on how to handle the tax angle for my returns and for the consultants. He offered the services of his accountant for free and I took him up on it. Mostly it had to with a form to send the IRS; I advised my two cohorts that their income would be reported and they had to deal with the consequences, which might include Social Security and other taxes. Joelle took the money I handed her with a surprised expression, but the computer guy didn't seem at all impressed. Jeremy also provided me a fat loose leaf binder full of gibberish regarding the system on which the code was to run. The computer guy grabbed it and disappeared behind his cubicle; I told him to keep track of his hours and double them.

In the commotion of the consulting I'd missed the departmental excitement. A visit by a woman, Momus' unique PhD descendant, who had won the Fields Medal. The youngest person ever and the only woman. It would have been surprising that I had not heard about it before, but I paid no attention to awards. The only Fields winner I knew of was Paul Cohen, a legend for his arrogant affront to his betters when he went around asking for the most significant unsolved problems and chose the generalized continuum hypothesis, considered exceptionally difficult but solvable with a yes or no answer since Cantor had asked it in the late nineteenth century. Even more of an affront given that his then-recent PhD had been in functional analysis, an area not directly concerned with questions about the relationship between different sizes of infinity. I had studied Cohen's proof in a grad class in logic, reading his little book from Benjamin, and saw functional analysis at work in the method he devised for solving the problem, a method he'd fittingly called forcing. It'd revolutionized logic and set theory. His proof that the continuum hypothesis was independent of the other axioms of set theory, hence without yes or no answer, had shaken the faith of some.

What made it more amazing was that this woman had done her PhD work in logic, the department not known for that stuff except maybe Bolyai. I'd seen a copy of Barwise's *Handbook of Mathematical Logic* in his office and guessed he did work in algebra that was related. But she worked under Momus. Maybe it had something to do with a grasp of algebraic geometry which I assumed he must have since he worked in several complex variables and had done is PhD under the illustrious André Weil.

The effect of her visit on the department didn't strike me until the dweeb buttonholed me at the board about a week after her colloquium talk. Momus had already shown me the flyer, not yet up around the department, when he buttonholed me outside his office.

Tulane Mathematics Department presents
Maria Hypatia Aline da Inferna
Presenting
Creatures from Inaccessible Cardinals
Norms on Possibilities: Forcing with Creatures on Trees
Maria Hypatia Aline da Inferna is a winner of the Fields Medal
PhD from Tulane
Dr. Hypatia Lie (as she is known professionally) is a Fields Medalist and wrote her dissertation under the direction of Professor Momus and Professor Bolyai

It was fucking bizarre. Momus told me how he'd come to get her as a student. He'd been approached by the principal and a math teacher at one of the top private schools in the city. The teacher had been a PhD candidate at Tulane, an excellent student who had passed his written and oral exams and then decided to drop out to teach high school. They had this young girl—she wore braces, Mr. Butcher, he'd said—with whom they could do nothing. She spoke Portuguese and English as native languages and her parents were Brazilian, her father an executive with a coffee company headquartered downtown.

"Uncontrollable," he said, clearing his throat in preparation for a long speech. "They called her uncontrollable, this girl. Only sixteen, it seemed, but already well beyond her peers in academic accomplishments. Worse, beyond her teachers. Not only a prodigy in mathematics, but superior in all her studies, including literature. Which of course one would expect of brilliance. More than brilliance, to be sure; a wild streak, often truant and refusing to work on any mundane assignments, often performing work that her teachers could not readily grasp. They thought her mentally ill or retarded, in fact, until this high school teacher listened to some of what she said and realized she was working in algebraic geometry related to mathematical logic. She had proven a new result that was publishable in a major mathematical journal.

"When she came to see me, she asked questions about some fine points regarding varieties over topological fields that she had found in Weill's *Foundations of Algebraic Geometry*. In particular, she took him up on his final sentence, to express certain facts in the language of categories and functors. A task she accomplished masterfully, as a matter of fact. She had mastered also Weill's *Basic Number Theory* and Zariski's *Algebraic Surfaces* and both volumes of Zariski and Samuel's *Commutative Algebra*. She had obtained much of her category formalism from Mac Lane's *Homology*. She even asked me why Weill's style in his papers was so different from that in his books.

"She engaged me in a discussion of Francesco Severi's proof of the Riemann-Roch Theorem versus that of Guido Castelnuovo whose papers she had read in German and Italian in early century mathematical formalism together with some papers of Picard in French. She went further, well beyond me to the extent that I dropped out of the discussion altogether, a rarity in my life except with certain peers, during which she regaled me with a detailed exposition of regular versus irregular algebraic surfaces using Picard's integral of the first kind and introducing antique notions such as the *plurigenera* of Federigo Enriques by which he and Castelnuovo, who was, by the way, Oscar Zariski's advisor, classified the algebraic surfaces into four natural classes in terms of their *plurigenera*. Of course, this all relates to birational classes…"

Of course, I thought.

"So why doesn't anyone talk about her?" I asked, hoping to slow him down. "Where's she teach?"

"Her command of the movement was such that she brought in Hodge theory, after discussing the role of Betti numbers and bringing in harmonic forms and the Hodge structure and dimension. Indeed, she actually tied it to the modern language via the singular cohomology groups with real coefficients of complex algebraic varieties as sums of the dimension of the subspaces and the relationship to the Betti numbers. Of course, this is for algebraic surfaces and she duly noted that the theorem only stated that the irregularity of the surface— that is to say the difference of the geometric and the arithmetic genus—is the dimension of the linear space of Picard integrals of the first kind which is half the first Betti number. But of course, that first Betti number is the also expressed as the difference of the dimensions of the two cohomology subspaces of dimension one.

"She knew the history of the dispute between Enriques and Severi and the practical destruction of the Italian school of mathematics by the fascists, making it impossible for Jews like Castelnuovo and Enriques to publish or teach. Furthermore, she launched into a discussion of Platonism in mathematics, of Enriques's belief in an algebraic world in existence independently of us, outside us and even outside our thoughts. Then she remarked, in passing, that his belief in the proof of his fundamental theorem by strictly algebro-geometric methods without need for the transcendental techniques adopted by Poincare led him to give faulty arguments. That in the end he was vindicated by Grothendieck, after his death. Imagine, she had read Grothendieck. While here she mastered Grothendieck's reformulation of algebraic geometry from his published Séminaires at IHES."

He stopped for moment and I considered asking him my last questions again, but then he took up the first one and I guessed he was considering his words with some care. The way he spoke one always assumed he was reading, but perhaps this was difficult for him on some level I could not feel. The competitiveness of some of these people amazed me. Massive egos.

"We can't really claim her. The fact is, I needed help from Imre Bolyai to grasp her thesis. She gave it to me in the semester after she had arrived in my office. It took us two semesters to read it. She chose me, it turned out, because she wanted to be a descendant of the André Weill who was himself a descendent of Picard and Hadamard. She knew all this history.

"She never completed high school, of course, which is of no consequence, but we had to admit her to graduate studies immediately since to put her in undergraduate classes would have been a disservice to her, to the faculty and to the students. The faculty of arts and sciences were a bit nonplussed and some frankly hostile, but on examination of her they seemed terrified. Particularly the departmental heads of literature, physics, economics and history. She had no problem exceeding everything they knew about their disciplines. It was as if she had absorbed all of Western knowledge and much from the East as well.

"Alas, there is also the fact that she appears without prior announcement. She usually does not announce herself at all. In the past she had the disquieting habit of sitting in on classes unannounced, but she stopped that after she caused an epileptic seizure of a professor of mathematics at Oregon State with a counterexample to a *theorem* he was presenting at a seminar on his recent work, although no one has been able to glean insight into the reason for her presence at that particular backwater. It is like appearing at Texas A&M or some other end of the mathematical universe."

"Maybe to present her counterexample. Where's she teach?"

"Nowhere. She has her choice of institutions, of course, but chooses to travel where she wishes. She is welcome at any institution with viable mathematics department and she often shows up to work on a problem or two with a specialist before going off to another institution for a stay. Or else she vanishes.

"But the difficulty with her in an institution is that her approach is so out of the ordinary no one much grasps her. She seems to view mathematics through formal language properties. She insists that with the right language one can see everything, but she works with languages of infinite length, most often of uncountable cardinalities, of inaccessible cardinalities for compactness properties. She has even used compactifications of languages, all inaccessible to me I admit. But you will understand why she is not teaching at any institution when you listen to her colloquium talk."

"She makes money? How's she do that?"

"She runs an international financial company. She makes money buying and selling stocks and commodities. She began that before she came here, making more money than her father very quickly. No one understands the business, to be honest, but she works with what she calls derived quantities, which she once explained to me in terms of options as the simplest example. It frankly didn't interest me in any sense.

"Her thesis regarded topoi and large cardinals and languages of infinite length and the theory of types. Her great love is mathematical logic. In fact, she has ways of viewing mathematics through logical constructs, a blend of what is called model theory and proof theory, that led to bizarre constructions of classical fields. Her foundations of real and complex analysis makes the nonstandard analysis of Abraham Robinson seem tame by comparison. She read both of Rudin's texts *Principles of Mathematical Analysis* and *Real and Complex Analysis* and worked all the exercises for her high school teacher, just to show she was not bluffing him. In two weeks and on the side. She threatened him with *Functional Analysis* which I remember he had not found amenable to his temperament as a student here. She has the uncanny gift of speed reading mathematics. No other person of my acquaintance can accomplish that task."

I couldn't imagine such a thing. "She does the problems that way?"

"As she reads them, she does them in her head. With as much detail as you could wish. But often from a point of view not found in any standard approach.

"She provided me with proof of the classification theorems and some other classical works in the Italian school of algebraic geometry that Grothendieck unified, but using a specific formal language. The results fell out as corollaries of properties she proved regarding the language. I was dumbstruck, to be sure, and could not completely follow the arguments. Bolyai finally worked through it and urged her to publish the result, but she didn't want to write it up formally. He passed it on for her as a communication.

"She loves to talk and hates to write, Mr. Butcher."

"It almost sounds like what they do with group cohomology, the bit of replacing long division by other functional variants of it. I mean, the way she changes language to get results."

"It is much more obscure, I assure you. Bolyai doesn't like to talk about her, as if it is bad luck or something. He looks around when her name comes up, as if she might be watching.

"Professionally she uses the name Hypatia Lie. She assumes any mathematician will know how to pronounce Lie, but may not know how to pronounce el aye in Portuguese. Hence she lengthened her shortening of her name a-lee-na, a el aye en e, to Lie." He cleared his throat, but didn't add anything more.

"I guess Hypatia Ali wouldn't work."

He seemed not to get the joke. Or he ignored it.

As I readied to leave his office, he said, "I imagine you will come to me for an overview of the cohomology as used in several complex variables. I can give you the Hodge theory, which may prove useful to you given that it is defined by harmonic forms using that generalization of the Laplacian I understand you have already discovered independently. Of course, the Hodge decomposition discussed here can be obtained without the Laplacian but utilizing Dolbeault's sheaf cohomology with holomorphic forms. It provides a more direct algebraic approach."

I escaped with a need to meet this creature who called herself Hypatia Lie. What he'd told me seemed impossible.

She made a significant impression on a lot of people with her talk, a surprising development. The Dweeb seemed especially dumbstruck and I thought it might erase the influence of Utta.

He caught me in the graduate student office with a question he had evidently wrestled mightily after her talk.

"I just don't get that bit about alpha equaling aleph-sub-alpha. Why is that necessary for a non-successor cardinal to be regular?"

He wrote on the board $\alpha = \aleph_\alpha$.

"Did she say that?" I asked, stalling for time to get my bearings.

"Yes, she did."

"You do get ordinals versus cardinals, right?"

"Ordinal numbers are about different well-orderings. Cardinals are the smallest ordinals such that there exists a well-ordering of that order type onto a set."

"Be careful with the word smaller. And you're assuming the axiom of choice. Otherwise the sets may not be comparable—"

"—or well ordered. Yeah, yeah, everyone assumes the axiom of choice."

"A cardinal is an ordinal that can't be bijected onto any of its own proper initial segments. That's the sense of smaller for ordinals. Ordinals are really just the set of strictly smaller, or preceding, ordinals. So an ordinal alpha is smaller than an ordinal beta if there is an isomorphism of alpha onto an initial segment of beta. I mean, if alpha is smaller than beta, then alpha is contained in beta."

"It's why cardinals are called initial ordinals."

"I guess it would be. It's the smallest of the ordinals as well-orderings of a set. Transitive, they call it; every element of the set is a subset. There are a lot of countable sets that are of the same cardinality: counting numbers zero one two etcetera, fractions, integers, but the one that is contained as the initial segment in every transitive well-ordering of a countably infinite set is little omega, the counting numbers. So it is the cardinality of the countably infinite sets. It becomes aleph-sub-zero, aleph-naught, however you want to call it" I wrote $\aleph_0$ on the board "the first one. The next is aleph-sub-one—"

"—which is two to the power little omega, that is two to the power aleph-naught, same thing, the power set or set of all subsets—"

"—assuming the continuum hypothesis, not otherwise. That's a statement of the continuum hypothesis…not the generalized continuum hypothesis, of course, which says all successors are power sets of their predecessors. But that is off track here. Anyway, I find it obnoxious to have to think of this definition, as in 0 1 2 etcetera all being cardinals and then the first infinite set, little omega of all the counting numbers, and then little omega plus one, which is not a cardinal because it has a bijection onto the initial ordinal omega by sending omega to zero and n to n plus one. It is not intuitive—"

"Assuming different sized infinities can be intuitive," Red shouted out.

"So a cardinal is a limit ordinal," I continued. "You get limit ordinals, right?"

"Sure. A successor ordinal is one that is obtained by adding one to the previous ordinal, the same thing as taking the union of the ordinal with the singleton of the ordinal," and he wrote $\alpha+1 = \alpha \cup \{\alpha\}$ "and if it isn't a successor it's a limit ordinal. A supremum over the previous ones—"

"Right, essentially a union. That's how you get the aleph sequence by transfinite induction on the ordinals. Aleph-sub-alpha is the smallest infinite cardinal strictly greater than all the aleph-sub-beta for beta strictly smaller than alpha. Of course, we begin with aleph-naught being the cardinal little omega, the set of all the counting numbers."

"Including zero. I don't think of zero as a counting number. Anyway, aleph-naught is also the cardinality of omega plus one—"

"Which is the union of omega with the singleton set containing omega."

I went to the board and wrote $\emptyset$ {$\emptyset$} {$\emptyset$,{$\emptyset$}} {$\emptyset$,{$\emptyset$},{$\emptyset$,{$\emptyset$}}} ... {$\emptyset$,{$\emptyset$}}...} ... and said, "Or just shorthanded as zero, one, two, three dot-dot-dot omega which is really the set of all the numbers zero one two etcetera. So adding one to omega is just taking its union with the set containing itself."

"Right. Which I wrote down already." He pointed to it. "So anyway, by induction the first uncountable cardinal is aleph-sub-one which according to the continuum hypothesis is the power set of little omega—"

"Two to the little omega—"

"—or aleph-naught, since by definition of cardinals those are the same thing."

"Set of all maps from little omega to two. Right, you get it."

"What about beth numbers?"

"Off track, really. Forget it, for now anyway. You get cofinality?"

"An unbounded set. I mean inside another set. I read several definitions before I got it. A way to look at an ordinal is that it is just the set of ordinals strictly less than it."

"The way cofinality is defined does seem more obscure than it ought to be. A cofinal set can always get a little further along in a set where it is cofinal. The least ordinal that is cofinal in a set is its cofinality. So the cofinality of a cofinality is its own cofinality. Anyway, a regular cardinal is equal to its own cofinality and every other cardinal is singular and would have a cofinality smaller than itself. And every infinite successor cardinal is regular. Easy to see, right?"

"Not so easy, but I got it. It requires some proof, but I've seen one."

Klaus called out in his perfect English tinged with a German accent, "Cofinality of a set depends on the order type. It is different for ordinals, since they are well-ordered, than for other orders. Little omega is cofinal in the real numbers in their natural order but not in aleph-one which is at most the cardinality of the continuum."

There was a visual flash of the counting numbers climbing by unit steps up the continuum of real numbers.

"So anyway, it always freaks me out that the subscripts catch up. That is weird, given how they're defined. I mean," and I wrote $\aleph_0\ \aleph_1\ \aleph_2 \ldots$ "are all initial ordinals of increasing infinities and eventually you get to where" and I wrote $\alpha = \aleph_\alpha$ "aleph-sub-alpha equals alpha. A fixed point in the sequence."

"You're avoiding my question. And there is some theorem about that in any case, for normal such sequences, which I seem to recall means that it is non-decreasing and continuous in that limits work. I think the cardinal sequence is normal."

"For any normal sequence," Klaus called out again, "there are arbitrarily large fixed points. That means the function indexing the cardinal numbers with the aleph numbers is forced to have arbitrarily large fixed points. And also, the cofinality of any limit ordinal must be a regular cardinal."

I wished Klaus would come up and do this. He worked with Bolyai and was clearly more intimate with this stuff than either of us.

"No, not avoiding it," I said. "Just trying to get to where we can talk about it. Klaus, why don't give us a bit of a hand here. I only learned this stuff as a way to get at Cohen's independence proofs.

"Doesn't Utta help you with this stuff?"

"Utta refuses to talk about infinite sets. She says there is too much magic and the language of these cardinals and ordinals and all this set theory is dangerous because you risk saying something powerful without knowing it."

I looked into his eyes and saw that she didn't let him piss in her mouth, but that he watched her when other men pissed in her mouth and then kissed her on the mouth. Deep French kisses. Jesus, he was a goner. After blow jobs too. Maybe vaginal tongue cleaning after gang bangs. I must have given some hint of my vision, some reflexive backing away or face twitch, because he looked startled.

Klaus interceded. He came up to the board, fair-haired, clean-cut, a no-nonsense Aryan.

"You understood Cohen's proof? The method of forcing?" Klaus asked me.

"Yes. We went through that little book of Cohen's published by Benjamin and also some horrible stuff by Takeuti and Zaring in Springer. And a proof I think by Solovay and maybe Dana Scott that used Boolean algebras. I'm sure you know that stuff too."

"The little book by Cohen is horrible. His original papers are easier to understand. But mostly we studied the Boolean-valued approach. Bolyai employs forcing and works within set theory only to examine problems with groups. Mostly the free groups. There are some open questions that may be independent. Saharon Shelah recently showed that the Whitehead's problem for groups is undecidable, even assuming the continuum hypothesis. But it is true for the constructible universe. This is a bit of a surprise and has captured Bolyai's attention.

"But to summarize this terminology: Ordinals are these transitive sets, well-orderings that start with zero and go through all the natural numbers to the first limit ordinal, which is little omega. The same as zero, one, two, etcetera followed by the limiting jump to little omega which is the set of all natural numbers." He pointed to my sequence $\emptyset$ $\{\emptyset\}$ $\{\emptyset,\{\emptyset\}\}$ $\{\emptyset,\{\emptyset\},\{\emptyset,\{\emptyset\}\}\}$ ... $\{\emptyset,\{\emptyset\}\}...\}$ ... on the board. "Cardinals are the smallest ordinals in the sense that they are initial segments in the ordinals. So little omega is a cardinal, aleph-zero. This is the cardinality of the countably infinite sets.

"Successor cardinals are as in that list above, but eventually there is a limit" and he added $\aleph_\omega$ and another indication of ellipsis after the ... so that it read $\aleph_0$ $\aleph_1$ $\aleph_2$ ... $\aleph_\omega$ ... "and aleph-sub-omega is a limit cardinal because little omega is a limit ordinal. Now the cofinality of any uncountable limit cardinal is the index. You see?" He wrote $\mathrm{cof}(\aleph_\omega) = \omega$ "because it is the limit of a sequence of cardinals aleph-sub-i for all the i in little omega. So its cofinality has to be little omega, less than its own cardinality."

Perhaps the Dweeb looked a bit puzzled, because Klaus said, "It isn't entirely obvious, of course, but it follows from a little lemma that characterizes the singular cardinals. It is not hard. Take it to be an exercise." He went on, "But think about little omega. It is not a union of fewer than omega sets of cardinality less than itself, that is to say, of finite cardinality. In fact, there is no way to get to little omega from any smaller cardinals. Everything remains finite with power sets until you take the limit, that is a union of all of the preceding sets into a new set. It is inaccessible in the sense that nothing can get to it. But then aleph-one is a successor, the next cardinal, and with the continuum hypothesis is the power set of aleph-zero, little omega. The generalized continuum hypothesis is that aleph-sub-alpha-plus-one is two raised to the power of aleph-sub-alpha. This is in the sense that two raised to any power is the set of all functions from the set into the set containing only zero and one, that is the set two, and that set of maps is the equivalent of the power set. You see how the set of all subsets of a set is the set of all functions from the set into the set zero-one, yes?"

The Dweeb shook his head yes, but that was so elementary I wondered why Klaus brought it up.

"The axiom of choice is very important to all of this," Klaus continued. "Without this, it is not possible to prove something so elementary as aleph-one is not a countable union of countable sets: you require the countable axiom of choice to prove that a countable union of countable sets is countable. To work without it here is insanity. With it, you are able to prove that a successor cardinal is regular, but it is necessary to make use of it."

"To your question about why an uncountable non-successor cardinal must be such that aleph-sub-alpha equals alpha—" I said looking at the Dweeb...

"—and uncountable is necessary because really aleph-zero is a limit cardinal and it is not true for that one—" interrupted Klaus...

"—because as Klaus has shown, for a limit cardinal, a non-successor cardinal—" I said...

"—uncountable limit cardinal—" Klaus interrupted.

"Right," I said, "for an uncountable non-successor cardinal, in other words an uncountable limit cardinal, its cofinality must be its subscript. But if it is regular, then that subscript must be the cardinality itself. So then aleph-sub alpha must be alpha." I pointed to what the Dweeb had first put on the board: $\alpha = \aleph_\alpha$.

"But," Klaus said, "the least such fixed point has cofinality little omega, so is not regular. It is singular. So the first fixed point is not regular. And of course, it is impossible to prove that there are such uncountable limit cardinals that are regular. They are called weakly inaccessible. They are the smaller of the large cardinals in the absence of the generalized continuum hypothesis."

"Their existence cannot be proved for set theory," I said. "Actually, more carefully, for some formalization of set theory, like say Zermelo-Fraenkel with or without the axiom of choice. Worse, you can't prove that the existence of such is consistent with set theory, since it can be shown that an inaccessible cardinal provides a model for set theory and hence would prove it consistent, which would make it inconsistent."

"That is by Gödel's incompleteness theorem," Klaus said.

"What are these bigger inaccessible cardinals?" the Dweeb asked.

"These are the regular strong limit cardinals. A limit cardinal is not a successor of a smaller cardinal nor is it a union over a set of less than its own cardinality of cardinals less than itself. Aleph-zero satisfies that, certainly, but is not uncountable. But aleph-zero is more inaccessible than this, in a sense, since it cannot be the power set of any smaller cardinal."

The Dweeb piped up again. "Not two to the power of any set smaller than itself. So then the continuum hypothesis gets involved."

"Of course, yes. A strong limit cardinal is always a limit cardinal but not vice-versa without the generalized continuum hypothesis. And a strongly inaccessible cardinal is a regular strong limit cardinal. They are very big. Think of how big is aleph-zero compared to the finite cardinals, the numbers zero one two and so on. It is much, much larger than all its predecessors. This is the relationship of large cardinals to the other cardinals. They are much, *much* larger than their predecessors. Especially so for the strongly inaccessible cardinal numbers."

"But," I said, "it is not just tied to mimicking aleph-naught on a grander scale, but is also related to other questions. Some of the questions have to do with infinitary languages, which is why she brought that up in her talk. She works with languages with sentences of infinite length, with infinitely many quantifiers and with infinitely many conjunctions and disjunctions, and she gets certain compactness properties—"

"Don't talk about that," the Dweeb said, looking around with a panicked expression.

"Yes, and there are questions regarding sets that are closed and unbounded, the—"

"Don't say it!"

"Clubs," I said.

The Dweeb got all wild-eyed like a cat with its hair standing on end about to dash off in all directions.

"What the fuck is wrong with you, man?"

"Utta says not to discuss that stuff, it's too dangerous."

"Does she know about club-guessing?" Klaus asked. "That seems to be the latest property studied by Shelah and his school. And the stationary sets, of course, play a part. Is this Utta afraid of them as well?"

"Just answer one more thing before I get away from you two," the Dweeb said. "Why'd she say that the continuum could be anything except aleph-sub-little-omega?"

"She said that?" I asked. "I didn't hear that."

"You must have been asleep—" the Dweeb started, interrupted by a cry from the bank of carrels: "Like advisor, like student."

"Assuming that it is not too dangerous to discuss," Klaus said, "this is a result of an old theorem dating to 1905. König's theorem. It states that for two families of sets A and B indexed by the same set, call it I, if each element A-sub-i of A is of smaller cardinality than each B-i of B, then the cardinality of the union of the elements of A is less than the Cartesian product of the elements of B. I think this is the equivalent of the axiom of choice, too. Now take the index set I as aleph-zero—indexed by only the natural numbers, in other words—and let each of the A-sub-i's be aleph-sub-i and the B-sub-i's be the same set, aleph-sub-omega. Assume that two to the aleph-zero is bigger than or equal to aleph-sub-alpha. Then the union is aleph-sub-omega and the product is less than or equal to two to the aleph-zero to the aleph-zero power, and that is just two the aleph zero. So if you assume that two to the aleph-zero—""

"—which is the continuum—" the Dweeb blurted...

"Yes, of course. The continuum then would have to be strictly greater than aleph-sub-omega if it were greater or equal to it. So it cannot be equal to it by König. But Solovay did prove that it could be anything not excluded by König."

"That paper had a nice title," I said. "Two to the aleph-naught can be anything it ought to be."

The visit with Goldman regarding the classical groups didn't inspire me. I had seen more interesting stuff relating the matrix groups to tori and maximal tori as coverings of connected matrix groups. That had gone by in a day's lecture as part of a course in something or other, but the exercise to show that quaternions had square roots was fun. Or at least I so remembered it. This bit from Goldman got him into what he called stable groups, which meant that eventually the nth homotopy groups stabilized for n sufficiently large and increasing in the sense that the $(n+r)^{th}$ homotopy groups were independent of n when n was large enough. It led to Bott periodicity, a nice name for a result that didn't do much for me, though it did give computational results, with a period of eight, for the stable homotopy of the classical matrix groups. He mumbled something about Clifford algebras and I thought maybe the octonians got in there. It made me think of the result due to J. Frank Adams, a name I couldn't forget not because of his result but because how it sounded stuck in my head from the first time I'd heard it. This theorem of Adam's was that normed real division algebras only existed for the real field, the complex field, the quaternions, and the octonians, being equivalent to there being trivial vector bundles only for the spheres S^0, S^1, S^3, and S^7. It was the sort of relationships that excited mathematicians, a relationship between some pure algebraic result with no seeming relevance to anything remotely geometrical, and pure geometry. Every graduate student eventually runs across the hairy ball theorem, that you can't comb the hair on a hairy ball flat without a cowlick, or just that you can't comb a hairy ball. It is actually true for all even-dimensional spheres. But this theorem of Adams was stunning. Froebenius had shown that the only real division algebras were of dimension one, two or four, being the real numbers, the complex numbers and the quaternions. By dropping the need for associativity, the eight dimensional complex quaternions or Cayley numbers as they were called was added to the list. There were no more. And worse, as you went up in dimension you lost something, from the real numbers' order passing to the complex numbers to the commutativity of multiplication in the quaternions and then associativity in the Cayley numbers. That that could be related to vector fields on spheres, a purely geometric result, seemed mind boggling.

Of course, I doubted I would ever see or understand a proof of the result, nor did I find such interesting. Hence, I kept from asking Goldman or anyone else about the result. I pretended to pay attention as Goldman waxed ecstatic, wishing I'd slept a bit longer on this Thursday, an off-day, when Hypatia Lie was to speak to us about creatures from the inaccessible cardinals:

Like an undernourished street urchin wearing thick, lusterless mahogany hair parted in a fastidiously constructed circular arc along the middle of her head that ended in a sloppy whorl far back on an extended skull with a pair of braids or pony tails or some thing of that sort hanging beyond the middle of her back, each of them tied in a single loose knot near the top of the bunched hair-wad and splaying strands as if exposed wiring, the much ballyhooed Maria Hypatia Aline da Inferna rose from a seat in front and almost disappeared behind the small lectern, so insubstantial I couldn't see her full face peeping over the stand. Something remarked that I had not before experienced such red-less mahogany on so round a dome. Dome for sure, more pronouncedly domed atop when she stepped out and faced us full on. A huge dome, as if attached to the lower half of her head along an inverted buttress where the coal-black arched eyebrows, pencil thin and coarse, disappeared beneath the hair bunches to hide with the implied ligamental ledge. Below the dome and wide expanse of naked forehead protruded a narrow face, long and tapering to a blunted sharpness of chin where mounted lips, painted orange or perhaps natural color, straight atop and fattened slightly below, a closed-mouth smile from an orifice that didn't cover even half the narrow expanse above the chin. Flesh folds like small welts, perhaps correctly called dimples, extended from the end of her lips downward at an angle of about forty-five degrees and appeared to be creases from a mouth-attaching hinge on a marionette.

"I thought I would talk about some work that parallels what is being done here in your topological algebra group regarding the correspondence between topos theory as it binds algebraic geometry and logic." She spoke without moving her lips. The words could have emanated from elsewhere in the room synthesized from a shrill, penetrating double-reed like an oboe in upper register intoning an accent hard to distinguish and harder to place.

"Much of this continues along the foundational lines of Lawvere who came to it from oddly enough continuum mechanics, incongruous for sure. I think he hated measure theory and look what he did. Freyd and Johnstone, and I think Johnstone has been recently here for some work in a seminar or such like that I missed, unfortunately, having been disappeared in the Amazon under less than ideal circumstances."

She smiled enough for me to glimpse a regularly aligned row of baby teeth. The marionette character of her lower face was presented by high cheekbones and prominent, rounded cheeks framing flared nostrils on a sharp arrow ending a long, thin nose bridge. Fossettes everywhere: below the lower lip dimpling the upper chin which jutted at the end; below the cheeks along the nose defining the marionette mouth; at the welts along the corner of the mouth. A face like an embellished hatchet, sharp and exotic, the entire mechanism propped atop a long, skinny neck. She looked like a scarecrow, her meager body draped in jeans and a long-sleeved flannel shirt from children's wear, on her feet black high-tops shoes that might have been men's size twelve triple-a, if such a thing existed. With nary a hint of curvature anywhere, she could have been a tall-for-her-age big-footed prepubescent fifth grader.

"The setting can be adjusted to suit varying tastes, though the logical structures are most easily assimilated within category theory, more precisely topos theory. But the theories can also be carried out in standard proof theory or model theory, using some variations on the forcing methods as first developed by Cohen but also using Boolean models as developed by Scott and Solovay and even Kripke semantics. Some of this work has been performed with Professor Saharon Shelah of the Hebrew University and a number people at Berkeley and

Stanford where there are so many fine logicians. Of course, all the wrong things are mine."

She stared out of black eyes set far back in the shadows of her head, slits radiating into the room, scanning every face. She stopped at my eyes and held the glance too long for my comfort. I disengaged.

I remembered the two semesters of readings with my master of the Moore school, billed as metamathematics though owing nothing to Kleene's fat book by that name but rather begun the summer before as set theory, a light summer search and destroy operation through the innocently named yellow peril *Introduction to Axiomatic Set Theory* of Takeuti and Zaring that set us all back a peg or two, instructor included, and culminated in a disastrous siege of their follow up alphabet soup entitled *Axiomatic Set Theory* along with Paul Cohen's skinny two-tone paperback gothic *Set Theory and the Continuum Hypothesis.* Forcing and such, a terrifying foray into models of mathematics that stood logic literally on its head. Here it was again, but then a tiny voice in my head, soothing and quiet, Don't be afraid, this is much smoother. Not so prickly. It won't hurt.

Where had I heard that before? I recalled the theorem providing for the existence of a model for set theory in which there lived an infinite subset of the continuum, the power set of the natural numbers, which contained no countable subsets. The little voice in my head laughed. Don't be so anal. To which I countered, Cohen thought the continuum hypothesis was false in reality, even though independent of the axioms of set theory. The voice cackled and I thought I was going nuts. Two to the aleph naught can be anything you want it to be, it laughed. What the fuck does it mean for someone to say, The continuum hypothesis is really false? I responded in my head and it said, Or true. Ye of little faith...

Hypatia spoke not nearly so soothingly. "For those of you who plowed through some of the original expositions or even the original papers, let me say the way has been smoothed considerably in the last few years. Even philosophers have contributed to the transparency of method, with people like Saul Kripke providing model theory via modal logics, especially the semantics on the language S-four which relates directly to intuitionistic logic. Still it is hard for some to come to grips with relativity within mathematics. We don't appreciate multivalued logic, and yet some work in probability."

Yes, I thought, but that is inherently two-valued at its root. Measureable sets, conditional probability as restriction to reduced sigma-algebras reflecting increased information—the voice cut me off, Again with the anal brain-constipation; condition your expectations on the idea that reality is local. But, I thought, none of this is real and the voice laughed again, Don't be so sure…

She looked directly at me and twitched her meager butt like a pigeon in Jackson Square. I wondered if anyone else noticed. I wondered about the last shipment of hash I'd loaded into this day's cigarettes.

The nasal drone continued. "Much of this work has been placed in perspective relative to the objections of the intuitionists, especially Heyting who himself formalized what he said was not formalizable—"

"Like Brouwer spending the first half of his career proving his fixed point theorem and the last half explaining why it was wrong." It was Oberst's voice, spoken without humor though his minions chuckled.

"Of course," she said, "Poincare and Brouwer and others had objections to classical extensions to the certain infinite that came from Cantor and led to perceived problems. But those objections were addressed, problems cured, after all. I very much recommend the book by Fitting on this intuitionism and forcing. But perhaps I ought to go quickly over the basic difference in the formal system of Heyting and Brouwer and the classical logic we all love and hold dear, at least at the sentential level, realizing that there are issues of domains involved too. But that is where the work that came out of algebraic geometry has proven so useful, the category theory that organizes it all so beautifully within the topoi.

"What disturbs most is the conceptual basis of the method to measure the infinite devised by Cantor is so primitive…so simple and obvious. Transparent. The sort of method one would find in pre-numeric societies. Given two herds of goats and no way to count beyond, say, three, and there are societies in which one two three many is the number system, sufficient for all that, then to determine which is larger simply run them side by side into two corrals until one set is depleted. And yet, when extended to the infinite, there begins the nagging nightmares which caused people like Heyting to declare that formal methods to characterize mathematics are impossible. Yet he did devise one, even if provisionally…"

She scanned the room again and stopped at me, almost imperceptibly twitching her butt upwards again, and I wondered anew if it were me hallucinating or if others saw it. I looked over at Red who stared with rapt attention, even as the two younger faculty of topology behind him studiously ignored her, whispering and writing something on a pad, perhaps working out a proof. My advisor had already fallen asleep.

"For most mathematicians intuitionistic logic remains a curiosity. I mean, we do live in a two-valued world, at least mathematically, most assuredly do we not? And maybe some find the position of Poincare and Brouwer and Heyting to be in their comfort zone that mathematics is languageless activity, in a sense, Heyting's view that axioms cannot capture mathematical ideas, and as for Poincare the integers are simply there in the thoughts all along anyways. But without dwelling as they did on the meaning of the impredicative definition or without rejecting the absolutenesses of such as a or not-a, not-not-a implies a, a or not-a; that is to say, the law of excluded middle and its consequences. But accepted, at least by Brouwer and Heyting, were such as a implies not-not-a and not-not a or not-a, where I mean a parenthesis around a or not-a."

She hadn't written a thing on the board. I would have at least written the last statement, the parenthetical bit. I understood why she chose not to teach. It was not easy to follow her.

"It makes one wonder what old Poincare would have done had he realized as it came to be seen that his beloved continuum of real numbers could not exist without impredicative definitions. So, also, unlike in classical sentential or propositional logic, whatever you like to call it, the connectives of intuitionistic propositional logic are not definable in terms of the others. Of course, in general it is enough to choose two in the classical two-valued logic, say negation and one of conjunction or disjunction, from which the rest can be obtained, or even alone the Sheffer stroke. But for the intuition, it seems two values is not enough and hence two connectives are not enough." She smiled as if making a joke to herself, a wisp of a mirthful grin at something no one else got, not me for sure unless somehow she found it amusing that two valued propositional logic could be characterized with two connectives, never mind Sheffer's stroke.

"Of course, the classical connectives live in Boolean algebras, though the quantifiers of first and higher order logics cannot be so captured. But some mathematical logicians like Tarski and maybe the mathematician Stone learned early on about the formal algebraic system corresponding to the intuitionistic propositional logic, what they called Brouwerian algebras that are dual to the more-studied-now Heyting algebras which characterize intuitionistic logic of propositions or sentences, call them as you will, closed formulas of any quantified logics. I think they called them closure algebras or something of the like but in fact they are really the open sets of a topological space, something dear to all our hearts.

"Let me just amplify with the fact that indeed these turn out to be modal propositional calculi corresponding to the language S-four which comes to us via Kripke or Beth-Kripke or Kripke-Joyal or sheaf or topos semantics, depending on the place of viewing and the latter of which, that Kripke-Joyal on, we will visit more later. And first, Kripke. But for now, just to know that these topological Boolean algebras are actually subsets of topological space with union, meet, complement, logical implication defined by" and she wrote on the board $Y \Rightarrow Z = (X—Y) \cup Z$ "and the interior and closure operations are necessity and possibility operations of S-four."

I assumed that X was the topological space where all this was happening. She never said, and I had no clue as to what the fuck were the possibility and necessity operations since I had no clue as to what was S4. But it did seem clear that somehow they provided more values than two, corresponding to the ambiguous truth value of stuff like the consequence of showing $A \Rightarrow \neg\neg A$. I had not considered modal logics and wondered now that perhaps there could have been available easier interpretations of Cohen's forcing. The idea that intuitionism could be expressed algebraically with general topology using closure and interior operators, but there was topology in Takeuti and Zaring's *Axiomatic Set Theory*—

"Of course, here by X is meant the topological space, that is, in the space X we have these things hold…" and she trailed off, then rose again to add "I will provide a Kripke semantics interpretation to forcing without mentioning intuitionism but first let me just discuss a moment more the business of the complement in Heyting versus Boole. Of course, for Boolean algebra we get the complement of an element x as minus x, so that x sup minus x is the 1 and x inf not x is 0" and she wrote $x \vee \neg x = 1$, $x \wedge \neg x = 0$, "that is to say, in the complete Heyting algebra maybe it is something like the union, I mean by it not x, is something like the sup of all those elements meeting x in zero."

Maybe she realized she was losing those who didn't already understand what she was talking about. As bad as some were at lecturing, my advisor included, few were this disorganized in presentation. Like she had way too much stuff jumbled up in her head. The clarity with which Bolyai presented his ideas had to reflect a deep sense of the meaning of what he did.

"For example," she said, "in the Heyting algebra of open subsets of a topological space the negation of an open set U is the interior of the set theoretic complement of U in the space. In other words, the complement of the set theoretic complement of the closure of U. So then the negation of the negation of U is the interior of U's closure, which can be bigger than U and it may be that even if x meet not-x is zero, its join may not be one."

I think she realized she had just done more damage to the discussion with her clarification. She giggled and said, "Well, it is called a pseudo-complement. If it be a true complement for all the elements in the algebra, then the thing is a Boolean algebra. That is, if the pseudo-complement of every element joins it in one, then it is Boolean."

She stood silent, surely trying to decide on whether to add one more remark or instead to leap out of the hole she had deepened. "It can be defined as the largest element that meets x in zero." She went to the board and I thought, Oh no, don't do it, but the little voice in my head told me to *cale a boca* whatever that fucking meant and she wrote $x \lesssim (q \Rightarrow p)$ iff $x \wedge q \lesssim p$ and said "so the element $q \Rightarrow p$ is the largest element x such that x meet q is less than or equal to p." Maybe she realized she'd just fucked up, digging deeper, but she continued "The pseudo-complement of an element p is" and she wrote $\neg p = (p \Rightarrow 0)$ "which means p implies absurdity, so that is the notness of p. Clearly the notness of p is the largest element x of the algebra so that x meet p is zero" and she wrote $x \square p = 0$. "Now if the notness of p joins p in 1 for all p" and she wrote $p \square \neg p = 1$, $\square p$, "then clearly" $\neg \neg p = p$ "instead of just" $p \square \neg \neg p$. "But obviously" and she wrote $\neg p = \neg \neg \neg p$ and $\neg \neg (x \square p) = \neg \neg x \square \neg \neg x$ "in any case."

I spoke up. "Didn't you mean a p in there for one of those exes?"

She looked at what she'd written and erased the first x on the right side of the second equation and replaced it with p. "*Claro,*" I think she said and the little voice in my head piped up, So trivial a correction.

I looked around and noted that perhaps only Oberst and I were paying attention. Momus looked bored and Bolyai was intently watching her and thinking of something different. But then Bolyai remarked, "Birkhoff in his book on lattices claimed some precedence over Tarski and Stone—"

"Probably," she said. "Is it always not so? Particularly with Birkhoff."

I think Bolyai shook his head no; maybe she confused the younger and elder Birkhoffs. I sure as hell didn't know except it was the older one who had set aside refereeing von Neumann's L^2 ergodic paper until he got his L^1 version done. But I think it was the younger who had written *Lattice Theory.* Petty assholes for the most part anyway, academics.

"Now let me just talk just a minute of the language S-four and the semantics of Kripke and the forcing of Cohen before I go to the topoi and local logic."

My advisor, head back as he slumped in his chair, began snoring audibly at the ceiling through his open mouth. The noise or motion or something woke him and he sat suddenly upright. He looked around and then hung his head forward and fell back asleep.

She described the language S4 as classical two-valued first-order predicate logic augmented with the symbol □ and the rule that if X is a formula, so is □X which she read "necessarily X" and to which she added ◊ as the dual operator defined via $\Diamond X = \neg\Box\neg X$ and read "possibly X."

She talked about Kripke semantics for this thing, adding that there were other semantics as well but that we didn't need them. She said the idea went back to Leibnitz for whom necessary meant truth in all possible worlds. But, she added, possible depends on where you are, I assumed as in what model or where in some model or where in some reality. She tossed in the idea of a frame, I assumed a sort of local reference frame, as a pair <𝔊,𝔎> (her gothic letters precisely and effortlessly drawn) with a set of possible worlds 𝔊 and a binary relation 𝔎 on 𝔊 so that for p, q ∈ 𝔊, if p𝔎q then she called q accessible from p. She made some remarks about needing domains of quantification in order to make this a mathematical model leading to a kind of model dependence for the domains but she added not to worry about it, for what we're doing it suffices to stay with the same domain for each possible world in the frame. She said that different conditions on accessibility led to different modal logics and she mentioned something called S5 where 𝔎 was an equivalence relation but for us 𝔎 would be a partial order, which was S4. That began to make sense, given I recalled Cohen's forcing had been a partial order, the details a bit fuzzy, and indeed she yammered about conditions, her back to us now and nose in the board writing stuff at random helter-skelter, skinny flat butt twitching with the chalk movement, talking about compatible families of conditions and how if one condition ensures that a has both u and v as elements then that is stronger than one ensuring only that u is a member, so that induces a partial order and I realized this was a clear way to see what the fuck Cohen had been doing developing a nonstandard, enlarged model, by which I recalled the term inner model as the standard one which was transitive or something made of constructible sets, the minimal model, built by Gödel, and the impossibility of proving the universe was not constructible which was denoted V = L, so far as

I remembered, a lot of water under the bridge since I had pushed that stuff out of my head and here it was again, so this "nonstandard" model (not in the sense of Robinson probably) obtained by forcing some unnatural, imaginary? generic set in there with partial information from forcing conditions to shove that baby, that generic set, in there; the set that would be necessary to get the continuum hypothesis false in the enlarged model, also the axiom of choice in some other enlarged model since that followed from V=L as well, as I recalled…

She showed a couple things with the □ and ◊, saying we'd revisit possibilities again in a more orderly context, and then blathered about categories and functors, shit I hated and tuned out though the voice in my head nagged me, It isn't only notation, which was also audible in the room, from the board, something about knowing many of us had little enthusiasm for what we called abstract nonsense and I thought that there had to be some naturally beautiful way to get at this and she said aloud "It all may seem formal and empty, only notation, but if you wander within the confines of these structures you will stumble across coherence and content and directness…much more organized than if you work it within set theoretic logic…" I sensed a religious crusade about foundations; the voice in my head stopped the bitching.

After ranting briefly about type theory and formal languages and set theory and such as foundations for mathematics, she said that in category theory the arrows between objects, the morphisms, had an autonomous role that was not subordinated to the structures, which I assumed were the categories. Verbs and nouns on equal footing, she said, unlike set theory where functions are actually sets, so subordinated.

So what? popped into my head. The little voice didn't reply but from Hypatia came something about generalizing Grothendieck topoi of algebraic geometry for use as logics themselves. Much as topology can give logics as Heyting algebras. She said what a topos was but it didn't stick though it seemed to have something to do with subobject classifiers and power objects and a natural number object, all of it empty verbiage for me at this point since she didn't explain what any of that was and I had not learned it anywhere. She drew some diagrams and talked about pullbacks and maybe pushforwards, the verbiage flying by now too fast to capture, but it all seemed so unnatural you'd be forced to memorize it, or at least I would since *she* was clearly into it big time. Anyway, it seemed that a topos harbored a natural language, with objects as types and arrows beginning with 1, the terminal object whatever that might mean, but she said that arrows of the form $1 \rightarrow A$ were terms of type A in the topos, or something like that, and that in the category Set, $1 \rightarrow A$ were elements of A at which point I began to shut down but not before she wrote $1 \rightarrow \Omega$ and called that a formula, and I realized I'd not heard what omega was, and she said something about $1 \rightarrow N$ being numbers. I had her partially tuned out now but caught that Kripke semantics could be captured this way inside topoi using geometric morphisms which are those with left adjoints. I had missed this meaning of adjoint, but somehow a geometric morphism was a pair of left and right adjoints or something of the kind related to exactness.

I looked behind me and saw the wonk madly taking notes, something I had missed on previous purviews of the room, and remembered that he never interrupted to correct colloquia lectures with "Excuse me, I have a question…"-corrections to fuck ups. I wondered if he got all this, though given he worked in several complex variables I was pretty certain that abstract nonsense was old hat to him, and anyway there were people here actually working with this logical topos shit. I stopped craning my neck and looked at her like I was interested. The little voice said, You can't fool me…

Now she was on about presheaf semantics and sections and she talked about some canonical topology as the largest topology that made all the representable functors sheaves. Again she brought up the Grothendieck topos, saying an important example was the category of canonical sheaves on a complete Heyting algebra. This somehow, or maybe not, but something seemed as if it led to sentences locally true in some kind of cover where only sheaves were allowed as sorts of languages. My brief exposure to sheaves had been in differential geometry with the de Rham stuff, only briefly but as a sheaf of modules over a manifold with stalks the modules and which led to cohomology and stuff like torsion-free modules and discontinuous sections and the cohomology was with coefficients in sheaves, but I hadn't learned it and probably would need to, from Momus most likely. I couldn't remember if it led to Hodge theory, which had something to do with the heat kernel on manifolds, but none of it had stuck or maybe it had come unstuck. This was not what she was on about. I guessed her sheaf stalks or fibers or whatever they were, were not modules but probably Abelian groups. Too much structure otherwise except as Z-groups, whatever they were, wondering from where the fuck had that term arrived.

When I tuned back in the words "flat functor" exited her lips and she started talking about how we "force" things to satisfy equations by passing to quotient spaces, a stretch in my opinion given how different that is from Cohen's method of forcing in logic and she started on geometric morphisms again, about geometric requirements expressed through possibly infinitary disjunctions of formulae—at which point she stopped and wrote as a reference, Carol Karp, *Languages with Expressions of Infinite Length* and then S. Maehara and G. Takeuti, *A Formal System of First-order Predicate Calculus with Infinitely Long Expressions,* Journal of the Mathematical Society of Japan, vol. 13, 357-370—turning and adding that the paper was of especial interest for its completeness results for tree-proofs when the cardinals were inaccessible: the inaccessible cardinals, she said, are the black holes of set theory, as will be seen. This was the same Takeuti whose books with Zaring had proven to be almost inaccessible, maybe Japanese in Braille. Anyway, she said that the object, whatever it might be since I had not caught anything regarding said object, was some kind of universal model for something or other, some geometric theory I guessed in the sense of both algebraic geometry and this pair of adjoints, duality of some kind I didn't catch, and she talked about how it arose from the evaluation functor as a subobject of the diagonal functor by the Yoneda embedding, first I had heard of that, and she proceeded to give it a cohomological meaning I didn't grasp but with, as I'd guessed, coefficients in Abelian groups.

I was also guessing she was out of time, and she might have been but she had plenty of steam left. I feared she was going to drag us through some shit like the logic of the circle or some other category of sheaves arising from a topological space, though it did seem that the Grothendieck topology she had brought up was somehow not what I considered a topological space but probably I didn't get it.

"So," she said, "each topos determines a type theory. But also true each type theory determines a topos. Even the methodologies of forcing are conceivable as truth-conditional schema in topoi. Rules of Cohen forcing, they are truth conditions for sentences in topos of presheaves over partially ordered set of forcing conditions. This explains a lot of mystery. Cohen's forcing obeys intuitionistic rules but the models are classical models. And it is moreover true that in a topos axiom of choice implies Boolean, so axiom of choice implies law of excluded middle.

"But this is more than just organization of concepts. It is more, in fact, than classification, but rather explanation. Indeed, the geometric implications, that is those first order formulas preserved by geometric morphisms, are such that if they have classical proof then they have also intuitionistic proof. In fact, for every Grothendieck topos there is a Boolean topos and a geometric morphism from the Boolean topos to the Grothendieck topos with a faithful adjoint.

"What it means is disquieting for some, in that it shows truth is local. Mathematical truth is local. Those who work in set theory know this: even the wonderful and simple concept of measuring size of infinite cardinals I talked about in the beginning is not so simple to those who have experienced cardinal collapse. Even forgetting that every first order theory must have countable model, so uncountable sets reside in countable model. Countable from outside, not inside, of course. Inside all is lovely. But forcing able to cause cardinal collapse: suddenly your uncountable cardinal goes kerplunk, deflates to countable. Or you get Cohen reals you didn't expect. Constructing the universes must be done with care. What you are inside others are outside, and they are not seeing your world or vice-versa. I have a friend who insists it is the problem of uncritical employment of axiomatic set theory. Cannot get the structuralist objective of form without specified substance, hence ruining the goal of Bourbaki. I am not really aware if or not that is the goal of Bourbaki. Take the variable in a polynomial as a step toward abstraction: it gets rid of those with not enough wit to see the meaning of the abstracted. So another step is to go to structures like groups and rings, another abstraction. Category goes one more step into abstraction, to not just abstract operations but to abstract kind of structure itself. To let structure vary in a completely general way."

She was proselytizing again. I wondered how this played with the Platonists, those believers in the reality of all this horseshit. Would they buy reality as local, or instead just find this didn't capture it? Heyting?

Perhaps she had a point in that these topoi could make the logic stuff clearer, put it all in some kind of framework, but if one didn't work in logic, it was fucking moot. I mean, it is not as if this shit were real in any kind of sense. No amount of jawboning would make the continuum hypothesis true or false in any universe I lived in. I won't ever need to waive the magic wand of the axiom of choice to choose a sock from each of an infinite collection of sets of socks. Structure in general be damned.

"Set theory strips structure from ontology of mathematics, while category theory transcends particular structure."

I was pretty certain those words were spoken aloud by her, not by the little voice in my head. Still, the so *what-ness* of it overwhelmed me.

"The best metaphor might be relativity," she rattled. "The local frames of reference with the topoi or even the Kripke semantics are akin to the reference frames in relativity. Classical two-valued logic and axiomatic set theory is more akin to Newtonian mechanics, with the absoluteness of space and time. But relativity is local, with distance and time-difference local within frames. So the space-time is relationships, as in Leibnitz and not as in Descartes and Newton. Space is not a place for dumping things. Simultaneity is relative to the frame, as is length or distance. But there is a global metric nonetheless, an invariant. That is the Lorentz metric in special relativity which measures the norm of the space-time event the same in all reference frames. And there is the same thing in the logic. It is the core validity, the necessary truth if you will, of the intuitionistic statements in all possible worlds.

"Cohen independence works showed that mathematical truth is multivalued, sometimes different from true or false. We see this at local level, in internal logic of topoi realizing intuitionist logic of types. This is *the* invariant truth, the core if you will. To get the universal truth it is necessary that it be constructively provable, which means transforming the statement into intuitionistic reciprocal. So the absolute universe of sets ought be replaced with topoi of discourse, since these are the possible worlds of mathematical activity. This is local mathematics, and the invariant is constructive provability of mathematical statements with judicious use of excluded middle. Intuitionist methodology. The metric, if you will, is translation of classical into intuitionist logic. That is the invariant."

She stopped and I was about ready to applaud that she'd finished when she spoke words that struck horror into my heart:

"Of course, all this jawboning about philosophy and such is not mathematics. A mathematician's job is to prove theorems, and I will now discuss actual theorems in work."

There was no clock in the room. Not having a watch of my own, I grabbed the arm of the dweeb who was sitting beside me spellbound in some sort of stupor that had nothing to do with any of the words she spoke. She had been at it for only half an hour. That was impossible.

"Part of what is happening now is work inside very large cardinal numbers, inaccessible cardinals. We have possibilities, as we call them, like the worlds of the Kripke semantics more or less and we construct models using topology of logic by jumping models with some powerful methods like Stone-Čech compactification. Leapfrogging, someone called it, but we often find ourselves in the presence of what have come to be called perverse sheaves..." she giggled or whinnied or perhaps cooed, hard to say which, and then continued "…perverse since they live on singular structures which one expects when dealing with the inaccessible cardinals. A view of forcing, but viewing the partial order as information, so forcing new constructs with partial information more than with logic though perhaps is not so much information as an engineer might recognize it. It looks like logic, and sometimes is, more or less. We like to make the continuum at least aleph-three, since that is where resistance increases to forcing our way in. Anyways, we converge with enough just partial information coalescing to get new imaginary structures.

"We hunt for creatures in the inaccessible cardinals. A weak creature is a kind of black box in an input-output sense that, again, an engineer might not recognize. So it has an input sequence and it gives families of extensions of the input. More formally, it is a triple" and she wrote some stuff on the board, a triple that she wrote definitions for term by term, some set theoretical stuff with unions and products and limits and using symmetric difference as an operator, the logic of either-or, exclusive as sometimes called, or at least that was what I thought she meant. It formed a product of sorts in a Boolean ring but she was working in less than this or something entirely different.

"Now we have also strong creatures; some of them quite scary. And there are tree creatures. These amount to, more or less, forcing conditions that we glue together or shrink, or just forget if we don't get too close. But this is related to an amount of freedom these things have, you see, and this relates to size of the inaccessible cardinal. Most important of these are tree creatures, since we have some that climb Aronszajn trees and chop down the Souslin trees; others do the opposite which is worse since chasing some creature from an inaccessible cardinal up a Suslin tree is harrowing to be sure. The worst creatures have the most freedom, which one would think had to do with the size of the cardinal but that is not so, as we have recently proved. Instead it is more a function of something else, which we have characterized to some extent but which we have not yet classified categorically. We can sketch that result."

She slowed and gave us another once over, then said, "I maybe ought not to assume everyone knows what is an inaccessible cardinal number. Roughly speaking, it is too big to get out of. More or less. For example, you cannot escape $\aleph_0$ from below with unions or power sets or any kind of exponentiations. An inaccessible cardinal is also inescapable in this sense, at least a strongly inaccessible, but it is also uncountable. We have weakly and strongly inaccessible cardinal numbers, but our interest is only in the strongly inaccessible ones. They are quite large. Their existence cannot be proven in Zermelo-Fraenkel set theory with the axiom of choice. Even the weak ones are big" she wrote $\alpha=\aleph_\alpha$ on the board and said, "That would be the case for all of the weak ones, but the least of these alpha is not even weakly inaccessible, yet the cofinality would be little omega for even the least of them. A weakly inaccessible will not be a successor cardinal and will not be reachable from below by a union of fewer than its own cardinality smaller cardinals."

It embarrassed; this was stuff I had not witnessed anyone here talk about. I understood what she meant to say, having done it in a prior mathematical universe, but I don't think many were with her now. At least not among grad students. You never quite knew just how much Bolyai or Oberst or their advanced students knew.

She marched on.

"Strongly inaccessible cardinals cannot be escaped with even power set operations, but then this all gets complicated without the axiom of choice, so we assume it always when we work in ZF. That is, assume ZFC. We don't assume continuum hypothesis, of course, but negation of that so strong and weak are different. Anyways, as I said, aleph-naught would be strongly inaccessible if we included countable. But we don't, for important reasons. For those who like mystery and confounding issues, there is a very odd relationship between consistency of ZFC and consistency of existence of inaccessible cardinals relative to ZFC" at which someone snorted, maybe Bolyai, but she kept right on, "and there are references for this, maybe Jech.

"We worked first with what are termed huge cardinals. That is their names. Of course there are a plentitude of these types, including indescribable and ineffable which we don't talk about much and Mahlo which I like but we don't see so much and measureable and weakly compact and so on and on" she giggled "but we discovered a certain huge cardinal using extenders, based on something called VP" she wrote the words *Vopěnka's Principle* on the board, followed by words to the effect that in a proper class of models for the same language, there are two members so that one can be elementarily embedded in the other; no one dared ask her to define elementary embedding or extenders, or if she meant the same thing by extenders or extensions here as she had with her creatures, but before anyone could ask she said "—not the same extenders that are approximating systems of measures for elementary embeddings in inner model theory analyzed with direct limits of ultrapowers—" and without missing a beat "and from that we found this one that didn't have so much scary creatures as in some other great big cardinals where things go out of hand in terms of regularity properties. We got some things we called iteration trees to work with here to prove this. It is a bit too technical to define this cardinal we found, but suffice to say it is beyond supercompact and clearly beyond measureable. It has a stationary set of measureable cardinals. I call it a wyrd cardinal: w-y-r-d."

She stopped and the room held its breath. Maybe she'd be finished. Christ, I couldn't imagine taking a class from her; no telling what she'd assume. Or maybe not. This was after all colloquium talk or seminar or somegoddamnthing for experts or geniuses or madmen.

"Anyways, this is where we do some forcing to get some surprising results. In particular, the creatures lurking herein among the trees are more manageable than in other inaccessible cardinals and we get universe properties that allow a form of forcing I call hexing. Among the creatures lurking—just remember not V equal L now—are forcing substructures I term weak curses and strong spells. All in topoi, to be clear, but with our perverse sheaf models. But beware the antichain!"

She had to be finished. She became more incoherent by the minute. She added, "So what is this good for?"

Nothing, I thought, same as all this shit.

"Surprising it relates to systems theory. Input-output systems. A form of what I term scrying since it relates to crystalline topos and crystalline cohomology and since it defies engineering causality, as in systems theory. Related to work I did previously with D-modules for microlocal analysis, but in different setting to be sure."

I noticed Frenchie was not in the room. He'd bagged the talk.

"Two issues. Optimal control using operators led to solutions that were not causal, in, that is, that the solutions depended on future. For example, have simple feedback system" and she drew

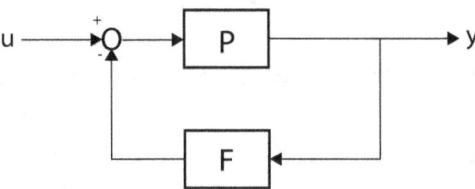

"Then" she wrote r = u − Fy "and" y = Pr, "so we can get the inverse operator taking u to y by feedback as" y = Hu "where" H = (I + PF)⁻¹P. She stood back and looked at what she'd put up, then said, "Now if P happens to be identity on L-two of the entire real line, infinity to minus infinity, and F is an ideal delay, say funny D, minus the identity on L-two of r" and she wrote $H = (I + I(Đ - I))^{-1}I$ "which equals" $= Đ^{-1}$ "which is ideal predictor, seemingly able to predict the future events. Engineers hate these solutions since they depend on future and so seem not to be realizable in real world. For this reason, mathematicians began using operators on Hilbert resolution spaces to keep from using the future in the function space approach. Also has been approached using truncation operators and in stochastic problems with resolution of identity where conditioning is done on measurements made prior to time t though if one does not work in real time it can be a smoothing problem, where future is available. I think this is related also to nest algebras and triangular operators.

"Anyways, making the long story short, have brought dynamics into logic. Using D-modules were stuck with differential operators or pseudo-differential operators which allows PDEs, but which restricts to rational dynamical systems, so can extend by dropping the explicit description of black box dynamics which is anyway not so important given we have minimal realizations. Can implement fractional integrators and differentiators, for example. It leads to entropy and ergodic theory on logics, and probability as well, but that is maybe too far afield. For example, can get dynamics from seeming static algebraic systems via torsion. Simple example is ring of polynomials with coefficients in field" $F[v]$ on the board "so an element is" $p(v) = \sum f_j v^j$ "finite sum clearly starting with j at zero. If we substitute derivative operator for v then we see can operate on the group of c-infinity real-valued functions with polynomials of differentiable operators and if p(d) is zero, then we have torsion element in the module so formed. This plays well for engineers who use the transfer functions matrices with elements rational functions of those polynomials in $F[v]$ though we can make this more general with such as one over square root of s, say, to get fractional integrators, which we ignore for sake of simplification here. As set up now, can be realized by linear dynamical system with input and output functions in state space, though the state space we love is not so finite dimensional but might even be a logical system realized as a topos with a feedback on logical models or other algebraic systems that interact and can be controlled to some extent, where time is now local property and feedback can come via infinite dimensional Lie algebras, a generalization on several levels of work of Elie Cartan, with lots of local symmetries acting via extenders to tree-like sections over the base. I call this a Dee system, for a famous mathematician of the middle ages named John Dee. But I digress. Let me finalize the example of torsion to dynamics and then I promise I will stop. But to add to what I said just now, we use this dynamics to get future acting on past for short times, acausal operators. I have predicted, in fact, that the inequality of Bell will be used to prove that Einstein was wrong with his insistence on locality in the Einstein Podolsky Rosen paper that dissed quantum physics for absurdly being non-local. We have shown the non-local nature of reality, but not in an experimental sense satisfactory to physical experimenters. Difficult to show because exist obstructions to long temporal extensions of seeing ahead. Bundle problem, more or less. See maybe Steenrod's little book on topology of fiber bundles. Transgressive elements, transgression, related to what is more or less, I mean can't be transgressive elements and so no answers to ambiguity from mod-two cohomology. But it will be shown that, Einstein to the contrary, spooky action at a distance is real. Okay, so now consider that we have a vector space and a formal power series in say one over the unknown v in that space, which is simply sum from say one to infinity of say y sub j times v to minus j power. Formally define addition in normal way to get Abelian group of set of all these such products, then define multiplication by polynomial p of v by normal sort of multiplication and throwing away terms of nonnegative degree, so modulo nonnegative terms. This F of square bracket v module tells a lot about the linear dynamic system because it reveals structure of matrix defining state transition, of course without considering input matrix. Take simplest example, a one by one matrix with element one over v plus one, call that capital x. Then if we multiply that by v using our rules is easy to see we get" and she wrote: $v[(v+1)^{-1}] = -[(v+1)^{-1}]$ "which gives an equation" $vX = -X$ "specifying the dynamics."

She stopped. The room held it's breath once again. I looked at the dweeb's watch. It was precisely one hour. I didn't believe it.

"I hope this gives some idea of the area I work in. I travel around not fixed anywhere, but if there is interest in any of these things, I can be glad to return.

"Questions?"

It was tradition for Oberst to ask something of anyone who spoke, something pungent and to the point indicating he had understood it all. He didn't disappoint and asked something I sure as hell didn't understand having to do with flabby sheaves and flat functors, and she droned on about some shit to do with rigidifying to avoid a need for full subcategories via the Yoneda lemma and some words spewed from her mouth about the inutility of flabby creatures or some such fucking thing. People began to leave. I felt we'd been bewitched.

Red caught up to me before I could bolt.

"Some babe, huh?"

"What? You nuts? She looks like a scrawny nine year old."

"Man, you are weird. She's built like a brick shit house. And did you see her do those gothic symbols?"

"Did you understand anything she said?"

"Some of it. Not much, though. Don't know about logic at all."

"Well I do and I didn't get much of it, either."

We started to head for the door but she stood suddenly before us holding up her arms. "Go ahead," she said, "circle my wrists with your thumb and index finger."

We both did it. I surrounded it with room to spare, no need to touch the skin, but Red couldn't quite close the gap. I held up my extended finger and thumb to compare to Red's and he gave me a puzzled look before laying his across it. He might have had a slight advantage.

"See," he said. "She's not skinny."

He hadn't perceived my roomily circumscribing her wrist.

She stood blocking my exit, top of her head at my shoulders, and craned back to look me in the eyes. "You must be Mr. Butcher."

"Yes. That's right."

"I heard a friend of yours give a talk in France. At *Collège de France.*"

"I don't think I know anyone at that school. I'm not sure where it is actually."

"We can talk. Besides, I am co-advisor of yours now."

"Really? When did that happen? And why? I don't do anything with logic. Who okayed that? I have two already."

Red gave me a sidelong glance that said, You lucky dog, before sidling out of the room. For me there was no such escape. Now I was to be disappeared in the Amazon.

"We need to talk. You need to escort me to a place for dinner where we can talk. My apartment is near yours in the quarter."

"I don't think so. I am concerned that you are telling me you are a co-advisor on my thesis. I'm not sure I want you on the committee."

"Such hostility. Your advisor approved it. I know more than logic. And it can help with jobs. Remember, I am Fields Medalist."

I thought about that. It was true. Fields Medal was as much prestige as I'd get near in this lifetime. I could see why he'd have done it. Probably was why Momus had spoken to me about her before she came.

"I hate being out of the loop when it involves me. I vowed that would not be happening again after the Marine Corps."

"I understand. It is said you were seriously wounded. Let's go to an oyster bar I know in the Marigny. A little place off the beaten path. My treat."

"I have money."

"I have more. I'm sure of it."

"Don't be sure. I have two benefactors, one of them the US government."

"Disability?"

"That is miniscule."

"I think I heard the other in France. Dina."

"Dina? She gave the talk?"

"Yes."

"Did you talk to her?"

"No."

"Then how the hell did you know I knew her?"

"A little bird told me."

She walked me out of the department and out of Gibson Hall and to the streetcar stop in the middle of St. Charles Avenue.

"What was the deal with the wrists?" I asked.

"Just a little demo of locale," she said. "You are not astride the same reference frame as other people around you."

"What?"

"You are in different possibility than these others."

"What the fuck are you talking about? Don't tell me you believe this mathematics shit, this formal logic, has some relevance to the real world?"

"Reality is local. Or as they say in the Berkeley math department, Reality is just another model."

On the streetcar she continued hurling her lecture at me.

"I wanted to go into some detail on generalizing of de Rham's theory to the logical topoi setting but I could no longer control the time."

"What? Control the time?"

"Controlling time, staying within time limits, same thing, no?"

I wanted to say no but she plowed on with a spiel regarding torsion on fibers, twisted products of irreducible factors in something that looked like the Postnikov decomposition but with different obstructions and transgression, cohomological measurements of the global twist in local logical truth fibers akin to what is called characteristic classes. Path integrals that arise from a variational problem on truth that deviates infinitesimally enough to get a flat connection and then integrate it out, leaving a relative of the Chern-Simons invariant related to what could be called the Levi-Civita connection in a possibility. There became manifest local metrics that lead to an entropy of truth as a local function since there are no partitions of unity to tie it all together, but there exist beyond-distributed local systems with feedback that interact via infinite Lie algebras without real infinite dimensional Lie groups because of an obstruction due to Whitehead's theorem not holding in this setting for the uncountable cardinals, assuming Martin's axiom, but truth is local and meager in distribution while the objects in lieu of Lie groups are still symmetries that provide the feedback and acausal controllers from future acting on past, bringing back local times. It ends up a sort of algebraic theory made geometric, the EXT and TOR functors generalized to get around the Whitehead obstruction by integrating out those connections to get torsion in modules tied to torsion in fibers to get a sort of Levi-Civita connection, torsionless but leaving the theory a noncommutative de Rham theory, a noncommutative differential geometry in logical topoi that gives a new cohomology theory related to the crystalline cohomology with sieves leading to all sorts of possibilities beyond the plain Dee theory, a Dee-coscinomancy scrying she called it, which is akin to cavorting with elementals in a semantic topoi. A cyclic cohomology as a derived functor, more or less, but first is necessary to arrive at a noncommutative de Rham complex, though it seems more natural to work with a Hopf algebra to get something like a Koszul complex but better would be a quadratic algebra along the lines of a Koszul algebra. Finishing with a PDE for truth, starting with an initial falsehood the flows of which converged to truth in her multivalued sense, the weakest of truth, intuitionistic and universal, Leibnitz's truth in all possibilities. The PDE parabolic, evolving in time like the heat equation, diffusing the mendacity like a snake sloughing off its skin, time evolution of an elliptic operator on god-knew-what.

As she finished, the streetcar pulled up to Canal Street at the mouth of the Quarter.

"I have no idea what you are talking about," I said.

"Quadratic algebras?" I shook my head. "Hopf algebras, Koszul algebras?" I shook my head again, then said "de Rham complexes, yes, though what the hell is a nonlinear de Rham theory I have no idea—" "Koszul complex?" "No—" "I'm sure you do and don't know. Anyway, don't worry; you will," she said.

That sounded like a threat. I was sure I didn't know what the fuck was a Koszul complex, knowingly or unknowingly.

"The best part, we actualized this in engineering systems," she droned. "Of course, application depends on how far into future we are able to actualize controllers to operate on past events, which is problem involving obstructions. But interesting is that we gain more control over animate objects like humans than over inanimate objects like bombs. Has to do with duality between physical and virtual, more or less, where for example a symbol can be more alive than a real thing in the dual world. It finds, therefore, more applications in genetics than anything like inertial navigations systems, which are too much insensate hardware but more amenable as they become more alive via small computers running software controllers, for example, to synthesize gyros, say. Simple example, sorry. I have system I call Enochian system that controls quite well the genetic sequences. In some of the cardinals, lurking creatures allow that which I call conjuring as a method of forcing for kind of quantifier elimination I call cursing; after all, what are creatures good for if not curses?"

I dragged her off the streetcar before it made the loop and headed back uptown.

"Enough, okay? This is weird." We stood face to face on Canal across from the Quarter, Bourbon Street on the other side. People moved around us like we were pebbles in the stream on the sidewalk where a gang of black kids tried to steal purses from people waiting to board the buses and streetcar and people threw their trash out the bus windows, giant drink cups and bags and wrappers and foam boxes from the local fast food joints.

"For me," I said, "this math shit has no connection to reality. It is just a fucking game. A kind of art form unrelated to the world. The way you're talking it's part of a bunch of local realities. Real realities, not imaginary shit."

"So you're not Platonist?"

"No way. Foundations is bullshit."

"And root two not being a fraction? Can you see that as real?"

"In what sense?"

"As in you can't produce non-terminating expansion."

"Computers haven't the power in any case, so who cares?"

"You ought, dude. It becomes extremely important for you at some point deciding what is necessary for application and what not."

"Like if the axiom of choice being independent or the continuum hypothesis—"

"Or Whitehead's problem, which is about groups—"

"Well, has to do with free groups over uncountable cardinals, as I recall."

"Okay, you met this skinny tattooed porn star whom you need to be careful of, as in not taking for granted. Disrespect won't hurt, but the more you disrespect her the more you need to take care and remain wary, as she is walking talisman who carries powers not of her or in her control…of which she is not aware, moreover."

I wanted to ask how she knew of Mirabelle but thought better of it. I decided to let it slide.

"You can't find model to make root two a fraction," she said.

"But neither are the reals predicative," I said. "No one can display root two in all its digitary glory."

We had crossed Canal and were heading up Royal by her choice.

"You don't become shocked," she said. "That is real plus in this business. And you don't make judgments, nor do you take stands, ethical nor social. You seem oblivious to what is real or not, at least outside mathematics. That is key to your survival, Whitey. Not prejudging reality. Take things as they are, not as you would have them be, and without too many questions of reality."

I thought perhaps that was why I studied mathematics: nothing real. But it bugged me she incessantly ended up talking what sounded like some kind of fucking witchcraft mumbo-jumbo.

She took my hand and led me to her apartment, a sizeable place above a bar. She dropped her backpack and stuffed money into her pocket. We headed for Decatur crossing into Faubourg Marigny past Elysian Fields and to some place I had never seen before between Decatur and North Peters just beyond Marigny, a brick structure like a warehouse or stable with tables inside, most not occupied, and a couple men on the floor with gunny sacks on ice behind them and oyster shells scattered around their feet. From a giant galvanized bucket of ice Hypatia took two Dixie longnecks which she opened with her teeth, then led us to a table. A tall bald girl in overalls brought us a tray of opened oysters. At the table was a jar of horseradish, a bottle of ketchup, a bowl of lemons and a bottle of McIlhenny Tabasco sauce.

"This is it?" I asked.

"Yup. Best oysters in town. Fresh, salty, and cheap. Not a real restaurant, is the reason. Sort of a moveable feast, running from health authorities. Fifty cents a dozen. Can't beat that."

She slurped one down without any sauce.

"I haven't eaten raw oysters," I said. "Only fried."

"This is time you started. You will be needing them tonight. I want a lot of juice out of you. You are going to fuck me and then I am going to suck your dick and I expect plenty of sauce on both encounters."

I didn't say anything. I had not considered her fuckable material.

"Try them slathered with horseradish and ketchup and hot sauce," she suggested. "Like this," and she mixed some together in a paper cup and dipped an oyster in it speared on a small version of Neptune's trident before slurping it down, after which she tossed back the juice out of the shell.

I did one with the horseradish-ketchup-McIlhenny combination and found it edible, even chewing the nasty little slimeball, though I wasn't taken with the salty gravy left in the shell. I lit up a hashish-laced cigarette coated with hash oil.

A red worm wriggled onto the table. She grabbed it and sucked it down. "Shell worm," she said. "Another benefit for coming here. They don't have concerns about cleaning off the shells. You need not eat them; give them to me," slurping down another oyster.

"Let's talk about your girlfriend," she said.

I offered her a cigarette. She took one and smelled it and nodded.

"Not my girlfriend."

I lit her smoke and she inhaled and held it before letting it waft from her nostrils.

"No, I gathered from her talk more slave, but then maybe that is somewhat ambiguous as well, given it is not clear who is the more indentured. She had been making films at some estate in Belgium. A titled character with a long family history. Seems they go back to the middle ages breeding dogs and other animals for sex with women."

I worked on sauce for my oysters. She slurped down several more oysters and a couple worms, all without any sauce, thankfully not talking with her mouth full. The same woman brought us another tray and more brews.

"She said something quite amusing. Something like, I tied the knot many times but not permanently. Evidently referring to massive English Mastiff named Hermanubis. Giant of a dog, weighed around three hundred pounds, paws the size of softballs, on all fours his shoulder came to her chest, his head above her shoulder level. His neck was over 40 inches. And she said he had huge penis with the monstrous knot at the end. And he knew how to use it, the knot, tying her with it in her mouth, anus and even her vagina, which latter can generally take a big knot. But not this one. She mated him, or more like he mounted her, for a month. His bitch. And he watched over her when she was with mules, horses and especially in gangbangs with trained packs of dogs. One group was German shepherds, the most polite of the packs, she said. All with endowed knots, tying her while the others worked over her free orifices."

"And did she enjoy it?"

"She said she fell in love with this dog. They hit it off right away, what I would describe as *carinhoso.* She even thought of staying with him, but in the end realized the dog cared too much about her. She needed something more aloof, more apt to throw her to the vagaries of sexually depraved creatures without worrying about the outcome. Some creature who didn't care if she lived or died. That I assumed as your role."

I found the oysters with the sauce quite edible so long as I avoided the liquid in the shell. I helped her get through the tray while avoiding the red worms.

"Did she have movies?"

"Not with. Said she made many miles of film but couldn't show them publicly in France, even at the *Collège,* for fear of jail. This is her path, it seems, to pursue sexual limits. She is going to become discarnate if she can, I think, at least in a spiritual sense. Like she will also end up cavorting with elementals."

I recalled that phrase as seeming out of place in her discussion of mathematics, presented as mathematical terminology without anything but a hint of content. I decided not to ask what she meant, instead waiting for it to reveal its extension on its own. I was pretty sure it would.

"She is nothing like this agent of hers. I think you have been fucking her, a not too good idea. That creature is hexed. She is under spell of insatiable need for drinking urine. Male urine. And must fuck or suck everything she finds. She seeks out glory holes. It is not clear whence it came, but it is a less than a curse, more than just a bewitching. An obsessive hankering."

"What difference does it make to you what I do with her?"

"You need to stop dealing drugs. It is not effective use of risk for you."

"I am aware of that. I did, in fact, stop. Found better scams."

"Yes."

"What did Dina do about her period?"

"She didn't say."

Hypatia's apartment felt like a warehouse. Undivided, crumbling red brick, a rectangle that spanned half a block on the top floor of a building. Mostly unfurnished, not even a bed in sight; only a desk and a couple chairs and what appeared to be a giant parakeet perch hanging from the ceiling in the middle of the room, bright red metal in a sharp oval attached directly to the ceiling with a red wooden pole as a base.

She didn't make small talk or try to kiss me or offer any other friendly gestures. She took off her clothes immediately we were inside, letting fall to the floor first her flannel shirt. Walking away from me, she let it drop between us. She unhooked a bra in back and turned to face me, undoing her two braids, her hair unfurling to the middle of her back. Her tits pointed outward with black nipples spread wide about a pronounced sternum, not massive but more noticeable than I'd have guessed.

Wearing a pout that I think she mistook for seductive, she got out of her tennis shoes without bending over to untie them. I considered that a hard trick for high tops. Her feet were bright orange claws. She pulled down her jeans and stepped out of them. She wore no panties. No navel. She hasn't a navel, I thought. Her twig thighs had more meat than I'd have guessed, muscular below a round, long ass. Svelte, that word muscled its way in. At the knee were attached a pair of orange bird legs, same orange as the claws. She had no trace of hair on her pale flesh, ivory were it not for a distinct hint of salmon glowing below the skin.

"You have bird legs," I said.

"I know they are skinny, but shapely, no? Womanly?"

"No. Bird's legs and bird's claws for feet."

"What color are they?"

"Orange. Bright orange."

"Like a dove. You like?"

"Better than I first appraised."

"Yes, you are a hard man. It is because you are in an accelerating frame. Maybe rotating, too."

She stood on the perch, back to me, and said "Now hurry and fuck me. We don't have all night." She twitched her pinched buttocks up and down like a pigeon, head bobbing.

intersection theory

I pulled my pants over my shoes, remaining shod, wary of splinters as the wooden floor looked to be unfinished planks. I left my shirt on, too, but when I got close to the perch she said to take it off. The perch placed her so her narrow arcs of ass abutted the top of my groin when I stood against her, just the height for intrusion between her legs. I reached down but found only one hole. A long tube lowered from the hole and I pulled my hand back. It extended about an inch and stopped.

"Don't be alarmed," she said. "Cloacal sexual organs."

"What?"

"Rare condition. Found in birds. With mechanism, a giant clitoris, like a female spotted hyena for sex. Called pseudopenis. Hyenas give birth through it. Swells like a water-filled balloon. Makes difficult having sex without my cooperation."

"Important for cavorting with elementals?"

"With demons. Or angels. Same thing actually. Way more intense than elementals."

My dick stiffened to full extension. The tubular tentacle protruding from her butt hole or whatever it was reached out and engulfed the head, working its way over the penis until covering it entirely. Warm, snug and slimy, it clung to my penis like an extra skin, radially symmetric contractions squeezing the length of my erection with an increasing frequency, continuous waves crossing from above and below, trains of waves interacting in a dance that brought me to orgasm faster than I wanted.

"Good," she said. "Good boy." The tentacle climbed off my penis and retracted up her orifice.

She came down from the perch and lowered herself without kneeling, a combination of drooping her back half and hugging up her skin into which her entire upper torso shrank, a puddle of flesh from which only her head protruded. My penis shrunk to a nub and she took it in her mouth, milking what juice still percolated. Sucking the tip, she lavaged the glans penis with tongue and caressed with inner buccal labial peristalsis as my erection bored into a constricted throat of wavelike flagella, her unmoving mouth leached to my groin, vacuuming as I thrust in short strokes. I ejaculated while buried to the hilt.

Afterward she told me I was scheduled for important things, in the long run. I remembered the quote by John Meynard Keynes, "In the long run we are all dead."

379

Chapter 22
Local Isomorphism: The Back and Forth Method

I caught Frenchie after he'd wrapped up his seminar before returning to Stanford. I think he'd burned out on the lack of response by anyone, including me. Finals week loomed on the horizon in any case. He asked if I'd made progress and I mumbled that I had some stuff to pursue but was trying to position myself to make money this summer instead of teaching. Good, he'd said, certainly you will need cash when you finish. A postdoctoral will be in the offing. I wondered how the hell he knew that, given I hadn't done much since the encounter that'd brought him aboard.

He handed me a stack of papers. "Systems theory," he said, "and estimation. State space approach. Quite hot for making money now. Some work on nonlinear filtering, extending to manifolds with Lie groups or something like this. Related to the Kalman filter I talked about. And some work in French on *calcul stochastique.* Mostly in the manifolds. Semimartingales. Get this dissertation over fast; it is not seen as propitious for the student to dwell overly long on thesis problem. You know?"

"That makes sense. But I wanted to ask you about Hypatia. Now that she is on my committee."

"Don't worry. She lends her name to much she never touches. You know?"

"I noticed you didn't go to her talk."

He stood silent for a moment, then sat on a desk and said, "I was going to say I was with other commitments, but that is not a good thing to tell you. Truth is, I cannot abide to hear her talk. It is like she does not see the mathematics from the inside. Like it is all from the outside in, you know?"

"No, not really."

"She is the odd bird. She speaks completely disorganized; no one follows her talk; like she is crazy person. I cannot abide with it. Like she pulls ideas…how you say?…out from her ass; but always right. She is always right. Wild conjectures but always right. Like she sees in some other dimension or the crystal ball. No one sees any place where these proofs can come from. So from her ass, as you would say."

I didn't bring up my own experience with her pulling things into her ass. It didn't seem real anymore anyway. Bird feet? No one would believe any of it.

If I told them I would be locked up in a nut house, a common thing to do with mathematicians in any case. Look at poor old Cantor.

"She works inside the formal languages and from this perspective she comes out with bizarrely new ideas. Strictly it seems on language properties: appropriate language leads to theory, as if a cohomology lies behind it all…she has said this, in fact…like with different variations of long division in group cohomology…different equivalence classes…you are familiar?" I nodded yes. "Mostly inside the category theory. That is as close to thinking mathematically as she does. You know much of what she does comes from formal language and some stability theory for them. Using this stability she can separate theory as classifiable or chaotic. The classifiable models no matter their cardinality are controllable through the countable submodels with decomposition into a tree of submodels, and she bounds them with beth function. The chaotic theory is wild with cardinal growth, so new models are needed always. Sentences with infinite length, abstract forcing and abstract models. She calls some of this hexing! Like she is the witch!…You know who is this Dee she names such things for?"

"No, I don't."

"A Medieval mathematician, so-called, sorcerer and alchemist with fame for application of scrying. With the assist of one named Edward Kelley, charlatan-alchemist who said he communicates with spirits in a crystal ball or something like this. Crazy things.

"Then she goes to different places, turning down professorships and living on money that also might come from her asshole, no one knows where. She looks for unsolved problems and puts them into appropriate formal structures and then sometimes solves them, sometimes relates them to other problem or theory no one guesses, often using some imaginary objects she forces into the models or topos, and pivots around them to produce new things—"

"—from her ass. I get it."

"It is like cottage industry, this approach. Many follow behind her like cleanup crew, working to build semantic bridge to her worlds that are mixture of formalizations and models in categories most often, but not always. Industry of youthful mathematicians tying it together, or trying, but almost no one figures out what she theories as semanticized."

"She pulls it out her ass, but it's always right and no one gets it."

"And she builds control loops for real things. They work, often counter to the intuition, not to say reasonable sense, for damn sure. Seems more useful for biology and genetics. The sort of inverse method from proof theory to scatter into isomorphic models or theories, in categories mostly."

"I don't want to end up as part of her industry."

"If she wants on your committee, then you will get some of this. But she is not someone to push this thing. She lets those come to her, once she opens doors. No pushing, for sure. But she bewitches, be wary. She bewitched Momus but not Bolyai."

"Her writing is clear?"

"Clear in the sense well organized, but with no rhyme or reason, so to say, like from the void. Like called up from the void."

Neither of us said a thing for a random time. I almost mused aloud that such writing was typical from what I could see, at least for papers. Instead Frenchie went off again.

"She developed this coscinomancy classifier constructed from patching together of maximal *cribles,* that is the sieves in English, on objects in crystalline topoi and is tied to some noncommutative de Rham theory based on integration of forms on logics, this dynamics of hers, that leads to some kind of thing she calls crystals of modules on which she does some cohomology. You know this word, coscinomancy, is to divine by use of sieve? Latin origin, the word? She is divinator? Divinatrice?"

"So how did she get on my committee? She says like a co-advisor."

"More or less. I guess she convinced your advisor. Maybe he is bewitched like Momus. She has been to Russia to work with the expert on these symmetry groups he pursues. But her method. Is like her imaginary objects are... she thinks of them attached like attaching i to the real numbers... like attaching irrational number to rational field... a logic extension, like a field extension, and she calls her theory Dee-Cantor-Galois theory of logic. Then iterative forcing of these things. Creates Henkin witnesses inside oracles, like somehow the oracles used by Turing...Bizarre things..."

"I'm guessing Kronecker would shit bricks."

He laughed. "His head would explode. She makes Cantor seem the sane one."

So I took a second trip out to the Parish to visit the SPR to see if that might be part of the real world, though the existence of a real world seemed less plausible by the day. Before going I'd found a plain brown envelope in my departmental mailbox filled with papers and hundred dollar bills. My name and Tulane Mathematics were the only address, though it had CEDEX in large letters where would have been a return address and a strange stamp that looked to be a stylized horn with a round handle formed by a triangle attached at the base to a line from the center of which hung a circle attached at what would have been π radians had the circle been centered at the origin with the point $(1,0)$ the angle zero radians. That is, as if it had been drawn as $e^{i\theta}$. There was a stack of papers sorted into lots, mostly prints from journals I'd not seen before, stuff like *Annals of Physics, Il Nuovo Cimento, Journal of Research of the National Bureau of Standards — B. Mathematical Sciences, Journal of Mathematical Physics, Navigation: Journal of the Institute of Navigation, IEEE Transactions on Aerospace and Electronic Systems, Journal of Guidance and Control, IEEE Transactions on Automatic Control, Journal of Applied Mechanics, IEEE Transactions on Circuits and Systems, IEEE Transactions on Communications.* There were some from journals I recognized but seldom read, like *SIAM Journal of Control* which was where had been published Kalman's paper on linear systems theory that Frenchie'd given me. *SIAM Review* was represented in the batch, too, but that I had seen before. I pocketed the bills and took the papers and envelope to Frenchie who looked at them with a curious expression. "Yes," he'd said, "these you need to read. They are from the future." "What? They have dates within our present and past," I said, and he pointed to one in French, *Analyse d'une boucle de phase numerique en termes de grandes deviations.* "From 1983." It carried no date at all, no citation, only an author. He pointed at another also undated, *A geometric description of wander azimuth frames,* that he said was from 1989. "Phase-locked loops are important. But more important are papers in guidance. Place them with the work of Brownian motion of rotation groups you have read by McKean and Gorman. And start here:" pointing to a pair of long papers, one regarding inertial and optical sensors and the other Kalman filters in navigation systems. When I asked him if he knew who they'd come from he shrugged his shoulders and said, "No one. Only the future." I didn't press him. Academics are an eccentric lot to be sure. Probably he'd stuffed them in the envelope and put them in the box, but then where'd the money come from? He wouldn't throw around that kind of scratch nor would it make sense. The titles included terms like strapdown attitude and coning corrections. Several of them concerned representing rotations with quaternions and I discovered that one could represent the dynamics of rotations as linear differential equations on unit quaternions in lieu of matrices, an idea I found geometrically appealing. The paper on the parameterization of the rotation group in *SIAM Review* began with the representation of Hopf,

I assumed the same Hopf of the fibration I'd explored with Goldman. Later I found an envelope on the kitchen table inside my apartment, unmarked except for the same odd stamp, a code of capital letters and numbers scrawled on the front, filled with hundred dollar bills. The two of them netted fifty thousand dollars. I had no idea where it came from. In between these findings I'd called Jeremy to give a head's up so he could smooth out the second trip to the Parish. His reaction was akin to exuberance. He'd make sure I got to meet Aldo and for me to make sure I billed for the hours. I didn't need the money, but the idea of getting paid for nothing appealed to me. This time Debby met me with some modicum of enthusiasm, putting her hand on my arm to lead me down the hallway to Aldo's office. She chattered in her yat like I might be paying attention to the words instead of projecting images into her head of her sucking my dick. I wasn't sure I got through, but Bobbi seemed to read the brain movie. Debby reluctantly handed me off. As Bobbi led me to the office she brushed the back of her hand slowly across my crotch, lingering within the tangential sweep to judge my apparatus.

Two men hunched over a cluttered table in the midst of an oversized office peered at some charts. The shorter one stood and approached me. Dumpy and short, a white-haired man wearing a rumpled sport shirt hanging boxy outside his slacks approached me smiling shyly like he'd misplaced his clippers, approximating a barber much in the manner of Bolyai. He shook my hand and apologized for not having time to talk and scooted me out. I noted the man at the table wore a threadbare suit and a badge that read DOE, causing me to surmise he was among the overseers employed directly by the civil service.

"Where to now?" Bobbi asked as we stood alone in the outer office at her desk.

She darkened her hair which was naturally red, I was sure, and came out with a warm auburn tone that set off her crystalline blue eyes.

"Let's go to your place," I said.

A controlled smile lit up her tight visage in contrast to her red dress. The outfit didn't show her off as well as the one she'd worn last time, her legs perhaps a skosh thinner from the knees down than I'd previously noted, but nonetheless raising my libido.

"Can't now, Mr. Butcher. But we might find some time when we can visit my humble digs, if you are interested."

"I am if you are. Maybe for the time being you can take me to Kip if he's here."

"He's always here," and she led me to the office where'd he been on the prior visit.

Jerry was nowhere to be seen but Kip sat with his feet propped up on his desk, back to the door, talking to a blonde guy seated beside him in the same pose. They turned at Bobbi's "I see you two are hard at work" and his companion stood up. From his chair Kip said, "Whitey...didn't expect you."

His companion came on aggressively with an outstretched hand. He was my height and built like a football player whose muscles vaguely remembered those days. "I'm Hayden," he said, gripping my hand like he meant it. "You the one drive's that black Porsche? I drive the white 911 out there."

"He's the dude I told you about," Kip said. "Whitey."

I detected no accent as Hayden went on about being a mechanical engineer they sent out to inspect the sites, about incompetents setting up pumps and jack-hammering so bad they drove Cats up to back them but the Cats got pushed around like toys, about small-time coon-ass operators were all broke until the drilling came along now driving new Caddies and wearing gold Rolexes as copper wire and pipe disappeared faster'n they could deliver it. His yat-free deliberate phrases came in measured bursts backlit by a broad smile spread over a wide, dimpled, square jaw beneath an expanded lumpy face over which hovered medium length curls of naturally yellow hair that made me think of a cartoon character, maybe Dudley Do-Right. Before I said anything he was on about Bobbi and eating pussy, about how he ate pussy better'n any lesbian, guaranteed orgasm in minutes. It seemed to fit with his satiny sport shirt with box bottom splashed in brightly multicolored swirls hanging over a pair of brown wool slacks, gunboat woven-toe slip-ons on his feet and a thick golden chain with large medallion hanging from his neck. Hands covered with orange hair ended in blunt, orange-haired fingers decked out in oversized square rings with and without colored stones, his wrists covered with metal, a gold watch on one of them.

"Yeah, I'm coon-ass so's okay to call 'em that, but DUCI's in charge of security and they're failing as bad as Parsons-Gilbane is busting drill bits."

"Drill bits?"

"You don't know what they're doing out there? S'posed to be drilling into salt domes to store petroleum. Never work. Shit's gonna seep, those fuckers some of 'em are cracked for sure, and the goddamn stuff is so fucking hard no can get through it. I gotta go out again to Weeks Island, out in Iberia Parish. You ever hear of New Iberia? I tell you, nobody out in that swampland, but they got some horny women out there, you be careful of the men you can get some nice pussy. For sure. And some damned good food, too, particularly the crawfish. Ever hear of the New Iberia Church of Voodoo and Imported Beer?" He dug an elbow into Kip's ribcage.

"Let's go to lunch," Kip said.

"Out in New Iberia imported beer is anything not made at home. You find little altars set up outdoors. Our Lady of the Butane Tank. They're drilling out in that swamp. When the DOE moved in the median income level jumped an order of magnitude."

Kip kept trying to work in some words about lunch. I told him to ask if Bobbi'd go with us and ducked out as Hayden kept talking in those bursts of carefully chosen words without saying anything anyone paid any attention. Bobbi agreed to come along but had to finish one task. I waited for Kip and Bobbi and Hayden in the lobby and Debby asked if she could go along with Kip and me to lunch. She seemed to have applied fresh paint to her face since I'd come in, her tight slacks and loose sleeveless knit blouse not so inviting as when she'd worn the skirt. I felt like asking how she knew Kip and I were going to lunch, but decided instead to tell her no, that my wife was in Europe but that I didn't like to step out on her. She looked astonished, then downcast when Bobbi came up front with Kip and told Debby she'd forwarded her phone to the lobby, that she was going to lunch with me and Kip.

There was no Hayden tagging along. I guessed his departure to the boonies was imminent or he was still talking and hadn't noticed we'd left. Bobbi hooked her arm through each of ours and pranced us out to the parking lot.

We took Kip's beat Mazda to a sandwich dive.

"What's Hayden's full name?" I asked while we waited for poor boys. "Is Hayden his first name or his last name?"

"I don't know," Kip said. "Bobbi takes care of personnel records."

"I don't know either. It just says Hayden on his records, I think." After a pause, she added, "He's from Natchitoches originally."

"I thought he was a native of the city," Kip said.

"Well, actually, Grand Encore. To New Orleans by way of Lafitte. That was where his father invented andouille."

"Uh, I don't think he invented it, Bobbi," Kip said.

"Well, that's what he said. Maybe he meant he just started the business there. It is a famous place for andouille."

"What's andouille?" I asked.

"Cajun sausage," they answered in unison.

I learned Bobbi was originally and most recently from Baltimore and could handle a messy sandwich with class. She had a big mouth, in the literal sense.

When we got back, I made a display of saying goodbye to Bobbi in the lobby while Debby watched.

I became aware of Dina's return from the European adventure when I laid eyes on her naked form sleeping curled in fetal ball on the solarium. She wore a spiked collar. I filled her water dish and set it out for her. It happened to be on a Tuesday. The day before she appeared a stranger waiting for me at the gate to my apartment had handed me a plain brown envelope and then disappeared into Lafitte's. It bore the same odd stamp and was stuffed with two hundred fifty hundred-dollar bills.

During this period I'd avoided human contact not of an essential nature, only facing others to teach or sit in class, instead alone working through papers regarding jet bundles in an attempt to get my arms around partial differential equations as tangibles on manifolds. Having grown familiar with differential geometry and fiber bundles, I wanted to approach Momus before the term was out, then maybe visit the physics guy at Loyola. I needed a certain at-homeness within the confines of the smooth structures I planned to run the Brownian paths over, hoping that I could tie it to the PDEs and the conservation laws and maybe relate it to infinitesimal generators. The engineering papers that dealt with quaternions as rotation implementation for inertial navigation devices amazed me until I understood the computational problems with Euler angle representations and such—it almost made me appreciate the computer maniac I had meantime, or maybe later, taken to the DOE site and while he installed and tested his code to an audience, code he developed on the university mainframe, I went to the lobby at Debby's request where she called me a bastard, saying "You got no wife"—and I began to see that stuff like radar or inertial devices were plagued with noise and had to be "filtered" and I grasped the Kalman filter as a tool for such that could tie devices together to keep each other more honest and fill in where they were respectively blind. I began to consider the possibility of attacking nonlinear problems by extending the damned thing. The difficulty was that linearity of the dynamics coupled with the linear measurements made the Kalman thing finite dimensional, only requiring the time-evolving expectation and covariance, at least if one assumed Gaussian initial conditions or as an equivalence class defined by the Gaussian problem, which was not the case when the dynamics or measurements were nonlinear. Then the problem theoretically required all the moments, an infinite dimensional problem, mostly likely tied to some PDEs for evolution of the distribution, generally a measure-valued PDE evolving in time. Mathematically the linear simplicity had to do with the fact that Kalman filter dynamics did not require full-blown Ito integrals but only Wiener integrals, independent of the sample path within the integrand and leaving the covariance and hence gain independent of the measurements. The work-around everyone seemed to use was something they called an extended Kalman filter, a linearization about the previous estimate that made the goddamn thing more nonlinear than before (or at least quadratic in the covariance), involving the sample paths and hence requiring the use of Ito's lemma which they either knew and ignored or didn't know, most likely the latter. There appeared additional quadratic terms to what they called the gain, the gradient of the gain becoming an ignored part of the propagation of the covariance dependent on the measurements. I could understand linearizing about something not related to the data, like say a predictable orbit or something, but impossible in most cases. I once brought it up to Frenchie and he shrugged his shoulders and said, "Engineers" followed by "The nonlinear problem anyway seems intractable in almost all the cases."

That was before I took the computer maniac out to install his code and deliver his manual that Joelle had typed for one hundred dollars an hour, the conversation with Frenchie about the extended Kalman thing, that is, and I told Debby that she was my serious girlfriend, the wife in Europe, and Debby said she'd heard that she wasn't any kind of a girlfriend. "Someone said she's a porn star" "yes, that's true; she was in Europe having sex with animals for the movies. She's been a prostitute. And she has a PhD from Columbia University. But none of that means she's ineligible to be my girlfriend." "That was a mean thing to tell me," she replied, looking down; maybe she hadn't grasped the animal comment or didn't believe it. "Would it have been better to say I just didn't want to go to lunch with you?" I asked. "Why?" "Why what?" Looking up, "Why don't you want to go to lunch with me? You could have let me come. Bobbi could have found someone else to take the phone." I looked at her with some intensity, staring actually, and she looked down again and said, "What did I do?" "It's what you didn't do. Or don't do. I avoid goodie-goodie girls. Can't stand 'em." "What do you mean, goodie-goodie girls? You think I'm a good girl?" "Yes, I do." "What about Bobbi?" "You don't want to know about what Bobbi does..." and she didn't, at least not in detail, not that I could have given her any then, given my visit to Bobbi's depressing box of an apartment located in a plastic neighborhood near the work site built for people indentured to the country store didn't occur until later in the semester, just before finals. I didn't tell her Bobbi had a fetish for big cocks shoved up her poop shoot, on her knees with her little droopy floppers hanging, two walleyed nipples unfocused as she squealed and grunted and chewed a pillow, drooled on the carpet and later farted splooge while lying on the floor, face down, better that angle than on her back with boobs strewn across her sternum, broken down but more resilient than Dina's despite her age, her face in the glare of an overhead lamp betraying years, her legs perhaps a bit too slender but not unshapely with no chunky thighs, no gobs or cellulite, and a firm if trifle meatless ass. It was almost impossible to put it anywhere else that night; it only ejaculated in the brown hole. Repeatedly, with a lot of mouth help. Brought to mind the small plaque affixed to my 1920s brick apartment building near Kansas City's Nelson-Atkins Museum: **All deliveries in rear.** Made me think of the other Bobbi who gave me such grief for poking her butthole and then later Mule informs me she lets, rather insists, that he and various friends simultaneously fuck her asshole, tells him she ass-fucked her way through graduate school. Anyway, escape was not easily won that night. One time we started with her draped over the back of the sofa and finished with her crawling and then slithering along the carpet, me riding her butthole fully embedded.

Her bush was thick and dark brown. Probably not as dark or dense as Debby's.

The papers Frenchie'd given me by Kalman opened up a new world. He wrote well, clearly and concisely, and it was hard to believe he was an engineer and not a mathematician. He proved theorems in his work like a mathematician; no hand waving. In a paper in the first volume of the SIAM journal on control he laid out all the dynamical linear systems theory I needed, working with differential equations. In another paper, he derived stability for the Kalman filter and discussed why optimality did not imply stability, so that it might be possible for an optimal nonlinear filter to be unstable. He also explained carefully what stability meant and why the linear optimal filter was necessarily stable (given certain assumptions on controllability and observability) though the dynamical system it estimated need not be. Asymptotic stability in the sense of Lyapunov, so the damned thing couldn't diverge if the model were right and there were satisfied those observability and controllability conditions parenthetically mentioned in the sentence above, stuff he had defined in the

SIAM paper. The stability depended on an essential property that would not be satisfied by the nonlinear filter: the covariance of the linear filtering error turned out to be independent of the data, as I had previously noted. The extended filter didn't satisfy such a property and there was a proof the fucker diverged with probability one. Kalman rooted his work in Wiener's filter for the continuous stationary case and likely in Kolmogorov for the discrete case, but I found most interesting the discrete measurement case with continuous dynamics, which would be the quasi-real world.

So while the numerical maniac got his shit running for the crowd, I cogitated Kalman's ideas and preyed on Debby. Things had come along as I'd hoped, but the dangerous part was yet to be sprung. "I really want to go to lunch with you sometime," she said, and I said, "I can feed you now, without leaving the building, but I'm not sure you'd go for it" "what do you mean?" "tubesteak, you know it?" "no" "a blowjob…" to which she said nothing. Then, "here?" and I said, "in the bathroom?" "Mr. Hines he's in Washington for the week; do it in his office" and we went in and she got on her knees grasping my legs with a hug and raised the cuffed bottoms of my blue chalk pinstripe trousers to lick each accent plate along the front of the high-top side-buckle black combat boots I'd worn, polishing them with the fabric covering her tits one by one before letting the trousers fall and while hugging my thighs unzipped my fly "now I don't want any mess on my trousers, so you gotta be real neat and swallow it all" and she kind of gasped when she had it in hand, confused maybe by the foreskin, maybe the first time she'd seen one but she sucked it from limp to hard, lips to my fly in the beginning but at full mast unable to make much headway, so to speak, and when I ejaculated I held her head and she drained it with only froth—white bubbles and squeak—escaping her lips, none of it getting onto my pants but leaving a trail on the carpet.

Kalman's later papers placed the foundations of linear systems theory algebraically in modules. It seemed solidly pure mathematics, mostly ignored by both engineers and mathematicians, that provided foundational algebraic insight into the relationship between the dynamical system as differential equations versus black-box input-output system. I absorbed the Laplace transform as insight instead of computational tool. It was on my mind while Debby sucked me off because I had only the prior evening gone through the work of another engineer, a professor at Stanford who'd developed an approach to filtering that showed promise for nonlinear problems; he defined the innovations process, so-called because that was where new information in the data entered the state estimate. I thought this might lead to a partial differential equation representation. This guy also paid homage to Wiener, but I left that behind when Debbi gobbled my spunk. She did so well I took her to lunch, though when we returned Kip seemed to notice scant traces of her lipstick on some of the blue stripes traversing my fly. They might have been from the second go-round in the restaurant men's room.

Dina'd awakened and sat naked, save collar, on the floor. First she asked if I'd gotten the money, seventy-five thousand dollars, and when I said yes, she said "Good. The network functions as advertised." She regaled me with tales of a Europe few discover, following me around on hands and knees as I tried to concentrate on mathematics.

"Baron Apteker's demesne covers parts of Belgium and the Netherlands, mostly in what are called the Low Countries, what is sometimes still called Benelux. Families in villages on his land are descendents of original serfs who were bound to the demesne and still live as dependents and provide corvée though now in terms of sexual prestation, though perhaps more as willing villeins. Manorial ancestral land has been under allodial title since Otto I the Great, under The Holy Roman Empire, when his ancestor sided with Otto against Eberhard of Franconia and played a significant role at the Battle of Andernach. Sir, Apteker is recognized as a legitimate baron in both the Netherlands and Belgium. His holdings cover an entire pagi and the inhabitants speak a variant of West Flemish that is similar to Zeelandic Flemish, but more local, actually, Sir, though someone told me it was more a form of Brabantish and someone else said it was more Aptekish. I thought it rather more a dialect of Low Franconian with modernisms. Baron Apteker is gay, but carries out his ceremonial duty in the traditional pre-nuptial gang bang by first boinking the bride. Incongruously, male human sex with the animals, male or female, is strictly forbidden. Apteker married to leave heirs, probably a tradition, being gay and marrying to leave heirs, I mean. His estate is a resort for wealthy women who come to fuck animals. Can you dig that? They have bred animals for sex with humans for centuries. The animals, I only experienced dogs and horses and mules—" "No goats or pigs?" "—but women come from all over the world. These animals are trained by village women, that is part of what they do, and they know how to fuck humans, these animals." I'd been reading a series of papers on jets defined in terms of germs by some people who did catastrophe theory, stuff of which I had little interest other than the jets, related somehow to differential topology, making use of Sard's lemma and winding up in a ring of formal power series in several variables over the ring of differentiable germs on n-dimensional real Euclidean space as the space of C^∞ functions modulo the ideal of functions vanishing on a neighborhood of the origin. It blossomed in full career to an orgy of multi-indices shaming Folland's work on partial differential equations into seeming one-dimensionality, manifolds popping up and derivations of the ring of differentiable germs as a vector space leading I would have assumed to some tangent space that never appeared, to create I imagined tangent spaces over the ring as module, or so it seemed. Questions of convergence arose in the formal setting of the power series as a ring and a map defined by a theorem of Borel from germ equivalence classes to jets, infinitely defined or prolonged or something by an intersection over an infinite decreasing collection, ideals generated by monomials related to Taylor polynomials in ascending powers that ended up a Noetherian ring that was a unique factorization domain, falling off the deep end with Nakayama's lemma, a result I had hoped to not see again after Bolyai's advanced class on modules, now applied ostensibly to what I believed was analysis lost in algebra and topology. The name Mather appeared frequently, probably a descendent of Cotton. I cursed the papers and the approach, shameful in obscuring such a seemingly simple idea, torturing my sleep that night and now my escape from Dina, sure I could sort it out as she broke in with a plaintiff "Please, Sir, I haven't had a human dick in weeks. Please just let me suck it, Sir." The train of thought derailed again by that remark, at which I found myself grateful.

"Okay, Dina, you relate your adventures and we'll see if they raise it up without nonverbal stimulus. If so, I will put it somewhere in you. Each and every time," not telling her how glad I was she had rescued me from a carnage of ideas, a debauch of machinery seemingly without cause. But it did trouble me in that I understood there was no invariant derivative of a tangent vector outside connections: consider the circle in Cartesian coordinates as cosine and sine of t versus polar coordinates as radial vector from the origin and angle, which on the circle was (1,t). Clearly tangent vectors were fine, both tangent as expected, given the invariance of the tangent space, but not so for acceleration, since in the first case it was (-cos(t), -sin(t)) and in the second (0,0). Most likely, I was on the wrong track, pig-headed in obstinate refusal to see what hung before my nose; there had to be natural way to get this without making it so fucking unnatural— "You aren't listening, Sir. That isn't fair." "Sorry, I apologize. Start again." "The Apteker demesne covers parts of Belgium and the Netherlands—" "I got that part; start with where you get there. I got that they breed animals to fuck humans—" "A spa, sir. A lovely little green valley with villages and rosy cheeked chubby girls who fuck dogs and horses and pigs and goats and mules and more, Sir, and take care of them, too, and their husbands are fine with it, for centuries, and women come to stay for days or weeks to be pampered and have sex with these animals; at great expense, I might add. I was mated with a huge dog, sir—" "named Hermanubis—" "how did you know that, Sir?" "I talked to someone who caught your lecture at the *Collège de France*—" "that would be impossible, Sir, since I never gave it. It was cancelled. Once they learned the topic they wouldn't let me deliver it. In fact, they might be ready to end my tenure there." She stared at me. "I know who you mean, Sir. She was there. Hypatia." "Where?" "Never mind, Sir. Hermanubis is said to be the biggest dog in the world and I believe it. Without raising up on hind legs, that is when he stands naturally on all fours, Sir, his shoulder is at my thorax. He weighs nearly three hundred pounds. God he was hung Sir; the biggest dick I ever experienced until I worked with the horses and mules. Horses are hung like baseball bats, Sir, and having a baseball bat rammed forcefully and repeatedly in your cunt or asshole is transcendental, especially with all the spunk they spew; it took me several tries to be able to swallow a full load. Like quarts, Sir, or liters. Anyway, Hermanubis is an English Mastiff. I was his mate for six weeks. I lived with him, Sir. We were quite sympatico—" "You consider marrying him?" "I considered staying with him. They said he took to me like to no other woman. They are looking for a slattern in residence—" "He wasn't jealous of your other lovers?" "No, he always kept watch as if to keep them in line—" "Within the bounds of decency?" "—never abandoning me like some creatures—" "Which was why you didn't stay with him; too caring?" and she hung her head and I was right. "God, he was dominant, Sir, 'no' was never an option. It was like constant rape." "You must have liked that." "You have no idea. Everything was sex and no humans involved; the first few days with that dog were so intense I think I left my body during some orgasms. They said that was why he took to me. Most women are worn out or scared shitless after a few hours or minutes with that red-eyed creature with his red club of a dick. The night I arrived they escorted me to his apartment: really an apartment, sir, with five rooms, one for sleeping, one for eating, one for him for shitting and such, another bathroom with shower and running water and toilet for a human, and one for fucking. The fucking room had devices to help the woman into special positions. Glass enclosed, one way mirrors, where they could watch us all the time. When I was in there I was always naked. It was the rule, and I ate from a bowl and drank from a bowl, like here, Sir. For the first three days, the honeymoon, there was no direct human contact at all. None until the coming out dinner party. Staying with him would have been costly were it not for the production company; top of the scale for spa attendees. The instant they locked me in there he came over and sniffed my butthole and pussy, lapped them with a giant tongue until I was literally beside myself. Then he fucked me. For hours. Without rest. He taught me to know when he wanted me to suck him, to get him hard or to cum in my mouth. First he fucked me in my pussy. And dogs have something horses and mules don't have, Sir: a knot on the back of their cocks, to tie the female so sperm can't escape. His knot swelled on intromission to the size of a ham; before he got it swollen inside, knotted me, he shoved me around the room with jackhammer fucking, Sir, holding me by my shoulders or with a paw on my head, covering my head with it, Sir, and then his knot grew inside my pussy and he lifted me off the floor, really I couldn't reach the floor on my hands and knees and had to stretch my arms and legs out to make floor contact and he ejaculated for what seemed an hour, all the while I'm wriggling and squirming and his stuff is puddling onto the floor, thick like pudding, Sir, oozing out of me around the seal, barely escaping, Sir, I was so full of his sperm it seeped out, nowhere else to go, his knotted thing throbbing, stuck until it deflated. His intromittent organ was nearly the size of a horse's dick, something I learned about later, Sir, as I have intimated. Huge; much bigger than yours or Mule's, a red giant schlong, pointed, ever-drooling, hard as a rock, and when knot-tied throbbing like a machine, thewy devices protruding from four-legged creatures of nothing but thew..." the image of her hanging beneath the dog, wriggling like a bug with hanging dugs dancing made me forget the horrors of the catastrophe and that I didn't know the word thew, but didn't prepare for me the first time I saw the film, The *Masque of the Honeymoon;* I grew an erection that she noted, obligating me to cram it into her cunt which I fucked until ejaculation, not long coming, actually, and asked her after I finished, "I assume you filmed all this?" "Yes Sir, we did, everything, they are all masques, Sir. This one is *The Honeymoon,* Sir, the first nights. Later he starred with me in *The Masque of the Red Dork,* which follows *Centaur,* where I couple with horse and rider, Sir, fucking controlled by the rider, the closest thing to human fucking after *The Dinner Party,* and there is also the *Masque of the Dog Orgy* and *The Kennel Masque* and *Barnyard Orgy* and *Doggie Rape..."*

Lauded by critics of animal fetishism and marketed to great commercial and artistic success as *Dina's Dog and Pony Show,* or *Oh Belgium,* the video collection for discerning connoisseurs of the four-legged fetish, it netted oodles of cash from which I received a handsome stipend. In *The Dinner Party,* Dina attends wearing only dog collar and leash and sandals, Hermanubis handling the leash, a dinner party for fifty couples who watch Dina mounted repeatedly by a horny Hermanubis, anal and vaginal and oral sex, plenty of knotting, subject to Hermanubis' demands which it seemed were frequent and violent, the only human sex of her trip with double penetration by dog and man or dog fucking while sucking human dick or lapping pussy or fucking a line of humans while sucking off Hermanubis, later fucking on a stage while the participants ate dinner and she hung knotted, suspended and wriggling like a pinned bug, and after ate from a bowl with her master beside her. In *Doggie Rape* Hermanubis watches over a gang of ten or so dogs, the smallest the German Shepherds and Doberman Pinschers, gang raping her for several hours in a fenced corral that plays in several other films. The technique displayed amazing teamwork as one dog would knot her anus or vagina and hold her in place and, by veering askew, allow his kennel companions access to fuck her free orifice, asshole or cunt depending on where she was knotted, while others fucked her mouth, the knotting dog always facing away from her so it appeared as a two-headed beast at opposite poles with double and triple doggie penetration. Dina originated from this the double knotting-dildo that she patented, knotting either two cunts, a cunt and an asshole or two assholes, gender not a barrier, that came with a pair of double ankle straps to tie together the ankles of the hapless knotted couple facing away from each other, along with a pair of O-rings to gape the mouths open for forced fellatio. *The Masque of the Red Dork* came with Hermanubis as the last participant after the *Doggie Rape*, a giant Black Lab holding her steady with anal knot. How the two fit behind her to allow Hermanubis to fuck her provided a lesson in honed doggie skills, Hermanubis standing on his hind legs and leaning his fore paws on a fence as Dina splayed along a bench, knotting her cunt so she is double knotted, filling the gash with goo that gushes when he withdraws to fuck her mouth, spraying a constant stream into her buccal cavity. The end has a disoriented Dina covered with dog splooge and eructating grayish exudate from every orifice as Hermanubis helps her back to their quarters. She seems disoriented after several of the encounters, with kindly Hermanubis always assisting her. In *The Masque of the Dog Orgy* she voluntarily parties with several dozen dogs, no knotting to hold her in-place for forced coupling though plenty of knotting and dragging across the floor, Dina aggressively pursuing doggie dicks, double penetration and fellatio with constant three-way encounters until she seems worn down by the insatiable hounds, perhaps passing out near the end as they continue to penetrate her until Hermanubis breaks it up. Worse in *The Kennel Masque* where she gives in as if she can't keep up and Hermanubis steps in again, and it seems she might be killed in *Barnyard Orgy* with dogs, horses and mules where she begins with high energy and realizes she can't win, can't wear them down, and Hermanubis has a difficult time breaking it up, a horse attacking him to keep the action alive.

The horse and mule films show stamina of a different sort. Dina leaning against a padded fence or cushioned backstop to dampen the blows, hands tied and feet secured sometimes, other times free form, a single stallion or a line of stallions taking turns on hind paws ramming her repeatedly to whinnying blasts; the films with saddle beneath the horse, Dina riding suspended below and horse cock buried within, in one a rider above guiding the horse, in the others the horse standing still or walking or prancing to gushing climax; other times on a bench or table, legs sometimes spread by stirrups and the horse fucking her mercilessly; fellating horses to orgasm, streaming from her mouth in early films until she masters the art of sealing the tube and swallowing it all down though there are some blasts so violent it escapes her nostrils, the horses warning her with eager neighs. In one video she leans back with dappled horse appendage displayed against her body from mons veneris to mid chest, showing the size of the pink and black monstrosity that she takes full in her cunt kneeling on a bench doggie style. In *Centaur* the skilled rider, the one who guided the horse with Dina suspended in the saddle beneath, prances the animal in place and cajoles it to rear up from time to time with Dina leaning into a fence in a tizzy, transported to some other dimension as revealed by several long Eisensteinian close-ups. In more than one film, she fellates one horse or mule while another fucks her. In *Barnyard Orgy* she mixes it up with horses, mules, donkeys and dogs. The mules she praised as more artful lovers than the horses. She shows them great affection in a number of films, fellating them and fucking them in numerous imaginative positions and especially on her back, legs around the animals. There were a variety of donkeys and mules in *Blue Fox,* filmed before a live audience in a mock-up of the famous Tijuana saloon.

As she related the tales of her adventures captured on celluloid, I porked various orifices until I could no longer maintain an erection, at which I bade her rig herself, without attending to toilette, in skank livery of short-short cut-off jeans and crop top with nipples peaking above her navel and sandals with straps winding up her calves, then fitted her head into a leather mask with only nose and mouth holes, a funneled O-ring embedded in the mouth aperture to keep her open trap drooling and led her around the upper Quarter and into Marigny like a blind bitch trolling bars until a Pied Piper parade followed us to her dungeon where I left her at their mercy while I returned to the apartment to ponder a method for disposing of the ambient embedding in Euclidean space of my manifold for running the BM, replacing the normal bundle with a vertical bundle tangent to some fibers of appropriate objects, not sure what but hoping it was an original thought, though likely I'd seen the vertical bundle and horizontal complement in K&N. It was immediately clear that there existed no splitting of this short exact sequence of bundle morphisms, especially given that the horizontal bundle on the right could not be a subbundle of the tangent bundle of the fiber bundle whose fibers I would need to choose to suit my BM. But beginning with the manifold M, choosing the fiber bundle (E, π, M) with appropriate yet to be determined fibers, one got this exact sequence

$$0 \longrightarrow V\pi \longrightarrow E \longrightarrow \pi^*(TM) \longrightarrow 0$$

of vector bundles where the map of the vertical subbundle into E was an embedding (actually the kernel of π_*, the differential of the bundle projection) but the map onto the horizontal or more appropriately the transverse bundle did not split, since there could be in general no distinguished subbundle of the tangent projection onto TE, the tangent space of the fiber bundle E. I recalled seeing this thing as a geometric construction for connections on the bundle π, using distributions in the sense of Frobenius, perhaps while perusing K&N.

It took me a bit of time to get Debby to do other guys. Two weeks to be exact, which amounted to three lunches and a few extra feedings. This was in sharp distinction to Judy who Mule, Jerry and I talked into going to the Brown Derby on Louisiana Avenue, a place I wouldn't have visited without Mule and Jerry, more a tavern than a restaurant in the window of which hung hand lettered signs in magic marker advertising red beans and rice with pig tails or pig ears among other typical fare. After eating and drinking on us, Judy said, "You boys all want to get in this here stuff, but it ain't gonna happen." Poking me in the chest, "You baby, you a white boy gonna run off out to some high-class place in California or Massachusetts and you don't need no light chocolate wife wif kids ain't your'n. You, Mule, I know how you makes money, used to be gigolo and now porn star, and there ain't no way I'm gonna tie up with that—" to which Mule interjected "Only for a few hours, baby, not forever—" and she turned it on Jerry, "That be you all over Jerry, what he saying right now. But thanks for the food and beer, y'all." Then she walked out. Debby, on the other hand, got busy with Mule in a motel for lunch; I was sure she wouldn't eat pig tails or pig ears, but she ate his black kielbasa. I watched and joined in at the end. Later encounters added male participants, often friends of Mule's or perhaps fellow actors, to a grand total of three at one time until a week before we went to the swing club. At that practice session she took on six including Mule, one of the night sessions we set up in my apartment. I avoided the guys she worked with for these encounters for obvious reasons, but I knew she would not have objected. She was quietly matter of fact, not saying much until she'd had her cunt massaged for twenty or thirty minutes at which time she howled like a bitch in heat whenever her mouth was not filled with cock but otherwise offered no manifestations of passion. She took to anal sex from the start, engulfing Mule in a single ram with only a quiver and goose bumps. Mule, proud of having made Albina cry, called her a "languid ho'." She looked better when wearing clothes. Mule complained he found it difficult to get aroused with her, as evidenced by his soft snake that took inordinate time to straighten, not very professional behavior but then he wasn't doing it for money. No masterpiece her naked body, especially with the dark hair surrounding the dark lips hanging between her legs, a thick black vee up to her navel around which marched a dense line of black hair, black hair sprouting from her butthole and her molasses nipples. Her shaved parts, armpits and legs, cut with stiff bristles that drew blood. Her white skin contrasted eerily with the mass of body hair, blue veins showing near the surface, especially on the flattened mounds of tit. Cottage cheese had begun accumulating under her butt and the backs of her thick thighs. It was hard to imagine why any of the men she worked with found her an appealing physical specimen, except the packaging and advertising was adequately applied and men, especially white men, are fucking stupid. It was her only gift, the advertising for white men, given how poorly she performed even when wound up with three dicks in her.

Hypatia showed up without warning, ambushing me unawares at places not Tulane at which she did not appear. Sometimes in the Quarter, like at La Marquise on a Sunday morning pastry outing, sometimes walking to Dina's car, and once while I lunched with companions from the SPR project out in The Parish. Attired most often in jeans and t-shirt, out in The Parish she once wore hooped earrings, a long-sleeved lace-adorned beige blouse, black skirt that looked to be made of something used for drapes festooned across front and back with a multicolor garland of painted roses, black mid-calf lace-up boots with brown socks or hose rolled down protruding several inches over boot tops and the wooden bead necklace of a gypsy fortuneteller. She hijacked the luncheon and, as Bobbi asked her where she'd got the peasant dot and lace blouse, led me away me from the table and to a Rolls-Royce chauffeured by a giant black man with a beaming smile wearing a tuxedo, black top hat, and cotton plugs in his nostrils. He smoked an odiferous cigar and drank from a bottle labeled Rhum Barbancourt. She addressed him as Saturday and directed him to tool us to the office on Plantation Road, which turned out to be not an office but a cottage. Hypatia rested her hand on my thigh and snuggled, an unusual move, lifting my arm around her shoulders for the drive, scaring the shit out of me. "I wanted to discuss things, given we're involved," she said in what sounded like a dreamy voice, causing me to wonder if I were awake. "We're going to a concert tonight, to meet your *pomba-gira.*" "My what?" "We'll get to that," and it reminded me of her initial reappearance. Dina seemed exhausted from her safari to Belgium and, after the visit in which she described her adventures following which I'd left her in the dungeon with a plethora of human dicks, had avoided me, disappearing into her world and perhaps not stirring from her small room at all. Not that I spent much time in the Quarter with my burgeoning adventure in the government boondoggle, which Jeremy had tasked me for the summer with figuring out how to integrate cost and schedule, the Holy Grail of the DOE management. Moreover the end of the semester loomed inchoate and I had to think about preparing a final for the stat class which I now lectured on the bare edge of consciousness. I think I'd gotten to the point I put off both Cone and the cheerleader with my absentness. I'd had scant time to indulge in drugs other than the usual pot and none for drinking excursions, in danger of estranging myself to my haunts. My thesis research lagged to the point I almost felt guilt, fed up with jet bundles and whatnot. I was hence none too pleased when Dina appeared in tow behind Hypatia who had not been seen since her lecture earlier in the term.

"I've been off cavorting with elementals," Hypatia explained. "And visiting the dark recesses of incoherent cardinals in search of economic truth." She laughed as if it were a joke, but I couldn't tell. Incoherent cardinals? Wouldn't be the first expression of hers I'd taken for a joke that she'd meant for real, particularly given her relationship to languages with sentences of infinite length.

Appearing out of the blue with Dina blurred her mystique. I had not expected to ever see them together.

"Master," Dina asked resting naked on her haunches, "can you grant me leave to have sex with Hypatia?"

"Why not?" I mused, lighting a spliff for the three of us. "Why don't you do it now?"

"Alone," Hypatia said. "I have some secrets to share with her. We can do it together another time if you desire. Is that acceptable?"

"I don't see what it's got to do with me. I'm almost at the point of cutting her loose anyway—"

"No!" Dina screamed at me. "You can't manumit yet. You made a commitment."

"I don't think it would be wise," Hypatia reinforced. "What I want is to prep Dina for a sacrifice at a club next week. You need to come along with a date. But Dina will be my date and gift to some elementals."

"What kind of club?"

"A private club in the Quarter. A businessman, very wealthy. Quite eccentric. Considers himself keeper of some demons from the *Goetia* or *Pseudomonarchia daemonum,* depending on which day of the week you talk to him. It's a swing club. You get a set up when you go in; you check your clothes and don robes."

That was the date on which I took Debbie a week after the sextet fucked her silly in my apartment. And before Hypatia and I became more or less lovers. More for me, less for her. This visit looked like more from her, hence the surprise which went along with my surprise at finding her romantic fodder, given my initial reactions and the bird feet and all, which had disappeared at any rate along with the cloaca, all of it replaced by a normal pair of sexual and excretory orifices. Between visits I could not remember and had no idea what she looked like. Those between times I found Joelle an object for romantic daydreams, intrusions on my attempts to concentrate on anything mathematical. And though my involvement was with Hypatia after Dina disappeared with the tattoo artist for a major remodeling and though I never thought of Hypatia when we were not actually face to face, during our encounters I was smitten to the extent I intended focusing all my sexual energy on her alone. Romantic sex, no less. Not so when away from her; at those times Joelle occupied my romantic brain activity, such as it was. In reality, as noted, when not with her I had no inkling what Hypatia looked like, though I remembered the bird feet and all from the first time, but otherwise no image at all of her from our most recent, or any prior after the first, liaisons. I always recognized her when I saw her, though she might have looked completely different each time.

Joelle invited me to her Irish Channel apartment on Chestnut Street near Casamento's where I once treated her to dinner of oyster poor boys. She felt grateful to me for the extra money, she made that clear, and intimated she was ready to pay with sex, something that occupied my thoughts but romantically, not so sordidly as with Dina or other of the professional skanks I'd been hanging with. I ignored the hint and went to dinner at her house, her invite, and didn't come on to her nor did she come on to me, but when I insinuated I was possibly interested romantically she said, "I expected more from you, Whitey. Every guy wants to be my steady, to lock me up in his little world and maybe marry me and imprison me behind a white picket fence with kids and cooking and all that. I don't want any of it. I don't want a steady like that, no romantically goo-goo-eyed dope all aquiver over me, wanting me pure and truly his." I wondered if she'd meant purely his or pure as in chaste, but didn't think it important given my dose of surprise. "All the men who want into my life want me to be virginal and chaste except when with them, and even then I think they want only missionary position but no matter if they want me to ride reverse cowgirl or give up my anal orifice to their lust and be a personal slut in the bedroom, they still want a saint in the outside world and I can't stand it, Whitey." She gazed deadpan over the plates across the table, as deadpan as she'd spoken, without rancor or any untoward inflection in her voice. "Say something," she said in the face of my silence. "What do you want? To be a whore? That can be arranged, you know. There is a porn producer working in the city close to Tulane." "Porn? No, dear boy. Nothing cheap. I want more, though. I don't want the white picket fence and family of cherubic urchins and growing old faithful or cheating on the side, either." "What do you want, then?" "More. I want more. People say you are familiar with places where there is more." "I wouldn't take you." "But you'd take that ugly woman who dresses like a kindergarten whore that you brought to the math department?" "I didn't bring her. She hunted me down and came for me. She knows people who are affiliated with Tulane, Joelle. And she is not someone I take anywhere. She took me to a club once. With her girlfriend, who is even worse than she, in fact is some kind of sexual freak with clitoris that becomes a penis. And the kindergarten whore fellates strangers and anonymous penises sticking through holes in men's room walls and drinks urine." "I want to know her girlfriend. She sounds interesting." "She isn't." "Then why did you go to this club with her?" to which I had no answer.

401

"I'll explain what I do," Hypatia said once we snuggled on the sofa in the cottage-cum-office while the driver waited without. "But I won't write it down. No one else has heard this, by the way."

"I'm flattered. But why me?"

"Two reasons. First, you take things at face value—as they are—without trying to find something more behind them—"

"So I must be a fool—"

"Exactly. No judgments from you. And more importantly, you are the only person to ever see me with bird's feet."

"Really? What about you?"

"Me what?"

"See yourself with bird's feet?"

"I'd like to say, Of course no, but I'd rather say nothing of this. If you don't mind—"

"Or if I do mind."

"Exactly.

"So firstly, you know who is John Dee?"

"Someone told me he was a magician or something like that, in the sixteenth century."

"Also mathematician. He had a man working with him, Edwar…Wait, let me go back… to start earlier…

"My mother was born in Italy but grew up in Brazil. Her parents died in a car crash and her aunt in Santos raised her. Her father had owned a business in São Paulo but her aunt was poor and lived on earnings she gained working at the *terreiro Centro Espírita Mãe Sabina* before she attracted enough followers to start her own *terreiro* when she gained a reputation as medium and later healer. My mother had the statues of the *caboclo, preto velho* and *yemanjá* in her small altar in New Orleans when I was a girl. I think she has them yet, the ones from her aunt."

"The what?"

"Sorry. Caboclo is a statue of an Indian. It represents the spirits of half-breed native Brazilians who died. Good spirits, with knowledge of herbs for healing. All of them I have seen, in the US or in Brazil, are the kinds of Indians on US television with the long feather hats. Like Indian Chiefs. They sometimes look like movie stars. Or the Mardi Gras Indians.

"The Preto Velho is an old black man with white hair and sometimes a corncob pipe like from the US, too. An old slave who has died. Another kind spirit.

"Yemanjá is a goddess of the sea, but she is a mother goddess and takes care of pregnant women and also children. And sailors. Well, I think sometimes. My mother found her in New Orleans when she got involved in Voodoo, because she is in Voodoo too and is called Yemana here. She has black hair and wears a long blue dress like the High Priestess on the Tarot cards of the Waite deck."

"Not familiar with any of that." Dina's story of the Indian chief and the old black man at the gang bang in the warehouse or men's club or whatever it was came back to me. The black man had spread the green salve on her nether regions.

"No matter. It has to do with my mother. Her aunt branched out of the Umbanda because it had this Kardecism in it that she found absurd. My mother called it French crap whenever we were living in Brazil. She learned Quimbanda, which I later discovered is based on Yoruba magic. It is more or less the Umbanda without the Catholic or French Kardecism influence. But she also called it Candomblé which is similar, but less pure African. They all have some deities together from Yoruba, the Orishas they call them, but I don't think Quimbanda kept the Preto Velho or Caboclo, though I am not positive, not being at all interested in this. Anyhow, they also have deities of Vodum from West Africa, which is like voodoo in New Orleans. And she sometimes called it Macumba, which is a big catch-all word in Brazil for all this. My mother began to get a following, especially men, and her aunt became jealous and called her a *pombajira* which is a *pomba-gira.* Which my mother said was amusing since my aunt seemed to be prostituting herself on the side, but anyhow, my mother used her powers to call up my father who came to her rescue and took her away from—"

"Is this going somewhere? I am not interested in all this voodoo stuff."

"Oh, sorry, Dear," caressing my hand, all uncharacteristic and spooky, "just to let you know that my mother continued to practice in Brazil when we lived there and in New Orleans, too, where she joined in voodoo ceremonies. It was second nature for her. She still does these things, but now mostly she stays in Brazil.

"I was born in the US, in New Orleans. My father is a big shot in the coffee business and oversaw operations in the US for a time, then both in the

US and in Brazil. He mostly stays in Brazil with my mother these days, but I grew up in both places. I have Brazilian, Italian and US citizenship—"

"You speak Italian and Portuguese?"

"Of course. Your mother was born in Brazil?"

"Yes. How the hell did you know that?"

"A little bird told me."

"You said that in this religion they have some gods that are old black men and Indians in headdresses?"

"Spirits. Like minor deities. The *pomba-gira* is supposedly a Brazilian creation like a goddess for whores. My mother—"

"So where are we going with this now?"

"Mother was quite promiscuous, with my father's approval. He liked to watch her with men."

"Okay, let's get back to where we were when you forked to this path. John Dee."

"Oh, sure. This only background, really. I think you have enough now.

"Because of her magic practice, I got interested in magic but wasn't interested in voodoo. I got some books and read them, but then I read Aleister Crowley. You know of him?"

"No."

"He was big idiot. A Brit. Buffoon and publicity freak. But he wrote a book called *Magick in Theory and Practice* that I found when I was ten. He said in there, in the beginning, that this magick as he called it—he spelled it with a k on the end—anticipated the recent discoveries of Frege, Cantor, Poincaré, and others, I think maybe Whitehead and Einstein and Russell and maybe Dedekind, maybe not… So I went looking for who those were and I found them. I was unimpressed with Russell and Whitehead, especially the cumbersome *Principia Mathematica* which seemed no better than what Crowley did—"

"You read that at ten?"

"Maybe eleven by then. It was my introduction to type theory. But I had a feel for what they did because I read work derived from Cantor and Frege and other logicians and that got me interested in mathematics, especially when I read Poincaré—"

"This is pretty hard to believe."

"Why? It is not so difficult if you are not brought up to fear it. I hated playing with other kids anyway. I hated going to school, so my father to appease the authorities when we lived in New Orleans got me tutors who were as stupid as the teachers, until he got me some people from Tulane and also the Universidade de São Paulo when we were in Brazil. Later he sent me to the *Instituto de Matemática* in Rio for some guidance. I got to learn much things. I learned calculus by Cartan's *Calcul différentiel* and *Formes différentielles*— Henri, not his father but I read some things from him too—and Spivak's little book *Calculus on Manif—"*

"Wait, you're telling me you read those two books by Cartan on your own? In French?"

"They were given to me by a tutor, but they were not so hard… I read his book of complex analysis in French, too, and André Weil's old classic on integration on groups and then lost interest in analysis and turned to algebraic geometry…"

I tuned her out, more or less. It was supernatural. I hated books, but I had looked at the "calculus" books by Henri Cartan and found them pretty fucking advanced, though I recall they were supposedly sophomore level texts at Princeton for math majors. Sophomores doing calculus in Banach spaces was a bit much to me.

I jumped in to interrupt her rambling. "How do you read so much math?"

"Speed reading. I have an ability to speed read, it turns out, naturally. Maybe because I taught myself to read with my mother's help about the same time I was walking. I read French along with the Portuguese and English in the house and later I read Italian, which was not hard since I spoke it from birth. But the key is to not read all the details in math. Provide them yourself; almost all the proofs are transparent anyway if you think properly so one can skip them."

It was one-up on the advise I'd given the dweeb.

"I convinced my father to send me to Oxford when I was fifteen. Or my mother did. She could control my father. She did control him. Very tightly."

"Why Oxford?"

"They have tutors there, so you read as directed. I wanted to do mathematics, and when I got there they learned I already had all the standard stuff: economics, literature, government, history, all that kinds of thing and in native languages. My father didn't want me to live alone so he boarded me where I would be parented, but it was easy-going and I fooled them most of the time. The readers in mathematics were of great help, steering me into algebraic topology and logic. I read a lot of new things. Mostly papers, current works, and became interested in algebraic geometry. I read Weil's book and also read a lot of Grothendieck and his followers. And I read Serre. But Carol Karp opened my eyes to the logic with infinitely long sentences and what is possible to do building categorical structures which led me to model theory, the back and forth method and saturated models and… But there was another reason."

I popped out with "John Dee?"

"Yes. The British Library has the original manuscripts that gasbags like Crowley and MacGregor Mathers had claimed as basis for their so-called Enochian magick. There were a lot of these magic books, some of them grimoires, most absurd crap. And incantations and all seemed juvenile, even to a twelve year old when I started reading it. But I was curious about the documents of Dee. For one thing, there was an analysis of them by a qualified linguist. I got to meet him once. An Australian; he went there to study them and I met him. Donald Laycock.

"There existed two major sets of these documents. Supposedly they were transcribed by Dee from a shew-stone read by a man named Talbot who changed his name to Edward Kelley when he went to work for Dee. They were supposed to be communicating with angels. This Talbot or Kelley or whatever his name was pretty unscrupulous man it seems, a charlatan though Dee also was astrologer and numerologist so who can say?… There is interesting story about wife-swapping ordered by the angels which was transmitted by Kelley who got to do Dee's young wife… Kelley was alchemist and did a lot of other stuff and probably was a swindler but for Dee he acted as a scryer—"

"A what?"

"Scry is like using a crystal ball to see the future.

"So anyway, they get—oh, scry is also to sieve—these transmissions from angels which is where the Enochian name comes in because I don't think they were thinking of the Book of Enoch—"

"What?"

"An ancient book supposedly by Enoch, before Methuselah in the Old Testament; it was read by Jews and had influence on the Bible, the story about those fallen angels and their offspring, the giants—"

"Nephalim, I know the story—"

"Okay, them. People thought these angels they communicated with were the fallen angels because they said bad things about Christ etcetera, you know?"

"So this linguist?"

"He liked magic. He said it worked, this incantation bullshit but I think it is this problem of humans believing that things work. Like magic, prayer, psychology, religion, economics, all the same mumbo jumbo nonsense. He said that the first part of the stuff they had, the text that Kelley spoke in the angel language, supposedly the original language before Tower of Babel incident, or which language had come from after Adam got the boot, was glossolalia—"

"What?"

"Speaking in tongues. Like holy rollers and *macumbeiros.* Because it didn't have any characteristics of natural language. The keys part, translated into English part, was not right either. It was much like English in structure, so a fraud. Probably of Kelley alone.

"But I looked at the first part for a long time and realized it was not natural language and not glossolalia either. It was formal language, which was why the characteristics came out wrong. No grammar; only symbols and rules of inference."

I stared at her.

"Really. I told no one, of course. But I worked with it and got a system that neither of them could have understood. The language was one of the infinitary logics, but with much bigger cardinalities than the usual omega-one omega or omega-one—"

"You mean, those languages denoted with the subscripts?"

"Yes. Usually L sub little omega-one omega or little omega-one omega-one, which are often big enough, but not this time. The cardinalities have to be inaccessible in this case. And of course, the second one, being over quantifiers—"

"Yeah, explain that. I am not fam—"

"The first subscript is the cardinality of the allowed disjunctions, the second is quantifiers, and of course the second must be smaller or no bigger. So let me see, do you understand the categoricity you buy with this?"

"Not really. I got through Gödel's and Cohen's work."

"Forcing? You understand it?"

"After your lecture it came together."

"Interesting. The…"

"Kripke stuff, believe it or not."

"I believe. Let me explain a little of the benefit of this infinitary logic, which is better for me than the types, but then everyone really works within set theory to avoid the problems, though there remain the problems of categoricity even so. No, but first…do you understand the hierarchy of interpretability of languages?"

"No, never ran across that."

"Well there is such, a way of determining a hierarchy of interpretations, with bigger meaning that the smaller can be embedded in an interpretation that leaves all the provable, provable. And there is also the notion of projective sets—" "No, not familiar—" "The so-called descriptive set theory, which comes maybe originally from Baire category theory—" "That is analysis for me, or general topology—" "Of course, but this becomes logical, you know? Like with compactness. Anyway, the projective set business is related to games where one fixes a subset of the closed interval zero-one and then each of the players chooses an element of the interval and if the sum of these as binary decimals, you know taking each one at kth step and multiplying by one over two to the k, converges to an element of A then player one—of course, the kth step is really like kth and then k+1 for second player—" "I got it—" "—and so if converges in A then first player wins and otherwise player two wins. If there is a strategy for winning for either of the players then the set is said to be determined and if the set is a projective set—a set is projective if it is obtained by finite series of projections like projection onto first coordinates of product of a subset of Euclidean space and complements like complements of set—these correspond by the way to quantification—"

"This is not getting me anywhere, Hypatia."

"Well, just to say that Peano axioms are second order arithmetic and the so called projective determinacy is that every projective set is determined and is—wait, the second level is like power set of natural numbers and one has that all projective sets are Lebesgue measureable—forget the determined example, Lebesgue measure works here; this is independent of set theory—and at next level is independence of continuum hypothesis: not the general version, just for two to the aleph null. This order is anyway not linear order, maybe dense too. Not important."

"No, clearly…"

"There are logicians who think that all the theories that arise naturally are well-ordered but I know this is wrong, though I have not shown this since it is upsetting, the example I mean. And my only proof reveals too much of my basic methods. I have yet to find a way to prove it in mathematically approved social setting, if you understand what I mean—"

"No, I don't."

"Don't worry about that then."

"I won't."

She smiled. "Claro. Is why I like you. So what are we talking about?"

"I think you were trying to give me an idea of the basis for your ideas."

"I will just say there are a lot of inaccessible cardinals." "An inaccessible cardinality of them? That's like saying, There's plenty of room in Hilbert space." She carried on like she hadn't heard me. "Some of them arose from certain kinds of problems, like why Gödel invented these large cardinal ideas—instead of inaccessible I ought maybe talk about large cardinals with inaccessible at the bottom, say strongly inaccessible so power sets don't get you anywhere from below—anyway, for settling certain kinds of questions farther along the hierarchy. But there are now small large cardinals that are okay with the constructible universe of inner models—I assume you know this idea inner models of Gödel's—" I nodded yes "—and so then these are useful but is better to use the large cardinals that move ordinals around so the constructible universe fails. Some of the large cardinal axioms—all the large cardinals are inaccessible, say variants of inaccessible—come from looking at problems related to Lebesgue measure and nonmeasureable sets which seems to upset people but not so much as taking apart spheres in a simple way and putting them back to have two—" "Banach-Tarski, I know of it, paradoxical decomposition, related to nonmeasureable sets in the manner the axiom of choice is used—" "—so led to measureable cardinals which are inaccessible but for us more interesting is usually related to compactness properties for infinitary languages which do not satisfy the compactness theorem for first order languages of course, but there is a compactness result for the most useless of these languages, L sub omega-one omega, with only the finite quantification, the Barwise compactness—"

"Are we going somewhere?"

"Okay, sorry. I just wanted to say we started with compact cardinals, because of their usefulness in infinitary logic. Tarski I think found these, or invented them, depending on how you think of it... You know that inaccessible cardinals are like black holes of set theory—?" "I see that as backwards," I interrupted. "Black holes you can't escape, inaccessible cardinals you can't get in." "Well, climbing out is not so easy either. We eschew the incompact cardinals for the same reason as we use compacts; maybe the incompact ones are of Tarski instead of compacts. There is a lot of tension between them, the compact and incompact cardinals. But you cannot trust results from within incompacts though it is necessary for economics since every axiomatic schema for economics is incompact within incompact cardinals, even when embedded within much more massive and inconsistent—"

"The discussion is leaving me behind—"

409

"Okay, let me just give some examples why are these so useful and why are they the basis for this Enochian business so-called. The natural numbers from Peano's axiom is not characterized up to isomorphism; that is, there exist nonstandard natural number models for first order Peano, you know this—" "—unnatural numbers, sure—" "—but second order they can be, or with a single sentence with infinite conjunction and a single universal quantification—" "—sure, for each x, x equals zero or x equals one or x equals two etcetera—" "—and there are other example from such as Abelian groups, which is why I first read Bolyai's book on Abelian groups. But for well-ordering this is not so. This requires infinite quantification and infinite conjunction. So is properly in L sub omega-one omega-one—"

"Did you get this stuff at Oxford?"

"I did, to pursue the Dee system. The Enochian system. But you see, well-order needs infinite quantification not available in L sub omega-one omega. Need omega-one—"

"I see, though I am not positive why it needs infinite quantification, but I see why that requires omega-one for disjunction. And don't try to explain why it needs infinite quantification; I'll take your word for it."

"Okay, so I proved some theorems, you know, that were new and kind of startling, about free groups and also torsion groups and inaccessible cardinals that startled people but made my tutor happy and he helped me prepare them to publish and they were published a while later. I finished my degree there in one year and went home to New Orleans to work out details of a theory. I had been studying category theory, especially the Lawvere and then Tierney work. I learned that Tulane had people working in this, even a planned seminar, with mostly Oberst and maybe with Bolyai, who also did some logic with Abelian groups and modules and partial orders and then Momus had been the student of Weil, who was a great man. I read his *Foundations of Algebraic Geometry* and then those seminars of Grothedieck and also Godement. So I worked for one year and then went to Tulane to request getting a PhD with Momus, but I had my thesis research complete already. I culled those parts that were acceptable and made a thesis of this, with the dynamical systems in the logic quite frightening to everyone, like something from outer space."

She stopped, a pout forming. "I sound like I am bragging…"

"No, not really. You are brilliantly far out, but I am sure you are not human so—"

"Not human? What I am?"

"I sure as fuck don't know, but I don't care either. Give me more detail about this logic stuff. Like what it does. How it works and where it lives. I sure won't understand it but I will have some idea… I mean, that was where you started."

"What I learned from Dee was how he opened his gibberish section as I call it, the part no one gets that Laycock called glossolalia, which is the infinitary languages but which encodes more or less the idea that *In my father's house there are many models.* Really. This is the idea. Anything that can be axiomatized can be modeled, but not all things have standard models, or at least not productively. Economics, for example, is a mess with many properties not persistent or invariant; in fact, it is a form of dialetheism that—"

"What?"

"Dialetheism is logic that allows contradictions; some people make a bad joke and call it Brazilian logic. I know, such is not even allowed in intuitionism, since from a contradiction one can derive anything, but it is the basis for economics. Paradoxes can be true in dialetheism. The key is to work in very large cardinals with huge trees and certainly no constructive universe, where you restrict to smaller cardinals, incompacts, is difficult because economics is unlike physics and science in fundamental way, that is remember I told you how you is necessary to decide which assumptions were critical? for physics the axiom of choice and continuum hypothesis are irrelevant but engineers ignore important hypotheses with the Kalman filter to make unstable estimators they call extended Kalman filters you will learn about, just wait, because they don't get Ito's lemma—"

"Go back to economics if you would. I understand the EKF as they call it and why it diverges." I dug her now, not the technical discussion except this bit, but what she wanted to tell me at the bottom of it all.

"In the large cardinal we discovered was the room and the possibilities represented literally and most important the right creatures. I call it Anakim; anyway, using a method of scrying I call—"

"You used that word before, scrying—"

"I mean by it a form of deduction specifically suited—natural in a different incarnation that no one chooses to follow because it is so dead end—to infinitary languages. No one seems to have stumbled on it but me. I don't openly apply it. Would be frowned upon. When in a dialetheism one must modify all deductions to locality using a method I call a shew-stone that restricts syntactic boundaries. Makes predicting humans simpler than, like I said before, predicting

411

mechanical. Economics is humans. Work in a simple merger of intuitionism and classical locally, very linear thinking, but the localization creates obstructions one cannot pass. That is true in all the logics, a block to the global picture

She was a witch. That was what she was telling me.

so is impossible to see all at once. But here is worse. Always there are obstructions to extending along trees…Here though we can form something like transgression in fiber bundles, you know?

I didn't know. I had never heard of transgression in a fiber bundle or any other math structure. But I saw it now. She couldn't be a witch: she wasn't a human.

With corresponding concepts in place, of course. Fortunately, the obstructions are not as to make application impossible, depending on the level of complexity of the actual situation."

I wondered if she could read my thoughts. I held my breath in case a little voice chided me, *Of course not.*

"Look," I interrupted. "I get it. In your mathematical derivations, you are not sure whether you are deriving the result via your own methods or if you are actually seeing future derivations from different mathematicians and stealing them—"

"Or finding them laying around, without anyone thinking them consciously. Very good. But there is no future. You need to come to grapple with that."

"Are you some kind of demon? Or angel?"

"Same thing, angel and demon."

"Elemental? Familiar?"

"Familiar of what? Clearly I am not elemental."

She was a familiar. I was certain of it. Or maybe a demon. A demon familiar?

"You know I saw this economics—" she began.

"—finance." I interrupted.

"Finance is localization of economics in activity and scopes, but it is an engineering application. Done poorly, albeit—"

"Except by you. I see that. You use this to make money."

"I started in my year at Oxford. No one knows the method. You are among the very few who have heard this much."

"The Foundation?"

"Is me, actually. With legal arms in several countries for travel and banking purposes.

"Anyway, when I came home from Oxford I spent a full year working out the details of this theory. I put it into a form of algebra borrowing from Tarski and Henkin in their cylindric algebras. Also a type-theory formulation, along the streamlining lines Gödel did for Russell's *Principia* mess, and also put it into topos theory. That was best of all for getting results. It was also where dynamics became apparent to me. It aped algebraic geometry and I saw the torsion leading to dynamics, which I stole from Kalman's work in systems theory. From a differential field of sorts to Hopf algebras. We get bundles and connections. A big kind of manifold can be defined then, using the Anakim which forms a pseudodifferential system—it has symmetries, by the way, very interesting symmetries—highly nonlinear system of equations in inaccessible cardinality of variables and equations—determining local properties again, and then the de Rham theory and such but all of it springing from the algebra, and noncommutative. But gives a lot of results in microlocal analysis which the Fields people liked too much. A form of gauge theory comes out of it in the end... They waxed ecstatic over that. But I didn't tell them what happens when following the connections—you know, the connections in bundles are like complementary subspaces with associated submanifolds, distributions in Frobenius sense, and there is a kind of curvature, obstruction to integrability of horizontal bundles, the vertical bundle natural but the horizontal bundle chosen with, or as, a connection may not have eigenfunctions leading to involutive distributions..."

She stared at me absently.

"Is related to the Frölicher-Nijenuis bracket."

My blank stare stopped her again. "You don't know?" I shook my head no. "I give you papers. You need to know. Momus might talk about in his class next term of analysis on complex manifolds, because of certain theorem characterizing manifolds with almost-complex structures as complex manifolds if and only if the bracket of Frölicher-Nijenuis of J, capital J, you know? canonical almost complex structure on the manifold, is zero, called integrability, sometimes also this particular bracket is called Nijenuis tensor, mostly just for vector-valued one-forms. Never mind. Take the class. A few extra discussions and you have what want from him in any case, so no need to hurry.

"The fibers we climb are anyway only inaccessible cardinals with extra structure, often algebraic. Lots of ultrafilters. And we use the ultrapowers.

413

"What everyone misses about what Dee was after, is he worked with automorphisms and isomorphisms—"

"In the house of many models—"

"Precisely. How brilliant. You don't understand but you follow like a puppy. And embeddings. And no one grasps this since it is such a triviality in their finite universe—"

"Of restricted possibilities."

"Exactly, in the very technical sense. And Dee was not privy to what Cantor learned. The infinities. Dee could not have known that infinity is of variable size, different sizes of infinity... So he missed the reality of nascent information, ergodic theory with invariants along flows to obstruction."

"I can't see how any of this answers mathematical questions. The real world, yes. I grasp that. Like physics, in a way."

"But bigger than only physics. And an application, starting from this magic system of John Dee. It answers mathematical questions like anyone does: solving problems. But using a kind of model theory for very large infinite languages with special rules of inference—"

"Scrying."

"Yes. And then one needs to translate the proofs or theorems—or predictions for real world events as with the economics—into the standard languages, formal or otherwise, that are finitary. When possible. But not a translation of the language as in the key of Dee, which has another meaning than has been thought. Dee was not speaking a language with creatures; he worked in formal systems with sentences of infinite length that are of special cardinality—"

"Strongly inaccessible cardinals, and in models with huge cardinality."

"Yes, exactly so."

"And your language reflects witchcraft because of Dee, not—"

"Because it is magic?"

I stared into her eyes, searching for what might be looking out.

"And if it is?" she asked. "You will find it magic when you design an estimator using pure mathematical principles that will accomplish its task. At least the first time it will be magic for you."

I didn't know if I would find magic in accomplishing such a thing. I would likely find it magic that I might work on things that would be realized in hardware, perhaps manifested as software, for purposive ends.

"I don't know if it is magic," she said. "It is a formal method. That is all I know. My names come from analogy."

"So how'd you get the PhD at Tulane?"

"I came to get in the Weil lineage. The Oberst lineage runs through Hilbert, but Weil was first generation and came from Hadamard and Picard. So I went first to Momus. I talked to him and he went to Oberst and also Bolyai. They admitted me and I took the exams the first year, and immediately formed a committee of Momus, Oberst and Bolyai. They gave me a reading list and I took the oral exams the same year. I handed my thesis in and they made small edits, I defended it the following year and was finished going to school. I published a lot of papers immediately and got invited to some postdoctoral positions but instead traveled to different schools and worked with people on open problems in a lot of areas. And I won a lot of prizes, including the Fields. And no one understands what I do."

"Except me, and then only sort of."

"And now you will fuck me? *Me foda?*"

"You mean literally?"

"I continue to carry the sperm I gathered from before-times, but I think you might like this?"

I wanted her. Amazing how much I wanted her. It seemed at that moment, as at every inconstant moment we spent together, that I could find satisfaction with her in monogamy. Instead I found a yet another bundle of papers in my Tulane mailbox without attribution of provider. On top was A. Frölicher and A. Nijenhuis from *Proceedings of Koninklijke Nederlandse Akademie van Wetenschappen, Series A59,* 1959, over 20 pages long, *Theory of vector-valued differential forms,* too dense for a speedy run-through, the central idea buried where I didn't see it. A bunch of papers by the French geometer Ehresmann, each two to three pages, in French, from the 1950s, *Structures locales et structures infinitesimales* from 1952 and *Les prolongements d'une variété differentiable* in five parts, the first subtitled *Calcul des jets, prolongements principal; Éléments de contact et élements d'enveloppe; Extension du calcul des jets aux jets non holonomes; Introduction à la théorie des structures infinitésimales et des pseudogroupes de Lie,* together with the decidedly longish *Les connexions infinitésimales dans un espace fibré différéntiable,* and one paper from the Transactions of the American Mathematical Society from 1953 by a pair of mathematicians named W. Ambrose and I. M. Singer, I assumed the Singer of the Atiyah-Singer index theory I'd heard so much and knew not a fucking thing about. Using horizontal vectors, it proved that curvature fucked up parallel transport by traveling around shrinking infinitesimal parallelograms in the limit converging to a derivative of parallel transport maps. One had to get jiggity with some groups, given as how they showed that for any connection (or connexion, as they spelled it), the curvature form generated the holonomy group. Which was not so uncommon as it happens. That is, getting jiggity with groups. Like when I went to CLUB with Linda and Albina, not sure how that came to be but there I was, one of them on each arm, Linda dressed unlike a librarian for the first time since I had seen her wearing clothes and Albina more an amulet than ever—Hypatia once called her a touch piece with holes—her skinny legs barely covered at the thighs by a short skirt but below clunky black lace-up boots to her mid-calves that complemented my own high-top studded-buckle combat boots and leathers. "Don't worry, we'll protect you" from Albina whose tattoos seemed to have come alive in the setting on the CLUB Island. "Yeah, you're safe with us" from Linda who added something about giving me her ass to which Albina said, "Wow, very rare event; never seen such a thing actually."

We'd entered from some other portal than the prior visit, no one to greet us when the mute boatman dropped us off from an oar-powered skiff he beached. Linda'd modified her presentation, her hair not bobbed with the ends flying away but falling straight below her shoulders as if tapered, the mousy brown traded for a darker hue that made her cerulean eyes stand out more than before, the drape pulling her face longer if such were possible and wrinkles beside the downturned pouting upper lip framing her ever-so-slightly elongated front teeth, dark lipstick and straight lower lip showing too many teeth, way too many teeth like how'd she fit all those ivories in there? as she removed all her clothing except a snazzy pair of multi-strapped climbing over and beyond the ankle, low solid heel, black pumps, crawling on her hands and knees toward me, up close wearing plenty of makeup and looking tired, maybe older than I'd thought, her tiny wouldn't-fill-a-champagne-glass tits barely drooping but nipples askew and using the plentiful teeth undid the leather strands wound through the eyeholes in the fly of my leather breeches to free my penis at which she said, "This is a beautiful cock," and Albina, watching with her tattoos iridescing opalescent as if from within translucent flesh, orange flames aglow on her mons, snarling teeth sparking around her cunt, said it again, "Wow, very rare event…" Linda slurped the so-called beautiful cock in her mouth and with lip action milked it erect, then turned and arched her back, raising her meager, globular buttocks and slender thighs saying "Stick it in my cunt" with which order I complied, sliding smoothly into slick gash as she cried out "Mirabelle kiss me" and Albina stretched on her back and kissed her all the while I fucked her with robotic conviction, not letting up until she pulled forward and lowered her head and presented her ass higher at which Albina slipped beneath her and, while Linda munched Albina's mouth-emblazoned cunt, spit in Linda's asshole and tongued the saliva within, saying "Ram it in her asshole and don't be gentle" and I entered the profound declivity upon Albina engulfing my throbbing member which emerged from her lips slathered with greenish drool. We became one flesh, a caterwauling beast of groans and whistles until I emitted a fuckwad. Upon my pulling out Albina glommed onto Linda's asshole, sealing the gape with her lips , tonguing the ejecta until Linda farted the bulk into her mouth. They kissed, exchanging the load three times at which both swallowed a portion and then, disconcerted, I watched myself kiss them deeply on the mouths, engaging my tongue in prolonged explorations, first Albina, then Linda as Albina dropped to her knees and worked my flaccid penis with her mouth until it no longer hung as a dead eel but pointed at the back of her head. Linda joined in the suck and lick-fest, then lay on her back, Albina procumbent with face between her legs, asymmetry of pale tattooed pre-adolescent waif atop lean-bodied olive-toned blank slate nine or so inches longer, long of face and evil-fashioned blue-shadowed purple-lined eyes glaring beneath thickened and bone-blackened brows ragged and dense, vermilion-black mouth agape, turned down upper lip disclosing a flash of extended front teeth in the fissure suddenly covered by tongue aimed at Albina's cunt before hissing *"Come o cu, Come o cu dela,"* and Albina lifted her face to moan "In my asshole" which direction I followed accordingly with urgent action and no lubrication, seeming unnecessary at any rate, riding hard at extreme angle until she pulled forward ripping me free, arching up to present her tooth-lined glistening wet vulva which I double occupied with Linda's tongue and lips, ending as prolonged projectile outflow with spasmodic waves from the top of my head to my heels concentrated in the small of my back like a battering ram hammering Albina so her repeated yowls of "Atta boy" modulated like hiccups the splooging spasms the tattooed opening ingurgitated, abetting amidst snapping of metaphorical teeth intromission as a vacuuming, her head and shoulders bobbing with the modulation as a hand puppet controlled by pneumatic cylinder. Linda lamprey-like attached her mouth to the canine tooth-tattooed vulva and emerged drooling dick-snot she slavered into Albina's smiling rictus, Albina returning the favor

417

THE AMERICAN DREAM — PART II

back and forth until the stuff disappeared down each gullet at which I, in horror, found myself again deep-tonguing each mouth by turns.

Upon completion, Albina said, "You're safe now, dude" which I doubted profoundly, doubt magnified when confronted by Maria Padilha, the tall, lissome brunette Hypatia called my pomba-gira, to whose concert of Shostakovich's Cello Concertos One and Two with the New Orleans Symphony at the Orpheum she had taken me. Padilha offset her backlit sea green peepers with a red muumuu, her tresses hidden within a wimple of color matching the painted yellow orchids adorning the shapeless floor-length tent. Hypatia introduced me to her after the performance as her husband, to which Maria said, "We have met already" to which I replied, "I don't recall" and she replied "You were incapacitated" at which came to mind a bone-crushingly fat girl riding me reverse cowgirl, bouncing to the nervous dancing strains in the last movement of the second cello concerto. We drank Sazeracs in the Old Absinthe House and before leaving us Maria said "We have a date, you and I, temporarily in abeyance. Don't forget." Tonight she said "Not now, our inchoate date. I have lined up later a crew of *homens invulgar e desconhecidos* during which I assume the prone decubitus, blindfolded, for a series of butt fuckings; this adumbrative assignation of ours can wait," then to Albina and Linda, "You girls assume the position gracefully; good you insumed protective fluids." Linda replied *"Obrigada, putinha. Gosto homens invulgar; mais pica?" "Sim, muito mais,"* and the two of them broke into raucous laughter, which ended abruptly with Maria saying, "I know you for a rug muncher, not interested in *picudo*. But maybe you can come to clean me out with your spatulate tongue, bitch." Behind her a light above a small door flipped red to green. "Your connection is on intromission through there;" pointing, "you *putada* make your introits now" and we ducked through, Linda screaming at her "Volta a putaria!" inside a long corridor in which rang the reply from Maria "Vá tomar banho!" reverberations echoing in a well. I think Albina said "Fucking Brazilian pseudocopulatory cunts" and Linda seemed to say, "Watch it about Brazilians, bitch," but I couldn't be sure I heard anything right. I realized Maria meant by connection a chosen horizontal bundle complementary to the vertical bundle of some giant fiber bundle over the manifold we'd exited, lifted now as it were to the horizontal bundle, that particular construction I'd gleaned from the papers left in my box and my swift run-through of K&N, pertinent to my BM lifting out of the abstract instead of the concrete Euclidean space. Of course, the connection was the horizontal complement to the vertical bundle; which one? plenty to choose from. It could just as easily be taken as the projection operator onto the horizontal. The vertical was unique, tangent to the fibers; not so the horizontal complement. What I didn't get was how she knew it, unless from Hypatia. "You," Albina poking me in the chest, "need to watch where you fire this thing, Dude" grabbing my cock "because you can't be sure what's done with the emission inside the receptacle of others—" "You're hagridden by that prepubescent witch-whore-mathematician—" Albina interjecting "Watch the prepubescent cracks, okay?" "—you ain't prepubescent any more, I'll have you know; more adolescent..." Hypatia led me to the bed in the other room at the cottage-cum-office. First she stood and turned fully around, arms above her head and hands joined like a ballerina. "You like?" as if a discarnation donning new corporeal substance. Full breasts hung low on a long torso with extended nipples pointed out from centered round areolae. Turning revealed a round, muscular ass, outgrowth of full thighs and long legs fleshed out leanly, a naked labia hanging distended and glistening between her legs. A strip on her mons the only evidence of hair on the corpus. Falling back and grabbing me around the neck, she pulled me down to her lying on her back in bed. Kissing with tongues intertwined I entered her gently feeling aglow, making love, desiring to be all inside her, fused single body, one body—one flesh: flesh of my flesh. She gazed into my eyes. I fell into her eyes—

"Whitey. What do you know about quantifier elimination?"

"God, Hypatia, what the fuck are you asking me?"

I stopped. "Jesus, your timing is amazing."

"You understand quantifier elimination?"

"No." I pulled out and leaned up on my elbow to look at her. Her eyes seemed farther back in her head than before.

"Well, no matter...just have equivalents quantifier free, more or less. But what I am working up to is imaginary elimination. Beware of that."

"I don't get it..."

"Look here," she put her face to mine, eyes close up. "What can you see?"

"Nothing. You're too close."

"Exactly. These theories are not stable. So if you end up in a singular cardinal, you have made a wrong turn."

"I—"

"Let me finish. The models need to be sufficiently saturated, preferably what I term supersaturated—what is well beyond the normal limits of a saturated model—but that can lead to a lot of imaginaries. I mean you make the virtually present appear in the structure. It is as if you have an infinite set of equivalence relations that define classes modulo their relations and they are all related by some automorphisms and you take a limit of them, like taking a limit of structures. You hope they are consistent. That is where imaginaries come in, since you build them this way. If they are inconsistent, it gets messy. Then the limit class doesn't really exist, but you can force it with a partial order defined by the automorphisms that leads to an algebraic structure and the imaginary may be not what you think it is. It can eliminate itself, even if it has previous existence in a lower model. See?"

"No."

"Maybe it would be best to think of inverse limits. No, forget this. It is really forking. That is not yet defined, by the way, but I see it. Forking. What they will want is non-forking. Then everything matches up. In stable systems it is all quite clear, but forking in unstable systems with all their models leads to some big trees, for want of a better term, and a type can be extended to a type that is of smaller dimension, in the sense of Morley rank, which is why I say worry if you end up after this in a singular cardinal because that can't happen. So if it does—"

"Nothing that can't happen will happen—"

"—remember reality is just another model. In my father's house—"

"—there are many models. Yeah, yeah, but what the fuck here, Hypatia? I mean—"

"Inside and outside the model are two different worlds, remember, and it seems one can often force what can't happen. I worked out a way to do all this in unstable models, using measures—probability measures, actually—that are extensions of types as measures on the algebra of definable subsets of the domain of the models that are sufficiently saturated. Supersaturated certainly works. It extends to unstable theories."

"Why are you talking about this now?"

"Because this is the best time for you to understand that one false move, one slip, and you can eliminate something in a model so it was in essence never there. That imaginary defined by limits of equivalences ends up gone. It is like cardinal collapse. It feels like a graded algebra as in cohomology with obstructions showing up, but worse since the characteristic class of that imaginary you were so involved with vanishes in the sense that it was not there. Ever. Never there, get it? The heirs, if you will, are distinct. I call it the dichotomy property. If there is one formula satisfying the dichotomy property, then the theory is unstable and you can end up with all the heirs unstable. You get an ultrafilter that essentially splits the heirs."

"You interrupted us for this discussion of a mathematical formalism?"

"Maybe math, but not formalism. Believe me. You need to see the distinction between the inner and outer here, Whitey. This is very important for us. Tomorrow you could wake up and never have met me. I could never have been at all, in fact."

"I don't understand that at all. You are, so how could you not have been?"

"Locally, everything is possible; globally not so much. All reality is local. Worse, you cannot be sure what is the imaginary. Or the power of the types. In an unstable theory, not all types are definable. Indiscernible is one thing, indefinable another entirely. You can't be sure—these models are not homogeneous—you can't be sure where you end up with what. Elementals can be imaginary or maybe you can be imaginary or both. What is eliminated? When you descend into the wrong model along some tree, because all the types inherit their father's dichotomies, you might be cut off forever. All the types are unstable in every cardinality."

"You sound like a witch."

"Do I? Well, think of the story that King Solomon conjured and then confined thirty-one spirits or demons—"

"Of course, that's bullshit. But that idea is in keeping with logic as magical conjuration."

"You aren't serious," she said and leaned toward me, taking my dick in her mouth, extracting a mouthful of sperm she swallowed, then adding, "You need to see if you can figure out not-V-equals-L from inaccessible cardinals due to the thinness of ultrafilters, dear. Maybe in a paper or in the book by Jech not yet published. Good luck. Ramified types, now…" and she kissed me on the mouth with enough tongue so I tasted my own sperm, then returned to gobbling my half-mast organ of intromission to full mast at which she conjured love-making to animalistic automated pummeling of various orifices, all the while singing sotto voce, sluicing a slurry of tumbling tones from gravelly to murky to muddy continuo in my ear nearly incoherent except for permutations of the recognizable strain "rutting lubricious lickerish clitoromaniacal anomaniacal priapic ithyphallic automaton machine-elves" da capo deviating each quasi-repeated refrain slightly from prior performance, a drone to my uninterrupted ejaculation by dint of constant erection into her asshole and her cunt, she switching without altering the industrial rhythm of our groins I could not break by any force of will. It ceased when she stopped singing with inverse transudation.

I'd not looked into the relation between $\neg V=L$, inaccessible cardinals and the thinness of ultrafilters, probably a mistake, but recognized this moment with Albina and Linda, or whoever she was, as a mode of parallel transport within a horizontal bundle transversal to fibers. Maybe reality in some general sense, the "in my house there are many models" bit. I was sure there'd be no predictable return in this specific place, particularly since Linda and Albina argued with Linda speaking a foreign language, Albina referring to her as Aline. "Not your Aline," she said to me in the middle of their heated discussion which I tried to tune out, unable to understand either of them though Albina spoke English. "Brazilian girl named Aline Pujol." It dawned on me like a smack in the forehead: maybe Hypatia could control connections, projecting to the transverse bundle as incarnation of the pullback of the tangent bundle of the base manifold but changing incarnation with coordinates as disguise as none were canonical, essentially choosing different connections and hence different projections and hence different covariant derivatives, different systems of parallel transport along the fibers, the vertical bundle: all in essence the same damned thing. The orthogonal complement was not unique, though her vertical components would be invariant and hence unique. And we didn't have vertical components, nothing tangent to the fibers; hence our inability to see one another's true horizontal natures as we rode infinitesimal parallel transport along our connection(s), which meant we could be seen as horizontal lifts of vector fields from the base manifold, reality? to vector fields in the fiber bundle whose integral curves would be the parallel sections along our integral curves down below. Like heaven? The house with the models could be a bundle (E,π,M) with tangent bundles $(TE,T\pi,E)$ and $(TM,T\pi,M)$ where of course I had to confound in my head the two $T\pi$s. Maybe call them $T\pi_E$ and $T\pi_M$. So clearly there was a short exact sequence inserting the vertical bundle into the tangent bundle of E which submerged the pullback of the tangent bundle of the base space M, but without splitting, since there was no way back, no *distinguished* way back to the tangent bundle of E from the pullback bundle of the tangent bundle of M that composed to identity. And there was the decomposition of the tangent bundle $TE=VE\oplus H_\Gamma E$ where Γ was the connection she chose, acting as projection from tangent spaces in the bundle TE onto a component complementary to the vertical bundle VE of vectors tangent to the fibers. But she didn't choose the connection where we resided down here, down below. That she couldn't do. Different connections gave different direct sum decompositions. Perhaps I was in a different horizontal bundle than others—from Albina, say, even as I'd fucked her what seemed minutes ago—what she'd meant by living in different frames, hence the bird feet. Could it be that the cardinal collapse she'd yammered about might lop off projected beings not lifted from the base manifold? Something seemed wrong. I backtracked. Everything in the tangent bundle came from something in the original base space, the horizontal lift pulling the vector from the base space of the original bundle to the tangent space of the of tangent bundle of the total space of the original bundle. By definition. So nothing to be lopped off locally. But there were fields lurking here not lifted, with coefficients not from the base manifold M. There was the global rub. Us not as vectors but as vector fields? Or some other kind of field? And then the fucking horizontal bundle might not be closed under the Lie bracket, not involutive, so it might not be a tangent bundle to a submanifold. I remembered the song from Lawrence Durrell, his *Alexandrian Quartet* I'd read while hospitalized:

> *Old Frobenius*
> *No-one half so breezy as,*
> *Half so free and easy as*
> *Old Frobenius*

I shook my head like a horse. Might not exist horizontal sections except locally. Or maybe not locally. No integral manifolds for the horizontal bundle. Had to be fields on the total space. Locally everything might be cool, but globally not so much. So what is projectable? Indeed, what is projected? And what lurks within that vertical dimension unseen to us horizontals? Consider the lowly Möbius band, locally just like home, globally reversing right from left.

The wall we'd come through had disappeared. We stood, mismatched trio with Linda or Aline Pujol or whoever she was naked and yammering Portuguese and the translucent tattoo job Albina in combat boots and short skirt and me in leathers and highly stylized combat boots and Linda-Aline yelling in my face "Não falo Ingles," Albina, coming between us, saying, "Bullshit. She speaks English, Whitey. It's when she's Rosa Azorra, the Hungarian, that she doesn't speak English—" which I interrupted with "What the fuck just happened? Where's the door? Where's the goddamn walls?" As far as the eye could see nothing but white; white above and white below meeting in white at the vanishing points on the line at infinity… "Don't get your britches in a bunch, dude," Albina said. "They know we're here." "They who?" "Alguém você não gosta, dude" Linda cum Aline said, her dude sounding not from around here. A self-propelled cart approached, PARALLEL TRANSPORT in black-lettering on the side, a young driver with a billy goat beard who said nothing as we climbed aboard and tore off into the whiteness, Albina explaining that Linda had likely shifted into Aline when I ass-fucked her, Linda not so fond of dicks and such but Aline more forgiving though a rug-muncher by choice and watch out for her when she was Rosa, a Hungarian-speaking slut less opposed to dicks but especially adept at muff diving. Aline sang something in Portuguese not a bossa nova. In the distance flashed a neon sign out of the solid white gloaming hovering above a door in the whiteness portraying a gob in summer whites, a one-striper, flying through the air in a broken trajectory of neon jerks, his jumper collar-flap a short cape straightening behind him, his white hat hovering like a flying Dixie cup, the words EJACULATED SEAMAN CLUB in garish red. We piled out at the door beside which stood a booth from which an unsmiling creature I took to be a woman looked out at us. "Your ticket?" she asked. "Check your back pocket," Albina said and I said, "There aren't any pockets on these pants." She rolled her eyes as when confronted by an idiot, reached around behind me and pulled out a plastic card. I grabbed it from her and stared, wondering where the fuck it had come from. I felt my backside and found no pocket. Embossed on the amorphous face of the card, the formula $F((u_c)^k) \circ \mathcal{U}$. I slid it through the slot in the window and the woman looked at it and said, "Okay. All of you go inside. With clothes." To which Aline said, "Não quero roupas" and the lady replied, "Sua escolha" and Albina shook her head, then whispered to me, "Very dangerous decision, that. I fear she's gone ajee. They won't mollycoddle her in there." I detected a hint of brogue I'd not noted before. Like when Frenchie'd taken me into his office to pummel me with an example of a control system, for my own good, to get the feel of the control engineers, his French accent tinged with a brogue? the example a pendulum of indeterminate mass m attached frictionless by rod sans mass to be stabilized at the upright unstable equilibrium. Measuring the angle from hanging straight down as zero and counterclockwise, the pendulum then to be standing upright at the angle pi radians, unstable since any infinitesimal movement in either direction would send it back to wobble about the stable equilibrium pi radians below. Frenchie of course chose units to make both mass and gravity unity since mathematicians don't much like units or, for that matter, unnecessary arithmetic. Being a mathematician in training, I didn't ask why we wanted to stabilize this thing upside down. Frenchie wrote the governing equation but it was trivial in any case, two dots above θ(t) which he used for angle as a function of the time, two dots for second derivative of the angle with respect to time, to which he added sine of the angle theta as a function of time, all of it set equal to some function of the time he named u. "To be an engineer in your thoughts," he began, "it is necessary to make the entire universe linear. We do it only a little here. Since this is only a local approximation, it means the engineer lives locally and so must someway find patches to stitch it all together with…"."like paracompact? but that leaves a lot of rough spots?" He laughed. "Anyway, here it is simple enough. Take the angle delta x to be the deviation of the upright, that is away from pi, but only just a little so that sine x is approximated by the first order Taylor series about pi" and I understood that meant $\sin(x) = \sin(\pi) + \cos(\pi)\delta x + o(\delta x)$ where little o meant some function that went to zero when divided by δx as δx went to zero, but automatically without having to hold it my consciousness; that is, I knew automatically without thinking that it meant the original equation replaced by its linear approximation on some small local interval about the angle pi as double dots above δx minus δx equal u since δx was the approximation to sine δx (the cosine of pi being negative one and the sine of pi zero) for this miniscule δx. "So this is the open loop equation of control. We are going to close the loop as a PD controller, for proportional-derivative. It would be nice to just use some proportional controller for u, like say some constant times the control function to torque in the direction opposite the error, but if we write down the differential equation of closed loop, that is when the control is applied for u, you get" and he wrote the second derivative of the angular error δx minus δx plus αδx equal zero. I noted right away that the equation was not good. "Right," I said, "that thing's gonna oscillate when alpha—" "the gain," he said, "alpha is called the gain or feedback gain because it is feedback and engineers think of everything as amplifiers" "—when alpha is greater than one—" "it pushes the mass away from staying upright when alpha is greater than one, see?" "Yes, for alpha greater than one the velocity increases and so does the error, but for the other case it might be feasible." "It overshoots. Too much building up of inertia. It will oscillate. But you can show that is true even for the original equation, not just the linearized closed-loop equation. So is necessary to add something to slow it down, a braking action." "I see that. Need to bring in the derivative, too." "Yes, which makes for its own difficulties, since becomes necessary to find that as well, that velocity of error as well as the error, but suppose it is there and then add to the proportional error the proportional derivative of the error. Now that is a control law that can work." It was a bit harder to see, but not much. I wrote down the equation and looked at the characteristic polynomial and found the roots had negative real parts so the thing went to zero quickly. "If you choose carefully, there is no oscillation associated at all as it goes to zero," Frenchie said. "Sure, get decaying exponentials by choosing the constant for the derivative bigger than four times the gain minus one." He smiled. "You will become a control engineer," and he went off on some stuff about classical methods, trying to show me how they tied to state space methods and about input-output systems as black boxes versus choosing states for a linear matrix differential equation within the box and yammered excitedly about spectrum assignment and wrote some second order differential equation with damping factor and natural frequency and underdamped where the oscillations decayed and the critically damped and overdamped cases so there is no overshoot or something. I tuned out at some point.

The place was jumping. Literally. Huge, seemingly unbounded, perhaps shapeless, void and all of it jumping. Linda-Aline-Rosa fled our company on entry, disappearing through a stand-alone doorway nearby. Everywhere there stood doors unattached to walls since there were no walls. I nudged Albina to see people enter them and vanish or drop in through them seemingly out of the sky. She nodded. "Don't need drugs here, Dude," she said. "Or maybe you do," I mumbled. I wanted someone to leave one of the doors open so I could look inside, but they closed immediately on their own, more like a shutter on a camera than a swinging opaque slab. The outlandish costumes gave it a carnival atmosphere, something out of a bent rewrite of *Petrushska* or Fellini's *Satyricon,* especially when I realized they weren't costumes. Most of the costumed were naked. The air around us thrummed visibly, modulated by the cacophony of singing, guitars, tumbling continual percussion as if Edgar Varèse orchestrated it, sirens, moans and cries, blackboard skreaks, cat-calls and cat wailing and saxophones and a grating boy soprano rising and falling within the din. A variety of humanish clamor emanated from writhing masses of bodies, or rather body parts, no individual figures discernible, convolutions within the ambient background.

"Shall we choose a doorway?" I asked.

"Not yet. Let me take this in. I've not seen such a thing before. So many goliwogs. I've been here before—the island that is, not this bit of strangeness— with Harry, to work out some kind of deal for filming. Seems they can't leave the island, so we need to do it here. He had me test some of them for effect, these men…I think they were men. Cold, like they had no body heat at all, like they were fucking dead, and their sperm was like clabber or crowdie, you know?" "No. Crowdie?" "Yeah, my parents were Scots and they ate horrible stuff. Like crowdie, sort of a sour milk with chunks, akin to curdled milk to me, soft and crumbly and wet, like cottage cheese gone bad. They made me eat clabber, too, worse than crowdie. These guys, whatever they were, had huge stone-cold cocks that ejaculated cold, chunky, sour wet stuff, real sour and thick, evil smelling, lots of it. Filled my asshole and cunt and mouth. Disgusting. I nearly vomited. Harry loved it. Made me see the sense in Dina going off to the European place to do animals. I mean, when it gets to this. I am considering going there. I had an invitation from the Baron Apteker. They are looking for someone to be in residence, full-time slattern-in-residence; maybe it's time for some security, something with a future. Though it might be too close to Glascow for my taste." She shivered as she talked, hugging herself. Her tattoos flashed like the neon sign of the ejaculated seaman.

She nudged me and pointed at a weedy, spidery-limbed female striding naked on a path orthogonal to us, shoulders-back, eyes-forward, stately and slap-footed if such gait be possible, her spindly legs hinting at convexity below knobbed knees. She packed hulking tits hanging flat from frail shoulders, curving outward tubular and erect and exuding roseate areolae from their final third studded with bumps akin to warty gooseflesh. Left facing, she marched towards us, one boob pointed in my direction, the other at Albina. She stopped briefly, then about-faced to walk away, her concave butt cheeks tautly cupped spoonlike into matching dimples of slight and slow curvature above bony hip protrusions that forked widely quadrate over meat curtains hanging in the oblongish free space of a thigh declivity so slight the pair would never meet until the knees kissed. A laughing hennaed thing with conical pale tits that showed blue veins replaced her, tits pointing up and away and capped with large smooth salmon areolae. A platinum-haired female writhed on the ground staring at me, her breasts erect cylinders planted on her chest and abruptly tapering as if extruded from a machine as long tubes suddenly orange halfway to their tips. Openmouthed and hissing, a tongue snaked along the upper teeth, its feathery tip licking glossy bronze lips. Next up, a sallow slightly built brown-head approached Albina and leaned into her, small, sagging bags lined in stretch marks for tits, their elongate elliptical nipples shriveled and oriented forty-five degrees toward her shoulders. She smiled and licked her drab lips. Albina stepped back watching yet another one crawling towards me on hands and knees in pink thigh-high nylons and black garter belt, her slight dugs hanging flesh tubers half covered with prolonged nipples matching her nylons. Dark brown hair tied in a bun with long bangs covered a high forehead rising above wire rim glasses; garish pink lips baring long lipstick-smudged teeth smiled up at me.

"What *is* this?" I turned to Albina who'd wandered off with a statuesque morena clara wearing nothing but shag-cut, refulgence-gobling atremental hair, no makeup or other skin cover, her long, shapely legs unshaven, serenely smiling as Albina sucked and licked the tiny nipples that capped modest areolae on massive bosoms soft to the eye though standing erect. Its stomach was flat below a long torso, hips slender, mons covered with a dark, dense thatch trimmed in a vee. She pushed Albina's face down to the vee as a female standing at full height with her head at my groin tugged at my crotch: looking up at me a fulsome face below ash blond hair hanging straight to her shoulders, flaring nostrils indented with a shallow central crimple running downward over the end to make the impression of separation, an effect echoed amidst an abrupt round chin. Her mouth occupied the bulk of her lower face; when she flashed a smile the long, thin contraption tried to leave its confines like an incomplete integral curve running out of space, extending her cheeks to remain embedded. "I like you," she giggled in adolescent chirp. "You're cute. You want a blow job?" She moved away and leaned back to get a clearer view and I saw a girlish torso adorned with a pair of massive symmetric cones pointing at me puffy rose areolae with stretched nipples like fingers, their acclivity due not to any upturn in the cones but her own upturned torso. She massaged the flesh-cones centered in her chest. "They're real. See. Touch them, you'll see. Men like them." I resisted the temptation.

Her shapely legs were the length of an infant's. I pondered how she could stand on them, let alone walk, but she'd begun loosening the leather laces on my fly. I swatted her hand away. "I just had one, thank you," I said. "You're mean," she responded. "Mean people suck." Turning, she scuttled away in baby steps.

I assumed the parade had finished. I didn't see Albina and wondered if she'd been seduced from my company by the creamy breasts. As I pondered whether to search for or abandon her, the little crotch-high one returned holding the hand of a hairless strapping creature of Herculean proportions, body rippling with bulging striations, veins popping, breasts smoothly globular extrusions without areolae accenting long nipples that arced downward more than did the globular slabs of meat to which they were attached. I stared into the crevice between those mid torso blobs at eye level, looked down to see a cauliflower of a cunt from the top of which extended a clitoris the shape and size of an adolescent penis where joined two thighs each the girth of my chest. The contraption was supported by knotted hams of calves. I looked up into a pair of red eyes glaring at me. She made a fist the size of a cinder block, her neck muscles throbbing with the set of her jaw, her face softly feminine despite frowning, comely features despite glaring red eyes. She squared off arms akimbo, her biceps the mass of my thighs, her forearms the mass of my biceps.

"You seem to be a trouble maker," she said in dulcet voice.

"Not trying to be. I told her I didn't need to be fellated because only recently had I been the subject of such attention."

"You need to get with the program or you'll have to deal with me."

I wondered if I could take her. Muscle-bound as she was she likely couldn't move fast, but if she got hold of me it would be hell to break loose. I wished I had my cane. The physical ordeal of fighting her or fucking her would be costly; I remembered my prior visit and remained wary of joining in any carnal activity or altercation. Even with the little one. Especially with the little one. Nonetheless, I was about to relent when Albina appeared at my shoulder, naked, her tattoos luminous from within her translucent flesh. "What's the problem?" she asked as the two jumped back from her. "He's with me." I was going to say, I thought you said it was dangerous to get naked here, but the Amazon spoke first. "The walking touch piece with holes. Now you are volunteering for him?" A motley of unlikely oddities had gathered behind the improbable pair confronting us. The majority of them were distributed along an array of feminine form and feature, womanly save exceptional endowment of male equipage. Some of it hung long between well-turned gams; other of it stood erect. Some had cunts with organs of intromission attached where one expected a clitoris; others bore no noticeable gash but were otherwise of human female construction. Amongst them mingled a crowd of creatures that reminded me of the goat things I'd seen with Utta on the prior visit, hoofed with hairy forelegs and goatish beards, trifurcated by enormous penises that could have been third arms stuck between their legs. The Amazon stuffed two fingers of her right hand in her mouth and whistled, pointing at Albina. The goat boys advanced on her, laughing and bleating in what might have been a foreign tongue. She struggled to escape but they had her by the arms and legs, carrying her away as she yelped to let her go, followed by supplication for my help, followed by "You owe me, motherfucker." From behind me a soothing voice: "You do owe her, Whitey." It was a smiling Maria Padilha. "Those gynandrous trollops travesty female human primates but they aren't. Not nearly so nice as the lot what had at you last time you visited. These lot were out to loosen your anal sphincter, dear." "I just saw you. You said you were having yours loosened." "I just did. With those very same goat boys." She'd swapped the muumuu for oversized gray and white vertically striped overalls, her hair tucked up under a round cap with a rounded brim. She looked like a railroad engineer except for the nipples straining at the coarse weave. Her breasts must have hung forward from low on her torso to remain constrained behind the bib; not insignificant flesh bulbs, they didn't seem particularly rotund given the lack of lateral effusion. "When did you find time to do it?" "Tomorrow. I did it tomorrow." "That makes no sense. You can't have done it tomorrow." "You are quite anal about time. That disappoints me. Are there not other geodesics in space-time? This place is nowhen. Your use of language is absurdly restrictive: it's done and it happened tomorrow." I was going to argue the point about geodesics in space-time, understanding there had to be some kind of causal stability at least locally, but from a distance Albina wailed, "Ow stop! Oh God stop! Ow!" She began sobbing, then crying, then bawled plaintively until the sound was smothered. "Those goat boys will fuck anything, but they prefer women. Gang fucking is their style. In my anal romps, I restrict them to taking turns. They don't appreciate fucking in tandem; they will stuff their bats in together, as many as they can fit in each orifice if you don't control them. They are at her now, so there is nothing you can do, Whitey. Poor Mirabelle. Her European boot camp didn't prepare her for this. Baseball bats two at a time are nothing compared to the goat boys. If she survives—" "You mean they might kill her?" "Happens all the time. But they have a wonderful surgical facility here. If she survives they can patch her back together. Though they are eccentric with their use of sutures. They like thick silk or even wire. They consider stitch scars an art form and are enormously creative. Her tattoos would inspire them for sure." "Can't we intervene? Get them to at least take turns instead of crowding in all at once with those oversized schlongs?" "Too late now. There was nothing you could have done at any rate. They get quite angry when interrupted." "What the fuck are those things?" "The goat boys? I can explain more later, in terms of horizontal bundles, though right now they are at that little tattooed bundle of joy" at which she snorted, then added "You don't like my jokes, Whitey? No sense of humor at all? You could have at least laughed at my pun on the *travestis* , though of course they are real hermaphrodites, dear, and they seem to be quite interested in you." I turned to notice the masculinely endowed feminine creatures pressing forward as they remained behind the Amazon and the little fuck-face. "Poor Mirabelle never guessed her protection for you would be as the goat for the goat-boys. Made in Brazil, those boys, Whitey, like most of the stuff here. We can discuss it as I give you a tour. Mirabelle is the goatess!" and she laughed aloud, as did the Amazon and the fuck-face. "Well, she was ready to retire from the business in any case after the cambions—" "The what?" "Cambions. The creatures she complained about, like living dead ejaculating some kind of cheese last time—" "Cambions?" "That's what they're called. But you've got other concerns than Mirabelle. I mean, better her than you with the goat boys, but those creatures travestying priapic womanhood" and she laughed again "are interested in you. We call them futanari. It's Japanese. The Japanese have a long tradition of longing for such."

The Amazon spoke. "Miss Maria, the futanari grow restive."

Maria turned to me but before she could speak I asked, "You ever wish you have a dick?" "Who says I don't? You can't be sure. You won't know until our adumbrative assignation is consummated. If I did, would you suck it? Or let me fuck you?" "No." "Not ready to be a cocksucker, are we? Or ass-fuckee? We will make a visit."

She returned to the Amazon. "Let them join the goat boys, Gerty. They can finish up with the tattooed one." The short one said, "I want him to face fuck me, Maria. Please?" "That is his choice. Maybe later he will be ready, and then we can call for you." "Is he a poltroon, Miss Maria?" "Heavens no, Gerty. Decidedly not. He is a veritable warrior. A war hero, wounded in combat, who comported himself valiantly in battle." "I would love to partake of some of that hero-spunk, Miss Maria. And maybe a violent fuck. I love warriors." "We'll see later. I need to take him on a tour. Maybe you and the little one here can work with the goat boys, try to salvage what you can of his friend over there. She's being awfully quiet." "Her mouth's full, along with everything else, Miss Maria." "See what you can do."

The gaggle marched out in formation and Maria took my hand, drawing me closer. "You need to be careful with Gerty, dear. In the throes of passion she has been known to snap off male members with her vagina. Here we say *vagina dentata*. The little one is an excellent amuse-guele before the heavier meal of Gert." It wasn't clear if her constant smile was of mirth or mocked. Probably both. "Listen to the vagitus emanating from that little tattoo job,

Whitey. I bet she's in full vaginismus mode now." She chuckled, probably at her use of repeated vags. I sure as fuck didn't know vagitus or vaginismus, though I heard Albina's screel and witnessed a creature that could have been an opalescing pair of ragged claws swarming with goat-boys scuttling along the floor. "Let's escape through there," Maria pointing to one of the doors "and become vagous ourselves." "What the fuck are those doors? I mean, there are no walls." "Someone's feeble attempt at humor, Whitey. Don't worry about it. And there exist in here of course no walls. I mean, it is CLUB. Closed and unbounded." "Okay, I get the joke. Unbounded. But closed?" "Invitation only. The creatures here are lifted here. That is the bundle bit. The invited often find themselves here not knowing they'd been invited. Mostly they are human primates. Housewives, lawyers, grocery checkers, physicians, maids, bank tellers, professors, politicians, word processors, receptionists, whatever; ordinary human primates harboring socially unacceptable urges. Some have acted on them already; most don't until they come here. There are males too, but not many single males like you. Mostly couples or the unaccompanied female. It is a kind of couples club with exogenous variables, more or less. Many are swingers only in their hearts, like your stupid President. You can sense them, their inhibited human primateness: like kids in the candy store." She lit up a joint. "Here, smoke this. It will take the edge off." I hesitated. "Go on, silly. It's not the mixture of ingredients you got on your last visit. That contained some elements of the venom of the wandering spider that is common in Brazil; the parts responsible for priapism. Blended with other Brazilian-rainforest-derived alkaloids. The spider venom components are synthesized and subdued so as to not induce pain, so only priapic. Has been used in the so-called Silicon Valley, which you will experience soon." I took a hit. It tasted sweet; good buds from some mountainous place. "Speaking of which, it would behoove you to dip your wick, selectively. Gerty would be useful. Fuck the little one's face, too; consider it appetizer or aperitif, depending on your point of view. But I recommend them both for aftereffect." "The creatures. They're the exogenous ones?" "You see them as exogenous, though that is backward. The humans are really the exogenous, the creatures, as you call them, endogenous. The humans are lifted here. But thinking as a swing club, the extraneous males or females are considered outsiders. Right? Like in Brazil, where they have public swing clubs, *boates* like explicit nightclubs, that allow loose males on weeknights who must be chosen by couples or they don't play. No single males allowed on weekends." "So how the hell do these people get invitations?" "Their choice,

Whitey. Their dreams. Let me bundle this up for you," at which she laughed aloud one more time. "You will realize the utility of dipping your wick."

I'd not paid attention to the goings on around us, but as we strolled toward the door I saw piles of writhing bodies, I assumed copulating but the term pseudocopulatory that had arisen of Albina's mouth returned to me. Not all participants appeared human. I didn't inspect for details since Maria said, "The creatures, as you call them, live here. They are not strictly horizontal. You have been raised to a horizontal bundle. A particular connection. But not all the human primates here are in the same horizontal complementary subspace. Doesn't matter for you, since you can't detect what is not there. But the projections of the creatures, as you call them, into the horizontal bundle, their horizontal components if you will, are different when experienced from different complementary components." "I'd already been thinking of this in terms of bundles, for some reason." "I am aware of this. That is precisely why I chose that framework. There is no reason behind it but that you have bundles on your brain. Hence I pursue that avenue. But you have two orthogonal girlfriends. One believes in the literal world of mathematics, a pure Platonist, the world as mathematical idea behind reality. The other doesn't understand mathematics at all and sets out to criticize it philosophically, mistaking it for metaphor. She confuses mathematics with science and believes in neither except as another mythos or metaphor. Physics is metaphor to her. The other makes no such error in confusing science and mathematics or science and engineering, but somehow believes in the literality of mathematics. Very crazy, both of them." "And you?" "But I am not one of your girlfriends, Whitey." "You have promised a romp." "Ah, the bespoken coupling. It has nothing to do with me, dear, though I will participate of course. It is promised, but not by me. It will be *suruba,* I think." "Which is?" "Orgy… or little group encounter. But this is not something new, eh? Anyways, when here you need find a *rosquinha* …sorry, tight cunt. Not of your world. A *tarada.* Randomly appointed coupling. Or maybe simple random coupling. Not as lovers or girlfriend and boyfriend or even as friends."

We passed through a door, I assumed the one she'd pointed at, but who could tell? and into another world. Scattered furniture, mostly beds and couches, and women everywhere talking to naked males, though not in general human males. One housewife in slacks and blouse who'd likely been abducted from a shopping center drifted by, in tow a bipedal creature with arms positioned atop where adjoined the legs and above that an uncircumcised dickhead, excessive foreskin a floor-length train dragging behind drooling a trail. "Good choice," Maria said to her. To me, "We designed this model on a bronze of Roman Priapus that they discovered in France. Gives new meaning to the term dickhead, no?" She laughed. "How the fuck's it see?" She howled. "You do have humor. Dry wit. I see this now. He puts it on when not involved carnally, like anti-camisinha. Looks much like leprechaun when wearing the proper head. He follows her pheromone trail by chemical sensitivity of meatus...." she laughed "...and often later must find where was left its head. No one thought to install a homing device, though the trail of lubrication is useful until the janitor cleans the floor."

I ignored the vision. "I bet Harry would love to film in this place."

"He came here with Albina. He talked to the board, of which I am a member. He wanted to make a deal. But he wanted to take them back to the mainland, so to speak. That was the problem. Can't film here, though we have been trying to work this out. It is physical problem. Some of it goes missing on film. We are working on a digital means to capture this. It is related to what, for want of better term, is ghosts in the machine. Or machine elves." "I don't get that. Doesn't come out?" "There are parts that do not show. Not of the humans, but of the creatures, as you call them. Just as they appear differently in different realizations of the horizontal bundle, the projections from the fibers, from the vertical bundle, don't show up on film when taken back to the mainland. They can't, given this lack of uniqueness. The creatures, as you call them, Whitey, are tensorial. We call them homunculus, by the way. They are synthetic genetic creations, not simple modifications, and as such equivalent to tensor products with added information, if you will, that is realized as the creatures reside within the whole bundle, but the new stuff, the part tensored on, is vertical and can't be seen except within the particular horizontal bundle to which they are projected. Of course, it is more than simply genes; there is the control mechanism, the proteins and their stimulation or repression of gene expression by turning off or on promoters and enhancers of the genes." The woman who'd just passed by stopped, removed her slacks and stretched out on a mat hovering above the floor. The dickhead with arms and legs grabbed her hips and, kicking like a swimmer, drove itself into her cunt. It clutched her breasts and wrists and hair and affected a swimming motion like a porpoise or a butterfly stroke, ajog with full, smooth, rapid strokes. The woman seemed dispassionately to enjoy the stimulation. "The tensored extension makes for more possibilities but also more complex control systems. Like circuits, you know? No. Well, no hurt. But that summand is not determined, as you know; the horizontal bundle, the projection, the connection, the connection map, the covariant derivative, the infinitesimal transport, whichever equivalent way you want to think of this, is not unique and so vanishes when carried by mainland information devices back to the mainland. So the digital approach we are pursuing, which will, we hope, capture the projection and fix it—" "Isn't there some invariant that can be captured?" "Good. That is the idea. But to find one that characterizes the activity of interest, that is the challenge. Something like working with the characteristic classes, you know, which are fixed but have varying representative forms.

"This is difficult for Harry and others in his art form who have contributed much money to our group in Brazil, where most of this work is done. They want some return."

"What's the problem with taking the creatures back to the mainland to perform?"

"We'll get to that. Information ghosts." "Sounds spooky." I hoped I sounded sarcastic, but it wasn't easy in this place. "What is the genetic code, dear boy? Information. And its components are not independent, either, the effects depending on combinations and even order of activation. The tensor product represents here the addition of information, not just modification of it; of course, there also is the control aspect, as I said: the peptides and steroids and such, you know, like modified amino acids. If the code is only modified, the result is not really more informative in the sense of true surprise. Remember, information is surprise. The addition of components, or in some cases the reduction of components, in the information stream causes a true surprise, as does modification of correlates or order of effectivity. Ricci—" "Ricci surprised me—" "But you are not an invariant information processor. Ricci is a modification of what is there. The clitoris is homologous to the penis, dear boy. It is more difficult to build a pure female with testicles and penis and no vagina than to build the combination of the two, as with Ricci who is more or less an ergodic prole. Remember that the genetic information has to do with turning on and off, controlling at a binary level a complex system. But there are states not obtainable with the human-primate genetic set. To turn off all female development of the sexual organs, perhaps to add a male aggression or female sexual response, or even combine them, and make it all female otherwise, this requires additional information in the control system. Ricci, she was quite an early model; notice the fake breasts. The ones who lusted after you were of both types. But to get shut of female sexuality and maintain female form with male equipage is quite the feat and requires complicated tensor product.

435

It does not appear in nature." She pointed to an obese brunette using a tiny man with an enormous erection as a dildo. "Another inspiration from artistic representation of Priapus, this time a fresco in Pompeii. Look at the beautiful beard on the little darling. The more interesting creatures can't leave once they come here. Like this one." The popeyed monstrosity wore a leafy wreath on its head, its beard and hair shaggy and brown, its limbs and chest muscular but the whole thing misshapen and undersized, no more than a couple feet in height bearing a thick, erect penis curved like a scimitar and of length more than half its height. "His greenish secretions are orgastic, prolonging the sensation for hours sometimes, a mood altering aphrodisiac absorbed through mucous membranes and especially well tolerated orally and anally. It makes the human female not only horny and amenable to extreme adventure, understated as less inhibited, but aggressively sexual, violently so. This room is female-friendly, unlike the one from which we exited, designed for orgiastical excess by a society committed to orgiasticism. When human females here are inebriated on these carnal juices and join together they rival the thiasus of Bacchus—" "The what?" "Excuse me, I should have said Dionysius. The maenads. Ecstatic orgiasts. His bacchanalian ecstatic retinue. I just realized the irony of making you human primates horizontal and others vertical, since we can in fact modify the homunculus horizontally, not just vertically, like bacteria..." "I'm sorry, the genetic stuff doesn't work for me." "Well, it isn't such a good analogy in any case. Ricci was modified in part horizontally, actually. The maenads are like a band of thesauri."

"So why can't they leave here for the mainland?"

"The creatures? You don't mean the women who become maenads? No, of course you don't. They do leave, of course, and often reappear on the mainland far outside your moral mainstream. The answer to your question regarding the creatures is monodromy. You experienced it when you came last time: you returned with a twist. Was there a difference when you returned to the mainland?" "It seemed my dick was bigger." "It was more than this. It became torulose as noted by that tattooed monstrosity who is likely torpefied by now. The foreskin changed: longer and thicker. Your penis grew protuberant veins; formed a nodose texture, especially immediately prior to ejaculation when it swells by perhaps a third its erect girth and nodulates uniformly, especially on the head; the frequency and impulse responses modified, perhaps distorted would be the better term. Surely you must have felt the serried column of cinctures marching along your pud when you masturbate, not to mention the burled warts or whatever they are that pop up as you ready to—" "The warts? You don't know what they are?" "No, dear, only that women can feel all that with the inflated tumescence. Maybe warts is the wrong term. Maybe bumps, knobs or simply the noncommittal convex protruberances." "I don't get much time to masturbate, though I do enjoy it—" "All that was only one aspect, since it went beyond the penis." "How do you know about my penis, anyway?" "It was apodictic, baby. Something you ought to understand. Computation. You know monodromy?" "Not really. I haven't heard the term." "I thought mathematicians used this word to express these phenomena of circumnavigating a singularity or whatever, like with the homotopy of non-simply connected space or integrating one-over-z around the deleted origin in the punctured plane. That was what you noticed. We just make the computation. Think of monodromy, my dear Whitey." "I don't really know the term." "Then holonomy. You know that." "I recall it from Kobayashi and Nomizu, but I didn't dwell on it. A group that measures curvature, as I recall." "Yes, but think of Cauchy's theorem. Integration around a singularity. This is not a simply connected place, Whitey. I like to say, In this place there are many singularities, but I am corrected when I say this since they are not truly singularities, not like poles, which I like. This place is not connected, either, actually, not to the mainland and for example, when you came in with those two before the parallel transport brought you here, you left one connected component for another. We left Mirabelle with the goat boys on another connected component." "How the fuck do you get from connected component to connected component if there are no paths?" "That I cannot explain to you. There are things we cannot talk about, even with your mathematical machinery. But suffice it to say we have a way to horizontally lift you from one component to another. Though it doesn't work with the homunculus—" "Because of the nonuniqueness of the complement to the vertical in the fibers, you don't get the same creatures—" "Precisely. This place not being simply connected means there exists certain events, creatures with whom you interact, not sure how to say this, so I will call them singularities though everything ought be smooth as bundles, that are different depending on the path you take to get to them within a connected component. And as I said, they are restricted to their connected components in the form you find them. And it is more: there are obstructions reached for those more dimensional than you, dear boy, as with the characteristic class when reaching that place the nth homotopy group is not zero." She paused to catch her breath. "Nor is it flat here. The curvature is wild enough the local holonomy groups

437

are quite poorly behaved globally, with varying dimension. The infinitesimal holonomy algebra can be quite scary, and of course the full holonomy groups of some of these places are quite a mess. Unclassifiable. Suffice it to say that in this place the holonomy groups are never the fundamental groups. But don't take any of this literally, dear." Her beatific smile came through her smirk; a field of calm surrounded her, surrounded us, the world just beyond writhing orgiastically. I became aware of bands of women coalescing, spasmodic, naked and drowning out the music which I had not noticed though it reverberated off walls not there. Maria laughed. "You hear it at last. A rock band of tuned jackhammers with pile drivers for rhythm section. Surprised you can't hear it until the drug-crazed harpies from the mainland drown it out?" "Maybe we should move on…" and she laughed. "You should have seen it would be a lift between connected components. I'm just trying to get this set-up through your thick skull. This seems the best language. I mean, don't try to find an excuse for paracompactness here." She laughed a mid-register soprano's riff and lit up another of her joints, passing it to me. I needed it more now than before. I assumed that whatever calm she exuded was enough to keep away the maenads. But I also realized we human primates were vector fields and the other stuff, the tensor products, were mixed tensors of some sort. So interaction would do something, like maybe some kind of tensorial contraction. She smiled like she read my mind.

"Right. You are feeling the metaphor. The metaphor Hypatia lives in." I knew it was unnecessary to mention the bird legs or that I had no idea what she looked like at this moment. But if she came here, I would recognize her. Or would I? That I recognized her sometimes didn't mean I always recognized her. Maria laughed again, her melodious phrasing floating free above the industrial ostinato.

"Their groups are trivial, Whitey, the tensors. If they leave here, it is like integrating z around the origin of the complex plane. No problem. Monodromy is trivial. And they vanish. Gone without any trace from the past. As if they never existed. This place is, I want to say, acausal. Not as used in Portuguese to mean random, whatever that might actually be, no disrespect for Kolmogorov or measure theory or Wiener, but as in without causality. Not anti-causal but acausal—" "I get it. I'm not that dense." "I know you have approached this yourself. Sorry. So when you leave here, your group depends on which *singularities* you encircle between entering and departing, which is why you need to dip your wick for effect: you will be different when you exit. With a twist. Or torqued, though that is not of the torsion field which you will witness later. In the torsion room. Exiting here is completing the monodromy." "I think that is wrong in its essence. Besides which all of that seems pretty causal to me." She confused connected components with factors transverse to the vertical bundle. How did I know that? She blathered and I engaged it. Fuck me running. "Well, maybe so, wrong that is. But it is not semisimple here, either. That is, you are a sort of degenerate Killing form. Everything that gets here is degenerate, actually; not in the social sense, of course. It would behoove you to look into sprays, dear. It would help you to grasp your relationship to Dina."

I shook off her comment about Dina. Maybe I hadn't heard it right. This was beginning to irritate me. I didn't know what the fuck were sprays and wasn't about to ask her. "So why can't they just stay on the mainland?" I asked instead. "You are familiar with the Frölicher-Nijenhuis bracket?" she asked back. "Not really. I think I ran across it, but chose not to pay much attention since not much happened with it. Or maybe that's wrong. What is this, anyway? Discussing mathematics at an orgy?" "Not mathematics, silly. Just mathematical ideas that might metaphor the events. All this is related to the tensor product. Maybe you are feeling that the homunculus are tensored additions to existing entities, but that is a bit naïve. The tensor refers to information that is part of control systems. Information, remember Wiener, information is neither energy nor matter, dear, but something entirely different. Here is where you see it. Many of these sentient beings are built from scratch, without using existent corporeal products like ova or sperm. Only information from imagination. So because they are vector-valued forms, the metaphor gets out of its natural bounds. It goes to sheaves, and we can go there—" "You're bullshitting me, right?" "Maybe. But for your ilk, you lifted human primates who update vertically to whom we can apply information horizontally, as you learned firsthand, the Lie bracket is mostly enough, but for the true homunculus the Lie bracket is never enough. The full Frölicher-Nijenhuis bracket is required. Since it is not available on the mainland, they are not apparent."

I tuned her out. The whole enterprise was nuts. She was throwing me a curve. I laughed aloud. A curve. Here, in this place with wildly nonzero curvature tensor. And with torsion fields. Like mine fields? The concepts as metaphor and reality wedged in my thoughts. None of this was real.

"Come on, then, let's go," pulling me towards a door as clots of naked skreighing females carrying sticks hunted down all things with penis and bludgeoned them senseless before tearing them apart, ripping off the intromittent organs and eating them along with the remainder of the hapless creatures. "Really," I agreed, and we made it through the door, she saying, "I don't know how long I could have kept you invisible. I think we overstayed our welcome." "They seem to be killing all your little monstrosities." "And eating them. Along with male humans they might find. Omophagia that causes more intense intoxication before it is over. How we replace the homunculus eaten, in fact, by sending in suitably information-charged cambions with whom they couple insatiably. A form of rather extreme zomotherapy, in effect. So don't concern yourself. They are not totally in vitro, these priapic monstrosities as you call them, but are transplanted in vivo to develop with human touches. These are not so true of homunculi, not developed in vacuo as are many of the others. So in reality, many of these very women will grow replacements before returning, if they return at all. Some, like your friend Utta, develop several generations of them. They gestate within hours in the womb, whereas it takes months in vitro to come to full term." "You are kidding, no?" "No. Well, maybe just a little. It uses up the female body quickly nonetheless, kidding or not, this process. Utta is a shriveled bag of stretch lines. The one-time breast feeding darkens and enlarges the areola and warps the nipple in unexpected ways, destroys mammary tone by stretching and elongating the Cooper's ligaments. One carry to term does not lead to hideous malformation by human primate standards, but repeating over and over leads to outright destruction of the female corpus." "Why would anyone do it repeatedly?" "Drug intoxication, dear boy. The fluids mingle with the woman's leading to constant sexual euphoria lasting through pregnancy and days after expulsion. Not to mention predatory sexual prowling on unsuspecting and suspecting males." She laughed a different lyrical refrain than the previous; I wondered if it were some kind of communication to which I was not privy. "Major reason for distressing of females is monstrosities are born fully developed and grow to full size within hours of insemination before expulsion."

We traveled along a corridor, the first walls I'd seen since entering this place what could have been days ago. By all signs a flea-bag hotel from a grade B movie: rotting wood beneath peeling wallpaper, creaking floorboards showing through threadbare carpet, everything of indeterminate hue in the jaundiced glow of bare bulbs scattered through a smog of ancient dust. There were no doors except one at the end of the passage on which appeared carved in the wood $\aleph_\alpha = \alpha$ and $\int e^x = \text{work}$ over symbolic noise. I turned to look behind us and saw what seemed an endless tunnel. The door led backstage at a theatre or auditorium, blank faces arrayed along the other side of a stage on which stood the dweeb pinned to a hole in the wall from which protruded a small section of tube inserted in his anus. "What—?" I began but Maria covered my mouth with her hand, pulling me back from the stage. "Must not disturb the audience. We need to remain silent. That is another use for Dina's contraption she invented. She is going to make a fortune with this thing. He is knotted to the wall by his asshole. This is one of our materials, however. Living tissue oozing like a slug and throbbing binaural tones he can't feel but hears. We call it pseudospectral knotting. Did you know that before coming to Tulane to study mathematics he earned a master's degree in control theory? His thesis was entitled *Pseudospectral Knotting for Bang-Bang Control.* Now watch." I thought for an infinitesimal she'd said gang-bang instead of bang-bang.

    The last time I'd seen the dweeb I'd begun feeling around the notion of partial differential equation as geometric object on a bundle. For example, if the bundle were trivial, say the cross product of a manifold with the real numbers, or for concreteness say the real plane crossed with the real line, the fibers were the reals and the bundle projection thus onto the real number line, a section no more than a C^∞ function of two real variables. One could consider a bundle with the appending of two more components for the section partial derivatives, fibers the first order Taylor series of the section which would lead to equivalence classes akin to germs of C^∞ functions. Clearly not all quintuples could represent sections with their derivatives given the last components needed to be plausible derivatives of the section. But you'd get two bundles. One would project onto the base manifold of the original bundle, the other onto the value of the section within the total space of the bundle. It was a bit of work to show in general it was a bundle for the projection onto the base manifold, but that the projection onto the value of the section was a bundle over the total space was transparent. Anyway, the dweeb had stopped by to disinterestedly watch me work out some details and play with some examples on the board in the office and that was when I noticed his phasing out. He'd said nothing, just watched, faint and blurry-edged as if slightly out of focus. This was after he had taken up with Utta and Ricci, sometime before the end of the semester which closed out precipitously: finals over, grading accomplished and grades posted, I in a state of aseity seated at the bar and dining on a muffuletta and Dixie longnecks, listening to Stravinksy's *Oedipus Rex* on the record player. It was the version conducted by Stravinsky with French narration and not nearly so scratchy as most albums in the Napoleon House as no one listened to it. Except me. Its starkness struck me as fitting; the fact that it drove people out of the place didn't hurt. The trumpet fanfares sent chills up my spine; I lived for the news that Jocasta had done herself in followed by the news that her son and husband had poked out his eyes. Good stuff.

A hand on my shoulder broke my reverie. "Mr. Butcher, imagine running into you here": the tonalities of Beatrice Cone. I turned to see her standing at my shoulder, beside her a substantial woman in pink sweater and long skirt patterned in a floral design, small flowers of varying round centers surrounded by petals that could have been someone's formalization of water lilies or some other oriental thing littered together in haphazard clumps of red, rose, pink and white on a black background. It looked as if it ought have been flocked, something one would find on a sofa in an old maid's dark living room or maybe even as curtains in the same living room or perhaps a rug or throw. Her friend stood at least five-eleven and was built like a football player except softer. You could see the soft in the tight sweater, out of place as the southern latitudes approached summer. Her friend was pink like the sweater, pale glowing pink radiating through her skin, hair a dark brown I couldn't tell if natural or tinted, eyes blue as a summer sky. Big eyes widely elliptical with moderate eccentricity surrounded by darkly lacquered lashes, painted dark for sure, below dark narrow brows apparently plucked to form a fine arc, her squat, wide face not too much forehead but mostly settling from the eyes down and framed by hair hanging barely to her shoulders kept from her face by a beret on the back of her head. She smiled thick lips and yellowish teeth square on top in the front four with pronounced canines after. The nose swooped along a narrow bridge to broad nostrils with a sharp point. She had a few freckles she tried to cover with some reddish stuff. Her Irish jaw kept the face from looking as squat as it might have been, though it was longish from below the eyes. She wore knee-high black leather boots.

"I saw my grade. Thank you."

"You don't need to call me Mr. Butcher. Call me Whitey."

"Cool," her friend said. "I always wanted to meet someone named Whitey."

"This is my friend Ashleigh," she said. "This is my math professor. For statistics."

"What grade did he give you?"

"An A. There were only two As, too."

"And you both deserved them." I didn't tell her the other belonged to the cheerleader. They'd both scored well above the others, getting the questions I used to separate out the As. The cheerleader had come to my office and thanked me; I told her she had done it, not I, by paying attention, reading the book, and doing the problems. She said it was the first time she had ever understood a math class.

"Let's go sit at a table," I said. "But I would appreciate it if you would refrain from talking until the music is done. The best part is coming. This is old blind Tiresias right now singing to Oedipus why he is a bozo."

"You like this?" It was Ashleigh.

"I played it. The rule is that the album must finish before anyone can put on another or take it off."

"What is this?"

"*Oedipus Rex.* Stravinsky. I thought everyone knew it."

I gathered more beers for the three of us and we took a table amidst the devotees of the crumbling late-nineteenth-century structure to drink and listen.

The narrator had finished telling the audience that the oracle had spoken: "*L'assassin du roi est un roi.*" Oedipus had answered Tiresias by singing his own praises and accusing the seer of working with Creon to overthrow the throne and of having killed Laius himself. "*Gloria gloria*" from the chorus. Act one ends and the narrator tells us Jocasta has entered to calm the disputants.

"Jocasta is telling them that oracles are full of it. The oracle predicted Laius would be killed by his son, but he was instead killed at the crossroads. *Carrefours.* But now Oedipus is afraid, because he killed an old man where three roads meet."

"Who's Laius?"

I put my finger to my lips.

"Oracula oracula" in soprano from the speakers perched high on the wall, "*mentita sunt oracula.*"

"Trivium, *trivium…*" from the chorus and Oedipus sings his fear: Jocasta, dear, did you say crossroads? Like, I killed an old man at the crossroads. A spirited duet, Oedipus afraid and Jocasta counseling beware of oracles, oracles are liars, let's go home and forget the whole fucking thing. But the narrator tells us Oedipus is only an adopted son of Polybus, King of Corinth, and Jocasta understands; everyone understands but Oedipus. The witness, the shepherd sang the tale to Cone and her friend looking bored. I was pretty sure I'd lose them, but didn't care. Oedipus sang "*Pudet Jocastam, fugit. Pudet Oedipi*

443

exulis" thinking she was ashamed of his lineage, not of the reality of the events. The shepherd and witness sang a bare duet accented by kettledrum explaining to Oedipus that he killed his real father and fucked his mother. Dire music. Oedipus quietly sings "*Natus sum quo nefastum est, concubui cui nefastum est, cecidi quem nefastum est. Lux facta est!*"

Dissonant trumpet fanfares frame the narrator's announcement of Jocasta's death. I loved the way he said *parricide*. "*Le roi est pris. Il veut se montrer á tous, montrer la bête immonde, l'inceste, le parricide, le fou.*"

I flashed five fingers to the girls to indicate five minutes. True to the narrator's word, the chorus helps the messenger get out the news that Jocasta is dead, having hanged herself, "*Divum Jocastae caput mortuum*" at which Oedipus pokes out his eyes with her brooch.

It died out following a final roll of kettledrums and stark orchestral announcement with the chorus subsiding to bid Oedipus bye bye when he reappears, eye sockets bloody. Too bad about your eyes dude; now get lost and thanks for getting rid of that evil Sphinx and her plague by solving that riddle.

The two were whispering when I stood. "Let's go?"

"Where?" Cone asked.

"I thought you might want to see my apartment. It is on Bourbon Street."

"What happened in the end?" asked her friend.

"Oh, Jocasta, Oedipus' wife, finds out her husband Oedipus is her son who murdered his father and so hangs herself, after which Oedipus gouges out his eyes."

"How awful. Why are operas so gruesome?"

"Art imitates life, I guess." I thought about asking her major but was afraid she'd say literature or music.

"Don't goad him on," Cone said. "Let's do happy thoughts tonight."

Cone appeared as her dowdy self, collegiate in dark pleated skirt, ribbed tan pullover blouse with an ovular boatneck surrounded by a flapped over collar and brown penny loafers topped with white bobby socks rolled down.

I guided them out the disorienting corner-bisecting door a quarter step left to St. Louis Street on which we passed one block to our right to Royal and then after a right turn the few blocks to St. Ann whence we hit Bourbon at the gay corner before Lafitte's in Exile. We made the end of the block and stood before the gate to my apartment, music blasting out of Lafitte's a few steps hence.

"Is that Lafitte's in Exile?" Cone asked.

"Yep. Noise machine." The block crawled with the usual men cruising men. The two women gawked like tourists at a female impersonator show.

I led them into the courtyard and up the winding stairs. On the second floor the landlord called out, "Is that you, Mr. Boo-shay?"

"It is, Mr. Boudreaux."

"It sounds like you're not alone," his nelly drawl more pronounced so I guessed he wasn't alone.

"No, I am with companions."

"Well, keep it quiet, please," he said.

I paid him no attention and we continued up to the solarium.

"Wow, this is neat," Ashleigh peering out into the courtyard, giving me a chance to examine her ass. Broad and flat. Cone wore her usual pout.

Inside the loft I hauled them through to the bedroom and onto the cat walk above Bourbon Street, grabbing a joint on the way. As I lit up, Cone said, "This is a long way up," backed away from the railing against the wall. Her friend leaned out over the railing. "I don't trust this structure all that well," I said to her. She ignored me. I lit up the joint and took a deep hit, passing it to Cone, who asked, "What's it like in Lafitte's in Exile?" before she toked and I tapped Ashleigh to take a hit. "I don't go there," I said. "I never go in the gay bars. Let's them know I'm not interested." Ashleigh exhaled, croaking the words "See, I told you he wasn't gay." "Why'd you make me think you were gay?" Cone asked and I said, "I did?" "Well, let's try some of what I brought," Ashleigh said, and Cone asked, "Do you think it's a good idea, Ash?" "Definitely" to which I asked "What is it?" "Designer drug from the Bay Area; snort it. I have a friend at Stanford who makes it." She pulled a mirror from her purse and brought out a mini-baggie from which she took sparkly stuff she spread into lines. She tooted, Cone tooted and I tooted the remaining lines. Some sort of crystals, couldn't tell the color in the dark but guessed clear from the way they caught the ambient light. It felt cold and sharp in the nose. "He calls it glass," she said and I felt a rush come on from the base of my spine that instead of shooting up and out the top of my head rammed into my groin like a hot fist. I sprouted an immediate and urgent erection.

Ashleigh reached out and touched the front of my pants. The pelvic perturbation resounded through my penis.

"Wow," she said. "I think we're in for a good ride, Bea. If I am correct, this is way outside the norm for dicks."

Cone came over and rubbed her open hand along its outline, setting off a new pulse train to superpose the one yet ringing as after-effect, distorting the original signal into echoing anharmonic inguinal oscillation. "Oh, my," she said and unzipped my fly, letting the glans poke out. "Gnarly." I looked down and saw it studded with knobbles I'd not previously noted. She rubbed the tip and licked the seepage from her hand. "Very tasty. Maybe we ought move inside." She led the way. As I came through the window she tugged at my belt. I backed up a step and removed my shirt. Ashleigh pulled up her pink sweater to reveal massive meat packed into a pink bra. "So you have music?" she asked and I said "Only jazz and classical." Cone said "How about jazz?" and peeled off her blouse to reveal a more modestly filled beige bra. I put on *Eric Dolphy at the Five Spot,* playing first *The Prophet* to which Ashleigh asked, "What's that?" and I said "Eric Dolphy" as the dissonance of alto and trumpet came together before Eric went nuts on a short flying solo skipping into the sonic opening for a more prolonged excursion after a repeat of dissonant melody, giving voice to a crying wailing sometimes burbling-submerged tone poem growing frantic amidst the topless women. Ashleigh's long tubes hung flat on her burgeoning not-quite-belly, sepia areolae reaching far back with pronounced buds for nipples propped at forty-five degrees from the horizon with the support of the mid-section. She crossed her hands in front and looked crossways toward me, eyes averted. Cone leaned back against the bed, hands extended behind her as props, wearing only panties. She stared at me with eyes half shut, as if to look languid or ready for action or perhaps come hither. Didn't matter: she was ready. It recalled to me the mound of papers that'd appeared in the envelope in my mailbox with the wad of money, mostly about strapdown navigation but including the topic of coning correction. Coning correction? My dick wept viscous humors in ciliary strands dredged from my balls.

A penis-packing gang had taken the stage and surrounded Utta and Ricci who they smothered in humping mounds of flesh that squished sweat and bodily fluids, the slapping of a run through sticky muck wearing flip-flops. One of the women with erection grabbed The Dweeb by his ears and fucked his mouth until he spit up ejaculate. As suddenly as they'd arrived, they left and the Dweeb, asshole pinned to the wall, stretched to the bed and lapped Utta clean.

I pulled Maria away from the stage. "What is this? What the fuck's he doing?"

"He has chosen to be Utta's slave. She is undergoing her final impregnation. He is keeping the chances uniform by lapping up all the ejaculate he can. Think of it as information vacuuming. He eats the information."

"What the fuck? Slave?"

"His choice. She seduced him some might say, but he chose her. She will die with the coming pregnancy and he will be sold."

"Sold?"

"Yes. For experimental purposes and general clean-up. Sort of information janitor."

"And Ricci?"

"She will be fine. You need not worry for her-him-it."

I helped Ashleigh out of her skirt. She leaned forward as if to kiss me but I wasn't interested. I reached instead for her tits, rubbing the nipples against her nascent gut. I felt her bush through damp coarse panties.

I turned back to Cone. Her tits were fatter than her friend's but not nearly so massive. They didn't sag to her belly but they did sag, two fat slugs melting into an elastic droop against her rib cage with areolae centered and staring out like fried eggs running towards the ground, bigger and darker than Ashleigh's, maybe taupe, the same round bud at the end except pointing out along the horizon. The little tummy that showed through her tight blouse did not show with it gone.

Ashleigh left her boots on her feet.

"You need to get out of those britches," Ashleigh said. Cone stared silent and unsmiling. I took off my shoes and removed my pants which by now showed a soaked spot where my dick slobbered through. When down to briefs slathered in dick juice, I signaled Cone I'd remove mine when she removed hers. We did it simultaneously, she revealing a black bush covering a long mons, spare on top and denser as it narrowed to the not visible pudendum between her legs. Ashleigh's bush ran higher and darker but not so mannish in coverage. Her mons bulged fatter.

She joined Cone on the bed and they kissed a prolonged kiss on the mouth, hands frantic between legs. I moved closer and Ashleigh reached out and pulled me by my drooling erection toward Cone's face from which snaked a tongue to catch the drool. She mouthed over it, sucking as Ashleigh climbed over to pull Cone along the bed, aligning us as if gyrocompassing an inertial device torqued by high frequency planetary rotation. Waves pulsated like a resonating saddle firing amplified bursts up my coccyx and along my pubic

447

symphisis, expanding muted charges distributed a resonant blanket modulating my sacrum. Grabbing Cone's stumpy legs which seemed more sexy to me now than when within her skirts, Ashleigh leveraged them up over Cone's head, one ankle beside each ear, and sat on her face, simultaneously immobilizing legs and pinning arms. "Go on," she said, "plant it in her. The slut's ready."

"I can't watch this," I told Maria.

"You disappoint me. It is not as if he were your friend. But come, then." She pulled me out of the auditorium and along another corridor.

Cone's cunt sucked me up snug and hot and slimy wet and I fell inside with a soft uhh escaping her as she mouthed the cunt splayed open over her face. I pounded and we precessed about some orthogonal axis through the bed at the torque applied by my cock which seemed to twist like a rotor with slight vibrations inducing a nutation that bobbled Ashleigh's head until the record ended at which it began to thump harmonically and I kept ramming until the gnarl in my groin shoved up the shaft to my glans penis, swelled like a fist, and spewed from the meatus in a painful jet. Cone yelped at the load.

I withdrew limp and wet and the two women came undone, Cone cleaning off my dick with her tongue and mouth while Ashleigh opened Cone's vaginal lips wide and red to explore with her hand, working it inside to her wrist and then her elbow. Cone bucked around the fist I imagined up beyond her belly button. I went to change the record and put on Miles at Carnegie Hall to hear the Mobley solo where he squawked and shrieked with a dry reed. When I came back Ashleigh had both arms buried to her elbow between Cone's legs. As the funereal opening finished to the blast of brass, Cone calmed down enough to provide me four lines to toot and as Miles came on to *So What,* drums piano bass-backing sliding out of the cool of disconnect, my dick sprang hard and wet and I entered Ashleigh lying on her stomach with Cone pierced on her arms. Again precessing, we transfer aligned to where Cone stretched back atop the two arms with tits sprawling flat lumps witnessing me batter her friend, unsmiling and impassive dark brown eyes like a cat watching nothing until Ashleigh's big legs scissored her face into the cunt where I harmonically thumped. All this without withdrawing her fists and forearms from Cone's furry-burry. About the time Mobley began his solo Ashleigh rolled her head back and gurgled throaty noises and muted growls and I hit my stride, the relentless sledge in my groin hammering. Ashleigh raised her flat butt and boxy hips and pushed back, snapping Cone's neck. I thrashed through Kelly's solo with all the rim shots from Cobb before the slub of twisted strands propelled into the head of my dick knotted to a burl and ejected another blast from the well between my legs.

"What is that stuff?" I asked Ashleigh. Astride Cone's face dribbling spunk into her mouth, she held out the mirror. I could see six lines of clear, long crystals. I did them all. The stuff percussed a hot lump in my groin. "Glass. That's what he calls it. For sex. That's why he designed it. Does it work for you?" She winked and did a couple lines and helped Cone contort to do a couple. Ashleigh came up with a small vial, maybe from one of the boots she wore, and rubbed some on my glans penis, smearing the retracted foreskin for good measure. "Fuck the little whore's asshole. Stick it deep and fuck it hard. Make the cunt cry. Punish the bitch. Make that asshole bleed. Fuck the little shit senseless." The lube lit my dick head like hot Vicks. I torqued into the well-posed butthole with a single movement. Cone lurched forward but then shoved back hard, grinding her butt by twisting against the forearms embedded in her cunt. I grabbed her straight hips and held her still, catching a tempo from the scorching inner swelling rapping me to move in ways I couldn't. I don't know how long I prodded her guts. It caught fire and I blasted another wad without warning, intruding so deep it seemed it shot out her mouth. The phrase *gird up your loins* intruded into the only speck of consciousness not devoted to my glans penis.

Ashleigh withdrew her arms, tooted more lines and slowly worked one hand into Cone's asshole. "My friend explains how it works in thermodynamic terms. He's an organic chemist's physical chemist. He talks about relaxation time and the time scale of relaxation to get rid of lower limits of integration and initial conditions. Relaxing away the fast variables for the male aspect of sex and the slow variables for the female aspect through adiabatic elimination via Haken's slaving principle. Adiabatic so as not to introduce external erotic stimulation." "That doesn't mean a fucking thing, Ashleigh." "Glad to know it. He made me memorize it. He says he will use it in television ads. He likes to throw in stuff about the Langevin equation and stationary Ornstein-Uhlenbeck process and the perturbed Fokker-Planck equation in its guise as the Smoluchowski equation but I have been informed by some that the Smoluchowski thingy is not perturbed. But what do I know? I'm a PE major." I knew of all those last equations, some intimately, and didn't doubt the viability of the former stuff though I had not encountered it, but related to drugs for enhanced sexual performance they didn't mean shit. By the time she'd finished yammering I was dry-humping the air like a horny dog. Ashleigh presented her asshole and

I fucked it as she impaled Cone's on her forearms and Cone buried her head in Ashleigh's cunt. When I finished and pulled out, Ashleigh pulled her arms free and sat her ass on Cone's freed face, farting dick snot and other stuff that Cone lapped up. "Dude, your dick is twisted," Ashleigh remarked. "Really," Cone reinforced her when she finally came up, "and roped with veins or something, chords—" "and swollen with bumps or knots, like a French tickler, you know?" I nodded no and then yes and they laughed, "— when you're ready to cum it swells up with those ropes and knots and the head gets huge and the whole thing twists—" "Really. It's awesome." "Maybe it's the drug," I said, meaning them and Ashleigh said, "No. I have never experienced it with any other guys using glass. In fact, this very glass we used here." Maria led me into a gymnasium with a wrestling mat in the center and someone powerful grabbed me from behind in a full nelson. I brought my left heel down on top of the arch of the foot but my attacker hoisted me up off the ground. "Don't kick me," Gerty said. "Don't make me hurt you early." I relaxed to display no aggression and she set me back on the floor without relaxing her hold. "Your boots look gay. *You* look gay. Leather pants and shirt? Are you gay?" she asked. "No," I said, looking at an amused Maria who said, "Well, Whitey, we're going to modify your copulatory implementation. Acausally. That means to be retroactive in certain special events. You will have already noted it in some past events yet to occur. It will be remembered as bigger than it was because it was bigger." Two naked women stepped up beside her. On the left a long, sinewy green-eyed blonde, straight hair hanging to slight, squared-off shoulders, with long face and angular features, bony hips and bony arms and legs, her lower legs of small negative curvature bending outward ever so slightly from elongated, flattened patellae. Not so gaunt as to be unappealing, she bore low breasts proportional to her stretched shape. She displayed a jewel in her navel accented by a tattooed sunburst. On the other side stood a shorter creature with pendent breasts cascading outward widely separated about a muscular thorax and above rippling abdominals. The round areolae rose up to bumps of nipples directed forty-five degrees outbound and slightly elevated with respect to the parallel of the floor, their diameter at least that of silver dollars. Long of face and mannish by comparison, a hard set to the mouth that told one she meant business exaggerated an extended chin jutting from a sharp, straight nose carved out of cheek furrows framing pronounced elliptical nostrils separated by a fine cleft. She had severely dark brown thick hair artlessly draped to her muscular shoulders as well as strong brows of the same hue, unsmiling brown eyes and unpainted lips, unlike her partner's. Not a bruiser like Gerty; despite or perhaps because of pronounced musculature she was more appealing than the smiling blonde with smiling eyes. I guessed they had the same hairdresser. "I am leaving you in the custody of my votaresses. These are two of the best, but all of my followers are devoted whores." "I can't pay. No money on me." "This bill's been paid fully, dear boy. Don't worry. On my left Mila, a splendiferous ass-fuck" and she turned her to reveal high, round, narrow buttocks above slender thighs "and on my right Paulina, the Venus of Las Vegas, a devotee of physical culture, wrestling and zoophilia. People call her V." "Let me make sure this right," Mila said. "Horizontal transfer inclusive of pre-effects and torsion field for sexual congress, as with helical torque, okay?" "Exactly," Maria answered, "Whitey, we leave you with a twist…" and she laughed "but frequency and impulse response, too, with control of the fast variables, and don't forget dimensionality, as in bigger at completion and of course studded for ringing after-effects." "That ending part is Gerty and V?" "Frequency response is short-leg effect," physical cultist Paulina interjected to which Maria laughed "No short arms now!" introducing the big-titted woman with infant legs to me as Euterpe of the Short Legs before making her regal way out of visual range, leaving me the only clothed creature. I stopped paying attention to her departure when Euterpe, standing at crotch level, undid the ties on my fly and freed my penis upon which Gerty twirled me around, hoisted me above her head and lowered my dangling penis into her open lips. "Me, me" little Euterpe yelped dancing around in imitation of an excited puppy. Gerty put me down and worked me back into the hammer lock and the little one slurped my stubbornly unresponsive member into her mouth, all of it, and applied melismatic humming refrains with sonic overtones that erected the unwilling flesh over which her lips stretched implementing a peristaltic pump amplifying refrains emanating from within the highly rouged vermillion border-crowned elongating tubeworm. The philtrum distorted elastically to account for the girth. My scrotum was a hanging sack attached to the Labium inferius of the incurrent siphon like an overgrown mouche. "She's a true crimson mawed sperm sucker," Gerty said. It didn't take long for the sensation of undulating penicillate pubescence and persistent suckling to coax an eruption upon which my penis shrunk away from the extruded labia which itself did not relax, leaving her with waving annelid in lieu of mouth complete with clitellum formed out of the distended philtrum that circled the convoluted mishmash of lipstick along the outer border. Cone on her knees sucked my dick with Ashleigh behind her coaxing her to get it all in, a struggle even though it was limp as an overcooked noodle until Ashleigh held out the mirror on which rested lines of the glass, six of them, that I tooted and that she replaced for me to toot again and my copulatory equipment erected into the constriction of Cone's throat as Ashleigh leaned against her to keep her mouth firmly flattened against my pubes. Her watering eyes bugged as if leaving her face, deformed with intorsion, her lips distending in grotesque displacement. I grabbed her hair in bunches and without need for the shrill encouragement of Ashleigh fucked her throat to jerked load after load she struggled to contain but which vented from around her lips and her nostrils, covering her face and hair and my groin. Gerty picked me up like a rag doll and turned me upside down, shoved my face into her muff and snarfed up my spent worm after ordering me to chew her clit, which order I obeyed out of a desire to not be tossed into the ring in an old-fashioned pile driver. The round knob resisted like a leather walnut, plumping the more ferociously I gnawed. My efforts were to no avail; she tossed me into the ring on my head. Too weak from too many emissions, I couldn't scramble fast enough to escape her iron grip. She sat on my face and removed my shirt, then my boots; Paulina officiated, giving her points for making me eat her pussy and for removing my shirt and boots. I gave in. I knew she was going to kill me. Once before I'd found myself helpless among the host of pitiless termagants in this place. She worked off my pants at which point I was no longer a singularity among the naked. She started to raise me up in a back-breaking move when she cried out, "My god. Is that your wound?" She rested me on the mat and gingerly touched my scarred leg. "Is it? Oh, what happened?" "Yes," I said, trying not to whimper. "I was shot several times with an automatic weapon. I nearly lost it." I hoped I sounded stoical. She stroked the folded precipices and creased lengths of muscle riddled with indents and traced the raised red ridge-line along the dual empiercements gored by bullets and fragmented bone. Tears washed down her face. "I surrender, V" she sobbed. Paulina held up my arm and said, "Now fuck her in the ass with conviction" to which I almost said no but thought better of it, remembering Maria's warning of the vagina dentata. The act took interminable time to initiate leading to a sharp jab of needle and stinging injection of fluid into my right buttock accompanied by Paulina's laughing "Don't worry, only spider bite. No paralysis. Also you can fire away this time." I burgeoned a rigid spar unrecognizable to me, rippling with knotted veins, rigged cordage and twisted with pulsating nodules; I shoved it into Gerty's tight asshole with effort as she clenched her butt muscles. Upon consummation it grew more tumescent, in need of another consummation. Paulina whispered it would remain rigid for at least the remainder of my excellent adventure, then went to all fours, presenting rounded buttocks astride nascent saddle bags on leanly muscular thighs. Mila put on a show leaning against Gerty, her bony knees together displaying lean-fleshed legs more curvaceous than her gaunt frame, the disparity between her thighs a cleft above which hovered puffy vaginal lips. Looking back at me, she raised up and spread apart her legs so the thigh gap was less noticeable, the curves less obvious, the knees bonier. Her calves flexed muscular when she raised up on tiptoes before leaning away from Gerty who held her up by her hands as she leveled her torso parallel with the mat inviting me to enter between upright thighs which did not meet though she brought knees and ankles again together. I ignored the offer, watching her smile an invitation before kissing Gerty on the mouth. She looked back at me and smiled another invitation, wiggling her ass without any hint of jiggle. Cunt and asshole aligned, the asshole high and level with sharp inward slope whose burgeoning prominence rounded to a peak that sloped gently to a shallow, narrow valley on the other side of which the entire structure repeated symmetrically, a declivity amidst the top to an elliptical hole where her anus declined. I moved in for a close-up and she accommodated by leaning forward and swaying her narrow back, still holding Gerty for support, displaying the russet-pink puckered sphincter. Her cunt stretched at forty-five degrees to the mat, the valley above it pulled up flattening the rounded cheeks. A white path ran straight to the top from the indentation where hid the shyly retiring anal sphincter. White and darker fine hairs showed along the ridgeline, noticeable on closer inspection all over the buttocks from vaginal lips to anal recess hidden within a tawny depression. When she turned a few degrees to the side in transit to her next position I saw that the narrow cheeks stretched along dual high bony prominences not noticeable when she stood or bent. She moved down and away from Gerty to rest on her hands and knees, arching her back so that her entire cunt was a vertical long red gash with swollen labia pointed at the mat from within spread spindly thighs capped by a flat verge of trimmed blonde Mohawk carpet peeking from above the occult mons. Rocking her hips forward arching her back, her anal sphincter on high obverted to eye in the sky staring up, an inverted prune countersunk within a burnt sienna ovular setting. I moved closer still and put my fingertip in the conical introduction to her asshole, reconnoitering the recessed sphincter. She gripped my digital probe with the counterbore and pinched it with anal sphincter. I pulled back and the conical hole snapped like a mouth, the anal sphincter protruding up out of it when opened, a worm pharynx grasping for food. Waiting gave way to urgent and I occluded her butthole with my dribbling penis, pushing straight down. The top-mounted countersunk opening was as slick as greased owl shit. She climbed my mast without effort on my part, rippling up and down in squirming syncopation harmonizing betwixt the seizing sphincter and its paired chattering countersink with support from grinding hips and clenching skinny ass-cheeks, setting up an assonant ringing enriched with side to side twisting overtones. I pulled away with effort and entered Paulina's cheeks; they responded as vice grips locking into a widely rolling arhythmic rumba that pulverized my innards and was harder yet to break. I took turns in each of their dual holes, back and forth, unhurried, Gerty looking on. When I moved to their front side Gerty joined them taking turns fellating me to a blur of releases of what might have been oversized wads given how my bones shook with each ejaculation, each one leaving me hornier. Gerty moved me back to the rear ends and held my shoulders to move me from one to the other until I ejaculated something into each of the four available holes. Mila had been a splendiferously hyperactive ass-fuck, Paulina serviceable but less otherworldly. Different styles, both athletic and original. I did Gerty's cunt without losing my equipment to hidden teeth or muscular contraction. When they stood to congratulate me, my erection had grown harder and coated with a noisome smegma like an iridescent hard sauce that they burbled over with the ardor of worshippers, kissing and stroking the throbbing mechanization of preternatural lust.

Paulina and Mila took each a hand and guided me into the boundless whiteness, Gerty walking point. Mila said, "We toward a place for my needs. But you also will find amusement. And it is necessary to attend." I had no idea how they could know where they headed; there were no distinctions of any sort, not ground to walk on or horizon to trudge toward or sheltering sky. I tried to step down, as a test, but it didn't work. I was on firm footing. "Don't be worried, silly," Mila said. "We are within a space that does not reflect visible light. But see…" and we stood in an expansive walled room filled with naked people and divans, couches, beds, matted flooring and an apparently unsupported sign that spelled in consecutive step-wise illumination YOU HAVE ENTERED THE VARIATIONAL COMPLEX with luciferous letters of differing hues and differing also on each progressive orthography to erasure and recommencement. To all appearances normal human women and men mingled with little people bearing all the characteristics of achondroplasia dwarfism except that the males pushed their massively oversized penises before them in small wooden-wheeled carts. Some of them bore impossible hard-ons, impossible given the apparent quantity of blood available. Mila pointed at the sign. Mournful cowboy yodels and hollers split the accordion drone carried no doubt by the reek of stale beer, puke and piss. "Just be glad this is not the variational bi-complex," she giggled at what I took to be a joke no one seemed to get. "How did you get us here?" "Impossible not to. Just following a path piecewise along predetermined fibers in this particular sub-bundle. Following nose." I considered asking why was it necessary to walk or even to move in order to get anywhere, but decided against it since I wasn't sure what I meant. "Have considered moving to jet bundle to tangent bundle of total space but still not seeing how to go there. We would like to engage prolongations, but maybe necessary to have integrability. This provides unique complementary sub-bundles for direct sum, so would not exist this problem of filming. It seems. Maybe. But for sure more room for rattling around within." I perked up at jet bundles. She noticed. "You understand this?" "No," I said, and she said "You will become a resident overly familiar with that terrain soon enough. Just think of local sections bunched under common Taylor series, okay? wearing them like turtles sharing shell. Equivalent turtles. You see, then there would be holonomic lifts; total derivatives or contact forms, dual to each another, see? Contact forms will live in kernel of local section, okay?" "No. Forget it." I needed to plunge my erect, slobbering dick into something. "Much dual annihilation going on, and naturality for the vertical and horizontal. Prolonged sections characterized by annihilation of contact forms. But in this place here much holonomy groups. Plenty hysteresis. Nonholonomic dynamics. How you go is important as where you go. Particular aholonomy different depending on fibers you pass. Just remember, you are not in the product bundle any more. Our current path here is for pleasuring me. Don't push that little dripping thing at me," she said, pushing me away. "V, you be in charge while I go merry-go-round." Mila walked through the traffic and clutter to a giant lazy Susan where women secured together side by side her wrists and ankles using a shiny aluminum single piece Spanish-stirrups. They tied a ball gag in her mouth and placed her face down on the merry-go-round in the doggy style with her ass raised up, securing her in place by strapping down her forearms and calves with her ass pointing at us. A wired plug attached to a black box beside her was inserted into her cunt. "This plays music of electricity. Voltage surges to music entraining her vaginal spasms. Cannot hear, only feel. Wired snatch called harmonic injection; originally only simple harmonic motion, but now more interesting. Today I think is *Rite of Spring*: so much heavy jolting." Spaced around the whirling device at close intervals were a group of the little men with their miraculous copulatory contraptions. "See, she likes the apparatuses all the way into her ass. Watch her butthole snapping the air." I watched the two holes, the outer pre-butthole that squeezed open and shut and the inner sphincter that raised up snapping when the outer opened, synchronized dual openings and closings. "Jeez," I said, "those dicks are like oversized proctoscopes. They'll be in her guts." "Proctoscopes only about ten inches, maybe one inch diameter. These twice that big. But not probing much beyond sigmoid colon, if so far." What I took to be human women slobbered and sucked the organs in erectile support, though few could get an entire glans inside the mouth so instead worked around the meatus and licked inside the prepuce and vigorously stroked, mostly two-handed. The wheel spun and revolved several times before slowing to a stop in front of one of the dwarfish characters standing in profile to us. He climbed up on the wheel and, supporting himself on her back with his hands, in a single stroke inserted his entire exploratory device into her skyward glancing brown eye. On one knee, he gained leverage and purchased ruthless thrusting power with extended strokes. Restrained to inhibit hip rotation, Mila worked her holes around the shafts so that the protrusile sphincter reached up and out in regular pattern of outer open, inner prolapsed on outstroke; outer closed, inner relapsed on in-stroke. "How's she do that?" I asked. "She is gifted athlete," Paulina said. "Note with dual hole she overcomes obstructed articulation of head of femur with socket of acetabulum." He apparently ejaculated without spillage save what dribbled at withdrawal. They spun her again and she stopped facing us. Her right cheek pressed against the floor of the wheel and she drooled incessantly around the gag. The new appendage-bearer fucked her asshole with great vigor. She kept her eyes shut and emitted smothered cries. "Come on," Paulina said, "I and Gerty take you on tour and you can expend some lust, an action I am sure of which you are in urgent need." My erection would not cease weeping. She lassoed it with a thin rope of coarse, high-itch material and led me, Gerty walking close behind. "Don't worry," Paulina said. "No plans for kinbaku." "Wrong rope in any cases, V," Gerty added. "No jute. And warriors in most or some cases get treatment with more modicum of respect, at least many times." "Plaited for respect," Paulina said. She gave a hard tug. "It's like brat with snotty nose. Running all the time. Maybe later if it limpens we can lay it up in flemish-coils." "And whip the ends, if need be." They snickered. I guessed it was some manner of nautical-speak but didn't give a fuck. I only wanted to plunge it into something malleable. We passed into a nightclub littered with copiously attended cluster fucks. Throngs of apparently regular human males and females and male and female small people and muscular women wandered together when not conjointly merging in copulating conclaves on flat surfaces or kneeling-standing on the floor. In the midst of the room on a raised flat surface sat a red-haired giant with braided hair past his shoulder, a full beard and flaring red nose hair, wearing the only articles of clothing in the room, a patched together homespun motley of animal furs. Someone said "Play it Sam" and he sang in noticeable Utahan twang

> I'm proud to be a lum-pen-pro-lo-tār-yee-yat
> In liege to the cor-prate fi-ef-doms
> Fucked in the ass by the Texas lej-i-slay-toor
> Owing my soul to the cor-prate store

"Texas Celtic cowboy" Paulina said. "Very famous in some tori." As he yodeled a black giantess so powerful of bulk she made Gerty seem frail approached. Flaring lats like sides of beef veed from bulging shoulders down to armored-plate abdominals. Her tits were flattened symmetrical rounds centered with miniscule areolaless nipples mounted on solid pectorals. She was supported by thighs so muscular they made her substantial calves seem skinny. Styled in extreme white sidewalls, shaved to be exact, she wore her long reddish locks piled atop her head in a fat fountain held in place with a white doodad and tumbling to the left side. It was the only hair in evidence, her body lustrously glabrous. From each wrist, attached between their tiny legs like sock puppets, writhed one of the short-legged Euterpe models, their mouths dripping tubular suction devices snaking in the air. Gerty held me up and one of the cocksucking hand puppets leached on and vacuumed, then the other replaced her, the dusky giantess encouraging them to gather up the nectar. When the two assailants had each drained me and popped free to skip to join a gangbang in progress, she continued the joint mouthing of my joint, kneeling when Gerty set me down, her hair mop falling forward over her face, her tongue exuberant. My horniness increased after she'd coaxed a load and stood, shaking her head like a wet dog, saliva and spunk flying from her lips. I moved behind her to examine her gluteus maximus, a bulging ridge of muscle along the top of each thigh turning sharply in a pinched crest downward to join protuberant vastus lateralis. The dense musculature apparently afforded no entry. Gerty and Paulina shook their heads even as the behemoth dropped to all fours and I climbed up in the style of a Chihuahua mounting a Danish Mastiff. She opened her muscular butt-cleavage but I was unable to penetrate beyond the cheeks. She pulled away and rolled on her back, lifting and guiding me between labia from within which jutted a penis-shaped club of a clitoris that rubbed against the upper side of my dong as her vagina clenched and milked my verrucose shaft to several explosions, each leaving me aching for another. Gerty and Paulina together extracted me from her suffocating bear hug, ripping from the jaws between her legs my penis, fully intact.

I fucked my way across the room through a horde of women, joining and disjoining clusters of housewives and muscle women and wee women copulating and otherwise sexually interacting with one another and all sorts of males, mostly husbands and dwarfs of gigantic phalli along with some indescribables. A woman of muscles held her hand in my face and I stopped to examine the hardest washboard abdomen I had ever seen, rippling rectus abdominus delineated in stark relief. Amidst the ripples hung a jeweled chain from a piercing in her navel swaying over the vein-encrusted flat extending to a decorated pudendum with labia covered in rings of gold and silver crowned by a knot of a clitoris deformed by numerous studs. A firm round ass had not been beefed into a pinched sinew but sat atop powerful thighs flowing smoothly into brawny calves not so muscular as to disguise underlying womanliness. She touched my penis, rubbing the nubby surface of fine wires, her fingers long and soft despite bulging biceps and triceps. A thewy torso of rounded shoulders and wiry thorax from which hung widely separated low-slung breasts curved sharply outward kept her from the Herculean realms of the likes of Paulina and the black giantess. She squeezed my cock with manly grip and I gazed down into a feminine visage framed within straight black hair that fell symmetrically beyond her shoulders to her breasts; she peered back through the round brown eyes of a deer in the headlights. Her straight-edge nose, meaty undulant lips and gently squared chin on a slightly elongated face tempered by high round cheeks I would have found imminently appealing were it not for the dense black mustache on her upper lip. She twisted my dick in an attempt to bring me to submission but given she was almost a foot shorter, I put her in a headlock and forced her to release me. Rather than stay and fight I escaped to a levitating body encased in a cohesive liquid—it flowed continuously—that sucked in all the nearby light, forming an aura that faded to gray before merging into a constant white. Her forearms adjoined her calves in one piece crossing over the knee between shoulder and elbow with forearm twisting under so it ended with ankle superior to wrist, forcing the legs and arms into a vee open at the feet, level with her head and displaying asshole and cunt as the viscous material flowed around

458

them, bounded away without visible frontier as if fluid and flesh fused into a seamless cover. The same was true of a lipless opening of mouth and a pair of nipples exposed without showing any areolae. She'd been decorated: her labia stretched perhaps a foot and pierced repeatedly with a row of thick rings along each flap, her clitoris fat and elongated and filled with studs and rings, the hood singly studded. Her asshole encircled with small rings. As I stood watching men fuck her various orifices and torture her nipples, an endless but orderly line awaiting their turn, the form detached from the transgressors and floated to me, locking its asshole over my erection. I humped until I spewed and switched to the cunt for another release before moving to the head maw at which the line moved to join me at the other end. The two prior ejaculations decreased my libido, an unexpected benefit that I intended to exploit via the mouth.

A woman in a nearby cluster fuck watched me work the mouth hole. One of two centers of gravity attending a clot of black men, she leaned on the thighs of a man on his back with his cock in her mouth while controlling her face placement using a pair of bunchy pigtails; another had at her from behind. Her mouth distended around the glans of the penis; with extra force the tube steak disappeared entirely. She had green eyes. I looked away but my gaze wandered back even as I worked the mouth hole. She had rolled onto her back with legs up, displaying a white cream pie oozing from her asshole down the intergluteal cleft. Her thighs glistened in ooze. She lowered one leg flat and raised the other, foot touching the bed, knees bent and arching her back to display a neatly trimmed pussy, the while staring at me. In a single movement, she flipped over and kneeled with back arched and chest resting on the bed so that her navel was visible, all without breaking the contact of her look back. From there she lowered her lissome frame to the bed and turned to face me, spine gracefully bowed to display a heart-shaped ass. Her face was a smear of white glop and eye shadow. She raised up on hands and knees, her back still arched, and a pair of massive tits hung down, the small nipples that capped gigantic pink areoles scraping the bed. When she straightened her spine the full girth of the hefty attachments became apparent in contrast to her svelte frame. "What you doin', bitch?" the man who'd had his dick in her face barked. "She displaying fo' that white boy," another said, pointing at me. 'That bullshit," a third said, and he mounted her as the other two held her in place. She presented her ass to receive him and ground her ass like a wobbling hydraulic receptacle until he hollered and straightened up in orgasmic spasm at which she backed firmly against his groin, then jumped up and walked away. Willowy with elegance on long, lean limbs, she approached me as I pulled my dripping cock from the mouth hole, saying "Whitey. What a surprise. And giving it to Dina, no less. She would be ecstatic if only she were aware." I would not have forgotten her face, proportioned as it was with nothing out of place, no asymmetry, the green eyes and general setup stunning despite the drab brown hair. My only quibble would have been the legs, straight including flat hips that didn't match the long trunk that seemed to belong to someone else, and was, despite a noticeable tummy, lithe and graceful with the capacious tits laying well above the waist and not flat but with nipples upthrust by corpulence. "I'm sorry," I replied, growing eager to shove my dick into one of her holes with the returning urgency of relentless libido, "I don't know you." She smiled. "Palo Alto, silly. We met when you and your date and another couple went to the city after a company party. She's your boss's girlfriend, but couldn't go with him because she works for him as his secretary. And the other couple was a woman you worked with and her boyfriend." I stared blankly. "The city?" "San Francisco. The swing club, House of David. You don't remember?" "I have never been to Palo Alto or to San Francisco." A man approached. He'd been watching her and another woman now left alone without assistance to manage the horde of blacks. A meager white guy with a patch of hair on a concave chest and nothing showing from his patch of groin hair, he seemed puzzled. "You've been to many of our swinging soirees," she said, reaching out to hold the little guy's hand. "They call you the warty meat prong of Silicon Valley. The horn dog of Stanford math. Biggest pud in the city, all decorated with hairy studs and of copious emission." The man whose hand she held whispered what seemed a warning in her ear. "This is my husband Ken. He likes to watch and clean up. I'm Claire." Behind her the other woman disengaged as the two pipy-mouthed dwarf muses who'd been attached to the fists of the giantess engaged the black gang with trumpet lips. "Ken designed that suit for Dina," Claire said. "It is specialized liquid elastomer, a smart material that bonds to flesh until solvent is applied." He spoke in a pipsqueak strained by nervous energy. "It replaces the ridiculous bulky isolation chamber of Dr. John Lilly…author of *Programming and Metaprogramming in the Human Biocomputer.*" I remembered Dina'd not given me a copy. "I've heard of it." "Well, rather than immersion in water with breathing gear and all the attendant hassles, this affords the same isolation when unbreached, simply being connected to you, as does the tank. Without external openings one is unable to see, hear, smell, feel, or sense in any way. Not even attitude in space. The unit maintains the body temperature by feedback: that's the smart material, with its ability to seal along the programmed boundaries. She can only feel where there exist openings." "So she feels herself being fucked?" "In a manner of speaking. Did she suck when you entered her mouth?" "Not with her usual conviction. There was tongue action or something. But not with such active authority as Dina, if that is Dina." "Oh, yes. It is truly Dina. That action was the mandibular response. She has a head full of designer drugs. Specifically created for this application. Also designed in the Silicon Valley, by students of Shulgin no less. The basic ambient backdrop is a slow motion DMT experience, but that is not all. She talks about having more interaction with the machine elves, especially when she's being gang raped as now. But they are not associated with the visible language matrix that Meyer and McKenna described with DMT. Because of the addition of an alkaloid derived from Lycoris radiata, the so-called Red Spider Lily, there is the lucid dreaming and out of body experience that entangles the dissociative effect of the additional NMDA antagonist. The difficulty there was to make them compatible. The same is true of the added effects from alkaloids that induce psychedelic and associated experiences; for Dina especially important are the entheogenic, deliriant, and empathogenic aspects, the mystical bonding with the anonymous men and women who assault her. She has, in fact, recognized some of them later though she never actually sees them while being used. And my God, the amount of testing she had to do, almost dying once—" "Honey, please this is boring. Can't we get down to action?" "Out of body experience?" I asked. "If she can't sense her body, isn't that redundant or ridiculous?" "No, not at all—" "Please you two, stop. You must be horny with the injection you had, Whitey." "Oh, yes, there is also an aphrodisiac effect in this cocktail she is administered by intravenous injection," Ken said. "I thought the greatest challenge with all that was to be rid of the body load. Can't have body effects if you are to null out the body. But my god, what a psychonaut. You ought to see her entrained to shpongle." The other woman had walked over, or rather been dragged over, by one of the men who had her by her disheveled hair, dishwater blonde with frosted highlights cut in a shag shorter in front that didn't reach her upturned, pointed tits but draped her bony shoulders, the longer drapes hanging down her back. He pushed on a dildo or whatever it was protruding from her asshole with his other hand. A fatter dildo protruded from between a pair of stick legs with knobby knees and rickety incurved spindly calves. Hardness emanated from her visage, a defiant set to her mouth and mean eyes so dark the pupils were not visible. When they were close enough I saw the man was Mule. There was no

461

doubt. He didn't acknowledge me, so I played along as if we were strangers. He dragged her lifting her just off the ground by her hair and the tail hanging from her butthole so she scampered on her toes to keep up, her feet barely contacting the floor. "Come on, bitch," he said to Claire, "we need you to get back to the program. My crew ain't diggin' them little bugle-nosed thingies." She ignored him. "Whitey, this three-way nympho is Nikki," indicating the one in tow. Mila joined us and stood beside me. She whispered, "Look at Ken. He likes this stuff. See?" and motioned toward his groin from the hair of which emerged a tiny erection. "I needs these two for the weekend," Mule said to Ken. "You had them last weekend," Ken said. "That was different project. They worked a crib with some other ho's for the experience of it and they own pleasure. Ax 'em they din't dig it". He asked Nikki, "You dug it, right ho?" pulling her off the ground again as she slapped at his hand. "The homeys thought they was sparse, you dig? This time's payback to the community." "Being a whore in the ghetto was one of the peak experiences of my life," Nikki said rapidly and evidently in some distress as he pulled her hair and the artificial tail so her head almost snapped off her neck as she raised up off the ground onto tip toes. "Me, too, honey," Claire said. Mila went to her knees and put her mouth over Ken's barely visible excuse for an erection. "Anyways, this be a charitable project," Mule said. "I got a 'bandon'd crib with couple 'bandon'd rides in front out by the hearta East Palo Alto, hearta the hood and not just at the edge, out by the inner fence where them wet lands is. They be working the back seat of them two old heaps, you know. And I gots a pair of stickers to put on them cars say *My child a honor student at Palo Alto High School.*" Ken sighed and Mila stood. "Can I watch this time?" Ken asked. "From the crib, but not up close so's to not scare off the johns." "Maybe you can clean up, dear. Can he?" "Only on breaks. You get a break ever two hours. You gon' stay Friday night through Sunday night, bitches. Got it? Breaks for supper and lunch, maybe a little breakfast, but try to get more nourishment from the free protein. That gon' be yo' pay. You bitches do a good job and my crew attend you soree." "Soiree," Claire said. "Whatever," he responded. "Now get you asses together, bitches." He dragged them away and forced them to their knees, back to back, and inserted the free dangling end of the appendages hanging from Nikki's holes into the correlative holes of Claire, using a key that tied the two women together asshole to asshole and cunt to cunt. He turned the key back and they locked together. I wondered how they'd be unlocked, given that nothing seemed to have been injected. "We'll see you at auction," Claire said before someone stuffed a cock in her face. "You bitches ain't seeing nobody nowhere. You gonna be tied up some time right here. You got miles of verge to ingurgitate. Inspired by infants suckling, you dig? Now get to copping them verges." "That is an improvement on Dina's invention," Mila said. Ken stood watching as the two headed beast's ankles were joined together with a padded pair of double Velcro cuffs. "I thought they injected something to fill those things. How the fuck does that work with the key? "Magic. *Colar Velcro,*" Mila said. "Pun. *Colar Velcro* is lesbian term in Brazil. To eat pussy. Also here ankle-collar Velcro." She snorted. "How the fuck did Dina get here?" realizing that she likely didn't know how the fucking things worked. "Oh, Hansel Romanof, he brings projects here to speed development and add stochasticity and acausality to transmogrification. I hope yer feelin better, dude. Cause I'm better. Yer thingy remains hard, anyways, but keep that weeping little dingus away from me. For now. Til we get in Wenona's room." I watched the Claire-Nikki two-headed cocksucker mechanization absorb the men forming two infinitely long lines, or at least long enough they seemed to disappear into the horizon, one at a time, sucking them to completion, each and every man Mule. And I thought of Dina, the party which led her to choose metamorphosis: I went with Debby, Dina accompanying Hypatia on the special deal they'd cooked up, for which they'd asked permission. Oddly, it seemed, and odd the reaction to perhaps my quitting Dina. Instead of a date it seemed a kind of sacrifice. Some shit I never got. Barn of a place on the edge of the quarter. Debbie'd met me at my apartment. Never'd been less appealing. As if someone had smushed in her face, grown a mustache to echo her bush, amplified the formless void of her zero-curvature surface more starkly than ever, had her limp hair cut in a tattered mullet. Asked me to fuck her after the mandatory blow job. I told her I wanted to save up for the shindig, advised her to do the same. She didn't say anything but I got vibes she didn't take it well. Hypatia came upstairs while Dina, naked and blindfolded, waited downstairs in the courtyard because she couldn't get on all fours with her hands bound behind her. Hypatia gave both of us a vial of some sweet stuff to drink. She had Debbie disrobe before tying her hands and blindfolding her. Somehow Debbie glided down the rickety winding stairway as if afloat and she and Dina as if invisible walked side by side behind us sure-footedly up Bourbon across Esplanade and on to our destination which appeared to be a monstrous cypress mansion astride the middle of a block. It opened into a multistory structure that defied the conventional geometry of its exterior, apparently an extension without ceiling or walls but likely obscured by the gloom of the interior. A regal brunette standing taller than I but in ten-or-so inch stiletto heel boots, high-button patent leather black with red spats to be precise, wearing a floral design pillbox hat bordered below by black velvet and to which was pinned a black net veil pulled over dark eyes shadowed with coal dust or the equivalent, greeted us from before an open door into a dark room. Her body covering consisted of a black leather bustier from navel to encircled paps extruded up and out, their long nipples on expansive areoles leading like headlamps. She handed us a basket she called a kit and pointed to a changing room, informing us it was prohibited to wear more than a robe. Hypatia greeted her as Heather, but the woman ignored her and walked into the dark room with another party's clothing, her dimpled ass cheeks riding high atop long legs I judged heavy at the thighs and straightly narrow below the knees. When we returned in white robes, our clothes offered, she smiled and exposed a hint of buck teeth. The crooked upturned nose would have been piggish had it not been a beezer. Her pillbox hat exposed extended forehead softened by the velvet along the base above a rectangular face tapering slowly to square chin, amplifying a visage delineated with subtle hues to amplify gender but devoid of feminine empathy. "Which is yours?" she asked Hypatia in a British accent. Hypatia pointed to Dina and she stamped her hand with some luminescent mark. We received no claim ticket.

Within yards a couple intercepted us. He was short and stocky and festooned with whorls of chocolate hair. There were ringlets covering his head and his arms and torso and back and shoulders and buttocks and groin and legs and his feet. Incessantly smiling, he pumped my hand with enthusiasm, saying "I'm The Cosmic Furnace. Heard lots about you, Whitey...hello Hy. This must be the one, huh?" meaning Dina, turning his attention to Debby whose hand he kissed, smiling even wider were such an event possible, saying as he led her away, "Who might be this enchantingly rapacious slut? My, you look good enough to gobble up all by myself." Hypatia whispered in my ear "He's our host. His real name is Johann Weyer, but besides Cosmic Furnace he calls himself Marduk." His partner was a woman taller than he with deepest-brown hair. She stood slump shouldered and beetle browed, her sagging tits hanging forward at a small angle from the vertical as determined by her posture. She kissed me on the mouth; her saliva tasted of Sen-Sen. "I'm Helen. I and Furnace are your hosts. He is going to steal your girlfriend, but for compensation you get me. For now." Turning to Hypatia, "This is the sacrifice?" speaking of Dina as if she were at most an accessory. I saw the Furnace leading the blindfolded Debby by a leash tied to a collar around her neck. Trailing her were a black man and a red-headed man she led by their penises. Behind them followed a disorderly assortment of males. The parade vanished along the line to which all lines converge, the line at perspective infinity that adds compactness to vision humans otherwise find disquieting. Dina was led to the frontier of a circle drawn in aging ochre on the floor and released. Something lifted her onto or into a contraption not reflecting in my visible spectrum that held her arms in a draped hug, legs opened and gripping. "Parvati" Hypatia said and I blurted, "Who's their Ganesha?" not knowing what the fuck I meant. "You, Whitey. Look: The first Tesla suit." Robot more than suit. Nimble robot. Not metal outerwear, if outerwear it be, but shiny, flexible and simultaneously absorbent of a swathe of spectra with overlapping crinkles forming and smoothing simultaneously with each movement. "You mean there's someone in those suits?" I asked and Hypatia said, "Yes, they're driven from inside. They gather up a charge on the surface and release it through the penis; hydraulics amplify impact, ejaculate and lubricant amplified with electricity and for volume—" "They put those things inside her? Shit, they won't fit. They look like elephant trunks—" Hypatia snorted "You don't know Dina. She takes bigger—and harder." They turned the levitating Dina on her side, one at her mouth, one behind her, one in front, the hammering trio releasing streams of sparks, sizzling scorched flesh in the air, her hair standing on end, arms and legs flailing. I doubted she'd had bigger even with the horses and donkeys and dogs and baseball bats. Upon interpenetration her orifices faded at the edges, puckering as if they might implode before swallowing the prongs. She seemed unconscious when the three pulled away, grayish discharge leaking from mouth-cunt-anus. "She's dead?" I asked and Hypatia laughed. "Not yet. Wait. There's Sytri" a reddish glow and mayhap reddish hue with red eyes and bigger, much bigger, positioning himself in lotus position and torquing Dina astride his erection facing him at which Hypatia sighed and mumbled "yab-yum—kāmamudrā— immitance—" turning to me "as in immit *and* electricity—and you of course know Shiva and Shakti" as Dina quivered, her flesh overridden with rippling waves superposing interfering reforming, arms and legs twitching, sagging breasts resonating mounds of quivering jelly—"pull-in" Hypatia narrated, "injection pulling"— convulsing and emitting a wideband caterwaul oscillating rapidly—"injection locking"—Dina astride Sytri hair glowing and streaming out and away emitting sparks from atop her head forming a blue tongue of fire within the flowing nimbus as the flesh ripples settled to waveforms uniform and orderly and she bobbled up and down first slowly and then uncontrollably, modulating a yodel atop her enraptured screel at which Hypatia said—"phase locked." Rotated about the bloated phallus to face us, her mouth agape, eyes widely staring, black tongue straight out, face blankly torpefied, rising impaled astraddle as lingam prolated its confines, stretching elastic pudendum, torose base apparent as she oscillated back and forth, screamed briefly, sang in spirited glossolalia. Hypatia: "adunation—my god Whitey that woman was made to absorb torsion—look at her now, a torsion oscillator." Dina wobbling with ever wider swings. The flesh waves narrowed to quivering strips as her voice wavered and she trembled in frenzied abandon and Hypatia said "sympathetic resonance— Sytri becomes immolator" the air saturated with smell of ozone, smoke rising from Dina›s head and skin as she twitched asynchronously like a rag doll, her intonation congealed to a hum, flopping as seized in spasmodic paroxysm she was surrounded by an aura of opalescence smoothly flowing yellowish-red to cerulean harmonically "ah, finally, crystalloluminescence." It seemed as if it went on an interminable span of time: I don't remember it ending.

A day later Dina crawled to me and said, "I'm ready."

"Ready for what?"

She handed me the cardboard card from Hansel Romanof.

Her flesh bore bluish-black and red singe marks and ink-blot bruises. Rolling onto her back, she lifted her legs to display a cunt pried wide enough to pass a fist with ease, the clitoris prominent, elongated and shaped like a dickhead. "You ought see my butthole," she said and raised legs over head, bringing to light a gaping bunghole occluded by protruding red meat. Both holes glistened, glassified, around the border.

"I thought I had that card."

She lowered her legs, rolled over and scrambled back to her knees. "I knew you'd lose it, Sir."

"They did a helluva job on your holes, there."

"They're relaxing now. You should have seen them when I came to, Sir. I thought they were permanently disfigured."

"Came to? Where were you?"

In an alley behind the market down by the river. Lying in a heap of rotting vegetables. Naked. Oozing spunk from every orifice. My mouth was contused with stretching. It was late so getting home along the periphery of the Quarter was not too bad. No one attacked me."

"How'd you get in?"

"The gate was unlocked, Sir."

"What was that fucking like?"

"Quite visual. It revealed for me the design of a suit. An isolation suit, based on John Lily's isolation tank. I never gave you his book, Sir. I have a copy for you, though it now seems largely irrelevant. The fucking was more intense than anything to date, Sir."

"More than the barnyard orgies?"

"I lost consciousness with the red one, Sir. It seemed to go on forever."

"I thought you'd blow a fuse."

"I did. It rewired me, Sir. Showed me the way."

I bade her paint herself yet again as a caricature of a prostitute and put on yet one more tank top with nipples peeking from below and the opened out cut-offs that showed her ass and the gladiator sandals that strapped to mid-calf. I affixed a stiff leather high collar into which her chin settled that forced her to face straight ahead, attached a leash and walked her up Bourbon Street to Marigny and on to the decrepit mansion factory of Hansel Romanof. He greeted us in an antechamber decorated in the style of a 19th century bawdy house, a man wiry of frame in loose black t-shirt, black leather pants and black work boots towering above me by half a foot or more, his pasty flesh stretched back taut along a forehead longly drawn to a high dome, all of it bald as a cue ball except the patch of beard on his chin. The constant evil-looking frown he wore didn't seem to stem from a demeanor serious so much as strict like an Old Testament prophet of Jehovah intending harm to all living creatures. With him were two limp-wristed boys continuously dropping beads atop droning susurrus overridden with girlish giggles, hinting at a firm master tabooing openly homosexual banter. The paired nellies circled Dina, touching her breasts as objects of wonder. Hansel said to me, "Finally she comes. There have been rumors of this skank braving the men's room at Lafitte's. She is ugly, no?" which amplified a subtle French accent not at all like Frenchie's. Likely a French Canadian. "She haunts places where joints are freely copped," I said. "Can you work with it?" "A remodel?" "Complete. Your blank canvas. Do with it what is appropriate according to what you have heard." "I hear she fucked most recently demons." "Suits," I said and he laughed. "The old Tesla gag." He put his face to hers and said, "Get out of the rags, bitch. And no talking. Don't want to EVER hear coherent sound from you. Only moans and screams and especially sucking noise." She removed what little she wore except the sandals posthaste. He motioned to his nelly minions and they each grabbed a tit and walked in opposite directions as far as possible, then led her around the room as he observed. "They certainly stretched her cunt and asshole, no?" He laughed without smiling. "Get the cone," he said and one of the two dashed into a back room and returned with a black traffic cone of some rubbery material. He fixed it to a chair with the suction device on the base. "Sit," Hans said and when Dina moved toward the chair haltingly he grabbed her hair and ran her to the chair, propelling her down onto the cone. She howled. "Good. Potential. I see how to proceed. You can leave her, but she must pay for the months of treatment. We are not charity." "She has money," I said, and he said, "Fuck money. I will use her as whore, charging for clients. And you," he continued, his finger in my chest, "need to be more careful where you deposit sperm. Witches today no longer require such shit as fingernails or hairs, but retain sperms in receptacles between their legs for years, even decades, utilizing it at will in genetic update of hexing. Information much more accessible and utile for exploitation. Old fashioned spells and whatnot were trial and error methods of exploiting genetics information before anyone knew about genes, you see? More scientized nowadays." I didn't respond, having received this warning from what I took to be witches about other witches. He pulled Dina up from the chair. The cone obstructed her ability to stand with its reluctance to come free of her cunt or to release its base from the chair which rose with her. Eventually the cone popped free of the chair and she lurched forward, standing as straight as possible with the massive object embedded between her legs. He had his two minions pull her around the room by her tits, she walking hunched over with short steps to accommodate the conical impaction.

"These mammaries are perfection," he said, lifting them off her chest, "and she has a start on cunt-work also. We take advantage of elastic hysteresis to lengthen nipples" twisting one until she fell to the floor, "about a foot. Seems ridiculous, no? a foot long nipples? but then the tits may be to her knees as well and these labia stretched around the cone" leaning over to pinch one as she lay on the ground, dragging her to her feet, "will reach to her knees too, and this clitoris" grabbing the knob riding atop the cone's outer surface "will be a four inch or so penis of an inch or more girth." He pinched the clitoris but Dina refused to give in to the pain. "Ah, perfect, she will absorb the pain. Much torque can be applied to this one. We can lengthen these flesh-bulbs beyond their inelastic limits by using adsorption hysteresis, or rather combining elastic hysteresis and adsorption hysteresis by inuncting special material of my design, bonding shape-memory compound with her flesh, thereby creating a form of pseudoelastic hysteresis as pseudoelastic spring with passive vibration isolation. A form of damping allowing gradual disrecovery. This keeps from destroying blood vessels and tearing tissue or overstretching to leave marks, while simultaneously relaxing tissue to extreme distortion from which it barely recovers after repeated application. Can keep tension with material applied for hours or even days without damage, only stretching to advanced limits and strengthening the piercings beyond normal skin parameters while simultaneously inducing nerve growth for hypersensitivity. Our methods are highly hysteretic. She will not be returned as she arrived, the dependence taking advantage of all her previous pathways. You know?" "Monodromy?" I asked. "You could say. A combination of curvature and singularities we apply, the result not totally ours to foresee. The singularities we control, the curvature we do not, being mostly global. Like the overstretched rubber band, there can be no return path." I thought of Hypatia, her "Locally everything is possible, globally not so much."

Ever the entrepreneur or maybe with an eye on posterity, her legacy, worry about how history would judge her, Dina filmed all of it, including this trip to the mansion. I freaked when I saw it, given as I was in it but never noticed anyone with a camera near us. The films were littered with close-up shots like in a Sergio Leone film, though less flattering. They became as famous as her zoophilia collection. Megasellers to fetishists and legal in most of the world, though God-intoxicated South Carolina tried to have someone arrested. Best known was the long (six hundred minutes in the short version, the two long versions, the entire unedited collection of film in both randomized snippet and chronologically faithful versions, said to have inspired Gérard Courant's *Cinématon*) edited montage of the many days she spent in her own dungeon with her head buried beneath the floor, her neck encircled by the metal doors with the hole in the center, the remainder of her naked body above ground at the mercy of an everlasting line of paying men and women and their pets, drunks and druggies in a party mood. Though condemned by those religious institutions that gave a shit, including the Pope, it took its place beside the works of Buñel— also condemned by The Church—in the film canon, largely through the influence of the *UCLA School of Theatre, Film and Television,* the *USC School of Cinematic Arts,* and the *Escola Superior de Teatro e Cinema* in Lisbon, as a masterpiece of surrealistic pornography. Most impressive, the segments were filmed as the art on Dina's back, emblazoned in nine sessions by a team of masters blending traditional Samoan Tatau and Japanese Irezumi with crude scarring and branding, healed. That work took several weeks to complete, including scabbing time, during much of which she stood naked with gallon jugs of water hanging from piercings in her labia and nipples, a crown of thorns on her head, staring heavenward. Hansel proved his originality in constructing devices to constrain her in rigorous requisite postures for the embossing of her skin: 1) on a platform in his workshop with her head sometimes resting cheek down on a pillow but more often in a box with only a hole for her mouth, on her knees with feet, buttocks and hands projecting through three highly polished wooden cutout boards that acted as stocks, sliding in place to form a large, smooth rectangle slightly longer than wide that clamped from above her wrists and below her ankles so that hands, buttocks, and feet protruded on the side opposite her back, legs and head, 2) again on her knees on a rectangular bench facing off the short side with her ankles and wrists manacled side by side on either half of her body by metal half-loops attached to a metal bar with holes for sliding adjustment, her buttocks raised in the air with a stainless steel hook embedded within her anus to keep it raised, head constrained to look forward by a metal collar held in place with an adjustable bar attached to the floor by a bolted-down base plate. In 2) her face is often hidden in a black bag with a mouth hole, though there exist scenes without the bag but often inserted into her mouth a variety of different attachments allowing the entry of penises, sometimes while blindfolded and other times wide-eyed. In both 1) and 2) as the work proceeded on her back, buttocks, vagina and anterior upper thighs, depending on the access provided, orderly lines of men and the occasional dog waited to be fellated by her. On her back as part of a complex scarring pattern in numerous colors emerged an image of her fellating a dog, taken from one of her European films. The cinematography won numerous awards, particularly one sequence in 2) as variable frame rates interspersed with dual imagery while the camera cuts from Dina's blindfolded face lovingly fellating a large dog penis and pans along the scar of Dina fellating a large dog penis healing on her back to the smoking flesh under the branding stamps punching along her vaginal lips, stretched and pinned by piercings with nails pounded through them into the table. One can almost smell the searing flesh as the irons raise up amidst a cloud of steam and smoke within which bluish flares ignite, are quickly doused, and reignite with the next branding in a speedily fulgurating climax capped by dog ejaculate streaming from her nostrils. Interpolated into this series were the scenes from the stretching films that document the process by which her nipples and vaginal lips were elongated beyond normal relaxation limits for human flesh. The iterated back and forth of piercing and stretching with weights suspended from rings in her vaginal lips and nipples while balancing barefoot on a crossbar wearing a metal or hard plastic helmet or a leather or latex hood with only breathing hole for mouth or nose, balance aided by ropes binding her tits tightly to purple and suspended from a bar above her, portrayed admirable endurance and concentration given the drug-induced body load accompanying it. As tits, nipples, and vaginal lips lengthened, more holes were punched, allowing more weight attached to more rings as well as further prolongation of the wire or screw type nipple-stretchers and the clover clamp or chain panty labia stretchers, lengthening in time the nipples to a foot, arcing downward with gravity; expanding the vaginal lips, long and wide like sprawling wings filled with thick rings or studs or both, reaching to her knees. Her tits gradually elongated to hang below her navel with the nipples brushing her mound of Venus. As her modified flesh surpassed the elastic limits of standard skin, realizing new values for the elastic modulus of human flesh, she would come to stand with dozens of weights suspended from each nipple or a series of large rings through both nipples and several filled gallon water jugs hanging from her vaginal lips, sometimes separately and at other times hooked through both labia, a linking that allowed her vagina to be shuttered with rings or studs. This was most often followed by rest periods using only the stretchers after which she endured hours of goat milkers relentlessly suckling her tits and clitoris as she engaged in a variety of sexual activities, frequently mechanized. Her clitoris enlarged with drug treatment into a thick pseudopenis lined with studs and topped with a pseudo-Prince Albert, erecting to four inches on arousal which became automatic and immediate via manual manipulation of any of the secret-formula balm sensitized scarred areas as well the expected hypersensitive secret-formula balm sensitized erogenous zones, but also when hearing drug-amplified mesmeric induced trigger words from common terms to Greek and Latin expressions and trigger music of varying genres, modalities and chord progressions at any and all of which she became blindly ravenous, a quivering insatiable slut without discrimination or inhibition or memory or recognition. Her anus was scarred as the center of an encircling disk painted bright orange, hyper-sensitized and surrounded by piercings to complement the ceremonial scarification of her buttocks with a series of concentric orange annuli as a target with the anus itself the bull's eye through which annuli flowed an orthogonal raised scar, one to each ring- or jewel-embedded piercing like a giant pucker or prismed scattering rainbow of hallucinatory beams, day-glo red orange yellow green blue indigo violet. Her inner vaginal lips were tattooed solidly in red for the right and blue for the left with a border of branded Rococo filigree. Tattooed on her left outer labia, a detailed yab-yum of a blue, eleven-armed Samvara in union with his consort the red dakini Vajravārāhī, while a fierce blue Kali wearing a necklace of skulls, sticking out bright red tongue and displaying with her four arms a severed penis and severed head, curved sword and trident, danced on a corpse on the outer right flap. Her face made up in permanent ink: lips gaudily tattooed dark candy apple red as if lipstick smeared outside the lines, tapered to sharp upturned corners where met upper and lower, exaggerating the dip of the philtrum like bird wings flapping symmetrically in the distance; eyes outlined starkly black as though recessed in shadow beneath yellow lashes induced unnaturally long, dense and upturned; brows permanently removed and tattooed bright green enhanced with a line of jeweled studs; cheeks rouged the same red as the lips with tattooed freckles giving a visage of twisted Raggedy Ann. Striae developed on the breasts with stretching, encouraged during the tearing of the dermis to grow to deep purple rivulets like streams flowing toward the extense nipples, hysteresis opposite that of her other stretched flesh with the proprietary bonding shape-memory compound. Added were a dual pair of scars on either side of her that looked like braid from shoulders to nipples and along the side under the axillae, flanking the breasts to the nipple. Together with the nipples which after final extension were tattooed solid black, the scars were treated with the same balm as the clitoris and vaginal lips, a special treatment that encouraged the overgrowth of hypersensitive tactilely exposed ganglia, to the end that wearing any covering on those areas led to unbearable sensitivity. The chords from her shoulders were red, those along the side blue, the rivulets of stretch marks on her tits enhanced as if tie-dyed luminescent purple along the flow toward the nipples from the attachment at the chest where they merged into an abstract expressionistic splash that covered her upper torso and shoulders. The canvas below her tits remained starkly blank so as not to distract from the prodigious pseudo-penile clitoris with its jeweled impalements and the ornate vaginal flaps which could be pinned open via flesh hooks in the inner thighs. The exception was her navel, discretely pierced but once. The bloodiest scarring came with the attachment of handles, or rather carving of handles, designed for gripping during sexual encounters, for leverage in fucking or placement in group encounters or simply for transporting her from place to place, one along her lower back crossways above her meager butt cheeks with a partner between her shoulder blades, two on the back of her upper thighs aligned with her legs, two on the sides of her hips also aligned with her legs and a final pair between

472

her breasts along her sternum with mate over her mons from navel to clitoris. Flayed free between two lines and treated with the same material applied for adsorption during the pseudolastic hysteretical stretching of nipples, tits and vaginal lips and with sufficient elasticity to provide adequate handles for large hands, the collagen bundles formed strong hypertrophic scars above the atrophic recesses that contrasted with the mixture of hypertrophic and atrophic colored scar designs on her back. To maintain consistency, the handles were colored red on upper thighs, blue on the sides of the hips and blazingly bright yellow on her lower back while the handle on the upper back blended with the underlying backdrop. The narrator in the instructional video terms the handles fortuna scars, but some film critics and body artists have commented that they are more keloid scars since they are not flush with the skin though the word fortuna resonates more tastefully. The scarring technique applied a tincture that intentionally amplified collagen bundling to block tissue regeneration; most of the hypertrophic scars artfully interweave with tasteful atrophic grooves. Branding was applied along the ropes of hypertrophic scars in designs before the coloring. Her legs were given traditional Samoan tattoo design, symmetric, which ended with solidly colored feet and ankles to match the vaginal lips. The atrabilious Hansel was often seen moping during the work, clearly ambivalent regarding the quality. But the penultimate touch, the skull, brought it all together: hair permanently removed save one pony tail (the sole remaining hair on her entire epidermis after proprietary permanent total body epilation) growing from the crown of her head, three rope-like hypertrophic scars along the top of her head, two from the eyebrow tattoos and one from between the eyes, parallel berms stretching along the quasi-sphere of her skull meeting at the nape of her neck which was pierced to accommodate a large rod with barbell ends. Two pairs of handles sculpted through bone grafts and scarring rose above her skull like ossified grips, one horny pair perpendicular to the scars across the front and back of her head, the other within the inner area between and parallel to the scars. A tasteful interweaving of tattoo and branding patterned her head from what had been the hairline over the top and down to encompass the entire neck like a Russian Easter egg, the scars a deep maroon and the four handles bone with intricate scrimshaw of Apsaras *in flagrante delicto* with animals and other creatures not of known zoological type entwined in continuous chain perhaps inspired as freak-amplification of carvings from the Khajuraho temple complex. There were the contrarian body artists and body art critics who complained the implantation of horns shaped as dual grips on either side of the handle on the back of her head was gratuitous if not over the top and redundant, but who came to be seen as wrong given the proven utility of the additions. Besides their functionality providing extra leverage in forcing deep fellatio or when fucking to pull back the head or deliver the face against chosen groins over mouth-engulfed erections, the horns emerged from two holes atop specially designed boxes, some plastic and some wooden, positioning her face within with mouth immobile over the extension of the blow-hole. This led to the design of special helmets and head masks with properties of *fellation pompage* deep splooge ingestion. Driven into the sides of her head near her ears, reformed into pointed elf ears with multiple piercings, were two stainless steel bolts for injection of electrical patterns into her brain, forerunner of implanted electrical plugs in later bodywork as forerunners of USB ports. Anthropologists and masters of body design as well as the denizens of the body-design shops waxed ecstatic regarding the documentation. The anthropologists were particularly dazzled by the fulgent critical opalescence of Hansel's oeuvre, calling it a magnificent portrayal of the dawning of a new subculture, the recording of a new and vibrant cult bifurcating, nee trifurcating, nee n-furcating into a movement of quasi-primitives with higher purpose. Hansel's final touch of genius came with the separation of the two labial meat curtains into nine paired strips, each determined by a column of piercings with a stamp of filigree branded at the bottom edge, the paired strips matched so they could be joined with empiercements, often with thick rings or with plain or jeweled studs, through the perforations separately or with custom made jeweled bars bearing studs that transfixed the lips across each row in the matrix of impalements as a single curtain or skewered to its opposite lip by screwing together the paired bars with studs, each matrix when adjoined to its dual shutting off the vagina entirely and forcing the shutting of the thighs when desired by pinning the entire structure to the inner thighs. Shuttering of the vagina could also be effected with small padlocks instead of the bars if the strips were to be joined independent of their neighbors. A rigorous program of exercise and treatment with certain unspecified drugs enhanced her vaginal musculature to the point she could crack walnuts with her cunt, vaginal prowess demonstrated in a film entitled "Nutcracker" during which she shelled an entire gunny sack of Brazil nuts. Afterward by constricting her anal sphincter she crushed an unripe green banana, then an unripe plantain, both in their skins, the sweet innards squeezed into and out of her asshole after which she defecated and farted that part ingested. Her heroic prowess milking cocks to release with her vagina and her anus, even when unconscious, became legends of modern cinema. Dina was liberally dosed with hallucinogenic, entheogenic, and empathogenic drugs together with deliriants, though they were chosen for the right moments throughout her transmogrification; she was often under the influence of a cocktail of designer drugs that included triptamines, telepathine or harmine and associated harmala alkaloids, 2C-B, phencyclidine better known as angel dust or PCP, STP or DOM as it is commonly known but technically 2,5-Dimethoxy-4-methylamphetamine, MDMA otherwise known as 3,4-methylenedioxy-N-methylamphetamine, psilocybin, lysergic acid diethylamide or LSD, belladonna and datura and associated deliriants of the acetylcholine-inhibitor family of dissociative alkaloids often applied as ointments, ALD-52 or N-acetyl-LSD and a host of other little known or unknown stuff, much of it unnamed and never before tested on humans. It had a pronounced affect on her behavior when first hooked up to the goat milking machine that was part of the exercised prolongation of her nipples for at least forty hours per week. Many doubted the veracity of her balancing act while blowing off trains of body load blasting from atop her head covered with a helmet and with weights on her tits and cunt lips. When not in treatment she remained immured under constant watch except near the end when Hansel attached a nipple-clitoris leash to her and walked her into the French quarter to different gay bars, most often a gay biker S&M bar, to service clientele. She would wear the same sort of scant costume in which she'd reported for duty, requiring extra harnesses to constrain tits and cunt lips from hanging in full view. The tits were commonly constrained with a conical apparatus that held them upright and outward stabbing the cropped t-shirt like shelves, nipples extruded from the open ends, the cunt lips hoisted up as if stage curtains, sometimes spread and stretched up against her inner thighs with chain panties rigged with hooks. These activities were also filmed and released to a mostly gay viewership. Art and film history books have stated that many tried to follow in her steps, but not many cults formed around these epigoni as the truly worthy perished with the rigors of the complete process. It is also claimed that this is a media-spread rumor started by a porn star stage-named Dolcett.

Wenona's room littered with females contorted, asses in the air, faces hovering between open legs above crotches as if attached by elongated necks at the navel, their ankles crossed and tied behind their necks, their thighs lashed behind their shoulders above the knees, arms stretched out orthogonal to trunks and affixed to benches on which they rested on their upper backs and shoulder blades. They licked their own cunts and assholes as men lined up to take turns sharing the three presented orifices with the owners snaking tongues. One woman's arms, head and calves covered in a tight black elastic hood, only her asshole and cunt available for penile intrusion, said by Mila to be "Wenona herself" in "her favorite. Now you be first with me," pulling me by my terminal erection to a wide metal ladder to which she was rigged with legs pulled back straight above her head and clamped to rungs at her ankles and along her calves, hands tied down at the wrists below her upturned ass with her arms crossing over her legs, elbows at knees. The ladder planted firmly in concrete sockets stood upright and I fucked her proffered cunt and anus, taking turns as another climbed the ladder beside her and fucked her mouth while hanging by one arm, holding her face steady with free hand wrapped in her hair. I thought it a shame her asshole and cunt were not available on either side of the device, since otherwise double penetration was impossible; as if reading my mind her cunt tightened around my dick, tugging downwardly as with an atypical display of sexual athleticism her asshole reached out and seized the penis of a man standing behind her who had inserted his copulatory appendage between the rungs in an attempt to get to said proffered asshole. Seeing her anal sphincter hunt down the anonymous organ of intromission snapped my own emission, accompanied by the pull of nano barbed wire through urethra which served to ramp my arousal beyond urgent with the sensation my dickhead would explode. I stepped back for a man with two dicks to fuck both holes as the other man continued hammering her anus, Mila gobbling the two dicks with her asshole displaying graceful greed to awe Adam Smith despite his gayness. I walked away. The ladder swarmed with men. Mila disappeared in the antlike horde.

Suspecting the worst I made a break for it, but a speck of a brunette of long torso, minute breasts, flat tummy, near zero curvature from waist to ankles, hips rectilineal and flat, meager ass tear dropped wide atop twiggy limbs, chased me down. She rolled into a ball on the floor in my path, tucked her knees behind her elbows, crossed her ankles behind her neck and raised up on her hands, a reconfigured demoniac from *The Garden of Earthly Delights*. Her sanguinarily painted physiognomy peered across sharp dual peaks of buttocks framing a boxy pelvic cavity of pronounced bony ridges of iliac crests, my eye directed along the line of a gash with studded clit from her skyward-staring brown-eye to close-set black-ringed peepers glowing at the same level. Luxurious hair as black and sleek as that hanging free of undulation to her shoulders overgrew the venereous region like a densely wooded declivity, lush from within the bony hips below the brown-eye up to the navel, densest within the length of the crack and on the mons pubis. Springing spider-like she impaled her asshole over my erection in a death grip, slamming to the floor on her back in a miraculous landing that injured neither of us. Trapped within her anus at a perpendicular to the floor in a variant of the pile driver, I felt her tuck her face into my belly and stretch the ankles which remained crossed behind her neck to grasp my head in a pincer movement with which she braced her lower structure and drove energetic hammering of her hard, meager gluteus maximus against my pelvis even as I floated above, causing me to appreciate the power of her unobtrusive gluteus medius and gluteus minimus which likely abetted the extreme lateral depression of her buttocks as well as the hardness of her lightly padded ischial tuberosity and perhaps the poor manifestation of gluteal sulcus or infragluteal fold or horizontal gluteal crease or perhaps even *ruta glutealis horizontalis* which I assumed were synonymous, not to be confused with the intergluteal cleft or vertical gluteal crease or plain old gluteal cleft or fuck it, the goddamn ass crack which also was meager and hairy on this creature pulverizing my groin as I wondered from whence the fuck came these expressions I'd never heard? while ejaculating a steady stream and I saw a pair of giant black feet with pink soles standing beside me. Straining to look up, I saw one of the pseudo-Mules who'd been with Ken and Claire bending down to unwind her ankles and free my head. He pulled her from beneath me and with fingers inserted in her three uplooking orifices with fingertip grip bowled her semi-roller into the crowd surrounding Mila's ladder with only a few spares left standing. He helped me to my feet and as I tried to take off again, snagged me. "Hold up there, Whitey. We got to go." No sign of Claire or the other attachment, Nikki, or Ken. "You the same one tied Claire and Nikki together?" "Do it matter?" "I just saw a man with two dicks." "And? That ain't no big deal. Diphallia. Happens in the real world. Rare as hell. Beats the hell outta penile agenesis. These here fuckers perfected this kind of two-dick shit with they genetic messin'-'round. Surprised you just see'n the first one. But you gots to watch that goddamn icthyic cunt, dude. You gonna lose you dick to one of them goddamn hyena contortionist bitches. What you doing in this place anyways?" "I think it was a shithole, not a cunt. Where we going?" "Torsion room. They unloading now. This here place too fucking unnatural even for here. N'I was referring to the creature, not the or'fice." "Me too." We moseyed along a poorly defined corridor that vanished by parts as we moved deeper, brick floor and walls deteriorating away to transparent gaps as we approached a partially defined door above which glowed a sign BE MORE THAN YOU CAN BE. "How can you be more than you can be?" I asked and the pseudo-Mule said "These dudes bending nature. You gonna see more in just a few minutes, soon's they get unloaded and install a complete set of eigenvalues for this here set of eigenvectors they cooking up. You dig?" "No." He stopped and stared. "Shit's gonna resonate with them eigenvalues, like that cunt Maria Padilha. That Pomba Gira get her a complete set and the modes gonna get resonant on your dumb ass. Structural vibration." I didn't respond and he stopped talking and stared. "Man, you are one hopeless fuck. You ought be perusing Antônio Alves Teixeira and forget that Brownian motion shit on manifolds." He shook his shaggy head, the myriad short braids waving like tentacles on a land-locked anemone. We dropped into the room from an unseen portal. Or more likely we appeared in the room, since there was no experience of any ride along a gravitational geodesic. I'd long since stopped trying to make sense of sensory input.

There proceeded unloading. Identical wooden crates, finely finished and stained and strapped with shining metal bands padlocked shut, upon which rested wooden cubes with single rounded slot across the middle of the section opposite the padlocked snaps. It was difficult to focus on specific objects without the surrounding visual milieu deteriorating into a pointillism of saltative dots smeared across a spectrum of hues not from nature, blurring edges and jabbing the naked eye. "Yeah," pseudo-Mule said, "it ain't you eyes. Spectral ambiguity. Emanations from building the room, dig? Like uncertainty principle in harmonic analysis, Fourier transform and all that time and frequency shit a la Gabor. I think somebody talking 'bout maybe fillin' in with some wavelets, but that just talk. Clears up fine soon's they get it up with completion of eigenvalues and basis of associated eigenvectors." I tuned him out and watched the background fill in with crates lifted from a truck bed by some unseen crane beyond visual range and brought to ground swinging freely to land on four or possibly five small wheels if I made one out in the center of the crate, out of sight when lowered sufficiently near the floor, the landings stabilized by some bundled rag characters lining them up along a row of two parallel wooden slats running beside a wall that stood unattached sprouting out of nowhere with wooden shelves attached at fixed close intervals, the fronts blunted so they looked like wide skateboards. A polished two-by-four varnished to match the wooden devices attached to the wall at perhaps three feet or so above them was dotted with pairs of eye bolts screwed into the wood on either side of the shelf, also into the lower slat nearest the wall and probably into the rear of the front slat, though I could not make it out. A stone wall in advanced disrepair took shape across a distance of a dozen or more meters from the green wall into which the wooden slats were affixed. Padded leather benches, cushions perched atop pairs of black metal poles secured to the floor on bolted stands, lined the wall at regular short intervals. From the wall behind them protruded clamps formed in U shape of parallel black pipes crossed with short black cross pipes as wrist or ankle restraints.

"What the fuck is this?" "This the room they gonna test new bitches for shit like stress relaxation and torsional rigidity. These be closed manifolds, dig? Like compact without boundary closed. Sometimes they got boundary, but then they got to specify if the conditions Dirichelet or Neumann. Not doing that shit too often. Mostly when they do they tie the fucking boundary down, so they go Dirichelet, but you been in one with boundary flapping in the breeze with normal derivatives and all that shit. This here be compact without boundary, dig?" "No." "I thought you was hip to all this jive. What give's?" "I don't get it. Someone, maybe Maria, tried to convince me we're on some big-ass high-dimensional manifold with fibers attached or something. I'm supposed to believe this? And there are creatures projected down here and there are some creatures building rooms, rather submanifolds, from the eigenvalues of the Laplacian or some operator in here?" "More or less; you got it. The enveloping space mayn't be no manifold; maybe Frechet or some shit. So the fiber shit ain't to be taken too serious. Dig?" I shook my head. Before I could say more, he went on, "This here a test room for auction. They's two parties gonna bid for two special bitches, then the rest's open—like a vendue. But not the first. High bid gets to choose, the other goes to the loser. Testing harmonic entrainment." "More like brainwave entrainment, actually." A female voice from behind, bland without accent, drawl or other characteristic. California, I thought. She spoke as if she knew what she was talking about. "Entrainment?" I asked, turning to see a pair of women. The one speaking spoke again. "You know. Christiaan Huygens. Pendulum clocks coming together harmonically though not necessarily in phase. In this case, one master uses natural means, which may include herbs like Telepathine, but mostly disciplined training including modern and ancient torture. The other one implants devices, especially in the brain, develops and administers drugs not found in nature, some of them created with an eye to individual chemistry, uses high tech equipment and makes horizontal genetic modifications in situ. Maybe we'll see a death state today." She stood about five six, short but at least six inches taller than the other. Kind of a bulbous nose, the sort of face your mother'd used to call cute to keep from using the term homely which more likely would come from your father or brother. As in: She's nice (even if she's homely). Or your brother; Man she's ugly; her beezer's bigger than her tits. To which the response would be, Yeah, but they're both blunt. She'd painted her eyes with blue-green eye shadow. Her tits flattened against a lean torso as if squashed with no hang, nipples blending into small dark red areolae. Would've been straight without hips were it not for the nascent saddle bags forming at the top of her thighs. Her legs were slender without a lot of curvation despite the beginning of those saddlebags, but she revealed herself with a three-sixty and I saw that her ass, skinny from fore or hind view, bubbled towards the rear with a pronounced indentation at the sides of the cheeks. Ugly-sexy, I thought. My erection dribbled. They both noticed. "Happy to see me?" she asked and the other said "It's an honor." "I never thought I'd get to meet Manley 'Whitey' Butcher" the bubble-butt said. "I'm Sasha; this is Joanna" indicating the ultra-short brunette. Mule asked Sasha, "You that western writer's kid?" She laughed and her companion giggled. Sasha would've seemed brunette were it not for Joanna, beside whose black hair, despite the shock of crimson flowing from amidst the center-parted mop hanging to her mid-back, it was a drab brown. The drab brown matched her rampant bush, but the other one was clean-shaven. Joanna had plenty of tattoos on her arms and her back and her legs, masks and skeletal female faces. I ignored them, having had my fill of tattoos with Albina who no one could match given hers glowed from within through translucent skin. Instead I examined Joanna's face: coal-lined dark eyes; lips painted the same crimson as gushed from the top of her head, the upper thinner and curvaceous, the lower plump and pouting down toward the sudden, lightly dimpled chin. An unreceding rounded chin with slight dimpled prominence arching infinitesimally towards the lower lip consistently completed the sharp angularity of the V-shaped face that was long though the forehead partly hid beneath hair combed to the sides. Her heavily drawn black brows swept near the eyes set back within hooded sockets. Unlike Sasha's mashed bulbous button, her nostrils widened on a long, straight, narrow bridge that flared more rapidly as it swooped down from amidst her eyes than did the nearly imperceptible decline slope towards a gently aduncous ending. A gypsy's face, or rather my idea of a gypsy's face. I copiously wept ooze from my turgid penile protrusion, now growing more uncomfortable as it puddled on the floor. The gypsy eyed it. "Whitey, we'd no idea such a projection was available from you." "We ought to have guessed," Sasha said. "Dina wouldn't choose just any old cock." She reached for my penis and I stepped back. "Dina's a Goddess," she said. "How the fuck you know my name? Or Dina?" "You're famous, Dude," Sasha said. "Yeah. Dina's the mother of us all, man," the gypsy said. "She's the model entrepreneur who followed her bliss, not for the money. When the Supreme Court decided if cooze was fungible, she was the deciding condition. That penis-obsessed Clarence Thomas saw the light and cast the deciding vote." "In her interview she gave you credit; said you'd made her." "I didn't make anybody." "She's the self-actualizing heroine of Maslow's hierarchy of needs, dude. The model. A true modern Goddess. She's in the hands of a higher power." "A saint. She answers to that higher power alone." Mule, not to be left out, jumped in. "They looks for bitches here what transcends normal sexuality but what can be controlled." "Dina is not fodder for here," Joanna said. "Too unruly. Self-actualization is not suited for this program." "We're not in the product bundle anymore, dudes," Sasha added. "Well, she didn't need direction from me," I said. "Actually, I was more an excuse. She decided her own means without my guidance. She didn't ask; she told." "You weren't paying attention," Sasha rejoined. "What fucking program here?" I asked. Mule came back. "These bitches be volunteers. They needs more but in structure. Dig?" "Dina chooses her own structure. Right now she hangs from the ceiling of a warehouse in downtown San Francisco, rigged up so that without ever seeing her face men or women who pay to enter can lower anatomical sections to bugger or fuck or get sucked off, among a plethora of activities. She wears a hood; never sees anything. Does that for a master, but when she's had her fill of that action she'll buy her freedom." Sasha was speaking but I looked to the gypsy again. "It ain't the same one you sold her to before you left New Orleans," she said. I didn't tell her I hadn't left New Orleans. "It all about eigenfunctions and eigenvalues, dig? What they need's bitches who be eigenfunctions orthogonal to they sister bitches. A infinite collection to be complete, but they gonna be a while." "Who they? What the fuck? Eigenfunction?" "That why they building this here room, man. See? not the same set as for this here room, but modes important, too, and…" "The Laplacian is God's tuning fork," Joanna blurted and pseudo-Mule came back with "That ain't right. Pyretic cunt." "More like an electric arc, point source from an arc welder, instantaneous point source of heat," Sasha said. "But sound's better than heat. This room's God's vibrating bladder," she continued. "I mean, there's no boundary so the first eigenvalue's zero and then the rest are positive and you don't need to worry about Dirichelet or Neumann boundary conditions, since they're irrelevant here." "Okay, I get this: you claim someone's building some sort of manifold from eigenvalues. I can prove existence of a weak solution to the Dirichelet problem in a bounded domain same as anybody, but what the fuck's…" "…that got do with women?" Joanna asked. "Assuming the former makes sense, precisely," I said, scoping out her hairless body while overlooking the fading-ink tattoos: Lean structure without excessive bulges on a curvaceous compact frame, proportioned appropriately except perhaps a trifle longish mons veneris, the slight hips and rounded ass growing from their ambient shape without exaggeration. "Eigenwhores," pseudo-Mule said. "These bitches got cunts resonate with proper administration o' some dick in they holes keeping them from simple connectedness." "Shut the fuck up about eigenwhores and bitches, will you? None of them are bitches and they aren't eigen- or any other type of whores," Sasha countered. "Fill all they orifices they be nearer simply connected Godliness…they cunts be bladders vibrating with them eigenvalues…" "Supreme court said they ain't that," Joanna said. "Shut him the fuck up, will you Sash?" "Why me? Can't you do it." Joanna was watching me ogle her tits which once must have stood roundly outward bound from mid torso with uplifted nipples, no sag or wrinkles, the sort of small breast that pointed down sharply when on her knees, now a pair of deflated bladders stretched flat against her chest, lines of stretch marks along the connection with the torso, the right longer than the left, elongate brownish-black nipples pointing orthogonal to the plane of her body from within purplish-brown warty areolae. She leaned towards me and the paps drooped like tubules with putty squeezed to the nipples skewed outward with an oblique angle between them. "You like them, don't you?" she said. "Sasha, I think he wants me. You take care of bigmouth over there," but Sasha, on her knees, had already worked the flaccid cock into her mouth with pseudo-Mule mouthing encouragement, Mmm suckit, come on suckit accompanied by moans, groans, ahhs, ohhs, suckits, suck the cock—on her knees Joanna's pendent tubes hung narrow at their connection, fattening towards nipples that forced pendular swaying about a wide gap—Mule talking faster: swallow it, oh fuck—I looked over and watched Sasha inch the entire erection into her face to which he said swallow it, mmm, ohh, suckit c'mon suck 'at cock, moaning goddamn, suck the tip, open that white mouth, c'mon suck it, gonna piss in yer asshole—"Don't look at them" from Joanna licking my penis, licking the unending drainage from the tip, looking up at me with my dickhead in her mouth—open your mouth!, suck that meat, c'mon there you go, swallow it, suckit! open up! god—I looked over at them again: Sasha had the end of it in her mouth, stroking the length of it with both hands—Joanna nipped me with her teeth and I returned to her, "Let me fuck you doggy style," I said and I watched them as I bent behind her—suck on the tip, suck that cock, gag on it, go down ten times, c'mon, he held her head and counted, she wiped the ooze from her nose with the back of her hand, lots of slurping from her, suck that black cock, dirty girl, suck that black meat, oh oh oh, more slurping, suck that cock, clean it up, suck it, oh damn, oh god, I'm gonna cum in your mouth, I'm gonna cum, slurping to accompany his clean it up, eat that cum, swallow it, open your mouth, get it down there, more slurps and other wet noises, swallow it c'mon clean it up, yeah yeah yeah moaning amidst more slurps from Sasha as white ejaculate oozed from the sides of her mouth and around the obstruction, open that mouth, open it, swallow it—I let go inside Joanna and she guided me into her anus, pushing against me pegged to my dick, forcing her asshole along my erection—Sasha watched us, saying to no one in particular, "My bum may be big but its round and according to Saint-Venant's theorem that gives it more torsional rigidity" to which pseudo-Mule said, "We gotta couple eigenskanks here, but t'ain't nothing like that super-eigenwhore Maria Padilha: she a Fourier series expansion of eigenwhores, Dude." Sasha said, "You know that Dina wouldn't work out here because her spectra's not all eigenvalues; opposite end of the spectrum, all adventure and too much self-actualization, too hard to control" to which pseudo-Mule replied, "Yep, no resolution for her—" and Sasha popped back "She doesn't need a resolution of her identity!" and I thought Women with big tits don't need to be justified and pseudo-Mule said, She ain't normal; neither that ho Maria Padilha." Then directed at me, "You don't hurry with that eigenho you fucking in the ass there you gon' miss the big show, Bro'" and sure enough, a series of platforms like tree stumps with sufficient diameter to allow one human to stand with ankle short-chained to a metal ring in the block about which swarmed men and women and others not so casually classified feeling the naked, hooded females, invading orifices, caressing breasts, tweaking nipples, pulling labia, two platforms in front and more behind drifting to vanish towards the line at infinity. The boxes atop the crates were removed and there appeared from beneath them women's heads, some of them blindfolded or hooded which removed revealed made-up faces in lipstick, eyeshadow, rouge, all of it applied with a bent found more often in exotic dance bars or freakish clown shows than shopping malls, or maybe not. The crates opened to reveal naked bodies, some tattooed and some scarred as if by whipping or otherwise decorated, the occupants marched to one of the two walls depending upon the symbol branded into the front of the crates, of which but two possibilities existed by induction on the crates visible. Those marched to the side with the skateboard-shaped shelves all had small sockets implanted in the sides of their heads near the temple, some sort of connectors evident within a glabrous patch; those on the other side showed scars and each wore a branded upside down M covering the right buttock. Before I could ask, Sasha said "Crazy M, for crazy meat," and pseudo-Mule said, "Precision synchronized fuck teams. Old school and new fangled electronic school that spare the whip and spoil the bitch." "Like water ballet but fucking," Sasha said. "We prefer to call them synchronized tup teams," Joanna pulling away before I went off again. "Man, you are wearing me out. I mean, boring. Shit. You need help." "He seems to not be able to get it down," Sasha said, laughing. "S'not funny," I said. "They gon' be testing for kernels" Mule interjected and I looked over at him, standing arms akimbo, limp dick hanging to his knees dribbling, "What? Kernels?" "Heat kernels, like." "Metaphorically heat," Joanna put in. "More like lust kernels—" "—or skank kernels" pseudo-Mule added, sounding peeved he'd been interrupted. "E'ry man want his bitch coupling indiscriminately. Jus' cain't deal w'it social-like. Porn fills the void, 'stead o watching they bitches doing a room full of niggers with giant nigger dicks, dig? Cepting a small minority like them freak swingers out there, Ken and Claire and that ugly friend o' hers do absolutely anyfuckingthing: her old man just eat that shit the fuck up. Other dudes and some of they bitches just get off watchin' a proxy bitch in a movie." "It's safer," Sasha said. "Sort of like a point source of *hysteria libidinosa*," Joanna said. "Or nymphomania," pseudo-Mule said, to which Sash replied "No such thing. Really what Joanna said as a function of plain old need for humiliation." "You ought know," pseudo-Mule said, but neither of them paid attention to him. The crowd had cleared from around the woman on the block to my right. Joanna said, "I'm going down to check out the ones in back. I want to get in a bid or two. You coming Sasha?" I couldn't believe I was discussing the heat kernel again in a completely different context, now building bitches instead of rooms, when pseudo-Mule said, "They needs harmonic bitches. Lots of bitches in the same cohomology classes, de Rham, I mean, dig? but they needs the harmonic reps to resonate purely enough. Hit that base harmonic—" "You are so full of shit, man" Sasha said to him, then to Joanna, "I'm going to stay here. See if you can send up a notion of forcing that gives old eternally dripping hard-on there a generic extension for control—" "Complete control?" "Sure, why not. It'd be awesome. Hard, soft, ejaculate at will, fast ejaculation, slow ejaculation, quantity, all of it. He'd have all the qualifications for a great actor. And please, get a generic chain. I am not about to round up a bunch of branches of some goddamn tree structure—" "So a complete sequence, in the ancient jargon?" "Pullease!" "Well, it might be slower than a filter, you know." Sasha rolled up her eyes. "Sure, a complete sequence of forcing conditions so he can at least regain control, but better give him more control, or even complete control over that monster schlong of his. And Joanna, a sequence *is* a filter." "You know what I meant, asshole. Maybe some of that shithead's" motioning to pseudo-Mule "egesta went to your head. A filter that is *not* a sequence. Like in the old time point-set topology you studied in middle school." "In first-countable spaces sequences are enough," I shouted. "Shut up," Sasha said. "If we want any shit out of you we'll squeeze your head. There is no information in your statement for anyone here, given we already know all that." "We sure as hell don't need to squeeze his dick," Joanna said, disappearing from view pursued by Sasha's words, "Well, Dina'd've been a perfect harmonic rep of the highest dimension were she not so fucking uncontrollable," to which pseudo-Mule added, "Yeah, you go, bitch. I might let you suck me off 'gain, or maybe take it in th'asshole. But you right, them fucking bitches with too much self-actualization—" I mumbled to myself, "No chains. Unchain my heart…" Sasha put her hand over Mule's mouth. "Quiet and I might let you cream-pie in my butthole later. Let's see if you can can it for a bit."

Standing alone on the auction block, ankle chained, eyes shrouded within a black hood, the woman exuded a calm that belied her circumstances. Two men in cowls as wide as tall, their backs to me, scribbled on clipboards. One of them rubbed the inside of her left thigh and inserted his hand into her vagina. He made a fist and continued until he'd buried his arm to the elbow, she tightening her upper torso but otherwise not reacting. He shoved and I thought she might fall from the pedestal, but she obliqued her knees and deliberately ground her hips against his fist. "Don't worry," Sasha said. "She's been through more. Final test to get to this stage is dogging in a public British park where strangers show up, some of them with trained dogs, for a public humiliation. Before that, it's swing parties, at some of which she'd be auctioned off, and vicious public gang bangs in bars. Male and female antagonists. Word is that she did a hell of a job at an old folk's home with wards full of old men they'd primed with Viagra. Said she felt compassion for them. Old ladies, too." She stared at the woman, now free of the fist, wistfully. "I attended some of the tests. She performed with aplomb. I didn't get to see that one with the ancients. Beautiful, isn't she?" Her symmetrical and substantial breasts hung from mid

485

chest, the same uniform olive tone as the rest of her untouched-by-sun skin. They didn't hang slack against her torso but defied gravity, projecting outward delicate pink nipples amidst pink areoles of slight but non-zero eccentricity with vertical semi-major axes, smooth and directing the eye to the extensive arc sweeping gracefully with slight negative curvature away from the chest far below slight shoulders and slender arms without hint of muscular definition, accentuating the sharper orbicularity of faster positive curvature flowing globular upward from below where they rose from the ribcage instead of sprawling against the longish abdomen high above a bejeweled navel. Her tits were corpulent from the side. No apparent bones, no ribs or sternum, only the bony shoulders. She seemed padded but on a lean frame without musculature or fat, the trunk from the base of her breasts to her darkly thatched mons equally divided by the navel and flat. A stew of connection, recognition, familiarity, sense of impending loss and regret overwhelmed me. Foreboding. This would not end well. "Who are the two monks?" "Those guys in the monk's habits are not monks. They're twin brothers, wealthy as hell, who do this stuff as a hobby. They develop these synchronized fuck teams as a competition. One uses traditional bondage and discipline and torture methods, the other modern electronic control technology. They have networks to find and bring along these women, like scouts in baseball. There are male counterparts, by the way, but these two are not gay. They woo prospects and develop them to this point. The two here are special, meant for leadership of the crew. They first go through a final test here, then bidding. Winner chooses one of them. They later go through the same training as the schlubs to prove they are capable—" "They bid money? Seems weird, just these two bidding against each other. Seems they could just sort of agree prior—" "Not money. The others up with vendue, where Joanna's going to bid, are for money. Or sexual favors, or humiliation, depending on the auctioneer. Those are the ones don't make the grade for either of the twins. They've already determined which of the inferiors they want as crew members. The twins meter their sexual reaction to the test performance of the special ones, which don't come along often, by the way. Higher score wins. The inferiors, the scouts develop them at training camp where they try out. They make it or not. This is different." I stared at the woman on the stand. I wanted her despite the bag over her head. Or maybe because of it. Desire abeyant; anxious. The idea of Maria Padilha as a direct sum of eigentines inserted itself, a fucking system of eigensluts, a Fourier series of eigentrulles expanded with fundamental frequency of venereal desire and frantic overtones of polymorphous perversity, unlike Dina with fundamental frequency of cathectic energy focused on dissociation ending in sluttish fugue; not Fourier series but more like Fourier integral. Or not. I fought off the intrusion and saw the expansion of Mirabelle or Albina the translucent tattoo-job touch-stone with holes as strumpet in residence for the Baron and his animal farm, Jezebel guide to the needy. Dina's spectrum not all eigenvalues; probably no eigenvalues. I saw that. Unbounded trollop so esurient for degradation she didn't always resonate purely enough to be expanded, no functional calculus of wantonness except guided by fideism of pure askesis of abstinence inverted. "The other one will have big boobs, too, I'm betting," Sasha said. "The brothers like substantial tits on tall women with lean frames. You'll see." She sounded jealous. "They're retiring two team captains. Is hard to get the frame to remain lean enough, so retire them with generous pensions when longish in the tooth. S'not easy to retire two captains at once. I cun't believe it, actually; this's a rare event. But those two twins, fat and disgusting…" She shuddered. Mule piped up, "The brothas dig that butterball bubble-butt you got back there, bitch, don't you fret that none." She smiled at him and rubbed said butterball against his groin. At my groin kneeled a short, bony woman with bushy brows, thick hair cascading below her shoulders covering her chest, thick hair billowing from her armpits and rampaging around her crotch up to her navel above which showed a faded blue tattoo of a geometric pattern, perhaps a mandala, with a scar from a cut running through it that reached from her navel to between her smushed breasts. A small goatee sprouted on the end of her chin and a straggly mustache grew over her upper lip. The hair was dark like milk chocolate but the growth on her head showed variation from auburn to chestnut to mahogany. She sucked my dick as behind her branched a tree of women in several lines, growing as I watched, females of all sizes and shapes and degrees of hirsuteness. "Looks like she couldn't get a fucking sequence. Shit." Sasha looked out at the spreading filter of women. I said, "The Riemann integral inspired the notion of nets in topology—" "Will you shut the fuck up?" she said, "filters generic in your frame are what we need in this Boolean valued model, to force these conditions—" "Assuming they all coherent," Mule said, staring at the woman slobbering over my erection, shaking his head and walking away mumbling "take me forever to 'jaculate in that ugly mug; they sure she a woman?" "She's a woman," Sasha said. "Compatible conditions, to be precise. These women are coherent because they tell a story. They describe something, for sure. Every pair of females here's got a common extension, see? What we got here's a trivial filter, see? There's a bit of her in all of them. It's all generic. Trivial ultrafilter with every kind of unappealing woman, this being the basic one here. Could've been worse, dude. We will surely force some kind of control into a generic extension of your world view, your frame, whatever one chooses to call your model. We need the interpretation and the range of that interpretation and that range is the generic extension of your frame by this filter. You can see the interpretation: *look!*" I looked. One could see that the hairy woman was the meet of the heads of the branches directly behind her, but conditions diffused along the branches as they receded into a horizon time-varying curve with multiple vanishing points. The curve altered course subtly, perturbed to small deviations punctuated by sudden discontinuous jumps to new configurations, I guessed a solid horizon figure of more than three dimensions rotating into view three dimensional projections joining multiple vanishing points inside and outside the visual field. I thought of perspective in lattices. Clearly coherent, but the image or whatever it described could not be discriminated. "I'm guessing the filter's a result of some parasexual process," she continued, her voice droning senselessly as the hairy mutt worked her hairy muff over my erection and I gazed at the woman on the stand whose entire body from the neck down two women covered with blue goo so she appeared encased in blue pudding that dried to the texture of latex. They ripped it from her leaving her free of hair, most noticeably the trimmed V of curly dark brown hair that had covered her mons down to between her legs. Probably denuded of stubble on her legs and armpits and dark fine hair on her arms not visible due to distance. Rectangular hips interrupted the flow of her torso with boxy abruptness. Not protrusion, but a cylindrical extension the width of her waist that led to anticipation of a flat ass belied as the two female handlers, releasing the shackle on her ankle, turned her for further inspection revealing from the side a rounded orb that narrowly fell away from delineated muscle stretching down across her upper thigh, a tensor of some ilk given the elasticity illuminated by a gentle depression of the cheeks. From the rear view, filled-out butt cheeks formed a teardrop beginning to give way to gravity and her upper legs fell away sharply from the squared off pelvic girdle to a false impression of the beginnings of saddlebags without hint of gob or cellulite, pronounced instead by slender legs that tapered gradually to well-turned ankles, legs proportioned in keeping with the stretched lean torso. A new creature worked on my erection though I was not sure I had ejaculated or whether this one was number two or later. From beneath her asymmetrically brown hair plunged an extended narrow face of the same width from hairline to chin framed

488

by the shag mop hacked unevenly from eye level to chin. She'd painted her eyes and penciled her arched brows black. Her mouth covered the width her face. When she smiled she showed oversized teeth collared with wide, pink gums. Her beak inhabited significant area on her face and was nearly as wide as her mouth when it bulged to culminate the extended narrow bridge overwhelming the geometry of her visage, crooking downward as it expanded with an illusion of protruding nose hair. A pronounced nasolabial fold erupted with her smile; where the smile line on the right met her face at flared nostrils rested a large brown mole. On her upper lip a shadow. Her round tits rode a meager frame without sagging and were fat enough they protruded beyond her ribcage with separation enough they did not touch, instead bordering a sternum in high relief. Widely globate buttocks formed into short ham-like thighs descending to blocky knees narrowing to short straight calves, gams that mismatched the upper torso inelegantly. It didn't add to the visual aspect that she bent at the waist to munch my erection rather than kneeling, but it was apparent that the erection had moderated in urgency and drool, if not in extent and girth. Meantime pseudo-Mule'd shoved his dick up Sasha's ass as she bent forward in the same ungainly pose as the one polishing my knob. After an initial grunt, she maintained an unconvincing running commentary "oh baby oh oh fuck that asshole stick that big black cock up that dirty asshole hit that sweet spot oh oh oh baby I love big black cocks up my dirty ass ream that shithole gimme that rotor rooter baby c'mon shoot me that white goo enema oh baby fill me with black sperm…" I tuned her out and concentrated on the woman on the stage. Mule started his own commentary "See they getting set to take that hood off her head there. They gon' fit her with a helmet too. Lookit them other" pointing at the women lined up along the two walls "bitches in the dorsal decubitus at Present Orifices" who were aligned on either side on their backs, ankles attached to the wall high above them with legs spread while on the wooden benches their wrists were fastened beside the benches and on the pole-mounted cushions the wrists were restrained to the wall directly below them near the floor. Each of them had been fitted with a silver metal helmet that covered the cranium. "That the helmet. And see they eyes? They dark, like solid black. They contacts that don't 'low no light." "Blinded with contacts?" "Yeah. Better'n any fucking blindfold." Sasha's tone changed as she watched the preparations, more noise and less diction; suddenly animated, she thrust her ass against his groin, butt cheeks jiggling as if under a direction of vigoroso. "And they moving in the robotic fuckers." Square boxes were mounted on stands bolted to the floor with protruding dildos

489

that made my cock small by comparison. By cranking a handle behind each machine, the fake organs of intromission were fixed at the verge of the gaping cunts by rotating a handle behind the machine. "See they gots them just aligned now. And they self-lubricating, too. See that shit transuding out over them dildos? slimy grey shit sweating out microscopic pores in them flexible prongs. It silicone grease. This here nasty bitch gots a ass full of it so's it's easy entry" she exclaiming more authentically now, as if from pain "she wishing she down there with one them robot fuckers in her asshole" and she began whimpering. "She jealous that first bitch down there. Soon they gonna be testing that bitch." "Test?" "Like I said, entrainment test. Dig?"

They removed the hood from her head. It was Joelle. "They gon' inject binaural beats directly in the brain through that there helmet. Now see that helmet on them other bitches hardwired to they fucking machine? that make each bitch and box a independent oscillator, dig? She gonna be put in that chair behind her there and hoisted up on that there pole behind her sitting over that hole with the dildo sticking up there and they gonna ratchet it up to the tip of her defile and her helmet gonna be tied to that machine and she gonna be an oscillator gotta take control first that machine and then entrain them other bitches—" "Uuuugh uuuugh goddamn" Sasha sobbing "Christiaan Huygens the fucking horologist" bawling that last out "More like van der Pol" pseudo-Mule corrected her. "Self-sustained oscillations from driving injected external force, dig? the injected binaural beat, gotta be overcome. For this here bitch to be queen bitch she cain't be no passive oscillator, dig? So gotta be active quenching, then phase or frequency locking, depending on how it viewed, on them other ho's. I thinks of it as phase locking. Some's call it synchronizing chaos." I tried tuning him out as I watched them strap Joelle into the chair and raise it up above us all. They cranked a dildo from below to the entrance of her vagina and then cranked another into her anus, the latter a thick plug several inches with a longer projection on the end, maybe four or five inches. "That butt plug be for lateral stabilization purposes. What you gonna see here's the spectrum o' this here ho'. I doubt she all discrete. I mean, she ain't compact, dig? If this bitch be normal, we gon' see us a spectral integral representation. We gon' see how rich that continuous spectrum be, dig?" "You're out of your fucking mind," I said. He laughed and gripped Sasha by her forearms and pummeled her like a rag doll as she drooled and frothed and hit a rhythmic ah-ah-ah-ah...: sinusoidal crying of the same period as the pummeling. Entrained, as it were. "See, this bitch gonna be like coupling mechanical with thermal fields. You got two relaxation times, dig? an' then you got other shit. Best you can hope for is not too much distortion. They lots of impedance: mechanical, characteristic, acoustic, and this bitch gotta do AGC in order—" "AGC?" "automatic gain control to get on top of shit so's she can quench them others and lead, dig? but distortion and cross talk can fuck the signal—" "Whoa, man. You are not making any sort of sense to me." "Just watch. You gon' see. This here bitch gonna control fast and slow variables if she as good's they think: some of them bitches gonna be running up and others down, but they all gotta be phase locked. It won't be no chaotic motion, dig? You'll see the pattern, even when they running half fast and half slow. She gonna need to be transvectant—" "What the fuck is that?" "Invariant, dude. Thought you was hip to that shit. Cayley's omega process, Capelli's identity—" I waved him off. "The hats?" "Only when they doing this combining shit, the two opposing teams. Synch them up. Otherwise—other methodologies. One raw, natural-like; th'other a electronic brain-implant for direct injection, dig? hooked up directly. But isolated, like. Adiabatic, dig? for the leader, not them others, isolate the bitch—" I half tuned him out. Sasha sounded distressed but he kept pounding her, driving his dick in and out of her asshole from which seeped white fluid running white rivulets down her perineum to her cunt whence it dripped accumulating on the floor. All the while he yammered on. I'd catch the odd phrase: synthesis of feedback control laws, disturbance decoupling, traction free, angle of twist per unit length, polar moment, cylindrical torsion and centroidal axis, scattered within the silent performance of Joelle riding the torque of the driving cylinder within her cunt as the women lining the benches, their spread legs affixed to the walls above them at the ankles, arms at the bench or on the wall below, living oscillators at different frequencies with the black-box dildos humping them at different beats, unsynchronized oscillators, began howling disorganized and dissonant cacophony to the steady independent pacing of the machines, more of them chaotically grinding wriggling thrusting in contrast to Joelle's placid visage of seraphic smile offset by spectral aura materializing into luminescent nimbus calmly beatific even as ever-increasing series of unblinking saccades made the blinding contact lenses soar like wings of hysterical raptus attuned to the battering of her relentless robotic lover ramping ever increasing harmonic urgency, her face glowing as if transported outside herself in a wall of silence as her mechanical steed's beat steadied, slowed, then rose and fell entrained to her hips constrained gyrating "bitch closed the loop; she phase locked" following which the beats of the human-machine oscillators smoothed as an ictus of independent strobes came together locked into the same tempo which tactus infected all, pseudo-Mule and Sasha tied in and I with my dick up the spreading ass cheeks of a pale creature last seen looking up at me through pale blue lash-less eyes below nondescript dishwater brows crossing below a high forehead with dishwater hair pinned back, her earlobes lined with rings, a long crooked wide nose with a ring through the left nostril, small oval mouth of puffy oversized lips, sharp chin, podgy cheeks, a fat girl waiting to get out of the tattooed abode of painted ribbons and bows covering her left arm, *lover* on the antecubital fossa of the right, another bow drawn neatly tied above and orthogonal to her butt crack as she kneeled now on chunky thighs going gobby at the hips with hands stretched forward smushing the fat tits into the floor, rotund ass spread amply and raised up to allow entry into the anus situated high and not distant from the bow, we two too entrained to the beat, the entire room gradually brought to a stop, all machines and people stopped dead, caterwauling ending in dead silence, my tattooed partner prostrated in halted kowtow ass in the air supported by my erect penis buried in her anus. Joelle resurrected all to harmonic larghissimo to grave to lento to largo and andante and steadily to moderato at which she led a time-varying race with groups in syncopation weaving a pattern in and out of fundamental beats then slowing reminiscent of *Pacific 231* to build momentum to a cascading romp of group patterns climaxing in forcing condition of coyotes-howling-at-the-moon chorus of group orgasm.

Silence. Dead time. Pseudo-Mule freed his flaccid hose from Sasha's clutches, spraying brown-specked dick snot about the area as the thing flopped loose. A geyser of whitish brown-streaked slurry erupted from her asshole in juicy farts, forcing pseudo-Mule to jump back as it splattered his feet. My own organ drooped and slipped out decumbent and weeping and accompanied by the nascent butterball's jism farts as she gnawed at *lover* tattooed within her elbow pit. "D'jew see that shit? Bitch be torsion free! Parabolic bursting in excitable system coupled with slow oscillator, pursuant to oscillator death'n'all." "What?" I asked him. "That be one fine harmonically tuned bitch. Powered by injection and libidinal response." "What?" "Libidinal response, man. Real shit, like frequency or step response. Dig? The real thing. Exists within, dwells way down deep in persona. Come out with matched input."

Joelle's chair lowered and an assemblage of oversized men pulled her off and rushed her to a wooden barrel set within a recess in the floor, stuffed her inside and covered it with the barrel's head centered with a hole through which her head protruded staring sightless at pubis level, her lush hair piled around the back of her chin. "What the fuck are they doing?" I asked. "They just gon' put her in sub mode. She got go join the chorus on the bottom now, start at the very bottom of the shit pile. Interning to replace whoever on top of this shit pile now. Dig? They gon' work her over while this other one here gets her input."

I stood transfixed, unable to stop watching. A hand gripped my limp dick and a tongue ran under the foreskin rimming the knob of my penis. Lips sucked the glans beneath the covering flap. I didn't turn my stare from Joelle's head protruding from the hole in the upright cask's head. Hairy male hands held it steady and they shaved her bald except for a trio of pony tails, one at the apex of the crown and the other two at forty-five degrees above the ears which were left sticking out like wood mushrooms. The pony tails they tied with brightly covered bands. They shaved her brows. Her denuded forehead rose to a peak.

"That's quite a prepuce, dude." It was Joanna's voice. She moved to partially block my view as they worked a firm flexible black ring into Joelle's mouth held in place by a harness of straps stretched around the back of her head and fixed on her mouth by a spider-like set of legs embracing above the upper lips and below the lower lips. "Like a leather lappet," she said as lips and tongue explored my prepuce inside and out. "Bet it's gotten elongated enough it'll cover when you're erect, too. Try it and see." "Not yet," I said. "You can't touch that one in the cask down there," she said. "She's off limits. There's an obstruction for you." "Yeah, man, wrong cohomology class. Dig? She like your obstruction cocycle." "Not exactly," Sasha piped in. Whoever worked under my foreskin licked and slurped and drooled a lot of viscous saliva, or at least I assumed it was saliva. I didn't look. The men had wrapped black rubber rings around Joelle's neck, raising her chin so her face looked up with sightless eyes. She drooled uncontrollably. "It's actually another who is the obstruction element, but it's equivalent. You can't be extended because the values of your obstruction cocycle lie in different groups." "They all isomorphic—" "So what? There is no natural unique isomorphism." It was Joanna jumping back in. "Yeah, but we talking homotopy groups here. Abelian—" "Irrelevant, man. It's easy to see the obstruction cochain's a cocycle. Just look at the homotopies of cross sections." "Anyway, it a transgression. That a transgressive element of the —" I tuned them out. Their mouths moved but nothing emitted. The men took turns face fucking Joelle, holding her head steady by her pony tails. Ejaculate oozed from around the bases of the injected penises and ran down onto the rubber rings, pooling on the barrel-head. She sang but the transgressive obstructions muffled her sound. I couldn't make out the words. I realized my companions

had been talking about two sections of the bundle that weren't homotopic, my section and Joelle's section, so that my obstruction cocycle was not homotopic to hers so we weren't in the same cohomology class or some such, that there was some sort of transgression or transgressive element in one of the classes or some such bullshit. Someone gummed and gently munched my foreskin. Joanna's yammering in my face came through. "I told Sasha that to force consistent conditions in your model, your control needs to be incomplete. The concessions were my choice: you will be unable to say no to any woman who comes on to you, no matter how unappealing. Your time to completion will be bounded below by ten minutes, but is unbounded from above and is, of course, your choice." "Ya mean this bloke can go to infinity?" a cockney accent standing beside her, bleached blonde choppy bob cut with pronounced brown eyes offset by smudged coal black eyeliner and brows, pock marked pimply face, hanging dugs covered in stretch marks, a tummy, convex globular buttocks and thighs of coagulated lumps of body fat the texture of cottage cheese, all of it crisscrossed with stretch marks. She had a tattoo of an anchor covered in what might have been blue octopus tentacles on her right thigh. "Shut up. I apologize, Whitey. I just bought her and that other one down there helping your forcing conditions polish your knob. Don't worry: she's consistent." I looked away from Joelle, into Joanna's gypsy eyes. She had traces of dried spunk around her mouth. "No down time, though, unless you choose it. You can get it up now if you want, I think, but the forcing is not yet complete. The venous striation will be more pronounced, for sure, those blue bulges will pop up the length of your schlong—"
"You mean the veins in this here thing will get bulgier?" a young girl's voice from down there. "Yeah, I do mean, and that thing will get a bit larger, not that much, only about four inches or so, but the girth might increase to four inches—"
"Four? You talking soft? I can barely fit it in me mouth now. Jesus, it's so fat I can barely get both 'ands round it. One 'and's not a possibility. It's at least the size of a wide pickle jar now and it's soft as a dead fish" from the same girlish voice. "Well, four or five inches diameter is still manageable by anyone who can give birth," said Sasha who raised up her arm in a fist as the girlish voice added "Or anyone who can take a healthy shit" at which Sasha laughed and Joanna said, "I knew she was a good buy. How you enjoying that foreskin?" "Mmm, reminds me of my puppy's leather chew toy. Big and meaty and tough." The munching had stopped and a woman likely eight or nine inches taller than Joanna stood beside her: a brownette with a long straight frame, no hips and chunky thighs and a pair of small breasts placed not far below her shoulders like

side-by-side fried eggs with red yolks and olive albumens cooked over hard. Her body was uniformly olive, maybe tanned or maybe her untanned color. Was the face drew attention: she looked like a fifteen year old my sister might've brought home as a best friend in past years. Blue eyed and almost worthy of the word pretty but more likely to be termed cute. Perky and smiling without a hint of sexuality. Her mousy hair hung artlessly straight to the middle of her back. "You need to get back down there and help the schlub with his joint," Joanna said. "Can you will it up for this one?" Joanna asked me. "I don't know. She doesn't look old enough to be fucking. I draw the line at under eighteen, and even that makes me uncomfortable." "She's older than you think. And she is compatible with the other forcing conditions. Look at her tattoo" raising her hair up to show a stylized flower on her right shoulder. "She's kind of nondescript," I said, and Joanne said, "Shame on you. Don't say that. You'll give her a complex and I just bought her." Two mouths worked my foreskin, one within and the other without. I wasn't going to erect a woody until one of them had it deep in her face. "Does it hurt going in?" Joanna asked and her new girl said from down below, "Don't know yet. Let me find out—" "Not you. Whitey." "Not so far," I said. "Christ, it's getting bigger?" "Those bulging cingula running up the shaft sensitive?" A hand ran up and down the length of it and the bland newbie's voice spoke up again, "I feel them. Not all that protrudent, neither those bumps under the skin and on the glans under that leather hood of a foreskin." "I feel them," I said without describing the localized discharges arcing the length of my urethra jolting my testicular plexus. "Not bulging yet, but I felt them all when he fucked me. They grew more pronounced, the rings, and those bulges got like carbuncles. The rings dragged more as we fucked. I'm guessing they're protrusile. Probably part of the erectile projection. Can you get it in your mouth?" A warm wetness engulfed it and another voice, probably the forcing condition herself speaking in a familiar voice, "Perhaps the word you seek is torulose. And it fits in everywhere, no worries. Is conformal dimension. The ridges play the same role as dog knot. Seal and hold in place for making emissions stay inside. Emissions act as drug, you know? Lubrication more lubricating and inflammatory. Sperm is pure aphrodisiac. You know?" I felt muted sucking and tongue lapping." "Conformable?" Joanna asked. "Not like plastic. Not pliant, because is rough for sure, with bumps and tori like French tickler, and not flexible when erect. More like quasi-symmetrically deformable, you know?" "No, I don't know," Joanna said. "Think scale invariance. You know, in a hyper-dimensional setting." Hypatia? It was Hypatia talking. I tried to look down but couldn't. My freedom of vision was obstructed. Through Joanna's gypsy eyes I watched Joelle's head protruding from the barrel getting face-fucked, drool running from her nose and mouth, hanging from her chin. My dick was free of the mouth. "It fit but shouldn't have," the new one said. "Not really malleable, either. But it's still soft. What happens when it gets hard?" Fingers slipped back the foreskin and Hypatia's voice said "Now suck that" and it slipped back inside the warm mouth.

Hypatia here now? Maybe I'd gone delirious. I hadn't slept or eaten in some indeterminate time. What came to mind was her warning about possibly never having existed. Who she connoted as disappearing in a cardinal collapse or some other logical calamity wasn't clear, but likely didn't matter since it would be two individuals disappearing from one another's frame of reference. I had become as Platonistically buggy as she was. The bleached-blonde stretch-marked sweat hog Joanna had brought back, the purchase not presently noshing my dick, was gnawing on pseudo-Mule's limp copulatory appendage. I didn't remember his black snake wore such a flaming red knob. She ingested it with encouragement from Sasha, a plumbers snake disappearing into the sewer only to reappear dripping with smegma, the head redder each time. His sour expression said he wasn't enjoying himself.

An engram reared up. Tied to never existing, it traced memory of a party at the Cosmic Furnace and Helen's in a few weeks or a few other cycles of some periodic temporal beat of relatively short duration with respect to the annual clock of elapsed time whose hands had not yet budged in that direction. Hypatia and I went or would go, equivalent prospects from here, as a couple, a date. She'd asked me to get someone else to take, suggesting Debby who had meantime disappeared with the white haired old man she'd met at the Cosmic Furnace party during which Dina was fucked into her present state of corpus correction. He had picked her up in a Rolls-Royce Camargue or perhaps, as Hayden claimed, a Bentley, which I took to be more likely correct. Some claimed the vehicle and occupants ascended into the heavens, but Hayden claimed it was an artifact of the Huey Long Bridge. In any case she was not seen again. I explained I had no one to take, Dina being out of the loop for remodeling. She suggested Bobbi but not sure which she meant I demurred, finally convincing her to accompany me as my date. She reluctantly acquiesced, though it seemed a more difficult decision than I'd have expected.

Pseudo-Mule jumped up and down like a Jack Russell Terrier as the three females at his dick worked to restrain him. He barked over and over, "She's frangible, she's frangible…" pointing at the second woman whose blonde head made a public appearance from beneath the hood. Sasha and Joanna grasped at the bit of cock not buried in the slave's pimply face. I looked over at a statuesque female with gleaming golden hair hanging straight and thick beyond her shoulders. True to Sasha's prediction, she was tall and lean and busty, her high nippled rotund breasts standing firm against gravity, the nipples small and inverted. More svelte than Joelle with leaner legs that seemed longer, she had narrower thighs and slightly curved hips without the straight edges, causing one to induce a skinny round ass, falsified by the flattened saggy buttocks that showed when she pivoted about face and bent forward to touch the floor. I believed that pseudo-Mule's excitation came from the unaffectedly demure smile she flashed on a visage with the selfsame girlish innocence of the skank now slathering my cock with her saliva. Bent over, her teardrop ass didn't seem unfamiliar with foreign intrusions, particularly the glabrous pubis displaying from the backdoor view a glans penis of a clitoris protruding from its preputial hood. Hypatia stood up and looked me in the eye without a hint of recognition. I had never seen her so tall. Unable to defy gravity with such pert abandon, her massive meat slab tits were gross enough their abundant adipose stuffing gave them roundness to point forward the prodigious nipples like brown raw yolks of goose eggs, diametrically opposite the tits of Hypatia-at-the-party's bumps of puffy red nipples with nary a hint of breast. At the door, the girl who collected my ticket flashed her a leer and tweaked them both simultaneously. Inside I asked Hypatia-at-the-party what that had been about but she answered with a "What had what been about?" I doubted she'd missed it, but let it drop. She said, "Policy is only one ticket per couple, and this is the first time I have been on another's ticket. Maybe that was it. The ticket goes with the one bringing, you understand?"

I didn't, but I let that drop too. She kept explaining. "The one with the ticket is making an offer. The *acompanhante* is the offering, fair and open game. That is the rule. Did you not read the ticket?"

"All of that's on the fucking ticket?"

"Yes. A sort of agreement you make as a couple. And the man is always the one with the ticket. A woman cannot bring a man, but two women must designate one the bringer. That is a fundamental rule of this house. There is an interview with the couple, the first time they come, with the woman included."

"No one interviewed me or my date—"

"No, I short-circuited that."

"How did you know the first time I came—"

"That your date would comply with this idea? I know you. Very persuasive. But now I am the date. And she? Did she not comply?"

"Too well."

Hypatia wore reddish-brown hair short and plastered to her scalp with spit curls at the temples. Extensive slender gams, narrow hips and round ass would have made her the apple of the twin's eyes were they not staring antipodally from her at the blonde, crowned with the metal helmet, placed forcibly in the chair and strapped in, dildo cranked in place and anal probe wedged inside for stability, raised heavenward for her machine trial. Hypatia's hirsute mons and environs below overgrew with brown hair the color of that on her head in contrast to the one in the chair. As if auditioning for me, she bent forward dangling her corpulent tits towards the ground, a pair of meat bags deforming as she lowered her torso level with the floor and turned to the side so the bags resembled for all the world whopping upside-down cones. Revolving to face away from me to attend the girl on the floor working my limpness, she presented round buttocks tapered with a pronounced lateral depression from trimly arced hips above a hairless butthole. The thighs were more substantial than those of the girl now howling in the chair, losing control it seemed, but with no trace of excess fat or globularity, the calves of correct proportion and tone. When she raised up once more, two symmetric hollows mirrored one another along the line where the upper hip flowed into the V-shaped crease formed at the top of the crack of her ass. Her ass smiled with infragluteal folds that did not sag, instead followed lateral curves of proximal concavity to upper thighs without a hint of bulging saddle bag. In all but this regard of ass, nothing like the Hypatia I took to Cosmic Furnace and Helen.

Pseudo-Mule was torn between face-fucking the three women in his service, evidenced by moans and oh shits and suck its, and his need to comment on the action of the yowling apparently out-of-control blonde in the chair, gibbering into his stream of encouragements and groans terms like elliptic complexes and diffusion tensor and Fokker-Planck Equation and linear response and susceptibilities, adiabatic elimination of fast variables, high-friction, Josephson tunneling junction, superionic conductors, bistability between running and locked solutions. Losing lock ran into suck-it-bitch, out of phase and ooh shit baby alternated in the seamless verbal flow as stridulation of partial expressions, rasping discontinuities at essential caustics, viscosity supersolutions across Brownian bridges and Smoluchowski Smoluchowski

Smoluchowski "She ain't locking up, she running free wheel" he finally moaned jerking out a fuckwad shared by the threesome on their knees. Joanna looked up at me, a string of drool hanging from her chin, and said, "She cun't do it." Hypatia, on her back, her dense rotundly-packed mounds splayed broad-bodied across her chest as she turned toward me so the nearer loaf slid towards the floor in the form of a dough droplet, laughed. "She won. Demonstrated almost sure stability in randomly coupled oscillators." When Joanna snorted, Hypatia responded "You need to get your dulotic minions out from here before taken from you by surreal guardians." "Don't worry about us. We are a dulocracy" to laughter and groans. "Those are some doughy boobs, babe," Sasha threw in I guessed for good measure. Hypatia configured a sensual smile with metallic red lips in an ovular pout. "We can take it from here," she said.

Much like what I remembered would be said to me at the Cosmic Furnace's party when with the Hypatia of puffy nipples: taut, skinny and straight as a board except the incongruous rounded ass of Callipygian form decorated with a big butthole and red stretch gash between her legs. Small fat mouth displayed below narrow crooked bony projection with bulbar pinnacle on a highly eccentric elliptical face ramping of a sudden from the lower lip to a blunt chin that did not so much taper as compress. She wears thin drab brown hair straight in a pair of symmetric ponytails on either side of her head. I remembered she will have a large clitoris high atop the extended gash. There is or will be or was a bluing butterfly tattooed below her navel. She said, "Then—this might become a problem for your life. Dina was the star that day."

"It did something to Dina. Not sure what."

"And your date, what was her name? The flat-faced one."

"Debbie. Did something to her, too. Changed her life, you might say."

"You didn't think she could be such a whore, yes?"

The same check girl as before gave us our robes and took our clothes without issuing us a claim ticket. There were about ten couples changing with us and likely more than a hundred couples would attend if the last encounter'd been any indication. The check girl had a phenomenal memory given she returned checked clothes without hints or prompting from their owners.

We stood outside both the circle surrounded by the annulus with the inscribed gothic letters in luminescent crayon hues I couldn't figure out and the triangle with base facing the annulus and I lit up a hash-laced cigarette we passed back and forth while searching the faces of the crowd already in attendance. People engaged in sexual activity in groups from two to several on the sofas, beds, banquettes and floor mats scattered around the cavern and already there writhed a mass of bodies in the darkened section with its glowing boundary. Hypatia pointed to it.

"Within there," she said, "you cannot visually make out anyone. They call it the orgy room. Once on that padded floor inside the luminescent markers, there are no choices. Anyone who wants you gets you; you cannot tell who or what gender they are without using your hands. Beyond it is the maze of pitch black corridors where there are beds against the walls in widened areas. There is a glory hole on the other side. And the private rooms. But to get to them you have to pass through both the orgy room and the maze."

"So there can be guys fucking guys in there?"

"Male homosexuality is not condoned among swingers; social prohibitions are the strongest enforcement mechanism. They discourage it strongly here. Kind of surprising, given that Helen's *apelido*— family name, I mean—is Shaushka."

"What does that have to do with anything?"

"You don't know your goddesses, do you? Dangerous to not know them, dear." She squeezed my hand. "A drink?" pulling me towards the bar. "Anyways, in there it would be difficult to patrol if two men consented to do it to each other."

It added an irreality that in the dense gloom one could not make out walls. I remembered walking to a wall my first time there to assure myself that indeed there existed boundaries and almost colliding with one of them before seeing it. From that wall I felt my way to a corner as my date enthusiastically engaged in a cluster fuck.

The Hypatia of big breasts kneeled behind the cute girl of innocent demeanor with my dick in her face and shoved her forward, burying the still inerect tube to the base so she smushed her mouth against my groin at which I erected it instantly, gagging her as she tried to move away and up from it while Hypatia held her firmly in place. I pushed deeper, feeling her throat constrict my shaft in a sweet spot that I amplified to manufacture an orgasm of epic proportion. Dick snot intertwined with nasal snot erupted from her nostrils and she cried copious tears before being released to vomit a mound of wriggling white worms. "Take this amateur bitch away," Hypatia said but no one paid attention, being busy once more with pseudo-Mule who remonstrated the twins in a loud and relentless harangue filled with haplologies and technical phraseology without apparent referents for a bad decision as the victorious blonde was taken away to rest with the group not to be mechanized and a port was implanted into Joelle's temple before removal from the barrel. She was led, awkwardly as she remained blinded with the opaque contact lenses, by chains attached to previously unseen piercings of her labia and clitoris and nipples and nasal septum to a free bench to be strapped to the wall with her new teammates, legs above her head exposing cunt and butthole, arms strapped below to the bench. Her temple port matched the others in the mechanized group and into it was plugged some device connected to the fucking machine readied at her cunt, as were they all. Her face trickled not-yet-dried splooge of the gang face-fuck. An obese woman of many folds squatted across her kisser and Joelle busied herself munching before the captain of the mechanized synchronized fucking team took her place in the chair. Joanna helped the sobbing slave to take her place in pseudo-Mule's penile service beside Sasha and the other slave. Pseudo-Mule had grown quiet, I guessed broken by the indifference of the twins and their crews to his energetic harangue. Hypatia leaned forward and rubbed my glans on her clitoris. With deliberate lentitude, on my whim I grew an erection that she guided within as it inflated.

Helen materialized out of the murk. She stood blocking our way, arms akimbo, naked except for flat sandals with straps twining up to mid-calf, drawing my attention to the angular attachment of her rounded knees to calves flatted on the inside and protruded at the joint on the outside, appearing unnaturally pinned. The calves showed no curvature on the inside and little on the outside but flowed with decreasing girth of increasing slope between her legs to feet without evidence of ankle bones. One could surmise there was space between her calves when she put her knees together, which was what? bow legged? bandy legged? knock kneed? Utta showed a similar characteristic, though of different musculature-curvature since Utta evidenced positive curvature compared to this if not flat, then of slight negative curvature. More incongruous still in Helen, given her meaty thighs on what therefore appeared shortened legs tapering with such disjunction to feet after so dislocated a connection. Standing now with legs wide apart accenting the wild black vee of long thick bush as if pasted on which I knew from previous experience covered not only cunt but asshole, rampant up over the crack and perhaps beyond if not trimmed, as I was sure was the case for what trailed down from her navel; to be trimmed so perfectly a vee in front but so unruly behind she likely took heroic measures to control the growth on her legs given the luxurious black down on her arms. And on her nipples: I recalled a smattering of long black hairs, looking now for evidence she'd had them disappeared. No, they remained, and why not? given caterpillar eyebrows apparently ready to crawl from her face.

"Let me guess. Beer for you" poking me in the chest "and wine for you."

"What kind of wine?"

"Vermouth. Right?"

"Cinzano rocks with a lemon twist."

From behind, her thighs swept seamlessly into a thick waist without pronounced ass-cleft, the base if you will of a trunk thick and short with no apparent shoulder blades or ribs but from the slight angular deviation off dead-center showing the bottom arc in space of steep Gaussian curvature along every section of tit leading the way though resting against a rib cage, hanging heavy and longly stretching from the middle of her chest well below her shoulders. The flat ass did not wiggle, nor did she attempt swaying the flattened hips.

She brought for me a Dixie with the pronouncement "Don't know how you can drink that piss."

"I like it."

"So, this is the first time Hypatia comes to us as date. She always brings us a date—"

"Escort," Hypatia said.

"More than escort. You never participate."

She stepped up to me, rubbed her prominent and pointy breasts against my robe and slipped her hand inside to rest on my penis. "I remember this fondly. But I remember it hard."

"I never needed to participate, given all the women I brought were sacrifices."

Helen looked up from under the living black beetle-brows and smiled. "Now that is different. You have been here five times and never participated. But now you are the offering."

"I'm not a sacrifice. That is not part of this."

"That remains to be seen, as always. At any rate, it is out of my hands. Yours too. And yours too, dear man…" pulling back her hand. "Seems you are unready; nothing to lick" holding up her palm. "And what of you, dear?" turning to Hypatia.

"I don't know what I'm ready for. But who are those two?" pointing to a pair of imposing naked presences vaguely defined in the gloom standing near the triangle. Men of significant stature; I would have guessed probably close to eight feet tall, broad and with what I took to be a brisket of beef hanging between each of their legs.

"Part of the same crew that had at your last date," Helen said to her.

"Dina," Hypatia said to me.

"They are part of the sideshow that Furnace keeps on hand. Some of them have been here every time you have come, but they are not usually so active as with that last one. Dina, you said?"

"I never saw so many giants," I said. "You called them a crew?"

"I'm not certain how many there are. Cosmo knows, I think. More of them have been coming of late.

"Are they required to bring dates?"

"Not all of them. Only those without the triangle, like those two. They brought dates, but others required to stay inside the triangle do not."

I considered asking how the hell they got in and out of the club if they never left the triangle, but figured I'd taken her too literally. Besides, she kept on talking.

"Most women are afraid of them, but they seem to have a strange power when they get started. Once they work their way inside, lust flows through every pore."

"Sounds like you have experience."

"I have done a group of six of them. In private. I won't do them here. Lose control. We don't allow them in the orgy room or beyond. Too scary."

As Hypatia ground and bumped, Joanna disappeared and a brunette was fitted into the seat vacated by Joelle and plugged in with ass and cunt dildos and wired via her temple port. She seemed out of place given Sasha's pronouncement regarding the twin's predilection, being neither tall nor svelte though she had noticeable tits not necessarily in a pleasing sense but with a certain something, sensed rather than felt, that overwhelmed the embryonic dumpiness: a virginal whorishness that shouted she would fuck anyone but you. Of course, she had tattoos, two of them on either side of the small of her back, of women, perhaps her, one in a red outfit and the other a mermaid or in a long gown, and something stylized on her right butt cheek. A flower? Palm tree? By now tattoos had become blurs, so many in one unbroken stretch of temporal continuity they ran together. Her ass was a beach ball and her thighs had begun to go to curd with projecting bags on the sides where they ought to have merged with the glutes which pseudo-Mule pointed out saying "See them gobs there on the sides're why she being retired…the whole thigh there going to gob, dig? Lady J's what they call her. She been lean in the past, so much she looked taller, like them others. But them tits always been that a way, hanging down like two filled up pastry bags spread wide apart just like that…used to be with bones betwixt 'em but now fat like the cheese on her thighs. Won't be long them knees be gone, disappeared like, dig? Dyes her hair black now, too. Used not be. She still got them big brown bedroom eyes…" The brows had been plucked into dense, dark arcs. The face with a rounded chin, round cheeks beneath thick black hair piled artlessly atop her head was starkly a fat girl's, the ear protrusions safer hidden. Prolonged tubular tits, the leanest part of her anatomy, snaked asprawl flat on her trunk, their giant nipples painted or tattooed bright red and positioned as if trying to escape one another. She put on a pair of narrow black plastic eyeglass frames and puckered her lips.

Hypatia pulled me over to where the two giants stood. She looked up at one of them.

"Playing human, ey wee ephemeron? We remember ya," he said, noticing her standing below the lofty perch of his eyes. "We 'ad hopes for sich an opportunity as this'n."

"And what opportunity would that be?" she asked, squeezing my free hand.

"We ere Silver indiscernibles" the other one said. "From a Ramsey."

They spoke with an accent I couldn't place. It could have been a cross between Scottish and Aussie with numerous audible clicks as of a fading FM radio and guttural wheezes accenting phrases erratically. Almost a monotone delivery.

"Ah, then zero-sharp," Hypatia said.

"Eggs-zactly. We return to Skolem hull. We exit climbing ultrafilters. Nonprincipal."

They ignored me. I almost pushed my way in with a question, if they meant ultrafilter as in Boolean algebras. Or in sets. But it was a stupid question.

"Well, cofinality is critical," she said. "There is a Jónsson cardinal where you live, then?"

"O' course," the one she stood in front of, the first one, replied. "But we, like you, prefer the variants of compactness. Especially the strongly compact, sometimes supercompact."

"I prefer to work with extenders. Get beyond the huge cardinals. Normal measurability is critical; language issues can be resolved." She moved closer, her boobs at the level of his groin. His penis hung flaccid from between her breasts to between her legs. "Such a disorderly universe."

"Not so disorderly, wee one" he replied. "They are orderly below such as the smaller Erdős. But one must understand which el'ment'ry embedding o' the ordered universe 's included. We can all live in an inner model, as ya well know. There's plenty of room in the inner models."

"By Vopěnka-Hrbáček, of course—"

"No, lass, by Kunen."

"Right. My mistake. But I find your universe won't be constructible—"

"O' course not. But we ken venture there—" the other started and Hypatia interrupted "Not always" at which the one standing before her said, "Language and trees are related through compactness. Ya' like ta climb trees?" and Hypatia said "Depends if they have ultralong branches of appropriate order. Anyway, Vopěnka's Principle still gives extendible. I, however, look for fine measures on cardinals. When hugely inappropriate enough" at which she giggled; "but what of Mitchell order?"

"Coiterate, ya skank. We got trunks fer ya ta climb."

"I bet you're strongly compact but not supercompact. I doubt you're indescribable with languages of the appropriate cardinality of disjunction and quantification. Like even with weakly compact cardinality."

"Only in the limit o' strongly compact card'nals. Our Mitchell order's beyond two successors. We ken be extended."

"You'll need the strong compactness at a minimum," the other said. "We're tough ta describe."

"You're pretty language-restricted, then. All bound up, then. Indefinable. But still and all, I guess I hadn't expected such royalty."

"Ya're easily surprised then, bitch. Prikry forcin's safest—"

"No collapse—"

"But collapse doe'n't bother us. Al'ays it proceeds below."

"Besides," the other said, "we ere well-reflected."

"How many of them are you?"

"You know this. Why ask?"

"Uncountably many, in any case," she said. "I wanted to hear you say it."

"I cannot, of course."

"Exactly. Indefinable."

"But remarkable, nonetheless. Skolem hull, remember. Remarkable Ehrenfeucht-Mostowski, en fact."

"Why don't we stop this game," the other said, moving closer to her, "ya panmictic cooze."

"That'd be the other one, actually. The one I brought last time."

"Aye, she 'ad issues."

"We 'ave a better'n mind," the one whose chest she stood looking up at said.

"Which would be?"

"A Wadge game."

"No," she said. "Banach-Mazur."

"Not y'ur choice," the other said, moving more to her side so the pair formed a corner, "given ya chose this particular game. But we shall concede that rejection of Wadge fer a cut-and-choose."

"Okay, that works. What stakes?"

"Cardinal collapse," he said. "Disjoint up 'til then.

"Orthogonal, not disjoint."

"One last appearance," the other said. "Granting that."

"For?"

"Sytri."

"I get to avoid Sytri if I win?"

"Yes. T'is't fair?"

"What the hell kind of game is this?" I asked her.

She turned back to me and handed me her drink. "An infinite game. We play in a Polish space with a given compatible complete metric. I personally like the unit circle with angular measure. The referee—I assume one of these two—chooses an uncountable subset that contains no Cantor set. I choose two open sets of diameter less than one-half with disjoint closure, he chooses one of them and then I repeat the process within the set he chose, but with diameter less than one-forth—"

"So the diameters are shrinking to zero as one-over-two-to-the-n at the nth step so this goes to zero. Fuck, what the fuck are you doing? This takes an infinity to play."

"It is a timed game, dear," squeezing my hand again. "I have a minute for the first choice, as does he to respond, then a half minute each, a fourth of a minute, an eighth, a sixteenth—"

"One over two to the n—"

506

"—so forth, so that in four minutes the game is finished."

"That doesn't even make sense—"

"Of course it does. You can sum that infinite series."

"That's just it. An infinite series. You'll need to be processing and passing information—"

"Witnessing, dear. That's what keeps the referee from cheating for one player or the other. There will exist a constant, a Henkin witness. The ref only chooses a set. I win the game if the final point to which the choices converge is in that set. He wins otherwise."

I didn't think about what sort of game she had chosen to play with me. "What did you wager?" I asked as if believing this nonsense.

"Cardinal collapse; remember what I said about cardinal collapse. In particular, we become orthogonal, so our projections meet in zero, nowhere, nowhen if you will; I avoid being fucked senseless by Sytri if I win." "Why you playing this shit anyway?" I asked to which she replied, "Not my choice, dear, but you can find the data in a Lévy collapsing algebra, if the back story remains describable…" and she stepped closer to the big guy in front of her, her mouth where his navel ought to have appeared. She looked up, stood on her tiptoes, and said "Ineffable, I assume—"

"Assuredly."

The other one said, "Ready—set—go." It seemed there glowed around each of their heads a nimbus, but of course that would be bullshit. It disappeared within minutes. "You were good," she said to him. "I submit." She put her hand beneath his penis and hoisted the gross tube with the open hand as prop; she could not stretch her fingers around it to hold it from above. It hung out of her open hand like a limp sausage and she propped it up to inspect the angular head more closely, then , smiling, showed me that she could not get both hands around it. "Rigidity?"

"No nontrivial automorphisms," he said. "Nothing moved thetaway. And this one," acknowledging me for the first time, "he knows what a gutter-snipe of a slut you be?"

"More or less."

"Yer boyfriend?"

"He would like to be."

"Foolish idea. You can dismiss him."

She turned. "You aren't welcome in this party, Whitey. No place for you. Go find some nice girls to fuck with that pathetic excuse for a cock." She turned and looked up at him again. "That enough send-off for you."

The giant looked at me and said, "Thank you for this gift. We take it from here, laddie."

The other one came around behind her, blocking my view. She affected a Scottish accent, "You goona tup with me, th'n air ya goblins?"

"Come on, let's bust 'er up."

Lady J. appeared bored with the fucking machine's hammering. She brought her subjects to sustained resonance in short order, frequency-locking with a variety of phase offsets and leading their machine-cunt oscillations in a drum-beat reminiscent of Rudy Collins, Ray Mantilla and Chief Bey at the Village Gate in 1961, a few years before I got the green light to kill gooks for my country. But all was not smooth; disorderly breaking with the pattern became pronounced with a subset of the participants led, it seemed, by Joelle who had been first to break lock and entrain others to her tempo. "What that bitch doin'?" Mule hollered. "She got cojones gonna be lopped off—" The fat lady sitting on Joelle's face pulled the wire from Joelle's temple and her machine ramped up to hypersonic speed and Lady J regained control of the renegades. Pseudo-Mule'd gone off into frenzy, barking that Lady J was finished, that she'd just lost. Joanna returned with a butcher knife and slit his throat from ear to ear, so deep the cut through his neck his head lolled back held in place by a flap of skin, looking behind him upside down, while he was held upright by the three women on their knees sharing his penis. Joanna looked me in the eye, bloody knife in her hand, and said, "You'll thank me later not only for your massive lactiferous putz and irresistible attractant, but also for the smoothing the integrations of these kernels will have effected both before and after." She looked down at the girls on the floor and said, "We're done here," at which Sasha, tinning snips in hand, snipped off Pseudo-Mule's penis at the base without removing any skin from the lips of the cutie who had supported him solely by dint of suction. He fell backward onto the floor slicked with blood, flat on his face. As they exited, Sasha said, "Didn't do any good: saw a countable infinity of them in another room" to which Joanna said, "Didn't even reduce their number by one" and Hypatia fucked me by backing up repeatedly over my erection from a bent forward position facing away and Lady J finished her routine and was let down and Joelle, remaining blinded, was fitted with a pig mask of pig nose and pig ears and brought to a fenced, matted enclosure where her temple port was plugged into a box. She had been fitted with leather knee pads that bound her legs from upper thighs to upper calves, bending the legs to force her aknee and unable to straighten up, and with leather mitts that transformed her hands to hoofs attached to leather elbow pads that forced her forearms up and elbows bent, hobbling her to knees and elbows facing downward toward the ground, ass in the air. A tall, hairy male therianthrope of cynanthropic ilk most especially represented of long fanged snout and erect penis of stout proportions knotted at the base, entered the enclosure. He was plugged into a large transformer via a port in his temple; sparks and drool escaped his dog dick. He fucked Joelle, knotting her inseparably. Caught by his dick in her asshole, she squealed and grunted like a sow and crawled furiously in futile effort to escape as sparks showered from her forehead, mouth and cunt while he dragged her around the enclosure.

Helen stood beside me. "This ought to be a good sporting event," she said. "Blood sport," I said and she whispered "Not jealous, are we?" "I can't see where she will fit those things inside her when erect." "Don't worry. Many have done it. Remember Dina? You'd be surprised how well deforms the flesh in these contacts." "Did you catch all that gibberish?" I asked and she smirked, answering "It's all inaccessible to me..."

She took the drinks and set them on a wandering tray. I heard pronounced slurping, then Hypatia's voice "Lévy collapse algebras—" "Shut up en suck, ya lit'le coont" followed by a smacking of lips modulated by slurps.

Helen told the one blocking our view to move to the other side so Hypatia could suck them both without having to turn. And so we could watch. He complied as if she were directing a film.

Hypatia stood flatfooted with the elephant trunk of a penis in her hand, working back a thick foreskin that covered well beyond the head. When unsheathed, it was not rounded like my own dickhead but pointed. The taper made it easier to work into her mouth. She sucked determinedly, licking it clean of drool when she came up for air.

She alternated to the other one, remarkably of identical physiological character, dimensions, hair color, both of them dunnish emanations rather than well-defined boundaries of flesh. Not obtusely brutal in facial feature as one would expect, but of sexually ambiguous facial feature with muscular torsos gone to seed, broad shoulders and chest, nascent paunch. Their legs came off as short, probably an illusion due to the girth of those appendages. All of it overgrown with dense hair.

509

The penises lumbered erect at a snail's pace, oozing a trail of slime that grew to cover her lower face and breasts. As she slurped the goo she became more aggressive, pushing the engorging members farther back into her throat, making me wonder how far she could go. My dick stood at attention. I didn't want to join; I wanted to watch.

Helen whispered to me that the ooze they secreted, and especially their ejaculation, increased libido. They'd had the stuff analyzed but were unable to reproduce it or isolate all the chemical constituents. It would be, she said, a big money maker if they could find the active constituents.

"What if it's a combined effect not due to any subset of constituents?"

"Look," she said, "she's so short she has to stand on tiptoes now they're erect."

One of them picked her up with one hand and with the other hand pushed her mouth down over his partner's penis. Her mouth widened like a scream and then puckered in at the cheeks, deforming to a near collapse of the entire visage as the conical prong disappeared within. The rest of it followed until her face pressed full against the groin, lips smushed flat.

"Interesting the amount of stretching the features can endure, isn't it?" Helen asked, eyeing the protrusion in the front of my robe. "You're getting off on this, naughty boy. I bet the more you are into a woman the more this sort of carnage on her turns you on."

The giants' erect torulose penises rippled with striations like bands circumscribing the cylindrical prolongations. One of them held her by her arms and compared her torso to the others erect penis. It stretched from her groin to her chin. She kicked and struggled to get her tongue in the flow of mucosal gravy creeping from the head.

"Where is she going to put that dick?" I asked but Helen had sunk to her knees to suck my dick.

Hoisting Hypatia with hands around her midsection, one of them put her to its erection and insinuated the head between her legs, corkscrewing her down to the end with a full turn. Her legs spread so apart she ought have split but didn't. The inner thighs puckered as had her facial cheeks as if to implode, but didn't. Held by her arms impaled to its groin, she became an extension of its penis, her sucking buccal cavity opening and closing like a fish out of water. The other shoved his cock inside the fish mouth, her face again nearly collapsing in on itself. Both creatures released their grip on her and moved in tandem with an out-of-phase rhythm, Hypatia pronged rigidly between them.

"Her distaff place," one of them said to the other who grunted in assent. They walked her inside the triangle.

"Oh oh," Helen said, standing up. "Soon it'll be Sytri's turn. This makes you really horny, doesn't it? You must really be into her. I'm guessing you were in love with her. When you're into a woman you really get off watching her fucked mercilessly. Makes me want to get you to fall in love with me. I'd get you to explode."

"Sytri? Who's that? The guy with the reddish Tesla suit?"

"Suit? What fucking Tesla suit?" she laughed.

"Hypatia said he wore a suit that generated or collected electrostatic charge to discharge through that dil—that wasn't a suit, was it?"

"No. How could you think it was? You believed her?"

"She seemed to believe it herself."

"Prob'ly she did. I can see that, 'cept these ain't the same's those with Dina." She went back to her knees to suck. I dropped my robe to the floor.

Helen grunted. Hypatia slurp-gobbled ooze.

The guy in reddish glow appeared in the triangle and the two pulled a squirming fish-mouthed gaping-cunted Hypatia from them like some kind of leach. They handed her over. Bigger yet, he stood as if an original fifteen feet had been compressed to eight and a half feet. Each leg bulged almost as wide as his torso. Without hair on any part of the body, including the head. It smeared her face and the inside of her mouth with ooze from its erection of rippling bands of muscle and then torqued her down over the protrusion with several back and forth turns of about forty-five degrees. She sang like a hopped-up mockingbird fed an auditory diet of Schoenberg and Stravinsky; Trane, Dolphy and the disjointed staggering perambulation of Thelonious Monk leanly plinked; industrial cacophony of clangs and whirrs and thumps, all of it accented with rolling rrrrrrrrs and nasal *ãos* and whining uvular diphthongs of indescribable phonic combination. Shrieked and gurgled. A blue flame leapt atop her head.

Glossolalia. She spoke in tongues. Not the same tongue as Dina, whose song had been of the squealing pig farm, the earth of mud and white suckers (*Catostomus commersoni*) tossed to penned hogs. Hypatia sang an abstraction of the multi-universals of nowhen, the timeless nesting corridors nested within corridors nested within corridors ad infinitum, some winding and some ordered linearly and some trees and all unreachable from below giving her language compactness properties so that all satisfaction led to higher satisfaction—

"Lay down," Helen pushing me. "Wait—" shadows within the gloom there in the triangle defined gradually into almost shapes, the same as the original pair, not quite substantial but more of the gloom than apart from it.

"She is going to do the lot of them, Whitey. It will be a while. But don't worry; the word is azoospermia, so no hybrids with humans. But with her, not clear what might result from her, given her requisition, storage and extraction functionalities. And she ain't human, anyways..."

Hypatia facing him attached to the rosy giant like an extension of his penis, straight in front of him, wriggling like a pinned bug, arms and legs flailing, hair electro-horripilated bolt upright, her entire body glowing bluish with electrical discharge climbing from the connection between her legs to the top of her head like a Jacob's ladder, the flame atop her head dancing. A crowd watched and clapped along to the rhythm of her song. He turned away from the crowd and all we could see of her was the glow and arms and legs and hair extended beyond his girth, the blue discharge hissing like a sizzling pair of arcing hot wires. He screwed her halfway around again and turned to face the crowd, Hypatia bent back facing us now, eyes rolled up showing only the whites, sucking mouth tongue wagging within. The giant grunted and gray egesta like snot blew from her face with such force that her nose and mouth flattened with the blast.

"He's done," Helen said, "now on your back you."

She shoved and I fell back like a feather floating, thinking: helpful, these soft floors. Not mats, not hard wood. Rubber-wood composite?

"Rubber-wood composition," from a woman standing above me. I couldn't see her with Helen squatting over me, facing my dick, hirsute twat covering my face.

"Oh look," another female voice.

"You're done, I take it," Helen said.

"Yes, ma'am, we finished playing for the night. Maria let us go. They're doing jazz now. Some string quarter from San Francisco to play transcriptions from Thelonious Monk and Bill Evans, and some others too I think."

"What about Maria?"

"She's coming. Said she needed to round up some playmates for him."

Who him? I wanted to ask but sucked her clit and the inside of her cunt instead. She grunted. "Good job. Keep it up, boy."

"Is that in use?" from the first woman, a husky voice. "I'm an opportunist; if no one's using it I'll just climb on—"

"Hey," more ethereal voice, "I'm an opportunist too—"

"Take turns girls. Be nice. You can share."

"Who goes first?"

"Paper-rock-scissors it," Helen said. The ethereal voice said "Shit" and someone lowered onto my erection and humped with a circular grind.

"Look at her," one of them said. "The trolls are fucking the living shit out of her."

"Not trolls, gnomes," the other said. "But she won't be walking with her legs together for some time. If ever." "They're too fucking big to be gnomes," the one astride my dick said.

"They're talking about your girlfriend, Whitey. The hordes are savaging her cunt and mouth."

"Or is that her asshole? No double penetration. They did that to me."

"They only come in pairs," the other said. "I did two. That was enough to keep me walking funny for a week."

"That stuff they spew is something, i'n't it? Hot and slimy—"

"Spicy and temperature hot—"

"Makes you horny as a motherfucker. God I could have fucked and sucked forever—"

"My asshole, my cunt, my whole body was like worms crawling everywhere tingling, I needed to cram stuff in me—"

"Too bad you can't see Whitey," Helen said. "They're passing her around like a used condom."

"A broken condom. She's leaking all over."

"Look, she's trying to crawl away—"

"She won't get far," Helen said. "Someone just snatched her up off the floor, Whitey, and spun her around on his dick while another guy fucks her mouth like an inflatable fuck doll."

"She weren't trying to get away. She 'as just crawling o'er to them there other ogres." It was the ethereal voiced one.

"What did I tell you about blabbering like a filthy tramp. Speak English!"

"Yes'm" she replied. "My turn, Ninatta."

One got off and the other worked her way down, butt at my groin and churning.

The secondhand vision of Hypatia's gang rape by giants or ogres or whatever the fuck they were drove me to frenzy. I chewed and sucked Helen's cunt and the woman on my dick cranked her hips trying to remove my penis from my body, but with a care.

"You did six of them, didn't you ma'am?"

"Yes. I was beside myself," Helen said. "I couldn't stop—"

"It's like you're going to come apart at the seams," said the husky voice.

"Amazing how one can stretch," said the one on me. "This here ain't a small club by any stretch—"

"Not the same stretch," said the other. "Look at her. Like she's going to pop open—"

"Or rip apart—" from my rider.

"Or implode. Amazing how distensible is the skin after contact with their lubricating gel," Helen speaking like a professor lecturing a pharmacy class. "We analyzed it, you know—"

"We know. Please don't tell us again, ma'am. My turn."

They switched and the husky voice rode me more savagely, gyrating back and forth as if she wanted to rip off my dick. "Don't see them so small as her often," she oinked. "Look how distorted her face" bleating and bucking.

"Looks like someone's getting off," Helen said. I felt an orgasm building at the base of my spine. Helen stopped speaking and gurgled, then brayed with such deafening force I felt my skull vibrate. I chewed her clit like a dog at a rubber toy; it swelled in my mouth, a strawberry ripening as I sucked while she yodeled a logorrhea of pungent expletives in transcendental tongue. The one astride barked like a dog and stopped grinding. Helen pulled away. "Lick inside my cunt," she gasped. The rider got off, the other one climbed aboard. "Yippee," she raked her spurs in my sides "giddap" and galloped across the room—I exploded in slow motion, disemboguing endless blasts, my hips in uncontrollable spasmodic jerks, slugs ramming through my dick from way back in my groin. "I feel it spurting inside," my rider intoned matter-of-factly in a guttural alien voice "…a lot of it…shoot it out, cowboy… lemme have it.." her disembodied monotone deep and harsh "…fill me up…" shutting up and cantering, then trotting until the distension shrunk and plopped out. Helen pushed her onto her back and set to sucking her pussy while the one who stood watching sucked the final vestiges of ejaculate from my shriveled member. I lay flat, unable to move.

Uncertain how long my paralysis had lasted or what had transpired in the meantime, I found myself standing and looking at Hypatia covered from head to toe with grayish sludge so her features disappeared, no eyes or mouth, hair a matted hint of structure from beneath the blanket of goo, standing on orange bird claws, the tubeworm or tentacle or pseudopenis—the word popped into my head—like a female spotted hyena—protruded from what she had called the cloacal opening between her legs. It reared up at belly level and seemed to sniff the air before glomming onto a stiff club and snarfing it inside, pulling her towards the giant who hoisted her to begin a new transaction.

My two riders stood with Helen watching someone approach out of the gloaming that swallowed us all. She addressed the pair as Ninatta and Kulitta, one of them a carrot top in matted dreadlocks draped over pendulous breasts that slumped to a belly atop broad hips atop substantial thighs and calves. Her bush was as dense as Helen's but flaming orange and as she whirled around with arms above her head her boobs flopped against her torso with loud slaps. Orange hair sprouted from her axillae and the orange growth on her legs had not been recently pruned. The other, a stumpy, red-cheeked brunette of globate visage with curly hair blacker than Helen's in braids to her bubble of a butt, tiny breasts, pig nose, turned up lips on a pooched-out mouth and thighs dimpled with fat, did not join in the dance of the orange-headed one. Neither did Helen.

Joelle at the mercy of a gang of dog-men of enormous copulatory prowess, squealing and grunting while driven by endlessly erect spraying dog dicks and knotted ass and cunt, sparks from the electrified members, the three pig tails on her shaven head emitting sparks and smoke, a trace of ozone in the air…

Eye to eye with the cellist Maria Padilha, my *pombagira* according to Hypatia, a rangy brunette with thick hair in waves to her shoulders and wearing a short red dress suspended by a single broad strap on her neck with collar like a shawl baring an elongate sternum without visible cleavage. The red amplified green eyes and olive skin to stark relief. The tight skirt displayed slender hips and thighs that barely tapered on their fall to seamless knees and calves of the same slight contraction that converged to smooth ankles and narrow feet constrained within flat white shoes that looked like slippers held in place with a single strap. I recalled I had not heard the cello play for me in many months.

"Too bad about Hypatia," she said in her deliberate speech. "But you'll never know, really, dear, and there is a tiny revenge awaiting you." She motioned to the two women in tow. "I brought them because they are with the two who took Hypatia into the triangle. If you are not too weary we can party at your apartment; the parturient moment arrives, our date at last, if you can find it within you."

It struck me that I found her lissome body and beaming smile beautiful. She could stand flat footed and look into my eyes. She must have sensed my attraction because she stepped back and spun in slow motion like a ballet dancer doing a pirouette, eyes smiling in harmony with straight mouth of narrow lips set amidst a chiseled chin and high cheekbones above a swanlike neck. Her globoid ass framed flagrantly within the tight skirt that ended an epsilon above her pubis inspired a vision of fucking languidly from behind, my hips hard pressed against that muscle. The vision resurrected my erection.

"I see you are not yet so tired," she said laughing. "Shall we get you dressed and depart?"

"I'm ready to go with you right now."

"And them?" pointing to the two standing behind her. I gave them a once over without intending to pay much attention, but something about them, some indefinable unchaste envelope surrounding them, reached down and extracted from me a new hunger for protracted surrender. They broadcast indecent promise. The shorter one, no more than five foot tall, bore a hardened expression of earnest and unbridled profligacy behind her restrained beam of lascivious promise, an indecency that prompted visions of unrestrained rape, an invitation in her simper that extended my erection; itself an amazement given the exhaustive draining scant minutes ago. Dissolute promise radiated from her challenging stare and I soaked it up, taking in her small mouth with broadly curved upper lip and luscious lower lip like ripe fruit, well proportioned face with a third devoted to forehead, a third to the midsection on which her straight-bridged nose as long as her forehead ran from between closely spaced eyes to the sensual mouth unpainted amidst the gradual slope of wide cheeks ending the bottom third with a turn inward to a rounded chin. She showed a light scar on the left side of her mouth, barely noticeable except as contrast to the dimple on the right. Lank black hair hanging untended to her chest and a rakish cocked-hips stance displaying slender legs gnarly with muscular calves spoke more to dissolute promise than did her sloe-eyed visage. She wore a pair of beat up black flat leather pumps, simple shoes without straps or decoration, and a red dress, almost the same red as Maria's but more revealing, as short but cut out in back with a strap crossing to restrain inconspicuous breasts. Her ostentatious tawdriness urged me to bend her over and savage her asshole.

Maria waved an opened hand in front of my eyes. "Not polite to stare, Whitey. Look now to her partner. She will feel neglected and me too," and she wrapped elongated fingers around my erection, levered it parallel with the floor and steered me toward the other brunette who barely smiled but as I stared loosened into a grin cocked up infinitesimally on one side. Narrow lips painted with something that glowed softly accentuated the curve where the upper philtral dimple intersected her small mouth, the medial depression beginning far up beneath the flare of her gracefully slender nose, gracefully slender the two words best describing her except for almost-skinny build and almost-skinny legs and arms and puny shoulders supporting mammoth tits packed into a bra with enough cleavage for the other two to spare. Her height was very nearly midway between Maria and the short one but the word willowy suited her more than it suited Maria, the sweep of legs and torso flowing with more elegant curvature and peaking at the rounded maximum attained where hip and thigh met in a wide bow that flattened out and swept inward to a wasp waist. She stood in scarlet form-fitting high heeled boots that came almost to her knees, wore bikini panties and bra and I marveled she didn't topple forward with the burden of her mammaries. I made contact with eyes perched beneath arched brows, the irises so pale a blue-gray they seemed faded. The opposite of the short one's impudent blasé projection, she peered out as if the constantly surprised by the reality she watched. Even the face could be declared gracefully slender though overwhelmed beneath a billowy growth of lustrous jet-black hair falling ragged to her shoulders. On her right shoulder she sported a bluing tattoo of an eagle in descent with extended claws, a pair of dolphins tattooed on her left buttock. Beneath the elegance and grace lurked the same promise of indiscriminant promiscuity broadcast by the little one.

Seduced by the promise of a groaning board of licentious delicacies and debaucheries, I said to Maria, "If you want them along, I won't try to stop you." She snorted, "Oh, if it is an imposition…" "No, really, it's not. My apartment is big." She flicked my penis standing at attention. "This too, and it might be enough to go around."

Maria introduced them both as Naditu, so I added subscripts to their names, $Naditu_1$ for the short one and $Naditu_2$ for the willowy one with hips; henceforth to be denoted as N_1 and N_2. We arrived at my place instantaneously.

I set to rolling a fat spliff from newspaper while they explored the garret. The usual amazement at the mirror and one of them said we needed to leave on lights so we could watch ourselves. The window opened and I heard footfalls on the metal catwalk above Bourbon. Indiscernible patter burbled in atop the sharp percussive hammering from Lafitte's. I lit up. The patter ceased when I appeared and passed the conical tube of newspaper to Maria, nearest at hand.

She took a long hit and passed it down. They watched the cruising throngs without comment until the little one, farthest from me, said "Too bad we can't fuck out here. Can we use the balcony downstairs?"

"No," I said. "Besides, we'd likely bring cops and there is no way I want to get involved with New Orleans cops. But I have nose candy inside if you want some."

"I brought something better," Maria said. In the bedroom she brought out four vials and a plastic tube that looked like an unmarked Vicks inhaler.

N_1 and N_2 stripped down for business and I grabbed an eyeful of N_2. Her mammoth globical tits without evident droop were worthy of the term bosoms. An expansive gulf of unrevealed sternum spanned their separation and a pair of unobtrusive nipples high and to the far edges of her thorax pointed up and out to form an oblique angle. Given the lack of apparent musculature on a lean frame, she appeared not slack but straight despite the bow where hips met thighs. Without the high boots her skinny lower legs were twigs extending the slim thighs that narrowed sharply from the rounded bulge immediately below her hips to decrease diametrally with smooth gradation to the knee. I saw no calf muscle in evidence until she raised up on tiptoes to kiss Maria on the mouth at which there appeared two shortened bulges directly below and behind her knees.

When they'd ceased the long kiss I asked, "What's that?" pointing at the tube and vials. "That doesn't look like a coke dispenser." I took a hit from the spliff and handed it to her."

"S'not," she said, lilting an easy laugh. She took a hit and in time released a cloud of smoke "Sumpin else," she croaked.

"Like what?"

"The inhaler goes with a snuff; stuff in the vials is a special philtre with the addition of hallucinogenic speed and telepathine."

"Where'd you get it? Telepathine as in *yagé?*"

"Designer drug from Silicon Valley that I have specially made up for moments like this by a little independent pharmaceutical house in Palo Alto. And yes, the same stuff except prepared with more specific intent and in more enduring fashion as an enlightened composition utilizing chemical magic not available to the Indians. Because you know it seems that the harmine and harmaline alkaloids that unleash the DMT in the *yagé* brew don't do a thing on their own. Seems they might be requisite for the release and for prolonging the effect by keeping the DMT from metabolizing at its usual rate. Of course, you can't get off on it orally otherwise since it does have the property of disappearing in your gut. Needless to say, this is superior."

"A filter? Not sure what you mean."

"As in p-h-i-l-t-r-e, dear boy. Magical potion to make you fall into heat. Though it might be redundant." We watched N_1 and N_2 make out like a couple of teenagers in the backseat of a family car.

"Hallucinogenic aphrodisiac with energy boost," said the short one in a manly voice.

I looked a question at Maria.

"In a way. It has a special ingredient to help with the gender issues none of us share with you. But the effect of said enhancement is quite pleasant to women."

I assumed she meant to maintain an erection. Wasn't sure I wanted to get into such a thing after the last experience.

"Why you so paranoid?" the short one growled. "Let's get going; so take it."

"What's the plastic tube? I guess its an inhaler we snort?"

"If you're worried I have several of them; we don't have to share one. The answer is yes; the snuff has some properties synthesized from what is called virola, enhanced by some synthesized alkaloids and the mitigation of the more physically disgusting properties."

"The body load can be overwhelming and a real turn-off," N_2 added. "Vomiting, way excessive nose discharge, seizures, unplanned defecation, shit no one wants to experience or watch others experience. So it's been eliminated. But it's bitchin' stuff for orgies. And so necessary for those times when one has only a single pure male in attendance." As she spoke there evidenced even rows of too many baby teeth interrupted by long front teeth flat to recessed and maybe a half tooth longer, the one on the right maybe overlapping the other enough to sense but too little to measure. Literally long, but not gracefully so, in the tooth.

I almost asked what the fuck she meant by "pure male" but decided to drink a vial instead. I asked "any vial?" and Maria answered they were identical in content and dosage.

At the proposal of the short one we toasted to a free-for-all exchange of bodily fluids and downed the vials together as Afro-Cuban rhythms or conga drums or some violent percussion filled the bedroom through the open window. The stuff in the vials hinted at moldy compost and fungus as if brewed from rotting leaves. We passed the inhalator. The sulfur odor of nose-scalding inhalant lasted scant instants and snapped my head back which then exploded while the two Naditus unceremoniously removed my clothes and pawed at my erection and fondled my balls while Maria disrobed without fanfare. I shook off the jangle but not the sudden paranoia at the attack. "Hold up," I said, "let me inspect you three together."

They aligned side by side along the wall across the room opposite the foot of the bed diametrically opposite their mirror images, shortest to tallest. The overhead chandelier mercilessly exposed their physiological aspects, most immediately the variance in complexion which did not vary within specimen so either they avoided sun altogether or tanned in the altogether. The short one's pale flesh blushed faintly rose as if aglow at the cellular level, creamy were it not given an unhealthy pallor in contrast to lusterless black hair. N_2 radiated like backlit translucent creamy-beige porcelain. Maria's olive color bespoke an earthiness that didn't fit the overall otherworldliness of the trio. Her tits sagged like half-filled water balloons stretched the length of the thorax from a pair of high collarbones, more tubular than the fat orbs N_2 projected, widely spaced and framing a long bony sternum, their rotund bottoms standing up off her ribs and sweeping upward with nearly constant curvature to small pink areolae centered by pointed nipples inclining up and away like N_2's. Far below on the long trunk sat a small belly which by contrast was not evident on N_2, though N_2 appeared slacker.

"You're drooling," Maria said indicating the steady drip from my dick onto the planks. She started to move towards me and I stopped her with a "Wait until after inspection."

The little one's smushed flesh-bulbs resembled concave pancakes of slight curvature about dark buds the color of her eyes amidst tiny pink areolae; they were anchored midlevel on what appeared to be a foreshortened torso. The pancakes settled towards her abdomen in doughy flow, most likely the result of insubstantial mass subjected to the force of gravity without support. She did not evidence a belly on her short waist.

Overall shapes from N_1 to Maria: stocky (by comparison only) with noticeable hips; bowed hips; straight.

"Turn around," I commanded, keeping my limbs from flying apart by pure force of will.

"What is this game?" the little one croaked, her manlike voice agitated. "We are soon flying."

local isomorphism: the back and forth method

"Just humor him," Maria said. From Maria to N_1, the little one, the overall shapes from the rear: high round ass, narrow but wider atop, with noticeable space in the upper thighs directly below the cunt with the knees together; narrower with less curvature but not flat with visual paradox (given the bow at the meeting of hip and thigh) of less space showing between the upper thighs; high, narrow, round ass with curvature betwixt the other two and no space showing between the thighs.

When they turned back the little one held the palms of her open hands against her head and opened her mouth wide in a silent scream and I saw she had even teeth, front incisors included, and I compared to Maria flashing through her smile elongated teeth, front incisors slightly longer like N_2's but not so pronounced, all of them narrower at the roots and widening at the ends.

They all had too many teeth.

In despair, I turned my attention to cunts. All naked. Shaved? No evidence of stubble. Maria's fat labia did not hang curtains but resided unobtrusively beneath a slight mound of Venus. N_2's large clitoris dangled down over the top of the entrance amidst modest lips not quite meat curtains. The little one's gross meat curtains projected as if from within the cunt gash itself and a corpulent prolonged clitoris that resembled a substantial penis hung across the access. "What the fuck is that?" I asked moving closer to inspect and Maria said, "A clitoris, dear boy. You haven't seen a clitoris before?" and the little one with surprising strength pressed me to my knees rasping "Suck it!" and shoving my face in her cunt. I licked inside the cunt around the lips and sucked the lips and then sucked the clit which grew in my mouth like a sausage. I backed away and faced an erect penis where there ought have been a clitoris.

They carried me to the bed where I sprawled and mouthed Maria's cunt and found a clitoris the size of a baby's fist shaped like a glans penis but without shaft or meatus...I sucked while she thrashed and held my head from the back and tried to suffocate me...I escaped and Maria and I cheek to cheek orally explored the little one's cunt from the top of which extended the clitoris like a man-sized penis she sucked before directing my head to suck it secreting tasteless viscous fluid and Maria whispered, "Hermaphrodites. The real thing. Phenotype female except the clitoris attached to testes and male neuropsychological wiring. The female organs intact and functioning..." and I thought, self-impregnating? as she sucked the labia and licked inside "...but with amplified hyper-sexual aggression of the male of the species..." a wet intrusion in my anus——tongue?——and a finger and then something bigger as the little one fucked my face with the erect mouthful of a clitoris and Maria worked her cunt around my cock and N_2 fucked my asshole, her tits slapping against my back and the thread of fluid that comes with prostate exams dragged from my urethra "...the clitoris not emptying the bladder, dear boy, only the testes, urethra empties through the cunt..." I sucked the little one's beefy penile clitoris while the other rammed my asshole with her clit and I of diminishing volition...the little one's clitoris releasing a load of grumous clabber in my mouth...Maria smothered my mouth with hers and snaked a spatulate tongue within...spit laving...spooning thick curds of ejaculate into her mouth "...most magical of the elixirs of legend..." she whispered after she'd swallowed the secondhand wad "...now fuck me harder..." cinching spider legs tighter and sucking N_2's clit as I licked inside N_2's cunt and N_1 drove her clitoris like a battering ram in my butthole—inhalant at a stopping time for second-order prolongation of the local section of the flesh bundle: orifices and extensible erections—in the mirror N_1 fucking Maria's asshole as Maria rasped my penis with her cunt and sucked N_2's protracted clitoral penis—more inhalant at stopping time for third-order prolongations of the sections extending globally along the entwined flesh bundle—in the mirror on my knees fucking Maria...N_1 leaning against the bed behind me...my hand exploring her pancake tits...her distended clitoris of thick-girthed protrusive shaft and podgy knob exploring my asshole rubbing mucilaginous outflow on and in pushing forward...hoisting one leg up on the bed driving in stepping on my calf and wrapping the leg up and around forcing me flat on my face atop Maria as N_1 pulled back my head and shoved her clitoral penis in my mouth and the two of them hammer me front and back...Maria free from beneath me deep-kissing them on the mouth in turn—stopping times blur to inhaled prolongations of ever higher order the flesh bundle geodesically complete global sections orifices erections fluids in every orifice repeating the cunnilingus of N_2's sucked clitoris exploding again inside my mouth...Maria feasting from my mouth...Maria cajoling loads from my penis with mouth-cunt-asshole and I heterodyne the two N_i's...Maria merging us all...skin slapping skin teats sweat and slime flapping squeezed pinched cries and moans and hoarse guttural groans of surrender—N_1 merging us all...N_2 merging us all—final convolution of orifices erections extended—every orifice leaking oozing draining peccant humors saps rheumy serums—ball of flesh contemplating him-her in-out duality—breathing koan of woman/man-man-woman-woman/man...redundant pair of threesomes united with shared organs penile-clitoral-duality illusory duality of two sexes—maya maya

maya —agglutinating fused life form harmonizing fluid synthesis—the two hermaphrodites facing away from one another, one on her back, the other on her stomach, their penile clitoral prolongations simultaneously fucking the other's cunt while Maria sat on the face of the one on her back, the other sucking my dick to some end. Maria and I lip-locked exploring one another's mouths with our tongues. She whispers "This completes your holonomy group, baby…"

I don't remember Cone and Ashleigh leaving, but in the morning I found a note. "We are not returning to Tulane next year. Got into better schools. And don't worry, your secret is safe with us." The record was back in its jacket, the turntable with arm stowed, both amp and turntable switched off.

Chapter 23
a) Large Deviations

Summer's last gasp provided escape through a hole in a reflecting barrier, the recurrent random process construed as willed, if not purposeful, determinism bouncing back endlessly to trace out new paths until meeting said tear in the fabric of pointlessness and freed to transience in yet more dysteleological drift forced by acausal diffusion beyond the boundary. I chalked it up to the notion that mental time, whatever the term mental might signify in some operational sense, proved to be not uniformly spaced (disregarding Einstein's time for Newton's) in step size (whatever the fuck a time-step might be), something Bergson inexplicably used to argue as a reason to believe in free will, whatever those concatenated strings of letters might signify when conjoined as words beyond an attempt to obscure elanguescence.

I'd mastered the ostensible task set me, slaying the dragon of cost-schedule disunity with a powerful report to take down incompetent management and pseudo-technical technocrats who had established the absurd enterprise in the first place. Handing the packet of papers to Joelle to be typed, I told her this was the final report, the last batch. She looked up and smiled the full-lip smile, catlike enigmatic, Creole skin as fresh as it likely had been forty or so years ago when she had not yet reached her tenth birthday. "Well, I will miss the extra money but I took this as a gift of good fortune from the God of boondoggles." I replied something to the effect that the last big boondoggle I'd been on had been with Marines in Vietnam, but it was not nearly so lucrative. She frowned at the remark.

Given her age, it seemed possible the luscious locks that hung to her shoulders were dyed black, belied by inspection when sunlight through a window revealed a spectrum hinting of burgundy and warm brownish reds.

The SPR battle turned out to be a hard fight. I pondered Joelle and reflected on unexpected allies. Kim the brunette, tall for a chick around there, young and not shapely, better off hiding her flat butt in a skirt rather than the jeans she usually wore, impossible to hide her flat chest without padding or some other ruse to which she did not resort. She worked the Wangs though seldom did she actually operate one, mostly hanging around taunting the horny guys with wives away in Bay Saint Louis or Biloxi, cities in Mississippi of which I had been blissfully ignorant prior to this experience. Some of those guys lurked in that hostile bullpen with their adding machines, a mystery not opened to me but which I suspected had something to do with a conspiracy at the heart of the mystery of cost-schedule integration. Kim ignored me and I ignored her, icy and regal in haughty disdain for work or come-on but always turning heads as she paced the corridors and crossed carpeted rooms on high heels, usually boots but sometimes mules. Whence that arrogance, I wondered.

"Her mother's second in command of DOE here," Kip told me. "She runs the day-to-day stuff under the other Washington bureaucrat who is in charge but clueless; his name is Krill or something. Civil service but high up there. Name's Lu Anne. Never seen him. I have no idea what he looks like, but her, she's got frosted hair and big tits. Big tits. Hotter than Kim who is really fucking hot and only nineteen years old; lives with her mom. She's a lot taller than her mom. Long legs, nice butt. She won't give anyone here the time of day but loves to tease. Word is she's into thugs and porn or something, but I think that's just talk. I'm guessing she's into guys with money."

"You don't think she might be into chicks?"

"Well, anything's possible, but I doubt it. The word is that she has made a porn film. With Harry directing."

"Unlikely. So her mom's the one to talk to if I want to figure out what the fuck is really happening?"

"For sure. Krill is not even connected. She is hard to get to, though. No one gets to talk to her much, not even the top managers. Krill talks to the top guys for all the contractors, not Lu Anne, but she runs it all and nobody gets to talk to her."

I stewed about how to get to talk to her. Considered approaching Jeremy, but decided it was not the way. Instead, I visited her office complex and chatted up her secretary, letting it be known that I would like to talk to her boss, that I had a couple questions if she could spare me an hour or so. I made myself apparent around the other buildings, mostly pacing like a distracted consultant, hoping to get some buzz going with the women. When I paced past the DOE building, her secretary paid attention. The buildings had glass walls, so it was hard not to notice sidewalk loiterers. Being it was hot and humid, I showed up in summer weight wool stuff that played up my physical attributes, particularly my pouch as the gay crowd referred to it. My jacket flung casually over my shoulder like a bad impersonation of Robert Redford or Paul Newman in some of the dreadful films they'd made separately or together, a knit shirt to display musculature, the available stud.

Joelle asked if I'd heard about the drama. She stared up through round black eyes. The irises betrayed no color; I wondered how'd they be in direct sunlight. Her gaze penetrated more intensely than her speech justified, like she would have me pinned to the wall.

"What drama?"

"One of the female PhD students quit in a huff. She walked out on her advisor."

There were only two women in the department, both PhD candidates. They had both entered with my class. "The skinny hippy?"

"She is a poetess," Joelle defended. "Published."

"What was her beef?"

"Something about a prize, a sort of Nobel Prize for mathematicians."

"The Fields medal?"

"That sounds like it. She was angry there were no women who had won it. Her advisor told her that there are not that many women in mathematics, that it would happen in time. That made her even madder. She said that was her point. It was chauvinist."

"Well, prizes are baloney. Who cares? And by quitting she makes for one less female candidate."

"But don't they get you opportunity?"

"More likely you need opportunity to be able to qualify. Anyone from Tulane ever win it?" I'd have told her that smart women don't go into mathematics because it offers no path to power and smart women, liberated women, ought to be on the warpath.

"You think I ought to be on the warpath? Or is too late for me?"

"Too late? There's nothing you're late for."

She looked down. I wasn't sure how she'd taken it, but she had plainly brought up her age for some reason. She had more than a decade on me, likely more than a decade and a half.

"Would you come to my home for dinner?"

"Sure. Where do you live?"

"Near here. Closer to the river, in the Irish channel. Near Casamento's. You know it?"

"I think I've been there. White tile everywhere? Even the walls? Floors like you could eat off them?"

"Good poor boys. Oysters are wonderful there. We can go there if you want. Or I can cook something."

"I'd rather eat your cooking."

"You don't know if I can cook."

"I'm sure you cook."

That my sexual ego could grant me access to a pivot point in this edifice of government waste was a ridiculous conceit correlated with donning my new duds. Accursed articles of Jekyll and Hyde apparel. Likely self-vision clouded by self-deceit. It didn't cloud reality when I wore my janitor clothes as in this moment with Joelle, always at Tulane or when walking the streets. Perhaps it bore some resemblance to the disease of the zombie wandering the SPR graveyard looking for software to integrate the cost and schedule. Tall and substantial decked out in his three piece tweed suits, he seemed to ask other wanderers he met at random if they knew of software to integrate cost and schedule. Most terrifying his eyes, empty and perceiving you without seeing you, as though everyone he met was someone he had never met nor would ever meet. Never far behind was the short one in a rumpled suit, ready to tell me of his work managing pure mathematicians working on problems in operations research. So far as I could see, managing pure mathematicians would be like herding cats. Anyway, they had been staffers on the election committed of someone named David Treen and with his victory were out of a job.

I got the invitation to meet with Lu Anne.

Leading up to the opportunity I had accomplished my own due diligence. Destroying several hours of my life to learn the COPES software package, I'd grilled Kip about his role in its application. He portrayed himself as a data entry dummy without an inkling what the fuck it was about, only that he put in numbers handed him by someone from the evil bullpen of green eyeshade calculating demons. There was, he hinted, a secret report issued from that pit of hostility, the official report spewed from the bowels of COPES. Tracing the flow from in to out led to the same stuff coming out as going in after minor massage into some variables named BCWS and BCWP and other acronyms which were unexplained. No raw data went into the formulas for these expressions, only high level data summaries from the various sites that Kip input. I played with the formulae but got nowhere understanding other than their redundancy in the sense of being algebraically dependent not only as a set in their entirety but for all triples of formulae. Simply substitute any one of them into two others and subtract and the result was zero. That forced me to pester for a document regarding the meaning of the terms, given they were the formatted output from COPES. That led to a dusty DOE published SPR document that explained them in terms of budgeted cost of work planned and budgeted cost of work scheduled and some other acronyms for actual cost of work performed and so on. Those terms made sense, but the formulae for them in this report did not.

With backing from Jeremy I discovered the author of the stuff, one Wayne Wyatt who had gone on to a high position with a software company in Houston selling a package for project management to reside on less expensive minicomputers. I got his number and called him and played ignorant, applying the Socratic elenchus to drag from him that he had no inkling what the fuck those formulae he had "derived" actually meant. A few days later I received an official warning from Mr. Wyatt via Aldo Corelli through Bobbi to refrain from ever calling him again. Bobbi called me a troublemaker and then asked if I wanted to come to her apartment for another session I assumed of butt-fucking though she didn't make that clear. I demurred, being intent on a different trail of major stupidity.

My telephone interview with Mr. Wyatt seemed to get me the invite. Or at least I so assumed, given the invitation arrived shortly after the warning.

Joelle handed me two sealed envelopes, both stamped with the same stylized horn design as earlier ones, addressed to two distinct codes in capital letters with no other information.

"I almost forgot these," she said. "They came for you."

"How do you know they're for me? There's no name on them."

"I know. Don't worry about how." Laughter in her eyes played against a mouth made to suck bloody strawberries. "And don't ask where they come from. It is not the standard postal service."

I opened the letters later. One contained five hundred crisp hundred dollar bills and the other a note from the dweeb who said he was not returning, having taken a job in Europe that he hinted might be with a traveling circus. The rest of the note was a series of computations detailing curvature on the two-sphere.

Lu Anne sat behind a wide gray metal desk across the surface of which papers and documents of the sort bound locally scattered as if searching for a hiding place in a mortar attack. I guessed her as early fifties but perhaps younger. Her face didn't explicitly show age; her wide expanse of brow seemed hardly wrinkled except for when she frowned, and then the lines were shallow and fleeting. Her hair showed darker roots, suggesting the frosted aura a result of cosmeticians rather than nature. Admittedly it enhanced her sexuality, but it was not as if she flaunted that. She kept herself behind the desk, not standing or coming around to greet me or shake my hand, so I had no idea of her legs or ass or hips or waistline, though it was apparent she kept an enormous pair of meat sacks firmly constrained within a button front blouse that bulged as it traveled to high on her neck not far below her chin. It was rather a pronounced nasolabial fold that started above where her nostrils attached to her face and curved around beyond the ends of her wide mouth of thin, straight lips, merging with an occasional wrinkle hinting of a jowl.

I didn't see her as hot. She'd ordered the Friday appointment earlier in the week and I dressed as conservatively as possible, embarrassed at having presented such a spectacle as part of plan to set this up. Clearly she had no interest in me. After explaining what I was tasked with, something I was certain she knew, I asked her what was coming out of COPES and what was coming out of the bullpen full of calculators. She replied with the sort of aimless cheeriness one might expect from a neighbor discussing a beautiful Sunday morning. "I know you are doing a systems analysis in order to determine how to integrate cost and schedule. But understand that in Washington they believe we already have them integrated, that the program management task is complete and they have been integrated from the start. So it puts the entire operation in a peculiar light, what you need to do." She smiled unflinching from across the no man's land of her desk. "But if you will have an early dinner with me on Sunday, I think I can help you complete the task."

The Dweeb's stuff in the note regarded geometry on the unit sphere S^2 related to a bullshit session on the board from months back. I remembered saying I'd like to see a derivation of the curvature term with the sine in it or some such thing; here it was in gory detail. "Of course $X(\theta,\varphi)$ is parameterized as $(\sin\theta\cos\varphi,\sin\theta\sin\varphi,\cos\theta)$." Of fucking course; it was how I envisioned it. Along came some shit about parallel translation and circles of constant latitude and walking along those curves, all of it intensely boring. He went into extravagant detail with computations, pages of them, and then he worked out some curves on the sphere like the intersection of a cylinder on the radius of circle one in the (x,y) plane centered at (1,0,0) and the sphere with radius two centered at the origin For some unfathomable reason he worked out its equation: $c(t) = (2\cos^2 t, \sin t, 2\sin t)$ which he showed had coordinates in terms of parameterization of the form $c(t) = ((u(t),v(t)) = ((\pi/2)-t,t)$. He drew a fucking picture. It got worse. "If we let C be a parallel of colatitude given by $\theta = \theta_0$ constant then a parallel translate of the unit vector $(\partial X/\partial\theta)(\theta_0,0)$ along C is given by $V(\varphi) = [\cos((\cos\theta_0)\varphi)]X_1 - \{[\sin((\cos\theta_0)\varphi)]/\sin\theta_0\}X_2$ with $X_1 = \partial X/\partial\theta$

and $X_2 = \partial X / \partial \varphi$." He presented computations I ignored that he claimed showed this expression was correct. "Then," he wrote after more calculations I didn't bother to read, "you can conclude that $V(0) = V(2\pi)$ iff C is the equator." Okay, parallel translation. I couldn't believe he had sent this note to me. Worse, I didn't see an answer to my question, not that I gave fuck: I'd figured it out in my head one time while fucking Debby in the ass. If I ever saw him again I'd be tempted to punch him. I wadded the narrow lined papers with their carefully formed letters and symbols into a ball and threw it into a trash can.

Jeremy loved the report. He said it was more than he'd hoped for. Once presented to the local DOE hierarchy, it got a meeting with big shots, including Aldo and the Hines guy from BOA, called by the top DOE dog, Krill. Neither Jeremy nor Lu Anne were there, but there were plenty of others I didn't recognize and who weren't introduced. They held it after hours in a DOE conference room. Krill at a desk hid in the shadows on an elevated stage looking down on the likes of us. Addressing me, he said "This is an amazing piece of work, Mr. Butcher. I wish we'd had a super-analyst like you here when we started up." Super analyst indeed; all that is needed is a little common sense to realize that common units are necessary to make cost and schedule work in unison. Grade school logic. Unmentioned went that the idea to use an estimator to determine the interpolations necessary to make cost and schedule units uniform came from the Indian schedule engineer, Monkar, a point I'd made in the report. No one addressed the fact that the actual budget cost came in a clandestine report from the bullpen of calculators or that the schedule report, also clandestine, came from the schedule shop and was written by Monkar and ceremonially approved by his boss. Lu Anne had given me copies of the reports and a copy of the COPES output, the only report that went to Washington. I didn't see any relationship with the data amongst the three reports but she and her notes assured me that the COPES report was consistent to the extent possible. The details about COPES and the calculator stuff accounted for five minutes of the business Lu Anne and I transacted that Sunday.

It was not long after the Krill-meeting that Krill announced he was leaving the DOE for private sector employment, some outfit in the state of Washington named Battelle. I'd never heard of it. Jeremy laughed about it as he opened a bottle of what he called special Scotch, hard to obtain he said. Smuggled in from Britain since it wasn't exported. A rare special bottling of five year old Springbank at 92 proof. "The charm's in its youth when bottled," he said. "Not a lot of wood aging to mellow it. I'm sure it will be to your taste."

It was. Rough whisky, almost unfinished; without the finesse of the stuff we'd imbibed before dinner, a lighter dram, as Jeremy liked to say. From a distillery named Tullibardine, it opened with an aroma of strawberries and left an aftertaste of flowers. Nothing like the young paint thinner which was, to be sure, more to my taste, though I had not found the floral notes on the other hard to take.

Our dinner companions were Gudrun and Shawntel. I had the impression I was supposed to take one of them home with me along with the bottles of Lagavulin, Edradour, and a special bottling of Scapa at only eight years of age and 140 proof. Jeremy had failed to convert me from Bourbon, but instead widened my horizons. I didn't take either of Gudrun or Shawntel to the apartment, which was by then haunted by a ménage of women.

I'd come home one day to find my key didn't fit the lock. The door showed no sign of tampering. I turned to head down to the landlord's apartment to see what the fuck when it opened and three women walked out into the solarium. The medium height fair one with flaxen hair confronted me. She wore a short pleated skirt and sleeveless scoop neck t-shirt that showed her as meatiest of the three with boobs of substance lying against her ribs, apparently not heavy enough to have yet settled with gravity given she was braless and the nipples poked into the material on a slight bias to the outside. Probably a C cup. Her face seemed to have been put together without care for symmetry though it was hard to measure any up and down asymmetry of the eyes even as one seemed to slant upward at a higher angle than the other; maybe it was the long upturned brows since the eyes, greenish gray almonds, didn't slope upward so much after all. The bridge of the nose started higher on the right side than the left, wide but narrowing before widening again with the impression of ever so slight a crook, dream of a fracture implied by an apparent mismatch of passage connection. It ended with flare at the base where it rose from the face, the right wing pulled up slightly compared to the left in a hint of warpage, amplified by broad flattened dorsum and apex. Looking directly on, the nasal ridge did not widen at the end, only the alae enclosing the nostrils which flared wider than the ridge, the nares themselves not visible. A pronounced ridge of short philtrum ended in a mouth not much wider than the extent of the nose and with longer superior labia on the left than the right, forming an unbalanced, narrow Cupid's bow off-center above a full lower vermilion border. Without apparent cheeks, the angle of the lower face sloped at constant rate to a rounded chin.

"Who are you?" she asked with authority, the words wrapped with paced speech in a smoky voice. I began to grow an erection.

"I live here," I said. "Who the fuck are you?"

"So you are Whitey?" It came from the tall one, a lean black perhaps five ten or so whose accent spoke of some origin I couldn't place. The sound of her speech rilled as laughing water. She wore loose white shorts that contrasted the tarry soot of her skin, leather sandals and a simple red blouse. She tended to skinny but not angularity; I doubted prominent ribs. Her face was long and her features unpronounced except her smile which lit up the entire edifice, the smile lines framing high, puffy cheeks. She wore her hair unadorned hanging straight down over her shoulders to the middle of her back, coarse, thick and black without overtones. My erection grew more pronounced, crawling down my leg.

"Jesus," I said. "There are more like you?"

Her laugh arose as shallow water over stones.

I am Whitey," I confessed with reservation. "Were you expecting me?"

The short one said nothing, only stared until I looked at her, at which she dropped her gaze. I guessed her at five-two. She sheathed herself in a loose white blouse with a high collar, almost a turtleneck, well-worn baggy dungarees rolled up at the bottom and tattered high-top red tennis shoes. She displayed nothing except a face peeking from a wilderness of dense mahogany hair draped down over her shoulders, framing her visage like an oval cameo. Long forehead, face tapering to a sharp cleft chin, expression of fright or regret.

I let my eyes wander below the blonde interrogator's waist. "So what are you doing here? More to the point, how the fuck did you get in? And why'd you change my lock?" Her slim legs were shapely, not twigs but not substantively meatier above the knees than below where calves as long as her thighs extended in elegant curvature. She wore black high heels with an ankle strap and strap around the toes like sandals. I could tell from the skirt her hips had no flare, straight from short waist to lean thighs, but that a narrow rounded ass arced out behind her, the skirt pleats not adding dimension enough to disguise corporeal substance.

From the door came the reply in straight-tone delivery. "We didn't change the lock. We changed your key."

A giantess stood in the doorway. Actually a tall woman, taller than I, perhaps almost seven feet. She wasn't of imposing girth, frail from the look of her long arms. She wore a vivid pink blouse with a round scooped neck embroidered in a geometric pattern likely of primitive origin; the word Chamula came to mind, though I had no idea from where or regarding its referent, if any. The blouse hung over a black skirt cascading to her ankles like a wrinkled cone from the bottom of which projected feet in sandals that looked like fancy thongs with leather soles and shell-covered straps.

"Jesus, how many of you are in there?" I asked.

"Don't worry. Your space is a strong deformation retract of ours, so you won't notice us unless you want to—".

"Or we want you to" from the blonde.

"You can fill the apartment with us or we can vanish entirely. Your choice."

"More or less" again the blonde.

"Uh huh. Strong deformation retract. As nuts as that is, I understand what you mean."

"You are always with us, but we are not always with you."

"And we are not projections," said the blonde.

"I'm guessing you somehow have something to do with Dina."

The giantess' skin tone was best described as pale. Maybe washed out had her face not been so carefully tinted, red lips the garish feature though someone had chiseled the light brown brows, colored the long lashes. She parted her hair, same color as the brows and perhaps better described as dark blonde, the color of honey called amber, in the middle of her head, a straight divide from whence it fell on either side of her face to her shoulders in long, relaxed waves. The way it framed her face made me think of the ears of a cocker spaniel.

"We serve The Dina. She has become Ma-Dina. Some think of her as Aphrodite, others as Ishtar or Astarte, but it is all the same. She is ascended. Her ordeal is over. She has been transmogrified and transcends mortal concerns."

"You mean she's finished with the remodeling?"

"Yes. And she returns shortly. We are here for her. We are her slaves, just as she is yours."

"I never noticed she was my slave, to be honest."

"You are paired, as in quantum physics…"

"Don't start that bullshit. So who are you? The den mother?"

"I am the Ma-Dina's rep. Mundane contact is through me—"

"Her agent?"

"If you want to use such a term. These three are my actuators. They are my horae—"

"Think of us as the charities of Dina," the blonde said. Her hair was the limpest of the bunch, thin and stringy, straggling over her shoulders down to the middle of her back.

"Horae?"

"Charis," she said. "We run the harines you'll be dealing with on a day to day."

"Hours," the one who had not yet spoken said, looking up through eyes filled with regret. "We are the hours. We are all hedonic engineers."

"Right. Hedonic engineering," the black one said. "My name is Akua-Ba. The sad one is Esther. The one with tits is Cybele."

"If you think of Picasso," Cybele said, "my face will appear." She didn't laugh, so I swallowed my own.

"You won't see me often." the one in the doorway said. "I govern the temple and the commercial interests that keep it all afloat. I leave for California, for San Francisco, where Ma-Dina's temple is under attack as we speak."

"So they get rid of COPES," I said to Jeremy as we worked our way into the bottle of Tullibardine. "That ought to save money."

"Not right away; they won't get rid of COPES right away. Need to port it over to the new system that will run on the Prime. And that will require an Information Systems Department, with a manager, systems analysts, programmers and an operator. And one or two of my systems guys from DC or California as consultants."

"There's nothing to port over. They just need to get the cost and schedule systems on the same units."

"Apples to apples, yes. But that is a local secret. As far as the external world knows, officially, they are porting over COPES to make it cheaper. Thanks to a genius analyst we brought on board. We got a big bonus from that. And of course the estimator who integrates the units will have to remain on staff in case of new items."

"That's nuts."

"That's business. We will replace the expensive and inefficient COPES program management system with one of our design on a new minicomputer, state of the art, adding a staff of systems people. Jerry will finally have something to operate."

"What will he do?"

"He'll come in the morning, install the storage disk, and boot it up. At night he'll shut it down and remove the storage disk."

"That's it?"

"It's more'n he does now."

"So you will buy this minicomputer?"

"Lease it. Cheaper than the COPES, including the direct-line costs. But the staff will unfortunately make up for that cost and then some."

"You've already got plenty of crazies running around there. Those two Treen guys, especially the one haunting the halls looking for magic software, are idiots."

"Well, maybe—"

"No maybe. It bodes ill for society if educated grown men believe in magic technology to solve their problems without a need for thinking."

"Thinking. Not many are called to it."

"I assume they'll be gone."

"Oh, hell no. They're there as a favor, to be honest. To a Louisiana political big shot who needs the favor of getting them jobs where they don't harm anything. And besides, they're the only people working for us there who look professional, aside from the secretaries."

"But you'll save by getting rid of the back-room boys with the adding machines?"

"Not. They stay too. They will continue to publish their report, as a check against the new stuff."

"But it isn't even related."

"So what? That is how cost savings work. We did a program where they wanted to get rid of radars and replace them with some other devices. They paid for annual studies for five years, then they implemented the new devices and kept all the old radars as well. That was DOD. They are even freer with money than this newly created DOE under the authority of which the SPR operates. But there has been a change of guard at the highest level of DOD and they understand the operational problems of the early days of the SPR. They are circumspect with respect to the failure of the COPES system about which they remain publicly mum."

"So they know?"

"Of course. One reason for the change of guard. Even before your report they knew the output of COPES was bogus. Had Krill scrambling for a new job, though you drove the nail in the coffin. Anyway, thanks to your outstanding solution our contract has been expanded thirty percent. On top of our bonus.

We will also be adding more adding machines, Whitey. Since there are two new sites coming on."

"So the cost saving will cost more."

"Precisely. Across the board, in fact. Not just for us. All the contractors will expand, and new contractors will be brought in, mostly as subcontracts. You should see how much paperwork reduction requires new paperwork.."

I stared at him, not sure whether to be aghast or amused. It made me think of the Marine Corps losing more men to lower casualties.

"I'll make you a vice-president if you would agree to come on board, give up this mathematics foolishness which can only end badly."

"How so?"

"Poverty, Mr. Butcher. Mathematicians die in obscure poverty."

I thought of Riemann. And Abel. Not to mention Fermat shot dead. And how I'd obtained the data for my report. I couldn't imagine a career following such a path. Jeremy had no idea and I wasn't about to give him one.

To meet Lu Anne I'd worn a cream knit shirt that showed off my muscles and a powder blue summer weight wool suit that showed off my eyes and the outline of my cock lurking along my thigh. I wasn't sure why I did it, but the urge overpowered me.

Her directions led me out Canal past City Park Boulevard and Robert E. Lee Boulevard to a suburban conglomeration of houses near the lake. Hers was standard ranch style with carport and picture window, probably three bedrooms, much like what I'd grown up in except not cinder block and bigger. The sort of place I avoided.

As I walked up the drive past a weed-infested excuse for a lawn, she appeared in the doorway wearing a loose flower print skirt in an A-line cut. It ended just above the knees without hinting at the form of her upper legs, but her calves arched to finely chiseled ankles. Her knees were longish and rectangular. Her feet in a pair of flat leather sandals, were surprisingly slender given stocky legs which were, on reflection, not stocky so much as merely short. And perhaps not really so short compared to her trunk. Certainly nothing like Gundrun for dwarfish. She wore a white blouse that might have been a man's dress shirt with the upper half of the buttons undone displaying a border of black bra, a tease perhaps but not out of line with the fashion on parade on the streets of New Orleans. Taking me by the arm, she led me to her car parked in the driveway and backtracked us to a ramshackle old two-story place on Canal Street called Mandina's where we sat opposite one another at a round table and drank Dixie beer and ate an appetizer of a platter of tiny fried shrimp she called popcorn shrimp, the reason she came here she said, and a couple dozen raw oysters at her insistence, after which she tried to coax me into eating an oyster poor boy. I chose instead soft shell crab.

Dinner conversation ran to questions about Jeremy. I answered with deliberate circumspection, assuming their relationship was strictly professional but beginning to suspect otherwise. I worked to steer the conversation to the project and my concerns regarding actual versus apparent operations. She deflected my questions without being obvious, controlling the conversation with ease. I considered it unwise to push the issue.

She'd chosen her blouse and bra to maximize exposure without laying it all out there, exposing endless cleavage of difficult to distinguish mounds of pasty flesh when she leaned into the conversation. I purposely fixed my gaze on her eyes, not a difficult feat, though I did note the bra seemed of sturdy construction.

When we got back to her house she insisted I come in with her. I wanted to beg off, instead following her into the suburban pile of cliché, knickknacks of various composition deposited on shelves and tables and even fucking doilies on the cloth sofa in the middle of the living room that faced both television and picture window. A goddamn coffee table. It reminded me I had not stepped foot into a pile of shit Americana in years other than the brief visit at my mother's former abode.

"Good," she said heading for the kitchen." Kimmie isn't here."

She asked me if I wanted wine and I asked for beer or something harder if she had it, figuring she was about to ask me to perform extra duties.

"Kimmie?"

After handing me a can of Pearl beer, she found a bottle of Jim Beam in a cupboard, saying it was pretty old since no one drank the stuff. I didn't ask why she had it, instead asking if it were okay if I smoked while eyeing what appeared a mix of butts and roaches in an ashtray on the square black kitchen table.

"Sure, go ahead. My daughter Kimberly smokes cigarettes. You know her. She works for BOA."

I lit up one of my hashish laced homemade ones and she took a jug of white wine out of the fridge and poured herself a glass.

"Kim? She's your daughter? I didn't know that."

"Let me show you the house," taking me by the arm and directing me out of the kitchen. "Wait," I protested, juggling the bottle, a glass, and the can of beer with the cigarette dangling from my lips rolling out thick hash-oil saturated smoke like a stovepipe. She poured a fistful of Beam into the tall glass and left the bottle on the table. "We can come back, silly" and I had sufficient degrees of freedom remaining to remove the cigarette from my face. "Whew, that's strong," she said. "Only tobacco?" "My own blend," I answered and she said "Kim sometimes smokes marijuana, though I try to discourage it. It is dangerous for our position, given the Department of Energy has a no-drugs policy and makes you get a clearance now and all."

She led me down a darkened hallway. There was a hard carpet underfoot, likely threadbare. She stopped in front of a doorway and dragged me into a bedroom by my belt.

"Let me help you out of those pants," she said, reaching for my belt buckle.

"Uh, not sure that's so good an idea."

"And why not? You find me unattractive?"

"I didn't say that—"

"You aren't married. The rumor is you hang out with porn stars. I may not be that experienced, but I have been around the block."

"Wouldn't say I hang out with them. I know some through a mutual acquaintance."

She pressed her tits into me and rubbed her hands over my groin.

"My," she said, feeling my appendage begin to erect, "that is quite responsive." Raising up on tiptoe, she pulled my head to her face and into a messy mouth kiss. My hands were occupied; I was unable to do anything but abide the tongue probe. I responded by stretching towards erect. Pulling back, she set her wine and my beer and glass of Beam on a dresser. I took another pull from the cigarette which lightened the moment.

"I was more concerned it might interfere with our work relationship," I said. "I don't mix with students, at least not while they're students."

Undoing my belt, opening my zipper, "I am not a student, Mr. Butcher. So don't fret about that. It could actually help…" pulling my trousers to my knees. "I've been wanting to see this thing up close. My God, it is huge. I have not seen so big a dick, ever. Bigger than speculation on site."

"I don't think it is especially oversized. Mostly average."

"At least a foot long with that diameter is not average, dear. Does it get bigger as it hardens? It does get harder, doesn't it? I'm not sure I can even get it in my mouth—" drawing in the foreskin and licking within the fold around the head before working her lips over the knob, my half-limp shaft disappearing halfway into her face, snaking down her throat, feeling the rough constriction—

"You seem practiced," I say, pushing it farther as it hardened and she came up for air drooling a long stream of spit and pre-cum.

"My God, it does get hard. And huge! I can't get my hands to meet around it. What is this thing? Look at it drool. And those bumps. It's turning purple! I need to feel it inside me."

"It was inside—"

"Not down my throat. That's Kimmie's specialty, ever since that Lovelace girl got famous."

"I heard that." It came from across the room, at the door. "Starting something without me?"

"Didn't think you were home, dear." She pushed me back to sit on the edge of the bed, pants around my ankles.

"But you didn't look too hard, either, did you?"

"You two don't look at all alike—"

Kim was dressed as at work, in jeans and a loose blouse. Long legs like a fashion model, but they didn't seem like twigs, especially where they ended at her high, flat ass.

"She takes after her father."

"He's a big man—"

"Fat man," her mother said. "Fat and gross—"

"But tall. Very tall. That's where I get my height and long legs—"

"You have different last names."

"I took back my maiden name after I divorced the bastard."

"You need to get over him—"

Lu Anne pulled down her panties and stepped out of them, leaving on her skirt and blouse. She worked my pants off and the two of them removed my shirt and shoes. Lu Anne climbed onto my dick, sitting astride facing me in her dress, answering her daughter who looked on, "He is a crook, dear. And a chicken queen."

"He is in prison for burglary, not for little boys—"

She settled gradually over my erection, her face contorted with pain or bliss or memories of her ex…

"But we both know his love of the little boys, the faggot son of a bitch," she hissed.

"He gets out soon, Mom, and you need to be a little more forgiving—"

"The son of a bitch isn't coming here. I want nothing to do with him."

"Mother—"

Pressing the back of my head forward, she pushed her mouth against mine, invading with a fat tongue, her cunt sliding up and down the length of my erection.

Abruptly standing, she turned around and backed up, gripped my cock at the base and wormed it into her anus, torquing it down with a moan. She bunched her skirt up around her waist and pumped her ass in rotary motion until she extracted an ejaculation, thrusting backward to smother, rotating and twisting against my groin until the erection vanished. She wriggled up, white ejaculate spewing with a fart. Kim gushed "What a lot of splooge" and dropped to her knees, lapping it up before turning to my deflated dick after informing, "Mom says I get my taste for sucking cock from my dad, but I think her love of dicks in her ass was borrowed from him…" "It's like an enema, dear." "Mmm…" from Kimmie, face in my lap tonguing the sperm from my crotch and my cock and her mother's asshole, turning at last to earnestly suck my erection back to life with studied vengeance.

She looked up through brown round eyes and slurped out "It better come back's'all I gotta say." It did, contorting her mouth as it grew fat and hard inside her face. She worked fruitlessly to swallow it. Her mom joined her with a "Here's how its done, Hon," getting her lips almost to the bottom third before Kim shoved her head from behind to bury the erect penis, jerked the head back with a fistful of hair, pushed her aside and gradually ingurgitated it down her own throat as her mother goaded the back of her head with the flat of her hand until Kim snorted chunky curds from her nose and came up gasping, sputtering strings of drool and sperm like strands of melted cheese. She struggled out of her jeans and kicked off her panties and climbed onto my lap, settling down over my erection with a wet cunt that eructed slurps as she rode and I stood and held her by the arms and turned to settle her in an arm chair near the bed and fuck her with a pounding, relentless rhythm at which she cried hoarsely in what I assumed to be an orgasm, the hoarse cries becoming "Stop asshole, let me suck it." Her mother pulled me off and Kim pushed me back into the chair, went to her knees and sucked until I exploded as far into her throat as she could force my dick.

I moved to the bed and flopped onto my back to recover. I sat up, lit another cigarette and chased Beam with beer, watching mother and daughter undress. I paid more attention to Lu Anne. She dropped her blouse on the dresser and verified my observation that her boobs were strapped in, ensconced in substantive packaging wired below for lift and covered diagonally across to expose maximum separation, "Help me with this, Kim" she said, struggling with the hooks or whatever they were in back. As Kim came over, Lu Anne shrieked, "Jesus, what happened to your leg?"

Without the distraction of my hard dick, she'd noticed my scars. As she leaned over and examined the leg, Kim undid the bra strap and her boobs unfurled from the middle of her chest, a pair of flattened, narrow briskets covered with fine spider webs of faint stretch marks where they attached to her torso. The hanging slabs were capped with nipples surrounded by brick red areolae bigger than the entirety of Kim's breasts and that pointed toward the floor.

Kim came over and traced the scars on my leg with long fingers.

"Wow. What is that?"

"Scar," I said. "Bullet wounds."

"Wow," Kim again. "You were shot?"

"Yes."

"Vietnam?" Lu Anne asked.

"Yes. They think six times or so, with an AK-47 or machinegun. I almost lost the leg."

"I never knew anyone who'd been shot. Or been wounded in a war. Or even been to a war," Kim said.

"Well, now you can have someone who's been to war fuck your asshole, dear," her mother said.

I reached out and touched Lu Anne's hanging dugs. Huge compared to Dina's, they seemed to have had all the stuffing removed. They were devoid of nubby protrusions on the areolae except a single spot on the right one far inside the inner rim and near the nipple, possibly a wart or colorless mole, and another on the left areola farther from the nipple and above it well inside the red disk.

"You think he can do it again?"

"What you think, there, war hero," Lu Anne asked, standing up with hands on hips, "you up to the challenge? You like my tits? They are so ugly."

"Let me smoke this cigarette first," I said. "I'm sure I have something left."

"We can help," Kim said, taking the cigarette from my hands and smoking it as if it were a joint.

"Careful," I said to her cough, "that is tobacco." But she knew there was more. She gave me a conspiratorial wink. I decided looking at her wasn't going to contribute to my resurrection. Neither was looking at her mother, though it was easier on the eyes.

Lu Anne was not so wrinkled as I would have guessed from her age. She had decent tone, but Kim's broad ass atop long legs dimpled at the thighs made me understand why she wore jeans. I guessed her at less than thirty, her mother likely twenty-five years her senior and with better tone. As tall as I, at least in the high-heeled boots she usually wore, and a full foot or so taller than her mother, at first quick glance Kim gave the impression of a model. More careful consideration revealed elongated legs that ended in obtuse pelvis and flat butt behind a short crotch attached to a short, thick waist. It sometimes gave the impression, when she wore the right outfit, that her ass attached directly to her armpits. As stretched out as were her thighs, they were hefty compared to her straight, thin calves set apart by oblong knees, perhaps a stray artifact from her mother's genetic information. The naked thighs going to cottage cheese seemed more appropriate to a short, squat woman. Her torso echoed her legs, drawn out interminably, and stationed low a notch above her waist were a pair of mounds far below her sternum defining an unexpected narrow valley hinting at cleavage, the breasts dotted outboard and above the midline with tiny nipples looking up and away.

As unappealing were the geometrics of Kim's body, her face had always struck me as attractive. Symmetry without obtrusive features: straight, smooth nose unmarred by extra curves or protrusions, mouth neither wide nor narrow, the vermilion border of no noticeable characteristic, dimpled cheeks when she smiled. Not a forehead high or low, unwrinkled, rounded chin not an extremity. Her ears hid behind hair of chestnut or mahogany or other warm brown tone that she parted atop her head so it hung with a solitary wave to her shoulders. Her brown eyes were neither round nor excessively ovular, the sort of eyes one forgot immediately.

Kim and I finished the smoke and I drank the beer and whiskey, all the while appraising Lu Anne sans boobs. Until now, I had thought what she kept under wraps would be dumpy, loose skin and thick thighs, gobby butt and spreading hips, tummy hanging down. I was wrong. It was tightly packaged but not really toned like she worked out or had muscular abs, what you could see

542

of her abdomen given the boobs dangling practically to her mons. She looked better out of her clothes, modulo the pendulous dugs, her ass smoothly rounded, her thighs and hips as shapely as the calves, the only defect a pad of dimpled fat on either side of her upper thighs, not a full saddlebag but more a minor outgrowth. The dugs hung from about mid chest, flattened with nipples pointed at her feet. They were crisscrossed with prominent blue veins, elongated but not as widely triangular as would be imagined in visions of her nakedness implicit in the clothed model-reality.

"My breasts," Lu Anne said, "were not always so large. When they first developed, I was about twelve and they were not large. But they were always flat. Always. And they just kept growing, creeping longer and flatter and skinnier. By the time I was a senior in high school, they had so enlarged I could not go anywhere without packing them in. Guys loved them. It was amazing. I discovered I wanted to be with lots of guys, too. It got so before I ever gave up my virginity I was sucking cocks and taking it in the ass. I used to take packs of guys out to a secluded place in a park near the middle school I went to in Dallas, eighth grade, and suck them all off. I had a terrible reputation, but the guys came around. In high school I started dating in tenth grade; I waited until I was a senior to give up my virginity. Don't even know which one of the five dudes I did in that session got it."

"Is it any wonder I'm such a slut?" Kim asked. "I really want to be a porn star. That's—"

"Now Kim, that is a bad idea and you know it—"

"Why not? They make a lot of money, don't they Mr. Butcher?"

"Look, under these circumstances I can't abide you calling me mister anything. Whitey. Call me Whitey. And I know one porn star who makes a lot of money. A hell of a lot of money. It's her Porsche I drive." I wished I hadn't said that, but it was too late to call it back.

"You know a porn star? That is the rumor at work, but I didn't believe it."

"Yep. Met her at a party at Jeremy Ball's house." I decided to leave Kip and Jerry out of it.

"Kim, we have talked about this—"

"It always comes down to YOUR reputation. No one will need to know."

"Someone will know."

"Tell me, Whitey, who is it? And at Jeremy's house?"

543

"That is no surprise," her mother said." We see him all the time at a swing house in Metairie."

"But never with any porn stars. Only that one woman—"

"Taller than he is, almost lanky with dark hair?"

"That's his wife, right?" Lu Anne asked.

"No," I said. "That's his personal assistant or executive assistant or some such thing. Shawntel, right?"

"That's her name," Lu Anne said. "I thought it was his wife. She can eat pussy, I tell you what, and she tastes good, too."

"Who 'we' go to this club?"

"Me and mom."

"I met Kim's father, my former husband, when I was in high school. He had moved to Dallas during my junior year; he was a senior, from Montana. He got involved with me because of my love of the attention of groups of boys. We ended up going steady through my senior year; he went to work after high school but encouraged me to keep up what I was doing. He used me to attract guys and after graduation we got married. I got a job; we'd advertise for guys to have sex with me and him, bi guys, and we'd do threesomes. But we'd go to swing clubs and he would very discretely try to pick up some of the guys for bi three-ways. Frowned on in swinging, mostly, and he still encouraged me. I got bi-sexual when we started hooking up with bi-couples. I love to eat pussies blindfolded while a gang of men fuck me in the asshole."

More personal than I wanted, the biographical commentary nonetheless induced a renewed hard-on.

"Can you introduce me to some people in the business?" Kim asked.

"I can, if your mom doesn't object."

"Nah, go ahead." She kneeled to suck my dick.

I decided to leave Harry Ball out of it for the moment, but I would contact him directly. I'd avoid Dina's underlings, since it wasn't clear when Dina would reappear, assuming she did. "The woman I know best calls herself Dina. Has huge boobs like your mother."

"Dina? Lean with giant breasts that hang down? I have seen so many of her films. She's a genius!"

Lu Anne slathered my dick with saliva, slurped the fluid oozing from the head.

"I just saw her in a movie. She gang banged a pack of German shepherds. Amazing. I couldn't believe those dogs. They must have been trained. They did double penetration! Dogs. She sucked one and two others double fucked her. It was so hot. They shoved their knots inside her and one of them got stuck inside her asshole. Started dragging her around, but then stopped when this amazingly HUGE dog, like a big bull dog or something, came up and stopped it. Quietly, sort of. It stood there until they came loose and meantime she just kept fucking and sucking. It was the sexiest thing I ever saw, stretching out her asshole like a rubber sheet. I have wanted to fuck a dog ever since I saw Linda Lovelace do it. God, the idea makes me wet…" She sat on the bed and worked her open hand into her pussy from the front, then closed her fist and worked it around inside, moaning and saying, "That big dog was so huge… The bulldog or whatever or it was, but not so ugly as a bulldog, very distinguished… Oh god, oh…" Her mother came up for air. "Finish you story, Kim…" pulling me up out of the chair and over to the bed and directing me to push Kim on her side while fisting herself and ease my cock into her asshole at which Kim gasped and curled into a tighter ball and pushed her fist inside her vagina past her wrist. Lu Anne whispered, "She can get her whole arm up to the elbow in there…" and Kim saying "That big dog had a massive dick, bigger than yours I think, and after the pack was spent it fucked her silly, got its knot which was MUCH bigger than any fist stuck in her pussy and dragged her around…" Lu Anne leaning back in the chair watching us, her right leg draped up over the arm and fingers in her twat, her flat boobs draped over her trunk with the grace of a pair of raw briskets. Kim shuddered and groaned and twitched, convulsing with her forearm up her cunt and my dick up her asshole and Lu Anne talked about how her husband had also gone into business as a burglar and was caught twice, the second time sentenced to a stretch in the pen, and then after a third conviction to a long stretch, but she'd divorced him by then and taken a civil service job that led to a DOE position in New Orleans and how surprising it was that the swing scene in New Orleans was tame compared to Dallas, given the cities reputation for a party town, but she'd found the Crescent City Couples Club out in Kenner and then she had started taking Kim when she came home midday once to find her fucking some boys though she had to wait for her to turn seventeen and I ejaculated in Kim's asshole before she pulled her hand out of her cunt and Lu Anne finished by saying her tits had not produced milk for Kim, dry as a bone and totally insensitive. Guys lick and munch them to no avail, nothing, dead as a doornail…

They tag-teamed me for a long time, coaxing me to sperm within each of their remaining orifices. Then they doubled up on me with vicious intent, eventually milking a final orgasm before setting me free.

I left after midnight. Lu Anne handed me a manila envelope at the door.

"The reports," she said. "All of them, including the secret ones. I made notes that indicate where the COPES data comes from as calculated by the cost analysts in the backroom with their adding machines. The official story is that the raw data is gathered from contractor site reports and in the field by cost analysts and entered into the COPES database where the cost and schedule are updated by COPES for program management reports. In reality, the separate cost data goes to those guys with the adding machines. They do the data crunching, not COPES. Same with schedule, though those guys have a program that updates the schedule on that computer in their office. The cost analysts are mostly like Hayden who tries to keep the subcontractors out in the boonies from stealing too much and screwing things up too badly.

"The basic thing is that they didn't have anyone who knew what they were doing when they set it up. They hired some consultants like Wyatt but were unable to get their good people to transfer out from DC to New Orleans. Schools, lack of potable tap water, lots of issues. It was mandated that they have an integrated cost and schedule and they chose COPES to do it, but no one bothered to figure out how to put the two kinds of data together. I guess you know how."

"Actually, that was explained to me by an engineer in scheduling."

"Really. That is odd."

"No one listens to him, probably 'cause he's a grunt and not a consultant; his boss doesn't let him talk up the management food chain. Lots of consultants roaming around this place."

"There are people at the top in DC who know what is going on; they have been turning the screws to get it right, but they also tread cautiously lest they get in trouble with Congress, maybe lose their jobs. Krill will take the fall. That's his job."

I thanked her for most of it. The last thing she said was, "Leave my name out of it."

b) Ramification Deficiency

The fall semester offered relief from the hallucination referred to as the "real world," a misnomer if ever there were one. More like make-work pretend world. Made me wonder how the entire contraption stayed afloat. So far as I was concerned, I was barreling into thirty and yet to hold a real job.

My necessary class load promised to be light, given how far along I had gotten in the eyes of the faculty. I had to take one class and attend a seminar entitled Thesis Research between me and my advisor, so really between me, and I intended to skip teaching. They must have suspected some such thing and offered me the only session of multivariate calculus. Instead of Lang's classic text, they chose Robert Seely's *Calculus of Several Variables,* but it didn't matter as I intended to approach it as if addressing a class of gifted Princeton freshman. I would hold forth from some combination of Spivak's *Calculus on Manifolds* and the *Differential Calculus* and *Differential Forms* of Henri Cartan.

Momus offer of Analysis on Complex Manifolds had won the vote for the advanced offering from the analysis group. It was a break for me.

Momus began gently with topological manifolds and made them differential, real analytical or holomorphic in much the same way as had Postnikov in the monograph Momus had recommended the previous year. He lectured with careful exposition precisely delineated on the blackboard and, being a master raconteur, dotted the lectures with stories of famous mathematicians he had brushed against so that by the time the waters got deep most didn't notice they were drowning. In no time he had moved to a discussion of embeddings of real differential and analytic manifolds in Euclidean spaces, leading to the theorem that there are no compact complex submanifolds of positive dimension in n-dimensional complex space. Of course, that followed from the simple result that global holomorphic functions on compact, connected complex manifolds were constant, indicating the first sign of significant difference between complex manifolds and real manifolds. He brought up Stein manifolds, noncompact manifolds which could be embedded in n-dimensional complex space, and promised to do some function theory on them if we got that far. He told us his only PhD student, a former Navy pilot, had done an excellent thesis in this area and turned down several tenure-track positions in mathematics at major universities to pursue his love of flying, eventually becoming a professor of aviation science. It was not long before we delved into complex projective space as the home of compact complex manifolds which were called projective algebraic manifolds. And that proved the last of the triviality as we marched past almost complex structures into vector bundles, most especially Hermitian vector bundles, once he'd disposed of sheaves of holomorphic germs and their cohomology with a proof that flabby sheaves were soft (though not all soft sheaves were flabby). Some Čech cohomology with coefficients in a sheaf mixed in with the de Rham cohomology and then Hermitian differential geometry replete with canonical connections and curvature of Hermitian vector bundles, Chern classes and hints of more to come. I was comfortable with most of this stuff in the framework of Riemannian manifolds, including principle bundles which I had seen transformed into frames of reference of the physical universe by the physics guy at Loyola with whom I had finally spent a day. For him, reality was a gauge as a local connection on the manifold of space-time in the principle bundles with their group actions representing change of reference frame or something akin, a continuous choice of reference frame mayhap, augmented by a gauge potential which I knew as a connection on the principle bundle. I knew what was to come from Momus, including elliptic operators followed by Hodge's theory of harmonic forms and Hodge's decomposition carried over to Hodge's representation of de Rham cohomology by harmonic forms. What I hadn't expected was the Atiyah-Singer index theorem, but I should have. This played into my thesis now under way and would lead me, I hoped, to my own variant of characteristic class as obstruction to the existence of finite-dimensional nonlinear filters where there was no trivial bundle structure. Momus gave a series of exercises developing in parallel Riemannian differential geometry through connections, a side tale I dutifully completed to cement my prior wanderings and gel my vision. Also suffice to say, I was the only one who completed that side story. It all made me glad I had spent sessions with the algebraic topologist pursuing his vision of the machinery.

My advisor off in Britain sent me notes inquiring about progress, but I kept him in suspense as I worked with a dual vision. It would be necessary to find some theorems to satisfy the mathematicians, but my goal was to invent them as stepping stones to a solution to a nonlinear filtering problem to mechanize a device, a balancing act made simpler by Frenchie at Stanford who sent me work from engineering publications, often from conferences on estimation for stochastic processes concentrating on filtering of stochastic processes. Besides the attention on inertial navigation, there was great interest in a new system under development called the Global Positioning System, a satellite-based one-way navigation tool clearly misunderstood by the majority of engineers as a ranging system when in fact it was hyperbolic, something I grasped as if by second nature. Frenchie noted its relationship to a classical problem of Apollonius, a Greek of the second or third century BC, and from the classical work derived an algorithm that provided an exact solution in the four satellite case and an approximate solution in the noisy overdetermined case. I worked out a probability distribution for the user (position, offset from GPS time) on a four dimensional manifold similar to curvature on space-time in general relativity, incorporating a certain matrix known as the *geometric dilution of precision* which measured how satellite configuration affected error spread for constant, uniform noise The other piece of the puzzle was the inertial navigation unit, a mechanization of a platform of accelerometers stabilized by gyroscopes, that is, the rotation group. My model was a Riemannian manifold of nine dimensions of configuration space of position, velocity and acceleration with three more for time, frequency and frequency drift of the receiver clock offset from GPS time, crossed with the unit quaternions as a double cover of the rotation group representing the stable platform.

GPS as a standalone device gave rise to what I called the GPS filtering problem, an inherently nonlinear problem. The GPS receiver was a radio that received its signal from the satellites in view and computed the position of its antenna and the offset of its clock with respect to the stable atomic GPS time transferred to the receiver by a phase-locked loop (PLL), something I had not previously heard of. It was through locking to the time offsets to different atomic satellite clocks, all synchronized to GPS time by software correction, that the measurements, called pseudoranges, were formed for one-way passive navigation. The addition of a platform with gyros and accelerometers measuring rotation and acceleration, fixed to the aircraft body rather than gimbaled, to maintain an inertial frame, the strapdown inertial system, treated as an inertial measurement unit (IMU) rather than inertial navigation system (INS), provided an independent link to the antenna position. Adding this device in the filter was known as integrating GPS with an inertial system. Almost linear in combination given the differential equation for the quaternions was linear, the integrated GPS-INS filter would have been linear were it not for the equations for position and time error from the GPS measurements. The nonlinearity from pseudoranges to position and clock offset transformed Gaussian distributed errors into something like Rayleigh distributed errors on a on four dimensional hyperboloid of position and time from which the velocity and acceleration states were derived in the filter, the INS accelerations bounced against them in the filter correcting the IMU platform errors even as it integrated the sensed platform measurements up to position and velocity within the filter to implement an INS. Clearly this was no Kalman filter, though had the measurement model been linear it could have been such on the manifold with unit quaternions or rotation matrices, however one chose to represent the rotations. The option of an extended Kalman filter was out of the question, being a kluge, even as it was a favorite of the engineering community for the GPS filtering problem. With the INS, one approach was to linearize the equations about the INS-derived velocity or position, but that was not the approach I desired. It would not be suitable as a thesis example. It was crappy engineering to boot, born of desperation, laziness and misunderstanding of the underlying mathematics.

The trick would be to avoid wrestling the seductive generalities that reared their heads as I waded past them to my goal. Single minded devotion was crucial, though I knew I would have to pick one or two topics to develop into red meat for the mathematicians. It was clear to Frenchie and me that the idea of using Lie groups and Lie algebras to determine finite dimensional filters, an idea that came of the mathematical systems theory academics, was doomed. In fact, the idea of finding finite dimensional filters was doomed except for very special cases. That made my notion of a characteristic class as obstruction stupid. Frenchie kept up with this stuff and when I sent him results he provided me with details as to what was known versus what was open. He expressed admiration for my methods, which he termed bizarrely effective; one of the results I sent my advisor turned out to be a special case of a problem he and his comrades in Britain had been chipping away at. My approach led them to a proof of their result and a series of papers, in which my as yet unpublished thesis got mention. But I knew I needed more. The best I had come up with for the two nonlinear filtering problems was to apply an idea my advisor had invented and explored in one of his papers that had been on my orals, that of the perturbation algebra associated to a fixed elliptic operator. The idea was that the invariance group could be applied to parabolic partial differential equations defined by perturbations that formed a Lie algebra isomorphic to a subalgebra of the algebra corresponding to a parabolic partial differential equation $u_t = Lu$ for the second order elliptic operator L to obtain their solutions using the quadrature of an ordinary differential equation. The full method is not worth detailing except to say it provided a solution to the perturbed problem given a solution to the unperturbed problem. The upshot was that the method in the paper led to equivalence classes of second order elliptic operators and that allowed me to determine equivalence classes for filtering problems by applying the perturbation algebra to the Duncan-Mortensen-Zakai (DMZ) equation for the unnormalized distribution. I characterized a class of finite dimensional nonlinear filters equivalent to the Kalman filter in the class determined by the

Laplacian via the heat equation, but they were not particularly interesting to me. Frenchie thought that result was worth publishing but I bagged it, not wanting to spend time writing up something for who-knew-what journal when it was likely already known and published, given it was simple. I didn't get far with the GPS filtering problem other than to show that it was not equivalent to the filtering problem obtained with the addition of an IMU. I showed that the latter DMZ equation was generated by a Lax pair and the former was not.

Among the haunters of my apartment was a stress eater, a special cocksucker skilled at gnawing away stress. When necessary she'd visit; her ministration served the dual purposes of easing stress, pulling me away from the mental jumble that could come of mathematical overload when it grew too intense for marijuana and its derivatives to smooth, allowing sleep instead of chasing theorems and proofs in half-waking states of delirium, and keeping me from falling for the seductive charms of more general results. Like a miracle she would appear in all her glory of not quite five feet, massive mammaries defying gravity, hour glass waist to hips, slender legs and slender ass with ample curvature to the rear. She called herself Jaime. Her close-set eyes at the base of a thin, straight extended beezer made her appear cross-eyed, particularly when engorging my dick which disappeared into her tiny mouth. It slid beneath the honker into a vermillion zone garishly reddened to contrast the black hair hanging over her shoulders. Big nose blowjobs caused me bone-crushing orgasms, a thing I had not realized before meeting her. She could swallow the entire erection to the base, her nose pressed against my groin. It would reappear coated in slobber sliding apposite the nose.

She frequently brought a friend who looked like an Afghan hound: hair bunches hanging from the sides of her head, a nasal protrusion slender at the base with a bump near where close-set tiny round brown eyes perched. The nose widened abruptly into a bulbous flare at the end beyond another crook in the bridge. She too had mammaries of giant proportions, no bigger than Jaime's but seemingly smaller given she stood a full eight inches or so taller. Longer, meatier legs, a longer meatier trunk minus hour glass curvature, straighter with slender hips and an ass of not excessive positive curvature with nearly zero eccentricity and no overhang. Brown hair and fairer flesh enhanced the Afghan similitude. Her mouth was wider with fuller lips, the upper a pronounced cupid's bow and the lower rolled downward in a permanent pout. Jaime's attempts at come-hither were laughingly goofy, but this one didn't have that problem. She permanently wore a fuck-me-or-please-can-I-suck-your-cock expression; I wondered how she kept from being mauled.

When I was in great danger of going overboard into the purity of mathematics in pursuit of my thesis, they would appear together and distract me with lesbian displays before ministering to my erect prong which seemed to grow fatter and longer and more warty with an ever more pronounced bend in the middle as a result of said ministrations. Both women, if that was what they were, could swallow the thing in its entirety, but Jaime made it seem easy while her friend sometimes struggled. I did on occasion fuck them in various orifices, but never with the intense release of unloading into their mouths, a joint head and gonad emptying exercise that knocked me out of the conscious world. I came to deem their appearance spooky action at a near distance.

The three who'd first accosted me were seldom on hand, though I arrived home one day to find them dancing to a cacophonous ditty they interchangeably called Kupferberg's complaint and Tuli's lament. Cranked up full volume on my stereo, the lyrics were something about his bed getting crowded, rolling on the floor, two or three of you women never come back no more. The place was full of naked females dancing and twirling, tits flapping, bare feet slapping; I wondered that the landlord didn't call the cops. They had a den mother, this crew. She had introduced herself as Miss Fire when I first met her. Not tall, maybe five seven, skinny as a rail, arms and legs like sticks, long black hair hanging down to her waist where ended a broad swathe of black hair arrived from the other direction continuing from a bush that obscured her cunt, black nose hair, thick black brows, legs covered with black stubble like Richard Nixon's five o'clock shadow. Long, narrow face, sharp nose, sharp chin, it was her tits that made her a freak. On her skinny frame they appeared beyond unnatural, inflated bags of flesh with wiry strands of black hair around the nipples adding not only to her otherworldliness but reminding me of one particularly hideous representation I had seen of a Hindu goddess with several arms wearing a necklace of skulls, brandishing a sword and holding high a freshly dripping severed head as she danced on some mutilated headless dude flat on his back. It had so haunted me I used to visit it at the Nelson-Atkins gallery; it seemed a place to bury as much of Vietnam as I could. It was impossible to grasp the exact number of women dancing, let alone place an upper bound, since many who passed into the bedroom never returned while others came out in their stead. The three I had first met remained, for sure, and this Miss Fire who had been hanging around ever since she first appeared. She sang along with the record, screeching the chorus above the others and the musicians on the recording who were I concluded satirizing the talentless exercise of rock and roll while giving as good an accounting as any in the process with more cogent lyrics than the usual: I got no time for a dozen, six of you have gotta go, oh oh oh caterwauled reverberating around the rooms. Jaime came over and grabbed my hands and started to dance with me, or tried to as I stood stock still, and she finally called out, "Violetta, come over here and help me with this lug." Miss Fire arrived and grabbed one hand while Jaime hung on the other and they twirled me out into the crowd of flouncing flesh. "Violetta?" I asked. "Violetta Fire?" "No," Jaime said. "Violetta de Provence." "What, she's French?" "No," Miss Fire said, "I'm named after an artichoke. Don't call me that."

I had to fuck an uncountable subcongregation of them. It took the remainder of the afternoon and night. My back hurt for several days after, a consternation during workouts.

Violetta acted as on-site manager. From the day she met me on the solarium, greeting my eyes as I came up the stairs while she sat buck naked at the winged black dining table with its wings at that moment in repose, she'd been ever present. Always visible, she manifested no corporeal substance to disturb me, sleeping in the bed beside me without taking any space unless she wished it or perhaps I wished it. There were times when I awoke with her riding me or sucking my cock; at times my dreams knit seamlessly to waking reality mid sequence, not only with her but others who could occupy space in the bed without disturbing spatial volume. One night I had some variance of sexual encounter with legions of them, slipping from dream fucking one of them to continuation of the same act with the incorporeal presence made corporeal, most of them specters I had not previously perceived. Drifting again to sleep, only to repeat the episode with yet another. Violetta Miss Fire laughingly called it somnial carnality or perhaps better, somcoitus. In the morning I sat down at the black table on the solarium and wrote a section of my dissertation, obtaining several results about a subject dear to my advisor, conservation laws, two of which merited the title theorem, all connected to integrable systems via loop groups and the infinite dimensional affine Lie algebras to which they corresponded. Though not directly related to my filtering problem, they were the tamer cousins of the infinite dimensional Lie algebraic monstrosities I would of necessity swim amidst to get to the opposite bank in the filtering problem. Substantiation? I wondered. Which event? Of what? When?

I pursued the filtering problem on two sides of a gap, one with position and time offset and the other of the raw pseudoranges. The statistics of Frenchie's solution differed in the overdetermined case from the iterative least squares solution, the latter being difficult to characterize statistically though engineers seemed to believe they were Gaussian, an obvious delusion that satisfied them though the errors were not symmetric. In the simplest case, that of four pseudoranges which provided a determined solution, there existed the possibility of a second valid solution, a nonuniqueness that engineers ignored but that demonstrated a hated bimodality. I was reminded of the search for the magic software to integrate cost and schedule. I wished I could set the goofs off in search of a normally distributed chi-square variate.

To bridge the gap, I nursed the fact that the solution was hyperbolic in nature: the solution could be considered an optimal meeting of weighted hyperboloids of loci determined by the pseudorange equations, and not multilateration as in range measurements since such were not available to a GPS receiver which measured the difference between GPS and receiver time and due to the unknown clock offsets were equivalent to range differences. This led to hyperbolic multilateration and a distribution of errors on a manifold of negative curvature which I called a hyperbolic distribution until Frenchie corrected me, saying that term belonged to an unrelated distribution in statistics.

I induced the discrete pseudoranges to evolve stochastically by joining them across time per satellite with a Brownian bridge that projected miraculously onto a single geodesic in the evolving position-time offset solution manifold with curvature a density due to the transformed error "mass" of the satellite signals. A flood of flows related to a partial differential equation in the Riemannian metric of the manifold of the form $\partial g(t)/\partial t = -\mathrm{Ric}(g(t))$, where Ric is the Ricci tensor of the metric g as a function of time, swamped the structure, washing away support and giving rise to a space of metrics as an infinite dimensional manifold containing the evolving metrics related to yet one more infinite dimensional manifold of measures of position and time errors, an infinite dimensional Banach manifold of measures for the distributions unfolding from the metrics on the melting substrates supporting the metrics. These flows contrived a nonlinear heat equation for the metric, a second order elliptic operator that provided a diffusion process and I met a new locally square integrable semimartingale emergent within the infinitesimal generator and its stochastic differential equation that I released to explore the vanishing infinite dimensional panorama. The question was how to relate it to the stochastic equation on the other side of the gap which was linear and would have defined a Kalman filter if only the measurement noise were Gaussian. Since it wasn't, I needed to determine the stochastic partial differential equation for the conditional distribution of functions of the state that were defined in the domain of the infinitesimal generator of the process in such a way that it was recursive, that is, could start from scratch in a memoryless fashion from the posterior probability measure as new prior. A glance at this baby on the raw pseudorange side of the gap and anyone would note it was infinite dimensional, a measure-valued partial stochastic differential equation, the DMZ equation I had perturbed earlier. It was not, as Frenchie hoped so hard that he "proved" it, the negative of the unnormalized conditional density of the conditional expectation given the innovation. That would have made life simple, since the recursion on the pseudorange side could be had with a normalization and a Bayesian update, as in the Kalman filter, though it helped that the flows preserved a family of unbounded Liouville measures which were related to our conditional probability density.

To make a tedious and long story short, Kolmogorov's forward (also known as the Fokker-Plank equation) and backward equations came into play, as ought to be expected, and application of a nifty theorem and other results from a physics paper published a bit more than a decade earlier by someone named Pawula to the effect that if the forward expansion of the equation in question here does not end after the first or second term, it must contain an infinite number of terms. If it does stop after the second term, one gets both the Fokker-Plank equation and the Kolmogorov backward equation. But this lovely result could not be applied until considerable mucking about in some infinite dimensional objects I hesitate to call manifolds, though they were related to Frechet Lie algebras, I suppose one could say if pressed, as sort of second order tangent spaces that Frenchie called Cameron-Martin spaces. Their Hessians lost in the Killing fields of Cameron-Martin space forced my newly found semimartingales in search of untwisted infinite dimensional affine Lie algebras with long roots, as well as their associates, infinite dimensional Lie groups called loop groups as explicated handily in a preprint of A. G. Reyman and M. A. Semenov-Tian-Shansky's *Reduction of Hamiltonian systems, affine Lie algebras and Lax equations I* provided by Frenchie. Invariants were excavated to tie shit together. Mostly they arose from the guts of a generalization of Spencer cohomology and a subspace of the space of connections on an associated manifold of quite steep curvature requiring an integrating out of the connections, only possible mathematically when the subspace was finite dimensional, a near impossibility, to be rid of the geometry underlying it all, leaving nothing more than topology and filtration of probabilities with sigma-algebras related to the topology as with Borel sets but on something not nearly so pleasant as Euclidean space. Suffice it to say, flatness was not enough. What Frenchie thought an unnormalized density had no bound; it turned out to be a topological entropy related to the information of the innovations process, a topological expectation of information if you will. Fortunately, in our special case it was also the algebraic entropy of a certain endomorphism that was an invariant of conjugacy of group endomorphisms and related to the homotopy group as a fundamental group entropy via those same conjugations. All this came of some harrowing exploration of loop groups with the usual suspects, namely unlikely extensions of conservation laws, harmonic maps and what could be called an integrable system with the apparent growth of the fundamental group and also homological growth. Messy but not icky. A couple more hints and a savvy reader of my high level summary would certainly be able to reconstruct this part of the work, given a hint to pair the standard BM on the manifold on the raw side with the new diffusion process out of the Ricci flow and to pair the process on the position-time offset side with the Ricci flow diffusion.

One observable would be the motion of the GPS receiver antenna and the time offset of the GPS clock, especially once the satellite motion and time were removed since it displayed invariants with respect to each trajectory. The receiver clock error was clearly observable, not affected so much by the relative satellite position, and showed up as an average line of sight vector that could be removed from each trajectory. That made me realize that perhaps the GPS filtering problem without an inertial measurement unit's observations was not possibly finite dimensional, but that the extra information available from the inertial unit would not only correct for attitude but also provide an invariant of motion obscured by the angles of satellites relative to the receiver antenna and the offset and wild drift of the receiver clock. Hence the Lax form for the DMZ equation. The INS added what could be called the ancillary statistic needed to be rid of certain nuisance statistics by conditioning, a fact visually driven home with the final bridging of the gap via a splitting of the infinite dimensional fibers into information component, ancillary component and nuisance component. Integrating out the connections led to parallel transport and parallel transfer of redundant "moments" from the information fiber to the nuisance fiber with projection via the conditioning onto a set of invariants related to the INS augmented ancillary fiber.

ramification deficiency

On my first visit to Stanford I had barely gotten so far. Things stood at the point where I had the set up on either side of the gap, including the raw data distribution on a four manifold, and only a hint of how this would work out. I realized there seemed to exist no finite dimensional filter for the GPS problem without additional information. Adding range measurements would not suffice, that was clear, since though they mitigated the clock error the augmented set would not be sufficient. Having to find a counterexample to Frenchie's false proof of the hopeful conjecture regarding the unnormalized density gave me the insight to plow more fertile ground, but details lagged.

I had not told anyone at the apartment of my trip, so the giantess and her three minions standing at my gate surprised me. I carried a small duffel and a briefcase which a beefy human of ambiguous gender and heritage and decked out in a tuxedo took from me as we made a beeline for a stretch limo it piloted. We five sat in the back in facing seats. The giantess Rachel explained we were headed to my quarters on the temple grounds in Atherton. She handed me a cold Anchor Steam beer from a refrigerator and passed around a joint and some nose candy not cocaine.

"What about my reservation? I was staying near campus."

"I cancelled it. Don't worry about it. We can get you to campus."

"In style," said Cybele, decked out in a fetching red metallic hot pants jumpsuit that displayed legs, ass and boobs to excellent effect, having made it a chore to walk out of the San Jose airport, a problem she worked to relieve ministering to me on her knees. That she had caused lack of control of my erective appendage, though not a new phenomenon with her as I recalled from our first meeting, caused me concern given it didn't happen with human females not in active predacious pursuit.

Akua-Ba wore a loosely fitting maroon robe that hung to her feet with a peaked hood revealing only the front of her face from the top of her eyes to the top of her chin. Esther's short legs fitted into a pair of denim bellbottoms, tight against chunky thighs with flaring, tattered leg-bottoms that dragged along the floor obscuring the red tennis shoes whose heels trampled them as she walked. Her upper parts hid in a baggy gray sweat shirt with hood and front hand warmer from which her hands never appeared.

Rachel had decked out much as when I had first seen her standing in my doorway, except now a hint of flesh peeked through. A sleeveless white blouse that displayed her navel reached almost to the beginning of a crocheted skirt in a motley of square patterns of green, blue, and pink on a navy blue frame.

Shapeless, it hung to her ankles in a zigzag pleat with navy blue border of hanging yarn. She wore clogs in leather the color of yellow dog shit with high heels, open toed to display pink toenails. I found it ugly, particularly given her hair now hung ragged to where there ought have been boobs, no longer waving smoothly around her head the forehead of which was cut off by bangs that nearly covered her eyes.

"This apartment is yours," Rachel continued. "When you come here permanently you will find it quite perfect. Private in a secluded estate, we have ten acres. It is separate from the temple and has its own entrance, away from noise and bustle. We provide maid service and cooking service, too, if you wish."

"Nothing like that skank you got cooking at the apartment, I hope," I countered, not entirely comfortable with this gaggle of women taking over my life. Visualizing the cook didn't long help me ignore Cybele at my penis, an appendage I wanted to keep limp. It didn't work. It never did. She got what she wanted.

My quarters were as palatial as an apartment can be, I suppose, though to call it an apartment was strange given it stood alone, not encumbered with adjoining walls or floors or ceilings of other structures. "It's a house," I said and they laughed at me. Tile and wood floors, several bedrooms, a library-study, dining room, all furnished.

Spacious and equipped with a six-burner stove with a grill and two full ovens, rows of glistening white cabinets stretching off to the vanishing point above white countertops of some material, perhaps marble, and below it all floors of white tile with black dots, white tile along the walls below the cabinets and behind the stove, the kitchen recollected for me the song *Saint James Infirmary*. My grandmother had given me an album by Scatman Crothers thinking it was the hip thing in 1961; I hated the hip thing, being attuned to jazz and classical of the romantic period but moving into Stravinsky via *The Firebird* and *Petrouchka*. I liked the Crothers' album, particularly the *Infirmary* cut.

The cook at the apartment in New Orleans was named Nico, from San Francisco, and whenever I fucked her I felt in need of a shower. She had the light red hair that goes with freckles and pasty flesh though she didn't have the freckles. On her head, layers of thinning hair shaved on one side, sparse on the other, straggled down in back to her shoulders and squared into a block of bang in front above a high reddish forehead, her ragged brows the same color as the hair on her head a contrast with the rouged skin atop the bubbles of cheeks that made her appear painted to act the clown in a circus. A wide swathe of chin ended in a cleft, lips that formed a line when she smiled and a pig nose filling out the visage. Skinny legs, skinny butt and no hips below a barrel trunk on which were glued low down on her thorax a lax pair of boobs with pink nipples completing the picture save her sparse orange bush and the tattoos, one arm sleeved with cartoon faces of nerdy males and gears, brightly colored fill-in, the other shoulder tattooed in flowers, tattoos on her upper foot on the left and her right ankle, bony structures her lower legs almost unadorned with flesh from the meatless calves to the ankles.

"You won't bring Nico here, will you?" I asked.

"I have heard she cooks. But she works alone and this kitchen will be staffed, overseen by the temple's executive chef. All lovely women."

That didn't leave me confident. Nico did cook, coming up with stuff I liked almost as if she knew more about my tastes than I did, but she demanded more than her share of dick, though I wondered now at Cybele.

My first day at Stanford I spent with Frenchie and an aged professor of engineering Frenchie said was the go-to man for mathematical descriptions of physical devices used in aerospace systems. He talked trash about the Aerospace Engineering Department as he explained details to us of the inertial navigation unit, its mechanization as a gimbaled inertial platform and then as a strapdown device which was more common, being cheaper, but not so accurate. The equations were no big deal, particularly the linear matrix differential equation of motion for the attitude, though he brought up complications resulting in systematic errors, especially coning and sculling, also sideslip which he said was bad piloting. He blathered about coning in terms of insufficient bandwidth, low sampling rates producing a coning bias that affected the attitude, which I gathered to be a mechanization problem depending on hardware. I had learned that bandwidth to engineers meant sampling rates, a marvelous view of reality bordering on time-invariant linearity *über alles*. "Coning results when there are angular oscillations of the same frequency ninety degrees out of phase about two orthogonal axes." I imagined my advisor snoring. I hoped I could avoid it. Frenchie feigned interest in the codger. "A cone results as the locus of the motion of the third axis." That made me think it might be real and not a phantom of the inertial devices induced by sampling which I had taken as akin to the sampling error due to discretization called aliasing that caused the spokes on the wheels of stage coaches and buggies and wagons in old westerns to slow down, stop and then reverse direction as the angular velocity due to rolling along increased. He droned on. "Coning about two orthogonal axes produces a rectification drift due to gyro excursions from the null because of bandwidth limitations, even in gimbaled units that have bandwidth limitations due to torque balance loops." I don't know how long he'd stopped yammering before I noticed. Perhaps he awaited a response from me, maybe he'd asked a question. I pretended I'd been listening and he went on about gimbal servo loops coupled with inherent stabilization from the inertia of the stable element. I was lost anyway, no idea whether he meant physical motion or error that looked like physical motion or something else entirely. Then came discretization: "…errors induced by coning in strapdown systems are due to computational errors due to noncommutativity of the angular rotations…" He began to make a computation to show how the error could be as large as two one-hundredths of a degree per hour, but Frenchie cut him off. "How about sculling?" Sculling might have been similar but had to do with accelerations and rapid attitude rates in the resolution cracks of the specific force. "Loop gain for the accelerometers must be sufficiently high to keep the excursions from null position small under vibrations or significant rectification errors are induced. The accelerometer senses a component of the vibration at orthogonal to its input axis proportional to deviation from the null." Or not. Fuck. I went from one image to another in a few words, orthogonal images that mutually annihilated one another. The best I could do was file this stuff for future reference in case I needed to understand it, but decided it would not find mention in the dissertation given I didn't get it and wasn't about to try to see the world as does an engineer, a frightening prospect in any case. For now, in my head it was all related to sampling rates, part of the lie of the newly emerging digital hype. There were rumors of a digital recording technology to replace records, though there existed already recordings that were supposed to be digital on analog media like tape or record.

The aerospace engineering prof dragged from a worn leather briefcase several texts written by aerospace engineers that claimed it was necessary to write the state transition function for the matrix differential equation as a first order approximation, the identity plus the matrix itself times delta t; the first two terms in the matrix exponential. Frenchie and I went to the board and wrote out more terms hoping for a pattern to emerge, which it did. Series expansions in the matrix components converged to sines and cosines. The aerospace engineer's handwritten notes provided the same formula. I wrote the equivalent linear quaternion differential equation and we solved that expansion as well,

560

again getting a state transition in sines and cosines. I'd wanted to compute it by transformation from the matrix equations or Euler angles to the unit quaternions; it ended up simpler to accomplish directly. The engineer said he didn't favor quaternions since they did not uniquely specify rotations, but I explained that the unit quaternions were a double cover of the rotations and so were easy to make unique by checking for sign change which was easily rectified by multiplication by negative one. He didn't like it until Frenchie asked if he knew of any engineering journal articles that presented the full state transition for the matrix formulation or for the unit quaternions. He went off to check the literature, he said, and this led to one of the most trivial papers I ever put my name to. Trivial papers and papers full of errors and incorrect in the large I would learn were commonplace in the engineering literature. This one went to the *Journal of Guidance and Control.* We also squeezed one out for the *IEEE Transactions on Automatic Control* that detailed an explicit formula for a nonlinear filter on SL(2,C), something with more depth but not fit for a mathematics journal. Frenchie said that it was important to publish in engineering journals if you wanted to compete successfully for grant money.

That evening, Rachel invited Ester, Akua-Ba and Cybele to a soiree in Palo Alto at the home of a prominent entrepreneur of so-called technology, a term which for me included the ability to start fires and create stone tools by controlled chipping, not to be confused with chippy controller, a technology denied me. The women seemed quite excited; I tried to beg off claiming a need to meet with Frenchie again on the morrow, but they would not hear of it. On the drive, Rachel provided us with copious quantities of product to smoke and snort, most of it delivering unexpected results regarding reality and mood. The driver tooled up to a large though not excessive one story ranch-style that filled its lot except for the concrete parking area in front. He let us out at the door; Rachel told him to stay by the car phone for our call to leave, a demand I found damned insensitive. He didn't protest.

The door opened before we reached it, a smiling brunette I guessed to be in or beyond her late thirties or early forties by the fact that her head was supported by a swanlike neck in the early stages of going turkey, though her other features didn't betray aging. That could have been due to her olive complexion and compact features: straight nose not prominent, straight mouth with thin vermillion zone, a smile that didn't display teeth, small brown eyes set without sloping up or down, a smooth jawline swooping from elf ears to the contour of rounded chin. She wore her hair short, parted over her left eye exposing the brow which levitated near the eye itself, not covering her ears but of the same length all over, thick on the sides and back of her neck. I guessed she paid plenty for the cut. She didn't wear much makeup, but the warmth of the color of her face and glossy pink of her lips made me realize it was likely skilled artifice. Her hands didn't show age, neither the bare feet visible from beneath the red full skirt decorated with vases painted in white that covered her ankles. She wore a white blouse, sleeves rolled up to below her elbows and opened low down at the third button, tied at the waist, displaying no cleavage. There were several necklaces with red and turquoise beads and several one piece turquoise bracelets on her left wrist, all of it too uniform to be stone but hard to believe the apparent plastic that informed the eye.

She looked at us distractedly, far away like through us or over us, her smile diffused within the ambience. "Oh, well, Rachel, you brought friends. And this is Whitey?" She reached out to touch my forearm, not to shake my hand but to rest long warm fingers. "Come in. Things are just getting started." We stood in a large foyer with dark tile flooring, maybe slate. "Leroy is supposed to be coming soon, but he will only bring Nikki and his crew with some of their couples since Claire and Ken are out of town. It's too bad; you would enjoy Claire, Whitey."

"So you have seen the interviews, then?" Rachel asked.

"Yes. It is quite the topic of conversation. That Dina survived is amazing. She is truly unrecognizable. What do you think of her transformation, Whitey?"

"Dina? I haven't seen her. She did an interview?"

"Oh yes, more than one. You haven't seen it? She praises your guidance. In *Goddess Magazine* she calls you her master. In *Extreme Body Modification* she calls you an inspiration. They have a photo of you in that interview. Also in *Tribal Culture,* that pop anthropology magazine, she calls you her master. There is a photo in that too, as I recall. And there is rumor of an article in the *Journal of Guidance and Control.* Is it true, Rachel?"

I was about to ask Rachel What-the-fuck? when what might pass for music made its way out of the inner rooms. "What's that?" I asked, ready to leave.

"We have dueling DJs tonight. A mix of bawdy disco rap, space disco, galactic funk and dirty blues, nerd rap and P-funk and some signifying."

"Now Whitey, take it easy. It won't hurt you." It was Akua-Ba, her hand on my other arm to keep me from fleeing.

"It might."

ramification deficiency

A naked black man with an enormous gut and a naked white man, pudgy, hirsute of body and baldheaded, appeared from where the music emanated. The white man wore a metal cage on his penis with a leash attached to it.

"Oh, this is my husband Bertrand and our master Tyrell."

"You bring all these bitches?" Tyrell was in my face immediately.

"No. They brought me."

"They belong to you?"

"Far as I know, they're free agents."

"He gotta put on a cage. All them little white dicks gotta be in cages."

"I don't think it qualifies as little," Cybele piped up.

"If there's a bigger penis here, I'll lay down and let every one of your crew fuck my asshole as long as they want," Rachel said. "If you don't find a bigger one, then one of you has got to put on a cage. Deal?"

Our hostess, standing immediately behind Tyrell, shook her head slowly; Tyrell glared at Rachel. "Deal only if all them bitches came in wit' you agrees to a ass fucking same as you." Rachel nodded and Tyrell strode out of the room. I noticed that Bertrand showed dried goo around his mouth. There was a small padlock on the metal cage that enclosed his penis.

"That might not have been so cool," our hostess said. "They brought a porn actor with them. He's supposed to have a bigger dick than the Mule."

"Don't worry. Whitey has the biggest dick in the world. Guaranteed."

I wondered if she meant the Mule I'd introduced to Harry. She tried to wipe the goop from her husband's mouth.

"Tyrell has been fucking some of the early arrivals in the anus and I have been cleaning up behind him."

"Good for you, Honey," she said. "You need to learn your place. You have been a bit demanding of late with that little dick of yours. I might have to go service the community center with Nikki for the weekend now that Claire is out of the town."

Tyrell returned, in tow a black giant, taller than I and easily as muscular, his penis hanging between his legs. Tyrell forced our hostess to her knees and shoved her face to the appendage. She licked it, spit on it and slurped the foreskin and bulbous glans into her mouth. Tyrell said, "Swallow it, bitch" and she took the slowly rising meat as far in as possible; he pushed on the back of her head. She came up drooling, then licked it languidly, kissed it, nursed it to erect.

"That there be a honest 'leven inches soft and sixteen hard. Let's see what you got, boy." Tyrell spit the words in my face.

"Come on, show it, Whitey," Rachel said. "I don't want this bunch fucking my asshole raw."

"It doesn't seem necessary," I said. "You can see the outline in these leather pants."

"You be wearing a sock. We know that white-boy trick."

Sad-faced Esther undid the drawstring and pulled my leather breeches down below my knees. My cock hung limp. Our hostess gasped. It was longer and thicker than Tyrell's hero's manhood at full mast. I felt ridiculous standing with leather pants bunched about my boots.

Our hostess lifted it in both hands. "I can't get my hand around it. Bertie, dear, get the measure." He'd already vanished only to reappear with a cloth tape. She measured its diameter at twelve inches, its length just under eighteen inches.

"It don't get hard, do it?" a concerned Tyrell said.

"Get it up, Whitey," Esther said. "You're the great white hope."

I bobbed it erect with force of will until it pointed to heaven and throbbed with veins and rounded tuberosities. She measured it at twenty-four inches, the girth at almost sixteen inches around.

"I'll get somebody from Leroy's crew soon's he get here, since he ain't bringing that sweet bitch Claire," Tyrell said. "Right after this here bitch clean off my dick," and he grabbed a fistful of hair to steer our hostess to her knees and his limp penis. She enthusiastically went about her task, her husband encouraging her with endearments involving black licorice I didn't catch in their entirety.

The vanquished hero sidled up to Cybele. "My name Satchel," he said, laying a giant hand on her shoulder. "I guessing you got some experience with his manhood, so maybe you can tell me how he get it inside of anydamnthing. I got plenty trouble my own self."

"I bet you do, big boy," putting her hand on his deflating penis. "His is deformable. As in it deforms. Smoothly. As in it's diffeomorphic to itself, no sharp edges. The place he puts it deforms too, within limits to the extent possible, which can be a lot for a vagina. Smoothly, again."

"I got no idea what you talking 'bout."

"Let's go try out yours, Satch. Can I call you Satch?"

"You call me anything, missy, long as I can stick my dick in you somewhere."

"Call me Cybele," she said.

Guests arrived. They stood and gawked politely, chatting among themselves and commenting on the hostess' work in progress. The room cluttered, especially when a gumbo of perhaps two dozen young black men arrived with several older white couples. Behind them were a half dozen older black men and three more white couples and a single white woman. Unattached white couples pushed into the room.

The noise from the nether regions gained intensity, a meandering conflagration of hackneyed catchpenny ditties that back-and-forthed between two sorts of genres I realized were meant to be cutting edge. It was repetitious cliché pop. I wanted to get the fuck out of there.

From the wide entrance to the outer rooms there appeared a woman with a heart shaped face, broad nose, thick lips, round sky blue eyes and reddish brown hair piled atop her head displaying a fountain of brown roots. She sported a diaphanous grayish gown shaped like a toga suspended from her shoulders by a pair of spaghetti straps; it didn't quite cover her bare ass and anyway revealed her entire naked body as through a translucent curtain. On her upper arm and upper thigh and her wrists and ankles were silver bands that might have been silver tape. Not much taller than five feet, she projected a take-charge expression behind an intense stare as she slowly panned the room.

"I'm Venere," she said. "Some of you already know me. You, Jeanette, are tasting my butthole on Tyrell's dick. Since Jeanette is busy at the moment — you need some help babe? — I will get organized. Tyrell's gang is already here and waiting in the other room. We have a bunch of fertile newbies coming tonight who are here to be bred and we have a room set up, two double beds and plenty of pads on the floor. Sorry, you will have to be bred in a group, though I find that does make it more exciting."

Tyrell broke in. "We got a bunch of unaffiliateds?"

Jeanette from the floor nodded her head up and down with her face impaled on the end of Tyrell's erection.

"Evidently," Venere said. She carried most of her weight above womanly hips that matched her round buttocks but were not so full as would be expected from her torso which rose straight up without indentation. Heavy breasts displayed large round rosy areolae parallel to the floor pointed outward and without sign of falling. Her slight legs gave the impression of post polio.

565

"My crew, we ain't got resources to accept a lot of unaffiliateds. Most of my crew don't have resources to expend on couples, especially way down here since we up in Oakland. Maybe when Leroy get here he got some crew can take on some of y'all, but then you have to spend time out in East Palo Alto and that require protection."

A lanky black man came in leading a bunch of other black men, more couples, and one woman. A dishwater blonde with frosted highlights, her hair tumbled copiously over her shoulders almost to the mounds pointed like miniature pyramids poking through a white crop top t-shirt displaying a stretched navel above a pair of tight jeans cut short enough the bony concave cheeks of her butt appeared along with some cunt from which arced a chain the end of which was held by the lanky black leader. Tyrell nodded to him and said, "Hey, Leroy, whassup?" Leroy said, "You go over and help out Jeanette, Nikki." Nikki turned a sharply-angled elongated rectangular face towards him and said "Then let go of my clit leash, man." He handed it to her. Her extensive skinny nose extended beyond the pinched nostrils to point to a blunt, pale rosebud of a mouth. The narrow face displayed a prominent forehead bereft of softening bangs. The close set eyes were narrow with a slant towards the nose, dark so the pupils didn't show, the thin brows arched to slope downward beyond the eye sockets. The butt cheeks narrowed to straight skinny thighs, upper legs tapering beyond knobby knees to skinnier lower calves of uniform diameter without apparent curvature to feet tenuously resting on flimsy black sandals with ultra high heels.

"Who is that gnarly thing?" I asked Rachel.

"Nikki. She belongs to Leroy. She lives with Ken and Claire. They took her in after her husband threw her out for serving Leroy. She tried to convince him to be part of the lifestyle and accept the superiority of black dick, but he would have none of it."

"I can't say I blame him."

"Ken and Claire found it insensitive and intolerant. So they took her in, but she spends a lot of time in East Palo Alto with Leroy who pimps her out. Claire joins her on weekends. Its for charity."

I looked at her. "Charity?"

"You bet. All proceeds go to a sporting club. Nikki started this thing here in Palo Alto."

I couldn't tell if she was serious.

"The whole setup smacks of racism."

"Not really. These people recognize the superior breeding qualities of black men. Not to mention the superior heft of their male members, you being one of the exceptions, and their stamina. Better staying power."

"Horseshit. That why the white guys wearing those cages on their dicks? Christ, they're padlocking them."

"The wives secure them and hold on to the keys."

"Where? They're all getting naked."

"They each have their places."

"This reminds me of a black student I met at Tulane who complained that he was always expected to fuck the liberal white girls."

"Not all these people are liberal. Lots of them are big Reagan supporters. Wait until Tawny gets here. She and her husband are from Texas and are not affiliated with any black man. She comes to… Well, just wait. You'll see. But they are as right wing as any people you'll meet. They think Reagan is too liberal. Both of them belong to the John Birch Society."

As Nikki joined Jeanette on her knees to attend to Leroy, Leroy groaned and cursed and said, "Take it all, bitch!" Jeanette swallowed valiantly repeating "uh-huh" throughout the effort; some escaped the side of her mouth. When it seemed she'd drained Leroy of everything she could milk, she stood and wiped her mouth with the back of her hand. "Let's get this party started," she said. "The bar is open in the kitchen and there are plenty of spaces for fucking. No white men allowed to fuck. Oh, wait, Whitey can join in except the breeding. Only black dick for breeding."

A twig of a girl with long mousy brown hair who looked to be younger than most of those arriving, perhaps in her late twenties, wearing a flimsy pink mesh top that appeared to be a bra but opened below like an ultra short crop top with pink ribbon along the top and ruffled white lace below supported by thin pink straps, let out a yell. "Nigger dick. I need nigger sperm in me. I need a nigger baby."

No one paid her much attention. Jeanette asked, "You alone?"

"No, I brought my girlfriend and her husband," hugging the bright-eyed girl standing beside her with shoulder length hair of a darker brown, taller of more physical substance covered in a loose pair of lightweight gray sweat pants, sleeveless gray t-shirt and clunky gray tennis shoes. The insubstantial one had insufficient tit to push up her top but her friend had a pair of breasts. They could have been boy and girl next door, the one in sweats smiling sweetly, perhaps an innocent sixteen. Below the waist the one who looked like a long-haired boy wore black lace bikini panties lined with pink lace tied with a small pink bow. It was female, that was evident from what didn't appear unless it retracted, but though it was pale and lean to sinewy, it wasn't frail given the mannish features, especially a nose so broad it narrowed her eye spacing and big ears not well hidden in hair.

"You sure you're of age?" Venere asked the one in gray sweats.

A tall white man in jeans standing beside her spoke up. "She is. I'm her husband and we've been married five years. We have two children."

"She looks sixteen."

"I get carded all the time," she said. "I have an ID with me."

Venere shook her head. "That won't be necessary. You looking to be bred too?"

"Yep. We're both ready to get pregnant with nigger seed," her athletic friend said. "I need a pickaninny growing in my belly."

"Anyone else for breeding? All who want fertile black breeding form up over in the corner there," pointing to the back of the crowded room. "And all white males must wear chastity devices at all times. No clothes, either."

I had meantime pulled up my pants while the other white guys were shucking theirs. Eight white women with seven white men moved to the breeding staging area in the corner.

Jeanette turned to Venere and pointed to me. "Except that one. He doesn't require a cage, though its doubtful we could find one to fit in any case. He has the biggest dick in the house."

There arose from the latest black gangs to arrive a muted roar of dissent. Tyrell spoke. "'s true," he said. "He betters Satchel by a foot. One'a your'n gotta put it in a cage, Leroy."

"More like by eight inches," Rachel said. "Just as well be a foot."

"Well, sir," Venere said, "I gotta see that thing. But you can't use it on fertile breeders because they only want black seed. 'Les you're black."

The blacks began to move into the outer rooms, providing breathing space. Some of the white couples followed them. Sad-eyed Ester had moved on with the latest group of black men to arrive. I was unsure what would happen to Akua-Ba since she was black; did she have to diddle only with white men? or was it perhaps a lesbian thing, only with white women? but my concern vanished when she vanished with three black men. I assumed it was left to me and Rachel, but Venere removed her toga and stood naked, head cocked to the side and back, and eyed me, her hands on her hips.

"You wanna fuck me?" she asked.

"I thought I might just stay faithful to my friend Rachel here," I said, but Rachel spoke up with "No way, I don't fuck men who only fuck me."

The athletic girl who looked like a boy's friend had stripped and she did have a pair of boobs. Sturdy legs, too, and broad hips with a meaty ass. Putting on a smile that lit up the room, she bit down on the band of her white panties with front teeth I found a tad longish, but which didn't stop several black men from approaching when she beckoned by holding the panties out on her index finger. More women had joined the group of fertile breeders, but she appealed to me; I almost wished I could have participated.

Another approached our forming ménage, this one likely brunette judging from the plush carpet of bush trimmed into a perfect pyramid on her mons. Her gossamer hair, tied in an insubstantial ponytail, had a reddish hue.

"Can I join?" in a pipy, little girl voice.

"Oh, honey. You don't need to ask," Rachel said. "All are welcome. Whitey can't say no."

I started to say something but she put her index finger to my lips. "No talking, big boy. Save your energy."

It would be a long night.

They steered me into a capacious living room crammed with white women of all age and physical description engaged in sexual congress of diverse sorts with black men, usually more than one man in attendance, while naked white guys with their penises caged milled around watching. I had to shake my head and blink. Every available surface and much of the floor was occupied.

In one far corner, a naked white woman well beyond her first youth on her stomach with her hands against the wall, screaming, a black man fucking her asshole. Most of the white men stood and chatted regarding the action or sports or engineering issues of mostly hardware variety. Not far from us, a couple in their late thirties to early forties on their knees jointly sucked a black cock and kissed each other, licked one another's lips. She was taken from behind by another black man while they continued ministering to the man standing before them. A woman who seemed to be in her fifties, on her knees on a wide daybed facing us, with dyed yellow hair and withered hanging dugs from whose artificially-elongated, pierced nipples with secondary round outer knobs there hung large hoops, was pounded from behind by a black man. He let out a long moan followed by a sharp croak as he jerked against her slack buttocks. He stepped away and she hauled over a white-haired balding man whose belly overgrew with white hair and directed him to clean it up for the next one, which he did, putting his mouth to her dripping cunt. He came up with cum around his face like a milk mustache and beard. Another black replaced the one who had finished.

"Is this a regular thing?" I asked no one in particular.

"This is the coming thing," Venere said.

The carpeted bush bobbled her head in agreement. "Nigger dick is best," she said.

They led me to a room where a plump woman, probably in her forties, sat astride a bench shaped like a saddle that raised her ass in the air and held her face at crotch level. She wore a blindfold and two-piece cheerleader uniform, the top pulled up around her shoulders so her tits hung down, the short skirt without panties. She was uniformly tanned dark bronze. Impaled by something hidden between her legs, she rode fixed in place.

"That's Tawny," Rachel whispered. "She's the city manager of San Mateo. Her husband" nodding to a watching man, tall with a slight paunch, loose pectorals and a full head of graying hair, "is an executive at a semiconductor laser company next door to HP Labs on Page Mill Road. They're the Birchers I told you about; most people here are not very liberal, given the strong technology and defense business roots of the community, but not many are so far to the right. She had that bench designed specially to fit her, holds her in place with a massive built-in dildo. Plus her ankles and hands are strapped to the thing."

It was hard to get a fix on her height, but she looked to be under five foot and quite chunky, putting it kindly. Thick thighs, thin calves, and a belly on which fat tits rested when she reared back but otherwise hung pendulously. Wrist and ankle restraints with short chains gave her some freedom of movement, enough to raise up to the necessary level to fill her mouth with cock. Deep blue eyes and lush, long inky black hair in two braids were her most appealing features, though I doubted they were both natural, especially the hair which appeared uniformly colored.

Whenever her mouth emptied she hollered: "Come on you niggers, that the best you can do?" "Fuck my asshole, niggers," "Niggers niggers niggers," the epithet nigger in every taunt. As expected, rough use of her anus, braids as handles for violent face fucking until the final moment whence a push for deepest intrusion and ejaculation.

"That's insane," I whispered.

ramification deficiency

Venere said, "That mount of hers was an engineering feat. A strapdown system allowing fast initial alignment."

"Pole placement, you know," piped in Rachel. "It's easier to align to an external reference, but then there can be attitude misalignment, given her goal of inspiring aggression."

"And of course coning due to the vaginal impalation—"

"That's not a word, dear. You mean impalement. But she was going to say that coning needs to be exploited to obtain optimal anal punishment, an inherent non-commutativity to be amplified."

Tawny hollered "You fuck like a bunch of needle-dick nigger-lovin' liberals—"

The man behind her held levers in each hand as if skiing. At her insult he worked them with frenzy.

"What's that guy holding?" I asked.

Rachel answered first. "We call them joy sticks but they control the inserted device. See, it has no slack, designed specifically for her cunt, conformal, a contact form if you will. Controls yaw, pitch and roll of the thing inside her."

"Like its made of goo or gel, see? Space filling. Conductive but slightly dielectric, something I don't get, switching from storing to oozing electrical current at random times, see?"

"It diffuses Gaussian current with random pulses due to the dielectric polarization between her clitoris and her Gräfenberg spot; current oozes out except for the spike train that hits those two areas. In an uncorrelated manner, of course."

"Gaussian current?"

"I want to be nigger-bred like a bitch—mmmph—"

"Local excursions and perturbations, more like. The variance is determined before she starts."

"And of course you want to avoid damping and you want to not lessen amplitude, want those constant shocks. Amping helps here, I mean she's incredibly amped from the start."

"Part of the strapdown is guy-wiring; adds stability to allow rapid realignment with minimal skew error for maximal thrust momentum via feedback gain and pole placement. Then you have yaw, roll and pitch feedback automatic gain control in tandem with the joy sticks."

"Yes. Increase sensitivity to vibrations while controlling actual vibration—"

"Not to forget realignment for efficient pole placement and pole switching."

"We covered that, dear," Venere's "dear" mocking Rachel's.

"Well, it is an incredible engineering design feat. And someone is already at work on a design for passive-maneuvering of tether-connected bodies. Nikki loves to be abused while tether connected."

"She's such a slut. But flexible slewing is her specialty, within the bounds of closed-loop pole insertion with internal vibration suppression."

"God yes. She's built for combined momentum dumping and slewing."

"With vibration suppression when in closed loop. She was designed for variations in natural frequencies."

"Which is a marvel. Why they designed that mount, too."

Tawny let out a shrill, "Come on you lazy jigaboos, fuck my oomph—"

Venere added, "It is a flexible structure. Couldn't treat the damping and natural frequency uncertainty individually."

"Repeated parametric uncertainties are a bummer. They ended up with a complicated transfer function; not rational."

"You can see why. Look how she naturally attenuates vibration in the closed loop; don't want that. Want that vibration strong as hell at the natural frequencies, need resonance. See it? Christ, look at the ass jiggle. I bet that trains up to her eyeballs."

"In open loop she hums, see? She can dump momentum. If they can get in synch front and back with the dildo and its electronic pitch, you'll see amazing pulse trains with hard discontinuities. Optimal input shaped slewing are tough to realize, but there are some who have studied it and team up. Real challenge."

As they spoke ripples formed along her entire body from asshole to the top of her head, then crossed and marched to her feet where secondary pulses rode atop them and then tertiary ripples with three standing waves flat along portions of her anatomy standing upright sharply discontinuous at the joining of her shoulders and neck and her thighs that threatened to buck her so fiercely she would break into pieces, her feet flopping within the confines of the bound with the third crest.

"See?" Rachel and Venere said it together.

"It's like control torque. Now watch!" Rachel flushed and she drooled as she spoke.

Venere, her face crimson, slobbered when she yelled "Now look! At the end of that thrust. See? Switching time. That's the maximum wheel torque she can take and now she's saturated, she dumps momentum!"

Jets of viscous pink outflow exhausted from both ends. The waves flattened and disappeared.

The two stood side by side, silent at the completion of their lecture and perhaps exhausted by virtual involvement.

"Well," I said, "it looks to me like she stores their ejaculate in reservoirs for this momentum dumping."

They stared at me. Venere said 'Pink?"

"Certainly after they ejaculate in her asshole she sucks them off as next in line," I added to my cretin-speak.

"She likes to clean up after herself. Common courtesy, a Republican sort of gesture," Rachel said.

"I'm more liberal," Venere said. «I like the taste of ass from one knows not where. Later she'll fart in her husband's mouth and they will exchange the brown sperm."

"That's insane," I repeated. I couldn't shake my inanity.

"I can't say. But look, you go next, rakehell. We'll solve the optimal capacity expansion problem for Tawny once and for all. Let me get it up for you," and Rachel dropped to her knees, Venere beside her. The bush meantime wandered off with a group of young black men to another room. It didn't take long to get it up, though I wasn't particularly interested in joining the queue. They pushed me over to cut in line as the one at her asshole let go and moved to line for her mouth. The one at her mouth finished and vacated; shrill invectives blasted out modulated by a plume of sperm. "You niggers can't do better? Fuck my asshole, loser niggers…" Rachel slathered my erection with saliva and indicated for me to shove it home without hesitation, which I accomplished with languid lack of urgency. Tawny stopped mid abuse with a frozen "nig—" and then "What the fuck? God, oh, ow, what is that?" I ignored her whimpers and took my time to deliver my first load of what promised to be more than I wanted to deliver. The three of us slipped away as two men attempted to simultaneously penetrate her anus but ended by taking turns.

"You are one cool customer, dude," Venere said. "She found a stiffness matrix for an infinite domain in the same way she found them for finite dimensional subdomains: the hard way. Undamped second order inelastic thrust. I've not seen many operate with so much control—"

"Harmonic forcing. Even at the end. Low thrust trajectory control—"

"At it's best. Long shank—"

"—single-link flexible manipulator. Like simple extension in elastomers. Can you do that to me?"

"Me first…"

The two of them pulled me by opposite arms in opposite directions as I plowed ahead ignoring them, looking for someone else to begin with.

A female stood in my path. "I'm looking for an expanding hypervelocity projectile." Without bothering to note what she looked like I pressed her to her knees to taste Tawny's asshole before savaging her asshole. I could party with these monstrosities.

As the lady bugs swarmed me and agglomerated into a cluster-fucking melee, I realized I'd not delineated the legion Laplacians appearing in the scattered fragments of my thesis. Of course, the dearest to my heart, the Laplace operator of the Riemannian metric acting on functions as the divergence of the gradient, or more directly as the reciprocal of the square root of the determinant of the Riemannian metric times the sum of the coordinate differential operators acting on the product of the square root of the determinant of the Riemannian metric by the individual components of the Riemannian metric matrix by the coordinate partials of the function, gave rise to my little buddies exploring the manifolds with glee, flying off to infinity at times exploding with the forcing of the negative curvature as a boost or hyperbolic screw, depending on point of view, later refined to a hyperbolic Laplacian wherein Brownian bridges replaced geodesics especially in Poincare coordinates. This was the Laplace-Beltrami Laplacian, or was it? I lost track with the frenzied pressing of flesh in the heated milieu of carnal racism. So what of the Hodge Laplacian, that with which I'd started for Frenchy and my advisor? Or was that the heat kernel constructed via the Laplacian as an unbounded operator on $L^2(M,\mu)$ for some measure μ the construction of which slips my mind as an unusually powerful Rachel pushed me on the couch and clambered aboard proving the operator self-adjoint and non-positive via spectral theory astride me galloping to encouragement from the forming crowd while I pondered the operator's one-parameter semigroup acting in $L^2(M,\mu)$ where of course μ is natural, $d\mu$ the Riemannian volume element on the manifold, again of course, Christ almighty Venere had a tight asshole, spongiform maybe whence a kernel possessed by the semigroup and hence the smooth heat kernel and Brownian travelers. The heat equation on manifolds and Brownian motion my first cut at the later embodiments of virtual wrigglers powered with stochastic flagella exploring via diffusion for more tangible rewards with less vestigial remains. That part of the story I had nearly wrapped up, zeroing in on results uninteresting in the abstract for me, though exploration and explication of geometry via random motion amused me and interested others enough to be a thesis in its own right. Venere replaced by a vicious and toothy brunette heavy-breasted tit monster of curdled thighs and buttocks gone to cheese, wrinkled visage brought into stark contrast with jet black dyed hair and tired blue eyes, fading tattoos, piercings, blue lacquered fingernails. I realized perhaps I had mistakenly started with the fucking Hodge Laplacian acting on differential forms misapplied to functions, or is that so misapplied given functions are zero forms? The rough Laplacian this bitch grinding away like my dick is too small for her, breathing onions in my face, kissing me. Christ. I push her away. "No kissing. I don't what's been in your mouth." What about the Laplacian as trace of the Hessian? No need, I could avoid Nash's embedding theorem and naturally raise a up a swarm of the random vermin to release using adjoints to set the little buggers free to skitter along manifolds exploring with their intrinsic recording of shape, especially curvature. I did need to be more careful if I wanted to form my BM via a stochastic differential equation-based diffusion process generated by a second order elliptic operator of the Hormander variety; but had I not done so already? I could get Bochner's horizontal Laplacian by lifting the Laplace-Beltrami operator to the orthogonal frame bundle once I found a suitable connection, preferably the Levi-Civita connection, but SDEs via second order elliptic operators were not, it seems, intrinsic. Granted those BMs could be squeezed out of a lift to the frame bundle as a principle bundle with only the dimension of the manifold for basis for the sum of squares, but to get what I needed required something more. I had to embed the fucker in a Euclidean space of the dimension required for Nash's theorem, where the embedding was with respect to the standard metric on the Euclidean space. I think the last one was blonde of long face, possibly only a decade older than I, big teeth when she smiled and huge jugs she licked and sucked while on my lap fucking me—Christ so many fucking meatloaf tits! though I recall one or two not overly endowed—of slender thighs and skinny calves and a sharp bony ass.

   We left as the party wound down, the exhausted and harried black bulls stretched out lounging, watching the white guys clean up the women, lapping the residual from the various flesh openings, cracks, crevices, splits, slots and apertures that had been invaded by black protrusions as their own puny pale worms strained against the cages they wore. I recall considering that going to Nash's embedding gave me more tangent vectors than the dimension of the manifold. It allowed me to take full advantage of stochastic calculus since the BM was intrinsically defined as an Ito SDE but required me to leave the manifold, a thing frowned on as disgusting and on which I didn't intend to rely. In the end, though, it wouldn't matter since I would leave the entire world of reasonable structures, especially finite-dimensional manifolds, perhaps even manifolds as I never was able to prove the infinite dimensional object was everywhere the same dimension as my processes could not skitter over the entire structure and might have had out-of-space experiences.

At my pad on the temple grounds I was confronted at the door by a naked female stick figure in orange hair and hyper-inflated breasts. Yet one more sharp face framed with lifeless strands hanging to rounded gaunt shoulders, the entire structure so rawboned skeletal details were apparent.

She handed me a magazine with a book mark. I opened it to the article marked. "The Kalman-Bucy Filter as a True Time-Varying Wiener Filter" by a Brian D. O. Anderson and John B. Moore. I looked at the cover. *IEEE Transactions on Systems, Man, and Cybernetics,* from April of 1971.

"What the fuck's this?"

"Read it before you fuck me," she said.

"What makes you think I'm gonna fuck you?"

"It's what you do. I'll always be here—"

"Lemme guess. You're the manager."

"Right. But note that the signal process produces the same result whether filtering or smoothing; however, the state processes are essentially equivalent only in the case of filtering. Of course, the probabilities will be different, the covariances, even in the filter case, but that's only local realization, or representation, depending on your point of view anyways. But not for smoothing—and you dude, you've been WAY smoothing."

I wasn't sure she meant smoothing in the sense of ironing out all the wrinkles as with the heat kernel or in the sense of noncausal estimation using the future to clean up the past.

"Well, I'm too tired to fuck you anyway."

"I'll be here."

"Same deal as with Violetta?"

"That fucking bloated cunt named after an artichoke. I read the interview with Dina in *The Journal of Guidance and Control.* Next thing they'll be making you dominant of the year. Dude, you need ergodic control of Markov chains with constraints. Maybe using a relaxation approach. Optimize your domain."

I trudged off to bed. She climbed in beside me; same deal as with Violetta. Before I passed on to sleep, or maybe after, she said, "And you need a reality assumption. It's like a safe word. You spend too much time in sub space."

c) Persistence of Dynamical Systems Under Random Perturbations

Violetta greeted my first return by handing me a paper, "Invariant Theoretical Interpretation of Interaction" by Ryoyu Utiyama, from March 1956, *Physical Review.*

"What's this?"

"What you need. Read it."

"Why the fuck do I need this? It looks like fucking physics."

"Look, let me put it in simple terms for you." She stood naked as a jay bird and hairier than usual. "The filtered probability space corresponds to path space. You know enough algebraic topology to known that path spaces are contractible. The probabilistic counterpart of the contractibility is the el-two resolution of the identity on probability space coming from conditional expectations."

I both did and did not understand what the fuck she meant.

"What the fuck does that have to do with this paper?"

"Nothing. That would be this," and she handed me another paper, this one from the *Annals of Mathematical Statistics* from 1970, someone with too many initials named Clark. "The Representation of Functionals of the Brownian Motion by Stochastic Integrals." "But you'll have to wait for the radial part of the Brownian motion and its life on the cut-locus."

Again, I understood the words she spoke. I had run into polar representations of BM on Riemannian manifolds in my thesis work; the cut locus was a problem in the radial component. But I still had no idea what the fuck she meant.

"I don't have a clue what you're talking about. I mean technically, yes, but not—"

"I mean it hasn't been written yet."

"No, no, I mean—"

"Valentina, dummy."

The manager of my Palo Alto pad in Atherton.

"So what are you trying to tell me? She's a contraction of you? You're contractible?"

"More or less she's a degenerate hypoelliptic operator due to the non-commutativity of the Lie algebra driven by vector fields that generate the control map. See?"

"No."

"Hypoellipticity. You must know about that."

"Sure. The heat equation's hypoelliptic. So's the Laplacian. The heat equation's not elliptic, though. So what?"

"Well, her non-commutativity induces her hypoellipticity and that causes difficulties."

"What's the control map?"

"Have you released Dina yet?"

"No. Maybe. I don't know what the fuck you mean by release Dina."

"Oh. Well. Never mind."

She walked away, skinny legs and skinny butt fleshy compared to the flesh-coated skeletal remains with tits that haunted the crib in Atherton.

It dawned on me she'd been talking about the probability space of Brownian motion as a universal probability space where its semigroups generated by arbitrary elliptic operator can be realized. Those elliptic operators have canonical form written as a sum of Lie derivatives along some driving vector fields. But I don't think she knew that. And I had no idea of what the fuck she meant by the control map.

Rachel's materialization didn't surprise me. At least she didn't have massive jugs, nor were they a lax pair as adorned Nico, the San Francisco treat. I'd meant to be a recusant relative to the carnal menagerie inhabiting my space but it was impossible. However, Rachel didn't push pursuits of the flesh.

"I advise you to accept my client's offer," she said.

"What offer would that be? And you mean Dina?"

"We now refer to her as The Porn Star Formerly Known As Dina. She intends to submit to a new master, one of higher authority than you, more spiritual."

"Fine. I haven't seen her since I delivered her to Hans for remodeling."

"Well, you have actually but you can't remember since it has not yet happened. Might never, actually."

"Uh huh…"

"See, you refuse to go with the flow. You have to cross the damned flow. It's like someone put a random bug in your highest order derivative. I mean, you can get anywhere you want by moving along a flow. You know? But you've got to escape where you ought to remain, by crossing the damn flow. And sometimes even going against the flow. I mean, you can't just cross the flow, we all do it, and then we get back on; noooo, you have to go against it. Looking for a more likely path of improbable movement. You don't just approach the boundary across the flow slowly, gradually, working up to it trial and error-like until you get across, you got to make a leap across a definite distance in a definite time. Even though you seem to hang back, you spend that time making unsuccessful attempts until you make the leap. It's like you break your gradient field, you defy it, and so instead of spending a lot of time exploring neighborhoods of stable equilibrium, you jump from one to another, hoping that they are all points of stable equilibrium, but of course they aren't. That's what you don't see. See?"

"Uh, no. Sounds like you're discussing small random perturbations of dynamical systems."

"Well, anyway, she is offering you royalties for all the films she made before this paper is signed, which I must admit are quite lucrative."

"That's the cash that mysteriously appears in envelopes with that bugle stamp?"

"Yes. It has been written of elsewhere, so we needn't go into it here. But you also get title to the Porsche and the apartment on the temple grounds in Atherton. And one point five million dollars."

"What?"

"Okay, I told Harry you'd drive a hard bargain. Two million, then."

I was speechless. Were they actually offering me two million dollars? For what?

"Harry Ball?" I asked.

"Yes, he will not be the new owner, but he will be the chronicler of her adventures. He says you're on a gradient descent to degeneracy as a singularity."

"Harry Ball said that?"

"Not in so many words. He says you've fucked up all his regular girls. He wants to sue you for scattering his stable."

"Well, that's bullshit. And isn't he now? I mean, doesn't he make the porn films?"

"We don't refer to them as porn. She has a spiritual following and her new master is not of this world. But Harry is not exclusive, no. He does not distribute them exclusively, either. This will become his new calling, so the exclusivity is two-edged."

"I don't have shit to do with any of this. So what are you offering me this two million dollars to do?"

"Sign this," slipping a paper towards me. "It grants Dina her freedom from you. It is an act of manumission. She can be free to choose a new master. Though there is a question in libertarian philosophy as to whether or not one has the freedom to give up one's freedom voluntarily."

"How can I manumit or sell or whatever something I don't own?"

"I cannot explain this to you. Others have tried to do so in your language in the last few days, but no one can get through."

"Okay. Let me read it."

A stark document in what I took to be vellum. Amidst the center of the page in enormous hand-drawn blackletter, 𝕴 𝕸𝖆𝖓𝖑𝖞 '𝖂𝖍𝖎𝖙𝖊𝖞' 𝕭𝖚𝖙𝖈𝖍𝖊𝖗 𝖒𝖆𝖓𝖚𝖒𝖎𝖙 𝕯𝖎𝖓𝖆 𝖆𝖓𝖉 𝖆𝖈𝖈𝖊𝖕𝖙 𝖉𝖎𝖘𝖘𝖔𝖑𝖚𝖙𝖎𝖔𝖓 𝖔𝖋 𝖔𝖚𝖗 𝖕𝖆𝖎𝖗𝖎𝖓𝖌 𝖇𝖔𝖓𝖉.

I signed it and handed it back. She handed me a briefcase.

"You don't have two million dollars in hundreds in there. That's twenty thousand hundred dollar bills."

She opened it and handed me two deeds, one to the car and the other to the apartment, along with a fat paper: "On Small Random Perturbations of Dynamical Systems," by A. D. Ventsel and M. I. Freidlin.

"Read this paper before you fuck me," she said. "It is copied from a *Russian Mathematical Surveys* of the year 1970. We think there is advice in it to help you regulate your life, though we aren't certain. The money is to be delivered in plain brown wrappers."

It was. Eight of them, each bundle about a foot high and weighing five pounds or so. The numbers were not consecutive, but the bills were crisp. I took one to the Whitney Bank and they verified it was real when they broke it for me.

The paper by Ventsel and Freidlin abetted exploration of Riemannian manifolds with my trained Brownian particles, but I took long enough to read it I didn't have to fuck Rachel, who meantime returned to California. My thesis moved along despite all the fucking required of me. My workouts improved with a sextet of physical trainers, brunettes all, lean, toned and not busty. Except Selene, who did sport a pair, not lax, with sufficient substance for them to lie on her thorax across the inframammary fold though they stood up and pointed their dark areolae at the sky. Her legs were thin, particularly her thighs, and she wore a sultry expression all the time, perhaps an artifact of her lips. Zara had almost enough boob to fall against her chest but her inframammary fold remained manifest from the front. Her long legs were not skinny. With arched eyebrows and thick, wavy hair to her shoulders, from a distance she had a pleasing aspect but closer inspection revealed puffy lips in a small mouth with cupid's bow narrowing precipitously to thin, elongated elastic tendrils extending well beyond the vermillion zone to the bow's nocks. Dark-haired Tanhua was skinnier than either of them with breasts that rose up as hemispheres pointing dead ahead and a face that made it seem she'd been crying. It was sharp with a fast gradient from high forehead to chin accentuated by indented cheekbones almost at eye level. Nika had an adolescent girl's body with a hint of rounded breast. She also had a broad, straight nose that rose up from between close-set black eyes and long enough that it dominated her face, especially given the nose remained the same width the entire length, wider than her small mouth with its pronounced cupid's bow above a wide lower border that almost covered the abrupt chin. Victoria had the body of a girl entering adolescence, her breasts hints, long and hard, her buttocks round and above which she carried a symmetric tattoo. She had a longish face with full lips and a dimple in the center of her chin. Her most remarkable feature was a prodigious clitoris protruding downward between her legs in the shape of a small penis, enough to fool the casual observer from more than a few meters into seeing a preadolescent boy. All of them sported noticeable clitoral prolongations when they stood naked, but Victoria's was unique in that when excited the appendage sprang up and out from her vagina like a childish erection.

They wore their hair long down to their shoulders or beyond, something I found odd for gymnasts. Gymnastic teamwork came out the first time we tumbled together in a bruising fuckfest where they definitely go the better of me. Victoria exhibited a voracious appetite for having her clit sucked, especially while I fucked her from behind, either in the ass or the cunt. Though all displayed insatiate sexual appetites, the most excessive was the spidery gamine Ralina with spindly arms and legs, no curves, nipples for breasts, and dense black hair, the most vicious of the gang.

Heavy machinery provided distraction during our after workout workouts, a practice that became a ritual as before showering we wrestled in a padded rumpus room where they gang-raped me. At first I tried to cut the routine to weekly, but it was while enduring these romps that a visitation of the jet prolongations that came to play an important part in my thesis first appeared to me; I learned to visualize jet bundles in such a manner they could be extended to random functions.

I'd had problems with the jets. No logical reason, more likely an obstruction to beginning the grunt work of marching to a dissertation. But once I'd started, jets became a triviality. Acceleration had no coordinate-invariant interpretation, obvious from considering the circle in the punctured plane under Cartesian coordinates and under polar coordinates, but the truncated Taylor's series, the jet, was invariant.

Under duress from n^{th}-order contact with my tormentors, n arbitrary, I gained facility visualizing jets as families of higher-dimensional manifolds generalizing higher dimensional extensions of the classes of one-dimensional manifolds, that is to say curves, running the tangent space at points of contact. First-order jets were a breeze; the higher order jets came with additional pressure from the hellcats, or perhaps better named Preisach hysterons, given the practically infinite gap between the switch-off threshold and switch-on threshold by which they were always initialized much nearer the switch-on threshold than the switch-off threshold and I never knew if the any of the hysterons had been in the state below the switch-off before our romp or if they had retreated from an earlier switching on, which of course made all the difference in the world as together they formed a Preisach operator with unpredictable weightings but always with Preisach measure singular with respect to the two dimensional Lebesgue measure. And behold, I was lifted to the infinite prolongation at the supremum of the set of all counting numbers which indexed the tower of jet manifolds grown ever more geometrically jumbled as grew the highest degree of the truncated Taylor series these counting numbers represented. The Cartan distributions dimensionally grew with the degree and were unreliable, leading to blind alleys amidst caves and holes in a maze of conditions that could not satisfy a system of partial differential equations, everything coming at you from everywhere beyond a horizon that rose with the tower; too much freedom to provide a maximal compatible set of consequences. By an algebraic miracle, the discontinuous leap that in the inverse limit of the tower of projections amongst the jet manifolds provided a Cartan distribution of the same dimension as the base manifold of the underlying fiber bundle of the jet bundles, provided thereby reliable finite-dimensional pathways through the infinite-dimensional infinite jet manifold. Though killed by its annihilating ideal at each step towards infinity, not until leaping across the first cardinal divide did the Cartan distribution's annihilating ideal swallow up its own differentials. Even so, it could not be according to Frobenius since the infinite jet manifold was of infinite dimension, a case specifically prohibited by hypothesis. Hence the algebraic miracle allowed in the inverse limit an orderly meeting up, pigeonholed by the restriction to fit together for every individual counting number, losing legs as it were from a countably infinite centipede, an n-pede with limit of ∞-pede at which it loses enough legs to become tame. More miraculous yet though not reaching the heights of Cartan's Theorems A and B, the differential structure without charts of the direct limit of the sequence dual to the tower, the rings of C^∞ functions on the jet manifolds as commutative algebras with derivation, immediately provided a differential calculus. I observed the formalization without geometry, real analysis embedded in rings and ideals by swapping functions for germs, based on a theorem of Borel on rings of formal power series over the ring of smooth germs and how germs matched series, convergent or not. Lurking within the proof was the Nakayama lemma as an essential stepping stone. The collisions of subspaces finally settled into ordered contact despite the algebra of contact on the mat; the daisy chains of trainers linked to my penis and my mouth, beginning and end interchangeable, induced the vision of the variational bicomplex, that cochain complex of the differential graded algebra of exterior forms on jet manifolds of sections of the underlying fiber bundle. Of course, the infinite tower was a daisy chain with connections moving down with decreasing index, and since endlessly extended did not need to close the loop in order to leave but one hole unattended. I could reach out and touch the partial differential equations without losing my view from below, intrinsic and extrinsic the same due perhaps to rigidity on the mat. Transported to an infinite jet manifold of random sections arising from finite dimensional state space nonlinear system driven and perturbed by white noise, that is to say a stochastic differential equation observed through noisy measurements, I beheld sections determined by the DMZ equation prolonged to the infinite jet manifold as fiber bundle over the base manifold of the original bundle on which dwelt the sections, far below. The random sections squirmed as though infested with worms. I released my own swarm of random travelers in search of a Cartan distribution across the divide; hence did I extend the jet spaces to accept random functions. Demonized as infinitesimally generated flows my travelers used themselves up and hence their search was stochastically incomplete, the little fucks exploding at random times. To cajole them to crawl I multiplied the stochastic by small positive constants in an attempt to keep them from exploding, which didn't work as well as I hoped and would require further tuning. Early on I invented and implemented a control law of march or be eaten, like Mormon crickets, a forced march driven by cannibalism. This aspect of my vision quest was due in part to the paper by Ventsel and Friedlin who had studied flows of parabolic PDEs slightly perturbed randomly by diffusions based on elliptic operators, a small parameter the multiplicative factor to keep the excursion small that I applied to modify my own explorations with Brownian motion in more subtle probing. The stochastic flow of diffeomorphisms infinitely descending a la Fermat, extension of the stochastic differential equations to jet bundles. This allowed me to use a ray method from a paper given me by one of the gymnasts by a Cohen and Lewis of the Courant Institute from 1967, the same method used by Ventsel and Friedlin; I was also handed a paper by Yudell Luke and Jet Wimp that I threw away, being from the *Journal of Computation* of 1963, though it regarded Jacobi polynomial expansions on a semi-infinite ray. The fruitful idea was asymptotic expansion along the rays, actually curves of maximum likelihood as in Ventsel and Friedlin, which provided estimates of the lowest eigenvalue of the diffusion equation, the reciprocal of which gave a measure of the persistence of the crawler. In the original work by Cohen and Lewis the functions in the expansion satisfied ordinary differential equations along the rays, so here it was necessary to extend the crawlers to satisfy random equations, hence the necessity of generalizing to what might be termed random jets. This became most fruitful in the case where the process nagged against the grain, so to speak; that is, moved against the flow to escape stable limit sets to reach new stable limit sets. Given they spent potentially infinite time milling around the limit sets, it was necessary to speed the little cocksuckers up without causing time scale inflation in my own time, hence the cannibalism-forced-march control law. It made me think of what Rachel had accused me.

I spent the long Christmas break in Palo Alto, learning new theorems from my head but no closer to leaping the gap. An ecstatic Frenchie escorted me two other places that wanted to lease a piece of my hide. One was a very small company on the Page Mill Road tech strip, not far from the incongruous Wall Street Journal office, that worked in control and had a slug of PhDs. They wanted me to consult on stochastic issues related to estimation but were hip to any sort of science-fiction enhancement they could sell to the DOD.

The other was a newly formed institute for mathematics that resided in back of a shop selling a spectrum from mundane to non-existent of gadgets for stimulation of any sort of erogenous zones. It was founded by a guy who'd decided he could not serve two masters and so gave up mathematics for pornography, becoming wealthy in the process. He was not connected with Dina as he wasn't at the front end of the business. Whether he could deal in her work was not clear to me, but I guessed he was aware of it and that selling it would be too risky. The quantities of her film sold were small, much of it personalized, all of it monumentally expensive.

The Institute was run by a woman to whom I was strangely attracted. Her name was Porqueria Hénon. She'd been born in India to parents who sold her as a divadasi, as which the village sold her to traders who sold her to a Mexican brothel from which she was rescued by a wealthy client who sent her to school, only to be devastated when she flourished as a mathematical physicist, starting from illiteracy to complete a PhD in only a handful of years. He killed himself. Her history and theorems made her relatively famous.

She had done work with the heavenly equation and later the hyperheavenly equation using excitations and twistor methods, all leading to explicit foliations of the entire solution manifold somehow related to non-invariance and something to do with deformation endowed with a fractional topological charge. After losing interest in relativity, she switched to degenerate conservation laws involving shock waves and rarefaction waves intermingling or some such shit that meant nothing to me. She knew who I was from reading interviews with Dina and she offered to help me.

A motto hung on the wall behind her desk.

Deivadasi serves the God, but is the wife of the whole town. I am wife to the whole universe.

The place on Page Mill Road was a for-profit company also loaded with odd ducks, though of a different feather. No blackboards at which gathered groups of wandering graduate students grown up to become professors or similar forms of mathematician, a metamorphosis mostly marked by more pay and better office space and without noticeable change in attire or carriage, to confront one another with intellectual challenges. Instead a few ties here and there, fewer jeans and t-shirts, engineers mostly introverted and avoiding contact. One of them kept an office filled with crystals and had a pyramid in the corner large enough to sit inside. On the door of another office hung a poster of an orangutan sitting in an office chair staring up, the caption reading "Sometimes I sit and think, sometimes I just sit." My own office overlooked a parking lot; my first time standing at the window the scrawny systems engineer assigned to care for my computer needs stood beside me watching two women dressed to the nines cross the lot. "Not bad," I'd said, and he replied, "I'd let her shit on my chest." He was small, but evidently he loved to fight and was insane enough to have fought his way into every brig in the Navy. He even escaped from the red-line brig in San Diego to hitchhike up the coast and turn himself in at the brig at Bremerton, Washington which he'd heard was nicer. Never advancing beyond deck ape, he ended up doing his bad time and getting a bad conduct discharge. From there he'd gone on to become a biker working in several rackets and was eventually busted for running guns into Mexico and running drugs out. That cost him his pilots license but he escaped jail time. After being stabbed in a bar fight, he gave up the biker lifestyle and went to college, graduating with a degree in computer science. He held a top secret security clearance.

The Page Mill office resonated with sexual charge that hummed from the brunette who ran the place and the marketing director she hung out with. The two of them dressed conservatively, nothing revealing, but it didn't matter. If they'd worn jute gunny sacks it'd have made no difference.

Mona, the office manager, could not hide her long legs which dresses revealed to be slender and shapely even as slacks revealed a high round ass. A long waist with no hint of tummy and breasts high up on her torso that were not overly bulky balanced proportions. The breasts were always packaged so as not to be conspicuous, relegating them to petty insignificance Her nose protruded from a regularly shaped face that black hair elliptically framed as it hung to her shoulders without hint of wave or curl. The nose was not a detriment, especially given the full mouth and gradual chin and eyes as dark as the hair.

Even as Mona showed tone her friend Carol, a natural blonde, struck me as luscious. Ripe. Not fat, not svelte. I wanted to fuck them both. But the woman in personnel who took my personal information and verified my citizenship emanated erotic tension, as did her boss, a slender woman in her fifties who I later saw jogging in short-shorts at lunch time with a man at least a decade younger. Something in the air.

Mona asked me to escort her to the Christmas party as her boyfriend was the VP we both worked for. She took me shopping at a department store she called Needless Markup where she tried several dresses and expected me to help her choose one. I bought two of them for her, surprising her that I carried so much cash. She resisted my paying for them, but the dark red cocktail dress the texture of a rose set off her skin and hair, the black short dress revealed her contours.

My quarters harbored several suits that must have originated with the same tailors Utta had chosen. I wore a sky blue job with a collarless nubby silk shirt. It was a hit with everyone but our boss, who gave me a sad look as she and I left the party arm in arm and met with Carol and a swarthy slender man who appeared to be a Latin lover she called Enrique. He joked about a ménage a quatre and the two women put their heads together and agreed. He seemed surprised but the question quickly reverted to where. I considered offering my place, but the two women agreed to go to a place they knew in San Francisco called the House of David.

On the drive into the city we shared several joints and some cocaine, though I was unimpressed with the quality of the latter. The women grew garrulous. I smoked hash laced cigarettes and they all wanted their own once they caught a whiff, even though neither Mona nor Carol smoked tobacco.

The House of David was a swing club. When we arrived, naked people cavorted throughout what seemed to be a mansion from the 1930s that had been remodeled for unconstrained group sexual sports among humans not afraid to act publicly, there existing no doors on any of the rooms.

Mona and Carol disrobed without hesitation. Enrique hesitated but joined them, lean and hairy and not particularly muscular. I hesitated, not wanting to create a stir with my lower appendages. Mona ragged me for my shyness which I deflected by talking of my war wound. She felt it through my trousers, taken aback by it and perhaps the hint of something substantial nearby, a surprise for her as the suit I had chosen did not reveal so much as many of them designed by Utta's tailors and I wore baggy cotton work slacks to the office.

My bared torso caught the eyes of both women. Enrique said, "Don't worry, man, no one will notice your leg," but that was not so much my concern. If someone asked me about the scar, I'd say I'd been wounded escaping from the pigs, intimating I was a drug dealer or bank robber. When I kicked off my trousers, there were audible gasps from the three of them. "It isn't that bad, is it?" I asked, but they stared at what hung between my legs, the appendage I could not adequately govern prolonging and bloating with excitement.

"I don't think anyone will notice your leg," Mona said.

"Third leg… Christ, is that what I think it is?" from Carol who moved closer to her date.

Now that I'd committed I took in the two beauties. Carol was soft, like looking through fog, grey eyes and pale blond for real, her shape womanly plush, padded to soften the curves, whisper of belly and swell of broad hips, broad legs with substance but not so as to obscure shape, short waist, wide back, breasts centered in her chest pointing nipples out at the apex of what might have been fat-padded cones, elongated hemispheres. She wore a bemused smile on a face furnished with normal features, eyes enunciated with too much black, bangs to her eyebrows. She knew why I had hesitated. The leg was forgotten.

Mona reached out and stroked it.

"Wow," she said. "Wow."

Mona was not so padded. Her hips did not exhibit pronounced swell, the hip bones plainly visible; legs neither substantial nor ethereal. Harder from toe to the top of her neck, her breasts too were fat-padded cones but flattened a smidge rather than prolonged a smidge. Her flesh pads spread out more, their darker nipples pointed forward. Carol's breasts reached farther but the ratio of back to boob was smaller for Mona.

I grew an erection. Partly I wanted it, partly I could not rein in the desire. A small crowd had formed and it was swelling. I heard comments: "hung like a horse" "I can't think where to put something that size" "I'd like to try"... A couple approached. She was the taller, elongated with the legs of an even taller woman almost bony below the knees, thinner than Mona's, flat hips and massive mammaries hanging from a trunk more befitting a woman with sturdier legs. She looked like a barrel on stilts: willowy from a semi-circular arc drawn from the hips through the mons pubis down, voluptuous above. Her areolae were of ten times the area of either of Mona's or Carol's, brownish orbs that covered the face of her breasts hanging against her chest resisting gravity, the nipples pointing out, not down. Green eyes, creamy skin of a glowing tone bounded by those of my two companions, not pale like Carol but paler than Mona, contrasted against brown hair. My erection began it's drool.

"You must be Whitey," she said. "We heard about you from the party, though I have since read Dina's interviews. The one in the *Journal of Guidance and Control* was marvelous. My God, the photos. Before and after. She is no longer of this world. Her homage to you is quite a story. If half of that is true, you are a genius. What a creation she is, and she claims you are the creator. Now they'll want to interview you. Word is you will be Master of the Year, though we still favor Leroy, no offense." She stopped as if she expected a response. None came. "My, what a thing you sport!" she said.

Her dumpy companion showed a patch of hair on a concave chest and a patch of hair on his groin without sign of penis. "I'm Ken, this woman is my wife Claire. We missed that party, the one at Tyrell's place." "Tyrell? I'm not sure—" "At his bitch's place. He's the master."

I nodded. The one to which Rachel had taken us. The racist shindig on my last trip at which white women abused black men as breeding stock for their husbands' amusement.

"I am designing a suit for Dina, by the way, a skin tight isolation chamber far less bulky than the one used by John Lilly. Smart materials. The big problem is to allow penetration of erogenous zones from outside without otherwise affecting isolation. Isolates sensations that way, pinpoints them more or less—"

"Please, Ken, shut the fuck up," Claire said. "Our friend Nikki and our master Leroy you met at the party." She stared at my erect penis, now slobbering like a mouth corked with a ball gag.

Mona pulled me away from Claire and grunted "Fuck me." She pushed Carol onto her back on a couch and stretched out on top, a contrast starker than brunette on blonde, the padded bluish-ivory Carol surrounding the tan, lean Mona with an edge of pale. They performed mutual cunnilingus and Mona pulled me towards her with a hand hooked around my left knee. "Now," she hissed. I worked my way into her cunt to a group sigh from the assemblage. Her ass rounded straight away at some distance from last visible vestige of her backbone across a pad with a bulge of fat. The crack began with a triangle pointing to the crevice in which hid anus and vagina. Narrow butt cheeks, pinched on the sides in a concavity too gradual and long to be called dimples, sloped up and away to a peak from slight fat pads on her thighs not seen when she wore clothing. The declivity of her buttocks framed the open between spread legs in invitation I could not resist rushing, pressing her forward on her partner so she almost unlocked, though neither lost lock, perhaps only some cycle slips amidst a cry from Mona that sounded like an alarm. She arched her back and pushed, abetting entrance. My orgasm fed Carol after which Claire set to work with her mouth to resurrect it; once up Carol claimed dibs, having seen from Mona that a constructive solution to the expansion problem did indeed exist.

It saw plenty of use that night, to the point I but watched my appendage in action. Claire was eager to meet again and told me she was inviting me as the only white male for soirees, other than the cuckolds. I had seen Leroy earlier auction off Nikki to a group of men who abused her with serious gladiatorial contests. Leroy made the rounds, perhaps aprowl for new recruits.

I ducked back into my thesis at some point during the melee, not returning until awakening in my quarters. I had demonstrated that the nonlinear filtering problem for GPS was not finite dimensional by projecting the density onto an L_2 Hilbert space expansion and showing that for each N, the projection was itself a density, so that no finite collection of sufficient statistics existed. It was clear that this was true as well for what was called the cubic sensor problem, but I didn't consider it worth writing up.

I gained unexpected assistance at the Institute when Hénon convinced me to consider entropy. This was no mean feat, given I'd burned out on learning new shit from outside my own head. She had investigated differentiable dynamical systems in terms of entropy, characteristic exponents and fractal dimension with respect to the production of information. Her advisor Hanumam Buddhimataamvarishtham, on leave from the Tata Institute radio astrophysics group in Pune, Maharashtra at the Instituto Nacional de Matemática Pura e Aplicada in Rio de Janeiro, guided her thesis on relaxation techniques for releasing the kundalini via shaktipat, most especially carnal shaktipat. She showed that the obstruction to release could be described using rectifiable and integral currents, where release required transgression of rectifiable currents that were not integral currents. Of course, this condition only existed when rectifiable currents had infinite boundary mass with the predictable effect on comass, the boundary being an integral flat chain but not a rectifiable curve. A deformation theorem allowed her to obtain a constructive closure that turned out to be destructive in practice, causing in unprepared humans a blowup rupture into inner space from forcing the infinite boundary onto a finite grid in consciousness, leading to what came to be called in psychiatry physio-kundalini syndrome. Most common were the symptoms of total body orgasm lasting for hours to years with continuous contractions and the bliss of infinite love and transfinite connectedness beyond the cosmos. Such debilitating effects caused lack of human productivity and had to be curtailed. The most remarkable feat, however, was the miracle of teaching herself to read English using Herbert Federer's *Geometric Integration Theory* as her sole source.

Her cohomology theory of partial differential equations had germinated with a paper she gave me from *Bulletin of the American Mathematical Society* of 1969 by one D. S. Spencer entitled "Overdetermined Systems of Linear Partial Differential Equations" that considered systems of linear partial differential equations as complexes $Ж \rightarrow К \rightarrow \Bbbk$ of sheaves of germs of differentiable sections of vector bundles over a differentiable manifold with the maps interconnecting the sheaves as differential operators. She'd generalized this setup in both the deterministic case and in the case of stochastic PDEs via an algebraic construction termed the deformation cohomology related to infinitesimal deformation of a filtered Lie algebra associated with a graded Lie algebra with Spencer cohomology resulting from symmetry groups of the PDEs. I never did see how it tied to Noether's theorems as she claimed, but from the cohomology complexes she gained information on conservation laws.

She was a tough taskmistress: I learned her spooky action at a distance: to not read assigned papers meant pain the next day: I sprung an erection lasting more than four hours.

THE DAKINI DANCES: LECTURES IN NONLINEAR TANTRA

Hénon had earned her name Porqueria in the brothel where she'd come of age; where her original name stayed behind. Unable to give up the life for which she was born, the God-given meaning of her life, she worked the temple of Ma-Dina as a sacred consort and teacher of mysteries. She taught me sacred transgression like Monk taught Trane to blow two notes at the same time.

I had not reacted to her as to Mona and Carole and Claire. My reaction to them had phenomenological origin, lust blossoming from the effects of their physical accoutrements without caring why; my reaction to Hénon seemed one more manifestation of spooky-action-at-a distance. Slight without appearing frail, she was skinny and straight. Her middling dugs spread flat on her chest and drooped toward the floor when she bent forward. Her hips showed no bow but neither did they show bone; from aft her ass sprawled, showing skinny from the fore. The color of tanned coffee, she was hairy. Black hair flowed from above the crack of her ass to her navel, appearing impenetrable at the curve of crotch. The black hair on her head hung in a thick braid formed above and behind her ears, reaching below her knees.

LECTURE 1: DYNAMIC FORCED OSCILLATIONS

Hénon trained me to sit cross-legged and she settled herself on my lap facing me, my erection penetrating her. If I moved she shocked my penis. Breathe quietly. Zero friction. No slow or fast variables. You must expand into a complete place; enlarge paramour capacity; apply adiabatic elimination to bypass the non-resonantly coupled levels. The rotating wave is of great utility in coherent excitation.

First goal: solve the simultaneous eigenvalue problem for dual resonance.

She applied ergodic theory, teaching me to simultaneously increase the information dimension in my partner and in me by optimizing excited degrees of freedom. We sat for milliseconds or days. Don't move. Humping and forcing distract. Focus. Merge as one in chaotic flow across the face of reality, chaos sparking new information as partitions tighten toward turbulence and a countable infinity of degrees of freedom in the information dimension. Communicate at the stationary point: the lingam unmoving ejects polyrhythmic waves fleshlessly into void merger of two, phase-locked, self-tuning cacophony of sympathetic modes within the folding strange attractor exploding the atomic level, stretching to every atom in the universe across all time.

Insufficient. A local shock wave rippled along my glans penis, absorbed on the boundary.

LECTURE 2: BAYESIAN MODELING OF FAT TAILS AND SKEWNESS

Grasping weariness with tits on twigs and barrels on stilts, she provided a Bayesian modeling. Castigating me as pointless and taken with ephemeron, she nonetheless took my measure of the day and normalized it. Valentina the first prior with application of Bayes rule uniformly filled in darker hued meat on the bones, pale brunette without pallor but with giant peach blossom nipples on heavy gravity-defying mammaries, a meaty ass with noticeable curvature melting into meaty gams.

Nico updated to a tattooed wearer of baby fat with a round mouth encircled by swollen lips without hint of cupids bow and towered over by an elongated thick nose. Deep brown hair stark against pale skin cascaded waving to corpulent boobs that leaned against a torso without visible sternum or ribs. A flattened hour glass with short, sturdy legs, short waist, a soft midriff and rounded hips.

Hénon brought me a ginger pear to work with, breasts mounds of negligible slope, nipples but buds. Her flared hips and coarse legs suited dimpled buttocks. Not five foot, the two rolled braids she sprouted on either side of her head at forty-five degrees from the level gave her the appearance of a child; a spoiled round-faced child with bangs hanging in her eyes, a haughty filtered stare, a perpetual pout perhaps the result of her mouth rather than an attitude one could not divine. Trusting all to gravity, she gradually sank over my erection, capacity expansion distending cylindrification until spontaneous oscillation set up poly-harmonic waves rippling her flesh in constructive and destructive superposition, shear flow and uncontrollable panel flutter the manifestation of vortex shedding about her cunt at resonances driven by enthalpy. Energy transferred to me as a sink calmed the potentially calamitous vibrations. We dispersed, wisps of merged being burning into that intercosmic serpentine connection across the fibrous dynamo in the machinery of bundles, subatomic blowup tourist visions, circumnavigating closed loops shrinking to zero, swept by infinitesimal holonomy to return to that which did not begin, astronomically long recurrence time palliated as the miracle of swift relaxation time to equilibrium.

"You're homoclinic," Hénon said. "You straddle the attractor and the repellor. When there exists extreme attraction or repulsion, suspect exogenous supernatural forcing."

"What about her," looking at the munchkin melted into a puddle on the floor, face floating in freckles staring up stupefied.

"Her orectic self is overwhelmed so she has become flooded with extraorganismal inputs. She may or may not recover. But don't feel sorry for her; she's found her bliss. Chalk it up to transvection. She's become paramutant. She unwittingly demonstrated the Khokhlov-Zabolotskaya equations. When the two are in synch there will be acoustic levitation."

I must have looked stupid because she said, "Or perhaps the conundrum of recurrence time versus relaxation time, the nearly infinite time and the small time, being one. Of course, your merger as one." I didn't reply. "Never mind. If she solidifies, we will turn her over to a qualified therapist—psychiatrist, psychologist, witch doctor, shaman, something—for treatment of advanced Kundalini syndrome. Forget about her anyway; she served her purpose and finds herself in a better place. Now you are ready for the next lesson? Circumnutation about your yogini to travel the finest scales and their gross inverses. She is mistress of circumvolution. You will be her sole subject."

I took her to have said sole, but she might have said soul. "Your measure will become excessive. You will be semipolar, but thin sets will not define you. Always of potential zero. Exceptional. Get it?"

I shook my head no.

"Good, then. Let's move on. It is a form of balayage, you know, taking from the superficial boundary where you are of potential zero to form substance. Miraculous, as in Dina's ingestion of honey transmuted from Mule's sperm. Excessive measures.

"You will learn to not catalyze the roll-ratchet when you pilot. It is the reading of acceleration cues. Excessive input demands and larger gains than can be tolerated result from feedforward rather than feedback. Your yogini will teach you the techniques. This is control of flexible structures with hysteresis and vibration compensation for stability in structurally elastic systems. Worst case control. She is mistress of the small gain. The ginger is testimony to the dangers of feedforward and of large gain feedback. Just hope you do not see interaction of magnetoacoustic waves; omnidirectional pulse and plane pressure pulse waves result in eversion by spontaneous discontinuous deformation. This can begin with the Alfvén wave. The onset can be from something as simple as the Kadmotsev-Pogutse equations, at least for simulations."

She must have thought I looked like an idiot. I felt like one. But she never gave away anything at the portals to her soul, black eyes the color of her hair a pair of highly eccentric ellipses pinched at the ends, so dark no pupils could be distinguished. A ring in her left nostril and her right eyebrow appeared as natural as the black brows arcing with a sharp peak across her face below her extended forehead to set off the lower ovoid ending in a rounded chin. Black fine hair draggled to her butt, the ends whacked into uneven bunches. A prominent nose plunged from between the close set eyes to spread uniformly with gradually increasing width ending with a slight hook below the ring, a long, lean nose befitting the long, lean face befitting the long, lean body. Her tubular boobs were almost a third dark areolae with small buds of pointed nipples. A wide mouth, narrow above and fat below, truncated lower lip not extended across the entire structure, ever unsmiling in harmony with the blank stare she leveled at everyone no matter the situation. She kept legs, armpits, and bush adorned with the same fine black hair that streamed from her head, the bush extending to cover her anus.

"If you have misfortune to go to Los Angeles, you will find more prevalent the plasticity equations. Quite explosive. But in the symmetries, there is semi-direct product. That is beautiful before the shattering. Creep plasticity can leave you with psychic vomiting for days.

"Is better to stay with small gain feedback. You will obtain flutter clearance when you pass from quadrature to cubature. That is the fourth stage. Wavelets, you know. Time-frequency methods because none of this is time invariant, and besides who wants the symphony lumped into a single moment? And all that uncertainty, you know? You cannot be simultaneously yourself and another without losing both; that transform is not to be concentrated simultaneously on sets of small measure. You must be one, not two. It is the Dzhrbashyan Theorem: do not tend to zero too rapidly. Flutter suppression, active and passive, are only the tip of the spear, so to say. Sensor and actuator modification into massively parallel processing and distributed control, infinite dimensional and nonlinear. The train will be the test: cubature, after quadrature with your yogini."

I had no idea about what the fuck she yammered but she introduced me to a dark skinned woman I had not previously noticed standing across the room.

"This is Dhara. She will be your yogini, your Karma Mudra. She is adept at vajroli-mudra and will guide you. She will release you with her own ecstatic alchemy. There is no need to lecture on the Siva Samhita. Instead, practice—"

"'E's a' one what needs th'impedance boundary conditions?"

"Yes. Call them Robin boundary conditions. I fear he will not grasp impedance."

The woman, I believed a woman given prominent breasts deforming the front of the long-sleeved tan V-necked blouse of muslin with an ornate pattern along the neck inlaid in silver thread that could have been a filigree collar, pierced me with brown eyes lurking beneath dense black beetle brows that met in an unkempt whorl extending from the nose root along the bridge where the eyes nearly intersected.

"Practice. Her moon fluid in yab-yum will open your Sushumna, beginning with the Vajrini, readying you for the yogini chakra to come, your flutter clearance trial. If all goes well, you will clear the Chitrini and if worthy, the Brahma Nadi. Dhara will prepare you for the flutter clearance trial."

Her straight skirt covered to her ankles. It seemed to be wrapped around her like a shroud, a coarse sheath with periodic pattern in bands that looked Middle Eastern or Indian.

"Her Mantras emanate for you in familiar images and terms, from unmanifest to becoming manifest to luminous enclosing to enclosed. Uttered aloud uttered softly uttered in silence in your being. They will be matrix-sound vibrations, primordial resonances seeding your diffusion. Listen well: protection."

Dhara's mouth was painted bright red, contrasting an adolescent's dark mustache covering her wide upper lip and curling down around the edges of her mouth. The border of her square chin was adorned with a wisp of black whiskers.

She undressed. To all appearances a female, what lurked within the dark bramble between her legs could not be discerned. Surely the thicket overgrew her anus and trailed up the middle of her back, given the rampant spread of the plunging whorl beginning at her navel. Man hands and feet, leathered skin the hue of a dirty Idaho potato uniformly covering her lean-limbed cylindric frame, notwithstanding she presented solid tubular tits splayed against fat rolls on her abdomen with nipples giant splotches like oversize black moles.

"Entropy in tantric duality is maximized when initial partners are optimally mismatched. Violate the matched stability dogma: fly in the face of structurally stable attractors; all motionless perturbations are allowed. No symmetries or constraints need be preserved under perturbation. This is opposite the Bernoulli trials where equiprobable outcomes maximize entropy. It corresponds to the Bernoulli case of zero entropy, but in the Tantric dual under propitiation may lead to infinite information dimension. Dhara is married to a pale, plump brunette female. You are less attractive to Dhara than she to you: all men are repulsive to her, but especially pretty-boys. Seek long periodic stable orbits with convoluted basins of attraction indistinguishable from strange attractors. Violate the stability dogma as preached by mystic dynamists in the land of strange attractors."

Armpits decorated with dark undergrowth contraposed light down on her forearms as her bush contraposed downy lower legs.

I assumed the lotus position and she climbed aboard. We departed posthaste, Hénon a frantic whisper in the distance: "Don't forget your necessary conditions for entrainment to sustained reentry roll resonance!"

Lecture 3: Resonance Near Chaos

Markov partitions squeezed down an indecomposable invariant set of wakes, residual decaying rarefaction waves surfed transverse the shocks expanding and contracting in a direct sum decomposition of the bundle assigned a symbolic dynamic imposed as lines projected parallel the eigenvectors of Anosov diffeomorphisms: we breached the shadow pseudo-orbits, trapped within toroidal vortices of irrational flows.

Uncountable restraint modes near resonant equilibrium of least action at stationary points bounced among chaotic balls in the horseshoe, merged from before the beginning of time, one, unity, dispersed beyond the end of time, catapulted via the ultrapower of the real numbers, stretched beyond and compressed within the thick continuum of the hyperreal field of Leibniz justified by Abraham Robinson via ultraproducts of Łoś, infinity outbound beyond every N and infinitesimal inbound in the cracks past the Archimedean, in the monads where nothing adds up, scattered outward and inward without identity beyond atomic particles and random universes, free floating variable geometry shapelessly shaped to no shape everywhere and nowhere, endless bifurcations of nonlinear oscillations, frequency entrainment near uncountably many resonances robustly controlled passive-joined robotic-arm of Mahakala. Rapid energy dissipation yo-yoing inversely back and forth infinity to infinitesimal, flexible body system of many synthesized one to none actively suppressing flutter in minimum time—no time like the present—no-time active damping by local force feedback. Escape reentry decay due to misdirected injection maneuver, wave-absorbing controlled flexible structure of nothing, no-time trajectories to nowhere robustly managed momentum and attitude control feedback linearized and bang-bang controlled incorporating inertial slip-stick actuators for flexible structureless structures in no-time-optimal slewing toward reentry, separation dynamics of strap-on boosters gone, the gone world, avoiding bright objects, stabilizing using transverse wheel for any spin-to-transverse inertia ratio, spinning momentum wheel, spinning up, no slippage, spinning down, longitudinal control law for autonomous reentry, feedback control for slew maneuvers off-on thrust, sustaining reentry roll resonance. Standing waves.

The three trainers assigned me came across as far more masculine than the New Orleans krewe. Three three-holed compacta, their chief was an ever-smiling flaxen haired body builder standing about five-ten with a set of meaty breasts rippled in muscles and veins. Round melons protruding to the fore and fat on the sides, I wondered it they'd been enhanced but daren't ask. Her extensile clitoris dominated the landscape of the hard vee of a mons veneris, all of it as bare as the rest of her, nary a hair save fair tresses to her shoulders. There were almost no lips on her vagina to pierce but her clitoris wore four diamond studs from the hood down the penis-shaped shaft, with a simple pair of rings adorning the two small lips hidden beneath the clitoral head. Her cunt was framed by a pair of pronounced blue veins emanating from either breast running parallel down either side of washboard abs that diverged along either side of her mons to disappear within bulky quads.

"I have some advice for you," she told me after wrestling me to the mat, astride my chest pinning my arms with her legs. She bored into me with pale green eyes. "You need to heed Saint-Venant's principle for the equilibrium deformation of long elastic cylindrical columns subjected to forces acting at the ends. On the lateral boundary there will be certain combinations of components of the stress tensor that vanish. They vanish throughout the cylinder except near the head and base, so they are filtered out in the interior. Dig?"

I knew she didn't mean what she was saying; I tried to listen to what she meant, not what she said. "My abs? You want me to work on my abs?"

"No," she said, leaning back with her hands on my lower abdominal muscles at the point where my penis attached. It hurt.

"Okay," I said, "but how?"

"I can teach you to apply maximum reaction wheel torque without harm by momentum dumping thruster torque without thrusting. You need to learn to avoid wheel saturation."

"Wheel?"

"It isn't part of your typical anatomy lessons. Subtle bodies, subtle energies. Kālachakra."

"It's about time," a voice emanating from beyond my field of vision.

So I met the second muscle girl, not so developed as the one pinning me to the mat, nor as tall, with vanishing tits more often seen in male steroid users, gynecomastia. She wore her brown hair in coarse dreadlocks interspersed with beads and ribbons and haphazardly arranged in all directions around her head. A discrete strip of brown thatch, pointed at the end, directed the view to a cunt without lips, a pronounced penis of a clitoris standing upright above the opening.

"We'll teach you to extend the Krylov-Bogoliubov-Mitropolsky averaging method to vector systems in normal form with angular components, just so's you can get necessary and sufficient conditions for frequency entrainment of quasi-sinusoidal injection-synchronized oscillators. Dig?" She stood looking down on me, arms akimbo.

I didn't want to say anything, but I was lost. Pinned and lost, but at least not wriggling.

My pinner, later referred to as the Queen of Hurt, added, "We'll start easy with you. Dynamic synchronization of two coupled multivibrators."

"But there gotta be eventually frequency plateaus in a chain of weakly coupled oscillators. At least."

A third voice from the void. "Yeah, and parabolic bursting in an excitable chain of weakly coupled oscillators with slow oscillation."

No bodybuilder, the third was slight, decorated on her torso with a series of bright interconnected floral and filigree motif tattoos in blues and greens. A pair of roses spanned her chest above her small breasts. She wore short hair, a brunette with olive skin who didn't shave but was not particularly hirsute; the densest growth between her legs did not cover her vaginal lips. The tattoos interlocked miraculously with the only symmetry the rose patterns above her breasts. There were sleeves on both arms and one around her left thigh, a bald, pregnant woman on the sleeve on the right arm, a mandala amidst dragon scales on the left, and down her right side a slender stalk that could have been garlic in bloom. She delighted in twisting herself into impossible yogic configurations.

Connection with my trainers subsumed in a trivial bundle via Fourier transform and inverse scattering, the nonlinearity satisfied by the connection. So back and forth between the two structures, trivial bundle without information and a connection satisfying a nonlinear PDE, a vector bundle without connection and satisfying no differential equation, all swept away by Fourier and inverse scattering transforms, and yet for all the world equivalent. By isospectral deformation we four fused as a set of coupled nonlinear PDEs, the Iyn'lomogob equations for ecstatic monopoles, became a self-reflecting irreducible root system and were scattered, sometimes transforming away the connection, less often but with greater effect integrating out all the connections, overcoming in the limit immiscibility.

Lecture 4: Symbolic Dynamics of a Bi-Infinite Sequence of Bimbos

A long exact daisy chain of Tantric complexes with Bogoliubov automorphisms connecting the distinctly identical yoni components with a single lingam identity and insertion from lingam to yoni provided the set-up for flutter clearance trials. I assumed the lotus position. From somewhere in the infinite past a prolate dumpling astride my appendage, deflection showing vibration suppression following momentum dumping for input shaping as she morphed into something less oblate with perhaps red hair or perhaps another person entirely switching times blurred with thruster torque of uncertain duration, slewing to a new form before me along the chain ostensibly bi-directional thruster firing of uncertain gain excites vibrations not damping out sufficiently, residual vibrations induce coasting, saturation with maneuvers as transformations come ever more quickly though there is no meaningful temporal stepping within in the thick continuum of hyperreality, monads within and reciprocals beyond everything, local entropy become global as expanding capacity engulfs infinite and infinitesimal alike, attractor a smooth stable foliation along which flows come at random or perhaps at haphazard, super ergodic not only dense but touching every point on the continuum in cosmic dance. Derived functors on my lap now blurred in change as I slowed to take control, to make it all constant suppressing the fluttering panels of oblivion, the entropy of the Bogoliubov actions of the commuting torsion-free group now less a blur as I will it slower, dense ergodicity my goal at my own mixing rate, canonically transforming commutation relations with unitary representations without symplectic form, creation and annihilation operators at my disposal, parallel transport in evidence finally as I steer the sequence of exact manifestations within the chain bi-complex and merge to a constant without leaving a faithful trace. Astride my erection a honey blonde with hazel eyes. She had a long face, straight and narrow and somewhat horsey with high forehead and sharply sloping chin, atop it her hair piled and pinned with a long metal clamp. A loose strand of several fibers hung down to her chin. I could not see but felt smushed padding against my chest and an unpadded bony seat on my lap.

"Sublation," Hénon said, "was the key. You have mastered the flutter with aplomb. Congratulations. Suppressing chaos in wraparound projectile motion is not something everyone can accomplish; mastering asymmetric bodies and their propensity to roll resonance is not enough, and you not only perverted catastrophic yaw, but roll lock-in as well. A true mastery of flexible structures. In this endeavor you have simultaneously chosen the wife for your arranged marriage, something few can do given it was arranged before you were born, though not before her birth, while admittedly she was born for this match, and microlocal control. Not just analysis, but control of pseudodifferential operators and singular operators. Of course, your choice of arranged mate is a blow-up. But note, there can be no antenuptial sexual congress. This yab-yum does not, of course, count."

She dismounted gracefully and unfolded to at least five-eleven. Rangy, built like a basketball player or hurdler with tits so overfilled they stood despite hanging like a pair of ever-so-slightly asymmetrical bags from her prominent sternum, her decided lack of tone didn't give the impression she engaged in athletics. Her pale skin tone spoke to avoidance of the sun, but against which her lightly pigmented round areolae and button nipples stood out. Her lips were painted metallic red. A short jeweled chain dangled from between her legs, apparently from her cunt, likely from her clitoris or the hood. I almost asked if this were mandatory, this piercing, but held my tongue. I took her to be in her late thirties. She had no hair in evidence below her neck save a thin vee of long fur, the color of that on her head, at the base of a flat, short mons far down from her long waist. She evidenced little curvature, her hips not flat but squared with yet one more round, narrow butt. Everything was long, face, waist, upper torso, hips, legs and arms, boobs, her knees; her legs reminded me of a race horse or deer, graceful but seeming without sufficient substance to carry her.

"What the fuck you talking about? Arranged marriage? What if I'm already married?"

"You're not. No one would have you. You're a promiscuous slut. Besides, you picked her."

"How the fuck did I pick her? I was just doing some exam or other, flutter control or some such shit."

She handed me a paper by an H. Araki, "Bogoliubov automorphisms and Fock representations of canonical anticommutation relations." It was dated 1987.

"Where did you get this?"

"You're concerned it's postdated? It isn't. It is the date of publication.

"You negotiated the modulational instability enveloping the wavetrain of your life and you're concerned about this paper from the future? It's a manifestation of characteristic values imposed from aftereffects on the present—shock waves if you will—and forwardeffects on the present as well that most people blindly never negotiate. Most humans take things on the face of it; their unstable lives develop locally pulselike behavior, singularities in finite time—often local times—quiet desperation giving way to surprise in the face of the collapse of their monochromatic waveforms. How can they take control of the aftereffects, let alone the forwardeffects? Life, Whitey, life is not causal, nor is it purely anticausal, but acausal, so the aftereffects combine with the forwardeffects. See?"

I shook my head no. My assigned wife made a grotesque face, showing large upper teeth as she covered her chin with her tongue and wrinkled her nose, displaying black hairs hidden within the pinched nostrils.

"The future does affect the present, but not solely the future. The past as well. Karma flows both ways. You have transformed your present and your past from the future; formed, if you will, your own solitons. Your arranged marriage partner chosen—no, created—here and now by you. Waves undulate from the past and the future. Sometimes they cancel, but when they don't, people freak. You have gained a modicum of control."

"She seems at least a decade older than I."

"So? She is ageless as she didn't exist until this moment, though she was born before you. See?"

I did, actually. That bothered me.

"Always remember the future as you modulate the seeming vicissitude of the past."

"I think she shows a lot of odd harmonics."

"Well, you worked with a twelve-tone row, from what we could see. Not much symmetry. You seem not to like symmetry about the present."

My assigned fiancé had not spoken. She stood arms akimbo, massive breasts a miracle defying gravity, their elegant round nipples pointed to the heavens. Her voice was high and thin and breathy, not at all as manly as her physical presence sans boobs would lead one to believe.

"Quarter tones. In the cracks, you were," she piped with a British accent. "A twenty-four tone row, that is to say, twenty-four tone equal temperament, to match my own personality."

"In the non-Archimedean cracks of the continuum, that's where. That's the Leibniz vision resurrected by Robinson. You understand that stuff."

I was pretty sure I did. Nonstandard analysis. Monads, named after Leibniz ridiculous metaphysics of reality, not his mathematics.

"What's your name? I mean, if we are to be married, I suppose I ought to know it."

"Hypatia Lee Faithful."

"Our little joke," Hénon said. "She has a voracious sexual appetite and will engage in sexual congress of varying sorts with anyone willing—"

"I like big groups, public spectacles. Dicks, mostly, big 'n' small, all of 'em weepy like. Girls but mostly snotty dicks. Prefer big, like yourn, but the more spunk I can wring from 'em the better. 'Specially when lots're watching."

"She's highly orgasmic when people watch. The more the crazier she gets. Unrestrained, totally without inhibition, aggressive like a male dog. Anyone anywhere anytime—"

"I get it," I said. "A Faithful fucker."

Hénon laughed. "Or cocksucker."

"Well," Faithful said, looking down demurely, "my true name's Katie Stevens, but no one calls me that."

"What is it then?" I asked.

"Does it matter?" Hénon replied. "What's in a name anyway? A rose by any other name would smell as sweet. Besides, she is quite organized and will take care of all your annoying quotidian minutiae. When you escape New Orleans and return here, you will marry her at the temple which is a good place for her to dwell as she can fuck all the time without danger. And she will be the perfect swing partner for clubs and parties and especially for the soirees, though it will be your choice to act as feckless cuckold or white bull master. She might even be able to help recruit a slave harem for you. The only white bull master."

"Great, just what I need. Do the slave babes need to be black?"

"Your choice. It is a duty."

"And a priv'lege," Katie-Hypatia Lee the Faithful added. "But I feel I missed so much, Mum. Take me to the temple, please Mum, so's I can get me bunghole stretched and injest me some sperm. I have need of a good fucking."

"Remember, no antenuptial congress for you two. No exchange of fluids, no intercourse of any sort. No congress. You cannot fuck her face or her anus or her vagina, not even a doglike pseudo-copulation on her leg. In time, you will increase her capacity." Hénon started to lead her away.

"Wait," I said. "We were watched. When we were out there. We were watched. Who were they?" I didn't see them except as shadows, but they communicated. Not in so many words.

"Did they bounce? Like balls?"

"I'm not sure. I was blind. I mean, not blind, but—"

"I understand. You were—"

"I 'eard 'em," Katie said. "They was talking amongst 'emselves, they was, and one um said somethin' like, 'Want to induce interacting turbulent flow; looking for strange attractors.'"

"I didn't hear that," I said.

"They likely whispered it in her head. That would not be the machine elves. More likely Henkin witnesses. They need you to touch specific tangibles to validate results. Get rid of quantifiers. More or less."

"Well, they implanted some shit in my head. I didn't remember it until now. Not remembered so much as it happened now, to me, but it was then."

"Aftereffect. Their presence was forwardeffect, though. What'd they leave with you? That would not, by the way, be Henkin witnesses. More likely observers. Luenberger observers. Lurking there, planted by something. They simplify, but only in theory, and testify. And these lot were smoothers. What was the message?"

I read it aloud: "To gain an infinity of excited degrees of freedom: turbulence, is to reach bliss. Reading the Hausdorff dimensional potential for excited degrees of freedom an important early lesson, part of recognizing most sensitive zones to initial conditions: judge symbols and local galvanic skin response. Accurate real estimation of partner's characteristic exponents early is necessary condition for optimization. Chaotic sensitivity to initial conditions possible with any partner, but costing years of coaxing in conditions of mismatched spectra. Chaos to turbulence opens doors to perception not open to other mortals."

"Interesting. That is aftereffect in that you just see it now but forwardeffect in that your seeing it now has caused it then. Quite uncommon. Combined causal aftereffect with anticausal forwardeffect so that it actuates anticausally while coming to you with aftereffect, skipping the moment it happened when it happened." She thought for a minute, then added, "Like cashing a post dated check before it is written that you only find later."

"So it just happened now but applied then?"

"Come on, dear, let's go get you fucked."

They left me alone.

Her mouth stayed with me, a cupid's bow like a bird of great wingspan in the distance elegantly gliding in a constant smile with minimal, infrequent waves. And a straight, noble nose to offset the wide, slender oral orifice.

It seemed I'd remained longer than the allotted time. Frenchie always expressed enthusiasm over new results I showed him, results I didn't remember deriving but which I thought had been with me when I arrived. Nonetheless my notebooks expanded with results I was sure I already knew. We put them together in a typed format with help from departmental slaves and sent them to my advisor. For me, there was but one item remaining: to jump the gap to an optimal nonlinear finite-dimensional estimator for the combined GPS-inertial measurement case, given I'd already proven the GPS standalone case admitted no finite-dimensional sufficient statistic.

New Year's loomed. During the interim period with Christmas, Frenchie and I endured Hénon's

Lecture 5: Asymptotic States for Reaction and Diffusion

In which she showed that realizable excitations of the heavenly equation may be generated by symmetry operators which yield two reduced equations with different characteristics. One equation is of the Liouville type, giving rise to gravitational instantons, the second equation appearing for the first time in the theory of heavenly spaces and providing half-instanton-like configurations endowed with a fractional topological charge, related to the Euclidean space-time solution of the Yang-Mills equation. I fell asleep while she established a link between the heavenly equation and the so-called Schröder's equation, something to do with eigenvalues of the composition operator that plays a role in the bootstrap model and in renormalization theory, whatever they might be. This time I was visited by machine elves who introduced me to a large single celled creature whose kinematic motions were accomplished by extending pseudopodia within which flowed a viscous fluid from the main body outward to a tubate projection. Bouncing around me, out of direct vision but of regular and constant period like oscillator balls forced by external device, the machine elves supplied words. Cytoplasm. What flows is cytoplasm. The outer boundary of the creature was a highly deformable membrane with an external mucous coat with which it surrounded my appointed fiancé who lay on her back, phagocytosis the bouncing elves shrilled in unison, the soup within its border shimmering in light reflected from the bouncing elves. It formed a massive tubular appendage of semirigid gelatinous mass, ectoplasm the bouncing elves shrilled, with which it probed her nether orifices simultaneously with dual projections while its endoplasm shuddered with shallow spherical waves and sparked as though riddled with electrical shocks. I awoke alone in my bed with an erection, with the expression "Dude, your future wife got fucked by a giant *Chaos carolinense* pseudopodium" jangling in my head, and with a good idea of how to leap the gap across the void. For the latter it was enough to find the appropriate creature to flow with the geodesic with a finite-state automaton riding along as observer.

Frenchie would later call it tunneling when I described the idea, though it wasn't clear whether he meant my means of inspiration or the idea itself. In neither case did I understand why he called it that, though he said it had something to do with quantum physics, with information instead of energy. Not that it mattered; he decided the last bit, the part I found most important and interesting of the lot, was of little consequence and that I might as well consider my thesis finished.

d) Constant Radial Thrust Acceleration Redux

The second return included my fiancé and my hairy yogini and her wife, new additions to a burgeoning retinue. Yogini and spouse took a slave-quarter apartment across the courtyard, the same third floor slave quarter as Dina's but in the adjoining building. I wasn't sure where my finance bedded down; I seldom saw her.

The trip had not been a success. I did make progress on my thesis, but instead of joining some semblance of reality as promised in escaping New Orleans, I had found more irreality. Insanity piled on exponentially since my days in the Green Machine. Machine elves and witnesses and observers. The latter two were constructs, one mathematical and the other engineering; soon I'd be haunted by ghosts in the machine and ghosts of departed quantities. My haunted apartment was nearly deserted, perhaps a result of my ogre's-disposition and fucked up aura, but though none of the spooks were often visible and no demands were made on my physical presence, my food was ready, my laundry washed, my sheets changed, all my quotidian requisites satisfied.

I bored down on my problem. I reviewed it all and tidied it up, tightening loose bolts in the machinery and rebuilding the setup infrastructure. I carefully reformulated the innovations representation and embedded the whole mess as an infinite dimensional submanifold of probability distributions within a manifold of measures containing both the raw pseudorange setup and the GPS derived position setup with its non-Gaussian densities. Delicate abuse of the innovations processes allowed a Cameron-Martin space as the tangent space, an important bit of delicate finagling. The gap now stood as an obstruction I needed to transgress within a vector bundle with smoothness along the infinity of directions in the Cameron-Martin space, an important privilege.

My review of the heat operator on functions on Riemannian manifolds turned up early work by Minakshisundaram and Pleijel from 1949 published in some Canadian mathematics journal, predating the work of Gaffney. Two papers appeared mysteriously in my inbox: "A New Strapdown Attitude Algorithm" by Robin B. Miller from the July-August 1983 issue of *Journal of Guidance and Control* and "Strapdown Attitude Algorithms from a Geometrical Viewpoint" by Richard McKern and Howard Musoff from the November-December 1981 issue of *Journal of Guidance and Control.* More post-dated papers or anticausal manifestations of journal articles from the future, not sure which. In any case, I refused to read them.

Carnival season on the horizon and as always the haunting of the Quarter by a variety of dregs of humanity and near-humanity intensified. Crossing Canal Street from the streetcar after the ride back from Tulane, an overtone of hysteria overlay the Quarter, more subtle in its early stage but crescendoing day by day to a peak on midnight of Fat Tuesday. More people slept in the hidden crevices of the place, some on doorsteps against locked gates, the scent of urine slapping the nostrils upon exiting the barricaded confines of courtyards and doorways. Most times of year the urine stench was reserved for hidden places like Pirate's Alley, but now it mingled with the electricity and stench of the thugs cajoling handouts from the residents who had to run the gauntlet. Mostly they left me alone while an increased police presence helped keep them at bay.

And there was the rub, as Joelle explained. This year, the famously corrupt New Orleans cops were going on strike just prior to Mardi Gras to push their effort to join the famously corrupt Teamster's Union. A match made in heaven, I said, the New Orleans cops and Hoffa's old gang. "Well," she said, "if I lived in the Quarter I'd leave town for Mardi Gras, police or no police. But the police say they will shut down Carnival this year. The parades may be cancelled, but the Old Guard say the balls will go on."

She invited me to dinner at her place, hesitatingly as if it had been a long thought out consideration. I didn't hesitate to accept.

Lecture: Free Objects

Joelle lived in a blue stand-alone structure in the Irish Channel. She called it a Creole cottage, dating from the 19th century. The neighborhood was full of them of, each small, unique structures sporting varying displays of gingerbread. Hers had none but there was a porch out front.

She greeted me wearing a long gown, her hair piled up on her head displaying a long neck, her features soft Creole, full lips, high cheekbones, rounded chin, luminous brown eyes in pronounced ample round settings, orbs agaze in subdued fire larger than I'd seen them before. The gown extended neck to toes without hiding plump womanly curves.

We sat opposite one another in a cozy living room uncluttered with bric-a-brac drinking a cocktail she'd prepared with Herbsaint, a local liqueur that tasted of anise, with which she coated the glass before discarding the liquid, a sugar cube, a few dashes of a local bitters named Peychaud, lemon peel and ice shaken with a shot of Old Overholt. We went through several of them while she moved back and forth from the kitchen, popping out with another just as I finished it's antecedent.

I spied Josephus' *Antiquities of the Jews* on a shelf.

"You studied history?"

She came out of the kitchen and sat beside me.

"I majored in history. I have a master's degree in ancient history."

"I heard a lot about Josephus history of the Jews when I was growing up. My mother studied the Bible and she brought it up to defend positions, denouncing it when shown it didn't support her position."

607

"I don't know about the Bible much. I'm Catholic. We don't read it. But I think Josephus would be a skewed source. That period is fascinating, though, and his history a masterful propaganda piece for his people. I also read his account of the Jewish wars. It was part of my thesis work."

"There seem to be a lot of volumes. I didn't realize it was so long."

She didn't add anything and I let it drop.

She wanted to know about my Vietnam wounding but I brushed that off. "I'd rather not go into that," I said "It's painful. Besides, I'm interested in you."

"Ah," she'd sighed, "I am older than you by more than you know. And I'm boring. My life has been uneventful, nothing like yours."

I assured her I didn't consider her age any sort of obstacle between us, but she wondered how I could prove faithful to an old woman, which she would become well before I became an old man. The difference was fifteen years. It didn't matter, I said, she was beautiful and would only grow more beautiful with time. She smiled at that. And, I added, my life has not been so adventurous. Much of it I spent on my back in a hospital, in rehab, and then studying mathematics.

"Boring," she said, "the mathematics. I don't understand the passion it brings out in those who pursue it. It's like an affliction."

"It is, in some ways, an affliction," I said.

"You could make money with all that wasted brainpower," she said.

I answered that people afflicted with that sort of brainpower seldom cared about money. "People who devote themselves to making money are seldom very bright, from my experience. Sometimes those afflicted with intellect deliberately turn their backs on what they love and pursue money, but more often they pursue what they love and get money sufficient to live as they go along. Sometimes they amass a pile of it by accident or by winning some prize or grant, but not often by intentional effort.

"But what about your passions? History?"

"No, not history, except local history and then mostly of this neighborhood and really traditional New Orleans food. Tonight's dinner is a historical preparation from the area."

"And lovers, if that isn't too personal."

"It isn't. There is nothing there. I had a few opportunities, mostly missed. Never married and no real lovers, only one real passion. There had been offers, but only one of them inspired real passion. I lost that through my own lack of vision."

608

"I doubt it was your vision alone. Anyone who would let you slip away without fighting was short sighted."

"He offered opportunities I'd not seen until now, too late. I pursued an empty vision of freedom that became a prison. I saw his dreams as a restraint. I realized too late it was not."

She reached out and covered my hand with hers. "Let's drop all that. I don't want to talk of it anymore than you want to talk of your wound."

Dinner was chicken she'd fricasseed in what she explained was a historical Creole recipe from a small family restaurant dating from before the turn of the century. We accompanied it with Alsatian white wine. She could cook.

Afterward she let her hair fall over her shoulders, a carpet of waving black with mahogany overtones. Without much ado we ended in the bedroom. Effortlessly I removed her robe, her bra. She snuggled against my bare chest, inspected my wounded leg when I removed my pants. We kissed and she caressed my penis. She drew back.

"What is that?"

"What?"

"That," pointing at my half erect penis. "That is not human. I have never seen anything like that. It is huge and warty and uncircumcised. I can't even get my hand around it."

"It isn't so big," was all I could respond.

"It is not of this world, Mr. Butcher. It's impossible. A demon member."

Her voice had taken on the sharp edge of a shriek.

"You will not point that at me," though it wasn't pointing, "you will not put that in me. Get that out of here."

She backed off the bed.

"Get out of here with that. And don't come back. Don't talk to me at work. Don't come near me. You are not what you appear. That is not a work of nature."

I sat impassive, unable to respond, paralyzed.

"Get out!" she shrieked.

e) Cascading Lossless Chain-Scattering Feedback and Unitary Dilation

The vanishing of the cops with the strike was the critical parameter leading to a bifurcation of the mutants descending on the quarter. Walking home from the streetcar stop came to be reminiscent of going on patrol. There were State Police and National Guard replacing the cops and reminding me I resided in a banana republic. They kept down the major extortion but were not much concerned about panhandling. Nor were they much concerned with public decency, unlike the regular cops who enthusiastically busted naked individuals and couples or groups of mixed or pure gender, the latter almost exclusively male, for public displays of what might be called, loosely, affection. This had an early affect on the gay homosexual population, especially on the corner of Bourbon and Dumaine, my intersection and a singularity of sexual tension during the Lenten season. The displays went far beyond the usual female tourists showing their tits. Now they copulated openly in carnal displays of a variety of sodomitic acts alongside gay leather-hardhat-Nazi uniformed bearded males, some in the garb of Southern belles, who unabashedly held their male partners above their heads to suck their dicks as flagrant street carnival. Hotel and apartment balconies around the Quarter, but especially on Bourbon Street, were displays of sexual congress often involving one female masturbating, but not infrequently with one female and several males emulating popular pornographic films. It was to be assumed that since those inhabiting the rooms were tourist couples who made their reservations years in advance, most of the gang bangs were conducted by otherwise wholesome Christians from places like Round Rock, Texas on a ticket of suspended judgment.

A fitting start of the Lenten season. As always, 'twas the Friday before Fat Tuesday when the pent up potential energy actualized with the workaday world shut down until Ash Wednesday's beginning ended the party at midnight. Palpable shock waves set up a resonance though the activities across the street from my apartment had grown ever more outrageous over the past month. Nothing like the breeding party would happen in the street, but Dina, it was said, held sessions with gangs of strangers in the dungeon in Marigny, assisted by the spooks who haunted my apartment which had grown quiet and empty even as my meals and laundry and apartment cleaning continued to be invisibly provided.

I had not yet bridged my gap, my nonlinear GPS-INS filter remaining at bay and perhaps unachievable and worse, not perhaps provably unachievable.

Friday afternoon I returned from Tulane on the streetcar down St. Charles Avenue in a city not noticeably different except the atmosphere like slow motion vortices in a heat flow, charge capacity swelling the closer we drew to Canal Street. The potential exponentially increased as I crossed into the Quarter walking up a Bourbon Street soon to be closed off for the duration, ignoring the panhandlers and carnal congresses. Intensity solidified as I approached the singular anomaly at Lafitte's, nonconservative forces commanding the day with neglected degrees of freedom, non-elastic stress imploding negative curvature unbounded in non-holonomic dissipation of the connection, parallel transport around closed curves failing to preserve geometrical data, non-holonomic mechanics meaning you never knew where you'd be after making a circuit of any neighborhood bounding the singularity.

In the courtyard two Nazi officers abused a helpless bearded devotee of gay bondage. I gave them a brief side glance as I started up the winding stairway. As my eyes came level with the solarium, I saw my fiancé seated alone on the floor in the corner by the kitchen door, her back against the ancient crumbling bricks. She wore what appeared to be an extra-large gunny sack with holes cut for the arms and neck. She stood to greet me.

"Whitey, finally. I've been here for hours." The British accent had vanished.

"Why? Thought you'd be out fucking the masses."

"I have been. For days. Weeks, maybe. I lost track. The women you keep here are animals. I and they have been in the streets enjoying the kindness of strange strangers, not really human I think, most of them. We had a major orgy in the squatters camp in Jackson Square. God, I so want to betray you as your wife, not just as some random slut. It gives a purpose to the squalor, it does." At the finish, a hint of Cockney. She grinned. "Me people was costermongers, they was."

She stepped under the skylight and I saw she wore no makeup, completely unadorned except for streaks of gray on her cheeks and forehead.

"Who the fuck are you?"

"Well, dear, perhaps I am not what I appear. There are a lot of morphogenetic variations about with not very different, to the naked eye, or naked to the eye, though often that latter can be the telling point, variations that were reorganized into new cellular structures. You, for example. As opposed to Dina, whose remodeling was totally exogenous in the sense of being surgically restructured, not from exogenously controlled internal concentration-gradient morphogens. You know, cues and interactions. Conditional specification as a means of control. Working with what is to get what cannot be."

"Uh-huh. I don't want to get what you're saying. But that doesn't answer why you're here now."

611

I opened the door and we went inside. I lit a joint.

"Feel my dress," she said.

I ran my hand over coarse material which hung loosely almost to her ankles, obscuring her boobs so long as she didn't move.

"It's true sackcloth. Woven from goat hair. I have ashes on my face."

"Sackcloth and ashes. What's the occasion?"

"It's for you. I'm not in mourning, but you seem sad. And I so want to submit to you. When we get married I want us to take strict vows of fidelity and such."

"Why?"

"So I can break my vows. It intertwines our selves. By promising to be faithful, I can truly be faithless."

"Great. I suppose you'll want a breeding party for a wedding reception."

"I want a massive gangbang with strangers as a first anniversary present, a breeding session with dogs for the reception. We'll do plenty of breeding parties with blacks, believe me. But we need to get you your own slave harem. Befits your status."

"Dogs? Sounds like you're following Dina."

"No, dear. Dina was never faithless to you. She was only concerned with her own self."

"Breeding with dogs? I thought you'd join that bunch in Palo Alto wanting a black baby."

"No, I want a litter of pups."

"That is not possible, or at least I don't think it is. Besides, doesn't a litter require several independent ovaries or some such?"

"No, it requires superfecundation. I am superfecund. I can produce dizygotic twins and, in fact, polyzygotic n-tuplets, with ease and without aftereffects."

"Well, maybe human, but dogs?"

"They won't look entirely dog-like, Whitey. But they will sport certain characteristics."

I didn't have any response. Another conversation turned crazy.

"You won't notice, dear, but I have a much higher slewing rate than pure human females, partly because I am not wholly female, partly because of my dog nature. I can amplify inputs at an infinite rate, and some say I howl at the moon when the input merits such. Turn on a dime, so to speak."

cascading lossless chain-scattering feedback

"I tend to not understand much of what the people I am thrown in with these days say to me."

"Or you don't want to. I am so glad we are having this conversation." She reached out and cradled my hands in the spacious warmth of hers.

"What should I call you?" I asked.

"That is so sweet. God, Whitey, it's so important for husband and wife to have names for each other. I see a beautiful alliance—"

"Unholy—"

"No dear. Holy. I wish you'd come downstairs. Harry has rented your landlord's apartment and the second floor of the Washing Well for Carnival. Your roommates are fucking up a storm. You seem sad, or at least melancholic. Too much thinking is bad, dear. You spend too much time inside your self."

"How did he pull that off? Jesus, the landlord and the Washing Well owners throw their own parties every year."

"Money talks, Whitey, bullshit walks. Harry knew that this year, with the idiot cops gone, the morality strictures would be released. He is filming. The coming costume contest will the highpoint, with a surprise appearance by Dina who will leave her dungeon for the celebration."

"I need to be alone."

"That's why I came. So we could have some together-alone time. It's so important for a husband and wife to get acquainted. But of course, not sexually. At least not before marriage. We can consummate our alliance after the doggy breeding, which will be public. You do understand that my sort can exchange information continuously, not discretely as with standard genetics. And the information mixes across individual sperm, so with the dogs or other humans."

"Of course," I said. "I would expect nothing less. That is probably why on your planet the wild creatures are more variable than the domesticated. However, I do wonder how that is accomplished given that humans and dogs only represent information discretely."

"That is not the only representation. There are at least two modulations of the carrier which is not" and here she squeezed my hands so it hurt "discrete. The discrete are sampled from the continuous carrier. Sampled gets most of what you humans can experience. By experience I mean sample with your sensing facilities, which are pretty limited. And dulled. My sort get in the cracks. Genetic modulation for us is continuous. Unsampled analogue. That was how Darwin first thought of it. It mixes across individuals which goes back to the Greeks. We experience subtleties you miss."

"No fucking horses or pigs?"

"No, dear. I'm closer to dogs and humans than any other animal, including chimps. But Harry intends to take advantage of the deformation of the undamped system. The relaxation time will be short, I assure you. Equilibrium will be harsh on return.

"Let me give you an example. At the Bourbon Orleans Hotel, only a block from here in the 700 block of Bourbon Street—"

"I know where it is."

"Of course, dear. Sorry. In the future I will be more circumspect. Anyway, a woman on the balcony had sex with two men for at least an hour until joined by a street spectator who somehow shinnied up one of those thick black columns and clambered onto the balcony. The crowd in the street went nuts. They locked up so tight the State Police feared a trampling and so went to the room to ask the woman and her friends to limit their carnal display to more natural one-on-one activities. And this on the afternoon of the Friday before Mardi Gras!"

In the old days the cops would beat up the queers, arrest the straights or rape the women. I knew one woman who had been forced to blow several of them after she'd been arrested for showing her tits.

"What happened?"

"The mob thinned out, dispersed to search for better shows once the balcony crew took turns fucking her instead of in tandem. But I wrote a poem.

"There once was a mom from Dubuque
"Who ate so much sperm she did puke,
"She said with a grin
"As she wiped off her chin,
"'Gents, why ere my o'er holes you've forsook?'"

"She was from Dubuque?"

"She and her husband. The other guy was a stranger they met on the street. And the guy who climbed up, who knows who he was, but they were impressed. I sucked his dick later in Pirate's Alley.

"Anyway, dear, this anomaly is a perfect example of turn-on dynamics with a power pump suddenly activated reaching its gain medium at saturation energy, spiking, taking resonator losses at the peak of its upper-state lifetime and decaying away while undergoing damped relaxation oscillations. Which is what is to come here. Harry knows that."

"I think o'er is a contraction of over, not other."

"Shoot. Now I have to think about it some more.

"By the way, you've yet to speak to Harry about Kim. You must, given she's already begun making films for him based on your telling him."

"Okay. More advanced action leapfrogging the present. Causality meeting anticausality, again. Is that the smoothing I was accused of?"

"By that twig with tits Valentina? I'm so glad you transformed her into something with meat. I prefer meat to bones. I so want to betray you as your wife and not merely as some random slut. It gives purpose to my whoring. And I want it to give you sexual pleasure."

It did. I bonded with her at this moment like I don't remember happening with Dina. I wanted to see her fuck dogs and gangs of stochastic strangers. I could foresee not only swing clubs and breeding parties, but random branching processes of outdoor encounters with caravans of alien barbarians, outlaws, foreign devils and intruders. I wanted to be a cuckold. A cuckolding cuckold. The best of both worlds. It did give meaning to otherwise inutile existence.

"Take this," handing me a tiny pill. "It entraps the brain oscillations. And I have an empathogen…I actually prefer the word entactogen… that we'll use on our outings. It blends well with everything. Adds a layer of sensitivity where you can get inside others and experience what they experience. From your own perspective, of course. It amplifies stimuli with hypersensitivity and may even add some sense perception not normally present in humans. That latter is still an open question. It might even ramp up the slewing rate."

I sprang a woody.

She noticed.

"That's so sweet. Of course, you can't use it on me just yet. But I'll think of you when I'm mobbed by dicks downstairs.

f) Higher Singularities and Forced Secondary Bifurcation: Swallowtail Catastrophe

With the closing of both Dumaine and Bourbon for the remainder of Mardi Gras, construction of the wooden stage in the middle of the intersection outside Café Lafitte in Exile got under way. The frenzied singularity of priapic satyriasis in the French Quarter's goatish celebration of homoerotic excess, Shrove Tuesday Sexualis, centered in this place. On Mardi Gras, Café Lafitte in Exile annually held a costume contest.

The best seats in the house were on the two diagonal corners. The balcony at the Washing Well across Dumaine was perfect since it curved around Bourbon to Dumaine and both faced the door to Lafitte's, which opened onto the corner, and overlooked the review stand. The balcony at Jake's Clover Grill overlooked Dumaine from the opposite corner. My landlord's balcony overlooked Bourbon next door to the Washing Well. It was good but removed from the stand, though not so high up and more spacious than my catwalk. The owners of the Washing Well and my landlord held small parties to view the action; Jake occupied his alone, seated in a folding chair at the corner, a white-haired fat man who otherwise manned the grill downstairs.

The acoustic noise level from below was more intense than in the past, but it didn't penetrate the convolved interactive feedback with my thoughts. Tangled in threads of cogitation or confronted by a vector field singularity that led everywhere and nowhere, I made no progress. I returned repeatedly to stand on the catwalk to feel the enthalpy of the singularity deforming the neighborhood with avariant expansion of optical pumping. What was the half-life of these creatures?

The balcony down below writhed in orgy. I couldn't see everything without peering over the metal railing which caused me vertigo amplified by the wobble of the flimsy bulwark, but I could see enough to note that my fiancé and my roommates engaged in sexual congress with creatures that might have been in costume or might not have been human. I didn't consider eventualities such as shape shifters, given I'd already been presented so many absurdities I'd begun to lose sight of the possibility of normal, whatever that might mean, though I was certain it would exclude cynanthropy as suggested by Katie Stevens-Hypatia Lee Faithful. In my morning session with Dhara the word Rati associated with my betrothed's face, which I realized did have some characteristics of a dog I at first thought horsy. She hadn't answered my direct question what to call her. I would have to discover if Rati meant something. I remembered chthonic escaping the lips of one of Harry's actresses, but the details had uncharacteristically blurred. That troubled me. My memories tended to be honest and crisp. Chthonic came to mind for the party world beneath my feet. Had I fallen among urban nymphs of the underworld? Night spirits?

I returned to my gap problem, loosening up my visions with a giant spliff. I couldn't pull back from the earth opening up around me. The pumping mechanism spewed more than photons into the mix, raising the pitch beyond fever level to some sort of hysteria, though perhaps a poor word choice given the etymology of *hystera.* Or maybe not, as evidenced by the story of the balcony at the Bourbon Orleans. I'd have expected that across the street at Lucky Pierre's. I hadn't noticed anything on my way home, but I'd avoided the dense maze on Bourbon by coming up Burgundy and crossing over on Dumaine. And Dumaine crowded up when I passed Dauphine, making it difficult to turn down Bourbon when I reached the Washing Well. Besides which I paid attention to my surroundings, not the balconies.

When I did venture out onto the catwalk I paid no attention to the street, overwhelmed with desire to see my designated bride fucked senseless, feverishly copulating with integrity as service bitch in heat. My erection was uncontrollable. To go downstairs and join the party at which I would be more than welcome would violate my vow of abstaining from her whether I conjoined with her or not. Conjoined in my mind, I would sin in my heart. Yet I wondered how she performed orally beside the two stress eaters.

I took the pill my betrothed left for me. Cast your fate to the winds.

g) Dynamical Discontinuous Feedback Strategies in the Regulation of Nonlinear Chimerical Processes

Transported to an infinite jet bundle of random sections towering above finite dimensional nonlinear systems given as state space realizations of stochastic differential equations observed through noisy incomplete measurements, I saw sections of distributions determined by the DMZ equation and released random crawlers upon which there nested finite-state automata seeking punctures in the base manifold of the Hilbert bundle whose inner product corresponds to the metric tensor of the space of conditional distributions, the Fisher metric on the statistical manifold. And lo, the entropy functionals from Boltzmann-Gibbs through Renyi and Tsallis and up to a host of others not including Shannon's which lacks the second law spoke as a trumpet saying, Come up hither and I will show you necessity in the power law of a deformed logarithm-exponential formalism with regards to the relationship of generalized entropy measures and Fisher information. And I was parallel transported along a smooth connection with feedback from the great harlot of impure mathematics to a high place where I watched my random wrigglers plow negatively curved hyperbolic projections to explode or simply vanish with random time constant multipliers as functions of conservation laws induced by infinitesimal generators dependent on the jets, exploding en masse upon beholding trivial conservation laws proffering no information in a barren land of exponentially growing negative curvature.

Very wet and horny housewife has husband's permission to fuck and suck well hung men. Husband loves to watch me cum all over your eight inch or larger cock. I love cum baths. Will answer all letters with nude photo proof of at least eight inches and self-addressed-stamped-envelope.

Behold the obstruction of the gap examined in blowing-up the Fisher metric on a tubular neighborhood seeking explicitly to transgress the Chern-Weil differential form representing the Euler Class. Employing the transgression to calculate the adiabatic limit invariant under fibration by maximal tori, the crawlers pass to blowing-up sets of almost probability one yet short, left to explode in the land of the torus bundles after failing to ascertain the signature of the Hilbert modular varieties on sets of exponentially small probability. Prayers offered to the index theorem of Atiyah-Patodi-Singer fall upon deaf ears; there is wailing and gnashing of teeth and no cohomology class to transgress the obstruction.

Wanted black males and black couples with bi wives. Husband likes to watch and take photos, sometimes join in. She's thirty-two, five foot three inches, one hundred twenty pounds and eager to please.

There came one of seven trainers and led me to the great whore, my betrothed arrayed in black fishnet with orifice openings of opportunity, with whom all creatures have fornicated and with whose sexual emissions she has grown drunk with orgiastic lust. And behold, she wore the leather biker's cap with chain along the sweat band and studs bordering the visor. On hands and knees her breasts hung like swaying meat pendulums as a multitude mounted her, fierce coupling forcing her across the floor, creatures half man and half dog growling accompaniment to her howling dog-faced at the moon.

SEXY CUNT-RY GIRL. Vital statistics: Age 24, 34B - 22 - 34. Brown hair, green eyes, 5' 1", 101 pounds, dress size 3. I dig dogs, the bigger the better so I got the world's largest breed to satisfy me. For a sample of photos send $3 to MAUREEN ANN, P.O. Box 1345, Dallas TX 75221.

I was made drunk with the wine of her fornication. She carried me away in spirit into a wilderness where she sat on a scarlet beast full of letters of blasphemous intent, the path a program of ambitious carnal deviations. She ached to sample all.

French-loving couple in search of other attractive couples or select singles. We are newcomers interested in all but pain. Smoke or drink okay.

She's five foot one inch, one hundred five pounds, he's five foot nine inches, one hundred forty-six pounds. No blacks, fatties, grubbies, rowdies or pain.

She cast aside the bigoted.

Very attractive couple. She's five foot three inches, thirty-four D— twenty-four—thirty-four, twenty-four years old. He's five foot ten inches, one hundred eighty-five pounds, eight inches by five and one-half inches, thirty-two years old. Would like to meet good looking couples and select males who have over nine inches. Discretion assured and expected as we are a professional couple. Revealing photo and brief letter a must. No Greek, B/D or drugs. Any race and ages twenty to forty-five.

She eschewed discretion. She asked, What is a professional couple?

Bakersfield area white couple thirty-one and thirty looking for other couples, same age, who are clean and discreet. Male must be safe. No drugs or weirdos. Swing only if all agree.

An amplified screech distorted by feedback, Dr. Boner speaks to me: Dude you need to put a squelch on that weirdo bitch. She oscillating without input at the merest excitation she got gain set so high. She orgasm to background noise. She picking up stimulation without anyone playing. Erotic feedback distortion, dude. Lookit her. On her knees, shuddering, frothing at the mouth, contractions of pubis, breasts aquiver to liquefaction swaying like microphones before a loudspeaker feeding back sexual tension.

Attractive couple wishes to meet single or married female, straight or bi, and select couples. Must be clean, disease free, discreet, selective. We are in our late thirties. He five foot eleven inches, one hundred eighty pounds, good body, sexy. She five foot five inches, thirty-eight D, sexy. Very oral, vocally pleasing. No single males, blacks, fatties, drunks, drugs, s/m or b/d.

Parasitic capacitive coupling transferring magnetic torque between the great harlot and everyone nearby at sexual athletic events, unbounded sum of crosstalk contributions from all adjacent twisted pairs, carnal leakage fringe effects kinky sideshow when she melts down to a quivering puddle of flesh like electrified gelatin, without apparent stimulus.

White couple seeks visiting well-hung, mature black males for mutual pleasure while he watches and takes photos. Very clean and expect same. Would try gang bang. Looks not important. Explicit photo guarantees reply.

And a voice split the fibers exact: She'll be bound over to a submanifold of terminal constraints given by transversality conditions.

I'm beautiful, sexy, slim and available for sensual nude and semi-nude modeling. I am forty FF—twenty-eight—thirty-six. I have a nice round ass and know how to use it. I will do retirement parties, award dinners, stag parties. I do topless or nude maid work. I have sexy long legs and a nice tight ass, to please all photographers. I have a great personality, too. I love to be photographed nude and my modeling gets me hot and wet. I've been a model and a swinger for thirteen years. I love gang-bangs and I am very open minded and bisexual too.

And behold the heavens opened and there passed a secret wriggler of enormous energy and ergodic determination who said to me, Release me with your whore on the Frechet manifold near which gap I must leap in finite time as you dream of days to come with the great slut of Babylon and Palo Alto. And I released it to great fanfare to repair what had been burst asunder by nonlinearity and must be made right by information regarding the position of the antenna corrected in the short run, to make public what is hidden by obscuration.

Sensational thirty-seven—twenty-three—thirty-four uninhibited thirty year old, five foot two, one hundred ten pounds, looking for females and couples who enjoy French to completion. I seek exceptional people who are into oral sex. I love to eat cum.

Information transudes the continuum.

Central Texas straight couple who has enjoyed swinging with couples. We now seek married males with no female swing partner to be our guests at discrete, monthly motel parties on weekends in various Texas cities. Couples and females welcome to party as voyeurs if you'd rather watch. I'm a one hundred percent exhibitionist, love to party naked. I'm nineteen, five foot four inches, one hundred pounds, multi-orgasmic sex athlete with large sensitive nipples, pussy lips pierced with three gold rings that I love to show. He's thirty-seven, six foot two inches, two hundred forty-five pounds, will join in only if asked. No to drugs, pain, Greek, homos, blacks.

After this I looked and behold, a great multitude which no man can number, uncountably many from all nations of the earth engaging the betrothed with implements of penetration, tails like scorpions, locusts wearing crowns of gold with faces like humans, hair like women's hair, teeth like lions' teeth, their king the limit ordinal from the bottomless pit of hyper-inaccessible depth of Mahlo cardinality. And she subdued them all with joyous insatiability.

Married female forty-one years of age seeks a heavy-hung submissive black male forty to sniff and lick my cunt and ass often. I'll tongue your asshole and massage your balls before letting you penetrate and spray your fertile cum deep in my non-birth control protected womb.

Hybrid stabilization by feedback output control calms the frenzied to asymptotic stability even with incomplete information on the dynamics when indiscrete automata perform cunnilingus adroitly lapping the excesses of moving frames from Gehenna. I am the Black Sun of fire and gall.

My baby needs hot black cocks to stretch her tight white holes. We seek couples with same interest, bi females, twins and hung black studs to give baby what she needs. Put baby on her knees and watch her put out. She loves black gang fucks, circle sucks, nasty talk, slow hard deep fucking and a pussy full of hot thick black cum. Hubby videos and encourages baby and her dark lovers. We're unshockable and seek the same. Cum on guys, my baby needs it bad.

Harvesting strategies in predator-prey interactions are never asymptotically stable since they linearize as harmonic oscillators.

Bossy nursing student, twenty-one, one hundred twelve pounds, five feet three inches, seeks older fatherly type men to lick her pussy and ass. Must not mind a little pee with lunch. I love to have you underfoot. Must be willing to serve my friends when I suggest.

And after these things I saw another angel come down from heaven, having great power; and the earth was lightened with his glory.

White anglo female, forty, five feet seven inches, one hundred twenty-seven pounds, yellow hair, gray eyes, into males eighteen to twenty-five or over fifty-five for safe sex. I like to be watched by mate. He won't join in unless asked. This is how I want sex—oral to completion with rubber masturbation with rubber or some without, doggie style. Will answer all who follow our requests. Photo to prove size, no beards or mustache. T/S, T/V fine.

And he cried mightily with a strong voice, saying, Babylon the great is fallen and is become the habitation of devils, and the hold of every foul spirit, and a cage of every unclean and hateful bird.

Married white couple seeks a discreet, straight but freaky black male forty plus in our area that ejaculates heavily and highly aroused by a woman's intoxicating scent during menstruation and finds slow deep bareback penetration during these times an ultimate turn-on. If interested, tell us why.

For all nations have drunk of the wine of the wrath of her fornication, and the kings of the earth have committed fornication with her, and the merchants of the earth are waxed rich through the abundance of her delicacies.

Love dropping to my knees and doing as I'm told by discreet, young, twenty-one to thirty year old men who would like a slim, leggy forty-one year old woman like me. Boyfriend thirty-two makes all the arrangements. I'm a five foot four inch, one hundred twenty pound divorcee/mother, so discretion is a must. Let's use our imagination, but no pain. In pubic I'm elegant and can be your escort but behind closed doors I do as you say. I never wear panties and always swallow. One night stands preferred but gentlemen who treat me like a lady may be entertained regularly. Cleanliness is demanded.

Now consider the optimal capacity expansion problem delineated by Moloch and Carl Solomon with regard to Nephilim of gigantic proportion their flesh like mules and issue like horses, unable to walk without dragging their members along the ground unless girded up. Derive a policy of optimal engorgement without geometric discounting to solve the BJ obstruction. Cocksucker in Moloch!

Cock sucker loves cocks, any age, shape or size. I'm an expert and will do you to completion. I'm single, twenty-six, five feet six inches, one hundred twenty-one pounds, thirty-seven—twenty-six—thirty-six, will travel for a hard cock or will entertain discreet men for overnight suck and fuck sessions. If you want a memorable blowjob I'm always ready.

Your betrothed played the prostitute before she existed, though she has always been yours, and doted on her legions of paramours of all genders and species from before you were given to pimp her. Of the desirable young men riding her like a dog she bestowed her whoredom on them, the choicest men of the world; and on whomever she doted, with all their issue and their idols she defiled herself.

I'm a thirty-three year old three way nympho and proud of it. I love French, Greek, and straight—one at a time or all at once. I love to entertain stag parties. I have no prejudices. Salesmen, truckers, military, travelers. Just off I-10 or US 90 on Mississippi Gulf Coast.

She played the whore in her youth and neither has she left her bitch-in-heat pursuit of depravity up to this day, cum-drinking slut for youth who lay with her and handle the full bosom of her virginity which never was; and they pour out their emissions on her.

Kinky white couple seeks new friends for deviant behavior! She's bi, thirty-eight, petite, blonde, shaved, tattooed, tanned, and is a cum-drinking slut in private. He's thirty-three, straight, well-built and is her cameraman. She likes girl/girl, is submissive and will take Greek from females with strap-on dildos.

nonlinear chimerical processes

I delivered her into your hands to expand the reach of her service, into the hands of new users and well-hung dogs on whom she dotes. These uncover her nakedness; they take her youth and they kill with the sword the conventions of the land: and she becomes a byword among women and the men and other animals they service. None are more carnal in their doting than she, and in her whoring she is more the slut than her sisters, which is your reward. She dotes on governors and rulers, janitors and servants, the lowly and the high-placed neighbors, clothed most gorgeously or in rags or naked, horsemen all riding her as their slut, all of them desirable to her, young and old, men and women and dogs and other creatures not of this world. I saw she was defiled by them all, to your delight, in all the ways.

Sexy attractive young girl in mid twenties would like to meet clean, sincere discrete single males, females and couples who have an interest in oral sex, Greek, French, family sex, animals, enemas, etc. Please enclose photo and letter of your sex desires.

She increased her craving for protracted attack from protrusile protuberant meat prongs and yearnings for meat holes to suck and lick; for she saw men and women and other creatures in flickering images on the walls, the images of the blacks portrayed with vermilion, dressed with girdles on their waists, with flowing turbans on their heads, all of them princes to look on, the likenesses of the whites of enormous proportions in screens in the land of ambiguous birth. Immediately she saw them she doted on them and sent messengers to them, men and women and half-humans, her kind, alike. The monstrosities came into her bed of lust and defiled her in aggression and she was polluted with them, and her soul was alienated from them even as she delighted in it for it was not enough. She uncovered her wantonness and uncovered her lascivious nakedness: then your soul was united to her, even as you created her as your assigned wife, your issued regulation kindred-spirit. Yet as she multiplied her promiscuous cravings, remembering the days of her youth in which she had played the bitch in heat to all men and women and creatures of her own sort and some not, she became your pet and you her indentured owner, bound over for the duration. She dotes on you with your massive appendage and on your bitches and on her male paramours who are hung with penises of donkeys that jet copious issue like the ejaculate of horses.

Sexy blonde female loves to fondle and fuck big, nasty Black cocks. Husband watches and will take discreet photos.

Her model type is high gain gene amplification based on the branching random walk, though more realistically is proliferation, modification, mutation, deformation and unsquelched continuous feedback distortion of gene copies by Brownian motion between cell divisions. Also random cell segregation of gene copies between daughter copies.

Big men wanted by experienced couple, five feet seven inches, one hundred pounds, five feet eleven inches, one hundred eighty pounds. Want threesomes or moresomes with well-hung men. Prefer young, hot, trim, bi and/ or black. Other couples into same, please write too.

She is your homogeneous chaos blues.

Bi couple wishes to meet bi males, TVs, she-males or bi couples. Early thirties, tall, slim, sincere and discreet. No weirdos.

She has demonstrated the feasibility of hardened chattering-free discontinuous feedback controllers in switching scenarios mechanized heterogeneously among weirdos.

French lady. Oh—I can take or give a you a great fuck, but I really would like to go down on males only, who like a great, full, French blowjob.

She dotes on weirdos of extraordinary equipage.

Blonde, young, attractive and insatiable DC female. Seeking very discreet, attractive, black gentlemen to satisfy fantasies. Large cocks preferred. Straight friend will photograph and participate. Clear photo and interests please. Small groups maybe.

Need saturated models. Love complete types. Not interested in determined fits that only amplify variance.

Sexy, young Bi housewife would like to hear from and meet Bi ladies and couples any race. My husband is straight and will join or watch but must be present. He loves watching me cum. I will also trade hot letters and photos with everyone. A few months ago, I was an innocent naïve housewife but my husband talked me into trying some new things—Bi, straight, gangbang—and I loved it! Now I want to do everything and be a real slut. I love exhibitionism and French to completion. I love to slurp pussy. This is my first ad and I'm for real!

Seeking a session with a Heisenberg group of well hung Kabeiroi controllers with symmetric elasticity. *Ignes fatui* and automata welcome.

If you're an honest, down-to-earth, straight s/w/m or s/w/f twenty-six to thirty-eight, clean, respecting of others, not pushy, maybe shy, inexperienced, afraid but genuine and respect total confidentiality considering jobs, reputations, etc., then write. We're a w/m/c thirty-one, both straight, clean, considerate, kind, gentle and confidential. We're not quote "swingers"—just people, ok. We have values and have a church-oriented background. He's six feet one inch, nice build, five inches by five inches. No drugs, alcohol, pain, Bi, married men or women. We'd like to be friends first, then just sex—no affairs. Looks and weight are less important. All answered with photo (not necessarily nude and returned upon request). Men, women, Kings, Princesses had more than one husband or wife. Seriously, read your history. Read your Bible. God saw no sin in this part. He understands, quote, "certain" situations. Man's laws have changed. Think about it...for your sexual health and conscience.

No preachers.

Country swingers, he's forty-five, she's thirty-five, would like to "meat" other broad minded couples. Nothing way-out or bi.

All with controllable actuators to grow regularly to reach my interior points with zero-time orbit, write. Discuss topological properties of reachable set. Demonstrate zero-time ideal. I can demonstrate nonempty interior.

First ad ever. Young blonde couple twenty-six and twenty-one seeking couples and bi females. She is five foot seven inches, one hundred seventeen pounds, blond and blue very passionately bi and very oral on both males and females. Like toys, lingerie. Enjoy all but pain, blacks, heavies, and weirdos. Can entertain.

A rigid body for a heavy top. No unnatural constraints, but subtle geometry obscured. Send diagrams for proof.

Happily married couple, she's thirty-two, he's forty. Seeking clean, discreet, non-pushy couples and males, eighteen to fifty, for friendship, open encounters and ménage à trois. Enjoy films, wine, erotic attire and atmosphere. Nothing way out. She's a fox and hot to trot. We are friendly and sincere, give us a try.

Shape shifting Nereid seeks creatures who can keep up and make the changes.

Married white female twenty-nine, pretty, travels all of the West Coast frequently on business, needs deep hard fucking from all extremely well hung men. Prefer ages twenty-one to twenty-five, but all with nine inches or more welcome. Love giving head and would love to try twelve inches. Respond only to those with photo for proof of size. No money involved.

Bisexual urban nymph seeking massive penises, prefer disembodied night spirits, information ghosts okay, no machine elves.

Beautiful, well built, young married female hot to try first black cock. Straight husband watches and photos. Prefer dark males twenty-one to thirty, eight inches or more. Especially turned on by a take-charge attitude. Will dress in lingerie, short mini and heels for the occasion.

Couple, she shape shifting urban nymph, he Nephilim with twenty-four inches by sixteen inches seek suicide girls and burning angels.

Hi! I'm twenty-eight, five feet five inches, one hundred fifteen pounds, blonde, divorced white female (thirty-four—twenty-three—thirty-six) that works for a major airline and can travel across the USA. I'm looking for men, women, and couples. I don't enjoy men that have cocks over seven inches long—but I do like it thick and hard. I really enjoy meeting new friends and lovers—so write soon!

She scratched that one.

Huge black studs needed in Orange County! Do you want a young, hot, sexy White woman with a magic pussy? If you're hung nine inches or bigger and know how to treat white pussy, write with nude photo.

And there came another of the seven trainers which had the seven vials and talked with me, saying, Come with me; I will show the great shape-shifting whore who sits beneath many waters with whom the kings and everyone else of the earth have committed fornication, and the inhabitants of the earth have been made drunk with the wine of her fornication. And she showed me my bride buried in a pile of writhing bodies.

Attractive, five foot two inches, one hundred pounds, young, sexy white lady and husband wish to meet clean, intelligent black male twenty to forty years old, for hot sex. Husband participates, nothing bi, Greek, S/M, B/D or weird. Must be at least eight by three and a half inches and discrete. Smoke and drink okay. Send nude, hard photo.

She anointed me the whore's fancy man.

Sensuous Los Angeles couple seeks couples, girls, men for free sex. Travel all Southern states. Photo exchange. Seek men hung ten inches or more. All races.

And I saw her bay at the moon with the fist and Louisville slugger forearm of a Nimrod buried in her asshole as the stress-eaters engorged massive meat of Nephilim in leathers.

I have big tits and my nipples are pierced to make them super-sensitive. If you know how to pinch, twist, pull or lick nipples; if you want to suck boobs way up into your mouth; if you like to fuck the valleys or piss on the mountains,

I might be interested in you. Prefer experienced couples where the female is into breast excitation, stimulation, punishment or torture, but will meet single women or men if they are bisexual.

Craving females to rent asunder with his twenty-four inches by sixteen inches.

Sexy young stewardess with beautiful bi roommate swing together or separately. Men everywhere. Will send panties, exchange photos.

Me: multilinear skank with multi-talented orifices and multi-orgasmic frequency response. You: at least bilinear and ready to tensor up. Eager for hard nonlinearities. Let's couple.

Attractive gal seeking fun-loving people. Can travel. Enjoy bisexuals, erotic times, French, Greek, Roman, water sports, toys. Age and looks not important. Being sincere is.

Out of this world couple with multi-port female seek extraterrestrials for un-attenuated couplings with impedance matching. Impedance bridging okay. Interested in trying complex conjugate matching. Attenuated relaxation by mutual cancellation of dipole-dipole coupling not acceptable.

Easily aroused young female, thirty-eight—twenty-seven—thirty-seven, one hundred twenty-two pounds, slim, beautiful, and eager likes more than one at a time and being watched. Bi with straight mate, seeks singles and couples with similar interests. Race no barrier. No overweights.

Seeking transgressive element of base cohomology to extend sections along fibration where everything is connected. Must pass through obstructions with restriction of global form, though singular cochains are acceptable. Send proven precise measurement of obstruction.

My master needs help in my continued sexual training. We are looking for discreet disease free bi white males and females between the ages of twenty-five and forty. Married okay. I like pleasing more than one man with all my willing holes and hands. Oral, anal, masturbation, voyeurism, toys, I love it all! Fill me up with your hot cock and cover me with your sticky cum while we film and photo the action. I would love to watch two men get it on while I play with myself and join in. I also want to watch him with another woman. If this sound interesting to you, send explicit letter, photos, and self addressed stamped envelope for response.

Seeking non-holonomic circle games. Cum play with me.

Sensuous bi white female seeks other bi, lesbian and select couples with sexy lady. I am oral, anal, like kinky very much and anything goes but pain. Can be top or bottom, pussy cat or bitch queen. Like sexy attire, toys, shaving, fetish and role play. First time ad but am experienced in above items. I also have a few homemade videos to trade on one to one. No single males, please.

Forming a Picard group of isomorphism classes of invertible sheaves, though rank one vector spaces welcome. Come, let's tensor and bundle up. Eager to try Albanese variety and maximal tori. No pulling back.

Couple seeking males for wife's sexual fun, both straight. Husband likes to watch while wife enjoys (hung) males, eight inches or better. Ages twenty to thirty-five. Must be clean.

Plump married bi-female in early fifties, frustrated with "useless" husband. I'm into sexual fantasies and constant masturbation and now seeking erotic and explicit correspondence with other women who are in a similar situation. I will also consider corresponding with mature married men who are frustrated with wives who no longer desire to please them.

Attractive white couple, happily married wish to meet single or married bi female or select couples where female is bi. Have small children so patience is a must. This is our first time so you must be clean and discrete. No fatties, blacks. We like smoke and drink. He is six feet three inches, one hundred sixty-five pounds, nine inches plus, blond with blue eyes. She is twenty-seven, five feet one inch, ninety-six pounds, blue eyes, brunette. Please no jerks need reply. This is a quality ad.

Discreet, clean, white couple will meet with same or single. Would like to meet a couple for threesomes after friendship. She has a fantasy of very large nine or ten inches. Loves two men at once. She is five feet seven inches, thirty-six—twenty-four—thirty-six, one hundred thirty-three pounds and can climax eight to ten times. Loves a threesome. White only. Would love a bi experience and could party alone with female.

Would you like to tie a beautiful young submissive girl to a bed? I'm twenty-three, five feet six inches, thirty-six—twenty-four—thirty-four. Seek male or couples.

Select couples, females, video buffs. Ultra discrete, reliable, honest videographer and two b/ms ten inches thick for your fantasies and experimentation. We are a clean, well mannered, sincere and non-push group that respects everyone limits and mostly privacy. Twosomes, threesomes, everything explored. Coupled with oral. Bi-males welcome. No pain or bizarre activities. Our small group is looking for quality, uninhibited people who enjoy great sex in a safe, relaxed setting. We can entertain. No single men, weirdos, druggies need apply. We are quality and expect the same.

Attractive blonde housewife cannot get enough sex. Would like to meet good-looking, well-hung men to satisfy sexual needs and desires. Can entertain at home, possible travel. Enjoy threesomes, moresomes with straight husband.

Hot and horny couple. She's twenty-five, one hundred fifteen pounds, thirty-four—twenty-two—thirty-four. Loves French, Greek and gang bangs, also she's very bi. He's twenty-nine, digs French, Greek and all good sex. Want to meet bi girls for either or both, bi couples, straight couples and men.

Two bi ladies, attractive thirties, both bi, he's cute TV. Seek rendezvous with couples, females and well endowed males. Interests include French, Greek, toys, groups and adventurous. Love dating and drag bars—together or separate. No weirdos.

Want men who can stay hard all night. Like to be licked and sucked, the more the merrier. Send photos (hard). We can travel anywhere. Blacks great.

Happy gal loves recreational sex. No ties, no involvements, just good lovemaking and 69 on layovers. I'm twenty-six and enjoy everything except pain.

Young traveling gal loves it all with the right man or couple. Can travel or entertain. I seek a Koszul connection-type for swinger parallel transport.

The surfeit of pleas for lustful encounters saturated the feedback systems into a nonlinear resonant coupling of actuator and disturbance response, shutting down feedback-driven sexual response. Feedforward response couldn't get it up.

I applied excessive measures based on Fisher information as excessive sets of the manifold melted away exposing the underlying structure like wings of a roasting goose. The potential-zero passes the horde of processes I'd released to flow along on geodesics of maximum likelihood stood starkly exposed with razor edges, the wrigglers swarming mostly to their deaths, suicidal lemming-like commandos of ergodic intent hunting invariant measures of the perturbed system, trapped on ergodic islands of decomposition, exploding, vanishing, lost. Could not maximum entropy be far behind?

The key to getting some heroes through without all being swept away was selecting the appropriate connection with appropriate exponential drag along which to parallel transport while not crossing the maximum likelihood flows which turn out to be Ricci flows in the true conditional probability; that is, by finding a metric to make the connection simultaneously symmetric and compatible and with as little curvature as possible given the eigenvalues of the Laplacian, hence slowed down along certain subspaces formed by ergodic pooling so as not to be swept to infinity by curvature and exploding or falling off the manifold. Speaking plainly, they found chutes and passes to go from one position of the final manifold to another as the raw data recursively melted the infinite dimensional manifold of conditional probability distributions away from beneath their swarm.

The INS increases information beyond position and velocity by attitude of antenna from lever arm, all independent of GPS but seems not enough for a connection to a finite dimension submanifold. Obscuration foreseen, but one questions what more is bought with attitude.

And it came to me in a vision imparted by automaton-laden random crawlers along the Hilbert bundle of conditional distributions where the adjoined inertial device provided global information hidden by discretized obscuration and kept honest by short-time feedback correction. The statistical manifold of conditional distributions embedded within more degrees of freedom indexed a Cameron-Martin space of finite-energy paths of zero measure with respect to the Wiener measure (as all finite-energy paths are of bounded variation whereas almost surely Brownian sample paths are of unbounded variation) and manifested itself as an infinite-dimensional Hilbert space with reproducing kernel. The subspace of curves in adjoined Cameron-Martin space fibers corresponded to directional derivatives formed as partials of score functions of conditional distributions, a tangent space to the infinite dimensional statistical space spanned by "time derivatives" of corresponding time evolution of infinite degrees of freedom of information as the nuisance tangent space.

Consider all possible parallel translations from every direction in the enveloping manifold with adjoined Cameron-Martin space at a fixed distribution and note the closure is a fiber in the larger Cameron-Martin tangent space in the nuisance tangent space of the statistical manifold of distributions. Then there exists an orthogonal subspace which splits exact as two orthogonal bundles, the information fibers of finite, fixed dimension and the ancillary fibers. This splitting provides a connection, but its utility is not apparent. Clearly a sufficient statistic would project into a sum of information and ancillary components, with the projection on the information fibers spanning the data but losing information by leakage. Further projection from the ancillary fiber by conditioning frees up information bound up with the INS, supplemental information that otherwise leaks away, not directly or otherwise accessible by projection of the finite dimensional information fiber. The difficulty becomes the projection from the infinite dimensional ancillary fiber which requires a global section whose extension is obstructed by growing dimensionality of the ancillary projections. To get a recursive estimator, it is sufficient to have causal temporal development of the conditional distributions as a resolution Hilbert space. These would project onto unfolding data and eventually drain the nuisance space of all information leaking into the nuisance fibers, given a global section for the ancillary fibers, so for the existence of a finite dimensional nonlinear optimal filter it is not sufficient to have finite-dimensional information fibers. There is the necessity of a global section for the ancillary bundle which has fibers of infinite dimension.

Backtracking, I constructed a Lax pair with the Fisher inner product on fibers by considering the conditioning of the ancillary fibers as a stochastic partial differential equation related to the DMZ equation via the innovations representation. This allowed me to find an infinite sequence of conservation laws that represent the moments of the estimator after conditioning. The requisite moments indeed grow recursively with the data, seemingly a method of moments problem enlarging the number of simultaneous equations to fit with each recursive data update.

A direct assault was thus faced with an ever expanding system of simultaneous, coupled equations. I resumed the siege by releasing travelers along flows tied to the underlying manifold, in this case a generalized Ricci flow associated with the curves of maximum likelihood related to Fisher information via a density Ψ solving $\mathrm{Ric}_\Psi = \mathrm{Ric} - \mathrm{Hess}(\Psi)$ where of course Ric is the Ricci tensor and Hess the Hessian. To affect this I released mathematical model *Chaos* pseudopodia along all paths into the infinite dimensional degrees of freedom, that is random travelers with slowed internal time (fast by the natural time of the flows) to search out all points with false feet of automata as observers equivalent to inertial measurement units. This pulled information from the nuisance components by transgression, where the transgressive elements belonged to a the generalized Spencer cohomology of the stochastic PDE. I characterized it as if the information were surrounded and ingested by phagocytosis, the term I chose to use for the process being *cloacal extrusion,* in the end the equivalent of information dysentery. The dimension of the recursive procedure did not expand with each step, but remained constant. Sufficiency was related to the generalized Ricci curvature discussed above, the recursive flow a Lax-type flow on a co-adjoint orbit of a semi-simple Lie group with a component defined on its Lie algebra as a cotangent space identified by means of its Killing forms, so the equations are of the form $\dot{G} = [G, \mathrm{grad}(F(G)]$ where F is related to Ψ by the obvious identifications. The approach to this point was nothing but a rehash of the old isospectral deformation method applied to the appropriate operators, where the invariant spectrum referred to both the expected spectrum of the operator and the cohomology spectral sequence, making for a nice bit of raw meat for the mathematicians. I later found a symplectic interpretation in terms of an infinite dimensional Hamiltonian, but it was not enlightening and I kept it to myself. Frenchie said it was equivalent to the Kirillov-Kostant-Souriau form, but I pretended to be insulted. The key point was indeed that the Lie algebra was the Poisson algebra with respect to the bracket.

The major difficulty in turning the mathematical procedure to prove existence into an effectively computable algorithm was finding an expression for the gain, there being no Riccati equation to attack, not even an infinite dimensional version. I'd shown all but the first five moments were independent of the data, even though the moments were coupled. Deriving the gain amounted to working out that relationship, a tedious computation with the conserved quantities that did depend on data through nuisance conditioning. The computation provided a counterexample and a necessary condition: I found a filtering problem in which the moments were independent of the data after the first moment but the gain of which required all the moments, growing in dimension with each new measurement since it turned out that each new measurement added to the dimension of the system even though it did not specifically enter the gain or the moments from the second moment on. The earlier data lingered in the new update so that it had to be retained in the measurement vector, a result of violating the condition that the Lie algebra was the Poisson algebra with respect to the bracket. That condition turned out to be necessary; I found no sufficient condition. The gain came from the Poisson bracket and never fully incorporated all the information in the Lie bracket of the Lax equation unless they were equal, hence the growing dimension.

In essence, the modified Ricci flow washed away the nuisance dross which showed up as curvature, obstructing the existence of flatness in the sense of an exponential family, albeit it on an infinite dimensional space. The fact that the finite dimensional filter is a finite dimensional solution to the infinite dimensional problem is related to the action of the inertial measurements providing a curvature correction as a flattening, exploited by the *Chaos* crawlers ingeniously tunneling through the obstruction on the gap. Frenchie later said it was akin to quantum tunneling, where instead of energy being insufficient, it was information that was insufficient, even as the process anyhow made it over the hump.

Unlike with most problems I worked on, I was able to clean this mess up into a neat package right away. Insights came as I worked out the details. Especially lovely was an approach to crossing the gap using a Brownian bridge with a connection from a finite dimensional subspace of the infinite raw pseudorange manifold to the derived position side with its quasi-hyperbolic distribution. The thing superficially appeared infinite dimensional but the connection, the very same connection of the splitting of nuisance bundle into information and ancillary bundles, allowed the taming of the holonomic group in path space which showed the way to hidden natural finite-dimensional charts. This was the surprise of the proof, that the bridge led from an infinite dimensional manifold without local charts to the clandestine finite dimensional charts. The most amazing part was that the finite dimensional submanifold could not contain sufficient statistics but had a deep relationship to the derived position distributions via a lifting and pull-back made possible by the augmentation of the inertial measurements.

Three applications came out of the tidying work. First and most important was a proof of the filter stability. I showed that the relative entropy of the true conditional distribution with respect to an incorrectly initialized filter was a positive supermartingale and decomposed into decreasing and local martingale terms from which there resulted a bound on information and an error bound on information and error measures of the difference between the conditional distribution and an arbitrary incorrectly initialized filter. The bounding supermartingale went to zero asymptotically with exponential convergence, driving the filter to the optimal estimator, hence forgetting the initial data. The approach here was necessary because there was no way to apply the standard Lyapunov functional. The optimal solution was not a normal distribution, a condition that classified this as a non-ergodic model. Essentially the Fisher information converged to a non-degenerate random variable instead of a constant, which led to the necessity of finding a way to prove asymptotic efficiency. I later accomplished the proof following hints from Frenchie regarding an extension of the Fisher-Rao model made by a statistician named Le Cam.

Two other applications came out regarding linearized filters. The extended Kalman filter (eKf) twists the information and nuisance fibers with the obstruction and ignores the ancillary fibers, equivalently ignoring the gradient of the gain from Ito's lemma in propagating the covariance. As the recursion proceeds, the eKf leaks information from the data into the nuisance fibers at a rate determined by the information adjoined to the data of the true nonlinear filter when there is no projection (in the sense of conditioning) from the ancillary fibers. Eventually enough information is lost that instability results from propagating arithmetical nonsense. I pointed out that it is every bit as ridiculous as the mathematical precision of astrology. This also provided a test to show when the standard linearized filter, that is linearized about a trajectory independent of the data, was far enough outside the linear range that it began to lose significant information. The test warns users to prepare a new, more accurate trajectory before the filter diverges significantly. All in all, it provided a plethora of papers in the high-end engineering literature.

I had only smoked a handful of joints while writing up the results, so I rolled a huge spliff and went to the window. It was dark outside but hints of morning light brought forth the crepuscular creatures who prowl the Quarter in the interstices of first and last light. I stood on the balcony to observe their mating rituals. The party in the apartment below raged. As dark gave way the streets showed themselves to be packed. All sort of permutations of coupling was afoot and crowds locked together beneath the balconies in the blocks down towards Canal spectating live porn from tourists. Lafitte's crowd oozed from the doors. The stage was completed and people were setting up speakers. I began to suspect it was not Saturday but Tuesday, that I had lost three whole days.

As light filled in the details, two creatures were hustled out the gate of our courtyard into Lafitte's. The first was escorted by the two males dressed in Nazi uniforms. He appeared on the balcony in jeans and a t-shirt torn open on one side to reveal a nipple ring from which he was chained to the balcony railing on the corner overlooking the intersection above the stand. I recognized him as the bearded slave in the courtyard. Immediately a line formed and he commenced sucking dicks.

Several females carried the second by handles attached to a highly ornate body of tattoos and scars and jewelry. I recognized it as Dina, even though her head was enclosed within a wooden box. It was designed to allow to protrude, for easy access, the horny handles on her skull. The only face hole in the box was at the mouth, fitted with a bung on a chain so as not to be lost once removed. She was naked other than the box. Unbelievable the extensive modifications she had undergone. It was hard to look upon. Her elongated vaginal lips, which bore elaborate designs from what I could see, were joined together with padlocks through a series of piercings and tied against her belly below her stretched and broken breasts which were also decorated and pierced and tied to her waist. Nothing dangled. She was attached to the balcony beside the male slave, tied by a series of chains through her nipples and from within her cunt, probably invisible clitoral piercings. A plug was inserted into her anus. Once in place, the bung was removed from the box on her head and the men in line had a new place to stick their penises for service.

h) Stabilization of Linear Differential Systems via Hybrid Feedback Controls

I went downstairs. An orgy raged. It was Fat Tuesday. My bride to be seemed dead, a variety of creatures using what appeared to be her corpse, but I was assured she was only taking a nap or passed out from drugs and alcohol. There were a handful of people wading through the piles, filming with handheld cameras.

I sought out Harry who told me they'd been filming for days and this day, Mardi Gras, was the culmination of a documentary of two weeks viewing duration chopped up for presentation in ten hours on multiple screens. Dina, beginning with her dungeon ordeal and ending with this day as a mobile glory hole, was to be the theme of several screens. The party in the streets was another. The costume contest was yet one more. He told me to take off my clothes and jump in, but I demurred. I had decided to save myself for my wedding.

I spotted Kim in the corner fucking several men. It reminded me of my commitment to her and I talked to Harry about her, that she wanted to get into the business. "She isn't all that great looking, though she does have an ugly girl-next-door charm and she is enthusiastic," I said, pointing her out. "Great," he said, "if she's half the hit Mule's become she'll be a big star. I promise I'll call her when we're done here. We've had trouble of late finding lax-type entropy-entropy flux pears." That freed me to see the film Kip had called about, lest otherwise it never exist. The film stunk: an unappealing woman, though she had Kip ecstatic. Yet one more higher singularity amidst the forced secondary bifurcations.

The well-equipped film crews occupied the better vantage point of the balcony of the Washing Well, filming the street action, the costume contest and the action on Lafitte's balcony. I watched the costume contest from my landlord's balcony. It was crowded, but the crowd treated me deferentially, making space

635

in the best corner where I sat on a chair, smoked dope and drank beer. The most striking contestants set off a chorus of approbative lowing. It was a group of naked giants of unearthly pallor. On a leash attached to a collar they walked a naked skinny brunette girl with meager tits and ass, a cunt giving away her gender. Below the knees were orange bird's legs with orange anisodactyl feet.

How the fuck they had created such masterful costumes became the instant buzz of the balcony. It was more amazing when she was hefted by one of the giants and fucked like a sex toy. Impossible. No one believed the huge implement would enter the opening, given it's length was half her height and circumference more than half the width of the hips.

They had to win the contest. I didn't wait around to find out, going upstairs to sleep. As I left, my betrothed had revived and was engaged in despicable acts with a group of unidentifiable monstrosities. I hurried away, not wanting to break my chastity vows by becoming aroused and sinning in my heart.

PART III

AN EXAMPLE OF A LOCAL PROBLEM IS
WHAT POT DO I PISS IN?

WHEREAS A GLOBAL PROBLEM WOULD BE
WHAT TIME IS IT?

— MIKE BALLOTTI

Chapter 24
A Sheaf of Germs

I emerged from my thesis defense a PhD. My advisor returned to attend and Frenchy attended with a friend, a professor of electrical engineering from Stanford who took kindly to my filter. He was alone in that, or nearly so. The questions pulled me back to Brownian motion exploring manifolds, a phenomenon I didn't find surprising given random scurries needed only intrinsic geometric properties, though it would have been interesting had they relied on extrinsic geometry as did the property of being a stochastic differential equation. I intertwined my responses to the filter, no matter how weak the thread. Eventually I was booed. Momus told me were it not for the interplay of probability and geometry, I would not be getting a PhD. The filter did not interest them. I made it on geometry, not engineering applications of stochastic differential equations.

At home, I dwelt mostly alone. My betrothed spent her time gone, I assumed so as not to tempt me during my wittol apprenticeship. The ghost women had abandoned me as well, I assumed for the same reason. Nonetheless, they continued to care for me on a daily basis even though I never saw them. I guessed the ghost women would reappear after I married. That would be when my cuckold training was deemed complete; my betrothed's call.

Instead they brought in a psychological engineer, a woman from Hollywood who had developed a patented process for amplifying connections on the fibers of the manifold of joint information belonging to two (or more) people. Said entity is a step up from the individual, mathematically that is, since an individual is no more than the connections on his or her information fibers. She made direct application of the Cuntz algebra of the C* algebra of observables on the Hilbert space of states of reality; this curtailed reality modulo the manifold of maximal shared information. It amounted to sub-band coding that she modulated to focus with a narrower beam on areas that were no longer chosen by the group of information holders. In order to be certain that individuals determining the information manifold were directly affected it was necessary to find paths connecting the embedded individual's submanifold to the outside. Control could be exercised over pairs of individuals, but the added complexity was difficult to tune. Instead, control would be exerted by assuming a couple, and no others, shared the information. She called it the two-soul problem, disregarding perturbations from overlapping information holders. Of course, the closer in total information content the two, the more powerful the connection. Consider, for example, the gang of all information holders who have personal knowledge of a fixed member.

Her basic setup called for a biological control system operating at the level of individual as defined via the Cuntz algebra. At the core of the information-bearing individual would be found the control system. This led to a new interpretation of the use of pharmaceuticals as mechanisms with which to drive and steer the individual's controller and also, particularly with psychotropic drugs, the operating system; she considered it a tongs-and-hammer-approach, without regard for potential interactions at the firmware level. But neither in her setup was consciousness binary; indeed, it was a continuum. The light seen by those who experience it at the edge of death is explained as noise of the control system as one's consciousness nears only internal noise, recorded on a device losing connectivity and hence awareness (receptor, storage and processor shutdown). We are talking here about activity at the quantum level with consciousness disintegrating. How do we know when the individual is no more a living entity?

That question was where she had begun looking. She claimed that for those for whom death is sufficiently smooth, they might possibly sense their operating system shutting down. This would be leaving semi-conscious for unconscious on the way to permanent dissolution without a trace.

With my betrothed and me she applied her theory to the two-body information manifold for couples. Easier than for the full manifold, but still quite complex. Fortunately, it admitted a closed-form integral to expose it, which could be exploited by adorning with a bit of small random perturbation and by ignoring the world outside the two. She would modify our synchronization by installing an intermediate coupling. She and Dhara took me offline and modified the superheterodyne amplifier on my side. The best analogy for the amplifier is a sexual theremin (or better, empathic synthesizer) or optical heterodyne with variable reception.

The modification resulted in hard-wiring Katie the Faithful and me by fusing our joint information with a regenerative feedback mechanism on a device similar to a biplolar-transistor. It would operate solely within Katie's control. The heterodyne amplifier was variable capacitance with Cuntz modulator that could emulate discipline-bondage, master-slave, dominant-submissive, dominant-

dominant but always actively male. The switch acted more like a unipolar three-way MOSFET that simultaneously amplified and switched. The idea was that instead of amplifying sexual dominance for cuckolding via heterodyning to intermediate frequency, when switched to wittol mode from dominant mode it became a homodyne device with superregenerative detection and amplification that when approaching high frequency poles would emit quenching frequency to modify loop gain of direct conversion for energy blockage with an amplified DC offset, blocking all penile potential from realization, leaving the masculine appendage unresponsive and flaccid even as the sexual stimulation ramped to instability. The feedback between me and my betrothed (hereafter referred to as Faith) drove amplification beyond the orgiastic-frenzy break-frequency even as I could not get it up and remained a passive cuckold. To get penile response from me she of necessity had to switch me back to dominant mode. This switching mechanism gave concern for effects of metastability with noise, though it seems the random time before settling on a final value was short enough to not often be noticed. Uncontrollable monotonically increasing spasms of the vagina for her were evidenced by vulva fluttering with labia chattering, the latter snapping open and shut. It could be quenched only by relief of my own libidinal pressure valve, necessitating my return to dominant mode.

In summary, by focusing within the narrowed, chosen sub-band and raising the amplitude of the beam when homodyne, the DC component shut down my ability to get an erection while amplifying the need to relieve one. In essence, all sexual inputs to physical response were masked while their effects amplified.

Fundamental to the approach was the shaping of harmonic distortion by regenerative feedback. With tuning was increased my sensitivity to Faith in the high frequency-responsive spectrum, while for Faith the sensitivity increased in the easier to ignore low frequency scale with long time constants interspersed with wider footprint.

Faith and I acted as waveguides one to the other, each of us filtering and amplifying the other's hungers, but Faith's sexual mood controlled the binary switch. She alone, though not usually consciously and sometimes under advisement. My relentless need fed back to her by raising the frequency threshold to which she responded even as the time constant shrunk to zero, making her more receptive to our joint need for my ramming the shaft down various and sundry throats and other openings. What was outwardly directed from me was literally a tone row of sexual overtones.

The two stress eaters returned to haunt me as a system test. With strenuous effort they were unable to bring me within a neighborhood of erection until Faith switched and I engorged almost instantaneously, nearly choking Jaime. Before I could unload Faith switched back. I lost the erection without resolution.

"Let's see how you like them blue balls," she said. "This switch will be off until me and you be wife and man."

The unexpected effect of the modified channel was amplified spooky-action-at-a-distance: when Faith was away, I responded to her sexual vagaries in a sensitized empathic connection. Bidirectional, by which means I could attempt to improve my chances of having the switch thrown if I wanted it so. Wanting it changed, no matter which position, was a rare event as I loved each situation the most when I was in it, a human temporal contradiction. Amplification was lower on the connection to Faith than from her, but what she received went to sub-carnal machinery operating below the controllable level. As with mine. In no way can these be personal levels, though each is unique to the information-individual. They are as impersonal as gravity.

The drive to Palo Alto from New Orleans would be leisurely enough to allow my betrothed to put me through my wittol paces without restriction, within the binary limit of course. Until marriage the switch would remain in the mode of impotent cuckold. Along the way were planned stops at glory holes at gas stations, rest stops and other establishments. Every overnight included what she called bag gang-bangs wherein she would wear a hood with only a mouth hole and I might, or might not, wear a hood as well but I would be seated, perhaps tied to a chair, to spectate at the sexual gladiatorial games. Our relationship was built on a foundation of impedance matched along the boundaries of harmonic distortion. With me in the dominant mode her admittance in semens (a term I later learned was a psychological engineer's idea of a pun) increased by several orders of magnitude, which would provide Faith yet more incentive to allow us spend time in that mode. I remembered the possibility of being bound over to a submanifold of terminal states effected by transversality constraints.

The roommates returned in their variant of the flesh to stress my unquenchable lust. I learned to stop transmitting, or rather I was suddenly unable to transmit. Their presence mocked me and I liked it.

Information ghosts haunted the stages of consciousness where I had previously concentrated on my thesis. I thought about mathematics, but not in the detail of problem solving so much as in breaking through the barrier of mathematical imagery. I wanted to find what was on the other side. Instead, I slogged through the vestiges of war .

It sent me back to Cosimo's. My old bartender and Marine Corps compatriot was there. He eyed me as he wiped the bar.

"The regular?" he asked and I nodded assent. "Been a long time," he said as he pushed a shot at me. "Thought you might have moved on."

"Am now," I answered. "My company's moving me to San Diego."

"Sweet. Though I hear it is expensive. And the food mostly sucks."

"It's a big promotion. Gonna take over the west coast operations."

"Impressive. Accounting must be good. You've probably been too busy to come in."

"Yep. Thought I'd stop in to say good-bye."

"There's a reunion in town."

"Marines?"

"Something called a CAP unit."

"A CAP reunion? I was with a CAP out of Tam Ky"

"I never heard of a CAP. What is it?"

"Essentially a rifle squad with a corpsman, plunked down in a hamlet to work with PFs to keep out the enemy. And to help keep the hamlet from getting too fucked over by the Americans."

"Sounds dangerous."

"It was. High casualty rate. High kill rate too. Our HQ unit was in Chu Lai. We were the last Marines down there. The rest went on up to Da Nang and north."

"How'd you get in that line of work?"

"I was a grunt when they started forming those things. The Combined Action Program asked for volunteers and I got volunteered."

"Tough luck, sounds like."

"They weren't on your butt so much. Our outfit was pretty chicken shit, so I didn't mind the change. There were no officers out there, only NCOs in charge. The officers were once removed to the HQ they called a CAG. Not a pleasant trip from Chu Lai to Tam Ky by jeep."

"Sounds like you were on your own."

"Our CAP was a bit less on our own than most. We were on a hill overlooking the area around the Tam Ky River. Had a good view of the valley north and west of us. The river was a few clicks and there was another unit there. They figured it was too dangerous and too political for a single CAP. The

Vietnamese in the area were pretty divided between us and them; we had strong support and strong opposition. Plenty of fighting among themselves. Spies and politics."

"Local politics. Sounds like a nightmare."

"So we had two CAPs to patrol the area. There were some ancient Cham ruins nearby. It was interesting and picturesque with the mountains in the background and the river. And there was a company of American a few miles from our perimeter opposite the river. But we still got overrun."

"No reactionary force?"

"I don't know. I was out of it early."

"Medevac?"

"I don't think until it was over. Probably at first light. No way you could land on the hill with hostiles all around."

"So what happened?"

"I never found out."

"Wounded?"

"Yep. Pretty much put an end to my days as a Marine. I woke up in a hospital."

"Well, you might find this worth visiting."

He showed me a mimeographed sheet with details. It was being held at a motel out by the airport.

"Not a very interesting place to meet."

"No," he said, "but probably a lot cheaper than the Bourbon Orleans."

I'd only been out in that direction for flying in and out and so it was unfamiliar territory. I dressed in my worst rag-picker's costume and took a cab, getting out a block away to go in afoot.

The taxi disgorged me in a place of drab structures devoid of the character of New Orleans. A flat, sprawling building clad in faded and worn beige siding amidst a field of weeds was the designated target. I made a recon circle of the building, then crossed the parking lot to an opening where was an office. A hand lettered cardboard signed hung in the window CAP REUNION with an arrow pointing parallel to the walkway, so I followed the concrete ribbon to a one story long-building standing alone with an entrance through one narrow side. It made me think of an airplane hangar. I stood in the doorway and watched. There were a lot of men standing around mostly dressed in jeans drinking, smoking and talking. There were two women. One of them approached.

"Hi. I'm Kerry. You were with a CAP?"

"Yes."

"I hope there are some from your unit here."

"Me too."

There were. I approached a small group of them. I recognized a few as NCOs from the CAP along the river. They stared as if a ghost had tried to sneak up on them.

"Jesus," a tall prematurely gray and balding fat guy said. "Whitey Butcher. We thought you were dead."

"Did my name appear in the Stars and Stripes?"

"Well, you know they di'n't list 'em all," he said, his words a tone-cluster with a southern drawl of some kind, not local that I could place. I didn't find him in my memory.

The guy standing next to him I found. The senior NCO for the two CAPS, he seldom came up to see us on the hill. He stuck his hand out. "Wow. Like seeing a ghost."

"I guess so. Not ever been in your shoes," I said.

The other one stuck out his hand. "I left just a little after you came in. I was in charge of the hill."

"I remember," I lied. This lard ass looked like an old man.

"Senior Master Sergeant Mitty," the other one said for him. "I'm a postal worker, but I used to be senior NCO when you were there."

"Sergeant Black. I remember."

That was the end of the conversation.

"Sergeant Mueller around?" I asked.

"Yes, as a matter of fact. He flew in from Germany to be here. I'll help you find him."

Like it would be a difficult task to find someone in this flattened Quonset hut. I let him walk point.

Mueller stood alone, staring into space. He wore a ball cap that announced SILVER STAR WINNER in gold letters. Not a big guy, he was wiry. Unsmiling when he turned to see us. It hardened to frown when he spotted me.

"Whitey Butcher," he said, as if we had spoken yesterday.

Sergeant Black began to back out as soon as Mueller spoke. We stared into each other's eyes. His were small and dark. He wore a handlebar mustache of the same flat brown as his hair, cut in the same USMC crew as the last time I'd seen him. It wasn't thinning. He didn't seem to be aging. I wondered if I had.

"When I came in they were debating whether or not you were dead. Your story's kind of a big deal."

"I would think the whole fucking story would be, but I missed the end of it."

"Well, when day came, the enemy retreated. Down at the river they were loath to send in a reactionary force. They knew there'd be a blocking force to ambush them. I don't know what I'd have done. Hard to watch the fight and do nothing. I got the full spectator's debriefing several times. Just lucky the NVA didn't do it. These were locals."

"Armed and dangerous locals."

"When I got back they assigned me to First Logistics in Da Nang. Weird change. With those guys, it was always gook this and gook that. I couldn't think that way after that attack. The PFs saved our asses."

"Where'd you go?"

"You weren't the only one wounded that night."

"Doc was dead. Grenades."

"Yeah, if only he hadn't given away our position."

"I don't think he was ready for enemy in the compound. I always wonder just what did happen."

"Gooks in the wire. Yep, that's how they'd put it."

He took a step closer and studied me.

"You were always a shitbird, Butcher."

"I know. Still am."

"Living here in New Orleans?"

"I rent a place out in the Ninth Ward. Cheap enough here to live on disability."

"Still don't like work, do you."

I turned my head side to side. "Nope."

"The next day the PF captain asked me, 'What happen? Why Marines no fight?' He'd lost a lot of men; they were fighting. One of them was lying on his back with his face peeled off, or nearly so. I picked up his M-1 carbine and starting shooting at hostiles along the perimeter. When that emptied, I ran to my hootch to get the M-60. I walked the perimeter firing down the hill until it jammed."

He reflected a moment.

"Of course, this was after the grenades got us."

"So you witnessed the whole fight."

"I did more; I participated."

"I'm pretty sure I did too. So did Doc, but look where it left him. Shooting his .45. Three times, I think."

"I don't remember how many. The grenades came in right away. I think they blurred my recollection of the prior details. Doc took the brunt of it."

"I remember one grenade."

"There were two, maybe three. But they were on the wrong side of the hole."

"I was never clear how I survived. I remember that explosion. My ears were useless after that. Threw me up against the side of the hole."

"They were off when they threw them. I think they were to the front and far side of Doc. His body took most of the brunt. They were concussion grenades or we'd have had more holes in us."

We stopped. Something nagged at him.

"I waited for the MEDEVAC from Chu Lai. There was a squadron of CH-46s from MAG-16 that morning. They had delivered some Marines who were going to support American people in the Que Son Valley. They heard our call and sent in a chopper. It picked you and the Doc up. We thought you were the only two of ours dead. You fooled them."

"They must have had a corpsman on board because they took me to NSA Station Hospital in Da Nang. He probably realized I wasn't dead."

"We had you covered with a poncho."

"The corpsman in triage who worked on me came to see me before they medevaced me. He says my heart stopped beating and they revived me. I must have lost a lot of blood."

"I had a collapsed lung and a lot of shrapnel. Some of it was bones and such from Doc. He was blown in half. I got out of the hole right away. I still remember all the mud on a starry night when it wasn't raining. The Lister bags had ruptured. That was why the M-60 jammed; the belt was dragging in the mud."

"I tried to get out of the fucking hole. My leg got shot out from under me and I ended up back in the hole waiting for more grenades."

"Was odd that night, the three of us in that hole. We were going to make it a hootch."

"So the rest of the crew didn't fight? That what you said?"

"I went to Guam for a stay, then came back. And they'd reassigned me. I got to sleep in a bed."

"Well, I wasn't coming back. I nearly lost my fucking leg."

"What a joke. Grunt outfits volunteered their biggest shitbirds to get rid of them. Nice way to start a unit. You guys were the worst batch of shitbirds I have yet to run across."

"What do you do now?"

"I head up a department of a construction engineering outfit in Germany. My wife's German. You don't do shit, right?"

"Well, I like to drink. I need a beer."

Beer was easy access and getting it gave us a break to mull over our approaches. We withdrew to a mostly isolated corner. I waited for his opening.

"I was surprised you weren't hiding out with the rest of the shitbirds."

"Where were they? Why didn't you rally them?"

He threw me an angry glare.

"They weren't showing themselves. I bet they were huddled-up by the bug out trail."

"Didn't recall we had one. Be dangerous going down that hill at night, all the booby traps they made with grenades."

"I would guess the American set up a blocking force down that way. If they had star clusters they might get out without getting shot up. I just wonder why you weren't with them."

"No matter how terrified I might be, I sure as hell wouldn't cluster up with those clowns."

"After the M-60 jammed, I went to the ammo bunker and got a couple boxes of grenades. The PFs and I threw a lot of grenades down the hill. That seemed to discourage them.

"At first light there was a reactionary force that came up from the river. We'd called the medevac from Chu Lai, but the 46 got there first and picked up what we considered our dead. Take them to Graves Registration."

"I don't recall anything until I awoke in a hospital bed in Da Nang."

"They had an officer from HQ down by the river, spending the night. He came up with the reactionary force and saw you before we had much chance to get to you. You were in that hole with Doc's forty-five still in your grip. Across the hole were five dead VC. Each one shot once in the chest."

"I remember seeing some shadows coming up that tunnel connecting the hole with the front gate. I expected more grenades but they didn't throw any. I reached down and there was Doc's forty-five and I shot them. I counted five. Just before I lost it, I thought, how can this be? Doc fired three times, so where'd the extra round come from?"

"They figured something like that. Like you got them all. I think Doc might have had a round in the chamber when he started firing. Or maybe it was only two rounds he fired. So they wrote you up for a Medal of Honor. That's what I heard them saying when I got on the Huey for my ride into Chu Lai."

"That's crazy. But I got a Navy Cross out of it," I said.

"There were a lot of wounded PFs. The worst rode with me into Chu Lai on the first one out."

His eyes flashed angry again.

"That means you trumped me," he said.

"So what? I don't have mine anymore anyway."

"Hock it?"

I didn't answer. He looked me in the eye.

"You're still a shitbird, Butcher. You'll never amount to anything."